PENGUIN  CLASSICS

THE RED AND THE BLACK

HENRI MARIE BEYLE, known through his writing as Stendhal, was born in Grenoble in 1783 and educated there at the École Centrale. A cousin offered him a post in the Ministry of War, and from 1800 he followed Napoleon's campaigns in Italy, Germany, Russia and Austria. In between wars, he spent his time in Paris drawing rooms and theatres.

After the fall of Napoleon, he retired to Italy, adopted his pseudonym and started to write books on Italian painting, Haydn and Mozart, and travels in Italy. In 1821 the Austrian police expelled him from the country, and on returning to Paris he finished his book *De l'amour*. This was followed by *Racine et Shakespeare*, a defence of Romantic literature. *Le Rouge et le noir* was his second novel, and he also produced or began three others, including *La Chartreuse de Parme* and *Lucien Leuwen*. None of his published works was received with any great understanding during his lifetime.

Beyle was appointed Consul at Civitavecchia after the 1830 revolution, but his health deteriorated and six years later he was back in Paris and beginning a *Life* of Napoleon. In 1841 he was once again recalled for reasons of illness, and in the following year suffered a fatal stroke. Various autobiographical works, *Journal*, *Souvenirs de l'egotisme* and *La Vie de Henri Brulard*, were published later, as his fame grew.

ROGER GARD was educated at Abbotsholme School, Derbyshire, and at Corpus Christi College, Cambridge. Before his death in 2000 he was Emeritus Reader in English at Queen Mary and Westfield College, University of London. Among his publications are books on Henry James, Jane Austen and the teaching of fiction in schools. He also translated Alfred de Vigny's *The Servitude and Grandeur of Arms*, and edited Henry James's *A Landscape Painter and Other Tales*, *The Jolly Corner and Other Tales* and a selection of his literary criticism, *The Critical Muse*, for Penguin Classics.

STENDHAL

The Red and the Black

Translated with an Introduction
and Notes by ROGER GARD

PENGUIN BOOKS

PENGUIN BOOKS

Published by the Penguin Group
Penguin Books Ltd, 80 Strand, London WC2R ORL, England
Penguin Putnam Inc., 375 Hudson Street, New York, New York 10014, USA
Penguin Books Australia Ltd, 250 Camberwell Road, Camberwell, Victoria 3124, Australia
Penguin Books Canada Ltd, 10 Alcorn Avenue, Toronto, Ontario, Canada M4V 3B2
Penguin Books India (P) Ltd, 11, Community Centre, Panchsheel Park, New Delhi – 110 017, India
Penguin Books (NZ) Ltd, Cnr Rosedale and Airborne Roads, Albany, Auckland, New Zealand
Penguin Books (South Africa) (Pty) Ltd, 24 Sturdee Avenue, Rosebank 2196, South Africa

Penguin Books Ltd, Registered Offices: 80 Strand, London WC2R ORL, England

www.penguin.com

First published in French, 1830
This translation first published in Penguin Classics 2002
025

Translations, introduction and editorial material copyright © Roger Gard, 2002
Le Rouge et le noir by Stendhal, texte établi par
Pierre-Georges Castex copyright © Garnier Flammarion, 1964
All rights reserved

Textual editing and Further Reading copyright © Robin Buss, 2002

The moral right of the translator and editor have been asserted

Set in 11/12.5 pt Monotype Fournier
Typeset by Rowland Phototypesetting Ltd, Bury St Edmunds, Suffolk
Printed in England by Clays Ltd, St Ives plc

ISBN-13: 978-0-14-044764-4

www.greenpenguin.co.uk

Penguin Books is committed to a sustainable
future for our business, our readers and our planet.
This book is made from Forest Stewardship
Council™ certified paper.

CONTENTS

CHRONOLOGY OF THE LIFE OF
HENRI MARIE BEYLE [STENDHAL]

1783 *23 January*. Born in Grenoble. The eldest child of Chérubin Beyle, an attorney and aspirant land owner, and Henriette (née Gagnon).

1786 Birth of Pauline, his favourite sister.

1790 His mother dies. Conflicts with his aunt and father. Private education, mainly with priests as tutors.

1796–9 At École Centrale in Grenoble, and excels in mathematics. 'I read Shakespeare continuously from 1796 to 1799.' Republican sentiments.

1799 Leaves for the École Polytechnique in Paris, but does not enrol.

1800 His cousin, Pierre Daru, obtains a post for him in the Ministry of War. In September he sees Milan and Italy for the first time and falls in love with it, and with Cimarosa and Mozart. He is appointed a sub-lieutentant in the Cavalry of the Army of Italy: but has no serious military experience. Meets Angela Pietragrua.

1801–2 On sick leave in Paris; resigns his commission and starts long, ongoing work on comedies for the stage.

1803 '*Vie galant*' in Paris.

1804–5 Reads much in Destutt de Tracy's *Ideology* (1801). In love with the actress Mélanie Guilbert; they live together in Marseilles while he tries a career in imports.

1806 Aided again by Pierre Daru, now a councillor of state, he is taken into the Napoleonic administration, and enters Berlin with the Emperor. Appointed to a post in Brunswick.

1807–9 More study of Shakespeare; reads Goldoni. Various literary work, at the same time rising fast in the Imperial service. Works in Vienna. Feels attracted to Madame (soon Comtesse) Daru. Misses seeing the battle of Wagram due to illness.

1810–11 Promoted to the Inspectorate of Buildings; presented at Court. During a 3-month stay in Italy becomes Angela Pietragrua's lover. Works on Italian painting, and other critical studies, as well as his comedies.

1812 To Moscow in the wake of the Grande Armée. Works there on his plays, but then takes part in the Retreat, which deeply shocks him and darkens his view of human nature.

1813 Complains of lack of recognition or promotion; but is present at the battle of Bautzen.

1814 Helps organize the defence of eastern France, particularly Grenoble, from allied advance. Subscribes to the declaration recognizing the Bourbon Restoration, but cannot get employment. Leaves for Milan.

1815 Publishes heavily derivative *Lives* of Mozart, Haydn and Metastasio; under a pseudonym, like most of his subsequent works. Lives on his pension. Unhappy in his affair with Angela Pietragrua.

1816–18 Enthusiastically lives the social and artistic life in Milan, and meets Byron, Monti, etc. Publishes a *History of Painting in Italy* and *Rome, Naples, and Florence in 1817* – the latter as 'de Stendhal'. Begins work on a life of Napoleon. The start of a grand unrequited passion for Matilde Dembowski. Avidly reads the *Edinburgh Review*.

1819 His father, with whom he had always been at odds, dies, leaving only debts. Meets the much-admired Rossini. Begins to write *On Love*.

1820–21 Suspected of being an undercover agent by both left and right, he is forced to leave Milan, and Matilde, for Paris.

1822 Publishes *On Love*. A certain amount of recognition follows. As a source of income he starts writing on the Parisian scene for English magazines. Travels in Italy and France. Member of several Paris salons, including that of the Delécluzes, where

Delacroix, Lamartine, Béranger, Mérimée, Constant, Balzac, Victor Cousin and Hugo all went.

1823 Travels in Italy and France. When not engaged in the literary, social, worldly life of Paris he visits England. The first of two pamphlets on *Racine and Shakespeare*, in defence of Romanticism. Publishes *The Life of Rossini*.

1824 Love affair with Comtesse Clémentine Curial.

1825 Death of Matilde Dembowski.

1826 Summer in England. Clémentine Curial breaks with him, he is pressed for money and in great distress.

1827 Publishes the novel *Armance* – a response to a Parisian literary joke about impotence.

1829 Publishes *Promenades In Rome*, and the first of his Italian tales, 'Vanina Vanini'. A love affair with Alberthe de Rubempré. In October conceives the idea for what became *The Red and the Black*.

1830 After welcoming the July Revolution, he is finally rather disappointingly, and after considerable difficulty, offered the consulship in Trieste. On leaving Paris, he proposes by letter to Giulia Rinieri, an offer eventually refused by her guardian. *The Red and the Black* is published in November, but dated 1831. 'Mina de Vanghel' and other stories and essays also published. The Austrian authorities distrust his liberal reputation and refuse him residence in Trieste.

1831 A month in Venice. Appointed consul in Civitavecchia, a town north of Rome, and accredited as Consul to the Holy See; for the rest of his life he fulfils his duties there, with the overseeing of trade, etc. and various diplomatic missions, but also with frequent lengthy leaves in Rome itself, and travels in Italy and France.

1833 Autobiographical work. Social life in Rome. More Italian stories, based on Renaissance manuscripts.

1834 Dictates two volumes (700 pages) of the unfinished masterpiece *Lucien Leuwen*.

1835 Awarded the Cross of the Legion of Honour. Begins writing the extraordinary autobiographical *Life of Henry Brulard*, but leaves it unfinished the following year.

1836 Goes to Paris on leave, which is eventually extended by him to more than three years. More work on Napoleon.

1837 Further *Italian Chronicles*. Publishes *Memoirs of a Tourist* – accounts of travels in France. Unfinished fragment of a novel, *The Pink and the Green*.

1838 More travels in France. Intimate with Giulia Rinieri again. Dictates *The Charterhouse of Parma* in seven weeks (4 November to 26 December).

1839 Publication of *The Charterhouse of Parma* in April and the beginning of a last, unfinished, novel, *Lamiel*. Returns to Civitavecchia; travels down to Naples with Mérimée.

1840 Sees Giulia again in Florence. Balzac delights him with great and imperious praise of *The Charterhouse of Parma*.

1841 An attack of apoplexy in March. Very lonely, though deeply attached to his two dogs. There are hints of another romance. Sick leave to return to Paris.

1842 Continues literary pursuits; but on 22 March, at seven o'clock in the evening, returning from dinner with the Minister of War, he collapses with apoplexy in the street, and dies at two in the morning without regaining consciousness. Buried in Montmartre. *Scrisse. Amò. Vissi.*

IN 1830

In October 1829, when he first had the idea for 'Julien', the tale that became *The Red and the Black*, Henri Beyle had lived near the centre of events in moving, even heroic, times. He was a man of his world. He had been a young officer in Napoleon Bonaparte's campaigns in Italy, and had later taken on considerable, though not very glamorous, administrative responsibility under the Empire, as well as pursuing literary work of many colours and kinds – plays that were never staged, the publication of heavily plagiarized musical and art criticism, books on travel and works of introspection. He had courageously participated in the atrocious retreat of Napoleon's Grande Armée from Moscow in 1812, as well as being the author of a most clever but obscure novel, *Armance* (1827).[1]

Beyle had been a dandy in Paris with no regular income; he had had a short career as a merchant: he was shortly to be appointed French consul in Civitavecchia, a small town just north of Rome. His life abounded with new starts, erotic escapades, friendships, aspirations and dissatisfactions. He had talked a lot and posed a lot. He would quite frequently fall in love, though in a curiously shy yet worldly way, about which he wrote a now famous treatise, *De l'amour* (1822). One gains the impression that people did not know quite how to take him, that he was perceived as a character, a wit and a thinker, that he was distinguished, but it was hard to say quite how. He loved using pseudonyms, of which Stendhal is one, but Louis-Alexandre-César Bombet was another. He was a funny man. He wore a toupee. He travelled a lot, was unmarried, not well off, had lived much in

Italy – he loved the country so well that he wanted *Arrigo Beyle, Milanese* to be carved on his tombstone.[2] At forty-six, which was considered much nearer to old age than it would be today, he was not quite a failure, but, in spite of all his varied experience and his intermittently fierce ambition, he had never shown anything that one could properly call a great success, let alone a display of startling genius.

Now, in about a year, in 1829–30, he produced *Le Rouge et le noir* (*The Red and the Black*), which, as well as being so obviously a thrilling double love story, pulsating with the energy of youth seen through the eye of experience, is one of the greatest European novels, and one of the most fervently admired.

The immediate germ of the book appears to have been its author's recollection of the sad story, in a *Gazette* of 1827, of Antoine Berthet, a handsome young peasant who had become tutor to a middle-class family. This and other little contemporary scandals involving murder and runaway heiresses, duels and the interpenetration of classes, fermented in Stendhal's imagination. As the twin subtitles of the novel ('Chronicle of 1830' and 'Chronicle of the XIXth Century') indicate, a larger aim was to draw on his long experience for a more general portrait of the manners and morals – the soul, really – of France at that time.

As the reader realizes from almost the first page, this is not a comforting portrait. It is satirical and sharp, even when locally affectionate; lively, but also a picture of corruption, grossness, illiberality and deceit in municipality, Church and state. A portrait of inauthenticity, of a tottering reactionary monarchy being undermined from above and below, profoundly shocked by and quailing from the titanic shadows of Napoleon and the Revolution, and riddled with fear, ennui, greed and short-term self-interest.

Even the liberals in opposition are part of the mess. In the very months the book was being produced – probably just before Stendhal was writing the thirteenth chapter of the second book – they rose and the Bourbons fell in the risings of July 1830, to be replaced by a *juste milieu*, the bourgeois monarchy of Louis-Philippe, not, to our distant political eyes, very much different or better.

No wonder that *The Red and the Black*, with its brusque style and bold accounts of moral transgression, was not very enthusiastically received when it was published. But good stories outlast particular sets of facts. Nowadays Stendhal's dramatization of 1830 through the strangely exemplary, rocketing career of the beautiful young peasant Julien Sorel seems not in the least gloomy or disaffecting – in contrast to a later book concerned with an in some ways comparable career, Flaubert's *L'Éducation sentimentale* (1869). Julien's tale is touching and engaging, romantic as much as cynical, and eventually sublime. History is only its medium.[3]

The picture of French Restoration society, though fascinating in itself, is not, of course, what readers go to the book for, any more than they read Jane Austen's *Persuasion* primarily for its devastating portrait of Regency Bath.

In art – as opposed to anecdote – there is a mysterious kind of suspense which survives pre-knowledge of the plot. There cannot be many theatre-goers who do not have at least some idea of what will happen in *Macbeth* – yet it is still exciting, awe-inspiring. (And if a work is unknown, a familiarity with the conventions of the genre will often guide the audience to a sense of what is likely to happen.

Yet there is also the legitimate – and important – suspense of the real first time, the privilege and excitement, not to be forgone, of not knowing what will happen next. Stendhal himself wrote of the urge to stay up all night with a novel. He also regarded revealing the plot in advance as theft; it is obviously so, and therefore: A WARNING:

First-time readers are advised to stop here.

– and perhaps return when the novel is finished. This is not the kind of book in which you need to be instructed before you read it.

STENDHAL'S MANNER

I

But, having read, one may desire to analyse, to think more about the mental set that drives the book and is at the core of Stendhal's vision of the world – and therefore his narrative method. His plain-seeming prose has, after all, been the subject of critical and scholarly commentary on an almost industrial scale (see, for only a few examples, the list of Selected Further Reading). Here a few details may suggest and affirm the ever fresh and vigorous nature of his genius.

We very often hear of Stendhal's *irony*; as with Jane Austen (whose work was probably unknown to him, but who has been called his severer elder sister) that quality has become part of a possibly formidable image.

Irony is not easy to define in the abstract, and I am not concerned to define it; but one of its features – as in *dramatic irony* – is that some thing (a person, an action, a sequence, a thought, etc.) is seen, at once or in quick succession, in more than a single way. Such a way of seeing, and presenting, is indeed central to the way *The Red and the Black* is told. What at first might look like a plain authorial tale, enlivened by free indirect speech, soliloquy and dialogue, is actually a tissue of intermingled angles and points of view. And the reader very soon acquires – and quite without stress – the sense that none of these viewpoints is automatically or authoritatively right, to be taken as flat and final, but that they achieve their truth in relation to each other and to likelihood. Perhaps that is why Stendhal's characters seem so free from authorial over-determination, the book so airy and light.

To take a famous passage (quoted at some length to retain a sense of the rhythm and flow) Julien, starting out in life, is on his way to the de Rênal household for the first time:

... This was the young man of nineteen – but so seemingly frail that one would have taken him for no more than seventeen – who, carrying his little parcel under his arm, entered the magnificent church of Verrières.

He found it sombre and solitary. To mark a festival, all the church windows had been covered with crimson cloth. The sun's rays shone through to produce a dim light, most pious and imposing. Julien shivered. Alone in the church, he established himself in the pew that had the finest appearance. It bore the arms of M. de Rênal.

On the prayer desk Julien noticed a fragment of printed paper, spread out as though to be read. He directed his eyes towards it and saw:

Details of the execution and the last moments of Louis Jenrel, executed at Besançon, on the . . .

The paper was torn off. On the other side could be seen the first words of a line, which were: *The first step.*

− Who could have put this paper here? said Julien. Poor devil, he added with a sigh, his name ends like mine . . . and he crumpled the paper.

Leaving, Julien thought he saw blood next to the holy water stoup − it was holy water that had been spilled: the refraction from the red blinds covering the windows gave it the appearance of blood.

Eventually Julien was ashamed of his secret terror.

− Am I a coward! he said to himself, *To arms!*

This phrase, so often repeated in the Surgeon-major's accounts of battles, represented the heroic for Julien. He raised himself up and walked rapidly towards M. de Rênal's house.

In spite of these fine resolves, from the moment he saw it twenty paces away, he was seized with an overpowering timidity. The iron grille was open; to him it seemed magnificent; and it was up to him to enter in. [I. 5]

Now this passage is often cited partly because, in *The Red and the Black*, coming to a place − to the Rênal house, the seminary, the Hôtel de La Mole − is a *motif*, a marker of Julien's progress, and partly because it contains unusual things: the proleptic menace in the red-blinded church, the near-anagram and *the first step*. These are elements in a web of delicate symbolic overtones that are purposefully touched on from time to time in what only seems to be a casually factual narrative − the controlled suggestiveness of light and colour, for example, of freedom and enclosure, of the heights of mountains and high-level lodgings, and of distance.

But in other respects the narrative texture is, particularly in its deft briskness, quite typical: first, we are given the character from above and outside, as it were, a sight of what the world's impression might have been (only *seventeen*!); then Julien's general response to the look of the church, his shiver and defiant choice of pew; then the strange voice of the paper, Julien's puzzlement, question and fright; then fresh defiance and resolution; then more sensitive doubts – then onward. What *happens* in the fiction is interwoven with the perceptions and feelings of a resolute but fearful boy, cheering himself up with the revolutionary and Napoleonic battlecry and mistaking bourgeois solidity for magnificence. However:

. . . Julien was not the only person whose feelings were disturbed by his arrival at the house. Mme de Rênal's great sensitivity was upset by the idea of this stranger who, by the nature of his duties, would find himself constantly coming between her children and herself. She was used to having her sons sleep in her room. That morning, many tears had been shed as she saw their little beds being carried to the apartment destined for the tutor. In vain she had asked her husband that the bed of little Stanislas-Xavier, the youngest, be brought back to her room.

Feminine delicacy was pushed to an excess in Mme de Rênal. She evoked for herself the most disagreeable image of a gross and ill-kempt being, empowered to scold her children solely because he knew Latin, a barbarous language for the sake of which her sons were to be chastised. [I. 5]

Here a statement of Mme de Rênal's mood and sensitivity flows into a quick flashback to that morning's painful but somehow pleasing little scene, which in its turn introduces the confident authorial appeal to commonly agreed values that '[f]eminine delicacy was pushed to an excess in Mme de Rênal' – and most of the rest modulates in and out of her mind. Again, a casually omniscient narrator is in play with character, scene and opinion.

Having seen Edmund Kean play *Othello* in London, Stendhal is said to have wondered at the way in which the great actor seemed to be discovering his words as he went along. But he himself is rather like that as a writer. And, as with an intermittent syncopation in music, or a dotted rhythm, the emphasis, even on re-reading, is often not quite where you would expect, the reader's attention is always kept fresh and alert. Sometimes, as in a famous sentence a few pages on from the passage just quoted, the shift of views is almost instantaneous: 'The children adored him: he did not care for them; his mind was elsewhere' (I. 7).

But Stendhal is not, I think, a Shakespearian writer.[4] Perhaps in spite of his own critical leanings, as expressed in two pamphlets on *Racine and Shakespeare* (1823 and 1825), Stendhal – unlike later novelists such as George Eliot, who pause to evoke and explore psychological states through metaphor – relies on a confident eighteenth-century vocabulary of the psyche, a vocabulary of entities such as *âme, ésprit, amour, transport*, or the condition of being *hors de [lui]* (beside oneself), etc., which exist somewhere between the very specific and the abstract, and which appear to be backed by an inherited confidence in their correspondence to the real. They are deployed with dazzling skill and sometimes give the impression of a strength derived from their usage reaching right back to the seventeenth century in France.[5] It is this that allows those sweeping *aperçus* and generalizations about the psyche that we may think of as characteristically French. Yet in Stendhal they always seem fresh, always new, always free – as though they were just being written. Mme de Rênal's *délicatesse de femme* (above) is a small instance. Elaborated pieces of wisdom such as, 'Love generated in the mind is doubtless more intelligent than true love, but it has only flashes of enthusiasm; . . . far from scattering the thoughts it is constructed by the power of thought alone . . .' (II. 19) are only larger and grander manifestations of the same impulse.

A danger in this swift and often paradoxical style might be a degeneration into what Turgenev, writing to Tolstoy about Dostoevsky, called 'backward cliché . . . an easy method of seeming original' whereby *man meets lion–blenches–runs*, is automatically turned into *man meets lion–flushes–advances*. But in *The Red and the Black* the pressure for fluent thought and exact expression, as opposed to mere verbal dexterity, is so powerful that this does not happen. Stendhal's demands on his prose are more like those of another great Russian, Pushkin – 'ideas and more ideas, without which brilliant expressions avail nothing'.

Valued highly by Julien and M. de La Mole and Mathilde is the spiritual and moral superiority of the spontaneous, the unexpected (the *imprévu*) – contrasting with a virtual horror of the predictable. In consonance with this, unexpected turns – which are nevertheless, as I say, the reverse of mere paradox because they create meaning rather than complicate it – are characteristic of the best Stendhalian manner. There is a famous moment in his later, unfinished, novel *Lucien Leuwen*, when the heroine, suddenly feeling jealous of a potential rival, studies her face in the mirror, finds it ugly and loves Lucien even more for the good taste she thinks he displays in loving her rival; but by then readers will have come almost to expect the drastic psychological beauty of such moments.

As these examples show, one of the great secrets of reading *The Red and the Black* intelligently – of course, this is true of many novels – is to be alert always to the questions *'Where does this come from?' 'Who is speaking?' 'Whom does this point of view serve?'* The questions sound simple; they may often turn out to be hard to answer; but the secret is to be continuously aware that they are pertinent.

Like any good comic satirical writer, Stendhal, even at his most dry, deep or despairing, puts the delighted reader into a state of exclusive collusion, a flattering sense that they together constitute an élite of two – or, perhaps, a meeting of the happy few. But it would be misleading to imply that this mode is limited only to the swift, often comic perception:

The pure air of the high mountains spoke to his soul of serenity, even of joy. The Mayor of Verrières was certainly still, in his eyes, the representative of all the rich and insolent people on earth; but Julien felt that the hate that had disturbed him, despite the violence of its onset, had nothing personal in it. If he should cease to see M. de Rênal, he would have forgotten him in a week or so – him, his château, his dogs, his children and all his family. I have forced him, I don't know how, to make a very great sacrifice. What! – more than fifty écus a year! – and only a moment before that I had got myself out of the greatest danger. That's two victories in one day; the second has no merit – I will have to find out why it happened. But time enough tomorrow for such tedious enquiries.

Standing upright on his great rock, Julien contemplated the sky, glowing with the August sun. Cicadas were chirruping in the countryside below the rock, and when they ceased all around him was silence. He could see twenty leagues of country spread out before his feet. From time to time, a sparrowhawk from the huge rocks above his head made itself visible, describing its vast circles in silence. Julien's eye automatically followed this bird of prey. Its calm and powerful flight impressed him – he envied that strength, he envied that isolation.

It was the destiny of Napoleon – would it one day be his? [I. 10]

Here the grander view that we are invited to share, standing right back after Julien's hotly youthful self-examinations, is that of a father.

Perhaps it is precisely because of these shifts of focus, because it is the characters who feel things and there is an all-dominant narrator, that for even largely unsympathetic characters like M. de Rênal, the Abbé de Frilair and even the mass of Julien's fellow seminarists, one may detect a less absolute scorn, and rather more understanding, than most commentators seem to feel?

MANNER AND STRUCTURE

More centrally, the shifting focus, coupled with an athletic spareness of physical description and scene-painting, is not only the manner of Stendhal's prose but is also writ large into the structure of the book.

At certain crucial points in the looping form of Julien's progression from place to place (A(Verrières)–B(Besançon)–C(Paris)–A/B), the narrative is suddenly elided, displaced or withdrawn – and always with a purpose.

When, after his desperately willed campaign to conquer the beautiful, naive and sensitive Mme de Rênal – already, even by this early stage so moving a presence for the reader, and surely one of the finest portraits of a young woman, as opposed to a girl, in literature – Julien at last forces himself to enter her bedroom, we might expect a scene of Machiavellian triumph, à la Pierre Laclos. Instead:

. . . Julien forgot his empty schemes and returned to playing the part natural to him: not to please so charming a woman seemed to him the greatest of misfortunes. His only response to her reproaches was to throw himself at her feet and embrace her knees. As she spoke to him with great severity, he melted into tears.

A few hours later, when Julien left Mme de Rênal's room, one could say, in the language of novels, that he had nothing left to desire. [I. 15]

The love scene itself, aside from a few references, is virtually absent, seemingly left untreated as a cliché which might obscure the real points being dramatized. The real points concern the characters' thoughts and feelings. The characteristic near paradox of 'it was precisely that which made Julien a superior being that stopped him enjoying the happiness that lay at his feet' is followed most powerfully by the religious implications for Mme de Rênal ('damned without remission' etc.). And for the reader the most resonant and vivid physical event between Julien and Mme de Rênal remains always the moment when he first grasps her hand in the garden at Vergy.

The same with the haughty and dazzling gothic dandy Mathilde. With her, as with him, and after another tense build-up, 'the language of novels' constrains their first, stringently comic, night together into a literary occasion of melodrama and farce – Julien confesses to being laden with 'All sorts of arms and pocket pistols' and Mathilde that 'I always have a supply of ropes in my room' – but also a literary occasion of the most painful kind:

After long-drawn-out doubts and hesitations, which to a superficial observer would have seemed born of a most decided hatred – so hard it is for even so strong a will to overcome the feelings of what a woman owes herself – Mathilde ended by becoming his complaisant mistress.

The truth is that their raptures were somewhat *willed*. [II. 16]

This elision in the description is not a disembodiment for reasons of prudery or suchlike – or even for the Henry Jamesian reason that we feel and see most when left the freedom to imagine – but because of the implicit valuation of what is significant in experience. The focus is on the exigencies of the excruciating psychological mess these brilliant young people – lovers? – have forced upon one another.

Perhaps the most powerful of all these (numerous) emphases by displacement, however, is at the very end. Here, the concern is not love, but violent death. Events have swiftly rushed, rather in the style of an overture by Stendhal's younger contemporary Hector Berlioz, to a brilliant first, and false, climax, and seeming conclusion. All Julien's ambitions are on the point of being realized with a huge worldly success – success in the style of a novel: 'Well, after all, thought he, my romance is at an end' (II. 34). But this is not the end; the ground shifts, there is a stutter from the past – and he must overturn his world and go on to face a very different fate. It is a fine day. The reader hears no drum roll and sees no guillotine, but:

Never had that head been so poetic as at the moment it was to fall. The sweetest hours he had known in the woods at Vergy long ago came crowding into his thoughts with wonderful intensity.

Everything passed off simply, appropriately, and with no affectation in his part. [II. 45]

This moving reticence needs no commentary.

JULIEN'S FATE

What the texture of the prose and its reflection in the structure of the book have in common is, of course, a kind of higher surprise. And this principle seems in a way central to Julien's fate.

Stendhal's engagement with Julien is not entirely dissimilar to that of Jane Austen with Emma – 'I am going to take a heroine whom no one but myself will much like.' The way forward in both cases has to do with a kind of instinctive generosity.

What unpromising material! – a sly, self-centred, devious, arrogant and coldly hypocritical young man, with a chip on his shoulder as big as an outcrop of the Jura. Yet his vindication (if, indeed, we do feel him vindicated – which is not always the case) is not primarily a matter of teasing out causes, and therefore excuses, and therefore compassion for an initially unprepossessing object, such as might be created in George Eliot or Tolstoy, but of coming to see that object's true nature.

Realizing this is complicated by the observation that many of the characters in *The Red and the Black*, particularly Julien, are deliberate role players rather than stable straightforward entities.[6] And, whether consciously or not, their identities shift.

But what kind of a hypocrite is Julien, and how consistent are his roles?

One of the key elements in his development from callow and frightened adolescent to triumphant and glamorous *arriviste* does *not* shift. It seems to be a constant substratum of his nature, which flares up from time to time: the reader will have noticed that with Madame de Rênal in her bedroom for the first time Julien 'forgot his empty schemes and returned to playing the part natural to him' – and that was the reason for his success. It is one of the larger ironies of his story that, except when he is obeying the instructions of Prince Korasoff and using Madame de Fervaques as a pawn in his struggle with another great role player, the perversely exquisite romantic intellectual Mathilde, this would-be calculator and cold exploiter progresses chiefly when he is moved or when he is in a panic.

Together with his looks, intelligence and capacity for work, it tends to be what he deems his weakness that advances him, not any accomplished hypocrisy. We see that Abbé Chélan takes to a lost boy, Amanda Binet is attracted by a flustered little peasant, he first excites the interest of Abbé Pirard by collapsing on the floor, M. de La Mole's 'deaf mute' steps on his heels and falls off his horse, and so on – though, of course, the experience is nothing like so neat as so pat a listing suggests, especially in the case of the Marquis, who in a complicated way, against his cherished aristocratic blood, as it were, is creating a second and more talented son.

Julien's *faiblesse*, and his failures in his self-imposed *devoir* as Machiavel-from-the-provinces, are sometimes genuine failures; but usually the duty he fails to do is swept aside by what is unforeseen – by his drastic flashes of warmth or honesty. The creepy person he *thinks* he should be would of course be able to sanction or overlook M. Valenod's gross greed, would never quarrel with the Mayor, would abase himself successfully in front of Abbé Castanède, and so on. But Julien can't do this; with them, he fails. It is what begins to make one love him.

This characteristic forms a constant counterpoint in Julien's story, rather as in that of his creator, who confessed to himself (in *Henry Brulard* [1835]) that 'I had and still have the most aristocratic tastes. I would do anything to make the people happy but I would rather . . . spend a fortnight of each month in prison than live with petty shopkeepers.' It has two interesting corollaries, and they are linked.

The first is that Julien's careerism never actually chooses to embrace either money or advancement. Is he really the clever calculator he pretends to himself that he is, or is he only taking often comical refuge behind one of the models or means of defence – Rousseau? Napoleon? the Church? – he can find in such a world? It is true that the lieutenant of Hussars, M. le Chevalier Julien Sorel de Vernaye – whose dizzy success the candid reader would probably admit to enjoying – does very temporarily blaze into brilliant fortune, but this is often because of his unruly instinctive capacities to feel and be generous, because someone likes or loves him, because of what he thinks of – and the narrator describes – as *faiblesse*.

Second, and accordingly, when, at the start of the long darkening climax of the book – in Julien's *peripeteia* – the letter supposed to have been written to the Marquis by Mme de Rênal confronts this chevalier with a public image of himself as an odious little Tartuffe, his world explodes. That the image is distorted, we know. But it is devastating because it is so nearly the truth; it exploits the fact that things happen to him because he is able to 'seek out and then seduce the most influential woman there', i.e. 'because someone likes or loves him'; it is the exact image of that possible other self he had set out to be, and often flatters himself he is just about to succeed in becoming. He cannot bear it. Whatever one's view of his subsequent actions,[7] the one thing that is undisputed about his rapt and doomed flight back to Verrières is that it cannot possibly benefit him in any worldly way. As to what happens there and afterwards, there are many opinions: my own is that the flight becomes, with all its blunders and fluctuations, an increasingly clear and courageous movement to distil truth and sincerity, and a tragic integrity fought out to the very end – an unlikely and unforeseen fate for an angry 'little hypocrite', but none the less luminously true. The cynical and disaffected plebeian outsider, who has become perhaps the real flower of his generation, now turns right inward. Julien could probably escape back into the world of Valenod, but of course he will not.

What! so that's all there is to it? Stendhal's protagonists so often exclaim after experiencing one of life's major crises. And now, for Julien, what matters at all? Well, love – and affection – do. His defensive pride persists to the end; perhaps only the women, perhaps only Mme de Rênal, can become indifferent to what the world thinks. But by this time it is increasingly difficult to distinguish pride from a peculiar and touching nobility.

Finally, as to the man of forty-six, as to his celebrated predictions that he would only be understood by the Happy Few in 1860 or in 1880 or in 1935, we may rejoice with Stendhal's shade. The admirers of this novel, so little admired by contemporaries, it seems – though Goethe acknowledged it and Balzac deeply gratified its author by his championship of *The Charterhouse of Parma* (1839) – have tended to be the leading spirits of their age. *The Red and the Black* has been read with passion by Baudelaire, Tolstoy and Nietzsche; by Proust and D. H. Lawrence and Valéry . . . And now, for many years, what would be eccentric, what would be shocking, would be not to be thrilled by Julien Sorel and his world.

ROGER GARD

NOTES

1. *but obscure novel, Armance*: Obscure not because of its manner, which is brilliantly lucid, but because the central characteristic of the hero's psyche is never revealed in the text.

2. *carved on his tombstone*: A wish eventually realized in 1892 – in Paris.

3. *only its medium*: On the subject of the difficulty of getting details right in history or biography, Stendhal later noted (in 1834) that '[the philosopher] M. de Tracy told me: there's no more truth save in the novel'.

4. *not . . . a Shakespearian writer*: Though the best account of this I have read, Chapter 3 of Geoffrey Strickland's *Stendhal: The Education of a Novelist* (Cambridge: Cambridge University Press, 1974), does not agree.

5. *seventeenth century in France*: In the Flammarion edition translated here, P.-G. Castex identifies multiple allusions to Racine buried in the text (and, of course, hard to indicate in a translation). Martin Turnell discusses this subject in *The Novel in France* (London: Hamish Hamilton, 1950).

6. *rather than stable straightforward entities*: This is made perhaps even a little too explicit when, in II. 42, Julien is surprised and amused by a small voice of negation in his head.

7. *his subsequent actions*: There is a very extensive historical debate about the interpretation of the whole of the end of the book – moving, essentially, from condemnation of Julien to admiration – which is very ably discussed in Roger Pearson's *Stendhal's Violin* (Oxford: Clarendon Press, 1988).

SELECTED FURTHER READING

Compiled by Robin Buss

Bloom, Harold (ed.), *Stendhal's 'Red and Black'* (New York: Chelsea House, 1991)

Hemmings, F. W. J., *Stendhal: A Study of His Novels* (Oxford: Clarendon Press, 1964)

Jefferson, Ann, *Reading Realism in Stendhal* (Cambridge: Cambridge Univesity Press, 1988)

Keates, Jonathan, *Stendhal* (London: Sinclair-Stevenson, 1994)

Pearson, Roger, *Stendhal's Violin* (Oxford: Clarendon Press, 1988)

Strickland, Geoffrey, *Stendhal: The Education of a Novelist* (Cambridge: Cambridge University Press, 1974)

Tillett, Margaret, *Stendhal: The Background to His Novels* (Oxford: Oxford University Press, 1971)

Turnell, Martin, *The Novel in France* (London: Hamish Hamilton, 1950)

Wood, Michael, *Stendhal* (London: Elek, 1971)

NOTES ON THE TEXT AND TRANSLATION

TEXT

The text followed is that of the first edition of *Le Rouge et le noir* of November 1830, edited for *Classiques Garnier* by Pierre-Georges Castex (Paris, 1964; revised 1989). Professor Castex has considered carefully the later corrections and commentaries made by Stendhal himself, which were the product of the author's desire to render the texture of the novel softer, more accurate and more pliable for contemporaries. After his first re-reading in 1831 he noted that, in reaction to the sonorous Romantic prose of Chateaubriand and others, he had been thrown into an 'abrupt, harsh, jerky, hard' manner – 'the author thought of nothing but pursuing his idea'. By 1835–6 he still thought the novel was written in 'too jerky a style' (as he said in *The Life of Henry Brulard*), and made emendations and comments that run to about seventeen pages in the so-called 'Civitavecchia Copy'. These were incorporated after his death by Jules Marsan. But, following the example of Henri Martineau, Castex prefers the lively unrevised spontaneity of the first printing – for all its brusqueness, repetitions and petty infelicities – and so has moved these interesting, though actually quite minor, interventions from the text to an appendix. Further, he tells us that, apart from the correction of a few obvious small lapses and errors, he has rejected the sometimes anachronistic emendations of other later nineteenth-century and modern editions, particularly in punctuation, and reverted to the original.

TRANSLATION

In a similar spirit, no attempt has been made to pretend that this is a book of modern English prose.

Reading inevitably involves more or less active interpretation by the reader; and a translation is a stronger act of interpretation because its results will coerce subsequent readers. It *must* interpret, and limit, at the basic level: words, ordinary words, like *bien* for example, often do not have one single, simple, 'faithful' meaning. Choices between the feeling, nuance and emphasis of a series of synonyms in a particular context, or between varying syntactical structures, etc., have to be made sentence after sentence – and the reader ignorant of the original language is thus shut off from the hovering possibilities and alternatives that might suggest themselves to someone who knows the language.

In an ideal world the translator would be one who was conscious of this, and who was also native in both French and English, loved and understood Stendhal, was steeped in the literature of both countries in the early nineteenth century, had the ear and the gift of pastiche, and an active conscience.

However, in the absence of most of these qualities, I have acted on my impression that one of the pleasures in reading the translation of a classic comes from hearing behind it the ghost of the original language. Probably the best model of an appropriate English manner is not a translation at all, but Robert Louis Stevenson's very subtly French narrator in his unfinished novel about a French adventurer in England, *St Ives* (1897).

So, when given the choice, I have leant towards a fairly literal, hard rendering of Stendhal's syntax and vocabulary, keeping close to the somewhat informal and conversational tone of the original while nevertheless, I hope, making the sense lively enough, and natural. 'Naturalness in manner and speech' was Stendhal's professed ideal, as opposed, perhaps, to the cultivation of a fine style. And, in contrast to most modern translations, I have kept to the original, French, method of marking off speech and internal speech. Stendhal very occasionally uses inverted commas when a phrase already in the text is repeated or cited from the past, but that is his only use of them. To indicate the beginning of a speech said out loud a dash – is used, most usually at the start of a new paragraph: otherwise he relies on one's sense of what is going on, plus the repeated use of prompt phrases such as 'he said to himself', etc., bounded by commas. I have followed this exactly, with the addition of one or two dashes.

It might be expected that the result would confuse a modern reader of English by its density and unfamiliarity, but the effect is in practice, I think, to produce a swifter, less formal narrative flow which easily engages the reader's active collaboration because it refrains from breaking up the rhythm and tidying up the text with constant quotation marks (which would tend to enforce a tiny pause on each, frequent, occasion). Also the text looks more authentic.

The same feeling has led me to stick, on the whole, and when they are easily comprehensible to the English reader, to the original titles and honorifics, etc. – Comte, Duc, Abbé, and so on – though sometimes it has seemed preferable to translate them.

The Red and the Black

CHRONICLE OF 1830

CHRONICLE OF THE XIXTH
CENTURY

Contents

CONTENTS

CONTENTS

Editor's Notice[1]

This work was just about to appear when the great events of July[2] intervened to give every mind a direction scarcely sympathetic to the play of the imagination. We have cause to believe that the ensuing pages were written in 1827.[3]

BOOK ONE

Truth, the bitter truth
DANTON[1]

CHAPTER THE FIRST

A Small Town

> Put thousands together
> Less bad,
> But the cage less gay.
>
> HOBBES[2]

The little town of Verrières could pass for one of the prettiest in the Franche-Comté.[3] Its white houses, with their pointed red-tiled roofs, are spread along the slope of a hill whose every undulation is marked by clumps of healthy chestnut trees. The river Doubs flows a few hundred feet beneath fortifications built long ago by the Spaniards, but now in ruins.

Verrières is sheltered to the north by a high mountain, one of the spurs of the Jura. The ragged summits of the Verra become covered in snow after the first cold days in October. A torrential stream dashing down from the mountain runs through Verrières before discharging into the Doubs, and supplies power to a large number of sawmills – an industry which is extremely uncomplicated, but which provides a certain well-being for the greater part of the inhabitants, who are more like peasants than townspeople. But it is not these sawmills that have made the little town rich. It is owing to the manufacture of a painted cloth, known as Mulhouse, that, since the fall of Napoleon, a general affluence has allowed the refurbishment of nearly all the façades of the houses in Verrières.

Hardly have you entered the town than you are deafened by the racket of a noisy machine of terrible aspect. Twenty massive hammers, falling with a boom that makes the street tremble, are raised up in the air again by a wheel driven by the torrential current. Every

II

day each of these hammers makes I don't know how many thousands of nails. Fresh, pretty young girls feed the gigantic hammer blows with little pieces of iron that are promptly transformed into nails. This crude-looking industry is one of those that most surprises a traveller penetrating for the first time into the mountains between France and Switzerland. If, on entering Verrières, the traveller asks who owns that fine nail factory which deafens people who ascend the main street, someone will drawl in reply: *Oh! that's M. the Mayor's.*

However short a time the traveller lingers in this main street of Verrières – which climbs from the Doubs towards the summit of the hill – it is a hundred to one that he will notice the appearance of a tall man with an important and preoccupied air.

At the sight of him all hats are swiftly raised. His hair is greying, and he is dressed in grey. He wears numerous Orders; he has a large forehead, an aquiline nose, and altogether his features do not lack a certain regularity: at first sight you may even find that he combines the dignity of a small town mayor with the sort of charm that may still be felt in a man of forty-eight or fifty. Soon, however, the traveller from Paris is disconcerted by an air of complacency and self-sufficiency, blended, in a way hard to define, with a sense of limitation and lack of imagination. One feels, in the end, that the gifts of such a man are confined to getting paid most precisely what is due to him, and to paying what he himself owes as late as possible.

Such is the Mayor of Verrières, M. de Rênal. After having crossed the road with solemn step, he enters the town hall and disappears from the traveller's view. But, if the latter pursues his walk a hundred yards further up, he will notice a rather fine-looking house and, through an iron railing next to it, magnificent gardens. Above this the line of the horizon is formed by the hills of Burgundy, and might have been designed expressly for the pleasure of the eye. This view enables the traveller to forget the tainted atmosphere of petty commercial concerns which had begun to stifle him.

He is told that the house belongs to M. de Rênal. The Mayor of Verrières owes this handsome freestone dwelling, which is just in the process of completion, to the profits from his great nail factory. His family, it is said, is Spanish, very old and, it is claimed, was established in the neighbourhood long before the conquest by Louis XIV.

Since 1815 he has blushed to be an industrialist: 1815 made him Mayor of Verrières.[4] The terraced walls which hold up the various parts of the magnificent gardens that descend, stage by stage, right down to the Doubs, are likewise the reward of M. de Rênal's skill in dealing in iron.

In France you do not expect to find anything like the picturesque gardens that surround the manufacturing towns of Germany – Leipzig, Frankfurt, Nuremberg, etc. In Franche-Comté the more one erects walls – the more one makes one's land bristle with stones piled up one upon the other – the more one acquires rights to the respect of one's neighbours. M. de Rênal's gardens, replete with walls, are admired the more because he has spent a fortune on the purchase of some little bits of land on which they stand. For example, that sawmill whose odd position on the bank of the Doubs struck you when entering Verrières, and where you noticed the name SOREL written in gigantic characters on a plank which dominates its roof – six years ago, that used to occupy the place where just now the wall for the fourth terrace of M. de Rênal's gardens is going up.

In spite of his pride, M. the Mayor had been obliged to make repeated diplomatic approaches to old Sorel, a hard and stubborn peasant; and had had to hand over a pile of golden louis to get him to move his works somewhere else. As to the *public* stream which turned the mill, M. de Rênal obtained permission for it to be diverted by means of the credit he enjoyed in Paris. This favour had come to him after the election of 182–.

He had given Sorel, five hundred yards down the banks of the Doubs, four acres for one. And, although this site was much more advantageous for his trade in deal planks, Père Sorel, as he was called since he became rich, had discovered the knack of obtaining a sum of 6,000 francs from the impatience and the *mania for ownership* that fired his neighbour.

It is true that this arrangement had been criticized by the deeper minds of the district. On one occasion, a Sunday about four years ago, M. de Rênal, returning from church in his mayoral robes, glimpsed old Sorel from a distance, surrounded by his three sons and smiling as he looked at him. This smile marked a black day in the soul of M. the Mayor; ever since then he knew that he could have got a better deal.

To be publicly esteemed in Verrières, the essential thing is, while building lots of walls, never adopt any plan brought up from Italy by those masons who cross the gorges of the Jura on their way to Paris every spring.[5] Such an innovation would give the rash builder a permanent reputation as a *hothead*, and would for ever damn him among those wise and moderate people who dispense reputations in Franche-Comté.

In truth, these wise people exercise the most tedious *despotism*; it is what is behind this nasty word that makes residence in small towns impossible for those who have lived in that great republic we call Paris.

The tyranny of opinion – and what opinion! – is as *stupid* in the small towns of France as it is in the United States of America.

CHAPTER 2

A Mayor

> Prestige! Is that nothing, sir? The respect of fools, the
> astonishment of children, the envy of the rich, the scorn of
> the wise.   BARNAVE[1]

Fortunately for M. de Rênal's reputation as an administrator, an
immense *containing wall* was needed for the public walk that stretches
the length of the hill a hundred feet above the Doubs. From this fine
position there is one of the most picturesque views in France. But
every spring torrents of rain used to wash over the walk, hollowing
out fissures that rendered it virtually impassable. This inconvenience,
felt by everybody, presented M. de Rênal with the happy need to
immortalize his administration by means of a wall twenty feet high
and seventy or eighty yards long.

The parapet of this wall, about which M. de Rênal had been
obliged to make three journeys to Paris because the Minister of the
Interior before last had declared himself the sworn enemy of the
public walk in Verrières, now rose four feet from the ground. And,
as if to defy all ministers past and present, it is now being dressed
with slabs of stone.

How often, musing on the parties I had left in Paris the day before,
and leaning my chest against these great blocks of fine bluish-grey
stone, my gaze has plunged into the vale of the Doubs! Further on,
on the left bank, there wind five or six valleys in whose depths the
eye can clearly pick out little rivulets. One can see them, having
cascaded from waterfall to waterfall, fall into the Doubs. The sun is
very hot in those mountains; when it shines at its height the traveller's
reveries are shaded by the magnificent plane trees on the terrace.

These owe their swift growth and magnificent blue-green foliage to the imported soil that the Mayor had put in behind his huge containing wall, when, in the face of opposition from the Municipal Council, he had the walk enlarged by more than six feet (although he is an Ultra and I am a liberal, I honour him for it), which is why, in his opinion and that of M. Valenod, who has the good fortune to be director of the poorhouse at Verrières, this terrace can challenge comparison with that of Saint-Germain-en-Laye.

For my own part, I find only one thing to complain of in LOYALTY PROMENADE – one reads this official name in fifteen or twenty places, inscribed on marble plaques which have earned M. de Rênal another decoration – I deplore the barbarous manner in which the authorities clip and pollard these vigorous planes back to the quick. They really ask no better than to be allowed to assume the magnificent shapes one sees in England, instead of being made to resemble the most common kitchen garden plants with their lowered, rounded and flattened heads. But a mayor's will is absolute, and twice a year the trees belonging to the town are mercilessly amputated. The local liberals pretend, though they exaggerate, that the hand of the official gardener has become more severe ever since the Curé Maslon developed the habit of claiming the profits from the cutting.

This young ecclesiastic had been sent from Besançon a few years before to keep an eye on the Abbé[2] Chélan and a few other local parish priests. An old Surgeon-major of the Army of Italy[3] who had retired to Verrières, and whose way of life was, according to the Mayor, Jacobin[4] and Bonapartist, dared to complain one day of the periodical mutilation of these beautiful trees.

– I like shade, replied M. de Rênal, with a touch of that hauteur appropriate to speaking to a surgeon who was a member of the Legion of Honour;[5] I like shade, I have caused *my* trees to be pruned to give shade, and I cannot imagine that a tree is made for anything else, when, unlike the useful walnut, it *doesn't bring in any money*.

Here is the mighty phrase that determines everything at Verrières: BRING IN MONEY. All by itself it represents the habitual thinking of more than three-quarters of the inhabitants.

To bring in money is the motive that rules everything in this little town you thought so pretty. The visiting stranger, charmed by the beauty of the fresh, deep valleys that surround it, imagines at first that the townsfolk are receptive to the *beautiful*. They speak of nothing so frequently as the beauty of their countryside: one can't deny that they set a high value on it; but this is because it attracts a number of visitors whose money enriches the innkeepers, and so, through the mechanism of local taxes, *brings in money to the town*.

One fine autumn morning, M. de Rênal was strolling down Loyalty Promenade, his wife on his arm. While listening to her husband, who was speaking with a grave air, Mme de Rênal's eyes anxiously followed the movements of three little boys. The eldest, who might have been eleven, often went too near the parapet, and looked as though he might be about to climb it. A soft voice would then pronounce the name Adolphe, and the child would abandon his ambitious intent. Mme de Rênal looked to be a woman of about thirty, but still rather pretty.

– He may seriously regret it, this fine gentleman from Paris, said M. de Rênal, with an offended air, his cheeks paler than usual. I'm not without some few friends at the Château . . .[6]

However, though I fully intend to talk to you about the provinces for a couple of hundred pages, I haven't the heart to subject you to the tedium and *astute manoeuvring* of a provincial conversation.

The fine gentleman from Paris, so odious to the Mayor of Verrières, was none other than M. Appert,[7] who, two days previously, had found a way to introduce himself not only into the prison and the poorhouse of Verrières, but also into the hospital, which was run on charitable lines by the Mayor and the principal local landowners.

– But, said Mme de Rênal timidly, what injury can this gentleman from Paris do you, since you manage the care of the poor with such scrupulous honesty?

– He has only come to *apportion* blame, and then he'll get articles put in the liberal press.

– You never read them, my dear.

– But these Jacobin pieces get talked about; and all this distracts us *and hampers our good works*.[8] As for me, I'll never forgive that priest.

CHAPTER 3

The Welfare of the Poor

A virtuous priest who refrains from intrigue is Providence's
gift to a village.   FLEURY[1]

It should be explained that the Curé of Verrières – an old man of
eighty, who, thanks to the invigorating air of the mountains, had a
constitution and a temperament of iron – had the right to visit the
prison, the hospital and even the poorhouse at any time. M. Appert,
who had a letter of introduction to the Curé from Paris, had had the
good sense to arrive in the inquisitive little town at exactly six in the
morning. Straightaway he went to the presbytery.

Reading the letter written to him by the Marquis de La Mole, a
peer of France, and the richest landowner in the province, the Curé
Chélan remained thoughtful.

– I'm old and loved here, said he at last in an undertone, and they
wouldn't dare! Turning to face the gentleman from Paris, with eyes
in which, despite his great age, there shone that sacred fire which
told of pleasure in the doing of a fine action that might be a little
dangerous:

– Come with me, monsieur, and in the presence of the gaoler, and
above all that of the overseers of the poorhouse, be so kind as to
offer no opinion at all about what we shall see.

M. Appert understood that he was dealing with a man of spirit: he
followed the venerable curé, visited the prison, the hospital, the
poorhouse, asked many questions, and, despite some strange answers,
permitted himself not the least sign of disapproval.

This visit lasted many hours. The Curé invited M. Appert to eat
with him; but he pretended to have letters to write: he did not want

to compromise his generous guide any further. Around three o'clock, the gentlemen went to complete the inspection of the poorhouse, and afterwards returned to the prison. There, on the doorstep, they encountered the gaoler, a six-foot giant of a man with bow legs, his mean face made hideous with alarm.

– Ah! monsieur, said he to the Curé when he saw him, this gentleman I see with you, isn't he M. Appert?

– What does that signify? said the Curé.

– Since yesterday I have had the strictest orders, which M. the Prefect sent down by a gendarme who must have galloped all night, not to admit M. Appert to the prison.

– I declare to you, M. Noiroud, said the Curé, that this traveller, who is with me, is M. Appert. Do you acknowledge that I have the right to enter this prison at any time of day or night, accompanied by anyone I choose?

– Yes, M. le Curé, said the gaoler in a low voice, lowering his head like a bulldog obeying reluctantly for fear of the stick. But, M. le Curé, I have a wife and children, and if anyone tells on me I'll be ruined; I've nothing to live on but my job.

– I'd be just as distressed to lose my own, replied the good curé, in a voice more and more filled with emotion.

– But what a difference! replied the gaoler eagerly; you, M. le Curé – one knows that you have an income of eight hundred livres, and a good sunny property . . .

These are the events which for two days, commented on and exaggerated in twenty different ways, had stirred up the spiteful passions of the little town of Verrières. At this moment they provided the subject for the little discussion M. de Rênal was having with his wife. That morning, in the company of M. Valenod, Director of the Poorhouse, he had gone to the Curé's house to express the most lively disapproval. M. Chélan had no one to protect him; and he felt all the implications of their words.

– Very well, messieurs! I will be the third 80-year-old curé to be thrown out in this neighbourhood. It's fifty-six years that I've been here; I have baptized nearly everyone in the town, which was only a village when I arrived. Every day I marry young folk whose grandparents I married long ago. Verrières is my family. But I said to myself when I saw that stranger: 'This man down from Paris may well be a liberal, there are far too many of them; but what harm can he do to our poor folk and our prisoners?'

The reproaches of M. de Rênal, and above all of M. Valenod, Director of the Poorhouse, waxed more and more severe:

– Very well, messieurs! throw me out, cried the aged priest in a trembling voice. I shall nevertheless live here still. Everyone knows that forty-eight years ago I inherited a piece of land that brings in 800 livres. I shall live on that money. I never make any savings myself from my position, messieurs, and perhaps that's why I'm not afraid when people talk of making me lose it.

M. de Rênal was on excellent terms with his wife; but not knowing how to reply to the question, that she repeated timidly to him: 'What harm could this gentleman from Paris do the prisoners?' he was just about to lose his temper completely, when she gave a cry. Her second son had climbed on to the parapet of the terrace wall and was running along it, even though it rose more than twenty feet above the vineyard on its other side. The fear of frightening her boy and making him fall prevented her from saying a word to him. Eventually, the child, laughing at his prowess, looked round at his mother and, seeing how pale she was, jumped on to the walk and ran towards her. He was roundly scolded.

This little incident changed the course of the conversation.

– I definitely intend to take Sorel, the son of the sawyer, into my house, said M. de Rênal; he can look after the children, who are beginning to get too rowdy for us. He is a young priest, or as good as, knows Latin well, and he'll be able to bring the children on – for he has a strong character, according to the Curé. I'll give him 300 francs and his board. I had some doubts about his morality; for he was the pet of that old surgeon, the member of the Legion of Honour, who got himself taken as a lodger at the Sorels' on the pretext of being their cousin. That man could very well have been nothing more than a secret agent for the liberals – he claimed our mountain air was good for his asthma, but there's no proof of that. He was in all *Buonaparté's* campaigns in Italy, and even, they say, voted *no* to the Empire at that time.[2] This liberal taught Sorel's son Latin, and left him a quantity of books he had brought with him. Indeed, I'd never have dreamt of letting a carpenter's son be close to our children; but the Curé, just the night before that row that has split us apart for ever, told me that Sorel had been studying theology for three years, with the idea of entering a seminary. So he's not a liberal – he's a Latinist.

This arrangement will be useful in more ways than one, continued M. de Rênal, looking at his wife with a diplomatic air; Valenod is so very proud of the two Norman horses he's bought for his barouche. But he has no tutor for his children.

– He could well take this one away from us.

– So you do approve of my scheme? said M. de Rênal, rewarding his wife with a smile for the excellent idea that had come to her. Very good, that's that, then.

– Ah, good Heavens! my dear friend, how quickly you make up your mind!

– That's because I myself have some character, as the Curé has been shown. Let's not deceive ourselves – we are surrounded by liberals here. All the cloth merchants are envious of me, I'm positive of that; two or three of them are getting to be really rich men. Very well! I wouldn't be at all displeased if they were to see M. de Rênal's children go past taking a walk under the supervision of *their tutor*. That will impress them. My grandfather used often to tell us how in his youth he had had a tutor. It could cost me a hundred écus,[3] but that can be put down as an expense necessary to support our station in life.

This sudden decision plunged Mme de Rênal deep in thought. She was a tall, well-formed woman who had been the local belle, as they say in the mountains. She had a certain air of naturalness and youth in her walk: to Parisian eyes, this unaffected grace, full of innocent vivacity, could even go so far as to suggest a mild sensuality. But if Mme de Rênal had been conscious of a success of that kind she would have been deeply ashamed. Her heart was a stranger to coquetry or affectation. M. Valenod, the wealthy Director of the Poorhouse, was thought to have paid court to her, but without success, and that threw a particular brilliancy on her virtue; for this M. Valenod, a tall and strongly built young man, with a rubicund complexion and great black sidewhiskers, was one of those boorish fellows, loud and full of confidence, who in the provinces they call a fine man.

Mme de Rênal, so timid, and with so apparently tranquil a nature, was shocked most of all by M. Valenod's constant bustling and bursts of noise. Her distaste for what in Verrières is called having fun had earned her the reputation of being excessively proud of her birth. She had no thought of that, but was perfectly happy to see that the townspeople called less frequently. We won't conceal that she was thought a fool by *those* ladies, because, not being in the habit of manipulating her husband, she let slip the most brilliant chances of making him buy her beautiful hats from Paris or Besançon. So long as she was let alone to wander about in her lovely gardens, she never complained.

She was a naive soul, who had never risen even to the point of looking critically at her husband and realizing that he bored her. She assumed, without quite saying it to herself, that no husband and wife had a more tender relation than theirs. She loved M. de Rênal most of all when he spoke to her of his plans for their children, of whom he destined one for the army, the second for the magistracy and the third for the Church. In short, she found M. de Rênal much less boring than all the other men of her acquaintance.

This conjugal judgement was sound. The Mayor of Verrières owed his reputation for wit, and above all for good breeding, to half a dozen pleasantries inherited from an uncle. The old Captain de Rênal had served before the Revolution with the infantry regiment of M. le Duc d'Orléans, and when he went to Paris had been admitted to the salons of that prince. He had seen Mme de Montesson, the famous Mme de Genlis, and M. Ducrest, the force behind the Palais-Royal.[4] These personages figured all too often in M. de Rênal's stories. But gradually the remembrance of things which required such delicacy in the telling had become a burden to him, and for some time now it was only on grand occasions that he repeated his anecdotes of the House of Orléans. Since he was also extremely polite – except on the occasions when one talked about money – he passed, rightly, for the most aristocratic figure in Verrières.

CHAPTER 4

Father And Son

E sarà mia colpa
Se così è?
MACHIAVELLI[1]

My wife really has an excellent head on her shoulders, said the Mayor of Verrières to himself as he walked down to Père Sorel's mill at six o'clock the following morning. Whatever it was I said to her in order to maintain my due superiority, I hadn't dreamt that if I don't secure this little Abbé Sorel – who they say knows Latin like an angel – then the Director of the Poorhouse, that pushy fellow, is quite capable of having the same idea and stealing him from me. In what smug tones he would talk of his children's tutor! . . . Now this tutor, once he is at my house, will he wear a soutane?

M. de Rênal was taken up with this speculation when he caught sight of a peasant in the distance, a man of nearly six foot, who, in the early morning light, seemed entirely absorbed in measuring pieces of wood disposed on the towpath along the Doubs. This peasant did not appear at all pleased to see the approach of M. le Maire; for the pieces of wood obstructed the way, and were placed there contrary to regulations.

Père Sorel – for it was he – was very surprised, and still more gratified, at the singular proposition put to him by M. de Rênal concerning his son Julien. He heard it, even so, with that air of melancholy discontent and indifference with which the peasants of these mountains are so adept at cloaking their cunning. Slaves in the period of Spanish rule, they still retain the facial expression of the Egyptian *Fellahin*.

23

Sorel's response at first was nothing more than a lengthy recital of the deferential formulae he had by rote. While he repeated these empty phrases, with an unnatural smile reinforcing the air of insincerity, almost of rascality, natural to his face, the busy mind of the old peasant sought to fathom what motive could have brought so considerable a man to take his worthless son into his own house. He was extremely dissatisfied with Julien – and it was for him that M. de Rênal offered the unlooked-for wage of 300 francs a year, plus food, and even clothing. This last daring demand, which Père Sorel had had the genius to put forward suddenly, had as quickly been accepted by M. de Rênal.

The demand impressed the Mayor. Since Sorel is not delighted and bowled over by my proposition as naturally he ought to be, it is obvious, said he to himself, that he has received offers from another party; and where could they come from if not from Valenod?

In was in vain that M. de Rênal urged Sorel to conclude the deal on the spot; the old peasant's cunning obstinately refused that; he wished, he said, to consult his son – as if, in the provinces, a rich father consults a penniless son other than as a matter of form.

A water-powered sawmill is made up of a shed on the bank of a stream. The roof is supported by a framework carried on four thick wooden pillars. Eight or ten feet up, in the middle of the shed, one sees a saw which moves up and down while a very simple machine pushes a piece of wood against it. A wheel driven by the stream moves these dual mechanisms: that of the saw, which goes up and down, and that of the device which gently pushes the piece of wood towards the saw, which cuts it into planks.

Approaching his mill, Père Sorel called out to Julien in his stentorian voice. Nobody replied. He saw only his older sons, giant-like men who, armed with heavy axes, were squaring off the pine trunks they were going to take to the saw. Completely absorbed in following precisely the black lines marked on the piece of wood, each blow of their axes would chip off enormous chunks. They did not hear their father's call. He turned towards the shed; entering, he looked in vain at the place by the saw where Julien should have been stationed. Then he saw him, five or six feet above it, astride one of the roof beams. Instead of carefully supervising the workings of the whole process, Julien was reading. Nothing was more antipathetic to old Sorel than this; he might have forgiven the slender build, so little fitted to manual labour and so different from that of his brothers; but this mania for reading was odious to him, who didn't know how to read.

He called to Julien two or three times, with no effect. The attention the young man gave to his book, much more than the noise of the saw, prevented his hearing his father's terrible voice. At last, despite his age, the latter leapt nimbly on to the tree trunk being worked by the saw, and from there to the cross beam supporting the roof. A violent blow made the book Julien was holding fly into the stream; a second blow, just as violent, and in the form of a box on the ear, made him lose his balance. He was about to fall twelve or fifteen feet down into the midst of the moving machine levers, which would have crushed him, but his father caught him by the left hand as he fell:

– Well, idler! – so you still read your damn books when you're supposed to be looking after the saw? Read them in the evening, when you go and waste time with the Curé, that'd be all right.

Julien, though stunned by the force of the blow, and all bloody, returned to his official station by the saw. He had tears in his eyes, caused less by physical pain than by the loss of his book, which he adored.

'Come down, you animal,[2] so I can talk to you.' The roar of the mechanism still prevented Julien from hearing the order. His father, who had descended, and didn't want the bother of climbing up the machine again, went to find a long rod for knocking down walnuts and rapped him on the shoulder with it. Julien had hardly touched the ground when old Sorel, driving him roughly in front, pushed him towards the house. God knows what he'll do with me! said the young man to himself. In passing he looked sadly at the stream where his book had fallen; it was the one he loved the most, the *Memorials of St Helena*.[3]

His cheeks were heavily flushed and his eyes lowered. He was a slight young man of eighteen or nineteen, weak in appearance, with irregular but delicate features and an aquiline nose. The great dark eyes, which in more peaceful moments proclaimed thoughtfulness and fire, were at that moment animated by an expression of the fiercest hatred. Dark chestnut hair worn very far down gave him a low forehead and, when he was angry, a wicked look. Among the innumerable varieties of human physiognomy,[4] none, perhaps, could be marked by so striking an individuality. A graceful, well-proportioned figure suggested more of litheness than of strength. From his early childhood, his excessively pensive air and his extreme pallor had given his father the idea that he wouldn't live long, or that he would live only to be an expense to his family. Despised by the whole household, he hated his brothers and his father; in the Sunday games on the public square he was always beaten.

It was less than a year ago that his pretty face had begun to earn him some friendly feelings among the girls. Scorned by everyone as a feeble creature, Julien had worshipped the old Surgeon-major who once dared to speak to the Mayor on the subject of plane trees.

Sometimes the Surgeon had paid Père Sorel for a day of his son's time, and taught him Latin and history – that is to say, what he knew of history, the campaign in Italy in 1796. Dying, he had left him his cross of the Legion of Honour, the arrears of his half pay and thirty or forty books, the most precious of which had just flown into that *public stream*, diverted through the influence of the Mayor.

Julien had scarcely entered the house when he felt his shoulder grabbed back by his father's powerful hand; he trembled, expecting some blows.

– Answer me without lying, shouted the hard voice of the old peasant in his ear, while his hand turned him round as a child's hand turns a lead soldier. Julien's great tear-filled eyes found themselves facing straight into the small spiteful eyes of the old carpenter, who had the air of wanting to read him to the depths of his soul.

CHAPTER 5

A Negotiation

Cunctando restituit rem
ENNIUS[1]

Answer me without lying, if you can manage that, little dog of a reader: how do you know Mme de Rênal, when have you spoken to her?

— I've never spoken to her, replied Julien, I've never seen the lady except at church.

— But you've stared at her, insolent villain?

— Never! You know that at church I see only God, Julien added, with a little hypocritical air, well adapted, he thought, to ward off further blows to the head.

— Anyway, there's something behind all this, replied the cunning peasant, and was silent for a moment; but I'll get nothing out of you, damn hypocrite. The fact is, I'll be rid of you, and my saw mill will be the better for it. You've won over the Curé, or someone, who has got you a fine job. Go pack your bag and I'll take you to M. de Rênal's place, where you're going to be tutor to his children.

— What will I get for that?

— Food, clothes and three hundred francs in wages.

— I don't want to be a servant.

— Animal — who talked to you of being a servant? would I want my son to be a servant?

— But with whom shall I be eating?

This question disconcerted old Sorel; he felt that in talking more about it he might commit some solecism; he worked himself up into a temper with Julien, covering him with insults and accusing him of greediness, and left him in order to consult with his other sons.

Julien saw them shortly afterwards, each leaning on his axe, in council. After having watched them for a long time, Julien – realizing that he could gather nothing from it – went to position himself on the other side of the saw so as to avoid being surprised. He wanted to think about this unexpected announcement which could alter the course of his life, but felt himself incapable of being sensible; his imagination was taken up entirely in picturing what he would encounter in M. de Rênal's beautiful house.

It would be necessary to give up all that, he said to himself, rather than be reduced to eating with the servants. My father will want to force me to; I'd rather die. I've got fifteen francs and eight sous saved up, and I'll free myself tonight. In two days, by side paths where I needn't fear any gendarmes, I will be at Besançon; there I will enlist as a soldier, or, if necessary, cross into Switzerland. But then there will be no more getting on in the world for me, no more ambition, no more of that fine career in the priesthood which could lead anywhere.

This horror of eating with the servants was not natural to Julien; to make his fortune he would have done far more painful things. He borrowed his repugnance from Rousseau's *Confessions*.[2] It was the sole book through which his imagination formed any idea of the larger world. The collected bulletins of the Grand Army and the *Memorials of St Helena* completed his Koran. He would have died for these three works. Never did he have faith in any other. Following the judgement of the old Surgeon-major, he saw all the rest of the books in the world as liars, written by scoundrels to gain advancement.

Together with a soul of fire, Julien had one of those astonishing memories so often associated with stupidity. To win over the old Curé Chélan, on whom he clearly saw his lot in life to depend, he had learned by heart the whole of the Latin New Testament; he also knew M. de Maistre's book *Du Pape*,[3] and believed in one as little as the other.

As if by mutual agreement, Sorel and his son avoided talking to one another again that day. At dusk Julien went to the Curé's house for his lesson in theology, but he thought it wise not to mention the strange proposition that had been made to his father. Perhaps it's a trap, he said to himself, I must seem to have forgotten about it.

Early next day M. de Rênal summoned old Sorel, who, after having made him wait an hour or two, finally arrived at the door making a hundred excuses mixed up with as many respectful bows. By means of rehearsing all kinds of objections, Sorel gathered that his son would eat with the master and mistress of the house, and, on the days that they had company, alone with the children in a room apart. More disposed to raise difficulties the more he perceived a genuine urgency on the part of M. le Maire, and anyway brimming with mistrust and astonishment, Sorel demanded to see the room in which his son would sleep. It was a large and well furnished room, but into it they were already busy carrying the three children's beds.

This circumstance cast a shaft of light into the mind of the old peasant; with even more self-assurance he demanded to see the clothes to be provided for his son. M. de Rênal opened his desk and took out a hundred francs.

— With this money, your son will go to M. Durand the draper and get himself fitted out with a complete suit of black.

— And even if I take him away from your house, said the peasant, who had suddenly forgotten his respectful manner, he'll keep the suit?

— Doubtless.

— Oh, all right! said Sorel in a drawling voice, there's only one more thing remaining for us to agree on: the money you'll give him.

— What! cried M. de Rênal indignantly, yesterday we agreed that: I will give him three hundred francs; I think that's plenty, and probably too much.

— It was what you offered, that I don't deny at all, said old Sorel, speaking ever more slowly; and by an effusion of genius which would only surprise those who don't know the Franche-Comtois peasantry, he added, looking fixedly at M. de Rênal: '*We've found better elsewhere.*'

At these words the Mayor looked disconcerted. He controlled himself, however, and after a skilled debate lasting a good two hours, in which not a word was said without calculation, the cunning of the peasant overbore the cunning of the rich man – who did not need it in order to live. All the many points which were to govern Julien's new existence were resolved; not only was his salary fixed at 400 francs, but it was to be paid in advance, on the first of each month.

– Good! I'll send him thirty-five francs, said M. de Rênal.

– To make a round sum, a rich and generous man such as that gentleman our Mayor, said the peasant in a *wheedling* tone, could go so far as to make it thirty-six francs.

– Very well, said M. de Rênal, but there's an end of it.

For the moment, anger gave him a firm tone. The peasant saw that he must go no further. Then, in his turn, M. de Rênal began to make himself felt. He certainly would not give the first month's thirty-six francs to old Sorel, who was very keen to receive it on his son's behalf. M. de Rênal had realized that he would have to recount the part he had played in the whole negotiation to his wife.

– Hand me back the hundred francs I gave you, said he crossly. M. Durand owes me something. I will go with your son and get him fitted out in black cloth.

After this vigorous action, Sorel prudently returned to his deferential phrasemaking; this took up another quarter of an hour. Finally, seeing that he certainly had no more to gain, he took his leave. His last respectful flourish ended with these words: I will send my son up to the château.

It was thus that the Mayor's underlings referred to his house when they wanted to please him.

On returning to his mill, Sorel sought his son in vain. Mistrustful of what might happen, Julien had left in the middle of the night. He wanted to deposit his books and his cross of the Legion of Honour in a safe place. He had taken all of them to his friend Fouqué, a young wood merchant who lived on the high mountain that dominated Verrières.

When he reappeared:

– God knows, you damn idler, his father said to him, if you'll ever have enough decency to pay me for your food that I've been advancing you for so many years. Pack up your scraps, and get off to His Worship the Mayor's place.

Julien, astonished not to have been beaten, made haste to go. But he was hardly out of the sight of his terrible father when he slackened his pace. He decided that to go to the church to perform a Station of the Cross would be of use to his hypocrisy.

That word surprises you? Before arriving at that ghastly notion, the young peasant's soul had had quite a course to run.

In his early childhood, the sight of some dragoons of the 6th returning from Italy wearing their long white cloaks and helmets with long black plumes on their heads – whom Julien had beheld tethering their horses to the grilled windows of his father's house – rendered him crazy for the life of a soldier. Later on, he had listened with rapture to stories of the battles at the bridge at Lodi, of Arcoli, and of Rivoli,[4] told him by the old Surgeon-major. He noticed the passionate looks the old man directed towards his cross.

But when Julien was fourteen, they began to build a church at Verrières which could be called magnificent for so small a town. It had, above all, four marble columns, the sight of which impressed Julien; these became famous thereabouts because of the hatred they excited between the Justice of the Peace and that young ecclesiastic the envoy from Besançon, who was supposed to be a spy for the Congregation.[5] The Justice of the Peace was on the point of losing his place, at least that was the local opinion. Had he not dared to have a quarrel with a priest who, nearly every fortnight, travelled to Besançon, where, they said, he saw Monsignor the Bishop?

In the midst of all this the Justice of the Peace, father of a large family, pronounced several judgments which seemed unjust; all bore against those citizens who read the *Constitutionnel*.[6] The right-thinking party triumphed. It was only a matter, it was true, of sums of three or five francs, but one of these petty penalties had to be paid by Julien's godfather, a nailmaker. In his anger this man cried out: 'What a turnaround! – and to think that for more than twenty years this Justice of the Peace passed for such a decent man!' The Surgeon-major, Julien's friend, was dead.

All at once Julien stopped talking about Napoleon; he announced his plan to become a priest, and could constantly be seen in his father's sawmill, occupied in learning by heart the Latin Bible the

Curé had lent him. That good old man, marvelling at his progress, spent whole evenings teaching him theology. In front of him, Julien uttered nothing but pious sentiments. Who could have guessed that this girl-like visage, so pale and gentle, concealed an inextinguishable will to die a thousand deaths rather than fail to make his fortune?

For Julien, to make his fortune meant first of all to get out of Verrières: he abhorred the district where he was born. Everything that he saw there froze his imagination.

From his earliest childhood he had experienced moments of rapture. Then, he would dream with delight that he would one day encounter the beautiful women of Paris, and would compel their attention by some famous deed. Why should he not be loved by one of them, as Bonaparte, while still poor, had been loved by the brilliant Mme de Beauharnais?[7] For many years, scarcely an hour of Julien's life passed without his telling himself that Bonaparte, an obscure and penniless lieutenant, had made himself master of the world with his sword. This idea consoled him for his sufferings, which he thought great, and redoubled his happiness when he had any.

The construction of the church and the Justice of the Peace's judgments suddenly enlightened him; an idea came to him which made him distraught for some weeks, and seized hold of him with the overwhelming force belonging to the first idea with which a passionate nature believes itself to have been inspired.

'When Bonaparte made people talk about him, France was in danger of invasion; military talent was necessary and fashionable. Today one sees 40-year-old priests with stipends of a hundred thousand francs, that is to say, three times more than Napoleon's famous generals. They need people behind them to support them. Look at this Justice of the Peace, so sensible, such a fine upstanding man until now, so established, who has dishonoured himself for fear of offending a young clergyman of thirty. It is necessary to be a priest.'

On one occasion, in the midst of this new piety, and after he had already been studying theology for two years, he was betrayed into a sudden eruption of the fire that consumed his soul. At M. Chélan's dwelling, during a dinner for the clergy to whom the good curé was presenting him as a prodigy of tuition, he found himself fervidly praising Napoleon. He bound his right arm across his chest, pretending it had been dislocated in moving a pine trunk, and carried it in this irksome position for two months. After this bodily penance, he absolved himself. This was the young man of nineteen – but so seemingly frail that one would have taken him for no more than seventeen – who, carrying his little parcel under his arm, entered the magnificent church of Verrières.

He found it sombre and solitary. To mark a festival all the church windows had been covered with crimson cloth. The sun's rays shone through to produce a dim light, most pious and imposing. Julien shivered. Alone in the church, he established himself in the pew that had the finest appearance. It bore the arms of M. de Rênal.

On the prayer desk Julien noticed a fragment of printed paper, spread out as though to be read. He directed his eyes towards it and saw:

Details of the execution and the last moments of Louis Jenrel, executed at Besançon, on the . . .

The paper was torn off. On the other side could be seen the first words of a line, which were: *The first step*.

– Who could have put this paper here? said Julien. Poor devil, he added with a sigh, his name ends like mine . . . and he crumpled the paper.

Leaving, Julien thought he saw blood next to the holy water stoup – it was holy water that had been spilled: the refraction from the red blinds covering the windows gave it the appearance of blood.

Eventually Julien was ashamed of his secret terror.

– Am I a coward! he said to himself, *To arms!*

This phrase, so often repeated in the Surgeon-major's accounts of battles, represented the heroic for Julien. He raised himself up and walked rapidly towards M. de Rênal's house.

In spite of these fine resolves, from the moment he saw it twenty paces away, he was seized with an overpowering timidity. The iron grille was open; to him it seemed magnificent; and it was up to him to enter in.

Julien was not the only person whose feelings were disturbed by his arrival at the house. Mme de Rênal's great sensitivity was upset by the idea of this stranger who, by the nature of his duties, would find himself constantly coming between her children and herself. She was used to having her sons sleep in her room. That morning, many tears had been shed as she saw their little beds being carried to the apartment destined for the tutor. In vain she had asked her husband that the bed of little Stanislas-Xavier, the youngest, be brought back to her room.

Feminine delicacy was pushed to an excess in Mme de Rênal. She evoked for herself the most disagreeable image of a gross and ill-kempt being, empowered to scold her children solely because he knew Latin, a barbarous language for the sake of which her sons were to be chastised.

CHAPTER 6

Ennui

*Non so più cosa son
Cosa facio.*
MOZART, *Figaro*[1]

With that liveliness and grace natural to her when she was far from the gaze of men, Mme de Rênal was stepping out of the French window giving on to the garden, when she noticed the figure of a young peasant near the main door – almost a child still, extremely pale and close to tears. He was in a clean white shirt, and under his arm he carried a very neatly folded jacket of violet ratteen.

This little peasant's complexion was so white, his eyes so gentle, that Mme de Rênal's slightly romantic temperament made her think at first that it could be a young girl in disguise, come to ask some favour from the Mayor. She pitied the poor creature halted at the main entrance and evidently not daring to raise its arm to the bell. Mme de Rênal stepped nearer, distracted for a moment from the bitter upset the tutor's arrival was causing her. Julien, facing towards the door, did not see her. He started when a soft voice said just next to his ear:

– What do you want here, my child?

Julien turned abruptly and, struck by a look so full of grace, forgot some of his shyness. Then, amazed by her beauty, he forgot everything, even his business there. Mme de Rênal had repeated her question.

– I've come as the tutor, madame, he said at last, much ashamed of the tears he was doing his best to wipe away.

Mme de Rênal was at a loss for words. They stood looking at one

35

another, standing very close. Julien had never encountered so well dressed a person – and, above all, a woman with so dazzling a complexion – who spoke to him so gently. Mme de Rênal gazed at the great teardrops which stood on the cheeks, at first so pale and now so pink, of this young peasant. Then she began to laugh; she laughed at herself with all the wild gaiety of a young girl, and could not fully grasp her own delight. What – this was that tutor she had been picturing to herself as a grubby, badly dressed priest, coming to chide and punish her children?

– Of course, monsieur, she said at last, you know Latin?

The word 'monsieur' so astonished Julien that he had to think for a moment.

– Yes, madame, he said timidly.

Mme de Rênal was so happy that she ventured to say to Julien:

– You won't scold the poor children too often?

– Me scold them? said Julien, much surprised, why should I?

– Then, monsieur, you, she added after a short silence and in a voice each moment more charged with emotion, you will be good to them – you promise me that?

To hear himself called 'monsieur' again, in full seriousness, and by so beautifully dressed a lady, was quite beyond all Julien's dreams: in all his youthful castles in Spain he had told himself that a real lady would only deign to speak to him when he was dressed in a handsome uniform. On her side, Mme de Rênal was utterly beguiled by Julien's beautiful complexion, his great dark eyes and his pretty head of hair, which curled more than usual because, to refresh himself, he had plunged his head in the basin of the public fountain. To her great joy, she found in this fatal tutor, whose harshness and forbidding air she had so much dreaded for her children's sake, the manner of a shy young girl. For so quiet a nature as Mme de Rênal's, the contrast between her fears and what she now saw was an event of great importance. At last she recovered from her surprise. She was disconcerted to find herself standing in this way at the door of her house with a young man almost in his shirtsleeves, and so close to her.

– Let us go in, monsieur, she said to him in a rather embarrassed manner.

In the whole of her experience Mme de Rênal had never been so deeply moved by so purely agreeable a feeling, never had so gracious a vision followed such disquieting fears. Well then, her pretty children, whom she cherished so, were not to fall into the hands of a dirty, growling priest. Hardly had she entered the entrance hall than she turned back to face Julien, who was following timidly. His wide-eyed look at the sight of so beautiful a house was another charm in Mme de Rênal's eyes. She could scarcely believe those eyes – it seemed requisite above all in a tutor that he be dressed in black.

– But it is true, monsieur, she said to him, pausing again, and mortally afraid that she had deceived herself, so happy did her belief make her, that you know Latin?

These words offended Julien's pride and dispelled the charm in which he had been living for the last quarter of a hour.

– Yes, madame, he said to her, striving to achieve an air of coldness; I know Latin as well as M. le Curé does, and even, as he is sometimes good enough to say, better.

Mme de Rênal found Julien's manner very disconcerting – he had halted some feet from her. She went up to him and said softly:

– It is true, isn't it, that at first you won't cane my children, even when they don't know their lessons?

So soft and almost pleading a tone from so beautiful a lady made Julien instantly forget what he owed to his reputation as a Latinist. Mme de Rênal's face was close to his, and he breathed in the scent of a woman's summer clothing, a bewildering experience for a poor peasant. Julien blushed deeply and said with a sigh and faltering voice:

– Have no fear, madame, I will do whatever you say.

It was only at that moment, when her anxiety for her children was completely dispelled, that Mme de Rênal was struck by Julien's great beauty. The almost feminine cast of his features and his embarrassed mien seemed not at all ridiculous to a woman so shy as herself. The air of masculinity commonly thought essential to good looks in a man frightened her.

– How old are you, monsieur? she asked Julien.

– Almost nineteen.

– My eldest son is eleven, continued Mme de Rênal, completely reassured, he will be like a friend for you, you will be able to talk with him sensibly. Once his father tried to beat him – the child was ill for a week, even though it was a very little blow.

How different from me, thought Julien. Only yesterday my father beat me. How lucky these rich people are!

Mme de Rênal was by now ready to catch the slightest nuance of what was going on in the tutor's mind; she interpreted this twinge of sadness as timidity, and hoped to cheer him.

– What is your name, monsieur? she asked him, with a tone and a grace of which Julien felt all the charm, though he could not have explained why.

– I am called Julien Sorel, madame; I am extremely nervous at entering a strange house for the first time in my life, and I will need your protection and forgiveness for lots of things in the first few days. I have never been to school, I was too poor; and I have never spoken to anyone except my cousin the Surgeon-major, a member of the Legion of Honour, and M. le Curé Chélan. He will speak up for me to you. My brothers have always beaten me, don't believe them if they speak ill of me to you. Excuse my faults, madame, I shall never mean any harm.

Julien became more confident during this long speech, and he looked closely at Mme de Rênal. Such is the effect of perfect gracefulness when it is natural to the character, and above all when the person it adorns is unaware of having such grace, that Julien, who was quite prepared to appraise feminine beauty, could have sworn at that moment that she was no more than twenty. At that moment he had the bold notion of kissing her hand. Almost at once he was frightened of the idea; a moment after that he said to himself: 'It would be cowardice in me not to carry out an action which maybe could be useful to me, and lessen the scorn that this beautiful woman probably feels for a poor worker only just plucked away from the mill.' Possibly Julien was a little inspired by the name of a pretty fellow that for six months or so he had heard repeated on Sundays by some of the young girls. During these internal debates, Mme de Rênal was offering him a few words of instruction on the means of making a start with the children. The violence of Julien's inner conflict had made him again very pale; he said constrainedly:

— Never, madame, will I strike your children. I swear it before God.

And in saying these words, he dared to take Mme de Rênal's hand and carry it to his lips. She was astonished at this action and, on reflection, shocked. Because it was very hot, her arm was completely bare under her shawl, and Julien's movement in carrying the hand to his lips had uncovered it entirely. After a moment or two she scolded herself; it seemed to her that she had not been offended quickly enough.

M. de Rênal, on hearing people talking, emerged from his study; with the same majestic and paternal air that he adopted when presiding over marriages at the town hall, he said to Julien:

— It is essential that I talk to you before you are seen by the children.

He showed Julien into a room and detained his wife, who wished to leave them alone together. The door closed, M. de Rênal sat down gravely.

— I am told by M. le Curé that you are a worthy individual — everyone here will treat you with respect, and, if I am pleased, I will in due course help to set you up in a little establishment of your own. I trust that you will see neither your relations nor your friends; their tone would not be suitable for my children. Here are thirty-six francs for the first month; but I insist on your word that you will not give a sou of this money to your father.

M. de Rênal was galled by that old man, who in this business had been more cunning than he.

— Now, *monsieur* — for on my instructions everyone will call you monsieur, and you will be aware of the advantages of coming into a household where things are done properly — now, monsieur, it is inappropriate that the children should see you in a short jacket. Have the servants seen him yet? he asked his wife.

— No, my dear, she replied with a deeply pensive air.

— So much the better. Put this on, he said to the surprised youth, handing him a frock coat of his own. Now let us go to M. Durand the cloth merchant.

39

When, more than an hour later, M. de Rênal returned with the new tutor all dressed in black, he found his wife sitting in the same place. She felt herself calmed by Julien's presence – in looking closely at him she forgot to be afraid. Julien thought of her not at all; in spite of his distrust of destiny and of mankind, at that moment his soul was no more than that of a child, and he seemed to have lived for years since that instant when, three hours ago, he had been trembling in the church. He noticed Mme de Rênal's aloof manner, and took it that she was angry because he had dared to kiss her hand. But the feeling of pride given him by contact with garments so different from those he had been used to wear so transported him, and he had such desire to conceal this joy, that there was something abrupt and foolish in all his movements. Mme de Rênal looked at him with amazement in her eyes.

– Some gravity, sir, said M. de Rênal to him, if you wish to be respected by my children and my household.

– Sir, replied Julien, I'm not at ease in these new clothes; me, a poor peasant – I have only ever worn short jackets; I will retire, with your permission, to my room.

– What d'you make of this new acquisition? M. de Rênal asked his wife.

With an almost instinctive impulse, of which she was certainly not aware in herself, Mme de Rênal disguised the truth from her husband.

– I am not nearly so enchanted as you with this little peasant – your kindnesses will make him into an impertinent fellow you will be obliged to send away before the month is out.

– Well, all right, we'll send him away! That will be a hundred francs or so it could have cost me, and Verrières will have become used to seeing that M. de Rênal's children have a tutor. That aim could not have been achieved if I had left Julien in worker's clothes. And in sending him away I will keep back, you may be sure, the complete suit of black I have ordered from the draper. He will have nothing but the readymades I found at the tailor's, and in which I've put him.

The hour Julien spent in his room seemed a short time to Mme de Rênal. The children, who had been told of the new tutor, overwhelmed their mother with questions. Then Julien appeared. He was another man. It would be untrue to say that he was grave: he was gravity incarnate. He was introduced to the children, and spoke to them in a manner which astonished even M. de Rênal himself.

— I am here, messieurs, he said to them in finishing his address, to teach you Latin. You know what it is to recite a lesson. Here is the Holy Bible, he went on, showing them a little volume in small print, bound in black. It is in particular the story of Our Lord Jesus Christ, the part which is called the New Testament. I shall often make you recite lessons — make me recite mine.

Adolphe, the oldest child, had taken the book.

— Open it at random, continued Julien, and give me the first word of a verse. I will recite by heart the Holy Book, the guide of our conduct in everything, until you stop me.

Adolphe opened the book, read a phrase, and Julien recited the whole page with the same ease as if he was speaking French. M. de Rênal looked at his wife with an air of triumph. Seeing the amazement of their parents, the children gazed wide-eyed. A servant arrived at the door of the salon; Julien continued to speak in Latin. The servant at first stood stock still and then vanished. Soon the lady's maid and the cook arrived near the door; by then Adolphe had already opened the book at eight places and Julien continued to recite with the same ease.

— Ah, gracious Heavens! loudly exclaimed the cook, a good and very pious girl — the lovely little priest.

M. de Rênal's self-esteem was nettled; far from thinking of how to examine the tutor, he was kept busy racking his memory for some words in Latin; at last he was able to produce a line from Horace. Julien knew no Latin except the Bible. He responded, knitting his brows:

— The sacred ministry to which I am called forbids me to read so profane a poet.

M. de Rênal quoted a fair number of supposedly Horatian lines. He explained to his children who Horace was; but the children, struck with admiration, paid but slight attention to what he said. They looked at Julien.

The servants still being at the door, Julien thought he should prolong the demonstration:

– It would be fitting, he said to the youngest of the children, that M. Stanislas-Xavier also indicate a page in the Holy Book.

The little Stanislas, very proud, read the first word of a verse as well as he was able and Julien repeated the whole page. So that nothing should be lacking to M. de Rênal's triumph, M. Valenod, the owner of two beautiful Norman horses, and M. Charcot de Maugiron, Sub-prefect of the district, came in while Julien was reciting. This scene earned Julien the title of 'monsieur'; the servants themselves could not refuse it him.

That evening, all Verrières flocked to M. de Rênal's to see the wonder. Julien answered them all in a sombre manner which kept them at a distance. His glory spread so rapidly in the town that, a few days later, fearing that someone would filch him, M. de Rênal proposed that he sign a two-year engagement.

– No, monsieur, Julien responded coldly, if you wanted to send me away, I would be obliged to go. An engagement which binds me without obligations on you is not just; I refuse it.

He managed affairs so well that, less than a month after his arrival at the house, M. de Rênal himself respected him. The Curé being at odds with MM. de Rênal and Valenod, there was no one to betray his ancient passion for Napoleon, and Julien spoke of him with nothing but horror.

CHAPTER 7

Elective Affinities[1]

They know not how to touch the heart without bruising it.

A MODERN WRITER

The children adored him: he did not care for them; his mind was elsewhere. Whatever the young monkeys did could never annoy him. Cold, fair, impassive and none the less loved because in some way his arrival had driven boredom from the house, he was a good tutor. On his part, he felt nothing but hatred and disgust for the superior society into which he was admitted – at the lower end of the table, it is true, which perhaps throws light on the hatred and the disgust. There were certain grand dinners when it was only with great difficulty that he contained his hatred for everything surrounding him. On one of these occasions, St Louis' Day at M. de Rênal's, when M. Valenod was holding forth, Julien was on the point of betraying himself; he escaped into the garden, under the pretext of looking for the children. What paeans to honesty! he cried to himself – one would think it's the only virtue; and yet what regard, what unworthy respect for a man who has obviously doubled and tripled his fortune since he took over the administration of poor relief! – I bet he's even profited from the funds meant for foundlings, for those poor things whose misery is even more sacred than that of the others! Oh! monsters! monsters! And me as well, I'm a sort of foundling, hated by my father, my brothers, my whole family.

A few days before that St Louis' Day, walking by himself and saying his breviary in a little wood called the Belvedere which overlooked Loyalty Promenade, Julien had vainly tried to avoid his two brothers whom he saw from a distance coming towards him on a lonely path. The jealousy of these coarse labourers was so provoked by their brother's fine black costume, by his air of extreme propriety, by the genuine scorn that he had for them, that they had beaten him up, to the point of leaving him senseless and covered with blood. Mme de Rênal, out walking with M. Valenod and the Sub-prefect, arrived in the little wood by chance. She saw Julien lying on the ground and thought him dead. Her shock was such that it made M. Valenod jealous.

He took alarm too soon. Julien found Mme de Rênal very beautiful, but he hated her because of her beauty; it was the first block on the road to fortune on which he had almost stumbled. He spoke to her as little as possible, trying to forget the transport that the first day had impelled him to kiss her hand.

Élisa, Mme de Rênal's lady's maid, hadn't failed to fall in love with the young tutor; she spoke of him often to her mistress. Mlle Élisa's love earned Julien the hatred of one of the valets. One day he heard this man saying to Élisa: You don't want to speak to me any more since that filthy tutor came to the house. Julien didn't deserve this slur; but, with the instinct of a good-looking young man, he redoubled the pains he took over his appearance. M. Valenod's hatred redoubled, too. He stated publicly that such vanity was not seemly in a young cleric. Save only for the soutane, Julien wore clerical costume.

Mme de Rênal noticed that he spoke to Élisa more often than usual; she gathered that these talks were caused by the paucity of Julien's tiny wardrobe. He had so little linen that he was often obliged to send it out to be laundered, and it was in these little concerns that Élisa was useful to him. This extreme poverty, which she had not suspected, touched Mme de Rênal; she would have liked to give him presents, but did not dare; that inhibition was the first painful feeling that Julien caused her. Up until then the name Julien had been synonymous for her with a wholly intellectual feeling of pure happiness. In distress at the idea of Julien's poverty, Mme de Rênal talked to her husband about making him a present of linen.

– What simplicity! he replied. How – make a present to a man with whom we're perfectly happy, who serves us well? It is when he's negligent that you must stimulate his zeal.

Mme de Rênal felt humiliated by this way of seeing things; she wouldn't have paid attention to it before the advent of Julien. She never saw the extreme neatness of the young abbé's turnout, otherwise so very simple, without saying to herself: How does the poor boy manage it?

Little by little she felt pity for all that Julien lacked, instead of being shocked by it.

Mme de Rênal was one of those provincial ladies one might very well take for a fool for the first fortnight's acquaintance. She had no experience of life, and no desire for conversation. Endowed with a delicate and discriminating soul, the instinct for happiness natural to all beings meant that most of the time she paid no attention at all to the doings of the gross people into whose company chance had thrown her.

If she had received the slightest education she would have been remarkable for her naturalness and liveliness of mind. But because of her status as an heiress she had been brought up by nuns who were passionate devotees of the *Sacred Heart of Jesus*,[2] their passion kept alive by a violent hatred for the French enemies of the Jesuits. Mme de Rênal had enough native good sense to forget very quickly all that she had been taught at the convent, because of its absurdity; but she put nothing in its place, and ended by knowing nothing. The premature flatteries of which she had been the object because of her status of heiress to a great fortune, and a definite inclination toward fervent piety, had given her a mode of life turned wholly in upon itself. With an appearance of the most perfect compliance with others and the abnegation of self – which the husbands of Verrières pointed to as an example to their wives, and was the pride of M. de Rênal – the settled habit of her soul was really the result of a most lofty disposition. The princess celebrated for her pride pays far more attention to the concerns of the gentlemen surrounding her than did this so apparently mild and modest woman to anything her husband said or did. Up until Julien's arrival she had not really had attention for anyone but her children. Their little illnesses, their griefs, their small joys, occupied all the capacity for feeling in this soul who, in all her life, had adored no one but God, when she had been at the *Sacred Heart* in Besançon.

Without her deigning to say this to anyone, an attack of fever suffered by one of her sons put her almost in the same state as if the child had died. When, in the early years of their marriage, the need to confide had driven her to intimations of this kind of distress to her husband, they had regularly been greeted by a burst of clumsy laughter, a shrugging of the shoulders, accompanied by some trivial maxim on the foolishness of women. This type of jocularity, above all when it bore on the illnesses of her children, twisted the dagger in Mme de Rênal's heart. This is what she encountered as successor to the forced and honeyed flatteries of the Jesuit convent where she had spent her childhood. Her education was accomplished by sadness. Too proud to speak of this kind of sorrow, even to her friend Mme Derville, she imagined that all men were like her husband, M. Valenod and the Sub-prefect Charcot de Maugiron. Coarseness, and the most brutal insensitivity to anything which did not concern money, status and decorations; blind hatred for all arguments which went contrary to them: these seemed to her the natural attributes of the sex, like wearing boots and felt hats.

After long years, Mme de Rênal was still not accustomed to these money men in whose midst she must live.

Hence the success of the little peasant Julien. She found a soft delight, all glowing with the charm of novelty, in the sympathy of this noble and proud soul. Mme de Rênal had swiftly forgiven him his extreme ignorance, which became an added grace, and the crudity of his manners, which she was able to correct. She found that it was worth listening to him, even when speaking of the most ordinary matters, even when it was a case of a poor dog being crushed as he crossed the road, by a peasant's hurrying cart. At the sight of this sad event her husband gave his loud laugh, while she saw Julien's beautiful black eyebrows, so finely arched, contract. Generosity, nobility of soul, humanity, gradually seemed to her to exist only in this young abbé. She felt for him alone all the sympathy and even admiration these virtues arouse in finely disposed natures.

In Paris Julien's relations with Mme de Rênal would swiftly have been simplified; but in Paris love is born of fiction. The young tutor and his shy mistress would have found the explanation of their situation in three or four novels, or even in some couplets from the *Gymnase*.[3] The novels would have outlined for them the parts to play, showed them the model to imitate; and sooner or later, although with no pleasure, perhaps reluctantly, vanity would have forced Julien to follow the model.

In some little town in the Aveyron or the Pyrenees the slightest happening would have been decisive because of the fiery climate. Under our more sombre skies, a poor young man who is ambitious only because his sensitivity of spirit gives him the need for some of the enjoyments available to wealth, can meet every day with a woman of thirty, genuinely modest, taken up with her children and far from finding exemplars for her conduct in novels. Everything proceeds slowly; in the provinces everything happens little by little, things are more natural.

Often, in considering the young tutor's poverty, Mme de Rênal was moved close to tears. One day Julien came upon her actually crying.

— Oh! madame, has there been some misfortune?

— No, my friend, she replied; call the children, and let us go for a walk.

She took his arm and leant on it in a way that seemed odd to Julien. It was the first time she had called him her friend.

Towards the end of their walk, Julien noticed that she was blushing profusely. She slackened her pace.

— Someone may have told you, said she without looking at him, that I am the sole heir of a very rich aunt who lives in Besançon. She heaps presents on me . . . My sons make progress . . . so wonderfully . . . that I beg you to accept a little gift as a token of my appreciation. It is only a matter of a few louis for your linen. But . . . she added blushing even deeper, and stopped speaking.

— What, madame? said Julien.

— It would be unnecessary, she went on, lowering her head, to speak of this to my husband.

— I am unimportant, madame, but I'm not low, replied Julien, halting, his eyes sparkling with anger, and drawing himself up to his full height, that is what you haven't sufficiently thought about. I'd be even meaner than a valet if I put myself in the position of concealing from M. de Rênal anything relating to *my money*.

Mme de Rênal was astounded.

– M. le Maire, continued Julien, has given me thirty-six francs on five occasions since I've come to live in his house; I'm ready to show my expenses book to M. de Rênal or to whoever it may be – even to M. Valenod, who detests me.

At the end of this outburst Mme de Rênal was pale and trembling, and the walk came to an end with neither one nor the other able to find a pretext for renewing the conversation. A love for Mme de Rênal became more and more impossible in Julien's proud heart; as for her, she respected him, she admired him; she had been rebuked. Under the pretext of making up for the humiliation she had unwittingly caused him, she allowed herself to pay him even more tender attentions. The novelty of these proceedings constituted Mme de Rênal's happiness for a week. Their effect was to soften Julien's anger in part; he was far from seeing in them anything resembling personal affection.

That's it, he said to himself, just like the rich – they humiliate you, and then think they can put everything right with a few monkey tricks!

Despite her resolutions in this respect, Mme de Rênal's heart was too full of the matter, and still too innocent, for her not to tell her husband of the offer she had made to Julien, and the way in which she had been repulsed.

– How, replied M. de Rênal, much nettled, have you been able to put up with a refusal from a *servant*?

And, when Mme de Rênal protested at this word:

– I speak, madame, as did the late Prince de Condé, when presenting his chamberlains to his new wife: '*All these people here,*' he said to her, '*are our servants.*' I've read you that passage from Besenval's *Memoirs*[4] – essential reading on matters of precedence. Everybody who isn't a gentleman, who lives in your house and receives a salary, is your servant. I'm am going to have a word with this M. Julien, and give him a hundred francs.

– Oh! my dear, said Mme de Rênal, trembling, at least don't do it in front of the servants!

– Yes, they could be jealous, and with good reason, said her husband, leaving and thinking about the amount of money.

Mme de Rênal sank on to a chair, almost fainting with unhappiness. He is going to humiliate Julien, and it's my fault! She felt disgusted with her husband and hid her face in her hands. She resolved firmly never to make any more confidences.

When next she saw Julien, she was trembling all over, her chest so constricted that she could not manage to speak a word. In her embarrassment she took his hands and pressed them.

– Well! my dear, she said to him finally, are you satisfied with my husband?

– How could I not be? replied Julien, with a bitter smile; he's given me a hundred francs.

Mme de Rênal looked at him uncertainly.

– Give me your arm, she said at last, with a note of courage new to Julien.

She was brave enough to go as far as the bookseller in Verrières, in spite of his terrible reputation for liberalism. There she chose ten livres' worth of books to give to her children. But these books were ones she knew Julien wanted. She insisted that there, in the bookseller's shop, each of the children write his name in the books that fell to his share. While Mme de Rênal was pleased with having made amends to Julien in this audacious way, he himself was amazed at the quantity of books he saw in the shop. Never had he dared enter so profane a place; his heart throbbed. Far from being concerned to find out what was going on in Mme de Rênal's heart, he thought deeply about the means by which a young student of theology could come to own some of these books. Eventually he had the idea that it might be possible, with some skill, to persuade M. de Rênal that he ought to give to his sons as an essay topic the story of famous gentlemen born in the province. After a month of manoeuvring, Julien saw his idea succeed – and to such a degree that, some time afterwards, in talking to M. de Rênal, he ventured mentioning a course of action that would be far more painful for the noble mayor;

it concerned taking a subscription out at the bookseller, and thus contributing to the fortune of a liberal. M. de Rênal fully agreed that it would be prudent to give his eldest son a *visual impression* of numerous works he would hear mentioned in conversation when he went to the military school; but Julien saw M. de Rênal baulk at going any further. He suspected a hidden agenda, but was unable to make it out.

– I believe, monsieur, he said to him one day, that it is highly unsuitable that the name of a prominent gentleman such as a de Rênal should appear on a bookseller's squalid subscription list.

M. de Rênal's brow lightened.

– It would also be a very bad mark, Julien went on in a humbler tone, for a poor student of theology if someone discovered one day that his name had been on the list of a bookseller hiring out volumes. The liberals would be able to accuse me of asking for the most infamous works; who knows, they might even go so far as to write the titles of such perverse books in after my name.

But Julien was losing the scent. He saw the Mayor's face resume an expression of embarrassment and dissatisfaction. Julien kept silent. I've got my man, he said to himself.

A few days afterwards, in M. de Rênal's presence, the eldest child asked Julien about a book announced in *La Quotidienne*:[5]

– To make sure there's no opportunity for the Jacobin party to triumph, said the young tutor, and to furnish me nevertheless with the means of satisfying M. Adolphe, a subscription should be taken out at the bookseller's by the least important of your people.

– Now, that's not a bad idea, said M. de Rênal, obviously delighted.

– At the same time it is necessary to stipulate, said Julien, with that grave and almost unhappy air that comes so readily to certain natures when they see the success of plans they have long desired to succeed, it is necessary to stipulate that the servant in question should not be able to take out any novel. Once in the house, such dangerous books could corrupt the women, and even the servant himself.

– You forget political pamphlets, added M. de Rênal in a lofty tone. He wanted to conceal his admiration for the crafty *mezzo termine*[6] devised by his children's tutor.

Julien's existence thus came to consist of a series of petty negotiations; and their outcome interested him much more than the marked preference for himself that was waiting to be read in Mme de Rênal's heart.

The moral situation in which he had lived all his life reproduced itself at M. le Maire's house at Verrières. Here, as at his father's mill, he profoundly distrusted the people with whom he lived, and was hated by them. Every day he observed in the talk of the Sub-prefect, of M. Valenod, of other friends of the family, how little their ideas corresponded to reality concerning things that happened under their eyes. An action that seemed to him admirable was precisely the one which would incur the blame of those around him. His inner response was always: What monsters, or What idiots! The laughable thing is that, with all his pride, he frequently understood absolutely nothing of the subjects about which they spoke.

In his whole life he had talked sincerely only with the old Surgeon-major; the little information he possessed was about Bonaparte's Italian campaigns, or surgery. His youthful hardihood relished accounts of the details of the most frightful operations; he told himself: I would not have flinched.

The first time that Mme de Rênal tried to have a conversation with him other than about children's education, he started to talk of surgical procedures; she went pale and begged him to stop.

Julien knew nothing else. So, in his daily life with Mme de Rênal a most peculiar silence came to prevail when they were alone. In the drawing-room, however humble his mien might be, she saw in his eyes an air of intellectual superiority to all who appeared at her house. But, finding herself alone with him only for a moment, she perceived him visibly embarrassed. She was uneasy, for her feminine instinct told her that in this embarrassment there was nothing tender.

On the basis of a peculiar impression taken from some story of good society as seen by the old Surgeon-major, Julien felt humiliated from the moment silence fell in female company, as if the silence had been his particular fault. This feeling was a hundred times more painful when they were alone. His imagination, full of overblown, almost Spanish, notions of what a man ought to say when alone with a woman, offered him, in his distress, only inadmissible ideas. His head was in the clouds, yet he was incapable of breaking out of that most humiliating silence. Hence his severe manner during his long walks with Mme de Rênal and her children was reinforced by the cruellest suffering. He mistrusted himself horribly. If by mischance he forced himself to speak, he ended up saying the silliest things. To complete his misery, he was conscious of his own absurdity, and exaggerated it. But what he did not see was the expression of his eyes; they were so fine, and spoke of so ardent a spirit that, like good actors, they sometimes imparted a charming meaning to that which had none. Mme de Rênal noticed that, when alone with her, he never said anything interesting except when, distracted by some unforeseen event, he forgot to think of paying compliments. Since the friends of the household did not indulge her by presenting her with new and brilliant ideas, she delighted in Julien's snatches of wit.

Since the fall of Napoleon, all appearance of gallantry has been severely barred from provincial manners. There is a fear of being deprived of one's post. The scoundrels seek the support of the Congregation; and hypocrisy has made most wonderful progress even in the liberal ranks. Boredom redoubles itself. There remain no other pleasures but reading and agriculture.

Mme de Rênal, wealthy heiress of a doting aunt, married at sixteen to a fine gentleman, had never in her life either felt or seen anything the least in the world like love. Only her confessor, the good Curé Chélan, had really talked to her of it – concerning the pursuit of M. Valenod – and he had created such a disgusting image that the word represented for her nothing but the most abject debauchery. Love as she had found it in the very small number of novels that had by chance come to her attention, she regarded as an exception, or perhaps quite out of this world. Thanks to this ignorance, Mme de Rênal, perfectly content and constantly preoccupied with Julien, was far from feeling the slightest self-reproach.

CHAPTER 8

Minor Events

Then there were sighs, the deeper for suppression
And stolen glances, the sweeter for the theft,
And burning blushes, though for no transgression.

DON JUAN, canto I, stanza 74[1]

The angelic sweetness that flowed from Mme de Rênal's character and from her current state of happiness was only a trifle disturbed when she came to think about her lady's maid, Élisa. This girl had received an inheritance, and went off to Curé Chélan to make her confession, telling him of her plan to marry Julien. The Curé was truly delighted at his friend's happiness; but extremely surprised when Julien said with a resolute air that he was unable to accept Mlle Élisa's offer.

– Be mindful, my child, of what goes on in your heart, said the Curé, frowning; I congratulate you on your vocation, if it is that alone which leads you to despise a very adequate little fortune. Fifty-six years have gone by since I've been the Curé of Verrières and nevertheless, in all likelihood, I am going to be dismissed. It grieves me – and yet I have an income of eight hundred livres. I let you know this detail so that you will not entertain illusions about what is in store for you in the priestly state. If you dream of paying court to those in power, your everlasting ruin is assured. You could make your fortune, but you must grind down the poor, flatter the Sub-prefect, the Mayor, the man of reputation, and cater to his passions: such conduct, which society at large calls knowledge of the world, might, for a layman, not be absolutely incompatible with salvation; but, in our calling, it is necessary to choose; one must make one's fortune in this world or the other, there is no middle way. Go now, my friend, think, and return in three days, time to give me a definite answer. I dimly make out, to my sorrow, a sombre flame in the depths of your being, which doesn't speak to me of the moderation and perfect abnegation of worldly advantage necessary to a priest; I predict good things for your intellect; but allow me to say this to you, went on the good Curé, with tears in his eyes, in the priesthood I would tremble for your salvation.

Julien was ashamed of his emotion; for the first time in his life he felt himself to be loved; he wept with delight, and went to hide his tears in the great woods above Verrières.

Why do I find myself in this state? he asked himself at last; I feel that I would give my life a hundred times over for this good Curé Chélan, yet he has demonstrated to me that I am no more than a fool. It is him above all that I ought to deceive, and he sees right through me. This hidden flame he talks about – it's my ambition to make my fortune. He thinks me unworthy of being a priest, and that at the very moment when I thought the sacrifice of an income of fifty louis would have given him the highest notion of my piety and my vocation.

In the future, went on Julien, I will rely only on those parts of my character I have tested. Who would have thought I would have found pleasure in shedding tears! – that I would love someone who shows me that I am no better than a fool!

Three days later, Julien had hit on the pretext with which he should have armed himself from the start; this pretext was a calumny, but what does that matter? He told the Curé, with much hesitation, that from the very first there had been a reason deterring him from the projected marriage which – because it was detrimental to another – he had been unable to explain to him. This amounted to impugning Élisa's conduct. M. Chélan was conscious of a certain worldly vehemence in his manner, very far from that which should animate a youthful Levite.

– My friend, he advised once more, become a good independent country dweller, worthy and educated, rather than a priest without vocation.

So far as language went, Julien responded very cleverly to these renewed remonstrances; he found words which a fervent young seminarist might have used; but his tone in deploying them, and the ill-concealed passion that shone from his eyes, alarmed M. Chélan.

It is unnecessary to fear for Julien's future; he worked out the correct diction for a cunning and cautious hypocrisy. Not too bad considering his age. As to the tone and gestures – he lived with country folk; he had been deprived of sight of the great models. Later, he needed hardly to come near these gentlemen before he excelled in gesture as well as words.

Mme de Rênal was amazed that her maid's new prosperity failed to make the girl happier; she saw her constantly going to see the Curé and returning with tears in her eyes. Eventually Élisa spoke to her about her marriage.

Mme de Rênal felt herself to be ill; a kind of fever prevented her from sleeping; she awoke to existence only when her maid or Julien was under her eyes. All she could think of was them, and the happiness they would find together. The poverty of their little house, where one had to live on an income of fifty louis, presented itself to her in ravishing colours. Julien could very well make himself an advocate in Bray, the sub-prefecture two leagues from Verrières; in which case she would sometimes see him.

Mme de Rênal sincerely believed that she was on the way to becoming insane; she told her husband of it, and eventually fell ill. The same evening, as her maid waited on her, she saw that the girl was in tears. She loathed Élisa at that moment, and had been short with her; she asked her pardon. Élisa's tears redoubled; she said that if her mistress would permit it she would tell her all her unhappiness.

– Well, tell me, replied Mme de Rênal.

– Oh, well, madame, he has refused me; some wicked people must have spoken ill of me, and he has believed them.

– Who has refused you? said Mme de Rênal, scarcely breathing.

– Oh, who, madame if not M. Julien? replied the lady's maid, sobbing. M. le Curé cannot overcome his resistance; for M. le Curé thinks that he ought not to refuse an honest girl, under the pretext that she's been a lady's maid. After all, M. Julien's father is no more than a carpenter; and himself, how did he make his living before entering Madame's house?

Mme de Rênal heard no more; an excess of happiness had almost robbed her of reason. She made her maid repeat time after time that Julien had refused in a definite manner, and one which would not allow him to change back to a wiser course.

– I want to try one last effort, she said to her maid, I'll talk to M. Julien.

After breakfast the next day Mme de Rênal gave herself the delicious indulgence of pleading her rival's cause, and of hearing Élisa's hand and fortune consistently refused for an hour.

Gradually Julien went beyond making constrained answers and ended by replying with spirit to Mme de Rênal's prudent arguments. She could not resist the torrent of happiness which flooded her soul after so many days of despair. She found herself ill indeed. When she was recovered and safely established in her own room, she sent everyone away. She was deeply disturbed.

Could I be in love with Julien? she asked herself at last.

This discovery, which at any other time would have plunged her into remorse and profound agitation, was now for her nothing but a strange spectacle, and indeed one to which she was indifferent. Her spirit, exhausted by all that she had been through, could find no further resources of sensibility to fuel her passions.

Mme de Rênal wished to work, but fell into a deep slumber; when she awoke she wasn't as alarmed as she should have been. She was too happy to be able to take anything badly. Naive and innocent, this excellent provincial woman had never tortured her spirit in the attempt to wring out a little sensibility from some novel refinement of feeling or of melancholy. Completely absorbed, before Julien's coming, by the mass of work that, away from Paris, is the lot of a good mother of a family, Mme de Rênal thought of the passions as we think of the lottery: certainly a delusion, and a reward sought by fools.

The dinner bell rang; Mme de Rênal blushed deeply when she heard Julien's voice as he led in the children. A little more cunning since being in love, she explained her colouring by complaining of a terrible headache.

– Typical woman, replied M. de Rênal, with a great laugh. There's always something to put right with those particular machines!

Although she was used to this sort of wit, her husband's tone of voice shocked Mme de Rênal. To distract herself she studied Julien's physiognomy; if he had been the ugliest of men he would have pleased her at that moment.

Careful to imitate the habits of the people at court, M. de Rênal moved to Vergy in the first fine days of spring; this is the village made famous by the tragic career of Gabrielle.[2] A few hundred paces from the wonderfully picturesque ruins of an ancient gothic church, M. de Rênal possessed an old château with four turrets and a garden designed like that of the Tuileries, with an abundance of box borders and alleys of chestnuts pruned twice a year. A neighbouring field planted with apple trees served as a place to stroll. Eight or ten magnificent walnut trees stood at the end of the orchard; their massive foliage rose to a height of perhaps eighty feet.

Each of these damn walnuts, said M. de Rênal when his wife admired them, costs me half an acre's produce – corn cannot grow under their shade.

The sight of the countryside was as if new to Mme de Rênal; her admiration for it was close to rapture. The emotion with which she was filled gave her intelligence and resolution. Two days after their arrival at Vergy, M. de Rênal having returned to town on mayoral business, Mme de Rênal hired some workers at her own expense. Julien had given her the idea of a little sanded path which would go around in the orchard and under the great walnuts, allowing the children to walk in the morning without getting their shoes soaked with dew. This idea was put into execution less than twenty-four hours after having been conceived. Mme de Rênal passed the whole day light-heartedly with Julien, directing the workers.

When the Mayor of Verrières returned from town, he was much surprised to find the alley complete. His arrival surprised Mme de Rênal also; she had forgotten his existence. For two months he spoke with irritation of the rashness involved in having carried out so important a *betterment* without consulting him, but was somewhat comforted by the fact that it had been done at Mme de Rênal's own expense.

She spent her days romping with the children in the orchard and chasing butterflies. Large nets of clear gauze had been made, with which one caught the poor *lepidopters*. That was the barbarous name Julien taught Mme de Rênal. For she had had M. Godart's fine work[3] sent from Besançon; and Julian told her the strange habits of these poor creatures.

They were pitilessly transfixed with pins on to a large square of cardboard, also set up by Julien.

At last there was a subject of conversation between Mme de Rênal and Julien; he was no longer exposed to the frightful torment that periods of silence gave him.

They talked to each other endlessly, with very great interest, though always about the most innocent topics. This active life, busy and cheerful, was to everyone's taste except that of Mlle Élisa, who found herself overwhelmed with work. Not even during the Carnival, she said, when there is a ball at Verrières, does Madame take so much trouble over her dress; she changes her outfit two or three times a day.

Since our intention is to flatter no one, we cannot really deny that Mme de Rênal, who had marvellous skin, arranged to wear dresses which left her arms and neck much exposed. She was beautifully formed, and this way of presenting herself was ravishing.

— You have never *been so young*, madame, said her Verrières friends coming to dine at Vergy. (This is a local phrase.)

The strange thing, which among us will scarcely be believed, is that Mme de Rênal took such pains with her dress without any deliberate object. She took pleasure in it; and, without her thinking much about it, all the time not spent chasing butterflies with Julien and the children was devoted to working with Élisa on her wardrobe. Her single journey to Verrières was the result of a desire to buy some of the new summer dresses arrived from Mulhouse.

She brought back to Vergy a young woman who was related to her. Since her marriage, Mme de Rênal had unsensibly become an intimate of Mme Derville, who before that had been her companion at the *Sacred Heart*.

Mme Derville laughed a great deal at what she called her cousin's wild ideas: by myself, I'd never think of that, she would say. When she was in the company of her husband, Mme de Rênal was ashamed of these unforeseen ideas, which in Paris one would call witticisms; but Mme Derville's presence gave her the courage of them. At first she spoke her thoughts in a tentative manner; when the ladies were alone together for a long time Mme de Rênal's wit was enlivened, and a long solitary morning would pass in an instant and leave the two friends full of gaiety. On this visit, the shrewd Mme Derville found her cousin much less vivacious but much happier.

Julien, on his side, had lived like a real child since his stay in the country, as happy to run around chasing butterflies with his pupils as they were. After so much constraint and cunning manoeuvring, alone, far from the observation of men, and by instinct not at all afraid of Mme de Rênal, he gave himself up to the pleasure of existence, so powerful at that age, and in the midst of the most beautiful mountains in the world.

From the moment of Mme Derville's arrival, Julien felt that she was his friend; he was quick to show her the view from the end of the new path under the great walnut trees. In truth, it is equal, if not superior, to the best that the Swiss or Italian lakes can offer; if one climbs the steep slope which starts a few paces away, one soon comes to deep precipices bordered with woods of oak that reach down almost to the river. It was to the summits of these sheer rocks that Julien, happy, free and – even something better – the king of his castle, led the two friends and rejoiced in their admiration of the sublime views.

– For me it is like Mozart's music, said Mme Derville.

The jealousy of his brothers, the presence of a despotic father full of ill temper, had spoilt the countryside around Verrières for Julien. At Vergy there were no such bitter associations; for the first time in his life there was no enemy to be seen. When M. de Rênal was back in the town, which often happened, he dared to read; soon, instead of reading at night, and even then having to be careful to hide his lamp beneath an upturned vase, he was able to give himself over to slumber; in the daytime, in the interval between the children's lessons, he went to those rocks with the volume which was the sole ruler of his conduct and the object of his rapture.[4] In it he found at once happiness, ecstasy and consolation in times of discouragement.

Certain things that Napoleon said about women, numerous discussions about the merits of fashionable novels in his reign, gave him then, for the first time, some ideas that any other young man of his age would have had long before.

The intense summer heats came round. They got into the habit of spending the evenings under an immense lime tree a few feet from the house. Beneath it the darkness was profound. One evening Julien was speaking energetically, rejoicing with delight in the pleasure of talking well, and in front of two young women; in gesticulating, he touched Mme de Rênal's hand, which was resting on the back of one of those painted chairs that are put in gardens.

The hand was very quickly withdrawn; but Julien conceived that it was his *duty* to ensure that this hand be not withdrawn when he touched it. The idea of a duty to accomplish, and of ridicule – or rather a feeling of inferiority – to endure if one didn't succeed in doing it, banished all pleasure from his heart on the spot.

CHAPTER 9

A Rural Evening

M. Guérin's Dido, a charming sketch.
STROMBECK[1]

When he met Mme de Rênal again the following day he had a peculiar look in his eyes; he observed her as though she were an enemy with whom he must do battle. His looks, so different from those of yesterday, undermined Mme de Rênal's self-control: she had been kind to him, and he seemed angry with her. She could not take her eyes off his.

Mme Derville's presence allowed Julien to talk less and concentrate more on what was in his mind. His sole concern, all day long, was to fortify himself by studying the inspired book that tempered and re-tempered his soul.

He cut the children's lessons very short, and later, when Mme de Rênal's presence recalled him wholly to the pursuit of his glory, he decided that it was absolutely necessary she should allow her hand to remain in his that very evening.

The setting of the sun and the approach of the decisive moment made Julien's heart beat strangely. Night came. He saw – with a joyful feeling that lifted a great weight from his breast – that it was extremely dark. The sky, full of heavy cloud blown across on a sultry breeze, seemed to threaten a storm. The two friends stayed out walking very late. Everything they did that evening appeared strange to Julien. They were delighting in this weather, which, for certain delicate sensibilities, seems to enhance the pleasure of loving.

At last they were seated, Mme de Rênal at Julien's side and Mme Derville next to her friend. Preoccupied with what he was about to attempt, Julien found nothing to say. The talk languished.

Shall I be trembling like this, and so ill at ease when the first duel comes my way? said Julien to himself – for he was too sceptical about himself and about others not to be conscious of the state of his soul.

In his mortal anguish, all possible perils seemed to him preferable to this. How many times did he not long to see some little matter come along which would oblige Mme de Rênal to go back into the house and leave the garden! The violence of Julien's effort to control himself was too great for his voice not to be profoundly altered; soon Mme de Rênal's voice began to tremble as well, but Julien did not notice that at all. The frightful combat that duty fought against timidity was too taxing for him to be able to observe anything outside himself. A quarter to ten chimed from the château clock without his having dared a thing. Indignant at his cowardice, Julien said to himself: At the exact moment when ten o'clock strikes, I will carry out what I have the entire day been promising myself to do this evening – or I go up to my quarters and blow my brains out.

After a final period of tension and worry, during which Julien became almost beside himself with his excess of feeling, ten struck on the clock above his head. Each stroke of this fatal clock echoed in his breast, and produced there an almost physical reaction.

At last, as the final stroke of ten was still reverberating, he extended his hand and took that of Mme de Rênal – who withdrew it immediately. Julien, not too well aware of what he was doing, seized it again. Though so fraught with emotion himself, he was struck with the glacial coldness of the hand he held. He pressed it with convulsive force. A final effort was made to free it from him; but at last it stayed in his.

His soul was flooded with happiness, not because he loved Mme de Rênal, but because a frightful torment had come to an end. So that Mme Derville should not notice anything, he felt obliged to speak; his voice was now powerful and resonant. Mme de Rênal's voice, on the contrary, betrayed so much emotion that her friend thought her unwell and suggested that they go inside. Julien sensed a danger: If Mme de Rênal goes back into the salon I will have fallen again into the dreadful state in which I have passed the day. I have held that hand for far too short a time for it to count as a solid gain.

At the moment when Mme Derville renewed her suggestion of going back into the salon Julien squeezed strongly the hand that had been abandoned to him.

Mme de Rênal, who had already risen, seated herself again, saying, in a dying tone:

— It is true I feel a little unwell, but the open air does me good.

These words confirmed Julien's happiness, which was just then extreme: he talked, he forgot to dissemble, he appeared to the two listening friends to be the most charming of men. Nevertheless there was still some lack of confidence in the eloquence that had suddenly come to him. He was in deadly fear lest Mme Derville, wearied by the wind which was building up before the storm, should want to go back by herself into the salon. Then he would be left alone with Mme de Rênal. He had found, almost by chance, enough blind courage to act; but he felt it quite out of his power to say the simplest thing to Mme de Rênal. However gentle her reproaches might be, he would be beaten, and the gain he had made annihilated.

Happily for him, that evening, his moving and incisive talk found favour with Mme Derville, who frequently found him as awkward as a child and not very amusing. As for Mme de Rênal, her hand in Julien's, she thought of nothing; she let herself live. Those hours that were passed under the great lime tree, which local tradition said was planted by Charles the Bold,[2] were for her an epoch of happiness. She listened with delight to the sighs of the wind in the dense foliage of the lime tree and the noise of the occasional drops that had started to fall on the lower leaves. Julien failed to notice a circumstance that should have reassured him greatly: after having been obliged to free her hand when she got up to help her cousin retrieve a vase of flowers that the wind had turned over at their feet, Mme de Rênal had hardly seated herself again than she gave it back to him with almost no difficulty, as though there had already been an understanding between them.

Midnight had sounded long since; they had to leave the garden; they separated. Mme de Rênal, transported by the happiness of loving, was so ignorant that she hardly reproached herself at all. Happiness robbed her of sleep. A sleep-like lead enwrapped Julien, mortally weary from the battles that timidity and pride had waged all day in his heart.

Next day he woke at five; and – what would have been cruel for Mme de Rênal had she known it – gave her scarcely a thought. He had *done his duty, a heroic duty*. Filled with the warmth of this sentiment, he locked himself in his room and gave himself over, with totally new pleasure, to studying the exploits of his hero.

When the bell for lunch made itself heard, he had forgotten all his gains of the previous evening, so caught up was he in reading the bulletins of the Grand Army. Going down to the salon, he said to himself lightly: It is necessary to tell this woman that I love her.

Instead of the looks filled with voluptuous sweetness he expected to encounter, he found the severe face of M. de Rênal, who had arrived two hours since and didn't conceal in the least his displeasure that Julien had spent the whole morning not attending to the children. Nothing could be so unattractive as this important man in a bad temper and thinking he was in a position to show it.

Each harsh word from her husband pierced Mme de Rênal's heart. But as to Julien, he was so immersed in ecstatic thoughts, still so preoccupied with the great events that for many hours had paraded before his eyes, that at first he could hardly bring his attention down to the level of hearing the harsh words being addressed to him by M. de Rênal. At last he said to him, rather brusquely:

– I was ill.

The tone of this reply would have annoyed a much less irritable man than the Mayor of Verrières. He had some idea of throwing Julien out on the spot; he was only restrained by his maxim that one should never be hasty in business.

This young idiot, he said to himself after a moment, has, in my household, built himself up some sort of reputation – Valenod could take him in, or perhaps he could marry Élisa, and in both these cases he would be able to laugh from the bottom of his heart at my expense.

Despite the wisdom of these reflections, M. de Rênal's displeasure none the less rung out in a series of coarse expressions that, little by little, angered Julien. Mme de Rênal was on the point of dissolving into tears. Lunch had only just ended when she asked Julien to give her his arm for a walk, when she leant on it with affection. To all that she said to him Julien could only mutter:

— *That's the rich for you!*

M. de Rênal was striding very close to them; his presence increased Julien's anger. He realized suddenly that Mme de Rênal was leaning on his arm in a demonstrative way; the gesture horrified him; he pushed her sharply away and disengaged his arm.

Fortunately, M. de Rênal completely missed this fresh impertinence and only Mme Derville noticed it — her friend dissolved in tears. At that moment M. de Rênal was occupied with throwing stones after a little peasant girl who had taken an unauthorized path across the corner of the orchard.

— Monsieur Julien, control yourself if you please; remember that we all have moments of temper, she said quickly.

Julien looked at her coldly with eyes that expressed the most perfect scorn.

This look astonished Mme Derville, who would have been even more surprised if she had guessed what it really signified; then she would have read in it a vague hope of the most atrocious vengeance. Such moments of humiliation are doubtless what create Robespierres.[3]

— Your Julien is very violent, he frightens me, whispered Mme Derville to her friend.

— He is right to be angry, replied the latter. After the amazing progress he has made with the children, what does it matter if he spends a morning not speaking to them? It must be admitted men are very hard.

For the first time in her life, Mme de Rênal felt some kind of desire for revenge on her husband. The extreme hatred against the rich that filled Julien was about to burst out. Luckily M. de Rênal called over his gardener, and remained occupied with him, barring off the unauthorized path across the orchard with bales of thorn. For the whole of the rest of the walk Julien failed to respond with a single word to the kind attentions of which he was the object. Hardly had M. de Rênal left them than the two friends, pleading fatigue, had each asked him for an arm.

Between these two women, whose extreme distress covered their cheeks with blushes and confusion, Julien's proud pallor, his sombre and purposeful air, formed a curious contrast. He despised the women and every tender feeling.

What! said he to himself, not even five hundred francs' allowance to complete my studies? Ah, how I'd send him packing!

Taken up with these harsh thoughts, the little he deigned to understand in the soothing words of the two friends irritated him as empty of meaning, silly, feeble, in a word, *feminine*.

Talking for talk's sake and seeking to keep the conversation alive, it occurred to Mme de Rênal to mention that her husband had come up from Verrières because he had made a bargain with one of the farmers for maize straw. (In that region they stuff the mattresses with maize straw.)

— My husband won't be rejoining us, added Mme de Rênal; he wants to finish off the renewal of the house mattresses with the gardener and his valet. This morning they put maize straw in all the beds of the first floor, now he's up to the second.

Julien changed colour; he gave Mme de Rênal a strange look and in a moment took her aside, as it were, by doubling his pace. Mme Derville let them get away from her.

— Save my life, said Julien to Mme de Rênal, you're the only one that can for you know the valet hates me like death. I must confess to you, madame, that I have a portrait; I've hidden it in the mattress of my bed.

At this speech Mme de Rênal paled in her turn.

— Only you, madame, can go into my room at this moment; search, without letting it be seen, in the corner of the mattress nearest to the window, and you will find there a glossy little black cardboard box.

— With a portrait inside! said Mme de Rênal, hardly able to hold herself upright.

Julien saw her demoralized air, of which he immediately took advantage.

— I have a second favour to beg of you, madame, I implore that you don't look at that portrait, it's my secret.

– It's a secret! echoed Mme de Rênal in a stifled voice.

However, although brought up among people who were money-proud and moved by financial considerations alone, love had already planted generosity in her soul. Cruelly wounded as she was, it was with an air of the most uncomplicated devotion that Mme de Rênal asked Julien the questions necessary for her to be able to accomplish her mission successfully.

– So, she said to him as she left, a little round box, of black cardboard, very glossy?

– Yes, madame, replied Julien with that hard look that danger gives to men.

She climbed up to the second floor of the château, pale as if she were going to her death. To crown her misery, she felt as though she might be on the point of fainting; but the necessity of doing a service for Julien gave her strength.

– I must have that box, said she to herself, redoubling her speed.

She heard her husband talking to the valet in Julien's room. Luckily they passed on to that of the children. She lifted the mattress and thrust her hand into the straw with such force that she grazed her fingers. But, though extremely sensitive to minor injuries of that kind, she was unaware of this one, for almost at the same instant she felt the smoothness of the cardboard box. She grabbed it and left.

Hardly was she free of the fear of being surprised by her husband when the horror inspired in her by this box made her feel really faint.

Then Julien is in love – and I'm holding the portrait of the woman he loves!

Sunk on a chair in the antechamber of the apartment, Mme de Rênal was prey to all the torments of jealousy. Her extreme ignorance was again helpful to her at that moment, for astonishment tempered her pain. Julien appeared and grabbed the box, without offering her thanks, without a word, and rushed to his room where he made a fire and straightaway burned it.

Napoleon's portrait, he said to himself, shaking his head, found hidden in the room of one who professes such hatred for the usurper! – found by M. de Rênal, so very much an Ultra and so very angry! – and, to complete my foolishness, on the white card behind the portrait, lines in my handwriting! – which could leave no doubt at all of my excess of admiration! – and each of these effusions has a date! – there's one from the day before yesterday.

My whole reputation gone, annihilated in a moment! said Julien to himself, watching the box burn, and my reputation is all I possess, I cannot live without it . . . and anyway what a life it is, good God!

An hour later, fatigue and the pity he felt for himself disposed him to a softer mood. He met Mme de Rênal and took her hand, which he kissed with more sincerity than he had ever done. She coloured with pleasure and, almost at the same instant, repulsed Julien with jealous anger. Julien's pride, so recently wounded, made him at that moment act like a fool. He now saw in Mme de Rênal nothing but a rich woman, disdainfully let drop her hand, and departed. He went for a stroll in the garden to think, and soon a bitter smile appeared on his lips.

– I walk here calmly like a man who is master of his time! I'm not doing anything about the children! I am exposing myself to M. de Rênal's humiliating words, and he would be justified.

He ran to the children's room. The caresses of the youngest, of whom he was very fond, soothed his smarting pain a little.

This one doesn't despise me yet, thought Julien. But soon he rebuked himself for this lessening of his pain as constituting a fresh weakness. These children caress me as they would caress the hound pup that was purchased yesterday.

CHAPTER 10

A Great Heart and a Little Fortune

But passion most dissembles yet betrays,
Even by its darkness; as the blackest sky
Foretells the heaviest tempest.

DON JUAN, canto I, stanza 73

M. de Rênal, who was proceeding through all the rooms in the château, returned to the one belonging to the children, accompanied by the servants carrying mattresses back. The sudden entry of this man was, for Julien, that drop of water which makes the vase overflow.

Even more pale, even more sombre than usual, he darted towards M. de Rênal. M. de Rênal stopped and glanced at his servants.

– Monsieur, said Julien, d'you imagine that if you had had any other tutor your children would have made the same progress as they have with me? If you can only answer no, continued Julien, without giving M. de Rênal a chance to reply, how dare you reproach me for neglecting them?

M. de Rênal no sooner recovered from his fright than he concluded from the unusual tone taken by the young peasant that he had in his pocket some advantageous offer and was going to leave him. Julien's anger mounted as he spoke:

– I can live without you, monsieur, he added.

– I'm truly sorry to find you so upset, answered M. de Rênal, stuttering a little. The servants were ten paces away, busy arranging the beds.

– That's not enough for me, monsieur, Julien – now beside himself – retorted; think of the shameful language you've used to me, and in front of the ladies, too!

69

M. de Rênal knew only too well what Julien was asking, and a painful conflict tore his soul. Then it chanced that Julien, in effect mad with anger, cried:

— I know where to go, monsieur, when I leave you.

At this announcement M. de Rênal had a vision of Julien installed at M. Valenod's place.

— Very well, monsieur, he said in a moment, with a sigh and an air like the one he might have adopted when calling in a surgeon for a major operation, I accede to your request. Counting from the day after tomorrow, which is the first of the month, I will give you fifty francs a month.

Julien felt a desire to laugh, and stood amazed: all his anger had vanished.

I haven't despised this brute sufficiently, he said to himself. That's undoubtedly the finest apology so base a nature can make.

The children, who had listened to this scene with open mouths, dashed into the garden to tell their mother that M. Julien was really angry, but that he was going to have fifty francs a month.

Julien followed them, out of habit, without even a look at M. de Rênal — whom he left in a state of profound irritation.

That's one hundred and sixty-eight francs, said the Mayor to himself, that M. Valenod has cost me. Assuredly I must have a couple of words with him about his plans for supplying the foundlings.

An instant later Julien was back face to face with M. de Rênal:

— I have a matter of conscience to discuss with M. Chélan; I have the honour to inform you that I shall be absent for some hours.

— Ah, my dear Julien! said M. de Rênal, laughing most insincerely, take the whole day, if you wish, and the whole day tomorrow, my good friend. Take the gardener's horse to get to Verrières.

— There he goes, said M. de Rênal to himself, to give Valenod an answer — he hasn't promised me anything, but you have to let young hotheads cool off.

Julien quickly escaped and climbed up into the great woods through which one can go from Vergy to Verrières. He had no wish to arrive at M. Chélan's house immediately. Far from wanting to subject himself to a fresh scene of hypocrisy, he needed to see clearly into his own heart, and to listen intently to the throng of feelings that disturbed it.

– I've won a a a battle, he said to himself as soon as he saw that he was in the woods and out of sight, so, I've won a battle!

This word painted his whole position for him in a brave light, and endowed his soul with a measure of calm.

– Here am I with fifty francs' salary a month – M. de Rênal must have been properly frightened. But what of?

This meditation on what could have frightened a happy and powerful man against whom an hour previously he had been boiling with rage, made Julien's calm complete. He was almost sensitive, for a moment, to the enchanting beauty of the woods through which he strode. Long ago, vast fragments of bare rock had fallen from the mountain side into the midst of the forest. Great beech trees had grown up nearly as high as these rocks – the shade of which produced a delicious freshness three steps from places where the heat of the sun's rays would have made lingering impossible.

Julien paused for breath for a moment in the shadow of the great rocks, then resumed his climb. Soon, by a scarcely distinguishable narrow path used only by goatherds, he found himself standing on top of a huge rock, and satisfied that he was quite isolated from humankind. This physical situation made him smile, for it represented to him the moral situation he burned to attain. The pure air of the high mountains spoke to his soul of serenity, even of joy. The Mayor of Verrières was certainly still, in his eyes, the representative of all the rich and insolent people on earth; but Julien felt that the hate that had disturbed him, despite the violence of its onset, had nothing personal in it. If he should cease to see M. de Rênal, he would have forgotten him in a week or so – him, his château, his dogs, his children and all his family. I have forced him, I don't know how, to make a very great sacrifice. What! – more than fifty écus a year! – and only a moment before that I had got myself out of the greatest danger. That's two victories in one day; the second has no merit – I will have to find out why it happened. But time enough tomorrow for such tedious enquiries.

Standing upright on his great rock Julien contemplated the sky, glowing with the August sun. Cicadas were chirruping in the country-side below the rock, and when they ceased all around him was silence. He could see twenty leagues of country spread out before his feet. From time to time a sparrowhawk from the huge rocks above his head made itself visible, describing its vast circles in silence. Julien's eye automatically followed the bird of prey. Its calm and powerful flight impressed him – he envied that strength, he envied that isolation.

It was the destiny of Napoleon – would it one day be his?

CHAPTER II

An Evening

> *Yet Julia's very coldness still was kind,*
> *And tremulously gentle her small hand*
> *Withdrew itself from his, but left behind*
> *A little pressure, thrilling, and so bland*
> *And slight, so very slight that to the mind*
> *'Twas but a doubt.*
>
> DON JUAN, canto I, stanza 71

It was necessary, however, to put in an appearance in Verrières. Leaving the presbytery, Julien ran by a happy chance into M. Valenod, whom he hastened to inform of his increase in salary.

On his return to Vergy, Julien delayed going down to the garden until it was shrouded in night. His spirit was tired out by the great number of powerful emotions that had agitated him all day. What shall I say to them? he wondered uneasily, thinking of the ladies. He was a long way from seeing that his mind was at just that level of concern with minor detail which usually absorbs the whole of women's attention. Julien was often unintelligible to Mme Derville, and even to her friend, and he in his turn did not understand more than half of what they said. Such was the effect of the power and, if I may put it so, the grandeur of the passionate impulses that convulsed this ambitious young man's soul. With this strange being, almost every day was a day of storms.

When he went into the garden that evening, Julien was ready to be interested in the thoughts of the pretty cousins. They awaited him eagerly. He took his usual place next to Mme de Rênal. The darkness soon became profound. He had an impulse to take the white hand

73

that for a long time he had seen lying next to him on the back of a chair. There was a little hesitation, but in the end it was withdrawn in a way that indicated some pique. Julien was inclined to let it be, and to continue blithely with the conversation, when he heard the approach of M. de Rênal.

Julien still had the coarse words of the morning in his ears. Wouldn't it be a way, he asked himself, of scorning this person – so heaped with the advantages of fortune – to get possession of his wife's hand in his very presence? Yes, I will do it – I, for whom he has shown such contempt.

From that moment, calm – so unnatural to Julien's character – swiftly vanished; now incapable of thinking of anything else, he anxiously desired that Mme de Rênal should genuinely want to give him her hand.

M. de Rênal angrily talked politics: two or three Verrières manufacturers had become decidedly richer than he was, and wanted to oppose him in the elections. Mme Derville listened to him; Julien, irritated by the talk, moved his chair closer to Mme de Rênal's. Darkness cloaked every movement. He ventured to put his hand very close to the pretty arm her dress left bare. He was confused, out of control of his thoughts, and, leaning his cheek alongside this pretty arm, dared to apply his lips to it.

Mme de Rênal trembled. Her husband was only four paces away; she quickly gave her hand to Julien, at the same moment pushing him from her a little. As M. de Rênal continued his complaints against the nobodies and Jacobins who were getting rich, Julien covered the hand which had been given to him with passionate kisses, or at least what seemed as such to Mme de Rênal. Yet the poor woman had had proof, on that fatal day, that the man she loved without confessing it loved someone else! During the whole of Julien's absence she had been prey to extreme unhappiness, which had forced her to think.

What's this! I'm in love, she said to herself, I feel love! Me, a married woman, I've fallen in love! – but, she continued to herself, I've never felt this dismal madness for my husband – something which makes me incapable of detaching my thoughts from Julien! And really, he's nothing but a boy who is full of respect for me! This will be a passing madness. What does it matter to my husband what feelings I may have for this young man? M. de Rênal would be bored by the conversations I have with Julien about things of the imagination. As for him, his interest is only in his business. I take nothing away from him to give to Julien.'

No hypocrisy had sullied the purity of this naive soul, bewildered by a passion such as she had never felt before. She was deceived, but without realizing it, and even then, her virtuous instincts were alarmed. These were the internal struggles that were agitating her when Julien appeared in the garden. She heard him speak almost at the same moment as she saw him sit beside her. Her soul was, in a manner, swept up by that sweet happiness which for the last fortnight had surprised her as much as it had seduced her. Nothing was foreseen by her. However, after a few moments she said to herself — so is it enough, then, for Julien to be present for all his offences to be wiped out? She was alarmed; and that was when she put her hand out of his way.

The kisses full of passion, the like of which she had never received, made her forget immediately that perhaps he loved another woman. Soon he was no longer guilty in her eyes. The cessation of her poignant sadness, daughter of suspicion, and the presence of a happiness of which she had never dreamt, sent her into raptures of love and wild gaiety. The evening was delightful to everyone, except the Mayor of Verrières, who was unable to forget the rich manufacturers. Julien thought no more of his dark ambitions, nor of his plans, so difficult to execute. For the first time in his life, he was enchanted by the power of beauty. Lost in a formless and soothing reverie quite alien to his nature, softly pressing a hand whose perfect prettiness gratified him, he half heard the rustling of the foliage of the elm stirred by the light night breeze and the distant barking of the dogs at the mill on the Doubs.

But this emotion was a pleasure, not a passion. Returning to his room, he thought of only one gratification — that of taking up his favourite book again; at twenty, the idea of the great world and the impact one might have on it carries all away.

Soon, however, he put down the book. Dreaming of Napoleon's

victories made him see something new about his own. Yes, I've won a battle, he said to himself, but one must profit by it – it is essential to crush the pride of this haughty gentleman while he's in retreat. That's pure Napoleon. I must demand a three-day leave to go and see my friend Fouqué. If he refuses, I threaten to break off our agreement again – but he'll give way.

Mme de Rênal could not close her eyes. It seemed to her that she had not lived until this moment. She was unable to tear her thoughts away from the bliss of the sensation of Julien covering her hand with ardent kisses.

Suddenly the frightful word *adultery* arose before her. All the most disgusting associations that vilest debauchery can impart to the idea of sensual love swarmed into her imagination. These associations worked to besmirch the tender and sacred image she had of Julien and of the happiness of loving him. The future portrayed itself in horrifying colours. She saw herself as an object of contempt.

This was a fearful moment; her soul was venturing into an unknown land. That evening she had tasted an exhilaration never felt till then; now she found herself suddenly plunged into excruciating unhappiness. She had no conception of such sufferings; they muddied her reasoning powers. For a moment she had the idea of confessing to her husband that she feared she was in love with Julien. That would allow her to speak of him. Fortunately, she met in her memory a precept delivered to her by her aunt long ago, on the eve of her marriage. It concerned the danger of confidences made to a husband, who, after all, is a master. In her excess of suffering she wrung her hands.

She was swept hither and thither by contradictory and pitiful imaginings. Now she feared that she was not loved; and now tormented by the frightful idea of a crime, as if tomorrow she were due to be exposed in the pillory in the public square at Verrières with a placard announcing her adultery to the populace.

Mme de Rênal had no experience of life; even when fully alert and in complete possession of her reasoning powers, she would not have perceived any gap between being guilty in the eyes of God and finding herself openly heaped with the noisiest manifestations of public contempt.

When she was allowed some respite from the frightful idea of adultery and all the ignominy that, in, her opinion, this crime brought in its train, and when she started to dream of the sweetness of an innocent life with Julien, as it had been in the past, she found herself flung into the horrible idea that Julien loved another woman. She pictured once more his white face when he was frightened of losing that portrait of her, or of compromising her by letting it be seen. For the first time, she had caught apprehension on that countenance, normally so calm and so noble. He had never shown himself moved like that for her or her children. Her suffering reached the highest intensity of misery that the human mind can naturally support. Without being aware of it, Mme de Rênal cried out loud, and so woke her lady's maid. Suddenly she saw the light of a lamp appear above her bed, and recognized Élisa.

– Is it you he loves? she cried in her distraction.

The lady's maid, amazed to find her mistress so terribly troubled, luckily paid no attention to this strange question. Mme de Rênal realized her indiscretion: I have a fever, said she to her, and I think I'm a little delirious; stay near me. Fully awake now because of the need for self-restraint, she found herself less unhappy; reason resumed the empire of which her half-conscious state had robbed her. To free herself from the maid's steady gaze, she ordered her to read the paper out, and it was to the monotonous murmur of the girl's voice, reading a long article in *La Quotidienne*, that Mme de Rênal took the virtuous resolution to treat Julien with perfect coldness when next she saw him.

CHAPTER 12

A Journey

> In Paris one finds elegant people, in the provinces there
> may be people of character.   SIÉYÈS[1]

By five o'clock the following morning, before Mme de Rênal was
visible, Julien had obtained three days' leave from her husband.
Contrary to what he had expected, Julien found himself wanting to
see her – he dreamed of her pretty hand. He went down to the
garden; Mme de Rênal made him wait a long time. But if he had
been in love he would have made her out behind the half-closed
shutters of the first floor, her forehead leaning against the glass. She
was looking at him. Finally, in spite of her resolutions, she decided
to make an appearance in the garden. Her natural pallor had given
way to the most vivid colouring. This simple and innocent woman
was obviously upset: a feeling of embarrassment and even of anger
transformed that expression of profound serenity – of being above
all the commonplace preoccupations of life – that lent such charm to
her heavenly face.

Julien quickly went up to her; he admired the beautiful arms that
a hastily thrown-on shawl allowed him to see. The freshness of the
morning air seemed to enhance the brilliance of a complexion that
her night's suffering had only made more sensitive to every impression. This loveliness, modest and appealing, yet informed by thought
in a way that one never finds in the lower classes, seemed to reveal
to Julien a capacity in his own soul of which he had never before
been conscious. Engrossed by his admiration of the beauties that
surprised his eager gaze, Julien had not a thought of the affectionate
welcome he expected to receive. He was therefore all the more taken

aback by the glacial coldness she sought to show him, and through which he believed he could even discern a wish to put him in his place.

The smile of pleasure died on his lips: he reminded himself of the rank he occupied in society, and above all in the eyes of a rich and noble heiress. In an instant his physiognomy expressed nothing but aloofness and self-reproach. He felt a violent resentment at having delayed his departure more than an hour in order to receive such a humiliating reception.

Only an idiot, he said to himself, gets in a rage over other people: a stone falls because it is heavy. Will I never grow up? When, oh when, will I acquire the sensible custom of giving these people my soul only in proportion to what they pay for it? If I want to be respected by them – and myself – I must show them that while my poverty engages with their wealth, my heart is a thousand miles away from their insolence, placed in a sphere too high to be reached by their marks of disdain – or of favour.

While these sentiments jostled in the young tutor's mind, his expressive features took on a look of suffering pride and ferocity. Mme de Rênal was much disturbed by this. The virtuous coldness with which she had wished to cloak herself gave way to an expression of interest, and an interest animated by all her surprise at the sudden changes she saw. The meaningless words one exchanges in the morning about one's health and the fineness of the day petered out between the two at once. Julien, whose judgement was unclouded by any passion, very quickly found a way to signify to Mme de Rênal how little he felt on friendly terms with her; he said nothing about the trip he was going to undertake, bowed to her and departed.

As she watched him go, cast down by the sombre pride she read in eyes that had been so loving the evening before, her eldest son ran up from the bottom of the garden and hugged her, saying:

– We've got a holiday, M. Julien's off on a journey.

At these words Mme de Rênal was stricken by a deadly chill; she was unhappy in her virtue, and in her weakness unhappier still.

This new development began to occupy her imagination entirely; she was carried far beyond the wise resolutions derived from the terrible night she had just endured. It was no longer a matter of resistance to so attractive a lover, but a matter of losing him for ever.

She was obliged to be present at lunch. To increase her affliction, M. de Rênal and Mme Derville talked of nothing but Julien's departure. The Mayor of Verrières had noticed an element of insolence in the firm tone with which the latter had demanded leave.

– This little peasant certainly has an offer from someone in his pocket. But that someone, even if should it be M. Valenod, ought to be somewhat deterred by the sum of 600 francs you'd have to find to pay him every year. Yesterday, at Verrières, there was a demand for three days' delay to think about it; and this morning, so as not to have to give me an answer, the little gentleman has left for the mountains. To have to bother about a low workman who plays up – see what we've come to!

Since my husband – who has no idea how profoundly he has wounded Julien – thinks he is leaving us, what should I myself think? Mme de Rênal said to herself. Ah! it's all over now!

So that she could at least weep freely, and not have to respond to Mme Derville's questioning, she complained of a shocking headache and retired to bed.

– That's women all over, repeated M. de Rênal, there's always something ailing those complicated machines. And he departed, bantering.

While Mme de Rênal was a prey to the cruellest manifestations of the terrible passion to which chance had subjected her, Julien blithely went on his way through the most beautiful scenery that mountains can afford. He had to cross the big range to the north of Vergy. The path he followed, rising gradually through the great beech woods, makes innumerable zigzags along the slope of the tall mountain which delimits the Doubs valley on the north. Soon the traveller's gaze, passing above the lower slopes which flank the course of the Doubs southwards, reaches right across to the fertile plains of Burgundy and Beaujolais. However insensitive this ambitious young man's soul was to this kind of beauty, he was unable to help himself pausing from time to time to survey so vast and so imposing a prospect.

At last he got to the summit of the great mountain which must be crossed, on this route, to reach the lonely valley inhabited by his friend Fouqué, the young wood merchant. Julien was in no hurry to see him, nor any other human being. Concealed like a bird of prey amidst the bare rocks which crowned the mountain, he would be able to see anyone approaching from a distance. He discovered a little grotto in the middle of the almost sheer incline of one of the rocks. He made his way towards it, and was soon established in this retreat. Here, said he, his eyes sparkling with joy, men can do me no harm. He had the idea of giving himself the pleasure of writing his thoughts down, a thing which everywhere else was so dangerous. A square piece of stone did duty as a desk. His pen flew: he was conscious of nothing around him. At last he noticed that the sun was setting behind the distant mountains of Beaujolais.

Why don't I spend the night here? he said to himself. I've got some bread, *I am free!* At the sound of this grand word, his soul was lifted up – for his hypocrisy entailed that he was not free even in Fouqué's house. His head couched on both hands, Julien sat in the grotto happier than he had ever been in his life, stirred by his reveries and by the joy of liberty. Without thinking about it, he saw the last rays of sunset fade one by one. In the midst of the vast obscurity his soul wandered, picturing what he imagined he would find in Paris one day. First of all there was a woman more beautiful and of much higher spirit than any he had been able meet in the provinces. He loved with passion, and was loved. If he was separated from her for a few moments, it was but to go off and cover himself in glory, and so deserve to be loved even more.

Even supposing he had Julien's imagination, a young man brought up among the sad truths of Parisian society would at this point in his story have been woken up by cold irony; great deeds would have evaporated with the hope of achieving them – to give place to the maxim, so well known, that says: Leave your mistress and – oh dear! – risk being deceived two or three times a day. The young peasant saw nothing between himself and the most heroic actions, save lack of opportunity.

But profound darkness had succeeded day, and he still had two leagues to cover in order to reach the hamlet where Fouqué lived.

Before leaving the grotto Julien lit a fire and carefully burned all he had written.

He amazed his friend by knocking on his door at one in the morning. He found Fouqué busy writing up his accounts. The latter was a tall young man, rather badly built, with large, hard features, an infinitely long nose and a great deal of good nature hidden beneath this unattractive exterior.

– So you've had a row with your M. de Rênal, is it that which brings you here so suddenly like this?

Julien told him his own version of yesterday's events.

– Remain here with me, said Fouqué, I see that you now know M. de Rênal, M. Valenod, Sub-prefect Maugiron and Curé Chélan; you've understood the finer points of character of those people; so you're in a position to take part in business transactions. You're better at arithmetic than me, you could take over my accounts. I make big profits in my trade. The impossibility of doing everything myself, and the fear of finding anyone I take into partnership to be a crook, is always stopping me from doing first-rate business. It was less than a month ago that I allowed Michaud from Saint-Armand, whom I hadn't seen for six years and met by chance at the Pontarlier sale, to make six thousand francs. Why shouldn't you have earned that six thousand yourself – or three thousand anyway? – for, if you had been with me that day, I would have bid for that cutting of wood, and they would all have let me have it soon enough. Be my partner.

This offer put Julien in ill humour; it disturbed his dreams. During supper, which, since Fouqué lived alone, the two men prepared themselves like heroes in Homer, he showed his accounts to Julien and demonstrated how profitable the wood trade was. Fouqué had the highest opinion of Julien's judgement and character.

When at last the latter was alone in his little pine-lined room: It's true that I could earn a few thousand francs here, he said to himself, then go back better equipped to the profession of soldier or priest – depending on the fashion currently ascendant in France. The little hoard I would have amassed would smooth out all sorts of small difficulties. Being solitary here in the mountains, I'd be able to do something to reduce the frightful ignorance I have about so many things that occupy the denizens of the salons. But Fouqué has renounced marriage, and has told me several times that solitude makes him unhappy. It is obvious that if he takes a partner who has no capital to pour into his business it is in the hope that he will obtain a comrade who will never leave him.

Would I then deceive my friend? cried Julien to himself, disturbed. This being, whose usual means of survival were hypocrisy and a total lack of sympathy, was unable to tolerate the thought of the slightest lack of delicacy towards a man who loved him.

But all of a sudden Julien was happy again: he had a reason to refuse. What! I'd idly lose seven or eight years! — I'd be twenty-eight; but at that age Bonaparte had done his greatest deeds. By the time I'll have made some money by running around obscure timber sales and currying favour with a few low-ranking rogues, who can say if I'd still possess that sacred fire with which one makes one's name?

The following morning, with great self-possession, Julien replied to the good Fouqué, who considered the question of partnership as settled, that his calling to the sacred ministry of the altar would not permit him to accept. Fouqué could not overcome his surprise.

— But d'you realize, he repeated, that I am making you a partner, or, if you prefer, I am letting you have four thousand francs a year? — and you want to go back home to M. de Rênal, who despises you like the mud on his boots! When you have two hundred louis in front of you, what's to stop you going into the seminary? I'll say more, I'll commit myself to finding you the best living in the district. For, added Fouqué in a lowered voice, I supply firewood to M. le . . ., M. le . . ., M. . . . . I let them have the finest heart of oak which they pay me for as if it were white wood — but never was money so well spent.

Nothing could conquer Julien's vocation. Fouqué ended up thinking he was a little crazy. On the third day, very early in the morning, Julien left his friend in order to spend the day among the rocks of the high mountain. He found his little grotto again, but he no longer felt peace in his soul, his friend's offers having taken that away. Like Hercules[2] he found himself placed, not between vice and virtue, but between the mediocrity consequent on assured well-being and all the heroic dreams of his youth. So I lack true resolution, he said to himself. This was the suspicion which gave him most pain. I'm not the wood out of which great men are fashioned, since I'm afraid that eight years spent earning my bread will rob me of the sublime energy required to do extraordinary things.

CHAPTER 13

Open Work Stockings

A novel: it's a mirror carried along the highway.

SAINT-RÉAL[1]

When Julien saw the picturesque ruins of the ancient church at Vergy, he realized that he had not once thought of Mme de Rênal since the day before yesterday. – When we parted the other day that woman reminded me of the infinite distance that separates us, she treated me like a workman's son. No doubt she wanted to emphasize to me how she regretted having let me hold her hand the evening before ... Still, it's very pretty, that hand! What charm! – what fineness in that woman's glance!

The possibility of making his fortune with Fouqué lent a certain ease to Julien's thoughts; they were less often distorted by irritation and an acute consciousness of poverty and low social standing. As though raised on a promontory, he was able to judge and, so to speak, stand aloof from both extreme poverty and the easy circumstances he still called wealth. He was a long way from being philosophical, but he was clear-sighted enough to feel *different* after his little excursion to the mountains.

He was surprised by the extremely troubled air with which Mme de Rênal heard the short account of his journey she had asked him for.

Fouqué had made plans to get married, and had endured some unfortunate experiences of love; long confidences on this subject had filled the conversations between the two friends. Having found his happiness too early, Fouqué had realized that he was not the only one to be loved. All his stories amazed Julien; he learned a great deal

85

that was new to him. His solitary life, full of dreams and mistrust, had placed him quite out of the way of those things which could have enlightened him.

For Mme de Rênal, life had been nothing but a series of torments during Julien's absence – all different, but all of them intolerable; she was now truly ill.

– And above all, said Mme Derville to her when she saw Julien reappear, indisposed as you are, you won't be going into the garden this evening, the damp air would make you much worse.

Mme Derville saw with amazement that her friend – who was always being scolded by M. de Rênal for the excessive simplicity of her toilette – had just acquired some open-work stockings and some charming little shoes from Paris. For the past three days Mme de Rênal's sole distraction had been in dressmaking and in getting Élisa to create a summer dress, as fast as possible, from a fine pretty material in the height of fashion. This dress was finished only a few minutes after Julien's arrival; Mme de Rênal put it on straight away. Her friend no longer had any doubts. She's in love, the poor woman! said Mme Derville to herself. She understood all the strange symptoms of the malady.

She watched her speaking to Julien. Pallor succeeded the most vivid blushes; anxiety was plain to see in eyes fixed upon those of the young tutor. Mme de Rênal expected at any moment that he would explain himself and announce whether he was leaving the house or staying. But Julien was far from speaking on this subject because he was not thinking about it. After some terrible struggles, Mme de Rênal at last dared ask him, in a tremulous voice that gave away her passion entirely:

– Are you going to abandon your pupils to find a place elsewhere?

Julien was struck by Mme de Rênal's uncertain voice, and her look. This woman loves me, he said to himself – but after this passing moment of weakness, which her pride rebukes, and when she no longer fears my departure, she will return to her high manner. This view of their respective positions came to him quick as lightning, and he replied with caution:

– I'd feel very much regret about leaving such lovable children, who are *so well born*, but perhaps it will be necessary. One has duties to oneself, as well.

In pronouncing the phrase 'so well born' (it was one of those aristocratic expressions Julien had learned recently) he was driven by a feeling of intense antipathy.

In the eyes of this woman, I . . . he said to himself, I am not well born.

Listening to him, Mme de Rênal wondered at his spirit and his beauty, and her heart was pierced by the possible departure of which he gave her a glimpse. All her friends from Verrières who had come to dinner at Vergy while Julien was away had competed with one another in complimenting her on the astonishing young man her husband had had the good fortune to discover. It was not that they understood anything about the children's progress. To know the Bible by heart – and in Latin, what's more – had struck the people of Verrières with a fit of admiration that should last a hundred years.

Julien, speaking to no one, knew none of that. If Mme de Rênal had been capable of the least self-possession, she would have praised him for the reputation he had earned, and – Julien's pride reassured – he would have become pliant and amiable, especially since he found her new dress charming. Mme de Rênal, also pleased with the pretty dress and with what Julien said about it, wished to take a turn round the garden; soon she pleaded that she was not in a fit state for walking. She had taken the traveller's arm, but, very far from increasing her strength, contact with this arm quickly robbed her of any she had.

It was dark; hardly had they sat down than Julien, claiming his established right, ventured to put his lips to his pretty neighbour's arm and take her hand. He was thinking of the boldness Fouqué had shown with his mistresses, not of Mme de Rênal; the phrase *well born* still weighed upon his heart. His hand was pressed; it gave him no pleasure. Far from his being proud of, or at least thankful for, the feelings Mme de Rênal betrayed this evening by all too obvious signs, her beauty, elegance and youthfulness found him virtually insensible. Purity of soul and the absence of any spiteful feelings undoubtedly prolong youth; in most pretty women it is the face that ages first.

Julien was ill tempered all evening. Up until then he had been angry only with circumstances and society; since Fouqué had offered him an ignoble way of securing a comfortable living, he was irritated with himself. Taken up with his thoughts – though from time to time he said a few words to the ladies – Julien ended up inadvertently letting go of Mme de Rênal's hand. This action caused turmoil in the poor woman's soul; in it she read her fate.

Had she been sure of Julien's affection, perhaps she would have been able to gather force enough to resist him. Terrified at losing him for ever, her passion led her astray to the point of reclaiming Julien's hand, which, in his fit of abstraction, he had left resting on the back of a chair. This action roused the ambitious young man: he would have loved it to have been witnessed by all those proud gentlemen who, at dinner, when he was at the bottom of the table with the children, looked at him with such patronizing smiles. This woman can no longer despise me: in which case, he said to himself, I should be receptive to her beauty; I owe it to myself to become her lover. Such an idea would never have occurred to him before his friend had treated him to his simple confidences.

The taking of this sudden resolution constituted an agreeable distraction. I must have one of these two women, he said to himself. He realized that he would much rather pay court to Mme Derville, not because she was more attractive to him, but because she had always known him as a tutor respected for his learning, and not, as he had appeared to Mme de Rênal, as a carpenter's assistant with a ratteen jacket folded under his arm.

It was precisely as this young worker, blushing to the whites of his eyes, halted at the house door, not daring to ring, that Mme de Rênal thought him most enchanting.

Continuing his review of the position, Julien saw that he should not dream of the conquest of Mme Derville, who had most probably already noticed the preference shown for him by Mme de Rênal. Forced to revert to the latter, What do I know about this woman's character? Julien asked himself. Only this: before I went away I took her hand and she took it back; today I withdrew my hand and she seized it and pressed it. What a fine chance to pay her back for all the times she has scorned me! God knows how many lovers she has had! – she's probably only decided in my favour because of the ease with which we can meet.

Such alas, is, the sickness of too much civilization! At twenty, a young man's soul – if he has had any education – is a thousand miles from that freedom of spirit without which love is often the most tedious of duties.

I owe it the more to myself, went on Julien's petty vanity, to succeed with this woman, since if ever I make my fortune and somebody reproaches me with having had the low occupation of a tutor, I will be able to make it understood that love cast me into this position.

Julien, who had again let go of Mme de Rênal's hand, now repossessed it, holding it tightly. As they went back into the salon around midnight, Mme de Rênal whispered to him:

– You're leaving us, you're going away?

Sighing, Julien replied:

– It is absolutely necessary that I go, for I love you passionately, and it is a sin . . . and such a sin for a young priest!

Mme de Rênal leant on his arm, so unconstrainedly that she could feel the warmth of Julien's cheek on hers.

The nights spent by these two beings were very different. Mme de Rênal was exalted by transports of the loftiest moral delight. A flirtatious young woman who loves early gets used to the dramas of love; when she comes to the age of true passion, the charm of novelty is gone. Since Mme de Rênal never read novels, all the little details of her happiness were new to her. No melancholy truth came to chill it, not even the prospect of the future. She envisaged herself being as happy in ten years' time as she was at that moment. Even the idea that had agitated her a few days ago, of virtue and of fidelity sworn to M. de Rênal, came along in vain, to be dismissed like an unwelcome visitor. I will not yield a thing to Julien, said Mme de Rênal to herself, we will live in the future as we have lived for the past month. He will be a friend.

CHAPTER 14

English Scissors

A young girl of sixteen had a rosy complexion, and she put
on rouge.   POLIDORI[1]

Fouqué's offer had in effect robbed Julien of all his happiness; he was
unable to decide on it one way or the other. Alas! perhaps I have a
weak character; I would have made a poor soldier for Napoleon. But
at least, he added, my little intrigue with the mistress of the house
will serve to distract me for a while.

Happily for him, even in this small matter his inner feelings
corresponded ill with his cavalier language. He was in awe of
Mme de Rênal because of her lovely dress. In his eyes this dress
was the avant garde of Paris. His vanity dictated that he leave nothing
to chance or the inspiration of the moment. Basing himself on
Fouqué's confidences and the little that he had read about love in
his Bible, he made a highly detailed plan of campaign. And since,
without admitting it to himself, he was very anxious, he wrote the
plan down.

The following morning Mme de Rênal was for a moment alone
with him in the salon:

– Haven't you another name besides Julien? she asked him.

Our hero had no idea how to reply to so flattering a question.
Such a contingency was not prefigured in his plan. If he had not had
this stupid notion of making a plan, Julien's lively wit would have
served him perfectly well, and surprise could only have added
quickness to his perceptions. He responded awkwardly, and regarded
himself as even more awkward than he was. Mme de Rênal forgave
him almost immediately. She saw a delightful candour in it. And an

air of candour was, in her eyes, precisely what this man, in whom people found such genius, lacked.

– Your little tutor inspires in me deep suspicion, Mme Derville said to her from time to time. I seem to see him thinking all the time and acting only circumspectly. He's very sly.

Julien remained profoundly downcast by the misfortune of not having known how to reply to Mme de Rênal.

A man like me must overcome this setback – and, seizing the moment when they were moving from one room to another, he believed it his duty to give Mme de Rênal a kiss.

Nothing could have been less appropriate, nothing less pleasant for him or for her, nothing more reckless. They were on the point of being seen. Mme de Rênal thought him mad. She was frightened, and above all shocked. This idiocy reminded her of M. Valenod.

What would happen to me, she said to herself, if I was alone with him? All her virtue returned, for love was in eclipse.

She managed things so that one of her children was always about her.

The day was tiresome for Julien; he spent the whole time clumsily carrying out his scheme of seduction. He never looked at Mme de Rênal without the look being a question; however, he was not fool enough to notice that he was very far from succeeding even in being agreeable, still less seductive.

Mme de Rênal could not get over her astonishment at finding him so awkward and at the same time so bold. It is the timidity of a man of wit in love! she told herself at last, with inexplicable joy. Can it be possible that my rival has never entertained his love!

After lunch Mme de Rênal returned to the salon in order to receive M. Charcot de Maugiron, Sub-prefect of Bray. She was working at a little tapestry frame set very high. Mme Derville was at her side. It was in this position, and in full daylight, that our hero thought it fitting to put out his boot and press Mme de Rênal's pretty foot, whose open-work stocking and charming Parisian shoe were obviously attracting the gaze of the gallant Sub-prefect.

Mme de Rênal was extremely frightened; she let drop her scissors, her hank of wool and her needles; and Julien's movement could pass for an awkward attempt meant to prevent the fall of the scissors, which he had seen sliding down. Happily, the little English steel scissors broke and Mme de Rênal made much of her regret that Julien had not placed himself closer to her.

– You noticed the fall before I did, you could have prevented it; instead of which, your zeal has only succeeded in giving me a great big kick on the foot.

All this deceived the Sub-prefect, but not Mme Derville. This pretty boy has such clumsy manners! thought she; even a provincial capital's notions of good breeding would not forgive such a blunder. Mme de Rênal found a moment to say to Julien:

– Be more discreet, I order you.

Julien realized his awkwardness and was flustered by it. He debated at length within himself as to whether he should resent the phrase *I order you*. He was stupid enough to think: She could say *I order* if it was something to do with the education of the children, but in response to my lovemaking equality is predicated. One cannot love without *equality* . . .; and his mind lost itself entirely in coining commonplaces about equality. He angrily repeated to himself a verse of Corneille that Mme Derville had taught him a few days before:

. . . Love
Creates equalities but seeks them not.[2]

Julien obstinately persisted in playing the role of a Don Juan – he who had a mistress – and was mortally stupid the whole day. He had only one sensible idea: tired out with himself and with Mme de Rênal, he pictured the coming of the evening when they would be seated in the garden, side by side in the darkness, with dread. He told M. de Rênal that he was going to Verrières to see the Curé; he left after dinner and returned only late at night.

In Verrières Julien found M. Chélan busy moving out of his house; he had finally been dismissed, to be replaced by the Abbé Maslon. Julien helped the good Curé, and had the idea of writing to Fouqué that the irresistible vocation he felt for the sacred ministry had at first prevented him from accepting his kind proposals, but that when he came to see an example of such injustice perhaps it would be more conducive to his eternal salvation not to enter into holy orders.

Julien congratulated himself on his subtlety in taking advantage of the dismissal of the Curé of Verrières to leave himself an open door for a return into business, should sober calculation triumph over valour in his breast.

CHAPTER 15

The Cockcrow

Amour en latin faict amor;
Or donc provient d'amour la mort,
Et, par avant, souley qui mord,
Deuil, plours, pièges, forfaits, remords.
BLASON D'AMOUR[1]

Had Julien really had a little of that cleverness he so gratuitously prided himself on, he would have been able to applaud himself the following day on the effect produced by his trip to Verrières. His absence had caused all his awkwardnesses to be forgotten. During the day he remained sulky enough; in the evening an absurd idea came to him, which he communicated to Mme de Rênal with unusual resolution.

Hardly had they seated themselves in the garden when, without waiting for it to get dark enough, Julien put his lips to Mme de Rênal's ear and, at the risk of compromising her horribly, said:

– Madame, tonight at two o'clock I will come to your room, I must tell you something.

Julien was terrified lest his request be granted; his role as seducer weighed on him so horribly that had he been able to do as he liked he would have retired to his room for several days and seen no more of the ladies. He realized that by his sage conduct yesterday he had spoiled all the good impressions of the day before, and was truly at a loss as to which saint to pray to.

Mme de Rênal replied to the impertinent announcement Julien had dared make with real indignation, quite unforced. He believed he heard scorn in her brief reply. He was sure that in this reply, uttered very low, the words *for shame* had a place. On the pretext of having something to say to the children Julien went to their room, and on his return sat himself by the side of Mme Derville, far from Mme de Rênal. He thus deprived himself of any possibility of taking her hand. The conversation was serious, and Julien sustained his part very well, save for a few moments of silence during which he racked his brains. Why can't I think up some brilliant stratagem, he asked himself, that would compel Mme de Rênal to give me those unequivocal marks of affection which three days ago made me believe that she was mine?

Julien was terribly dismayed by the almost desperate state into which he had run his affairs. But nothing would have embarrassed him like success.

When they parted at midnight, his gloomy mood made him think that he enjoyed Mme Derville's contempt, and probably nothing much better from Mme de Rênal.

In such bad humour and deeply humiliated, Julien could not sleep at all. He was a thousand miles away from the idea of renouncing all deceit, all his schemes, and living on a daily basis with Mme de Rênal, to be satisfied like a child with the happiness each day brings.

He tired his brain out inventing clever stratagems – a moment afterwards finding them ridiculous; he was, in short, most unhappy – when the château clock struck two.

The sound woke him up as the cockcrow woke St Peter. He realized that the most painful emergency had now arrived. He had thought no further of his insolent proposition since the instant he had made it; it had been received so badly!

I told her I'd go to her at two, he said to himself as he got up, I may well be inexperienced and as coarse as you would expect from the son of a peasant – Mme Derville has made me understand as much – but at least I'm not weak.

Julien was right to praise his own courage, for never had he imposed such fierce constraint upon himself. While opening his door he was trembling so much that his knees gave way under him, and he was compelled to support himself against the wall.

He had no shoes on. He went to listen at M. de Rênal's door, through which he could distinguish snoring. He was distraught. So there was no further excuse for not going to her. But, good God! what was he going to do? He had no plan, and even if he had had one, he felt so upset that he was in no fit state to carry it out.

At last, suffering a thousand times more than if he had been marching to his death, he arrived in the little corridor that led to Mme de Rênal's room. He opened the door with a trembling hand, making a frightful noise.

There was light, a night light burning in the fireplace; another snag he had not foreseen. On seeing him enter Mme de Rênal sprang swiftly out of her bed. You wretch! she cried. There was some confusion. Julien forgot his empty schemes and returned to playing the part natural to him: not to please so charming a woman seemed to him the greatest of misfortunes. His only response to her reproaches was to throw himself at her feet and embrace her knees. As she spoke to him with great severity, he melted into tears.

A few hours later, when Julien left Mme de Rênal's room, one could say, in the language of novels, that he had nothing left to desire. Indeed, the love he had inspired and the unexpected impression made upon him by such compelling loveliness had given him a victory that his clumsy manoeuvres could never have achieved.

But, victim to a bizarre pride, he still aspired, even in the tenderest of moments, to play the role of a man used to subduing women; he made tremendous efforts to spoil what was most lovable in himself. Instead of being sensitive to the transports he aroused, and to the remorse that increased their intensity, he constantly had the idea of *duty* before his eyes. He dreaded fearful remorse and eternal humiliation if he deviated for one moment from the preordained model he wished to follow. In short, it was precisely that which made Julien a superior being that stopped him enjoying the happiness that lay at his feet. He was like the girl of sixteen with a charming complexion who, going to the ball, is silly enough to wear rouge.

Appalled when Julien appeared, Mme de Rênal soon became prey to the cruellest anxieties. Julien's tears and desperation tried her sorely.

Even when there was nothing more she could refuse him she

pushed Julien far from her with genuine indignation, and then threw herself into his arms. No design was apparent in any of this behaviour. She considered herself to be damned without remission, and sought to hide from the vision of hell by covering Julien with fervent caresses. In a word, our hero's happiness would have lacked for nothing, not even passionate sensibility in the woman he had just overcome, had he known how to enjoy it. Julien's departure did nothing to arrest the raptures she experienced in spite of herself, and her combats against the remorse that racked her.

— My God! To be happy, to be loved, is that all there is to it? Such was Julien's first thought when he got back to his room. He was in that state of amazement and deep uneasiness into which a soul descends when it gets what it has desired for a long time. Such a soul, in the habit of desiring, now finds no more to desire but has as yet no memories. Like a soldier coming off parade, Julien was studiously occupied in reviewing all the details of his conduct.

— Did I let myself down in any way? Have I played my part well? What part? That of a man who is accustomed to shine in front of women.

CHAPTER 16

The Following Day

He turn'd his lips to hers, and with his hand
Call'd back the tangles of her wandering hair.
DON JUAN, canto I, stanza 170[1]

Fortunately for Julien's sense of his own glory, Mme de Rênal had been too agitated, too amazed, to register the fatuity of the man who had so suddenly become all the world to her.

Seeing dawn approach, she urged him to leave:

– Oh! dear God! she said, if my husband hears anything I am lost.

Julien, who had time for the making of phrases, recalled the following one:

– Would you then begrudge your life?

– Ah! very much at this moment! but I don't begrudge having known you.

Julien considered it a duty to his dignity to go back deliberately in broad daylight, and with no precautions.

The incessant care with which he scrutinized his slightest actions – with the inane idea of appearing as a man of experience – had but one advantage: when he saw Mme de Rênal again at lunch his behaviour was a masterpiece of discretion.

As for her, she was unable to look at him without blushing up to her eyeballs, yet unable to exist for a moment without looking at him; she was aware of her confusion, and redoubled her efforts to conceal it. Julien raised his eyes to hers only once. At first Mme de Rênal was pleased at his prudence. But soon, seeing that the look was not repeated, she became alarmed: Can it be that he no longer loves me? she asked herself. Alas! I'm too old for him; I'm ten years older than he is.

While passing from the dining room to the garden she squeezed Julien's hand. In his surprise at so marked a sign of love he looked at her passionately, for at lunch she had seemed to him wonderfully attractive, and, though his eyes were lowered, he had passed the time detailing her charms in his mind. This look consoled Mme de Rênal; it failed to rid her of all her fears; but her fears almost completely rid her of compunction towards her husband.

At lunch, this husband had noticed nothing; but such was not the case with Mme Derville: she thought Mme de Rênal on the point of succumbing. The whole day long her bold and clear-sighted friendship abounded with hints designed to paint the danger Mme de Rênal was running in lurid colours.

Mme de Rênal burned to find herself alone with Julien; she wanted to ask whether he still loved her. Despite her consistent sweetness of character, she was several times on the point of making clear to her friend how much she was in the way.

That evening, in the garden, Mme Derville arranged things so well that she was able to seat herself between Mme de Rênal and Julien. Mme de Rênal, who had created for herself a delightful image of the pleasure of pressing Julien's hand and carrying it to her lips, was now prevented from even saying a word to him.

This disappointment increased her agitation. She was eaten up with regret concerning one point. She had scolded Julien so thoroughly about his rashness in coming to her room the previous night that now she was in fear that he would not come tonight. She left the garden early, and went to establish herself in her room. But being unable to contain her impatience, she came to press her ear against Julien's door. In spite of her uncertainty and the passion that tore at her, she was not brave enough to go in. This action seemed to her the ultimate baseness – for that is what is said in a provincial proverb.

The servants were not all in bed yet. At last, prudence forced her to go back to her own room. Two hours of waiting became two centuries of torment.

But Julien was too faithful to that which he called his duty to fail to carry out, point by point, what he had laid down.

As one o'clock sounded, he slipped softly from his room, assured himself that the master of the house was soundly asleep and appeared in Mme de Rênal's chamber. This time he found greater happiness in his lovemaking because he thought less insistently about the part he was playing. He had eyes to see and ears to hear. What Mme de Rênal said to him about her age reassured him somewhat.

– Alas! I am ten years older than you! How can you love me? said she – with no particular motive, but because the idea oppressed her.

Julien failed to understand her uneasiness, but he saw that it was real, and almost forgot his fear of being ridiculous.

The idiotic idea of being thought of as an inferior lover on account of his obscure birth also disappeared. And as soon as Julien's demonstrations of delight started to reassure his timid mistress, so she recovered a little happiness and the capacity to see her lover more clearly. It was fortunate that by this time he retained almost none of that artificial air which had made yesterday's encounter a victory but no pleasure. For if she had detected his concern with playing a part, the disheartening discovery would have permanently taken away all her happiness. She would have been unable to discern anything else but a sad effect of the disproportion between their ages.

Mme de Rênal had never theorized about love, but in the provinces, whenever the subject is raised, disparity in age is – second only to disparity of fortune – one of the great staples of wit.

In a few days, Julien, yielding to all the ardour of youth, was desperately in love.

– It must be acknowledged that she has an angelic sweetness of spirit, and no one could be lovelier, said he to himself.

The idea of being obliged to play a part had almost completely gone. In an hour of abandon he even went so far as to confess all his anxieties to her. This confidence wrought the passion he had inspired to a climax.

– Then I never had a happy rival! exclaimed Mme de Rênal to herself delightedly. She ventured to ask him about the portrait he set such store by; Julien swore to her that it was of a man.

When Mme de Rênal had stored up sufficient calm to be able to reflect on matters, she could never get over her amazement that such happiness was possible, or that she had never suspected it.

Ah! said she to herself, if only I had known Julien ten years ago, when I was still thought attractive.

Julien was very far away from reflections like these. His love still partook of ambition; it derived from the joy of possessing so noble and so beautiful a woman – and he a poor creature, so unhappy and so despised. His adoring actions, his transports at the sight of his lover's beauty, eventually succeeded in calming her down a little about the difference in their ages. If she had possessed just a little of that knowledge of the world in which a woman of thirty in more civilized countries would have long since rejoiced, she would have shuddered for the long continuance of a love that seemed to thrive only on novelty and the delighted gratification of self-esteem.

At the moments when Julien was oblivious to his ambition he took huge delight even in Mme de Rênal's hats, even in her dresses. He could never tire of the pleasure of their scent. He would open her mirrored wardrobe and remain for whole hours admiring the beauty and the order he found there. His lover, leaning on him, would gaze at him; he himself gazed at the decorative objects, the chiffons that on the eve of a marriage make up the collection of wedding presents.

And I might have married such a man! Mme de Rênal sometimes reflected; What a soul of fire! What an enchanting life it would have been with him!

As to Julien, he had never found himself so close to the devastating material of feminine artillery. It's impossible, he said to himself, that they can have anything lovelier in Paris! At those times he could find no objections to being happy. Frequently his mistress's heartfelt admiration and her loving raptures would make him forget the futile theory that had rendered him so limited and so nearly absurd in the first moments of their liaison. There were times when, in spite of his code of hypocrisy, he found a wonderful pleasure in confiding to the fine lady who loved him his ignorance of a host of minor social usages. His mistress's rank seemed to raise him above himself.

On her side, Mme de Rênal derived the sweetest moral gratification in instructing thus, in a host of little things, that young man full of genius whom everybody thought would go so far one day. Even the Sub-prefect and M. Valenod could not refrain from admiring him; they seemed to her less stupid for that. But Mme Derville was far indeed from expressing similar feelings. Despairing at what she thought she saw, and seeing her sensible advice become odious to a woman who had quite definitely lost her head, she left Vergy without offering the explanation that they were wary of demanding from her. Mme de Rênal shed some tears about this, but soon it seemed that her joys redoubled. Because of the departure she found herself in intimate contact with her lover almost all day long.

Julien gave himself all the more willingly to the delightful society of his friend, because every time he was left too long in his own company Fouqué's fatal proposition would return to disturb him. In the first days of this new life there were moments when he who had never loved, who had never been loved by anyone, found such sweet pleasure in being sincere that he was on the point of laying bare to Mme de Rênal the ambition that up till then had been the very essence of his existence. He would have liked to have been able to consult her on the curious temptation that Fouqué's proposition constituted for him — but a minor incident was to inhibit all frankness.

CHAPTER 17

The First Deputy

O, how this spring of love resembleth
The uncertain glory of an April day,
Which now shows all the beauty of the sun
And by and by a cloud takes all away!

TWO GENTLEMEN OF VERONA

One evening at sunset, seated by his lover's side in the depths of the orchard and far from any interruptions, he was sunk deep in reverie. Can such delightful times go on for ever? he wondered. His mind was full of the difficulty of getting a position in life, and he was deploring that most unhappy necessity which, for a young man who has no money, cuts off childhood and spoils youth's first years.

– Ah! he cried, Napoleon truly was the man sent by God for the youth of France! Who will take his place? Without him what can those unfortunates do, even those better off than I am who have just enough money to procure a decent education but insufficient cash at twenty to buy a place from someone and push themselves into a career! Whatever we do, he added with a deep sigh, that fateful memory will always stop us being happy!

He quickly saw Mme de Rênal frown and take on a cold and disdainful air; this kind of thinking seemed to her appropriate to a servant. Brought up in the knowledge that she was very rich, it seemed to her understood that Julien was the same. She loved him a thousand times more than life itself and cared nothing for money.

Julien was far from divining these thoughts. The frown brought him back to earth. He had sufficient presence of mind to adapt his words for this noble lady, seated so near him on the grassy bank, and make her understand that he had heard the speech he had just repeated during his visit to his friend the wood merchant. It was the reasoning of impious men.

– Indeed! Well, don't mix yourself up with that type of person any longer, said Mme de Rênal, retaining somewhat of the chilly air that had suddenly taken the place of an expression of radiant tenderness.

This frown – or rather chagrin at his lack of discretion – was the first check inflicted on the dream that had been sweeping Julien away. He said to himself: She's good and sweet, she has a lively affection for me, but she's been brought up in the enemy camp. They are obliged to fear above everything the class of talented men who, having received a decent education, haven't enough money to launch themselves into a career. What would become of them, these nobles, if it was given to us to fight them on equal terms? Myself, for example, if I was mayor of Verrières, and well intentioned, and honest as M. de Rênal is at heart! – how I'd see off the Abbé and M. Valenod and all their frauds! How justice would triumph in Verrières! It's not their abilities that get in my way. They constantly fumble about.

Julien's happiness had, on that very day, been on the point of becoming permanent. What our hero lacked was to dare to be sincere. He should have had the courage to give battle, and *on the spot*; Mme de Rênal had been disturbed by Julien's words because the men of her acquaintance kept on repeating that the return of Robespierre was possible, above all on account of young men of the lower classes being too well educated. Her aloof manner was maintained for some time, and seemed very marked to Julien. Actually, her distaste for his unwelcome speech had been followed by the fear of having said something indirectly disagreeable to him. It was disquiet about this that was strongly evident on features so pure and candid when she was happy and away from the company of bores.

Julien no longer dared to let his reveries run free. Colder and less in love, he discovered that it would be rash to visit Mme de Rênal in her room. He would rather she came to his; if a servant saw her going about the house there were twenty different pretexts to explain the incident.

But this arrangement also had its drawbacks. Julien had received books from Fouqué that he, as a student of theology, could never have requested from the bookseller. He dared open them only at night. Often he would have been well pleased not to have been interrupted by a visit, the tension of waiting for which, even on the night before the little scene in the orchard, would have put him quite out of the state of mind for reading.

To Mme de Rênal he owed the capacity to understand books in a completely new way. He had the nerve to ask her about a crowd of trivial things, ignorance of which totally baffles the intelligence of a young man born out of society, whatever natural talents have been granted to him.

This loving education, supplied by an extremely ignorant woman, was a joy. Julien directly came to see society as it is today. His mind was not cluttered with accounts of what it had been at other times, whether a thousand years ago or sixty, in the age of Voltaire and Louis XV. To his inexpressible pleasure, a veil fell from before his eyes and he at last understood what went on in Verrières.

In the foreground there appeared some very complicated intrigues, woven during the last two years around the Prefect at Besançon. These had been sustained by letters sent from Paris, and penned from the most illustrious quarters. They were concerned to ensure that M. de Moirod, the most pious man in the district, became the First, and not the Second, Deputy to the Mayor of Verrières.

His rival was a very wealthy manufacturer whom it was absolutely imperative to drive back into the position of Second Deputy.

At last Julien understood the hints that he had overheard when the high society of the district came to dine at M. de Rênal's. This privileged body was deeply concerned with the appointment of the First Deputy, of which the rest of the town, and above all the liberals, suspected not even the possibility. What made it important, as everyone knew, was that the eastern side of the main thoroughfare of Verrières ought really to be moved back more than nine feet, because this road had become a royal highway.

Now, if M. de Moirod, who owned three of the houses scheduled to be set back, did become First Deputy and so subsequently Mayor

– should it come about that M. de Rênal be nominated to the Chamber[1] – he would avert his eyes, and unobtrusive minor repairs could be made to the houses abutting the public thoroughfare so that they would last another hundred years. Despite M. de Moirod's high piety and acknowledged rectitude it was a certainty that he would be *pliant*, for he had many children. Among the houses that ought to be set back, nine belonged to the best people in Verrières.

In Julien's eyes this intrigue was very much more important than the history of the battle of Fontenoy,[2] the name of which he encountered for the first time in one of the books Fouqué had sent him. There had been things that had amazed Julien ever since he had started to spend evenings with the Curé five years ago. But discretion and humility were the prime qualities required in a theology student, and it had always been impossible for him to ask questions.

One day Mme de Rênal gave an order to her husband's valet, Julien's enemy.

– But, madame, it's the last Friday in the month today, replied the man with a peculiar look.

– Go then, said Mme de Rênal.

– Well, said Julien, he's off into that hay store which used to be a church, and has recently been restored to religious use; but what to do? – that's one of the mysteries I have never been able to make out.

– It's a very salutary institution, but decidedly odd, replied Mme de Rênal; women aren't admitted; all I know is that everyone there uses familiar forms of address.[3] That servant, for example, will meet M. Valenod there, and that individual who is so stupid and so proud won't be at all put out to hear himself addressed in familiar fashion by Saint-Jean, and will reply in the same tone. If you really want to know what goes on, I'll ask for the details from M. de Maugiron and M. Valenod. We pay twenty francs per servant so that they won't cut our throats some day.

Time flew by. The memory of his mistress's beauties distracted Julien from his dark ambitions. The necessity of not mentioning serious or rational topics, since they belonged to opposing parties, augmented, without his suspecting it, the happiness he owed to her, and added to her acquisition of empire over him.

On the occasions when the presence of children who might understand too much reduced them to speaking only the language of cold rationality, Julien, looking at her with eyes sparkling with love, listened with perfect docility to her discourses on the world as it really was. Often, in the middle of a tale of some clever doubledealing in the matter of a road or a supply contract, Mme de Rênal's mind would suddenly start to ramble almost into a state of bemusement; Julien was forced to scold her, for she allowed herself the same intimate gestures with him as with her children. This was because there were times when she was under the illusion that she loved him like one of her children. Didn't she have to reply to his naive questions on a thousand straightforward things which a well-born child would know by the age of fifteen? A moment later she would look up to him as her master. His intelligence began to frighten her; she believed she could see more precisely every day in this young abbé the great man of the future. She saw him as Pope, she saw him as a first minister like Richelieu.[4]

– Shall I live long enough to see you in your glory? she said to Julien; there is a place ready for a great man; our monarchy, our religion have need of one.

CHAPTER 18

A King at Verrières

Are you worth no more than to be cast aside like the dead
body of a nation, a nation without a soul in whose veins
blood no longer flows?

THE BISHOP'S DISCOURSE in St Clement's Chapel

On the third of September, at ten o'clock in the evening, the whole
of Verrières was roused by a gendarme galloping up the main street.
He brought a message that His Majesty the King of — would
arrive the following Sunday – it now being Thursday. The Prefect
authorized – that is to say, demanded – the formation of a guard of
honour; and the greatest possible pomp must be displayed. An express
messenger was sent to Vergy. M. de Rênal arrived in the middle of
the night to find the whole town buzzing. Everyone was busy claiming
their rights; those with the least to do were hiring balconies to view
the entry of the King.

Who should command the guard of honour? M. de Rênal immediately realized how important it was, in the interests of the houses due
to be set back, that M. de Moirod should take command. It would
lend weight to his claim to the position of First Deputy. He had
nothing to say about M. de Moirod's piety – the man surpassed all
others in that – but he had never been up on a horse in his life. He
was a man of thirty-six, timid in every way, who feared falls and
ridicule in equal proportion.

The Mayor called for him at five in the morning.

— You understand, Monsieur, that I'm claiming your advice as
though you already occupied the post into which every right-thinking
man wants to put you. In this unfortunate town the manufacturers

make a lot of money, the liberal faction has millions, it wants power and it knows how to make weapons out of anything. It's our duty to consult the interest of this king, of the monarchy, and above all the good of our blessed religion. To whom, Monsieur, d'you think we should confide the command of the guard of honour?

Despite his terrible fear of horses, M. de Moirod ended by accepting the honour like a martyr. 'I shall know how to strike the right note,' he told the Mayor. There was just time enough to arrange the refitting of the uniforms that had been worn seven years previously for the visit of a prince of the Blood.

At seven o'clock Mme de Rênal arrived from Vergy with Julien and the children. She found her drawing room full of liberal ladies preaching the union of parties and come to beg her to make her husband give their husbands a place in the guard of honour. One of them protested that if her husband was not selected the shame would bankrupt him. Mme de Rênal quickly sent everyone away. She seemed much preoccupied.

Julien was surprised and, more than that, annoyed that she made a mystery of what was agitating her. I should have foreseen this, he said to himself bitterly – her love for me is eclipsed by the joy of receiving a king in her house. All this fuss dazzles her. She will love me afresh when the preoccupations of her class no longer muddy her brain.

The amazing thing is that he loved her all the more for this.

Upholsterers began to fill the house, and for a long time he tried unsuccessfully to get a chance to talk to her. At last he caught her as she was coming out of his room – his, Julien's – carrying one of his outfits. He made as though to speak to her. She refused to listen and fled. – I'm an idiot to love such a woman, ambition makes her as mad as her husband.

She was that, and more. One of her great desires, which she had never confessed to Julien for fear of upsetting him, was to see him cast off his grave black clothing, even if only for a day. With a diplomatic adroitness truly wonderful in so straightforward a woman, she had arranged – first with M. de Moirod and then with M. de Maugiron the Sub-prefect – that Julien be named for the guard of

honour in preference to five or six young sons of wealthy manufacturers, at least two of whom were of exemplary piety. M. Valenod,
who had counted on lending his carriage to the prettiest women of
the town and showing off his beautiful Norman horses, was persuaded
to provide one of these horses for Julien – the creature he disliked
most in the world. But all the guards of honour owned, or had
borrowed, one of the beautiful sky blue coats with silver colonel's
epaulettes that had shone so brilliantly seven years before. Mme de
Rênal yearned to get a new one, but she had only four days to send
to Besançon and obtain the uniform dress, the arms, the hat, etc. –
all of that which qualifies a guard of honour. What was amusing
about this was that she found it inadvisable to have Julien's uniform
made in Verrières. She wanted to surprise him – him and the town.

The business of the guard of honour and public opinion once
settled, the Mayor had to busy himself with an important religious
occasion – for the King of — did not want to pass through Verrières
without a visit to the celebrated relic of St Clement, preserved at
Bray-le-Haut, a mile or so out of town. A large body of clergy was
desired, and this was the most difficult business of all to deal with;
M. Maslon, the new curé, wished at all costs to avoid the presence of
M. Chélan. In vain did M. de Rênal argue how rash that would be.
The Marquis de La Mole, whose ancestors had so long been governors
of the province, had been chosen to accompany the King of —. He
had known the Abbé Chélan for thirty years. He would certainly
have asked for news of him when he arrived in Verrières, and if he
found that he was out of favour he was just the man to go and seek
him out in the little house to which he had retired, accompanied by
as many of his entourage as could be mustered. What a mortification!

– I am dishonoured here and at Besançon, replied the Abbé
Maslon, if he appears among my clergy. A Jansenist,[1] great God!

– Whatever you may say, my dear abbé, replied M. de Rênal, I
won't expose the administration of Verrières to an affront from M.
de La Mole. You don't know him; he is right-thinking enough at
court; but here in the provinces he's a mischievous satirical joker, a
mocker who only likes to embarrass people. He's capable of covering
us with ridicule in the eyes of the liberals, just to amuse himself.

It was not until very late on Saturday night, after three days of negotiation, that M. Maslon's arrogance bent before the Mayor's foreboding – which was transforming itself into courage. He was obliged to write an affable letter to the Abbé Chélan begging him to assist, should his infirmities and his great age allow, at the ceremony of the relic at Bray-le-Haut. M. Chélan asked for, and received, a letter of invitation for Julien to accompany him in the capacity of Sub-deacon.

From Sunday morning onwards, thousands of peasants came in from the nearby mountains, flooding the streets of Verrières. It was a lovely sunny day. At last, towards three o'clock, the whole crowd became excited, for a great beacon had been seen alight on the summit of a rock two leagues from town. This signal announced that the King was about to enter the departmental territory. At that instant the pealing of all the bells, and the repeated discharge of an old Spanish cannon belonging to the municipality, signified public joy at this great event. Half the population climbed up on to the roofs. All the women were on the balconies. The guard of honour put itself in motion. The brilliant uniforms were admired by everyone, everyone recognized a relative, a friend. Everyone scoffed at the apprehensions of M. de Moirod, whose cautious hand was hovering all the time over his saddle bow, ready to clutch at it. But one phenomenon outshone all the others: the leading horseman of the new troop was an extremely good-looking boy, very slim and recognized at first by no one. But soon a cry of indignation from some, and a stunned silence from others, announced a general sensation. This young man, mounted on one of M. Valenod's Norman chargers, was seen to be young Sorel, the carpenter's son. There was an outcry against the Mayor, especially among the liberals. What! – because this little peasant dressed up as an abbé was tutor to his brats, he'd had the gall to appoint him to the guard of honour at the expense of M. This and M. That, wealthy manufacturers! The gentlemen in question, said a banker's wife, really ought to confront this insolent little person, born in the mud. – He's the underhand kind and he's carrying a sabre, replied her neighbour – maybe he'd be mean enough to cut their faces open.

The comments in noble circles were more penetrating. The ladies wondered to themselves if this striking impropriety originated with the Mayor alone. On the whole, justice was done to his contempt for lack of birth.

While he was causing all this talk, Julien was the happiest of men. Naturally bold, he conducted himself better on horseback than most of the other young men from this mountain town. He read in the women's eyes how much he intrigued them.

His epaulettes shone brightest because they were new. Every moment his horse danced, and he was at the peak of happiness.

His joy had no limits when, passing by the ancient rampart, the noise of the little cannon made his horse prance out of rank. By great good luck he did not fall off, and from that moment he felt himself a hero. He was Napoleon's orderly officer charging a battery.

One person was happier even than he. At first she had watched him pass from one of the windows of the town hall; then, climbing into a barouche and making a quick detour, she had been in time to tremble when his horse broke ranks. Finally, her barouche driving at full gallop from another of the town gates, she arrived at the spot on the highway where the King must pass with his guard of honour, and was able to follow them twenty paces to the rear, in a noble cloud of dust. Ten thousand peasants cried Long Live the King! – when the Mayor had the honour of holding forth to His Majesty. An hour later, as the King was about to enter the town – all the speeches having been heard – the little piece of artillery began to fire at a great rate. But an accident ensued, not to the gunners, who had served their apprenticeships at Leipzig and at Montmirail,[2] but to the future First Deputy, M. de Moirod. His horse gently put him off into the sole muddy patch along the main street – which was a disgrace, since he had to be pulled out of it for the King's carriage to get through.

His Majesty alighted at the beautiful new church, which was decked out in all its crimson hangings for the day. The King was to dine; and immediately afterwards to climb back into his carriage to be taken to venerate St Clement's famous relic. Scarcely had the King got to the church than Julien galloped off to M. de Rênal's. There, with a sigh, he abandoned his beautiful sky blue coat, his sabre, his epaulettes, and put on his shabby little black jacket once more. He remounted his horse and in a few moments was at Bray-le-Haut, which covers the top of a very fine hill. – See how enthusiasm increases the numbers of these peasants, thought Julien. In Verrières one could scarcely move, and here there are more than ten thousand around this old abbey. Badly damaged by vandalism during the Revolution, it had been magnificently rebuilt since the Restoration, and there was already talk of miracles. Julien joined the Abbé Chélan, who scolded him severely and handed him a soutane and a surplice. He dressed quickly and followed M. Chélan, who was about to wait upon the young Bishop of Agde – a nephew of M. de La Mole, recently appointed, who had been charged with showing the relic to the King. But this bishop was not to be found.

The clergy were getting restive. They awaited their chief in the dim gothic cloister of the old abbey. Four and twenty curés had been assembled to represent the ancient chapter of Bray-le-Haut, which had been composed of the same number of canons prior to 1789. Having deplored the youth of the Bishop for three-quarters of an hour, these priests considered that it would be appropriate that M. the Dean should withdraw to inform Monseigneur that the King was about to arrive, and that it was high time to repair to the choir. M. Chélan's great age had made him dean. Despite the irritation shown with Julien, he made a sign for him to follow. Julien wore a surplice very becomingly. By dint of who knows what churchly art of dressing, he had made his flourishing curls lie down flat; but, by an oversight that redoubled M. Chélan's annoyance, beneath the long folds of his soutane the spurs of a guard of honour could be seen.

When they arrived at the Bishop's quarters, two great big footmen in heavily braided uniforms only just deigned to inform the aged curé that the Bishop was not to be seen at present. They were scornfully amused when he tried to explain that in his capacity as dean of the noble chapter of Bray-le-Haut he had the privilege of admittance to the officiating bishop at all times.

Julien's proud temper was appalled at the insolence of these lackeys. He set off searching through the dormitories of the ancient abbey, rattling all the doors he came to. One very small one gave way to his attempts, and he found himself in a little cell in the midst of Monseigneur's valets, who were dressed in black with chains around their necks. Seeing his hurried air, these gentlemen assumed he must have been called by the Bishop, and let him pass. In a few strides he found himself in a vast and immensely sombre gothic hall, panelled throughout in black oak; with one exception, the ogival windows had been bricked up. The crudity of this work was not at all disguised, and formed a sad contrast to the venerable magnificence of the panelling. The two great sides of this hall – which is celebrated amongst those interested in Burgundian history, and which Duke Charles the Bold[3] had built about 1470 in expiation of some sin or other – were decorated with elaborately decorated wooden stalls. There one could see all the mysteries of the Apocalypse, carved in woods of variegated colour.

This melancholy magnificence, degraded by the sight of bare brick and untreated plaster, impressed Julien. In silence he halted. At the other end of the hall, next to the one window that let in the light, he noticed a travelling mirror framed in mahogany. A young man, dressed in a violet robe and a lace surplice, but bareheaded, was standing three paces away from the mirror. Such a piece of furniture seemed strange in such a setting – doubtless it had been brought from the town. Julien perceived that the young man had an irritable air; with his right hand he was gravely performing blessings in the direction of the glass.

What can this mean? wondered Julien. Is this young priest accomplishing some preliminary rite? Perhaps he's the Bishop's secretary . . . He'll be offensive, like those lackeys . . . Good God, never mind, let's try.

He stepped forward and quite slowly traversed the length of the hall, his eyes set constantly towards the single window and his attention fixed on the young man, who went on making blessings with deliberate gestures, but endlessly, without pausing at all.

As Julien got nearer, he made out the air of annoyance more clearly. The richness of the lace-embroidered surplice brought him to an involuntary halt, a few steps from the magnificent mirror.

It's my duty to speak, he said to himself at last; but the beauty of the hall had aroused his feelings, and he was ruffled by the anticipation of harsh words that might be addressed to him.

The young man glimpsed his reflection, turned round and, suddenly dropping his air of annoyance, said in the gentlest of tones:

– Ah, well, monsieur, has it been sorted out at last?

Julien stood there astounded. As the young man turned towards him, Julien saw the pectoral cross on his breast: this was the Bishop of Agde. So young, thought Julien; at the most six or seven years older than I am!

And he was ashamed of his spurs.

– Monseigneur, he replied timidly, I am sent by the Dean of the Chapter, M. Chélan.

– Ah! he has been highly recommended to me, said the Bishop in a tone so polite that it redoubled Julien's fascination. But I must ask your pardon, monsieur, I took you for the person who should be bringing me back my mitre. It was badly packed up in Paris; the silver webbing towards the top is horribly spoilt. It would have the most disagreeable effect, added the young bishop sadly – and still they keep me waiting!

– Monseigneur, I'll go to look for your mitre, if Your Lordship permits.

Julien's fine eyes had their effect.

– Do, go then, monsieur, replied the Bishop, charmingly polite; I need it straight away. I'm most awfully sorry to be keeping the gentlemen of the chapter waiting.

When Julien reached the middle of the hall he turned round towards the Bishop and saw that he had gone back to making blessings. What can this possibly be? Julien asked himself – no doubt it's a church preliminary needed for the ceremony that's going to be performed. When he got into the little room where the valets were he saw the mitre in their hands. These gentlemen, giving way in spite of themselves to Julien's imperious look, surrendered My Lord's mitre.

He felt proud to carry it; while crossing the hall he walked softly; he carried it with respect. He found the Bishop seated in front of the mirror; but, from time to time, his right hand, though tired, gave another blessing. Julien helped him put the mitre on. The Bishop waggled his head.

– Ah! it sticks, he said to Julien with a satisfied air. Would you step back a moment?

The Bishop went quickly to the middle of the hall; then, walking back towards the mirror with slow steps, he reassumed his air of annoyance and gravely dispensed blessings.

Julien stood still in astonishment; he was tempted to interpret this, but dared not. The Bishop stopped, and looked at him in a manner that quickly lost its gravity:

– What d'you say to my mitre, monsieur, is it all right?

– Very good, Monseigneur.

– It's not too far back? – that would look a bit stupid; but one cannot wear it low over one's eyes like an officer's shako.

– It seems absolutely fine to me.

– The King of — is accustomed to venerable clergy, and no doubt very solemn ones. I wouldn't want, especially in view of my age, to have too unserious a look.

And the Bishop started to pace round again giving blessings.

It's obvious, said Julien, daring at last to understand, that he's rehearsing making blessings.

After a few moments:

– I'm ready, said the Bishop. Go, monsieur, and inform the Dean and the gentlemen of the chapter.

Shortly afterwards, attended by two of the most ancient priests, M. Chélan entered through a very grand and magnificently sculptured portal that Julien had not noticed before. But this time Julien kept to his place, the last of all, and could only glimpse the Bishop above the shoulders of the clergy, who crowded and squeezed through the portal.

The Bishop slowly traversed the hall; when he reached the threshold, the curés formed themselves into a procession. After a minute of confusion, the procession started to move, chanting a psalm. The Bishop came last, between M. Chélan and another very elderly priest. Julien, as being attached to the Abbé Chélan, wormed his way quite near to Monseigneur. They followed the long corridors of the abbey of Bray-le-Haut, damp and gloomy in spite of the brilliant sunshine. Eventually they arrived at the portico of the cloister. Julien was speechless with admiration for so beautiful a ceremony. The ambitions reawakened by the Bishop's youth disputed with that prelate's sensibility and exquisite manners for possession of his heart. These manners were in a different category from M. de Rênal's, even at his best. The more one rises toward the front ranks of society, thought Julien to himself, the more one finds delightful manners.

They entered the church by a side door; all at once an astounding noise echoed around the ancient vaults. Julien thought they were collapsing. It was the little piece of cannon again; it had just arrived, dragged along by eight horses at the gallop; straightaway the gunners of Leipzig set it up and fired at the rate of five shots a minute, as though the Prussians had been in front of them.

But this stirring sound no longer moved Julien, he dreamt no more of Napoleon and military glory. So young and to be Bishop of Agde! thought he. But where is Agde? And how much would it bring in? Two or three thousand francs, maybe.

The Bishop's servants appeared, bearing a magnificent canopy. M. Chélan grasped one of the poles, but in fact it was Julien who took the weight. The Bishop positioned himself underneath. He had contrived – truly – to give himself an air of agedness; our hero's admiration knew no bounds. What couldn't one achieve with such skills! he thought.

The King came in. Julien had the good fortune to view him very close to. The Bishop addressed him with unction, not forgetting to add a little flutter of nervousness, very pleasing to His Majesty.

We won't give here yet another description of these ceremonies at Bray-le-Haut; for a fortnight they filled the columns of all the journals in the department. Julien learned from the Bishop's discourse that the King was descended from Charles the Bold.

Later on it became part of Julien's duties to check the accounts of how much this ceremony had cost. M. de La Mole, who had had his nephew made a bishop, had made him the generous gift of discharging all the expenses. The ceremony at Bray-le-Haut alone cost 3,800 francs.

After the Bishop's discourse and the King's response, His Majesty took his place under the canopy, then knelt with great piety on a hassock next to the altar. The choir was surrounded by stalls, and these stalls were raised two steps above the flagstones. Julien was seated at the feet of M. Chélan on the last of these, somewhat like the trainbearer next to his cardinal in the Sistine Chapel in Rome. There was a *Te Deum*, clouds of incense, infinite firings off of muskets and artillery; the peasants were intoxicated with happiness and piety. Such an occasion destroys the work of a hundred issues of the Jacobin papers.

Julien was six paces from the King, who prayed with actual fervour. For the first time he noticed a small man with a spirited expression who wore an almost undecorated coat. But over this extremely simple costume was a sky-blue riband.[4] He stood much closer to the King than the many other lords, whose coats were embroidered with so much gold that, to use Julien's expression, you couldn't see the cloth. He learned a few moments afterwards that this was M. de La Mole. He thought his air haughty, even insolent.

This marquis would not be polite like my lovely bishop, thought he. Ah! the ecclesiastical condition makes one gentle and wise. But the King is here to venerate the relic, and I don't see any relic. Where would St Clement be?

His neighbour, a little clergyman, informed him that the venerable relic was at the top of the building, housed in a *chapelle ardente*.[5]

What is a *chapelle ardente*? Julien said to himself.

But he did not choose to ask for an explanation. He redoubled his concentration.

Etiquette ruled that the Bishop ought not to be accompanied by the canons on the occasion of a visit by a sovereign prince. However, in setting out for the *chapelle ardente*, Monsignor d'Agde called the Abbé Chélan to him; Julien ventured to follow.

Having climbed a long stairway, they came to a very small door with a magnificently gilded gothic frame. The work appeared to have been done only yesterday.

In front of the door were assembled four-and-twenty young girls drawn from the most distinguished families in Verrières. Before opening the door, the Bishop sunk to his knees in the middle of these very pretty girls. As he prayed out loud, they seemed flooded with admiration for his beautiful lace, his gracefulness and a face so young and so gentle. The sight robbed our hero of what sense he had left. At that moment he would have fought for the Inquisition, and with passion. Suddenly the door was open. The little chapel appeared as though brimming with light. One could see more than a thousand candles on the altar, divided into eight divisions separated by bouquets of flowers. The fragrant smell of purest incense billowed in clouds from out of the sanctuary door. The freshly gilded chapel was very small, but very high. Julien saw that on the altar there were candles rising up more than fifteen feet. The girls could not restrain a cry of wonder. The only people admitted into the little vestibule of the chapel were the twenty-four girls, the two priests and Julien.

Soon the King came in, accompanied only by M. de La Mole and his Grand Chamberlain. Even the guards stayed outside, on their knees, presenting arms.

His Majesty tumbled rather than threw himself on to a prie-dieu. It was only then that Julien, pressed against the gilded door, saw – under the bare arm of one of the girls – the elegant figure of St Clement. He was recessed under the altar and dressed as a young Roman soldier. At his neck was a great wound from which blood seemed to flow. The artist had surpassed himself: the dying eyes, full of unction, were half closed; a budding moustache graced the charming lips which, half open, seemed still to be in prayer. At the sight of this the young girl next to Julien wept hot tears, one of which fell on Julien's hand.

After a moment of prayer in the deepest silence, disturbed only by the distant ringing of bells in all the villages for ten leagues around, the Bishop of Agde asked the King's leave to speak. He concluded a short and very moving discourse with a few words that were all the more penetrating for their simplicity.

– Never forget, young Christians, that you've seen one of the greatest kings on earth on his knees before the servants of this terrible and omnipotent God. These weak servants, persecuted and slain on earth – as you can see from the ever bleeding wound of St Clement here – these servants triumph in Heaven. You will, won't you, young Christians, forever remember this day? – you will loathe impiety. You'll be faithful for ever to this great God, who is so terrible yet so good.

At these words the Bishop raised himself up in authority.

– You will promise me this? he said, throwing out his arms, inspired.

– We promise it, responded the girls, melting into tears.

– I receive your promise, in God's dread name! added the Bishop in a voice of thunder. And the ceremony was over.

Even the King was in tears. It was not until a long time afterwards that Julien summoned up the nerve to enquire where the saint's bones, sent from Rome to Philip the Good, Duke of Burgundy, actually were. He was informed that they were concealed within the graceful figure of wax.[6]

His Majesty condescended to allow the young ladies who had waited upon him in the chapel to wear a red sash, on which were embroidered these words: HATRED TO IMPIETY, ETERNAL ADORATION.

M. de La Mole had 10,000 bottles of wine distributed among the peasantry. That evening in Verrières the liberals found excuses for illuminations a hundred times finer than those of the Royalists. Before he left, the King paid a visit to M. de Moirod.

CHAPTER 19

Thought Brings Suffering

The grotesque nature of everyday events conceals from
one the real suffering of the passions.   BARNAVE[1]

While putting the ordinary furniture of the room that M. de La Mole
had occupied back into place, Julien came across a thick sheet of
paper folded in four. He saw at the bottom of the first page:

To His Lordship M. de La Mole, Peer of France, Chevalier of the
Orders of the King, etc., etc.

It was a petition, in the crude handwriting of a cook.

Monsieur le Marquis,
I have had religious principles all my life. I was exposed to exploding shells
in Lyon during the siege in 1793 of execrable memory.[2] I am a communicant;
every Sunday I go to mass at the parochial church. I have never failed in
my Easter duty, even in 1793 of execrable memory. My cook – before the
Revolution I had some servants – my cook observes Fridays. I rejoice in a
general esteem in Verrières, I presume to say merited. I walk under the
canopy in processions, at the side of M. le Curé and M. le Maire. On
important occasions I carry a large wax candle bought at my own cost. For
all this the certificates are at the Ministry of Finance at Paris. I ask M. le
Marquis for the lottery office in Verrières, which cannot fail to be vacant in
one way or another, the holder being very sick, and anyway voting wrong
in the elections, etc.

DE CHOLIN

In the margin of this petition was a recommendatory note signed *De
Moirod* that started with the line:

I had the honour to speak *yestday* with the deserving character who makes this petition, *etc.*

So, said Julien, even that imbecile de Cholin shows me the path to follow.

A week after the King of — had departed, what chiefly emerged from the innumerable lies, idiotic interpretations, ridiculous discussions, etc., etc., concerning, in succession, the King, the Bishop of Agde, the Marquis de La Mole, the 10,000 bottles of wine, and poor horse-fallen Moirod – who in his hopes of a cross did not leave his house for a month after his accident – was the extreme lack of decorum that had *catapulted* Julien Sorel, carpenter's son, into the guard of honour. On this subject one should have heard the wealthy manufacturers of painted cloth who, morning and evening, would talk themselves hoarse in the café making speeches about equality. That proud woman, Mme de Rênal, was responsible for the abomination. Why? – the fine eyes and fresh cheeks of little Abbé Sorel told you why.

Shortly after the return to Vergy, the youngest of the children, Stanislas-Xavier, developed a fever; all of a sudden Mme de Rênal sank into a frightful state of remorse. For the first time she thought critically about her love affair in an ordered way; she seemed to comprehend, as if by a miracle, into how grievous a sin she had let herself be drawn. Despite her deeply religious temperament she had never considered, until now, the magnitude of her crime in the eyes of God.

Long ago, at the Convent of the Sacred Heart, she had loved God with a passion; now, in this predicament, she came to dread Him as fervently. The struggles that tore her heart apart were the more terrible because there was nothing rational in her fears. Julien found that the slightest reasoning irritated rather than calmed her; she saw in it the language of Hell. However, since Julien was himself extremely fond of little Stanislas, he was more welcome to her when he came to talk to her of the boy's illness: this soon took on a grave aspect. From then on, her endless remorse robbed Mme de Rênal even of the ability to sleep; she kept an austere silence: if she had opened her mouth it would have been to confess her crime to God and to men.

— I beg you not to speak to anyone else, said Julien to her when they found themselves alone; let me be the sole confidant of your suffering. If you still love me, don't speak: your words cannot rid our Stanislas of his fever.

But his efforts to console her had no effect. He did not know that Mme de Rênal had it fixed in her mind that, in order to appease the anger of a jealous God, she must hate Julien or see her son die. It was because she felt that she could not hate her lover that she was so wretched.

— Get yourself away from me, she said to Julien one day; in the name of God, leave this house: it's your presence here that is killing my son.

God is punishing me, she added in a whisper, and He is just; I worship His justice; my crime is appalling and I continue to live without remorse! That's the first sign of a flight from God; I deserve a twofold punishment.

Julien was deeply moved. He could see neither hypocrisy nor exaggeration in this. She thinks she is killing her son by loving me — yet she loves me more than she loves her son. That, I have no doubt, is the remorse that is destroying her; that is real nobility of feeling. But how have I been able to inspire such a love — I, so poor, so badly brought up, so ignorant, sometimes so crude in my manners?

One night, the child became much worse. Towards two o'clock in the morning, M. de Rênal came to visit him. The child, devoured by fever, was very flushed and could not recognize his father. Suddenly Mme de Rênal threw herself at her husband's feet: Julien saw that she was going to tell everything and ruin herself for ever.

Luckily this strange action disconcerted M. de Rênal.

Goodbye! Goodbye! he said, and turned to leave.

No, hear me, cried his wife, on her knees before him and trying to hold him back. Learn the whole truth. It is I who am killing my son. I've given him life, and I'm taking it away. Heaven is punishing me — in the eyes of God I am guilty of murder. I must destroy and humiliate myself — perhaps the offering might appease the Lord.

If M. de Rênal had been a man of imagination, he would have understood everything.

— Romantic tosh, he cried, avoiding his wife, who was trying to embrace his knees. Romantic tosh, that's all this is! Julien, have the doctor called as soon as it's light.

And he returned to bed. Mme de Rênal fell on her knees, half fainting while repulsing Julien, who wanted to help her, with convulsive movements.

Julien stood there amazed.

So this is adultery! he said to himself ... Can it be that those deceitful priests ... are in the right? That those who commit so many sins have the privilege of understanding the true anatomy of sin? How extremely odd! ...

For twenty minutes after M. de Rênal had left, Julien watched the woman he loved, her head pillowed on the little child's bed, unmoving and almost unconscious. Here lies a woman of the loftiest spirit reduced to the depths of misery on account of knowing me, he thought.

Time's passing by. What can I do for her? I must decide. It is not a question of myself any more. What do I care for men and their shallow pretences? What can I do for her? ... Leave her? But then I leave her alone, suffering the most terrible grief. That automaton of a husband might well do her more harm than good. He'll say some wounding thing to her, because he's so clumsy; she could go mad and throw herself from the window.

If I leave her, if I stop watching over her, she will confess everything. And who knows, possibly, in spite of the money she should bring him, he will make a scandal. She might tell it all, good God! to that b— of an Abbé Maslon, who's using the illness of a 6-year-old child as a pretext to stick around this house, and not without some purpose. In her misery and her fear of God she forgets what she knows about the man, and sees only the priest.

— Go away, said Mme de Rênal suddenly, opening her eyes.

— I'd give my life a thousand times just to know how I could serve you best, answered Julien: never have I loved you so much, my dearest angel — or, rather, only from this moment have I begun to adore you as you deserve. What will become of me, far from you and knowing that you've come to such grief through me! But it isn't a question of my suffering. Yes, I'll go, my love. But, if I leave you, if I cease to watch over you, if I'm not constantly between you and your husband, you will tell him all, you will ruin yourself. Think with what ignominy he will drive you from his house; all Verrières, all Besançon will be chattering about the scandal. All the guilt will be put on you; you will never recover from the shame . . .

– That's what I ask, cried she, straightening herself. I'll suffer, so much the better.

– But, with such an abominable scandal, you will do him damage, too!

– But I abase myself, I throw myself in the mire; and, perhaps that way, I will redeem my son. Such a humiliation in the sight of the world is perhaps an overt atonement? As far as my feeble mind can judge, isn't that the greatest sacrifice I can make to God? . . . Perhaps He'll accept my humiliation and let my son go! Show me a more painful sacrifice and I will run to it.

– Let me punish myself. Me – I'm guilty, too. Would you like me to become a Trappist? The rigour of that life might appease your God . . . Oh! Heavens! if only I could take Stanislas's fever upon myself . . .

– Ah! you love him, too, said Mme de Rênal, rising and throwing herself into his arms.

In the same instant she pushed him away with horror.

– I believe you! I believe you! she continued, falling to her knees again; Oh, my only friend! oh, why aren't you Stanislas's father! – then it would not be such a terrible sin to love you more than your son.

– Will you let me stay, and from now on love you only as a brother would? That's the sole rational atonement, and it might succeed in appeasing the wrath of the Most High.

– And me, she cried, rising and taking Julien's head between her two hands, gazing at it at arms' length – and me, would I be able to love you only as a brother? Is it in my power to love you as a brother?

125

Julien melted in tears.

— I'll obey you, he said, falling at her feet, I'll obey whatever you say; it's the only thing left for me. My mind's struck blind; I don't know which way to go. If I leave you, you will tell your husband everything, you will ruin yourself — and him with you. Never, after such shame, would he be made deputy. If I stay, you will think I have caused the death of your son, and you will die of sorrow. Shall we see what my absence is like? If you want, I will punish myself for our fault by leaving you for a week. I will go into a retreat anywhere you choose. To the abbey of Bray-le-Haut, for example: but you must swear that while I'm gone you'll say nothing to your husband. Remember that should you speak I can never return.

She promised, he departed, but was recalled when two days had passed.

— It's impossible for me to keep to my undertaking without you. If you aren't there all the time to bind me to silence by your looks, I'm bound to speak to my husband. Every hour of this detestable existence seems to me to last a day.

Finally Heaven had pity on this unhappy mother. Little by little, Stanislas passed out of danger. But the surface had been smashed, her reason had grasped the extent of her sin; she could not restore her former equilibrium. Her remorse stayed with her, and it was of a quality only to be expected from so sincere a heart. Her existence became a heaven and a hell: a hell when she didn't see Julien, heaven when she was at his feet. I entertain no illusions, she would tell him, even in those moments when she dared give herself over wholly to her love — I'm damned, irrevocably damned. You are young, you've given in to my seductions, Heaven may pardon you; but myself I'm damned. I know it from a sure sign. I'm terrified: who wouldn't be terrified at the sight of Hell? But in my heart I don't repent. I'd commit my sin all over again if it was there to be committed. If Heaven would only refrain from punishing me in this world through my children, I'd have more than I deserve. But you — she would cry at other times — you at least, my Julien, are you happy? Do you feel that I love you fully enough?

Julien's suspicious nature and his painful pride, which above all needed a love full of sacrifices, could not resist the sight of so great and so indubitable an offering, made to him every moment. He adored Mme de Rênal. She's a beautiful and noble being, I'm the son of a worker, she loves me ... I'm not attached to her like a lackey ordered to play the part of a lover. This anxiety dispelled, Julien fell into all the extravagances of love, into all its deadly uncertainties.

– At least, she cried, seeing his apprehensions about her love, I'll make you truly happy for the few days that are left to us to spend together! We must be quick; tomorrow I may no longer be with you. If Heaven blast me through my children, it would be useless for me to try to live only for the love of you, and not to recognize that it's my crime that's killing them. I could not survive the blow. Even if I wanted to, I couldn't; I'd run mad.

– Ah, if only I could take your sin on my head, as you so generously offered to take Stanislas's burning fever!

This great moral crisis transformed the nature of the feeling that united Julien and his mistress. His love was no longer simply adoration of her beauty, and the pride of possessing it.

Henceforth, their happiness was of a higher kind; the flame that consumed them burned brighter. They had times of ecstasy filled with wildness. To the world their passion would have seemed greater. But they never recovered that delightful serenity, that cloudless felicity and easy happiness which had marked the first stages of their love – when Mme de Rênal's sole fear had been that Julien did not love her enough. Their happiness at times took on the appearance of a crime.

Mme de Rênal would suddenly cry out, even in the happiest and seemingly most tranquil of moments, and, pressing Julien's hand convulsively: – Ah! Almighty God! I see a vision of Hell ... What terrible torments! And I've deserved them, totally. Then she would hug him, clinging to him as ivy clings to a wall.

Julien tried fruitlessly to calm her distracted soul. She took his hand and covered it in kisses. Then, relapsing into sombre reverie: – Hell, she said, would be a mercy to me; I'd have a few days still to spend with him on earth – but Hell in this world, the death of my children ... Yet possibly at that price my crime might be forgiven me . . . Oh! Almighty God, don't grant me mercy at that price. These children have in no way offended Thee; I, I alone am the guilty one: I love a man who is not my husband.

Then Julien would see Mme de Rênal achieve periods of apparent calm. She made an effort to control herself, she tried not to poison the existence of him she loved.

Between remorse and pleasure, these two poles of love, time passed for them with the speed of light. Julien lost the habit of thinking.

Mlle Élisa went off to visit Verrières to deal with a little lawsuit in which she was involved. There she encountered M. Valenod who was much incensed against Julien. She had a loathing for the tutor, and often spoke of it to M. Valenod.

– You'd be the ruin of me, monsieur, she said to him one day, if I was to tell the truth . . . On important things the Masters always stand together . . . You never forgive certain things poor people might say . . .

After these ritual phrases, which M. Valenod's active curiosity soon discovered the art of abridging, he learned things most mortifying to his self-esteem.

The most distinguished woman of the district, she whom he had surrounded with so many attentions – unfortunately in the sight and knowledge of everyone – for the last six years this woman who was so proud, whose disdain had so often made him blush, had come to take a little plebeian youth disguised as a tutor for her lover. And, so that nothing should be lacking to the discomfiture of M. Valenod, Director of the Poorhouse, Mme de Rênal adored this lover.

– Also, added the lady's maid with a sigh, M. Julien did not go to any trouble making this conquest, he did not emerge from his usual coldness towards Madame at all.

Élisa had sure knowledge only from when they were in the country, but she thought the intrigue went back further.

No doubt it's because of that, she added spitefully, that he wouldn't marry me some time ago. And it was me – what an imbecile! – who went to ask Mme de Rênal's advice, who begged her to speak to the tutor.

That very evening M. de Rênal received from town, with his newspaper, a long anonymous letter which told him in the greatest detail what was going on in his house. Julien saw him go pale while reading this letter, written on bluish paper, and dart some wicked looks at himself. All evening the Mayor persisted in this troubled state, and it was useless for Julien to try to flatter him by asking for explanations of the genealogy of the best families in Burgundy.

CHAPTER 20

Anonymous Letters

> *Do not give dalliance*
> *Too much the rein: the strongest oaths are straw*
> *To the fire i'the blood.*
>
> *The Tempest*

As they were leaving the salon around midnight, Julien found the opportunity of saying to his lover:

– Let's not see each other tonight, your husband is acting as though he suspects something; I could swear that that long piece of writing he was sighing over was an anonymous letter.

It was lucky Julien locked himself into his room. Mme de Rênal conceived the wild idea that his warning was merely a pretext for not seeing her. She completely lost her head, and went to his door at the usual time. Hearing some noise in the corridor, Julien immediately put out his light. Somebody tried to open his door – was it Mme de Rênal or was it a jealous husband?

Very early next morning, the cook, an ally of Julien's, brought him a book. On its cover he read these words in Italian: *Guardate alla pagina 130.*[1]

Julien trembled at this rashness, turned to page 130 and found a letter pinned in there – written in haste, stained with tears, and without the least care taken over spelling or presentation. Mme de Rênal was usually very punctilious in such matters, so that he was touched by this detail and his attention slightly diverted from the frightening rashness of the deed.

You didn't want me to come to you tonight? It's at these moments that I think I've never seen into the depths of your soul. Your eyes scare me. I'm frightened of you. God above! – can it be you've never loved me? In that case, let my husband discover our affair, let him imprison me for ever in the country, far from my children. Perhaps God wishes it so. I would quickly die. But you would be a monster.

Do you not love me, then? Are you sick of my follies, of my remorse, infidel? D'you want to ruin me? I'll provide you with an easy way. Go and show this letter to everyone in Verrières – or, rather, show it to M. Valenod alone. Tell him that I love you – no, don't utter such a blasphemy, tell him that I adore you, that life only began for me the day I first saw you; that in the most doting moments of my youth I never even dreamed of such happiness as you have brought me; that I've sacrificed my life to you, that I will sacrifice my soul. You know that I will sacrifice even more.

But what would he know of sacrifices, that fellow? Tell him, tell him to gall him that I defy all spiteful people, and that there's only one unhappiness left for me in the world, that of seeing changes in the one man who keeps me clinging to life. What joy it would be to me to lose it, to offer it up as a sacrifice, and not to have to fear for my children any more!

Don't doubt, dearest friend, that if there is an anonymous letter it comes from that odious man who for six years has pursued me with his loud voice, his stories of the jumps he's made on his horse, his fatuity, and the perpetual enumeration of his superior qualities.

Is there an anonymous letter? – villain, that's what I wanted to discuss with you; but no, you did right. With you clasped in my arms – perhaps for the last time – I'd never have been able to discuss it calmly, as I do now, alone. From now on our happiness will be less easy to arrange. Will that be tiresome for you? Yes, on the days when you haven't received an amusing book from M. Fouqué. The sacrifice is made – tomorrow, whether or not there's an anonymous letter, I shall tell my husband that I've received one, and that he must at once shower you with gold, find a decent pretext and send you back to your family without delay.

Alas! my dear, we will be separated for a fortnight, perhaps a month. Go! – to do you justice, you'll suffer as much as I will. But in the end, it's the only way to ward off the effect of that anonymous letter; it's not the first my husband has had, and concerning me, too. Alas! – how I used to laugh at them!

The sole aim of my conduct is to make my husband think that the letter came from M. Valenod; I have no doubt he was the author. If you leave this house, don't fail to go and settle in Verrières. I'll see to it that my husband gets the idea of spending a fortnight there, to show the idiots that there's no estrangement between him and me. Once at Verrières, ingratiate yourself with everyone, even the liberals. I'm sure all the women will run after you.

Don't go and quarrel with M. Valenod, nor crop his ears as you once said you would; on the contrary, be very charming to him. The essential thing is that at Verrières they believe you might go into Valenod's household, or someone else's, to teach the children.

That my husband would never stand for. And if he should resign himself to it, well! at least you'll be living in Verrières, and I'd see you sometimes. My children, who love you so much, would go to visit you a lot. Great God! I feel I love my children the more because they love you. What shame! How will it all end? ... But I'm wandering ... Anyway, you know how to conduct yourself; be gentle, polite and, I beg you on my knees, don't show your scorn for these crude folk: they'll become the arbiters of our fate. Don't imagine for a moment that, in his dealings with you, my husband won't conform in every respect to what is prescribed by *public opinion*.

It's you who are going to supply me with the anonymous letter. Arm yourself with patience and a pair of scissors. Cut the words you'll see below from out of a book; then stick them with licked gum on the sheet of bluish paper I'm sending you – it came from M. Valenod. Be prepared for a search of your quarters: burn the pages of the book you've cut up. If you don't find the words ready made, be patient and compose them letter by letter. To spare you trouble I've made the anonymous letter rather too brief. Alas! if you don't love me any longer, as I fear, how overlong mine must seem to you!

ANONYMOUS LETTER

Madame

All your little doings are known; but those people who have an interest in repressing them have been alerted. Through the vestige of an attachment for you, I urge you to cut yourself off completely from the little peasant. If you are wise enough for that, your husband will think the notice he received was a deception, and will be left in his error. Consider that I know your secret; tremble, unhappy one; from now on you must *quick march straight ahead* in front of me.

When you have finished sticking the words of this letter (do you recognize the Director's way of talking?), come out into the house and I will meet you.

I will go down into the village and return with a troubled face — I shall indeed be deeply troubled. Great God! I'm taking all these risks, and all because you *believed you made out* an anonymous letter. Then, with an averted face, I will hand my husband this letter that an unknown person gave me. You, go and walk with the children on the woodland way and don't come back before dinner time.

From the top of the rocks you can see the turret on the dovecot. If the business goes well I will put a white handkerchief up there; if it goes the other way, there will be nothing.

Ungrateful boy! Won't your heart find a way to tell me if you love me before you start on this walk? Whatever can happen, be sure of one thing: I will not live for a single day after our final separation. Ah! wicked mother! — Those last two words I've written here mean nothing, dear Julien. I don't feel them — I can think of nothing but you at this moment — I've only written them so as not to be blamed by you. Now that I see myself on the brink of losing you, what is the point of disguising the truth? Yes! even if my soul seems foul to you, I will not lie to the man I adore! I have too many deceits in my life already. Go along then, I forgive you if you no longer love me. I have not time to re-read my letter. To my eyes it is a very trifling thing to pay with a life for the happy days I have been allowed to spend in your arms. You know that they will cost me more than that.

CHAPTER 21

Dialogue with a Master

Alas, our frailty is the cause, not we;
For such as we are made of, such we be.
                                        Twelfth Night

For an hour Julien pieced the words together with a childlike pleasure. Coming out of his room he encountered his pupils and their mother; she received the letter with so much naturalness and courage that he was frightened by her calm.

— The gum's dry enough? she asked.

Is this the woman whom remorse has driven so wild? he thought. What can she plan to do now? He was too proud to ask; but perhaps she had never delighted him more.

— If this turns out badly, said she, everything I possess will be taken away. Bury this little collection in some spot in the mountains; perhaps one day it will be my only resource.

She handed him a spectacle case in red morocco, stuffed with gold and a few diamonds.

— Now go, she said.

She hugged her children, the youngest twice over. Julien did not move. She left him at a rapid pace, without looking at him.

From the moment he had opened the anonymous letter, M. de Rênal's existence had been blighted. He had never been so upset since a duel he had almost been forced to fight in 1816, and, to do him justice, the prospect of being hit by a pistol ball then had made him less unhappy than he was now. He examined the letter in every way: Isn't that a woman's handwriting? he asked himself. If it is, what woman wrote it? He considered all those he knew in Verrières without being able to fix his suspicions on any. Had a man dictated the letter? What man? An equivalent uncertainty there; he had earned the jealousy, and therefore no doubt the hatred, of most of the men he knew. I must ask my wife, he said to himself out of habit, lifting himself up from the armchair into which he had sunk deep.

He was scarcely on his feet – Great God! he cried, striking his brow, it's her that I must distrust above all; she's my enemy now. And tears of anger came to his eyes.

By way of fair reward for that aridity of heart which is involved in all the practical wisdom of the provinces, the two men of whom at that moment M. de Rênal was most fearful were his two most intimate friends.

– Besides those two, I have maybe ten friends – and he passed them in review, estimating the level of sympathy he might be able to exact. To all of them! – to all of them! he cried to himself with rage, my awful predicament would give the greatest satisfaction. He believed himself very much envied for his good fortune, and not without reason. Quite apart from his grand town house, that had just been honoured for ever by the King of — sleeping there, he had fixed things up wonderfully well at his château at Vergy. The façade was painted white, and the windows decorated with beautiful green shutters. For a moment he was cheered by the thought of such magnificence. In truth this château could be seen from three or four leagues away – to the great disadvantage of all the neighbouring country houses, or so-called châteaux, that had been abandoned to the humble grey tints bestowed by the passage of time.

M. de Rênal could count on the tears and sympathy of one of his friends, the parish churchwarden; but he was an imbecile who would burst into tears at everything. Yet this man was his sole resource.

What affliction can compare with mine! he cried to himself with rage; what isolation!

Can it be possible! this man – truly to be pitied – said to himself, can it be possible that I have not a single friend from whom I can ask advice in my misfortune? – for my wits are all scattered, I know that! Ah! Falcoz! Ah! Ducroz! he cried bitterly. – These were the names of two childhood friends he had alienated through his aloofness in 1814. They were not nobles, and he had wished to discontinue the equal terms on which he had lived with them from infancy.

One of them, Falcoz, a man of wit and feeling who was a paper merchant in Verrières, had bought a press in the chief town in the department, and founded a journal there. The Congregation had resolved to ruin him: his journal had been proscribed, his licence to print withdrawn. In these unhappy circumstances he ventured to write to M. de Rênal for the first time in ten years. The Mayor of Verrières believed it his duty to answer in the style of an ancient Roman: *If His Majesty's minister did me the honour to consult me on this matter, I would say to him: Ruin all the printers in the province without compunction, and make printing a monopoly, like tobacco.* M. de Rênal now recalled the terms of this epistle to an intimate friend – that at the time had been applauded by all Verrières – with dismay. Who then could have said that with my rank, my wealth, my decorations, I would one day regret it? He passed a frightful night in fits of anger, sometimes against himself, sometimes against everything around him – but, luckily, it did not occur to him to spy on his wife.

I'm accustomed to Louise, he said to himself, she knows about all my concerns; were I free to marry tomorrow, I could not find anyone to replace her. Then he comforted himself with the idea that his wife was innocent; such a way of looking at things excused him from having to display some character and arrange matters better – how many women had he not seen slandered!

But what's this! he burst out suddenly, pacing up and down erratically – Am I to endure her mocking me with her lover as though I were a nobody, a vagrant? Must the whole of Verrières be allowed to snigger over my complaisance? What don't they say about Charmier [a notorious local cuckold]? Isn't there a grin on every face when he's mentioned? He's a good lawyer, but who says anything about his way with words? Ah! Charmier! they say, Bernard's Charmier – characterizing him so by the name of the man who has dishonoured him.

Heaven be thanked, said M. de Rênal at other moments, that I don't have a daughter, and that the means by which I will punish their mother won't ruin my children's standing in life a bit; I could surprise this little peasant with my wife, and slay both of them; in which case maybe the tragic nature of the story might free it from ridicule. This idea attracted him; he pictured it in all its details. The penal code is in my favour, and, whatever happens, our Congregation plus my allies on the jury will save me. He examined his hunting knife, which was extremely sharp; but the notion of blood frightened him.

I could thrash this insolent tutor mercilessly and chuck him out; but what a scandal in Verrières and even the whole department! After Falcoz's journal was condemned, when his editor-in-chief came out of prison, I had a hand in making him lose a post worth six hundred francs. They say this scribbler has dared to raise his head in Besançon; he could pillory me cleverly, and in a way it would be impossible to bring before a court. Bring him before a court . . . The scoundrel could insinuate in a thousand ways that he was telling the truth. A well-born man, who asserts his rank in life as I do, is hated by all the plebs. I shall see myself in those abominable Paris papers; oh my God! what an abyss! to see the ancient name of Rênal plunged into the mud of ridicule . . . Should I ever travel, I would have to change my name; what! abandon this name that's my glory and my strength. What a pitch of misery!

If I don't kill my wife but simply throw her out in ignominy, she has her aunt in Besançon, who will consent to putting her whole fortune at her disposal. My wife will go and live in Paris with Julien; they will learn of it in Verrières — and again I would be taken for a dupe . . . The unhappy man now saw from the paling of the lamps that it was beginning to get light. He went into the garden for some fresh air. By then he had almost decided not to make a scandal, above all because of the idea that an outcry would flood his good friends in Verrières with joy.

The walk in the garden soothed him somewhat. No, he cried to himself, I won't deprive myself of my wife, she's too useful to me. He pictured with dismay what his household would be like without his wife; the only other relation he possessed was the Marquise de R——, old, foolish and spiteful.

An idea full of good sense occurred to him, but carrying it through required a greater force of character than such small amount as the poor man possessed. If I keep my wife, he said to himself, I know myself, one day, when she annoys me, I will reproach her with her crime. She's proud, we'll quarrel, and all that will take place before she has inherited from her aunt. Then how they'll mock me! My wife loves her children, in the end everything will come to them. But as for me, I'll be a byword in Verrières. Ho! they'll say, he didn't even know how to revenge himself on his wife! Wouldn't it be better for me to just have my suspicions and leave it vague? But in that case I bind my hands, and cannot reproach her later on.

A moment later, gripped again by wounded pride, M. de Rênal carefully recalled all the methods mentioned when, in the billiard room of the casino or the Club of Nobles in Verrières, some sprightly talker interrupted the game to make fun at the expense of a deceived husband. How cruel these jokes seemed to him just then!

God! why isn't my wife dead! Then I'd be proof against ridicule. Why aren't I a widower! I'd spend six months in Paris in the best society ... After the fleeting happiness provided by this notion of widowerhood, his mind returned to ways of finding out the truth. Should he sprinkle a fine layer of bran by the door to Julien's room, at midnight, after everyone had gone to bed? The next day at dawn he'd find footprints.

But that way's no good, he cried immediately in anger, that slut Élisa would notice it, and the whole household would soon know I'm jealous.

In another story told at the casino, a husband had made certain of his misfortune by sealing a hair with pieces of wax on to the doors of his wife and her gallant.

After so many hours of uncertainty this means of illuminating his fate seemed decidedly the best, and he was thinking of how to go about it when, at a curve in the walk, he met the wife he would like to have seen dead.

She was returning from the village. She had been to hear mass at the church in Vergy. A tradition, very doubtful to the cold gaze of reason, but to which she gave credence, had it that the little church in use today was once the chapel of the lord of Vergy's castle. The whole time that she had meant to devote to prayer in this church she had been preoccupied by this idea: She obsessively pictured her husband slaying Julien while hunting, as if by accident, and then that evening making her eat his heart.

My fate, she said to herself, depends on what he comes to think while listening to me. Perhaps after these crucial few minutes I won't find another chance to speak to him. He isn't a wise man, ruled by reason. If he was, I might be able to predict, by the light of my own feeble reason, what he'd do or say. He'll decide our common destiny, he has the power to do it. But what this destiny will be lies in my abilities, in the art of moulding the attitudes of this headstrong man, whom anger makes blind and incapable of seeing half of what is going on. Great God! I have to summon up some art, some self-possession, but where can I find them?

On entering the garden and seeing her husband at a distance, her calm returned as if by magic. His hair and ruffled clothes proclaimed the fact that he had not slept.

She handed him a letter, the seal broken, but refolded. Without opening it, he stared at his wife with crazy eyes.

– Here's an abominable object, said she. A nasty-looking man, who pretended to know you and be under an obligation, handed it to me as I was going round the bottom of our lawyer's garden. You must grant me one thing – you must send this M. Julien back to his family instantly. Mme de Rênal hastened to come out with this sentence, perhaps a little prematurely, in order to rid herself of the awful prospect of having to say it.

She was seized with happiness at seeing the joy this produced in her husband. She divined from the fixed look he directed at her that Julien had guessed correctly. And instead of being painfully concerned about this very real misfortune, she thought: What genius, what perfect aplomb! And in a young man still without any experience! What won't he be able to do in the future? Alas! by then his success will make him forget me.

This little act of admiration for the man she adored entirely relieved her distress.

She congratulated herself on her conduct. I have not been

unworthy of Julien, thought she, with a sweet and private delight.

Saying not a word for fear of committing himself, M. de Rênal examined the second letter, made up, if the reader recalls, of printed words stuck on to a sheet of paper of bluish tint. – I'm going to be ridiculed in any case, he said to himself, overwhelmed by fatigue.

– Still more insults to look at, and always about my wife! He was on the point of heaping her with the coarsest reproaches, from which the prospect of the legacy from Besançon only just restrained him. Eaten up by the need to take it out on something, he screwed up the paper of the second anonymous letter and strode off at a great rate, feeling the need to get away from his wife. A few moments later, he returned nearer to her, and calmer.

– It's essential to take action and send Julien away, she said to him straight away; after all, he's only a working man's son. You can give him a few écus' compensation, and for the rest he's very well read and will easily find a place – at M. Valenod's, for example, or with Sub-prefect de Maugiron – they have children. So you won't do him any harm at all . . .

– You speak there like the fool you are, cried out M. de Rênal in a tremendous voice. What sense can you expect from a woman? You're incapable of considering what's rational; your carelessness, your laziness only give you the gumption to chase butterflies – feeble creatures that it is our misfortune to have in our families! . . .

Mme de Rênal let him speak on, and on he went for a long time; he *passed his anger*, as they say there.

Monsieur, she replied at last, I speak as a woman who has been outraged in her honour, that is to say in her most precious part.

Mme de Rênal had maintained an unruffled self-possession for the whole of their dreadful conversation, on which depended the possibility of continuing to live under the same roof as Julien. She tried to find the suggestions she thought best suited to guiding her husband's blind anger. She remained impervious to all the insulting reflections he addressed to her, she didn't really hear them, but thought instead of Julien. Would he be satisfied with me?

At last she said: This little peasant – on whom we have heaped attention, and even gifts – may well be innocent, but even so he's the occasion of the first insult I have received ... Monsieur, when I read that vile note, I swore to myself that either he or I would leave your house.

— D'you want to cause a scandal that will dishonour me, and you as well? That really would delight the fine folk of Verrières.

— That's so, there's widespread jealousy of the success your prudent dealing has secured for you, your family and the town ... Fine, then! I will advise Julien to ask you for leave to spend a month with his friend Fouqué, the wood dealer in the mountains, an apt friend for a little peasant.

— Kindly refrain from doing anything, replied M. de Rênal with a fair degree of calm. What I require above all is that you do not speak to him. You will show your temper and set him at loggerheads with me — you know how touchy the little gentleman is.

— That young man has no tact at all, replied Mme de Rênal. He may be learned — you'd know about that — but at bottom he's only an ordinary peasant. Myself, I've never thought much of him since he turned down Élisa; — there was a fortune on a plate; and all on the pretext that she sometimes pays secret visits to M. Valenod.

— Ah! said M. de Rênal, raising his eyebrows to an extraordinary degree, Julien told you that?

— Not exactly; he's always talked to me about the vocation that impels him toward the sacred ministry — but, believe you me, the prime vocation for these common people is to get their bread. He simply gave me to understand that he wasn't ignorant of those private visits.

— But me, I was ignorant of them! cried M. de Rênal, flying into a temper again, and emphasizing every word. Things happen here that I know nothing about ... What! there's been something between Élisa and Valenod?

— Oh! that's an old story, my dear friend, said Mme de Rênal, laughing, and perhaps it wasn't such a bad thing. It was at the time when your old friend Valenod wouldn't have minded letting Verrières think that he'd set up a little love affair between himself and me — wholly platonic, of course.

— I had an inkling of that at one time, cried M. de Rênal, hitting his head with rage and proceeding from discovery to discovery. And you told me nothing about it?

– Should I have made a quarrel between two friends because of a little puff of conceit on the part of our dear director? I don't know where you could find the society woman to whom he hasn't sent a few very sprightly, even perhaps rather flirtatious, letters.

– He's written to you?

– He writes a great deal.

– Show me these letters instantly, I order you; and M. de Rênal grew six feet taller.

– Certainly I'm not going to do that, she replied in a gentle tone verging on the nonchalant, I'll show you them some other time when you're less excited.

– At this very instant, damn it! cried M. de Rênal, carried away with rage, yet feeling happier than he had been for the last twelve hours.

– Do you swear to me, said Mme de Rênal very solemnly, never to have a quarrel with the Director of the Poorhouse about these letters?

– Quarrel or not, I can take the foundlings off him; but, he continued furiously, I want these letters instantly; where are they?

– In a drawer in my bureau; but you may be sure I'm not going to let you have the key.

– I'll find out how to open it, he cried, running off towards his wife's room.

And indeed, using an iron stake, he did smash the precious whorled mahogany writing desk, ordered from Paris, that he had so often rubbed with his coat-tail when he imagined he detected some smudge on it.

Mme de Rênal dashed up the 120 steps of the dovecot; she tied the corner of a white handkerchief to one of the iron bars of the little window. She was the happiest of women. Tears in her eyes, she gazed towards the great woods on the mountain. Doubtless, said she to herself, from beneath one of those leafy beeches Julien will see this sign of good omen. For a long time she strained her ears, then cursed the monotonous drone of the cicadas and the song of the birds. Without this inopportune noise, a cry of joy from out of the vast rocks could have reached her. Her avid gaze devoured the enormous slope of dark greenery formed by the treetops, unbroken as a meadow. Does he not have the wit, she said to herself, brimful of emotion, to devise some signal to let me know that his joy is as great as mine? She came down from the dovecot only when she grew fearful that her husband might come looking for her.

She found him in a rage. He was scanning M. Valenod's insipid phrases – phrases that were little used to being read with such emotion.

Grasping a moment when her husband's fumings gave her a chance of being heard:

– I keep on coming back to my idea that it would be a good idea for Julien to go away for a while, said Mme de Rênal. However much talent he has for Latin, he's only a peasant, after all, who's frequently coarse and lacking in tact; every day, thinking he's being polite, he makes me extravagant compliments in poor taste which he has learnt by heart from some novel . . .

– He never reads 'em, cried M. de Rênal; I'm sure of that. D'you think that as head of the household I'm blind, and know nothing of what goes on under my roof?

– Well, if he hasn't read those silly compliments somewhere, he has made them up, and that's even worse. He will have talked about me in that fashion in Verrières; . . . and, without going so far away, said Mme de Rênal with the air of making a discovery . . . he'll have talked like that in front of Élisa, which is the next best thing to having spoken in front of M. Valenod.

– Ah! cried M. de Rênal, causing the table and the whole room to shake with one of the greatest blows of the fist ever given, that anonymous letter with print and Valenod's letters are written on the same paper.

At last! . . . thought Mme de Rênal; she affected to be shattered by this discovery and, without daring to add a single word, went to seat herself at a distance on a divan at the end of the salon.

From then on the battle was won; she had considerable difficulty in restraining M. de Rênal from going to speak to the supposed author of the anonymous letter.

– How is it that you don't see that to make a scene with M. Valenod without sufficient proof would be the most blatant of mistakes? You are an object of envy, monsieur, and who's to blame for that? Your talents, your wise administration, your tasteful building works, the dowry I brought you, and above all the inheritance we expect from my worthy aunt, an inheritance whose importance is infinitely exaggerated – they have made you the first man in Verrières.

– You forget my birth, said M. de Rênal, smiling a little.

– You're one of the most distinguished gentlemen of the province, Mme de Rênal resumed quickly; if the King was at liberty to act and be able to do justice to birth, no doubt you would have made an appearance in the Chamber of Peers or some such. And it's in this position that you propose to give envy something to work on?

To accost M. Valenod about his anonymous letter is to proclaim to all Verrières – what am I saying? – to Besançon, to the whole province, that this middle-class person, perhaps rashly admitted to the intimacy *of a Rênal*, has been able to find a way of offending him. Had these letters you've just discovered shown that I had responded to Valenod's advances, your duty would be to kill me and I would have deserved it a hundred times over, but your duty would not be to show anger towards him. Do you think that your neighbours don't lie in waiting for a pretext to pay you back for your superiority? – remember that in 1816 you helped with certain arrests.[1] That man who hid on your roof . . .

– I think that you have neither esteem nor affection for me, cried M. de Rênal with all the bitterness such a memory awoke in him – and I have not been made a peer! . . .

– And I conclude, my dear, replied Mme de Rênal, smiling, that I shall be richer than you are, that I have been your companion for twelve years, and that with all these qualifications I should have a voice in the council – above all in today's business. If you prefer M. Julien to me, she added with ill-disguised contempt, I am quite prepared to spend a winter with my aunt.

This phrase was said *most happily*. It contained a firm pressure cloaked in politeness; it decided M. de Rênal. But, according to the custom in the provinces, he went on talking for a long time yet, going back over all the arguments; his wife let him talk, his tone still betraying his anger. At last, two hours of pointless verbiage exhausted the powers of a man who had been subject to fits of choler for a whole night. He laid down the lines of conduct to follow towards M. Valenod, Julien, and even Élisa.

Once or twice in the course of this great interview, Mme de Rênal was on the point of feeling some sympathy for the genuine unhappiness of this man who had been her companion for twelve years. But true passions are egocentric. In any case, she was expecting any moment to hear a confession about the anonymous letter he had received the previous evening, and that confession did not come. Mme de Rênal lacked any precise knowledge of the ideas that might have been put in the head of this man upon whom her fate depended. For, in the provinces, husbands are the masters of opinion. A husband who complains covers himself in ridicule, a thing every day less dangerous in France; but his wife, if he does not allow her any money, sinks to the status of a working woman on fifteen sous a day, and even then right-minded people are disinclined to employ her.

An odalisk in the harem may love the Sultan with all her strength; he is all powerful, she has no hope of sapping away his authority by a series of little manoeuvres. The vengeance of the master is terrible and bloody, yet it is martial, generous, a dagger blow puts an end to all. In the nineteenth century a husband kills his wife with blows of public scorn; he closes all the salon doors.

The apprehension of danger was powerfully reawakened in Mme de Rênal when she returned to her quarters; she was shocked at the mess she found in her room. The locks of all her pretty little boxes had been smashed; numerous parquet tiles had been levered up. He would have no pity on me! she said to herself. To ruin the variegated parquet like this – which he loves so much; when one of the children goes on to it with wet shoes he flushes with anger. To ruin it for ever! The sight of such violence quickly dispelled the last scruples she had entertained about her over-rapid victory.

A little before the dinner bell, Julien came back in with the children. At dessert, when the servants had retired, Mme de Rênal said to him very drily:

– You expressed to me a wish to go and spend a fortnight in Verrières. M. de Rênal is very willing to give you leave. You may go when you deem it appropriate. However, so that the children don't waste their time, their work will be sent to you every day, for you to correct.

– Certainly, added M. de Rênal sharply, but I don't give you more than a week.

Julien divined in his physiognomy the anxiety of a deeply troubled man.

– He still hasn't made up his mind, he said to his mistress when they were alone for a moment in the salon.

Mme de Rênal quickly told him all that she had done since morning.

– Tonight the details, she added, laughing.

The perversity of women! thought Julien. What delight, what instinct drives them to betray us!

– I find you at once made intelligent and blinded by your love, he said to her with a certain amount of formal coldness; your behaviour today has been very fine; but is it wise to see each other tonight? This house is paved with enemies; think of the violent hatred Élisa has for me.

– That hatred much resembles the passionate indifference you seemingly feel towards me.

– Even if I were indifferent, it is my duty to save you from the perils into which I have plunged you. If by chance M. de Rênal were to speak to Élisa, one word could make him understand everything. Why shouldn't he hide himself next to my room, well armed . . .

– What! not even some courage! said Mme de Rênal with all the loftiness of a nobleman's daughter.

– I shall never descend to a discussion of my courage, replied Julien coldly – that would be low. The world can judge me by my actions. But, he added, taking her hand, you cannot conceive how attached I am to you, and how great a joy it is to me to be able to take leave of you before this cruel absence.

CHAPTER 22

Modes of Behaviour in 1830

Words have been given to man to hide his thoughts.

R. P. MALAGRIDA[1]

Hardly had Julien arrived in Verrières than he reproached himself for his injustice to Mme de Rênal. I would have felt contempt for her as a poor little woman if, through weakness, she had failed in her scene with M. de Rênal! But she conducts herself like a statesman, and then I go and sympathize with the loser, who is my enemy. That's bourgeois pettiness for you; my vanity is shocked because M. de Rênal is a man! – that huge and illustrious company to which I have the honour to belong; I am no better than a fool.

M. Chélan had refused all the lodgings that the most prominent liberals in the district had vied with one another to offer him when his dismissal had driven him from the presbytery. The two rooms he had rented were encumbered with his books. Julien, wishing to demonstrate to Verrières what it is to be a priest,[2] went to fetch a dozen planks of pine from his father's place, which he then carried on his own back down the length of the main street. He borrowed some tools from an old schoolfellow, and had soon put up a sort of bookcase, in which he arranged M. Chélan's books.

– I thought that you had been corrupted by the vanity of the world, said the old man, weeping with joy; this is something that does much to redeem the childish vanity of that ostentatious guard of honour uniform, which made you so many enemies.

M. de Rênal had ordered Julien to stay at his house. Nobody suspected what had happened. The third day after his arrival Julien witnessed no less a personage than M. the Sub-prefect of Maugiron climb right up to his room. It was not until after two hours of insipid chit-chat and lengthy jeremiads on the wickedness of men, on the lack of probity to be found in those individuals in charge of public funds, on the dangers of this to poor France, etc., etc., that Julien began to see the point of the visit. They were already on the landing, and the poor semi-disgraced tutor was ushering out, with appropriate respect, the prefect-to-be of some happy department or other, when it pleased the latter to concern himself about Julien's career, and to praise his moderation as regards his own advancement, etc., etc. At last M. de Maugiron, squeezing his arm in the most paternal manner, proposed to him that he should leave M. de Rênal and go into the household of an official who had children to *acculturate*, and who, like King Philip,[3] thanked Heaven, not that they had been given to him, but that they had been born in the vicinity of M. Julien. Their tutor would enjoy eight hundred francs in salary, payable, not month by month, which is not aristocratic – said M. de Maugiron – but quarterly, and always in advance.

It was Julien's turn: he had waited through an hour and a half of tedium to speak. His response was perfect, and above all as drawn out as a pastoral homily; he let everything be understood, yet said nothing plainly. In his speech there was to be found respect for M. de Rênal, deference to the public of Verrières, and gratitude to the illustrious Sub-prefect. The said Sub-prefect, astonished to find a greater Jesuit than himself, tried in vain to obtain something concrete. Julien, delighted, jumped at the opportunity to practise his skills, and began to reply again in different terms. Never did an eloquent minister, wishing to use up the last period of a session when the Chamber seems to be starting to rouse itself, say less in so great a number of words. Scarcely had M. de Maugiron left than Julien started to laugh like a wild thing. To take advantage of his surge of Jesuitical verve he wrote a nine-page letter to M. de Rênal, in which he told him all that had been said to him, and humbly solicited advice. – That joker didn't even give me the name of whoever made the offer! It will be M. Valenod, interpreting my exile to Verrières as the effect of his anonymous letter.

His missive despatched, Julien, happy as a hunter marching into a plain full of game at six in the morning on a fine autumn day, went out to ask counsel of M. Chélan. But before he had arrived at the good curé's rooms, Heaven – which seemed intent on bringing him joy – threw M. Valenod under his feet. M. Valenod, to whom he did not conceal the fact that his heart was desolate; a poor boy such as himself should devote himself wholly to the vocation that Heaven had vouchsafed his heart – but in this base world, vocation was not all. To cultivate the Lord's vineyard with propriety, and not to be unworthy of a multitude of learned fellow labourers, instruction was necessary; it was essential to spend two expensive years at the seminary at Besançon; it was therefore indispensable to make savings, which was easier with 800 francs, paid quarterly, than with 600 francs which ate themselves up month on month. On the other hand was it not the case that Heaven, in placing him beside the issue of a Rênal, and above all in inspiring in him a special attachment for them, was it not that Heaven seemed to direct that it was not meant to be that he should abandon this educational task for another? . . .

Julien attained such a degree of perfection in this kind of eloquence – which has replaced the decisive action of the Empire – that he ended up by boring himself with the sound of his own voice.

On arriving back he found one of M. Valenod's footmen, in elaborate livery, who had been looking for him throughout the town with a card inviting him to lunch the same day.

Never before had Julien been in this man's house; only a few days previously he had been thinking of little else but how to assail him with a flurry of blows with a cane while avoiding police prosecution. Although lunch was not scheduled until one o'clock, Julien felt it would seem more respectful to present himself from half-past twelve onwards in the work room of M. the Director of the Poorhouse. He found the latter parading his own importance amid a mass of dispatch boxes. His huge black whiskers, his enormous amount of hair, his smoking cap worn askew on the top of the head, his vast pipe, his embroidered trousers, the chunky gold chains crossed every which way on his chest – all these appurtenances of a provincial money man who fancies himself a ladies' man, did not impress Julien at all; he thought only the more of the caning he owed him.

He requested the honour of being presented to Mme Valenod; she was at her toilette and could not receive him. By way of compensation, he had the privilege of assisting at that of M. the Director of the Poorhouse. They then proceeded to Mme Valenod's quarters, where she introduced her children with tears in her eyes. This lady, one of the most respected in Verrières, had a large manly countenance to which she had applied rouge for the great occasion. She displayed a world of maternal feeling.

Julien thought of Mme de Rênal. His habitual mistrustfulness meant that he was susceptible only to that sort of nostalgia evoked by contrast, but here he was seized with it to the point of tears. The mood was increased by the sight of the Director of the Poorhouse's mansion. He was given the tour. Everything there was magnificent and new, and one was told the price of each article of furniture. Julien found something ignoble in all this, smelling of misappropriated funds. Everyone, down even to the servants, had an air of putting on confident looks in order to avert contempt.

The Inspector of Taxes, the Officer of Indirect Taxation, the Head of the Gendarmerie and two or three other public officials arrived, accompanied by their wives. They were followed by a selection of wealthy liberals. Lunch was announced. It occurred to Julien, already in a terrible mood, that on the other side of the dining-room wall might be found poor people, shut up there, whose helping of meat had perhaps been *siphoned off* to pay for all this luxurious bad taste that was supposed to bowl him over.

Perhaps they are going hungry at this very moment, he said to himself; his throat tightened, he found it impossible to eat, almost impossible to speak. It was much worse a few minutes later; in the distance there could be heard snatches of a popular and, it must be admitted, rather coarse song, being sung by one of the inmates. M. Valenod glanced at one of his men in magnificent livery, who went out – and soon there was no more singing to be heard. At that moment a footman offered Julien some Rhine wine in a green glass, and Mme Valenod was careful to tell him that it cost nine francs a bottle, from the makers. Julien, holding out his green glass, said to M. Valenod:

– They're not singing that low song any longer.

– Good Lord! I should think not! cried the Director triumphantly, I've had the scroungers silenced.

This reply was too much for Julien; he had the manners of his station in life, but not yet its sensibility. Despite his so frequently rehearsed hypocrisy, he felt a large tear flow down his cheek.

He attempted to hide it with the green glass, but that made it impossible for him to do justice to the Rhine wine. *To stop the man singing*! he said to himself, Oh dear God! – and Thou sufferest this!

Luckily, no one noticed his sentimentality in such poor taste. The Inspector of Taxes had struck up a royalist song. During the din of the refrain, sung in chorus, Julien's conscience said to him: Here, then, is the filthy good fortune that is coming to you, and you will enjoy it only in these conditions and in company like this! Perhaps you will get a post worth twenty thousand francs, but that means that while you gorge yourself with food, you will stop a pathetic prisoner singing; you will give dinners with the money you have filched from his miserable allowance, and during your dinner he will be even more wretched! – Oh Napoleon! in your day, how sweet it was to rise to fortune through the dangers of battle! – but to heap up the sufferings of the poor in this low way!

I confess that the weakness displayed by Julien in this soliloquy gives me a poor opinion of him. He was fit to be classed with those yellow-gloved conspirators who pretend to alter the whole manner of arranging affairs in a great country, but do not want to have to reproach themselves with making the slightest scratch.

Julien was rudely recalled to his role. It was not to muse and say nothing that he had been invited to dine in such good company.

A retired painted cloth manufacturer, a Corresponding Member of the Academy at Besançon and of that at Uzès, addressed a question to him from one end of the table to the other, asking if what was commonly said about his amazing progress in New Testament studies was true.

Suddenly a profound silence reigned; a Latin New Testament found itself as if by magic in the hand of the learned member of the two Academies. On Julien's response, a half-verse in Latin was read at random. He recited on from there: his memory proved faithful, and the marvel was applauded with all the boisterous energy of a table at the end of a dinner. Julien looked round the glowing faces of the ladies; many of them were not unattractive. He picked out the wife of the melodious tax inspector.

— Verily, I am ashamed to speak in Latin for so long in front of the ladies, he said, gazing at her. If M. Rubigneau — the member of the two Academies — would have the goodness to read out a Latin phrase at random, I will attempt, instead of responding with the ensuing Latin text, to construct an impromptu translation.

This second test crowned him with glory.

There were numerous wealthy men there who were liberals, but who, as happy fathers qualified to obtain scholarships, had suddenly become converts since the last mission.[4] Despite this subtle political move, M. de Rênal had not been willing to receive them in his house. These fine men, who knew Julien only by reputation and by having seen him on horseback at the entry of the King of —, were his most clamorous admirers. — When will these idiots leave off wanting to hear biblical language of which they understand nothing? he wondered. But, on the contrary, the style amused them by its strangeness; they laughed at it. It was Julien who became tired.

He gravely rose as six o'clock sounded, mentioning a chapter of Ligorio's[5] new theology that he must learn by heart by tomorrow in order to recite it to M. Chélan. For my calling, he added pleasantly, is to make people recite lessons and then recite them myself.

There was much laughter, much admiration; that kind of thing passes for wit in Verrières. Julien had already risen, everyone else got up as well in defiance of decorum; such is the power of genius. Mme Valenod kept him another quarter of an hour; he really must hear the children say their catechisms. These were full of the most amusing confusions, of which only he was aware. He prevented himself from pointing them out. What ignorance of the first principles of religion! thought he. At last he bowed, and believed he might escape; but he must endure a fable by La Fontaine.

— This author is truly immoral, remarked Julien to Mme Valenod — in one of his fables, the one on Messire Jean Chouart,[6] he presumes to pour scorn on that which is highly venerable. It has been most strongly censured by the best commentators.

Before he left, Julien received four or five invitations to dinner. – This young man does the department honour, his wine-flown fellow diners shouted all at the same time. They went so far as to talk of a grant to be voted out of municipal funds to enable him to continue his studies in Paris.

While this rash notion echoed around the dining room, Julien had nimbly reached the outer door. Ah! the scum! the scum! he whispered to himself three or four times in succession, taking pleasure in breathing the fresh air.

At that moment he felt completely aristocratic – he who for so long had been so offended by the patronizing smirk and complacent superiority he thought to lie behind all the politenesses he was offered at M. de Rênal's. He could not help feeling the great difference. Even if we forget, he said to himself as he walked along, that it is a matter of money stolen from the poor, and that then they are even forbidden to sing! – even then, would M. de Rênal take it into his head to tell his guests the price of each bottle of wine he is offering them? And this M. Valenod, going over the list of his possessions to which he eternally returns, cannot speak of his house, his estate, etc., when his wife is there without saying *your* house, *your* estate.

That lady, apparently so conscious of the joy of possessions, had just made a frightful scene during dinner with a servant who had broken a stemmed glass and *spoiled one of her sets of twelve*; and the servant had replied with the utmost insolence.

What a crew! said Julien to himself; they could give me half of what they've stolen and even then I wouldn't live with them. One day I would forget myself; I wouldn't be able to stop myself expressing the scorn they make me feel.

Nevertheless it was necessary, following Mme de Rênal's orders, to attend numerous dinners of the same kind; Julien was fashionable; he was forgiven his guard of honour's uniform, or, rather, that daring episode that was the real cause of his success. Soon the great question in Verrières was to see who would win the contest to secure the services of this learned young fellow, M. de Rênal or the Director of the Poorhouse? With M. Maslon these gentlemen had formed a triumvirate that had tyrannized the town for a number of years. People were jealous of the Mayor, and the liberals had things to complain of; but, after all, he was a nobleman and born to rule, whereas M. Valenod's father had not left him an income of 600 livres. With him one had to pass from the pity inspired by the shabby apple green coat by which everyone knew him in his youth to envy for his Norman horses, his gold chains, his suits sent down from Paris, for all his current prosperity.

In the eddies of this world so new to him, Julien believed he had found one worthy man; he was a geometrician called Gros,[7] who was believed to be a Jacobin. Julien, who had sworn never to affirm anything except what seemed to him false, was forced to behave as though he had his suspicions about M. Gros. He received great bundles of children's work from Vergy. He had been advised to see his father frequently, and conformed to this melancholy necessity. In a word, he was rebuilding his reputation pretty well, when one morning he was much surprised to find himself awoken by a pair of hands being pressed over his eyes.

It was Mme de Rênal, who had come to town on a visit, and who, leaving her children busy with a favourite rabbit who was travelling with them, and running up the stairs four at a time, had arrived in Julien's room an instant before they did. The moment was delicious, but very brief: Mme de Rênal had disappeared by the time the children came in with their rabbit – whom they wanted to introduce to their friend. Julien warmly greeted all of them, even the rabbit. He seemed to have found his family once more; he felt that he loved these children, that he loved to chatter with them. He was struck by the softness of their voices, by the naturalness and nobility of their little ways; he had the need to cleanse his imagination of all the vulgar mannerisms, all the disagreeable thoughts, in which he existed in Verrières. There it was perpetually fear of failure, always opulence and misery grabbing at one another's hair. The people with whom he had dined would make confessions, in the middle of talking about their roast, that were humiliating to them and nauseating to those that heard them.

– You, you aristocrats, you're right to be proud, he said to Mme de Rênal. And he told her of all the dinners he had been subjected to.

– Then you're quite the fashion! She laughed whole-heartedly, thinking of the rouge Mme Valenod thought herself obliged to put on every time she expected Julien. I believe she has designs on your heart, she added.

The lunch was delightful. The presence of the children, however constricting it might have appeared, in fact increased their mutual happiness. These poor children could not sufficiently express their joy at seeing Julien again. The servants had not failed to inform them that he had been offered 200 francs extra to *acculturate* the little Valenods.

In the middle of the meal, Stanislas-Xavier, still pale from his grave illness, suddenly asked his mother how much his silver knife and fork and the goblet from which he was drinking were worth.

– Why do you ask?

– I want to sell them and give the money to M. Julien so that he won't be a *dupe* for staying with us.

Julien hugged him, tears in his eyes. His mother wept openly, while Julien, who had taken Stanislas on to his knee, explained to him that one shouldn't use the word *dupe* in this way, it was lackey's talk. Seeing the pleasure this gave Mme de Rênal, he tried to explain, with vivid examples that amused the children, what it was to be a dupe.

– I see, said Stanislas, it's the crow who's fool enough to drop his cheese, to be grabbed by the fox who's flattered him.[8]

Exhilarated with happiness, Mme de Rênal covered her children with kisses – which she could hardly do without supporting herself on Julien a little.

All of a sudden the door opened; it was M. de Rênal. His severe and disgruntled face made a queer contrast to the gentle merry-making that his presence chased away. Mme de Rênal went pale; she felt herself not in a state to deny anything. Julien launched into speech and, talking very loudly, began to tell M. the Mayor the incident of the silver goblet that Stanislas wanted to sell. He was sure

the story would be ill received. From the first M. de Rênal frowned at
the very word silver, out of habit. The mention of that metal, he would
say, is always the prelude to some demand being made on my purse.

But here it was not only silver that concerned him; his suspicions
had been aggravated. The happy spirit that animated his family when
he was away was not calculated to soothe a man ruled by so ticklish
a vanity. When his wife spoke in praise of the graceful and ingenious
way in which Julien conveyed new ideas to his pupils:

— Yes, yes! I know, he makes me seem disagreeable to my own
children; it's easy for him to be a hundred times more lovable than I
am, who, in the end, am the master. In these days everything tends
to throw discredit on *legitimate* authority. Poor France!

Mme de Rênal did not pause in the slightest to examine the finer
points of her husband's manner to her. She had just seen the possibility
of spending twelve hours with Julien. She had a multitude of little
purchases to make in town, and declared that she absolutely must
dine in a chophouse; whatever her husband might say or do, she
stuck to her idea. The children were enchanted at the very word
chophouse – which conventional modern delicacy pronounces with
such relish.[9]

M. de Rênal left his wife in the first dress shop she went into; he
had to go and pay some calls. He returned even more morose than
he had been in the morning; he was convinced that the whole town
was thinking about Julien and himself. In truth, nobody had yet
given him a hint of anything offensive in public gossip. What had
been repeated to M. the Mayor had been solely concerned with
knowing whether Julien would stay with him at 600 francs, or accept
the 800 offered by M. the Director of the Poorhouse.

The said director, meeting M. de Rênal socially, gave him the *cold
shoulder*. This behaviour wasn't just stupid; in the provinces there is
little thoughtlessness: feelings are so rare that they are made to flow
underground.

M. Valenod was what one calls, a hundred leagues from Paris, a
loudmouth: that is, a type naturally insolent and coarse. His triumphant
career since 1815 had confirmed his beautiful disposition. In Verrières
he reigned, so to speak, under M. de Rênal's orders; but, being much

more active, blushing at nothing, mixing himself up in everything, ceaselessly bustling about, writing, talking, overlooking humiliations, making no claim to personal dignity, he had ended up rivalling the influence of his master in the eyes of the Church authorities. M. Valenod had, in effect, said to the food suppliers: give me the two most stupid among you; to the lawyers: show me the two who know least; to the medical officers: point out two charlatans. When he had assembled the most shameless examples of each profession, he had said to them: Let's rule together.

The manners of these people pained M. de Rênal. Valenod's coarseness was proof against everything, even being called a liar in public by the little Abbé Maslon.

Nevertheless, in the midst of this prosperity, M. Valenod felt the need to shore himself up against the gross truths he knew only too well everyone had a right to charge him with, by little shows of insolence in petty matters. His activity had redoubled as a result of the anxieties left by M. Appert's visit – he had made three journeys to Besançon; he wrote several letters by each courier; he sent others by anonymous messengers who passed by his house at nightfall. Perhaps he had made a mistake in getting the old Curé Chélan dismissed; for this vindictive proceeding had caused him to be regarded by many pious women of good birth as a deeply wicked man. And services rendered on that occasion had put him in a state of absolute dependency on the Vicar-general, M. de Frilair, from whom he was receiving strange commissions. This was the stage his conduct of affairs had reached when he gave way to the temptation to write an anonymous letter. To crown his embarrassment, his wife had declared to him that she wanted to have Julien in her house; her vanity was smitten by the idea.

In this situation, M. Valenod foresaw a crisis in relations with his old ally M. de Rênal. The latter might give him some hard words – that wouldn't matter; but he could also write to Besançon and even to Paris. Some minister's cousin might suddenly descend on Verrières and grab the poorhouse. M. Valenod thought of making an agreement with the liberals; that was why several of them had been invited to the lunch at which Julien had performed his recitation. They could give him powerful support against the Mayor. But the elections would come along, and it was all too obvious that the poorhouse and an unfavourable vote did not go together. The story of these machinations, very well understood by Mme de Rênal, was told to Julien while he gave her his arm in strolling from one shop to another, and it had gradually taken them to Loyalty Promenade, where they spent several hours in almost as much tranquillity as if they had been at Vergy.

Meanwhile, M. Valenod tried to put off the crisis with his old patron by adopting a bold front towards him. That day the ploy succeeded, but it increased the Mayor's ill temper.

Never had a man's vanity, at odds with all that is harshest and most shoddy in petty money-grubbing, produced so wretched a state as that in which M. de Rênal found himself when entering the *chophouse*. Never, by contrast, had his children been so gay and so joyous. The comparison crowned his irritation.

— I'm not wanted in my own family, I can see that, he declared as he entered, in a tone he strove to make imposing.

For all her reply his wife took him aside and expounded to him the necessity of getting rid of Julien. The hours of happiness she had just had with him had lent her the ease and confidence needed to follow the plan of action she had been thinking about for the past fortnight. What really upset the poor Mayor of Verrières at the deepest level was that he was aware that people joked publicly about his fondness for *the ready*. M. Valenod was as generous as a thief, while he — he had shown more prudence than ostentation in the last five or six collections for the Brotherhood of St Joseph, for the Congregation of the Virgin, for the Congregation of the Holy Sacrament, etc., etc., etc.

Amongst the gentry of Verrières and its environs, as adroitly classified in the records of the collecting brethren, and ordered according to the amount of the offering, M. de Rênal's name had more than once been seen to occupy the bottom line. It was in vain for him to plead that he *earned nothing*. On this matter the clergy do not appreciate pleasantries.

CHAPTER 23

The Frustrations of a Public Servant[1]

Il piacere di alzar la testa tutto l'anno è ben pagato da certi quarti d'ora che bisogna passar. CASTI[2]

But let us leave this little man to his little fears. Why had he taken a man of feeling into his house, when what he required was the soul of a lackey? Why doesn't he know how to choose his servants? The usual process in the nineteenth century when a powerful, well-born person meets a man of feeling is that he murders him, exiles him, imprisons him or humiliates him so badly that the fellow has the stupidity to die of sorrow. It is by mere chance that in the present case it is not yet the man of feeling who suffers. The great misfortune of the small towns of France and of elected governments – like that of New York – is of not having the power to forget the existence of beings like M. de Rênal. In the climate of a town of 20,000 inhabitants such men make public opinion, and public opinion is terrifying in a country that has the Charter.[3] A generous man endowed with a noble spirit who might have been your friend, but who lives a hundred leagues off, judges you by the public opinion of your town – which is created by idiots whom chance has caused to be born noble, wealthy and conventional. Woe to him who is out of the ordinary!

As soon as possible after dinner they departed for Vergy; but two days later Julien saw the whole family back in Verrières.

Not an hour had elapsed when he sensed that, to his great surprise, Mme de Rênal was making a mystery out of something. She broke off her conversations with her husband when he appeared, and almost seemed to wish he would go away. Julien did not need telling twice. He became cold and reserved; Mme de Rênal noticed this, but sought

THE RED AND THE BLACK

no explanation. Is she about to find a successor for me? wondered Julien – She who was still so intimate with me even the day before yesterday? But they say these great ladies are like that. They're like kings – never such kindness shown than to the minister who, on returning home, finds an order for his disgrace.

Julien noticed that in the conversations abruptly broken off at his approach there was much mention of a big house belonging to the town of Verrières – old, but vast and commodious, and situated opposite the church in the busiest part of town. What connection could there be between this house and a new lover? Julien wondered. In his troubled state of mind he repeated to himself Francis I's neat verses, which seemed fresh to him because he had been taught them only a month since by Mme de Rênal. At that time how many vows, how many caresses had given the lie to each of these lines!

> Ladyes alle fickle be
> Hee who trusten mad is hee.[4]

M. de Rênal posted off for Besançon. The journey was determined upon in a couple of hours, and he seemed much distressed. On his return he threw a large packet wrapped in grey paper on to the table.

– Here's that tiresome business, he said to his wife.

An hour after that, Julien saw a bill-poster carrying the fat packet away; he followed him hurriedly. – I'll find out the secret on the first street corner.

He waited impatiently behind the bill-poster, who was pasting the back of the poster with his big brush. Hardly was it on the wall than Julien's desire to know was met by a very detailed notification of the public auction for the rental of the big old house so frequently alluded to in M. de Rênal's talks with his wife. It was announced that the bidding for the lease would be at two o'clock the following day, in the town hall, at the extinction of the third candle. Julien was mightily disappointed; it occurred to him that the interval was pretty short: how could all the rival bidders be notified in time? But otherwise this poster, which was dated from a fortnight before, and which he read right through in three different places, told him nothing.

He went to see the house in question. The porter, not having noticed him come up, was saying mysteriously to a neighbour:

— Pooh! pooh! it means nothing. M. Maslon promised that he'd get it for 300 francs; and when the Mayor played up, M. the Vicar-general Frilair ordered him to go see the Bishop.

Julien's arrival seemed to embarrass the two friends considerably, and not another word was said.

Julien could not fail to attend the auction of the lease. The badly lit hall was crowded; but everybody was *eyeing up* everyone else in a strange fashion. All eyes were fixed on a table where Julien saw three small candle ends burning on a pewter platter. The auctioneer cried out: Three hundred francs, messieurs!

— Three hundred francs! That's too bad, muttered a man to his neighbour. (Julien was standing between them.) It's worth more than eight hundred; I'll cover that bid.

— That'd be spitting in the wind. You'll only get M. Maslon, M. Valenod, the Bishop and that terrible Vicar-general Frilair on your back — and all that bunch.

— Three hundred and twenty francs, cried the other.

— Bloody idiot! commented his neighbour. And look, there's a spy for the Mayor just here, he added, pointing at Julien.

Julien turned sharply, ready to rebut this; but the two Franche-Comtois paid no attention to him. Their calm attitude restored his own tranquillity. At that very moment, the last candle stub went out and the auctioneer's drawling tones allocated the house, for nine years, to M. de Saint-Giraud, Chief Secretary to the Prefecture of —, at 330 francs.

When the Mayor left the hall, the remarks started up.

— That's thirty francs Grogeot's rashness has cost the town, said someone.

— But, someone else replied, M. de Saint-Giraud will get back at Grogeot — and he'll know it.

— What a scam! said a fat man on Julien's left: that's a house I'd have paid eight hundred francs to use as my factory myself, and it would have been cheap at the price.

— Huh! a young liberal manufacturer answered, isn't M. de Saint-

Giraud a member of the Congregation? Haven't his four children got scholarships? Poor chap! So the town hall at Verrières just has to give him another five hundred francs, that's all.

— And to think the Mayor can't stop it! remarked a third man. He's an Ultra, we know that, but he doesn't steal.

— He doesn't steal? replied another; no, it's the birdies who steal. All that goes into a great communal pot, and the lot's shared out at the end of the year. But that's young Sorel over there, let's go.

Julien went home in extremely ill humour; he found Mme de Rênal very low.

— You've come from the auction? she asked him.

— Yes, madame, where I have had the honour to be taken for the Mayor's spy.

— If he'd have listened to me he'd have gone on a journey.

Just then M. de Rênal appeared; he was looking glum. Dinner passed without a word. M. de Rênal ordered Julien to accompany the children to Vergy. The journey was melancholy. Mme de Rênal said consolingly to her husband:

— You must get used to this sort of thing, my dear.

That evening they sat in silence around the domestic hearth; the crackle of burning beech logs was the sole distraction. It was one of those moments of sadness that occur in even the most united families. One of the children cried out joyously:

— Someone's ringing! Someone's ringing!

— The Devil! if it's M. de Saint-Giraud come to pester me on the pretext of thanking me, cried the Mayor, I'll tell him where to go; it's too much. It's Valenod he should be under obligation to, and it's me who has compromised. What can I say if those damn Jacobin journalists get hold of the story and make me out to be a M'sieur Noinety-Foive?[5]

At this moment an extremely handsome man with great black whiskers came in, led by a servant.

— Your Worship the Mayor, I am the Signor Geronimo. Here's a letter that the Chevalier de Beauvaisis, attaché to the Embassy at Naples, gave me when I departed. That was nine days ago, added Signor Geronimo gaily, looking at Mme de Rênal. Madame, the

Signor de Beauvaisis, your cousin and my very good friend, tells me that you know Italian.

The good humour of this Neapolitan turned a dull evening into one of great gaiety. Mme de Rênal was absolutely determined to give him supper. She stirred the whole household into activity; at all costs she wanted to distract Julien from the epithet of spy that had rung in his ears twice that day. Signor Geronimo was a celebrated singer, a well-bred man, yet extremely light-hearted – qualities that today are scarcely ever found together in France. After supper he sung a little *duettino* with Mme de Rênal. He told delightful stories. At one in the morning the children protested when Julien suggested they go to bed.

– Just one more story, said the eldest.

– It's my own story, little mister, replied Signor Geronimo. Eight years ago I was a young pupil like you, at the Conservatoire in Napoli. I mean I was your age; indeed, I did not have the honour to be the son of the illustrious Mayor of Verrières.

This made M. de Rênal sigh, and he glanced at his wife.

– The Signor Zingarelli, went on the young singer, exaggerating his accent a little and making the children burst into laughter, the Signor Zingarelli was a mightily severe master. He is not loved at the Conservatoire; but he always wishes people to act as though he were. I slipped out as often as I could; I used to go to the little theatre of San Carlino, where I would hear the music of the Gods: but – oh, Heavens! – how could I manage to raise the eight sous it cost to get into the pit? A vast sum, said he, staring at the children until they laughed. Signor Giovannone, Director of the San Carlino, heard me sing. I was sixteen years old. – The boy is a treasure, he said.

– Dear child, would you like me to offer you an engagement? he came to ask me.

– And what will you pay me?

– Forty ducats a month. – Gentlemen, that's a hundred and sixty francs. I thought the Heavens had opened.

– But how can we fix it that the terrible Zingarelli will let me go? I asked Giovannone.

– *Lascia fare a me.*

– Leave it to me! cried the eldest child.

– Exactly, my young master. Signor Giovannone said to me: first of all, *caro*, let's have a little bit of a contract. I signed: he gave me three ducats. Never had I set my eyes on so much money. Then he told me what I had to do.

Next day I asked for an audience with the terrible Signor Zingarelli. His elderly footman let me in.

– What d'you want from me, you rogue? asked Zingarelli.

– Maestro, I told him, I'm heartily sorry for all my misdoings; never again will I get out of the Conservatoire over the iron railings. I'll work twice as hard.

– If I wasn't afraid of ruining the most beautiful bass I have ever heard I would shut you in prison for a fortnight on bread and water, you scamp.

– Maestro, I will become the model for the whole school, *credete a me*. But I beg one favour of you – if anyone asks that I sing outside this place, refuse to let me go. I implore you, tell them that you can't.

– And who the devil d'you imagine is going to ask for a wicked little scruff like you? Is it likely I would ever give you permission to leave the Conservatoire? Are you trying to make fun of me? Be off with you, go away! he said, trying to give me a kick up the b—
– and beware of dry bread in prison.

An hour after that, Signor Giovannone called to see the Director:
– I've come to ask you to make my fortune for me, he said to him – let me have Geronimo. He can sing in my theatre, and this winter I can marry off my daughter.

– What d'you want to do with that scamp? said Zingarelli. I don't agree; you mustn't do it; and anyway, even if I did consent, he would never leave the Conservatoire; he has just promised me that.

– If it's only what he wills that signifies, said Giovannone solemnly, pulling my contract out of his pocket, *carta canta*![6] – here's his signature.

Immediately the furious Zingarelli hauled on the bell rope. – Will someone throw this Geronimo out of the Conservatoire? he shouted, boiling with rage.

Well, they threw me out, me shouting with laughter. The same evening I sung the aria *del Moltiplico*. In it Polchinello wants to get married, and counts on his fingers the things he will need in his household, for ever losing track of his sums.

– Oh! if you'd be so kind, monsieur, you might sing us that aria, said de Rênal.

Geronimo sung, and everyone wept with laughter. Signor Geronimo did not retire until two in the morning, leaving the family enchanted by his good manners, his willingness to please and his gaiety.

The following day M. and Mme de Rênal provided him with the letters he needed for the Court of France.

So, there's deceit everywhere, thought Julien. There goes Signor Geronimo on his way to London with 60,000 francs' worth of engagements. If it had not been for the cleverness of the Director of the San Carlino, perhaps his wonderful voice would not have been known about and admired until ten years later . . . My God, I'd rather be a Geronimo than a M. de Rênal. He's not so honoured in society, but he does not have to endure the chagrin of ordering auctions like that one today – and his life is full of gaiety.

One thing greatly impressed Julien: the solitary weeks he had spent in M. de Rênal's house in Verrières had been a time of happiness for him. He had experienced distaste and melancholy thoughts only at the dinners he had been given; alone in the house, could he not read, write and reflect in peace? He had not been perpetually dragged out of his glowing dreams by the cruel necessity of paying attention to the workings of an ignoble mind, and the need to deceive it by manoeuvres or hypocritical speeches.

Is happiness as close to me as that? . . . The expenses of such a life would be slight; I could, as I chose, marry Élisa, or become Fouqué's partner . . . But . . . the wanderer who has just climbed a steep mountain sits on its summit and feels perfect pleasure in resting himself there. Would he be so happy if he were compelled to stay there for ever?

Mme de Rênal's mind had begun to entertain fatal thoughts. In spite of her resolutions she had told Julien about the whole business of the auction. – He'll make me forget all my vows! thought she.

Had she seen her husband in danger she would without hesitation have sacrificed her life to save him. She was one of those noble and romantic spirits for whom to realize the possibility of a generous action and leave it unperformed it would be a source of remorse almost equal to that of committing a crime. At the same time, there were dark days when she could not rid herself of the image of the happiness she would taste if, suddenly becoming a widow, she could marry Julien.

He loved her sons more than did their father; despite his strict discipline, they adored him. She knew very well that in marrying Julien she would have to quit Vergy and all its beloved shades. She saw herself living in Paris, continuing to give her sons the education everyone admired so much. Her children, Julien, she herself – all in perfect happiness.

The strange effect of marriage as it has become in the nineteenth century! The tedium of matrimonial life inevitably kills off love, even when love has preceded marriage. None the less, says the philosopher, among those rich enough not to have to work it soon creates profound dissatisfaction with all the more tranquil joys. And, among women, it is only the desiccated souls who are not predisposed to love.

This philosopher's thought leads me to excuse Mme de Rênal; but in Verrières no one excused her and, without her suspecting it, the whole town was interested in nothing but her scandalous love. Because of this great affair people were less bored than usual that autumn.

The autumn and some of the winter passed very quickly. It was time to leave the woods of Vergy. High society in Verrières began to feel indignant that its anathemas made so little impression on M. de Rênal. In less than a week a number of solemn personages – who rewarded themselves for their habitual gravity by the pleasure of running errands of this kind – implanted the cruellest suspicions in him, though using the most circumspect phrases.

M. Valenod, who was playing a tight game, had obtained a place for Élisa in a noble and very respectable family, where there were five women. Élisa, fearing – as she said – that she would not find a place for the winter, had asked this family for only about two-thirds of what she received at M. the Mayor's. On her own initiative this girl had come up with the excellent scheme of going to make her confession to the old Curé Chélan and to the new curé at the same time, so she could tell both of them the details of Julien's love affair.

At six in the morning, the day after his arrival, the Abbé Chélan spoke to Julien:

– I'm not asking you anything, said he. I beg you, and if needs be, will order you, to say nothing; I insist that within three days you leave for the seminary in Besançon, or for the house of your friend Fouqué, who is still willing to offer you a magnificent future. I have anticipated everything, arranged everything – but it is essential that you go, and do not return to Verrières for a year.

Julien answered not at all; he was considering whether his honour ought not to consider itself offended by the pains that M. Chélan had taken on his behalf – after all, he wasn't his father.

– I'll have the honour to visit you again at the same time tomorrow, he at last said to the curé.

M. Chélan, who counted on being able to take a high hand with so young a man, said a great deal more. But taking refuge in the humblest bearing, and wearing the humblest expression, Julien did not open his mouth.

Eventually, he left and hurried to warn Mme de Rênal, whom he found in despair. Her husband had just been speaking to her with a certain degree of frankness. The natural weakness of his character, bolstered up by the prospect of the inheritance from Besançon, had determined him to consider her as perfectly innocent. He came to talk about the peculiar state of public opinion he had encountered in Verrières. The public was mistaken, led astray by envious people, but what should they do?

For an instant Mme de Rênal had the fantasy that Julien could accept M. Valenod's offers and remain in Verrières. But she was no longer the timid and simple woman of the previous year; her fatal passion, and her remorse, had made her more lucid. Soon, as she listened to her husband, she felt the sorrow of knowing that a separation had become inevitable, at least for a time. Away from me he will go back to those ambitious plans that come so naturally to one who possesses nothing. And as for me, great God! I'm rich! – uselessly so for my own happiness! He'll forget me. Lovable as he is, he will be loved, and he will love. Oh! miserable woman . . . But what am I complaining of? Heaven is just – I did not have the the the virtue to forgo my sin, and my judgement deserted me. It only needed me to bribe Élisa on to my side, nothing could have been easier for me. I failed to take the trouble to think for a moment – wild dreams of love occupied me wholly. I'm doomed.

Julien was struck by something when telling Mme de Rênal the terrible news of his departure: that he encountered no selfish objections. It was obvious that she was holding back her tears.

– We need resolution, my friend.

She cut off a lock of her hair.

– I don't know what I'll do, she said to him, but if I should die, promise me you won't forget my children. Far or near, try to make decent people of them. If there's another revolution the throats of all the nobility will be cut, their father might well flee abroad because of that peasant who was killed on the roof. Watch over the family . . . Give me your hand. Farewell, my love! These are our last moments. Having accomplished this great sacrifice, I trust I will have the courage to look to my reputation in public.

Julien had expected despair. The simplicity of this leave-taking moved him.

– No, I'll not receive your farewells like this. I will leave; they would have it so; you wish it yourself. – But, three days after I've left, I will come back to see you in the night.

Mme de Rênal's existence was transformed. So Julien truly loved her – he had himself conceived the idea of coming back to see her! Her racking pain was transformed into one of the most vivid sensations of joy she had ever felt. Everything became easy for her. The assurance of seeing her lover again deprived these last moments of their power to harrow. From then on, Mme de Rênal's behaviour, like her features, became noble, resolute and perfectly conventional.

Shortly afterwards M. de Rênal came back in; he was beside himself. At last he told his wife about the anonymous letter he had received two months before.

– I mean to take it to the casino and show everyone that it's from that infamous Valenod, the man I raised from beggary to become one of the richest citizens of Verrières. I'll shame him publicly, then I'll fight him. It's become too much.

I could become a widow, great God! thought Mme de Rênal. But almost at the same moment she said to herself: If I don't prevent this duel, as I certainly can, I will be my husband's murderess.

Never had she worked on his vanity with so much skill. In less than two hours she made him realize that he must show more friendliness than ever to M. Valenod, and even take back Élisa into his household. Mme de Rênal needed courage in resolving to set eyes on the girl again – the cause of all her pains. But the idea came from Julien.

At last, having been set on the right path three or four times, M. de Rênal came all by himself to the idea – financially most troublesome – that what would be most disagreeable of all to him would be for Julien, in the midst of the stir and gossip of all Verrières, to settle there as tutor to M. Valenod's children. It was obviously in Julien's interest to accept the Director of the Poorhouse's proposals. It would, on the contrary, redound to M. de Rênal's own glory if he should leave Verrières and enter the seminary at Besançon, or the one at Dijon. But how to convince him of that? And then, what would he live on?

Realizing the imminence of a financial sacrifice, M. de Rênal was in even greater distress than his wife. For her part, after this conversation, she was in the state of a sensitive man who, tired of life, has just taken a dose of *stramonium*;[7] he acts only by reflex, so to speak, and takes no interest in anything. Thus Louis XIV as he lay dying found himself saying: *When I was king.* A wonderful remark!

As soon as it grew light the following day, M. de Rênal received an anonymous letter. This one was in the most insulting style. The grossest epithets applicable to his state leapt from its every line. The work of some envious underling. This letter forced his thoughts back to a duel with M. Valenod. Very soon his courage mounted to the point of thinking of immediate action. He left the house alone, went to the gunsmith to secure some pistols and had them loaded.

In reality, he said to himself, even if the Emperor Napoleon's severe administration were restored to the world, I personally do not have a sou's worth of pilfering to reproach myself with. I may have more or less closed my eyes, but I have some fine letters in my desk authorizing me to do so.

Mme de Rênal was terrified by her husband's cold rage – it brought on again the fatal imaginings of being a widow which she had fought off with such difficulty. She shut herself up with him. For several hours she talked to him, to no effect; the new anonymous letter had decided him. Eventually, she succeeded in transforming the courage needed to administer a slap in the face to M. Valenod into that of offering Julien 600 francs a year for his maintenance in a seminary. With a thousand curses on the day he had had the idea of taking a tutor into his house, M. de Rênal forgot the anonymous letter.

He consoled himself somewhat with an idea he did not mention to his wife: with a bit of management, and availing himself of the young man's romantic notions, he hoped to persuade him – and for a lesser sum – to refuse M. Valenod's offers.

Mme de Rênal had much more difficulty demonstrating to Julien that, in sacrificing the 800-franc engagement – publicly offered to him by the Director of the Poorhouse – to her husband's convenience, he could accept compensation without dishonour.

– But, said Julien again and again, I've never had, even for a moment, any intention of accepting those offers. You've made me too accustomed to a life of elegance; those people's coarseness would kill me.

Julien's will was bent by the iron hand of cruel necessity. His pride supplied the illusion of accepting the sum offered by the Mayor of Verrières solely as a loan, and he made out a note entailing repayment over five years, with interest.

Mme de Rênal still had a few thousand francs hidden in the little grotto on the mountain.

She tremblingly offered these to him, feeling only too sure that she would be angrily refused.

– Do you wish to make the memory of our love abominable? he said to her.

At last Julien left Verrières. M. de Rênal was very happy: at the crucial moment of accepting money from him Julien found the sacrifice too difficult. He refused point blank. M. de Rênal embraced him with tears in his eyes. Julien had asked for a certificate of good behaviour from him, and in his enthusiasm he could not find terms grand enough to exalt his conduct. Our hero had five louis in savings, and counted on asking Fouqué for a matching amount.

He was greatly moved. But by the time he was a league from Verrières, where he was leaving so much love, he thought only of the joy of seeing a capital, a great military town such as Besançon.

During this short absence of three days, Mme de Rênal was taken in by one of love's cruellest illusions. Because between herself and the final unhappiness there was to be this last meeting with Julien, her life was tolerable. She counted the hours, the minutes, that separated them. At last, during the night of the third day, she heard the agreed signal from far off. Having gone through a thousand dangers, Julien appeared before her.

From that moment she was to have only one thought: It is the last time I shall see him. Far from responding to her lover's eagerness, she became like a scarcely animated corpse. If she forced herself to say she loved him, it was with an awkward manner that almost indicated the opposite. Nothing could distract her from the cruel idea of an eternal separation. The suspicious Julien thought for an instant that he had already been forgotten. His irritated words to this effect were received only by great tears flowing through silence, and almost convulsive squeezings of the hand.

– But, great God! how d'you expect me to believe you? Julien responded to the cold protestations of his lover; you would show a hundred times more sincere feeling to Mme Derville, to a mere acquaintance.

Petrified, Mme de Rênal could only reply:

– It's impossible to be unhappier . . . I hope I shall die . . . I feel my heart icing over . . .

These were the most extended responses he could get out of her. When the approach of day made his departure necessary, Mme de Rênal's tears suddenly ceased. She watched him fix a knotted rope to the window, without saying a word, without giving herself up to his kisses. In vain did Julien say to her:

— We've come now to that condition you have so ardently wished for. From now on we live without remorse. You'll no longer see your children at death's door as soon as they have the slightest indisposition.

— I'm upset that you aren't able to give Stanislas a kiss, she replied coldly.

Julien ended by being profoundly impressed by the absence of warmth in the embraces of this living corpse; he could think of nothing else for several leagues. His soul was riven, and before passing over the mountain, as long as he could see the belltower of the church in Verrières, he kept looking back.

CHAPTER 24

A Capital

What bustle, how many men of affairs! What plans for the
future in twenty-year-old heads! What distractions from
love!   BARNAVE

At last he glimpsed dark walls on a faraway mountain; it was the
citadel of Besançon. How different it would be for me, said he,
sighing, if I was arriving in this noble military town to become a
sub-lieutenant in one of the regiments charged with its defence!

Besançon is not only one of the prettiest towns in France, it abounds
with sensitive and intelligent people. But Julien was only a little
peasant boy, with no means of getting to know anyone of distinction.

He had borrowed a townsman's suit from Fouqué, and was
wearing it as he crossed the drawbridges. Full of the history of the
siege of 1674,[1] he wanted to see the ramparts of the citadel before
shutting himself up in the seminary. He was nearly arrested by
sentries two or three times; he had penetrated into areas that the
military engineers had forbidden to the public so that they themselves
could sell the hay for twelve or fifteen francs a year.

He had been busy admiring the height of the walls, the depth of
the excavations and the menacing air of the cannon for several hours
when he passed by the front of the principal café on the boulevard.
Here he stopped in amazement; he could very easily read the word
'café' written in bold letters above an immense pair of doors, but he
could not believe his eyes. He fought down his nerves; he plucked
up courage to enter and found himself in a room thirty or forty paces
long, the ceiling of which was at least twenty foot high. That day
everything seemed enchanted.

Two games of billiards were in progress. The players circled round tables jammed with spectators; the waiters sang out the scores. Clouds of tobacco smoke billowed from every mouth, enveloping them all in a blue haze. The height of these men, their hunched shoulders, their heavy gait, their enormous whiskers, the long frock coats draped around them – the whole scene compelled Julien's attention. These noble scions of ancient Bisontium[2] communicated only by shouts; they put on the airs of fearsome warriors. Julien stood and stared; he mused on the size and splendour of such a capital city as Besançon. He thought he would never have the courage to order a cup of coffee from one of the haughty-looking gentlemen shouting out the billiard scores.

But the girl at the bar had noticed the charming features of this young countryman halted three steps from the stove, his little parcel under his arm, and studying a fine white plaster bust of the King. This young woman, a tall Franche-Comté kind of girl with a very fine figure and dressed in absolutely the right fashions to do credit to a café, had already called out twice, in a muted voice meant to be heard only by Julien – Monsieur! Monsieur! Julien's eyes met two of the largest and most melting blue eyes, and he realized that it was he who was being addressed.

He moved determinedly up to the bar – and the pretty girl – as though marching on the enemy. During this great manoeuvre his little parcel fell to the ground.

What disdain our provincial would inspire in those Parisian schoolboys who by the time they are fifteen have already learned how to enter a café with such distinction! But those children, so stylish at fifteen, by eighteen have become *common*. The passionate timidity to be found in the provinces is sometimes overcome, and then it imparts strength and purpose to the will. As he approached the beautiful young girl who had deigned to speak to him, I must tell her the truth, thought Julien, becoming brave through his conquest of shyness.

– Madame, I'm visiting Besançon for the first time in my life; I'd very much like to have a roll and a cup of coffee, and pay for it.

The young woman gave a little smile, then flushed; on this pretty young man's behalf, she dreaded the billiard players' ironic looks and jokes. He'd be scared and wouldn't come back.

– Sit down here next to me, said she, indicating a small marble table almost completely hidden by the vast mahogany bar which jutted out into the room.

The young woman leant forward over the bar, which gave her the chance to show off her wonderful figure. Julien saw this: all his ideas changed. This beautiful girl came to put a cup, some sugar and a roll in front of him. Knowing very well that the arrival of a waiter would mean the end of her tête-à-tête with Julien, she put off calling for some coffee.

Julien, thoughtful, compared this fair-haired and sprightly beauty with certain memories that often stirred in him. The memory of the love he had inspired banished much of his timidity. The beautiful girl had only a moment; she studied Julien's eyes.

– This pipe smoke makes you cough, come and have breakfast here tomorrow before eight in the morning: I'm almost alone then.

– What's your name? said Julien, with the caressing smile of pleasure succeeding shyness.

– Amanda Binet.

– Would you let me send you, an hour from now, a little parcel about the same size as this?

The fair Amanda thought for a moment.

– I'm watched here: doing what you want could get me into trouble. Never mind, I'll just go and write my address on a card so you can stick it on your parcel. Then you can send it without a worry.

– My name is Julien Sorel, said the young man; I have no relations in Besançon, and I know nobody.

– Ah! I see, she said delightedly – then you've come to the law school?

– Alas! no, Julien replied; I'm being sent to the seminary.

Complete discouragement quenched the light in Amanda's features; she called a waiter over; she felt up to that now. The waiter poured Julien's coffee without looking at him.

Amanda was taking money at the bar; Julien was proud that he had dared speak: at one of the billiard tables a quarrel developed. The assertions and denials of the players ringing through the immense room made an uproar that nearly stunned Julien. Amanda had fallen into a reverie, and stood with lowered eyes.

– If you like, mademoiselle, he said to her bravely all of a sudden, I will say that I am your cousin.

His little air of authority pleased Amanda. This young man's not a nobody, thought she. Very quickly, without looking at him since her eyes were busy watching for anyone approaching the bar, she said:

– I'm from Genlis myself, near Dijon; you can say that you're from Genlis too, and my mother's cousin.

– I'll certainly do that.

– Every Thursday in the summer, at five o'clock, the gentlemen from the seminary pass here in front of the café.

– If you think of me as I go by, hold a bunch of violets in your hand. Amanda gazed at him in astonishment; this look transformed Julien's courage into rashness – even so he blushed enormously as he said to her:

– I think I have fallen violently in love with you.

– Then speak lower, she said to him, alarmed.

Julien thought of retrieving phrases from a battered volume of *La Nouvelle Héloïse*[3] he had found at Vergy. His memory served him well. And for a good ten minutes, feeling pleased with his bravery, he had been reciting *La Nouvelle Héloïse* to an enchanted Mlle Amanda when suddenly the fair Franche-Comtoise put on a glacial air. One of her admirers had appeared at the café entrance.

He came up to the bar, whistling and rolling his shoulders; he looked at Julien. At that moment the latter's mind, as ever running off to extremes, was filled with the idea of a duel. He went very pale, pushed his cup away, put on a confident air and gazed hard at his rival. When this rival bent his head, pouring himself a glass of brandy at the bar like an old customer, a glance from Amanda ordered Julien to lower his eyes. He obeyed, and sat motionless in his seat for two minutes, pale, determined and thinking only of what might now transpire; he was genuinely fine at that moment. The rival had been amazed at Julien's look. His glass of brandy having gone down in one gulp, he said something to Amanda, shoved his hands into the side pockets of his large frock coat and went over to one of the billiard tables, emitting little snorts the while and staring at Julien. The latter rose from his seat in anger; but he did not know the correct procedure for being offensive. He put down his little parcel and, with as swaggering an air as he could manage, began to march towards the billiard tables.

In vain did Prudence interject: With a duel on your arrival in Besançon, your career in the Church is gone.

— What does that matter? — I'll never let it be said that I ducked an insult.

Amanda noted his courage; it made an admirable contrast with the naivete of his manners; in a flash she found herself preferring him to the big young man in the frock coat. She got up and, giving the impression that her eyes were all the time following someone passing in the street, rapidly stationed herself between him and the billiard tables.

— You mustn't look so cross at that gentleman, he's my brother-in-law.

— What does that have to do with it? He stared at me.

— D'you want to make me unhappy, then? Certainly he looked at you, he may even come and speak to you. I told him you're a relation of my mother's, and that you're from Genlis. He's from Franche-Comté and hasn't ever been further than Dôle, on the road to Burgundy; so you can say anything you like to him, don't worry.

Julien still hesitated; so, her barmaid's imagination supplying her with plentiful inventions, she added very quickly:

— Certainly he looked at you, but that was just when he was asking me who you were; he's someone who's *prickly* with everybody, he didn't mean to insult you.

Julien's eyes followed the alleged brother-in-law; he saw him buy a ticket for the pool being played at the billiard table farthest away. He heard his rough voice crying in a domineering tone: *Right! I'm in.* Julien stepped nimbly past Mlle Amanda and started towards the billiard tables. Amanda seized him by the arm:

— First come and pay me, she said to him.

That's all right then, thought Julien; she's frightened that I might leave without paying. Amanda was as upset as he was and was very red; she gave him his change as slowly as possible, while repeating in a whisper:

— Leave the café at once or I won't love you; but I do love you a lot, really.

Julien did leave, but slowly. Isn't it my duty, he kept on saying to himself, to go and stare in my turn at that coarse personage, and snort? This quandary kept him lingering on the street outside the café for an hour; he was watching to see if the man came out. But he did not appear, and Julien departed.

He had been in Besançon only a few hours and already he had acquired a source of regret. The old Surgeon-major had once given him a few fencing lessons, in spite of his gout; it was the only piece of useful knowledge Julien could find that might be of service in his anger. But this drawback would have been as nothing if only he had known how to quarrel any other way than giving a slap; and if it came to a fist fight, his rival, a huge fellow, would have beaten him and left him on the ground.

For a poor devil like me, said Julien to himself, without anyone to protect him and without money, there's not much difference between a seminary and a prison. I must leave my townsman's outfit for safekeeping at some inn, where I will put on my black suit again. If ever I get let out of the seminary for a few hours, I could very easily see Mlle Amanda again in these townsman's clothes. This thinking was admirable; only Julien, while passing in front of all of the inns, did not dare go in any one of them.

Finally, as he walked past the Hotel Ambassador for the second time, his nervous eyes met those of a stout woman, still young, with a high colour and a happy, jolly air. He went up to her and told her his story.

— By all means, my pretty young priest, said the hostess of the Ambassadors, I'll take care of your clothes for you, and get them brushed regularly. In this weather, it's not a good idea to hang a cloth suit without touching it. She produced a key and led him into a bedroom, advising him to make a note of what he had left there.

– Heavens! how sweet you do look like that, M. Abbé Sorel, said the stout woman when he came down again to the kitchen, I'm going to make them give you a fine dinner; and, she added, lowering her voice, it'll cost you only twenty sols, instead of the fifty everyone else pays; for you've got to look after your *little treasury*.

– I have ten louis, replied Julien with a certain amount of pride.

– Ah! Heavens! cried the good hostess in alarm, don't say it so loud; there are plenty of crooks in Besançon. They'll get that out of you in less than no time. Above all, don't go into cafés, they're full of scoundrels.

– Is that so! said Julien, whom these words made thoughtful.

– Never go anywhere but here, I'll give you your coffee. Remember – you'll always find a friend here, and a good dinner for twenty sous; that's saying something, I believe. Go sit yourself down, I'll come and serve you myself.

– I don't know that I can eat, replied Julien, I'm too nervy, I'm going straight to the seminary after I leave you.

The good woman did not let him go until she had filled his pockets with provisions. At last Julien set out for the terrible place; leaning through her door, the hostess pointed him the way.

CHAPTER 25

The Seminary

> Three hundred and thirty-six dinners at 83 centimes, 336
> suppers at 38 centimes, chocolate for those that are allowed
> it; how much might one make on this deal?
>
> The VALENOD of Besançon

He saw the gilded iron cross over the door from far off; he approached it slowly – his legs seemed about to give way under him. Here then is this hell on earth from which I shall not be able to escape! Eventually he made up his mind to ring. The sound of the bell echoed as if in a deserted place. After ten minutes had gone by, a pale individual, dressed in black, came to open the door to him. Julian looked at him and immediately lowered his eyes again. This porter had a most peculiar physiognomy. The bulging green pupils of his eyes were rounded like those of a cat, the eyelids' unwinking set denied the possibility of any human warmth, the thin lips described a semi-circle around protruding teeth: yet this physiognomy betrayed not so much a criminal nature as that complete lack of responsiveness which is even more terrifying to the young. The only feeling Julien's rapid survey could discern in this long, sanctimonious countenance was a profound contempt for anything anyone might say that did not concern the life hereafter.

With an effort Julien raised his eyes again and, in a voice that quavered from the throbbing of his heart, explained that he wished to speak to M. Pirard, the director of the seminary. Without a word, the black-clad man gestured for him to follow. They climbed two flights of a wide staircase with a wooden rail whose warped steps sagged right down on the side opposite the wall, and seemed about to collapse. A small door crowned by a large black-painted deal funereal cross was negotiated with difficulty, and the porter showed him in to a low, dark room where the whitewashed walls were decorated with two large pictures blackened by time. There, Julien was left alone; he was terrified and his heart thumped violently; he would have been happy to find the courage to weep. A deathly silence reigned throughout the building.

At the end of a quarter of an hour – it seemed to him a day – the porter's sinister face reappeared at the threshold of a door at the other end of the room and, without deigning to speak, he made a signal for him to advance. Julien entered a chamber even larger than the first, and very ill lit. Its walls too were white; but here there were no furnishings. Only as he passed a small corner near the door did Julien glimpse a deal pallet, with two wicker chairs and a little armchair made of un-upholstered planks of pine. At the other end of the chamber, next to a little window glazed with yellowing panes and decorated with ill-tended vases of flowers, he saw a man dressed in a shabby soutane seated in front of a table; he seemed angry and was picking up small slips of paper one after another from a heap, arranging them on the table after having written a few words on each. He did not notice Julien's presence. Julien stood motionless in the middle of the chamber, where the porter, who had departed closing the door, had left him.

Ten minutes went by in this way; all the time the ill-dressed man went on writing. Julien's agitation and dread were such that he felt himself on the point of collapse. A philosopher might have commented, perhaps mistakenly: This is the violent impression ugliness makes on a soul created to love beauty.

The man writing lifted his head; Julien perceived this only after a moment, and then, even when he realized it, he remained rooted there as though the terrible gaze fixed upon him had dealt a mortal blow. His tear-dimmed eyes could barely make out a long face covered all over with red blemishes – except on the forehead, which had a deathly pallor. In the midst of red cheeks and a white forehead glittered two small dark eyes fit to daunt a hero. The forehead's massive contours were outlined by a head of thick, flat hair, as black as jet.

– D'you want to approach – yes or no? the man said at last peremptorily.

Julien advanced falteringly, near to collapse and paler than he had ever been in his life, and at last came to a stop three paces from the little deal table covered in slips of paper.

– Nearer, said the man.

Julien moved forward again, holding a hand in front of him as though seeking something for support.

– Your name?

– Julien Sorel.

– You are exceedingly late, he said, fixing him again with his terrible eyes.

Julien could not endure this gaze; stretching his hand out as though for support, he fell full length on the floor.

The man rang a bell. Julien had lost only the use of his eyes and ability to move; he heard steps approaching.

Someone lifted him up and he was set on the little deal armchair. He heard the voice of the terrifying man say to the porter:

– He's fallen down in a fit, it seems – it's the limit.

When Julien managed to open his eyes again the man with the red face was continuing with his writing; the porter had disappeared.
– It's essential that I be brave, our hero said to himself, and, above all, hide my feelings: he felt terribly sick; if I'm taken ill, God knows what they'll think of me. At last the man stopped writing and looking sideways at Julien:

– Are you in a fit state to answer me?

– Yes, monsieur, said Julien in a weak voice.

– Ah! that's lucky.

The black-clad man had risen half to his feet and was searching impatiently for a letter in the drawer of his pine table, which creaked as he opened it. He found it, sat down slowly and, gazing once more at Julien in a way that seemed about to tear out what little life he had left:

– You're recommended to me by M. Chélan, who was the best of parish priests, virtuous man that he is, and my friend for thirty years.

– Ah! it's M. Pirard to whom I have the honour of speaking, said Julien in a sinking voice.

– So it would seem, replied the Director of the Seminary, looking at him irritably.

The gaze in the little eyes increased in intensity, followed by an involuntary contraction of the muscles at the corners of the mouth – the countenance of a tiger savouring in advance the delights of devouring his prey.

– Chélan's letter is short, said he, as though talking to himself. *Intelligenti pauca;*[1] the way it is these days, it's impossible to write too little. He read aloud:

I send to you Julien Sorel, of this parish, whom I baptized some twenty years since; he is the son of a rich carpenter, but who gives him nothing. Julien will be a notable worker in the vineyard of the Lord. Memory and intelligence are not lacking, and he is capable of thought. Will his vocation endure? Is he sincere?

– *Sincere?* repeated the Abbé Pirard looking at Julien with an air of great surprise; however, the look was now less completely devoid of humanity; *sincere!* he repeated, lowering his voice and resuming his reading:

I ask you for a scholarship for Julien Sorel; he will deserve it by submitting to the necessary examinations. I have introduced him to a little theology, the old and sound theology of Bossuet, and Arnault, and Fleury.[2] If this person does not suit you, send him back to me; the Director of the Poorhouse, with whom you are well acquainted, offers him eight hundred francs to be tutor to his children. – As for me, I enjoy inner peace, thanks be to God. I have reconciled myself to that terrible blow. *Vale et me ama.*[3]

The Abbé Pirard, speaking more slowly as he got to the signature, pronounced the word *Chélan* with a sigh.

– He is at peace, said he; surely, indeed, his virtue deserves that reward; God grant it to me in like circumstances!

He looked up to heaven and made the sign of the Cross. At the sight of this pious action Julien felt some relief from the deep horror that had chilled him from the moment he had entered the building.

— I have here three hundred and twenty aspirants to the most holy of estates, the Abbé Pirard said at last, in a severe yet not inimical tone; only seven or eight have come recommended by men like the Abbé Chélan; therefore among these three hundred and twenty-one, you will be the ninth. However, my patronage involves neither favour nor indulgence: it means a redoubling of effort and of vigilance against vice. Go and lock the door.

Julien forced himself to walk, and managed not to fall. He noticed that a little window near the entrance gave on to the fields. He saw the trees; the sight did him good, as though he had glimpsed some old friends.

— *Loquerisne linguam latinam?* [Do you speak Latin?] Abbé Pirard asked him as he walked back.

— *Ita, pater optime* [Yes, most excellent father], answered Julien, reviving a little. Surely never had any man in the world seemed less excellent to him than M. Pirard during the last half hour.

The conversation continued in Latin. The expression in the Abbé's eyes softened; Julien regained some self-confidence. How feeble I am, he thought, to let myself be imposed upon by these shows of virtue! This man will prove an ordinary scoundrel like M. Maslon; and Julien congratulated himself on having hidden nearly all his money in his boots.

The Abbé Pirard examined Julien on theology, and was surprised at the extent of his knowledge. His surprise increased when he questioned him more closely on the sacred scriptures. But when he came to questions of Patristic doctrine, he realized that Julien hardly even knew the names of St Augustine, St Bonaventure, St Basil, etc.

In fact, thought Abbé Pirard, this is obviously that fatal leaning towards Protestantism with which I have always reproached Chélan. A profound — a too profound — knowledge of Holy Writ.

(Julien had just been talking, without being asked about the subject, of the *actual* times when Genesis, the Pentateuch etc. had been composed.)

To what does this endless pondering of the scriptures tend? thought Abbé Pirard, if it's not to *individual interpretation* — that is to say, to the most frightful Protestantism? And beside this dangerous knowledge, nothing from the Fathers that might counterpoise the tendency.

But the Director's astonishment was boundless when he came to question Julien about the authority of the Pope. He was expecting to get the doctrines of the traditional Gallican Church, but instead heard the young man reciting the whole of M. de Maistre's book.

What a strange man Chélan is, thought the Abbé Pirard; has he introduced him to that work to show him how to parody it?

It was useless questioning Julien in order to find out if he seriously believed M. de Maistre's doctrines. The young man answered only by rote. From that time Julien really was very good, he felt that he was in control of himself. After a very extended examination it seemed to him that M. Pirard's severity towards him was only pretended. And indeed, if the Director of the Seminary had not for the last fifteen years imposed principles of gravity and austerity upon himself with regard to his theological students, he would have embraced Julien in the name of logic – such clarity, accuracy and precision did he find in his answers.

Here is a strong and healthy mind, he said to himself, though *corpus debile* [the body is weak].

– D'you often fall down like that? he asked Julien in French, pointing to the floor.

– That was the first time in my life – the porter's face petrified me, added Julien, flushing like a child.

The Abbé Pirard almost smiled.

– You see the effect of worldly appearances; you're used to smiling faces, it seems – those veritable showplaces of falsehood. Truth is austere, monsieur. But our task here below, isn't that austere also? It is essential that your conscience guards vigilantly against this weakness: *excessive sensitivity concerning vain exterior graces*.

If you had not been recommended to me, said Abbé Pirard, returning with marked pleasure to the Latin tongue, if you had not been recommended to me by such a man as the Abbé Chélan, I would speak to you in the vain language of that world to which it seems you are only too well accustomed. The entirety of the scholarship for which you ask is, I should tell you, the most difficult thing

in the world to obtain. But Abbé Chélan has deserved little indeed
for his fifty-six years of apostolical labours, if he is unable to dispose
of one scholarship at the seminary.

After saying this, the Abbé Pirard advised Julien not to join any
secret society or congregation without his consent.

– I give you my word of honour, said Julien open-heartedly, like
a gentleman.

The Director of the Seminary smiled for the first time.

– That word is not at all in place here, said he, it's far too redolent
of the empty honour of worldly men that's conducive to so many
faults – often to crimes.[4] You owe me a religious obedience by virtue
of paragraph seventeen of the Bull *Unam Ecclesiam* of St Pius V.[5] I
am your ecclesiastical superior. In this house, my very dear son, to
understand is to obey. How much money have you got?

Here we go, said Julien to himself, that's what this very dear son
is about.

– Thirty-five francs, father.

– Keep a careful written record of how you spend this money;
you'll have to render an account of it to me.

This exhausting interview had lasted three hours; Julien called the
porter.

– Go and put Julien Sorel in cell no. 103, the Abbé Pirard ordered
the man.

As a great mark of distinction he was according Julien a separate
lodging.

– Take his trunk there, he added.

Julien looked down and saw that his trunk lay exactly opposite
him; he had been gazing at it for three hours and had not recognized
it.

When he arrived at no. 103, which was a little closet eight foot
square on the top floor of the house, Julien found that it gave on to
the ramparts, and that over those one could see the fine-looking plain
that is separated from the town by the Doubs.

What a delightful view! cried Julien; but as he uttered this exclamation he was devoid of the feeling the words expressed. Such
violent sensations as he had experienced in the short time he had

spent in Besançon had completely exhausted his powers. He sat down by the window on the single wooden chair in his closet, and immediately fell fast asleep. He heard neither the bell for supper nor that for Benediction; he'd been forgotten.

When the first rays of the sun woke him next morning he found himself stretched out on the floor.

CHAPTER 26

The World, or What the Rich
Don't Have

> I am alone upon the earth, and no man deigns to think of
> me. All those I see being successful possess an insolence
> and a hardness of heart which I do not feel at all. They
> loathe me because of my easy good nature. Ah! soon I shall
> die, perhaps of hunger, perhaps of the sadness of seeing
> such cruel men.   YOUNG[1]

He hastened to brush off his coat and go down – he was late. An
assistant master scolded him severely; instead of trying to justify
himself, Julien crossed his arms over his breast:

– *Peccavi, pater optime* (I have sinned, I acknowledge my fault, O
father), said he with a contrite air.

This debut was a great success. The sharper ones among the
seminarists saw that they were dealing with someone who was not
without some elements of their calling. The recreation hour came
and Julien found himself the object of a general curiosity. But this
was met with nothing but reserve and silence from him. Following
the maxims that he had evolved for himself, he considered his 321
comrades as enemies; in his view, the most dangerous of all was the
Abbé Pirard.

A few days afterwards, Julien had to choose a confessor and he
was given a list.

Eh! good God! what d'they take me for? he said to himself, Do
they think I don't know enough to *get the message*? – and he chose
Abbé Pirard.

Without his suspecting it, this move was decisive. A very young
little seminarist, a native of Verrières who from the first day had

188

declared himself his friend, told him that if he had chosen M. Castanède, the under-director of the seminary, he would probably have acted more prudently.

— The Abbé Castanède is the enemy of M. Pirard, who is suspected of Jansenism, the little seminarist added, leaning close to his ear.

All our hero's first moves, which he thought so wise, were — as in the choice of a confessor — blunders. Led astray by all the presumption characteristic of an imaginative man, he mistook his intentions for accomplished deeds and believed himself a consummate hypocrite. His folly went as far as self-reproach for his successes in this art of the feeble.

Alas! it is the only weapon I have! In another age, resounding exploits in the face of the enemy would have been my way to *earn my bread*.

Pleased with his own conduct, Julien looked round about him; everywhere he found the semblance of purest virtue.

Half a dozen or so of the seminarists lived in the odour of sanctity, and had visions like those of St Theresa, or of St Francis when he received the stigmata on Mount *Vernia* in the Apennines. But this was a great secret, concealed by their friends. These poor young men with their visions were nearly always in the infirmary. A hundred or so others united a sturdy faith with indefatigable hard work. They persevered to the point of making themselves ill, but without learning a great deal. Two or three were distinguished by genuine talent, among them one called Chazel; but Julien felt remote from them, and they from him.

The rest of the 321 seminarists were composed entirely of gross young creatures who were not even sure of the meaning of the Latin words they repeated all day long. Nearly all were peasants' sons, and they preferred to earn their living by reciting a few Latin words than by tilling the soil. It was after realizing this that, in the first few days, Julien predicted rapid success for himself. — In any kind of service there have to be intelligent men because there is work to be done, he said to himself. Under Napoleon I would have been a sergeant;[2] among these future curés I'll be Vicar-general.

All these poor devils, he added — manual labourers from infancy

– have lived on curds and black bread until they arrived here. In their cottages they ate meat only five or six times a year. Like the Roman soldiers who thought war a recreation, these crude peasants are charmed by the delights of a seminary.

Julien never descried anything in their dull looks but bodily needs satisfied after dinner, and bodily pleasures looked forward to before the meal. Such were the men among whom he must distinguish himself; but what Julien did not know, and what they refrained from telling him, was that to be first in the different courses pursued at the seminary, on dogma, ecclesiastical history, etc., was in their eyes nothing but the sin of *vain conceit*. Since Voltaire, since two-chamber government, which is at root only *lack of faith* and *individual judgement*, and engenders in the minds of the people the unfortunate habit of *distrust*, the Church in France seems to have understood that books are the real enemy. In its eyes, heartfelt submission is everything. To succeed in one's studies – even religious studies – is suspect, and very rightly so. What hinders a clever man from going over to the other side, like Siéyès or Grégoire?[3] The anxious Church clings to the Pope as to its last chance of salvation. The Pope alone can aspire to paralyse individual judgement, and make an impression on the sickly, wearied minds of worldly people with the pious pomp and circumstance of his court.

Julien, half divining these several truths – which, however, everything said in the seminary tended to deny – fell into a deep melancholy. He worked very hard, and rapidly succeeded in learning things that were very useful for a priest, completely false in his eyes, and in which he had no interest. He believed there was nothing else he could do.

Have I then been forgotten by everyone else on earth? he wondered. He was not to know that M. Pirard had received and thrown into the fire several letters postmarked from Dijon, from which, despite the proprieties of a very conventional style, there escaped signs of a most vivid passion. Great remorse seemed to be battling against this love. So much the better, thought the Abbé Pirard, at least it was not an irreligious woman this young man loved.

One day Abbé Pirard opened a letter that seemed half washed out with tears – it was an eternal farewell. At last – it informed Julien – Heaven has granted me the grace to be able to hate, not the cause of my sin – he will always be the thing I hold most dear in the world – but the sin itself. The sacrifice is made, my dear. Made not without tears, as you can see. The salvation of others to whom I am bound, and whom you have loved so much, prevails. On them, a just but terrible God can no longer avenge their mother's crimes. Farewell, Julien, be just in your dealings with men.

The end of this letter was almost completely illegible. An address in Dijon was given, yet a wish was expressed that Julien should never reply, or at least that he would make use only of language a woman recalled to virtue could read without blushing.

Julien's low spirits, in conjunction with the second-rate nourishment supplied to the seminary by the contractor of dinners at 83 centimes, was beginning to affect his health, when one morning Fouqué suddenly appeared in his room.

– I've succeeded in getting in at last. I've journeyed to Besançon five times – not your fault – to visit you. Always wooden faces. I stationed someone at the seminary door; why the devil d'you never go out?

– It's an ordeal I imposed upon myself.

– You look to me to have changed a lot. At last I'm allowed to see you again. Two lovely five-franc écus have just shown me what a fool I was not to have offered them the first visit.

The two friends' conversation ranged over everything; Julien changed colour when Fouqué said to him:

– By the way, did you know? the mother of your two pupils has been taken with the most tremendous piety.

And on he talked, in that detached manner which makes so singular an impression on a passionate soul whose dearest concerns are, unwittingly, being thrown into confusion.

– Yes, my dear fellow, into the most exalted devotion. They say she goes on pilgrimages. But, to the eternal disgrace of Abbé Maslon, who spied so long on poor M. Chélan, Mme de Rênal wants nothing to do with him. She comes to confess at Dijon or at Besançon.

– She comes to Besançon? said Julien, his brows flushing all over.

— Pretty often, replied Fouqué with an inquisitive air.

— D'you have any *Constitutionnels* with you?

— What d'you say? asked Fouqué.

— I asked whether you have any *Constitutionnels*? Julien replied in the calmest of tones. They sell here at thirty sous a copy.

— What! even in the seminary — liberals! cried Fouqué. Poor France! he added, adopting the hypocritical voice and soft modulations of Abbé Maslon.

This visit would have made a deep impression on our hero if, the very next day, a remark made to him by the little seminarist from Verrières who seemed to him so childlike, had not led him to make an important discovery. Ever since he had been at the seminary his conduct had been nothing but a series of false moves. He laughed at himself bitterly.

In truth, the major actions of his life were astutely managed; but he did not pay attention to details, and details were the only things the clever people in the seminary valued. Thus he was already known among his comrades as a *sceptical mind*. He had been betrayed by a host of little things.

To their eyes he was guilty of the monstrous vice that *he thought, he judged for himself* — as opposed to blindly following *authority* and example. The Abbé Pirard had been no help at all to him; he had not once addressed a word to him out of the context of the confessional, and even there he listened more than he spoke. It would have been far otherwise had he chosen Abbé Castanède.

From the moment Julien realized his folly, his boredom departed. He now wanted to discover the whole extent of the damage and, to that end, emerged slightly from the disdainful and obstinate silence with which he had rebuffed his fellows. This was their chance to pay him back. His advances were greeted with scorn, verging on derision. He realized that since his entry to the seminary there had not been a single hour — above all in the recreation periods — that had not involved consequences for or against him, that had not augmented the number of his enemies or conciliated the good will of a few genuinely virtuous seminarists, or at least those a little less coarse than the others. The damage to be repaired was very great, the task very difficult. From then on, Julien's attention was fully alert; he set about designing himself a completely new persona.

His eye movements, for example, caused him a lot of difficulty. It is not without reason that they keep the eyes lowered in such places. How presumptuous I was in Verrières! said Julien to himself. I imagined myself to be really living; I was only preparing for life; here at last I am in the world as I'll find it until I have played out my part, encircled by genuine enemies. What an immense trial, he added, this perpetual hypocrisy is; it makes the labours of Hercules look pale. The Hercules of modern times is Sixtus the Fifth – who for fifteen years fooled forty cardinals with his humility, after they had all seen his youthful energy and arrogance.[4]

So learning counts for nothing here! he said to himself scornfully; progress in dogma, in sacred history, etc., matters only in appearance. All that is said on the subject is designed to make fools like me fall into the trap. Alas! my only merit lies in my rapid progress, in my facility to grasp this stuff. Can it be that deep down they estimate it at its true value – judge it as I do? And I had the stupidity to be proud of it! Those places at the top of the class I've always won have only served to get me relentless enemies. Chazel, who knows more than I do, always throws some idiocy into his compositions that relegates him to fiftieth place; if he gets the first it is through absent-mindedness. Ah! how useful a word, a single word, from M. Pirard would have been to me!

From the moment Julien was disillusioned, the drawn-out exercises in ascetic piety, such as the rosary five times a week, performing canticles to the Sacred Heart, etc., which had seemed to him so deadly boring, became the most interesting fields of action. Thinking about himself rigorously, and above all trying not to overestimate his capacities, Julien did not even attempt at first, like the seminarists who served as models for the others, to constantly perform actions that would be *significations* – that is to say, demonstrative of some type of Christian perfection. At the seminary there is a method of eating a hen's egg that displays the amount of progress made in the devout life.

The reader, who may be smiling, might be so good as to recall all the blunders in eating an egg made by the Abbé Delille[5] when he was invited to dinner by a great lady of Louis XVI's court.

Julien tried at first to arrive at the *non culpa*, which is the state of the young seminarist whose mode of walking, whose ways of moving his arms, eyes, etc., have certainly nothing worldly about them, but do not yet advertise the person as being absorbed by the idea of another world and the *pure nothingness* of this one.

All the time, Julien would find sayings of this kind scrawled in charcoal on the corridor walls: What is sixty years of travail when weighed in the balance with eternal bliss or the eternal boiling oil of hell? He did not despise these any more; he understood that he should keep them constantly in front of his eyes. What will I be doing all my life? he asked himself; I'll be selling places in Heaven to the faithful. How will that place be rendered visible to them? – by the difference between my appearance and that of the laity.

After several months of incessant application, Julien still retained the air of *thinking*. His ways of moving his eyes and setting his mouth did not proclaim an implicit faith, ready to believe all and maintain everything, even unto martyrdom. With anger Julien saw himself worsted in this kind of thing by the coarsest peasants. They had good reasons for not having a thoughtful air.

What pains did he not take to achieve that physiognomy of fervent, blind faith, ready to believe all and suffer all, that one meets with so often in Italian monasteries, and of which Guercino has left us laity such perfect representations in his religious paintings?[6]

On the high feast days the seminarists were served sausage with their sauerkraut. His neighbours at table noticed that Julien was indifferent to this delight, and this itself was among his leading crimes. His comrades saw it as an odious indication of the most stupid hypocrisy; nothing made him more enemies. Behold this middle-class type, this high and mighty one, said they, who affects to despise the finest treat, sausage with sauerkraut! Shame on the scoundrel! the snob! the lost soul!

Alas! the ignorance of these young peasants, my comrades, is an immense advantage to them, Julien would cry out in moments of discouragement. When they come to the seminary there is no necessity at all for a teacher to free them from the fearful number of worldly ideas that I brought with me, and that they can read in my face, whatever I do.

Julien studied the coarsest of the young peasants who arrived at the seminary with an attention bordering on envy. At that moment when they were rid of their ratteen jackets in order to put on the black robe, their education was limited to a boundless respect for money, *dry and liquid*, as they say in Franche-Comté. This is the sacramental and heroic way of expressing the concept of *ready cash*.

Happiness for the seminarists, as for the heroes in Voltaire's novels, consists above all in having a good dinner. In almost all of them Julien found an innate respect for a man who wears a coat of *good cloth*. This sentiment estimates *distributive justice* – of the kind handed down by our courts – at its true value, or even below that value. What is to be gained, they would frequently ask each other, by going to court against one of the *fat*?

That is the term in the valleys of the Jura to denote a rich man. From it one may guess their respect for the richest thing of all: the government!

In the eyes of the Franche-Comté peasantry it is unwise not to give a respectful smile at the mere mention of M. the Prefect's name: and lack of wisdom in the poor is quickly punished by a lack of bread.

Having been at first almost suffocated by his feelings of scorn, Julien in the end experienced pity: the fathers of most of his comrades would often have returned home on a winter's evening to find no bread there, nor chestnuts, nor potatoes. Is it then very surprising, said Julien to himself, that in their eyes the happy man is first of all he who can command a good dinner, and then he who possesses decent clothes? My comrades have a settled vocation, that is to say that they see in the ecclesiastical life a long continuance of this happiness: to eat well and have warm clothes in winter.

Julien happened to overhear a young, imaginatively gifted seminarist say to his friend:

– Why shouldn't I become pope like Sixtus the Fifth, who had been a swineherd?

– Only Italians are made pope, the friend replied; but, for sure, they cast lots among people like us for the appointments of vicars-general, canons, and possibly bishops. M. P—, Bishop of Châlons, is the son of a cooper – that's what my father is.

One day, in the middle of a lesson on dogma, the Abbé Pirard sent for Julien. The poor young man was delighted to get out of the physical and moral atmosphere in which he was immersed.

In the Director's room Julien encountered the same welcome as had so terrified him on his first coming to the seminary.

– Explain to me what is written on this playing card, Abbé Pirard said, looking at him as though to make him wish the earth would swallow him up.

Julien read:

Amanda Binet, at the Girafe Café, before eight. Say that you're from Genlis, and my mother's cousin.

Julien saw the magnitude of the danger; the Abbé Castanède's spies had stolen this address from him.

– The day I entered here, said he, gazing at the Abbé Pirard's forehead because he could not face his fearsome eyes – I was much afraid. M. Chélan had told me that this was a place full of delation and all kinds of spitefulness; spying and denunciation between comrades is smiled upon here. Heaven wishes it so, to show young priests life as it is and inspire them with disgust for the world and its vain shows.

– Is it me you're preaching at? said the Abbé Pirard, furious. You little scoundrel!

– At Verrières, Julien coolly continued, my brothers would beat me up when they could find a reason to be jealous of me . . .

– Come to the point! the point! cried M. Pirard, almost beside himself.

Intimidated not at all, Julien went on with his speech.

– The day I arrived in Besançon, around midday, I was hungry and went into a café. My heart was full of repugnance for so profane a place; but I thought my dinner would be cheaper there than at an inn. A lady, who seemed to be the owner of the establishment, took pity on my novice's air. Besançon is full of scoundrels, she told me, I fear for you, monsieur. If something bad should happen to you, fall back on me, send a message to me before eight o'clock. If the porters at the seminary refuse to do it, say that you are my cousin and come from Genlis . . .

— All this prattle will be checked on, cried Abbé Pirard, unable to keep still and pacing up and down the room.

— Take him back to his room!

The Abbé followed him and locked him in. Julien immediately examined his trunk, at the bottom of which the fatal card had been hidden like a treasure. Nothing was missing, but many things had been disarranged; and yet the key had never left his possession. What a lucky thing, Julien said to himself, that all the time I was in the dark here I never accepted the permits of leave M. Castanède offered me so often, with a geniality I now understand. Maybe if I had had the weakness to change clothes and go to see the beautiful Amanda, I would have been lost. When they despaired of taking advantage of the information like that, they made use of it as a denunciation, so as not to waste it.

Two hours later the Director sent for him.

— You have not lied, he said to him with with a less severe look in his eyes; but to keep an address of that kind is a rash mistake of which you cannot conceive the seriousness. Unhappy boy! Ten years from now, perhaps, it will bring trouble on you.

CHAPTER 27

First Experience of Life

The present moment, great God! 'tis the Ark of the Lord.
Woe to him that lays hand upon it.   DIDEROT[1]

The reader will be so kind as to excuse us for giving only a very few clear and precise facts about this period of Julien's existence. Not that these are lacking, very far from it; but what one encounters in a seminary is perhaps too dark to harmonize with the discreet tones we have tried to maintain in these pages. People living today who have suffered certain things may recall them only with a horror that paralyses all other pleasures, even that of reading a story.

Julien had little success in his attempts at evolving hypocritical mannerisms; at times he fell into a state of revulsion, even utter demoralization. He was not succeeding, and moreover was not succeeding in so very low a career. The slightest help from outside would have been enough to hearten him – the difficulties to be surmounted were not so great; but he was alone like a ship abandoned in the middle of the sea. – And even if I did succeed, he said to himself, then to have a whole life to spend in such frightful company! Gluttons who dream of nothing but the bacon omelette they are going to devour at dinner, or men of the kind of Abbé Castanède, for whom no crime is too black! They may well achieve power – but, good God, at what a cost!

The human will is mighty, I'm always reading that; but is it strong enough to conquer such distaste as this? The labours of great men used to be straightforward; however terrible the danger, they found in it something beautiful; but who, except me, can comprehend the ugliness all around me?

This time was the most testing of his whole life. It would have been so easy to enlist in one of the fine regiments of the garrison of Besançon! Or he could turn himself into a Latin teacher; he needed so little to live on! – but then there would have been no more career, no more future about which to dream; it would have been a death. Here's the detail of one of his dispiriting days.

– In my asinine pride I have congratulated myself so often on being different from other young peasants! he said to himself one morning. Well, I've now lived long enough to understand that *difference breeds hatred*. This important truth had just been demonstrated by one of his most galling failures. Every day for a week he had worked away at charming one of those pupils who lived in the odour of sanctity. He had walked with him in the courtyard, humbly listening to nonsense fit to send one to sleep standing up. Then suddenly the weather turned stormy, thunder growled and the saintly pupil cried out, rudely pushing him away:

– Look, it's everyone for themselves in this world, and I don't want to be burnt by thunder: God might well strike you as an unbeliever – a Voltaire.

Julien – his teeth clenched with rage and glaring open-eyed at a sky now streaked by lightning – cried to himself: I deserve drowning if I slumber in the tempest! Let's on to conquer some other little pedant.

The bell rang for the Abbé Castanède's course on Church history.

That day Abbé Castanède informed these young peasants – who had been so terrified by the grinding toil and poverty of their fathers – that the government, so formidable an entity in their eyes, could only have genuine and legitimate authority by virtue of its being delegated by the Vicar of God on earth.

– Render yourselves worthy of the Pope's beneficence through the sanctity of your lives, by your obedience, become *as a rod in his hands*, he continued, and you could obtain a magnificent posting where you would rule at the top far from all interference; an unassailable position, where the government pays a third of your emoluments, and the faithful, swayed by your preaching, the other two-thirds.

Coming out of his classroom, M. Castanède lingered in the courtyard.

– What people say is certainly true of a curé: the job's worth what the man's worth, he told those who made a circle around him. I myself – me talking to you now – have seen parishes in the mountains where the perks alone were worth more than a town priest's whole living. There was as much actual money, without counting fat capons, eggs, fresh butter and a host of agreeable little extras; and the curé is top of the pile, nobody contradicts him: no fine meals to which he is not invited, fussed over, etc.

Hardly had M. Castanède gone up to his quarters than his pupils split up into little groups. Julien was not of them; they avoided him like a scabbed sheep. In every one of the groups he saw a pupil toss a coin in the air and if he guessed right, heads or tails, his friends would be able to tell whether he would soon be one of those curés enjoying rich pickings.

Then came the anecdotes. Such-and-such a young priest, ordained only a year before, having offered a tame rabbit to the servant of an aged curé, had managed to get himself requested as priest, and, little more than a month after – the curé having very rapidly died – had replaced him in the fat parish. Another had succeeded in getting himself designated as successor to the curé of a wealthy market town by means of attending all the meals of the old priest – who was paralysed – and slicing his chicken for him gracefully.

The seminarists, like all young men in every career, exaggerated the effects of any little ploys that were a bit out of the ordinary and caught the imagination.

I should join in these conversations, Julien said to himself. When the talk was not of sausages and fat parishes, they discussed the secular parts of Church doctrine; the different relationships between bishops and prefects, between mayors and curés. Julien noticed the idea of a second God emerge, but a God more to be feared and very much more powerful than the other; this second God was the Pope. It was said – but in hushed tones and when one was very sure not to be overheard by M. Pirard – that if the Pope did not take the trouble to appoint all the prefects and mayors of France, that was because he had delegated this chore to the King of France in naming him the Eldest Son of the Church.

It was about then that Julien thought he might gain some advantage from his study of M. de Maistre's *Du Pape*. Most certainly he impressed his comrades; but this again turned out badly. He offended them by expounding their own opinions better than they could. M. Chélan had been as unwise for Julien as he was for himself. Having given him the habit of reasoning with precision and paying no attention to empty words, he had neglected to inform him that in someone who was little esteemed this practice was a crime; for all good reasoning is disagreeable.

Julien's eloquence was thus another offence. Forced to take notice of him, his comrades arrived at two words to express the sum of the horror he inspired: they nicknamed him MARTIN LUTHER; above all, they told themselves, because of that infernal logic which made him so proud.

Many of the young seminarists had fresher cheeks than Julien's and might be thought prettier fellows, but he had white hands and was unable to hide certain habits of cleanliness and delicacy. In the deplorable institution where his fate had cast him this advantage was not an advantage at all. The grubby peasants in whose midst he lived pronounced that he had very debased morals. We are afraid a multitude of details about our hero's misfortunes would bore the reader. As an example, the more energetic of his comrades decided to make a habit of beating him up; he was forced to arm himself with an iron compass and let it be known that he would use it – though only by gestures. Gestures could not figure in a spy's report nearly as vividly as words.

CHAPTER 28

A Procession

Every heart was moved. It seemed as though the presence
of God had descended into the narrow gothic streets, which
were decorated on each side, and well sanded by the cares
of the faithful.

YOUNG

Julien had tried his very best to make himself insignificant and dull
– but he could not please, he was too different. Yet, he said to
himself, all these professors are shrewd men, picked out of a thousand;
how is it they don't appreciate my humility? Only one of them
appeared ready to take advantage of his willingness to believe everything and seem to be deceived by everything. This was the Abbé
Chas-Bernard, the Director of Ceremonies at the cathedral, where
for the last fifteen years he had been led to expect a canonry; whilst
awaiting this, he taught pulpit oratory at the seminary. During the
period of Julien's blindness there this was one of the classes in which
he had most habitually excelled. The Abbé Chas had gone out of his
way to show him friendship, and, when the class came out, would
gladly take him by the arm for a few turns round the garden.

What is he driving at? Julien would wonder. He felt astonished
that Abbé Chas should talk to him for hours at a time about the
ornaments possessed by the cathedral. It had seventeen gold-laced
chasubles, in addition to the mourning vestments. High hopes were
being entertained of the ancient Présidente de Rubempré; this lady,
who was ninety, had preserved her wedding dress, made of superb
Lyons cloth embroidered in gold, for at least seventy years. Just
imagine it, my friend, said Abbé Chas – stopping abruptly and
opening his eyes wide – these fabrics have so much gold in them that

202

they stand up on their own. It is widely believed in Besançon that, under the Présidente's will, the cathedral's treasures will be increased by more than ten chasubles, not counting four or five copes for high festivals. I could go further, added the Abbé Chas, lowering his voice, I have my reasons for believing that the Présidente will leave us eight gorgeous gilded candlesticks, thought to have been bought in Italy by Charles the Bold, Duke of Burgundy, whose favourite minister was an ancestor of hers.

Now what is this person trying to get at with all these old furnishings? wondered Julien. This clever build-up has been going on for ages, and nothing comes of it. He must be tremendously suspicious of me! He is cleverer than all the others – you can see through to their hidden agendas within a fortnight, easily. Oh, I understand – this one's ambition has been on edge for the last fifteen years!

One evening, in the middle of arms drill,[1] Julien was summoned to the Abbé Pirard, who said to him:

– Tomorrow is the festival of *Corpus Domini* [Corpus Christi]. M. the Abbé Chas-Bernard needs your help in decorating the cathedral – go, and obey.

Abbé Pirard called him back and added, with an air of commiseration:

– It's up to you whether you wish to make use of this occasion to wander in the town.

– *Incedo per ignes* [I have hidden enemies], replied Julien.[2]

The next day, as soon as it was fully light, Julien walked to the cathedral with lowered eyes. The look of the streets and the bustle beginning to spread in the town did him good. On all sides, housefronts were being draped for the procession. The whole of the period he had spent in the seminary appeared to him no more than an instant. His thoughts dwelt on Vergy, and on that attractive Amanda Binet – whom it was possible he would meet, since her café wasn't far away. From far off he saw the Abbé Chas-Bernard at the door of his beloved cathedral: a portly man with a cheerful face and a candid air. Today he was triumphant:

– I've been waiting for you, my dear child, he cried as soon as he saw Julien in the distance, consider yourself welcome. Today's task will be long and hard, so let's fortify ourselves with a first breakfast; the second will be due at ten, during the High Mass.

— I ask, monsieur, said Julien with a solemn look, not to be left on my own for an instant; be so good as to mark, he went on pointing to the clock above their heads, that I got here at one minute to five.

— Ah! those little devils at the seminary have scared you! You flatter them by paying any attention to them, said the Abbé Chas; is a road the less beautiful because there are thistles in the hedges at its side? Travellers march ahead and leave the nasty spikes to rot where they stand. In any case, let's to work, my dear friend, to work!

Abbé Chas was right in saying that the job would be hard. The previous evening there had been a grand funeral ceremony in the cathedral; there had not been time to prepare anything; so it was necessary — in a single morning — to drape all the gothic columns that divided the aisles and the nave with a kind of red damask, up to thirty feet high. His Lordship the Bishop had called in four decorators by mail coach from Paris, but these gentlemen could not do everything and, far from lessening their Bisontine colleagues' clumsiness by encouragement, they redoubled it by laughing at them.

Julien saw that he must get up on a ladder himself, and his agility served him well. He put himself in charge of the local decorators. Abbé Chas was delighted to see him flying from ladder to ladder. When all the pillars had been draped with damask, there arose the problem of setting five enormous bunches of plumes on the great baldaquin over the middle of the high altar. A richly gilded wooden crown is supported by eight great spiralling columns of Italian marble. But to reach the centre of the baldaquin, right above the tabernacle, it is necessary to step along an ancient wooden frame, forty feet from the ground and possibly worm-eaten.

The prospect of this difficult climb had quite dispelled the gaiety of the Parisian decorators, so brilliant until then; they peered at it from down below, talking about it a great deal, but not going up. Julien grabbed the bunches of plumes and climbed the ladder at a run. He stuck them very handsomely on the ornamental crown, right at the centre of the baldaquin. As he descended the ladder, Abbé Chas-Bernard clasped him in his arms:

– *Optime*, cried the good priest, I'll tell Monseigneur of this.

The meal at ten o'clock was very jolly. Never had Abbé Chas seen his church so lovely.

– My dear disciple, said he to Julien, my mother used to hire out the chairs for this venerable basilica, so that in a way I was brought up in this great building. Robespierre's Terror ruined us; but, at eight years old, as I was then, I was already serving at masses in secret, and was given meals on the days of the mass. Nobody could fold a chasuble better than I, never did the lace get damaged. Since Napoleon restored religious observances, I've had the good fortune to regulate everything in this venerable metropolitan church. Five times a year my eyes have beheld it dressed up in these beautiful decorations. But never has it appeared so resplendent, never have the damasks been so well put up, so tight against the pillars, as today.

– At last he's going to tell me his secret, thought Julien, he's talking about himself now; he's becoming expansive. Yet this man, so evidently elated, let fall nothing indiscreet. – And this when he's worked so much, at that, and is happy, said Julien to himself – and the good wine hasn't been stinted either. What a man! what a fine example to me! He *takes the biscuit*. (Which was a piece of slang he had got from the old surgeon.)

When the *Sanctus* of the high mass rang out Julien made as though to take a surplice to follow the Bishop in the grand procession.

– What about the thieves, my dear boy, the thieves! cried Abbé Chas, you're not thinking about them. The procession will go; the church will be deserted; and we'll keep watch, you and I. We'll count ourselves pretty lucky if we lose only an ell or two of the lace round the bottom of the pillars. That's yet another gift from Madame de Rubempré; it came down from the celebrated count, her great grandfather; it's pure gold, my dear friend, added the priest, whispering in his ear with obvious exaltation, nothing false about it! I charge you to keep guard on the northern aisle – don't leave it. I myself will take care of the southern aisle and the nave. Pay attention to the confessionals; it's there that the thieves' female accomplices wait for the moment we turn our backs.

As he finished speaking, the quarter before twelve sounded and immediately the great bell made itself heard. It rang out out a full peal; the richness and solemnity of its tone moved Julien. His imagination stirred from its earthly bounds.

His exaltation was enhanced by the odours of incense and rose petals, strewn in front of the holy sacrament by little children arrayed as St John.

The solemn sounds of this bell should really have awoken in Julien thoughts of nothing but the hours of twenty men paid at fifty centimes, assisted perhaps by fifteen or so of the faithful. He should have considered the wear on the ropes and on the wooden frames, or the danger to the bell itself, which crashed down every second century, and have calculated ways of reducing the pay of the ringers or of paying them by some indulgence or other benefit – deriving from the riches of the Church, but not diminishing its purse.

Instead of entertaining such prudent thoughts, Julien's soul, lifted high by those full-bodied and masculine sounds, wandered in realms of the imagination. He will never make a good priest or a great administrator. Spirits stirred in this way are at best fit to produce an artist. Here Julien's presumptuousness is revealed in the full light of day. Fifty or so of his colleagues in the seminary – having been alerted to the hard realities of the world by public hatred and the Jacobinism they had been shown was lurking in ambush behind every hedge – would have thought of nothing except the wages of the ringers. When they heard the great cathedral bell they would have calculated, with the genius of a Barême,[3] whether or not the degree of feeling stirred in the public was worth the money paid for ringing it. And if Julien had become concerned with the material welfare of the cathedral, his imagination, overshooting the goal, would have worked out how to save forty francs on building while missing the chance to avoid an expenditure of twenty-five centimes.

While, in the loveliest weather in the world, the procession moved gently through Besançon, pausing at the shining altars of repose that local authorities had vied with one another to erect, the church remained in deep silence. Half light and an agreeable freshness reigned there; a scent of flowers and incense embalmed it still.

Silence, profound solitude, the freshness of the long naves, made

Julien's reverie the sweeter. He had no fear of being disturbed by the Abbé Chas, who was busy in another part of the church. While his mortal frame paced slowly down the northern aisle confided to his charge, his soul had almost flown. His tranquillity was the more complete for his having assured himself that there was only a scattering of pious women in the confessionals; his eye looked on without seeing.

Nevertheless, this abstraction was half penetrated by the sight of two very well dressed women on their knees, one in a confessional, the other very near her on a chair. He looked without seeing – but, whether from a vague feeling for his duties, or from admiration for these ladies' noble and simple attire, he noted that there was no priest in the confessional. It's odd, thought he, that these beautiful women aren't on their knees in front of some altar of repose – if they're devout; or, if they're from society, seated in some advantageous position in the front row of a balcony. How well made that dress is! What grace! He slackened his pace in order to observe.

On hearing the sound of Julien's step in the depth of the great silence, the lady on her knees in the confessional turned her head a little. Suddenly she gave a little cry and started to faint.

Her strength failing, she slumped backward from her knees; her friend, close by, threw herself forward to help. At the same moment, Julien was able to see the falling lady's shoulders. A twisted collar of large natural pearls caught his eye. What sensations flooded through him when he recognized Mme de Rênal's hair! – for it was her. The woman trying to hold up her head and prevent her from falling right down was Mme Derville. Julien, beside himself, dashed forward; Mme de Rênal's fall might well have dragged her friend down had not Julien supported them both. He saw Mme de Rênal's face, ashen and absolutely bereft of emotion, drooping on her shoulder. He helped Mme Derville lift this charming head on to a straw chair for support. He was on his knees.

Mme Derville turned and recognized him:

– Be gone, monsieur, be gone! she said in a voice full of intense anger. It's vital she doesn't see you again. Indeed, the sight of you would fill her with horror, she was so happy without you! Your behaviour is atrocious. Get away; if you have any shame left in you, leave at once.

This speech was made with such authority, and Julien felt so feeble that moment, that he took himself off. She has always hated me, he said to himself, thinking of Mme Derville.

At the same time, the nasal chant of the leading priests in the procession echoed through the church; it was coming back in. The Abbé Chas-Bernard called out to Julien, who did not hear him at first, several times; eventually, he arrived at the pillar behind which Julien, half-dead, had taken refuge, and took him by the arm. He wanted to present him to the Bishop.

– So you find yourself unwell, my child, said the Abbé, seeing him so wan and almost unable to walk; you've worked too hard. The Abbé gave him his arm. Come, sit down on this little sacristan's bench behind me; I'll conceal you. By then they were at the side of the great doors. Calm yourself, we've a good twenty minutes before Monseigneur appears. Try to compose yourself; when he passes by I'll lift you up, for I'm good and strong in spite of my age.

But when the Bishop went by, Julien was trembling so much that Abbé Chas gave up the idea of presenting him.

– Now don't be cast down, he said to him, I'll find another opportunity.

That evening he had ten pounds of candles taken to the seminary chapel – saved, he said, by Julien's exertions, and the speed with which he had extinguished them. Nothing could be less true. The poor boy was himself quite extinguished; he had not had a coherent thought since seeing Mme de Rênal.

CHAPTER 29

The First Promotion

He knew the times he lived in, he knew his department,
and he's rich.   *The Precursor*[1]

Julien had not quite emerged from the deeply pensive state into
which he had been plunged by the events in the cathedral, when one
morning he was summoned by the severe Abbé Pirard.

– Here's M. l'Abbé Chas-Bernard writing in your favour. On
the whole I'm not entirely displeased with your conduct. You're
extremely imprudent and even stupid, without appearing so; however, up until now your heart has been good, even generous; you
have a superior mind. Altogether, I detect in you a spark that should
not be neglected.

After fifteen years of toil I am on the point of leaving this
institution: my offence is to have left the seminarists to their free
judgement, and to have neither protected nor disabled that secret
society of which you've spoken to me in the confessional. Before
departing, I'd like to do something for you; I would have acted two
months ago, for you deserved it, had it not been for that denunciation
based on Amanda Binet's address found in your things. I'm going to
appoint you tutor in the New and Old Testaments.

Thrilled with gratitude, Julien actually had the notion of sinking
to his knees and thanking God; but he gave way instead to a more
natural feeling. He went up to Abbé Pirard and took his hand, which
he carried to his lips.

– What's this? cried the Director angrily; but Julien's eyes spoke
still more persuasively than his deed.

Abbé Pirard looked at him with amazement – the amazement of

a man who, for long years, had been unused to encountering delicate feeling. This tribute undermined the Director; his voice changed.

– Well, well! yes, my child, I've become fond of you. Heaven knows, it's in spite of myself. It's my duty to be just, to have neither hatred nor love for any individual. Your career will be a painful one. I divine something in you which offends the vulgar. Jealousy and calumny will pursue you. In whatever place Providence places you, your colleagues will never be able to see you without hating you; and if they pretend to love you, it will be to betray you more certainly. There's only one remedy for this: have recourse solely to God, who has given you this propensity to be hated as a correction to your presumption; be sure that your conduct is pure; it is the only safeguard I can see for you. If you stick to the truth with unconquerable rigour, sooner or later you will confound your enemies.

It had been so long since Julien had heard a friendly voice – his weakness must be forgiven: he melted into tears. Abbé Pirard opened his arms to him; the moment was a comfort for both of them.

Julien was wild with elation; this promotion was the first he had gained; its advantages were enormous. To conceive of them one must have been condemned to pass whole months without a moment of solitude, in immediate contact with comrades who were at best importunate, and mostly intolerable. Their shouts alone would have been enough to disorder a delicate constitution. The rowdy joy of these well-fed and well-dressed peasants did not know itself to be joy – did not find itself complete – without their shouting it out at the tops of their voices.

Now Julien dined alone, or nearly so, an hour later than the other seminarists. He had a key to the garden, and could stroll there when it was empty.

To his very great surprise, Julien saw that they hated him less; he had expected that, on the contrary, the hate would be redoubled. His private desire not to be talked to, which was too obvious and earned him many enemies, was no longer seen as the sign of a ridiculous hauteur. In the eyes of the gross beings who surrounded him it became a reasonable expression of his dignity. The hatred declined appreciably, above all among the youngest of his comrades who had become his pupils, and whom he treated with much politeness. Gradually they even became his supporters; it was now in poor taste to call him 'Martin Luther'.

But what is the good of specifying his friends, his enemies? The whole scene is ugly, and the truer the picture the uglier it is. Yet, these men are the only teachers of morality the people have, and what would become of the people without them? Will a newspaper ever be able to take the place of the curé?

From the moment of Julien's new dignity, the Director of the seminary was careful never to speak to him except in the presence of witnesses. This course was prudent for the master as well as for the pupil; but it was above all a *test*. The unvarying principle of Pirard, the severe Jansenist, was: Does this man have merit in your eyes? – then put obstacles in the way of everything he desires, and everything he undertakes. If the merit is genuine he will know very well how to overcome, or avoid, the obstacles.

It was the hunting season. Fouqué had the idea of sending a stag and a boar to the seminary on behalf of Julien's family. The dead animals were deposited in the passage between the kitchen and the dining hall. There, they were seen by the seminarists on their way to dinner. They were a great object of curiosity. The boar, stone dead as it was, frightened the younger ones; they stroked his tusks. Nothing else was talked of for a week.

This gift, which put Julien's family in that class of society to which one owes respect, delivered a mortal blow to envy. He possessed a superiority blessed by fortune. Chazel and the most distinguished seminarists made advances to Julien, and almost complained of him that he had not let them know of his family's fortune, and had thus put them at risk of betraying lack of respect for money.

There came a military conscription, from which Julien was exempt on account of being a seminarist. This fact upset him deeply. – There it goes for ever, the moment when twenty years ago a heroic life would have opened for me!

He walked alone in the seminary garden and heard a conversation between two masons working on the containing wall.

– All right then, must be off, it's a fresh draft.

– In that *other's* day,[2] 'twas fine! – a mason ought to be officer, be a general, has bin known.

– Have a look now, then! – Only beggars join up. Anyone that has *a bit* stays home.

– Born poor, stay poor, there you go.

– 'Bout that, is't really true what they say, that t'other one's dead? chipped in a third mason.

– 'Tis the fat ones say that, mark you! – t'other did frighten 'em.

– What changes we've seen, how well work went on in 'is day! And they say the marshals betrayed 'im. There's treachery for you!

This talk consoled Julien somewhat. As he departed he repeated to himself:

The only king whose memory is cherished by the people![3]

Examination time arrived. Julien answered brilliantly; he noticed that Chazel himself was keen to display all his learning.

On the first day the examiners, appointed by the famous Vicar-general de Frilair, were extremely put out by always having to place this Julien Sorel first, or at the very least second, on their list – he who had been pointed out to them as Abbé Pirard's Benjamin.[4] Bets were made in the seminary that Julien would take first place in the general exam table, which carried with it the honour of dining with Monseigneur the Bishop. But at the end of a session in which Julien had been questioned about the Fathers of the Church, a clever examiner, having asked him about St Jerome and his passion for Cicero, went on to speak of Horace and Virgil and other profane authors. Unknown to the others, Julien had learnt a great number of passages from these writers by heart. Carried away by his success he forgot where he was and, at the repeated request of the examiner, passionately recited and paraphrased several of Horace's Odes. Having allowed him to betray himself for twenty minutes, the examiner suddenly changed face and reproached him bitterly for the time he had wasted in these profane studies and the useless or even criminal ideas with which he had filled his head.

– Monsieur, I am a fool, and you are quite right, said Julien humbly, recognizing the clever stratagem of which was the victim.

This examiner's trick was thought dirty, even in the seminary; which didn't prevent M. de Frilair – that capable man who had organized the structure of the Bisontine congregation so sagely, and whose reports to Paris made judges, prefects and even generals of garrisons quake – from putting the number 198 by Julien's name with his powerful hand. He was delighted thus to mortify his enemy, the Jansenist Pirard.

For ten years, his great aim had been to take the directorship of the seminary from Pirard. That priest, himself adhering to the line of conduct he had pointed out to Julien, was sincere, pious, devoted to his duties. But Heaven, in its rage, had given him a bilious temperament which made him feel injuries and hatred keenly. None of the affronts offered him were lost on his fiery nature. He would have resigned a hundred times, but for the conviction that he was useful in the post where Providence had placed him. I hinder the advance of Jesuitry and idolatry, he told himself.

At the time of the examinations it was probably two months since he had spoken to Julien, yet when he received the official letter giving the result of the competition and saw the number 198 put next to the name of the pupil he regarded as the glory of his house, he was ill for a week. For this stern character the only consolation was to concentrate all his means of surveillance on Julien. With delight he found in him neither anger, nor plans for vengeance, nor discouragement.

A few weeks later, Julien was startled to receive a letter; it had a Paris postmark. At last, he said to himself, Mme de Rênal has remembered her promises. A gentleman who signed himself Paul Sorel, and claimed to be his relative, sent him a letter of exchange for 500 francs. In addition, if Julien continued successful in his study of Latin literature, a comparable sum would be sent each year.

It's her, it's her goodness! thought Julien tenderly, she wants to console me; but why not a single word of affection?

He deceived himself about this letter; Mme de Rênal, guided by Mme Derville, was entirely taken up in her profound repentance. Often, in spite of herself, she thought of the strange being her encounter with whom had revolutionized her existence, but she was determined not to write to him.

If we spoke seminary language, we should hail this remittance of 500 francs as a miracle, and say that it was M. de Frilair himself who was heaven's instrument in making Julien the gift.

Twelve years previously, M. l'Abbé de Frilair had arrived in Besançon with the slimmest of portmanteaux, which, according to the legend, contained all he had. Now he found himself one of the richest landowners in the department. In the course of his rise to prosperity he had purchased half of an estate, the other half of which had descended by legacy to M. de La Mole. Hence a great lawsuit between these two figures.

Despite his brilliant existence in Paris and his employments around the Throne, M. le Marquis de La Mole felt it would be dangerous to struggle in Besançon against a vicar-general who had the reputation of making and unmaking prefects. Instead of asking for a present of 50,000 francs, disguised under some name or other that would look feasible in a financial statement, and conceding this squalid lawsuit of 50,000 francs to M. de Frilair, the Marquis became annoyed. He believed himself to be in the right: a brilliant reason!

For, if one may ask: Does there exist a judge who has not a son, or at least a cousin, he would like to see advanced in the great world?

To enlighten even the blindest – a week after the first judgment he obtained, M. l'Abbé de Frilair borrowed the Bishop's coach and himself took the cross of the Legion of Honour to his lawyer. M. de La Mole, somewhat thrown out by the self-possession of his adversaries, and feeling his legal advisers weaken, asked for advice from the Abbé Chélan, who put him in touch with M. Pirard.

At the time of our story these contacts had been going on for several years. The Abbé Pirard brought his passionate nature into the affair. Constantly talking to the Marquis's lawyers, he had studied the cause, and, finding it just, had openly become the Marquis de La Mole's proponent against the all powerful Vicar-general. The latter was outraged at this insolence – and coming, moreover, from a little Jansenist!

– You see what it's like with this Court nobility who pretend to be so powerful! the Abbé Frilair would remark to his circle. M. de La Mole hasn't sent a single cross to his agent in Besançon, and limply lets him be thrown out. Yet, I'm informed by my correspondents, this noble lord doesn't let a week go by without parading his blue riband in the salon of the Keeper of the Seals, whoever it might be.

In spite of all the Abbé Pirard's activity, and though M. de La Mole was always on the best of terms with the Minister of Justice, and above all with his departments, all that he had been able to effect after six years' effort had been to not lose his case completely.

Being in ceaseless correspondence with Abbé Pirard over a concern that both pursued with passion, the Marquis ended up developing a taste for the Abbé's turn of mind. Little by little, despite the immense difference in their social standing, their letters took on the tone of friendship. Abbé Pirard kept the Marquis informed of the movement to force him, through a series of insults, to hand in his resignation. In the rage inspired by the despicable trick, as he called it, used against Julien, he told the Marquis that story.

Although he was very rich, this great lord was not at all a miser. Never once had he been able to get the Abbé Pirard to accept anything, not even reimbursement of the postal costs involved in the lawsuit. He jumped at the idea of sending 500 francs to his favourite pupil.

M. de La Mole went to the trouble of writing the accompanying letter personally. This made him think about the Abbé.

One day the latter received a little note urging him to go without delay to an inn in the suburbs of Besançon on urgent business. There he found M. de La Mole's steward.

– M. le Marquis has ordered me to bring you his barouche, this man informed him. He hopes that after reading this letter it will be convenient to you to leave for Paris four or five days from now. I shall employ the interval you'll be so kind as to specify in a tour of M. le Marquis's estates in Franche-Comté. After which, on the day that suits you, we'll leave for Paris.

The letter was brief:

Disencumber yourself, dear sir, from all the mischievous manoeuvrings of the provinces – come to breathe the tranquil airs of Paris. I send you my carriage, which has orders to await your decision for four days. I myself will stay for you in Paris until Tuesday. I need only a yes from you, monsieur, to accept on your behalf one of the finest livings in the district of Paris. The wealthiest of your future parishioners has never seen you, but is devoted to you more than you could well believe; he is the Marquis de La Mole.

Without ever realizing it, the severe Abbé Pirard loved this seminary full of enemies – and to which he had devoted all his thoughts for fifteen years. For him M. de La Mole's letter was like the arrival of a surgeon's ordered to carry out a painful yet necessary operation. His removal from office was certain. He arranged to meet the steward three days from thence.

For forty-eight hours he was in a fever of uncertainty. Finally he wrote to M. de La Mole, and composed a letter for the Bishop which was a masterpiece in the ecclesiastical style, if a little long. It would have been difficult to find phrases that were more irreproachable and which breathed a more sincere respect; yet at the same time this epistle – calculated to give M. de Frilair a trying time in front of his patron – detailed all the matters for serious complaint, going right down to the minor dirty tricks that, having been endured with resignation for six years, were forcing the Abbé Pirard to leave the diocese. His wood had been stolen from his shed, his dog had been poisoned, etc., etc.

The letter completed, he ordered Julien, who at eight in the evening was asleep like all the other seminarists, to be roused.

– You know where the Bishop is to be found? he said to him in fine classical Latin; take this letter to Monseigneur. I'll not conceal from you that I send you among wolves. Be all ears and eyes. No prevarication in your answers; but reflect that whoever puts the questions will probably feel a real delight in having power to harm you. I am content, my child, to give you this experience before leaving you – for I will not hide that the letter you carry is my resignation.

Julien stood without moving; he loved the Abbé Pirard. Prudence might very well say: when this honest man leaves, the party of the

Sacred Heart will demote me and very likely throw me out. He could not think of himself. What inhibited him was the difficulty of phrasing politely something he wanted to say, but for which he could not really summon the wit.

— Well, my friend! — aren't you going?

— It is only that it is said, monsieur, replied Julien timidly, that during your long period of office, you have not put money away on the side. I have six hundred francs.

Tears prevented him from going on.

— *That also will be noted*, said the former Director of the seminary coldly. Go to the Bishop, it's getting late.

It chanced that M. l'Abbé Frilair was on duty in the Bishop's salon that evening; Monseigneur was dining at the prefecture. So it was to M. de Frilair that Julien delivered the letter, though without knowing who he was.

Julien was amazed to see this priest boldly open a letter addressed to the Bishop. The Vicar-general's handsome face soon expressed surprise mingled with a lively pleasure, and his gravity greatly increased. Julien, who was struck by his good looks, had time to inspect him closely while he read. It was a face that would have had even more gravity had it not been for the excessive subtlety evident in certain features — features that might even have gone so far as to suggest deceit, had the possessor of this fine countenance let them out of control for a moment. The prominent nose kept a perfect straight line and unfortunately gave an otherwise highly distinguished profile an irremediable likeness to the physiognomy of a fox. For the rest, this abbé — seemingly so fascinated by M. Pirard's resignation — was turned out with an elegance which much appealed to Julien, and which he had never before seen in a priest.

Julien did not discover the Abbé de Frilair's special gift until later. He had the knack of amusing his bishop — an affable old man who ought to have lived in Paris and regarded Besançon as a place of exile. This bishop had poor eyesight and was passionately fond of fish. Abbé Frilair picked the bones out of the fish served to Monseigneur.

Julien was watching in silence as the Abbé read the resignation over again, when suddenly the door opened with a crash. A richly clad footman bustled quickly by. Julien had just time to turn towards the door; he saw a little old man wearing a pectoral cross. He bowed very low: the Bishop gave him a friendly smile and passed through. The handsome priest followed him, and Julien was left alone in the salon, free to admire its pious splendour.

The Bishop of Besançon, a man of intellect who had been tried, but not destroyed, by the long-drawn-out miseries of the Emigration,[5] was more than seventy-five years old, and worried himself extraordinarily little about what might happen ten years from now.

— Who was that seminarist with the clever look I believe I saw as I went by? asked the Bishop. Oughtn't they to be in bed at this hour, according to my ruling?

— That one's very much awake, I assure you, Monseigneur — and he brings a great piece of news: the resignation of the sole Jansenist left in your diocese. At last, the frightful Abbé Pirard has taken the hint.

— Well, well! laughed the Bishop, I defy you to replace him with a man as good as him. And to show you his full value, I invite him to dinner tomorrow.

The Vicar-general tried to insinuate a few words on the choice of a successor. The Bishop, little inclined to talk business, replied:

— Before putting another one in, we ought to know something of why this one goes out. Let that seminarist come and see me — there's truth in the mouths of babes.

Julien was called for: I'm going to find myself between two inquisitors, thought he. He had never felt so brave.

As he entered, two large valets even better turned out than M. Valenod himself, were disrobing Monseigneur. The prelate felt he ought to question Julien about his studies before coming to M. Pirard. He conversed a little about dogma, and was much impressed. Soon he turned to the humanities, to Virgil, Horace, Cicero. Those are the names, thought Julien, that have earned me my number 198. I've nothing to lose — if I can, I'll shine. He succeeded: the prelate, himself an excellent scholar, was delighted.

At the prefecture dinner a justly celebrated young woman had

recited the poem 'Mary Magdalene'.[6] The Bishop was in the mood
to talk about literature, and he very quickly forgot Abbé Pirard and
all business matters, while discussing with this seminarist how one
might tell whether Horace had been rich or poor. The prelate cited
many of the Odes, but his memory was sluggish, and immediately
Julien would, with a modest air, recite the whole poem; what particularly struck the Bishop about this was that Julien never departed
from a conversational tone; he would say twenty or thirty Latin lines
as though speaking about what went on in the seminary. They talked
for a long time of Virgil, of Cicero. Eventually the prelate could not
refrain from complimenting the young seminarist.

– It would be impossible to have studied to better effect.

– Monseigneur, replied Julien, your seminary can provide you
with one hundred and ninety-seven persons much less unworthy of
your high approbation.

– How can that be? asked the prelate, astonished at the number.

– I can bring official proof to substantiate what I have the honour
to say before Monseigneur . . . At the seminary's annual examination,
answering on exactly the same the topics as have just now earned me
Monseigneur's praise, I came number One Nine Eight.

– Ah! It's Abbé Pirard's Benjamin, cried the Bishop, chuckling
and looking at M. de Frilair; we should have expected this; but it's
excellent tactics. Would it be true, my friend, that they woke you up
to send you here?

– Yes, Monseigneur. I've only ever been out of the seminary on
one other occasion, to help M. l'Abbé Chas-Bernard decorate the
cathedral on Corpus Christi day.

– *Optime*, said the Bishop. What, so it was you who showed so
much courage in setting the bunches of plumes over the baldaquin?
They make me tremble every year; I'm always afraid they might
cost a man's life. My friend, you will go far; but I wouldn't want to
cut off your career, which will be a brilliant one, by making you die
of hunger.

And at the Bishop's order biscuits and Malaga were served. Julien
did them justice, and the Abbé de Frilair, who knew how his bishop
loved to see jovial and hearty eating, did even more.

The prelate, more and more pleased with the conclusion of his evening, talked for a while about ecclesiastical history. He saw that Julien did not understand. He passed on to the moral climate of the Roman Empire in the age of Constantine. The end of paganism was accompanied by that state of unease and dubiety which now afflicts the melancholy and exhausted minds of the nineteenth century. Monseigneur observed that Julien was ignorant even of Tacitus's name.

Julien frankly replied, to the prelate's amazement, that this author was not to be found in the seminary library.

— I'm really much relieved, said the Bishop gaily. You dispose of an embarrassment: for ten minutes I've been searching for a means of thanking you for the delightful evening you have afforded me, and in so unexpected a manner. I never expected to find a learned doctor in a pupil from my seminary. Although the gift may not be very canonical, I would like to present you with an edition of Tacitus.

The prelate sent for eight volumes in very fine bindings, and insisted that he himself write a Latin compliment to Julien Sorel on the title page of the first. The Bishop prided himself on his fine Latinity — and he ended by saying, in a serious tone which suddenly cut across that of the rest of the conversation:

— Young man, *if you are wise*, you will one day possess the best living in my diocese, and not a hundred leagues from my episcopal palace; but you must *be wise*.

Julien, loaded with his books and in a state of astonishment, left the Bishop as midnight struck.

Monseigneur had not said a word to him about the Abbé Pirard. Julien was amazed above all at the Bishop's extreme courtesy. He had never had any idea of such urbanity of manner, allied to such natural dignity. He was particularly struck by the contrast when he saw the sombre Abbé Pirard again, awaiting him with exasperation.

— *Quid tibi dixerunt?* [What did they say to you?] he called out in a powerful voice the very moment he saw him.

Julien tangled himself up slightly translating the Bishop's discourse into Latin:

— Speak French, and repeat the Bishop's own words, adding

nothing and omitting nothing, said the ex-Director of the seminary, with his harsh tone and deeply inelegant manner.

– What a peculiar gift from a bishop to a young seminarist! said he, flicking through the pages of the magnificent Tacitus, the gilded edges of which seemed to horrify him.

Two o'clock was sounding when, after a complete and detailed account had been delivered, he allowed his favourite pupil to go back to his room.

– Leave me the first volume of your Tacitus, where Monseigneur the Bishop's compliment is, he said to him. That Latin line will be your lightning conductor in this house after my departure . . . *Erit tibi, fili mi, successor meus tanquam leo quaerens quem devoret* [Because for you, my son, my successor will be as a roaring lion seeking whom he may devour].

The following morning Julien found something odd about the way in which his comrades spoke to him. It made him only the more reserved. Here's the effect of M. Pirard's resignation, he thought. It is known all through the place, and I'm thought of as his favourite. There must be something insulting in this behaviour – but he could not make out what it was. On the contrary, there was an absence of hatred in the eyes of every one he encountered while going through the dormitories: What do they mean by this? – it's a trap, no doubt – we'll play close to the chest. Finally the little seminarist from Verrières said to him, laughing: *Cornelii Taciti opera omnia* [The Complete Works of Tacitus].

At this, which had been overheard, all the others competed in paying compliments to Julien, not only on the magnificent gift he had received from Monseigneur, but also on the two hours of conversation with which he had been honoured. Everything was known down to the finest details. From that moment, envy disappeared; people paid abject court to him; Abbé Castanède, who only yesterday had been supremely unpleasant to him, came to take him by the arm and invite him to dine.

By virtue of the fatal composition of Julien's character he had been much pained by the insolence of these gross creatures; their grovelling gave him a feeling of disgust and no pleasure.

Around midday Abbé Pirard left his pupils, but not before treating them to a severe lecture. – Do you aim for worldly honours, he said to them – a crowd of advantages in society, the pleasure of giving orders, the pleasure of mocking the laws and behaving insolently to everybody with impunity? Or do you rather aim for eternal life? The least advanced of you has only to open his eyes to distinguish between these two ways.

Hardly had he left than the devotees of the *Sacred Heart of Jesus* went to intone a *Te Deum* in the chapel. Nobody in the seminary took the former director's lecture seriously. It was said on all sides that he was furious at his dismissal; not a single seminarist had the simple-heartedness to believe in voluntary resignation from a post that allowed so many contacts with the big contractors.

The Abbé Pirard proceeded to establish himself in the finest inn in Besançon; and, under the pretext of some non-existent business, proposed to spend two days there.

The Bishop invited him to dinner; and, to tease his Vicar-general, did his best to make him excel. They were at dessert when there arrived from Paris the astonishing news that the Abbé Pirard had been appointed to the magnificent living of N—, four leagues from the capital. The good prelate offered his sincere congratulations. In the whole of this business he saw a piece of *excellent play* that put him in a good humour and gave him the highest opinion of the Abbé's talents. He presented him with a magnificent Latin testimonial, and forced silence on Abbé Frilair, who was indulging in some remonstrances.

That evening Monseigneur conveyed his admiration to the Marquise de Rubempré. This was tremendous news to Besançon's high society, which became mazed in conjectures about this extraordinary favour. M. Pirard was already seen as a bishop. The most discerning thought that M. de La Mole was now a minister, and from that day on allowed themselves to smile at the imperious airs affected by M. l'Abbé Frilair in society.

On the following morning Abbé Pirard was all but followed around in the streets, and shopkeepers come to their doorsteps as he went to canvass the judges concerned with the Marquis's cause. For the very first time he was politely received. This stern Jansenist – indignant at everything he saw – laboured long with the advocates he had chosen on the Marquis de La Mole's behalf, then left for Paris. He had the weakness to remark to two or three friends from the college who had gone with him as far as the carriage – whose coats of arms they admired – that, having administered the seminary for fifteen years, he left Besançon with savings of 520 francs. These friends embraced him, weeping, and said between themselves: the good Abbé might have spared us that fib, it's too ridiculous.

Vulgar people, blinded by love of money, were simply incapable of understanding that it was through his sincerity that the Abbé Pirard had found the strength to struggle alone for six years against Marie Alacoque, the Sacred Heart of Jesus, the Jesuits and his bishop.

CHAPTER 30

An Ambitious Man

There's only one style of nobility left, and that's the title
of *duke*; marquis is ridiculous – at the word *duke* people
turn their heads.   *Edinburgh Review*[1]

The Marquis de La Mole received Abbé Pirard without any of those
little grand seigneurial ways that are so polite, yet so insolent to
those who understand them. That would have been to lose time, and
the Marquis was too much involved in affairs of state to have time to
spare.

For the past six months he had been intriguing to persuade both
the nation and the King to accept a certain ministry,[2] which, in
recognition of his efforts, would make him a duke.

Year after year the Marquis had vainly demanded a clear and
condensed statement of the progress of his lawsuit in Franche-Comté
from his Besançon lawyers. But how could the famous lawyer explain
things when he did not understand them himself?

The little slip of paper the Abbé handed him explained everything.

– My dear abbé, said the Marquis – having run through all polite
formulas and personal solicitations in less than five minutes – my
dear abbé, in the midst of my apparent prosperity, I lack the time to
deal adequately with two little things that are none the less rather
important: my family and my business concerns. I take care of the
fortunes of my house in a broader context, and I can advance them
considerably; I take care of my pleasures – and that's what should
come first, at least in my eyes, he added, having detected a look of
surprise in those of Abbé Pirard. Although a man of experience, the

Abbé was astonished to find an old man talking so openly of his pleasures.

– Doubtless there is work done in Paris, continued the noble lord, but it's done when perched on the fifth floor – and from the moment I approach a man he takes an apartment on the second, and his wife starts receiving once a week; consequently there's no more work done, nothing but attempts to be, or seem to be, a figure in society. That's their sole concern as soon as they have enough bread to eat.

To be more specific: for my lawsuits, even for each case taken separately I have lawyers killing themselves with work; one of them died on me only the day before yesterday, of chest trouble. But as to my affairs in general, would you believe, monsieur, that for the last three years I have given up any idea of finding a man who would deign to think seriously about what he was doing when writing on my behalf? In any case, all this is only by way of a preface.

I have high regard for you, and, I dare add, though seeing you for the first time, I like you. Would you consent to be my secretary, with a salary of eight thousand francs, or quite likely double that? I'd gain by the arrangement, I assure you; and I'd make it my business to hold your fine living for you for the day when we no longer agree.

The Abbé declined; but towards the end of their conversation the genuine plight in which he saw the Marquis to be suggested an idea to him.

– I've left a poor young man buried in my seminary, who, if I'm not mistaken, will be harshly persecuted. If he was nothing but a simple monk, he'd already be *in pace*.[3]

Up until now this young man knows only Latin and Holy Writ; but it's not impossible that one day he will employ his great talents either in preaching, or in the direction of men's souls. I don't know what he will do; but he has the sacred fire, he could go far. I'd planned to give him to our bishop, if only one had ever come to us who had something of your manner of seeing men and affairs.

– Where does your young man come from? enquired the Marquis.

– He's said to be the son of a carpenter from our mountains, but I rather think he's the natural son of some rich man. I've seen him receive an anonymous, or pseudonymous, letter with a letter of exchange for five hundred francs.

— Ah! It's Julien Sorel, said the Marquis.

— How d'you know his name? asked the Abbé, amazed; and, as he blushed at the question, the Marquis replied:

— That would be telling you.

— Well! said the Abbé, you might try to make him your secretary — he has the energy and the wit; in short, you could try the experiment.

— Why not? said the Marquis; but is he a man who will let his palm be greased by the Prefect of Police, or someone else, to spy in my house? That's my only reservation.

After favourable assurances on this from Abbé Pirard, the Marquis produced a 1,000-franc note:

— Send this travel permit to Julien Sorel; get him to come to me.

— It's easy to tell that you live in Paris, said Abbé Pirard. You don't realize the tyranny that presses on us provincials, and especially on those priests who aren't friends of the Jesuits. They wouldn't let Julien Sorel go, they'd know how to cover it up with the cleverest excuses, they'd reply to me that he's ill, that letters got lost in the post, etc., etc.

— One day soon I'll obtain a letter from the Minister to the Bishop, replied the Marquis.

— I'd forgotten one word of warning, said the Abbé: though he's low born, this young man has a haughty spirit. He will be of no use if his pride is ruffled; you would make him stupid.

— That pleases me, said the Marquis, I'll make him a companion for my son, will that do?

Some time after this Julien received a letter in unknown handwriting, and carrying the Châlons postmark; he found in it an order on a Besançon dealer and instructions to report to Paris without delay. The letter was signed with an assumed name, but on opening it Julien had experienced a thrill: a leaf from a tree fluttered at his feet; it was the sign he had agreed with the Abbé Pirard.

Less than an hour afterwards, he was summoned to the Bishop's Palace, where he found himself welcomed with a truly paternal kindness. Constantly quoting Horace, Monseigneur made him the cleverest compliments on the lofty destiny awaiting him in Paris, compliments which seemed to invite, by way of thanks, some explanation. Julien could say nothing, primarily because he knew nothing, and Monseigneur conceived a great regard for him. One of the Bishop's assistant priests wrote to the Mayor, who hurried along in person to bring a passport that had been already signed, but on which the traveller's name had been left blank.

Before midnight that evening Julien was at Fouqué's house; that sage spirit was more surprised than delighted at the future that seemed to await his friend.

– It'll end up for you, said this liberal voter, with a government job that'll oblige you to do something which will be vilified in the press. I'll hear of you through your disgrace. Remember that even financially speaking it's better to earn a hundred louis in the honest wood trade, where one is one's own master, than to receive four thousand francs from a government – even if it's King Solomon's.

Julien saw nothing in this but the petty-mindedness of a country merchant. At last he was to figure on the stage of great events. The happiness of going to Paris, which he imagined to himself as crammed with clever people, scheming and hypocritical, but polite as the Bishop of Besançon and the Bishop of Agde, eclipsed all else for him. To his friend he professed himself deprived of the freedom to choose by the Abbé Pirard's letter.

Around noon the next day he arrived in Verrières the happiest of men; he counted on seeing Mme de Rênal again. First he went to visit his first patron, the good Abbé Chélan. He met with a severe reception.

– D'you consider yourself to be under any obligation to me? said M. Chélan to him, not responding to his greeting. You'll dine with me and meanwhile another horse will be hired for you, and you'll leave Verrières *without seeing anyone else here*.

– To hear is to obey, replied Julien in the best seminarian manner; and there was no further talk but of theology and fine Latin.

He mounted his horse, rode for a league, then, seeing a wood and no one around to see him enter, slipped in. When the sun set he sent the horse away. Later on he went to see a peasant who agreed to sell him a ladder, and to carry it behind him as far as the little wood overlooking Loyalty Promenade in Verrières.

— It's a poor draft dodger . . . or a smuggler, said the peasant to himself as they parted, but what's that matter! My ladder's well paid for and, myself, it's not as though there aren't bits of my life that have *had their moments*.

The night was very dark. Around one in the morning, Julien entered Verrières carrying his ladder. As soon as he could, he got down into the bed of the stream which crosses M. de Rênal's magnificent gardens at a depth of about ten feet, and is contained between two walls. With his ladder Julien easily climbed over it. What kind of reception will the guard dogs give me? he wondered. That's the whole question. The dogs barked and bounded towards him; but he whistled softly and they greeted him with wagging tails.

Mounting in this way from terrace to terrace, though all the gates were locked, it was easy for him to get right up underneath the window of Mme de Rênal's bedroom – which on the garden side is only nine or ten feet above ground.

On the shutters was a little heart-shaped opening that Julien knew well. To his great chagrin this chink was not lit inside by the glimmering of a nightlight.

Great God! on this very night Mme de Rênal isn't in this room! said he to himself. Where can she be sleeping? The family's in Verrières, for I met the dogs; but here in this room, with no nightlight, I might find M. de Rênal himself – or a stranger – then what an explosion!

The wisest thing to do was to give it up; but Julien had a horror of doing that. – If it's a stranger, I can run like hell, leaving my ladder; but then suppose it's her, what reception can I expect? She has fallen into a state of repentance and high piety, I cannot doubt that; but nevertheless she has some remembrance of me, because just now she's written to me. This argument determined him.

His heart shrinking, yet resolved to see her or die, he threw some pebbles against the shutter; no answer. He leant his ladder by the side of the window and tapped on the shutter himself, softly at first, then harder. Even though it's so dark someone could fire a shot at me, thought Julien. This reflection resolved the wild enterprise into a question of courage.

This room is empty tonight, he thought, or whoever's sleeping there is awake by now. So there's nothing more to be done about that; the only thing is to try not to be heard by people sleeping in the other rooms.

He climbed down, set his ladder against one of the shutters, climbed up again and, passing his hand through the heart-shaped aperture, had the good luck to find quite speedily the latch wire that locked the shutter. He pulled this wire; and it was with tremendous elation that he felt the shutter no longer fast and yielding to his pressure. I must open it little by little and get my voice recognized. He opened the shutter wide enough to let his head in, and said in low tones: *It's a friend.*

Cocking his ear forward he assured himself that there was nothing stirring in the silence of the room. Even so, there was certainly no nightlight, not even a half extinguished one in the fireplace – a very bad sign.

Beware of a pistol shot! He considered for a moment; then he tapped on the glass with one finger; no answer; he tapped louder. Even if I end up breaking the glass, I must go through with this. As he tapped very sharply he felt that in the midst of the extreme dimness within he could see a kind of white shadow crossing the room. Then – no doubt of it – he made out a nebulous shape that seemed to be advancing on him very slowly. All of a sudden he saw a cheek pressed against the window where his eye was.

He jumped, and recoiled a little. But the night was so dark that, even at this distance, he could not make out whether it was Mme de Rênal. He feared a first cry of alarm; he heard the dogs prowling around the foot of his ladder, growling a little. – It's me, he repeated rather more loudly, a friend. No answer; the white shade had vanished. Please open up, I must speak to you, I'm so unhappy! – and he struck the glass as though to break it.

A sharp little click was heard; the window latch yielded; he pushed the crossbar and leapt lightly into the room.

The white phantom retreated; he grabbed its arm; it was a woman.

All his courageous resolutions fled. If it's her, what will she say? What sensations flooded through him when he recognized from a little cry that it was Mme de Rênal!

He enfolded her in his arms; she trembled, and had hardly strength to push him away.

— Wretch! what are you doing?

Her choked voice could scarcely articulate the words. Julien sensed the most genuine indignation.

— After fourteen months of cruel absence, I've come to see you.

— Get out, leave me this instant. Ah! M. Chélan, why did you stop me writing to him? I'd have been able to prevent this outrage. She shoved him back with really extraordinary strength. I repent of my sin; Heaven has deigned to enlighten me, she repeated in a voice broken up with emotion. Get out! fly from here!

— After fourteen months of misery, I won't leave you, certainly not without having talked to you. I wish to know everything you've done. Ah! I've loved you well enough to deserve that confidence . . . I wish to know everything.

In spite of herself, this tone of authority had some power over Mme de Rênal's heart.

Julien, whose passionate embrace held her close, and prevented all her attempts to free herself, relaxed the pressure of his arms. This movement reassured Mme de Rênal a little.

— I'm going to draw the ladder up, he said, so that it won't betray us should some servant come poking round, woken by the noise.

— Ah! get out — instead of that, get out, said she with real fury. What matter men to me? It's God who sees the terrible scene you thrust upon me, and who will punish me for it. You basely abused the feelings I had for you — but which I no longer have. D'you understand that, Monsieur Julien?

He drew the ladder up slowly so as not to make a noise.

— Is your husband in town? he asked, using the intimate form *tu* — not in order to defy her, but carried away by the habit of old.

— Don't speak to me like that, I beg of you, or I'll call my husband. Already I'm only too guilty for not having thrown you out regardless.

I pity you, she added, trying to wound the pride she knew to be so sensitive.

This refusal of intimacy, this manner of roughly breaking a bond so tender, on whose existence he still depended, transformed Julien's passion into a delirium.

– What! can it really be possible you no longer love me! he asked, in those heartfelt tones that are so difficult to hear and not be moved.

She did not answer; for his part, he began to weep bitterly.

He genuinely had no strength left for speech.

So I am completely abandoned by the only being who has ever loved me! What can I live for from now on? From the moment he no longer had to fear the danger of meeting a man all his boldness had deserted him; everything had departed from his heart, save love.

He wept for a long time in silence. He took her hand – she made as if to free it; yet after some almost convulsive efforts she let it rest in his. It was profoundly dark; they found themselves sitting side by side on Mme de Rênal's bed.

What a difference between this and fourteen months ago! reflected Julien; and his tears redoubled. So all human feeling inevitably falls prey to absence!

Embarrassed at his silence, and in a voice choked with tears – I beg you to be kind enough to tell me what's happened to you, he said.

– There's no doubt, replied Mme de Rênal in a hard voice, the tone of which seemed to imply something wry and full of reproach towards Julien, that my straying was known in the town at the time of your departure. There was such rashness in your conduct! Some time afterwards, when I was in despair, the estimable M. Chélan came to visit me. For a long time he tried to have me confess, uselessly. One day he had the idea of taking me to the church in Dijon where I'd made my first communion. There, he was courageous enough to speak first . . . Mme de Rênal was interrupted by her tears. What a moment of shame! I confessed everything. This worthy man was so good as not to overwhelm me with the weight of his reproaches: instead, he suffered in sympathy with me. About that time I wrote you some letters I dared not send; I carefully hid them, and when I was too overcome by unhappiness I shut myself up in my room and re-read my own letters.

Finally M. Chélan persuaded me to give him them ... Some, written a little more sensibly than the rest, had been sent to you; you didn't reply to me at all.

— Never, I swear to you, never did I get a letter from you in the seminary.

— Great God, who could have intercepted them?

— Imagine my unhappiness – until the day I saw you in the cathedral, I didn't even know whether you were still alive or not.

— God gave me the grace to realize how I'd sinned against Him, against my children, against my husband, went on Mme de Rênal. He's never loved me as I thought then that you loved me ...

Julien threw himself into her arms – really with no aim, but not in control of himself. But Mme de Rênal pushed him back, and resumed with considerable firmness:

— My estimable friend M. Chélan enabled me to see that in marrying M. de Rênal I had pledged all my affections to him, even those I wasn't yet conscious of, and had never felt before a certain terrible affair ... After the great sacrifice of those letters, that were so dear to me, my life has continued with some tranquillity, if not exactly happily. Don't disturb it; be a friend to me ... the best of friends. Julien covered her hands with kisses; she learned from this that he was still weeping. Don't cry any more, you're giving me such pain ... Tell me in your turn what you have done. Julien was unable to speak. I want to know what your life was like in the seminary, she went on – then you must go.

Without thinking much of what he was saying, Julien spoke of the innumerable intrigues and jealousies he had encountered at first, then of his more peaceful life after he had been made a tutor.

It was just then, he added, that after a long silence on your part, which undoubtedly was meant to make me understand what I see only too well today, that you love me no longer, and that I've become an object of indifference to you ... Mme de Rênal squeezed his hands ... It was just then that you had the sum of five hundred francs sent to me.

– Never, said Mme de Rênal.

– It was a letter stamped in Paris and signed Paul Sorel, to divert any suspicions.

There arose a little discussion as to the possible origins of this letter. The moral atmosphere changed. Without knowing it, Mme de Rênal and Julien abandoned their tragic tone; they reverted to that of loving friends. In such thick darkness they could not see one another, but the tones of their voices betrayed everything. Julien put his arm round his lover's waist; the movement was highly dangerous. She tried to escape his arm whilst he, rather adroitly, diverted her attention at that very moment to an interesting part of his narrative. The arm was forgotten, and stayed in position.

After many conjectures about the origin of the letter enclosing 500 francs, Julien had taken up his story; while speaking of his life in the past – which interested him so little compared to what was happening at that moment – he developed rather more self-control. His attention was concentrated entirely on how this visit was going to end. Then you must leave, a dry voice kept on repeating to him at intervals.

What disgrace for me if I'm shown out of here! he said to himself, it will be a shame which will poison my whole life, and she would never write to me. God knows when I'll come back to this part of the country. From that moment, all disposition of grace vanished from his heart. Sitting next to the woman he adored, almost clasping her in his arms in profound darkness in this room in which he had been so happy, knowing that she had been crying for some time now, and feeling her sobs from the movement of her breast, he had the misfortune to become a cold schemer, almost as cold as when in the seminary courtyard he had found himself the butt of some aggressive pleasantry from one of his comrades who was tougher than him. Julien protracted his tale, speaking of the wretched life he had led since leaving Verrières. So – said Mme de Rênal to herself – after a year's absence, deprived almost entirely of tokens of remembrance, while I myself forgot him, he was thinking only of the happy days he found at Vergy. Her sobs redoubled. Julien marked the success of his story. He saw that he should try his tactic of last resort: he moved abruptly to the letter he had received from Paris.

— I've taken leave of Monseigneur the Bishop.

— What, you're not returning to Besançon? You're leaving us for ever?

— Yes, replied Julien in a decided manner; yes, I abandon the land where I am forgotten even by the person I loved most in my life, and I abandon it never to see it again. I go to Paris . . .

— You're going to Paris! Mme de Rênal cried out quite loud.

Her voice was almost muffled by tears, and showed the extremity of her distress. Julien needed this encouragement: he was about to try something that might turn everything against him; and prior to this exclamation, being unable to see, he had absolutely no knowledge of the effect he was producing. He hesitated no longer; fear of future shame gave him complete control of himself; he added as he rose:

— Yes, madame, I leave you forever, be happy; farewell.

He went a few steps to the window; he was already opening it. Mme de Rênal dashed towards him and threw herself into his arms.

Thus, after three hours of talking, Julien obtained what he had desired so passionately for the first two. If it had come just a little earlier, this return to tender feelings, this eclipse of Mme de Rênal's remorse, would have issued in divine happiness; brought about as it was by manoeuvre, it was no more than a pleasure. Julien absolutely insisted, against his lover's wishes, on lighting the nightlight.

— D'you wish, he asked her, that I be denied the memory of the sight of you? — That the love that is surely in those charming eyes be lost to me? — The whiteness of this pretty hand invisible? Remember, I have to part from you for what may be a long time!

Mme de Rênal had nothing to oppose in this argument — it made her melt   But dawn had begun to sketch in the distinct outli   rees on the mountain east of Verrières. Instead
⸱   rt, Julien, intoxicated with pleasure, suggested
                ⸱ spend the whole day hidden in her room
                      ⸱owing night.

                            ⸱lied. This fatal relapse robs me of all
                            ⸱ne wretched for ever — and she pressed
                            ⸱ is no longer the same; he has his
                            ⸱ed him throughout this business,

and he is behaving very resentfully toward me. If he hears the least noise I'm lost, he'll throw me out like the miserable sinner I am.

— Ah! there's one of M. Chélan's phrases, said Julien; you didn't speak like that before my cruel departure for the seminary; you loved me then!

Julien was rewarded for the self-possession that produced this remark: he saw his lover swiftly forget the risk that the presence of her husband made her run in thinking of the much greater risk of seeing him doubt her love. Day broke rapidly and flooded the room with light; Julien found all the voluptuous pleasures of satisfied pride once more, now being able to see this charming woman in his arms, and almost at his feet — the only one he had loved, and who a few hours previously had been completely dominated by the fear of a terrible God and devotion to her duty. Resolutions that had been fortified by a year of constancy had not been able to resist his valour.

Soon a noise was heard within the house; something she had not thought of struck Mme de Rênal.

— That spiteful Élisa will be coming to the room, what shall we do with that enormous ladder? she asked her lover; where to hide it? Suddenly she cried out with a kind of playfulness — I'll take it to the attic.

— But you have to go through the manservant's room, said Julien, astonished.

— I'll leave the ladder in the corridor, then I'll call the servant and send him on an errand.

— Think of something to say in case the servant passes the ladder in the corridor and notices it.

— Yes, my angel, said Mme de Rênal, giving him a kiss. And you, think of hiding quick under the bed if Élisa comes in while I'm away.

Julien was astounded at this sudden gaiety. So, he thought, the approach of real danger, far from troubling her, gives her back her gaiety because she has forgotten her remorse! What a truly superior woman! Ah! this is a heart in which it is glorious to reign! He was delighted.

Mme de Rênal took the ladder; it was obviously too heavy for her. Julien went to help her; he was admiring her elegant figure, far indeed from suggesting strength, when all at once, without help, she took up the ladder and lifted it as if it had been a chair. She carried it rapidly to the corridor of the third floor, where she rested it along the wall. She summoned the manservant, and, to allow him time to dress, climbed up into the dovecot. On her return to the corridor five minutes later, the ladder was nowhere to be seen. What had become of it? If Julien had been away from the house this danger would not have worried her at all. But, at this moment – should her husband see the ladder! – the situation was potentially disastrous. Mme de Rênal ran about everywhere. At last she discovered the ladder under the roof, where the servant had carried it, and at the same time concealed it. This circumstance was very strange, and at any other time would have alarmed her.

But what does it matter, thought she, what does it matter what may happen in twenty-four hours, when Julien will have gone? – won't everything then be horror and shame for me?

She had a vague idea that it was her duty to quit this life – but what did it matter! After a separation she had believed to be eternal he had returned, she had seen him again, and what he had endured to come to her showed so much love!

In telling Julien about what had happened with the ladder:

– What should I say to my husband, she asked him, if the servant tells him that he found the ladder? She thought for a moment; it will take them twenty-four hours to discover the peasant who sold it to you – and, throwing herself into Julien's arms, hugging him convulsively – Ah! to die, to die like this! she cried, covering him with kisses; but you mustn't die of hunger, she added laughing.

Come; first of all I'll hide you in Mme Derville's room, which is always kept locked. She stationed herself as a look-out at the end of the corridor, and Julien flitted by. Be sure not to open if someone knocks, she adjured him, turning the key; in any case, it'll only be the children amusing themselves playing together.

– Make them come into the garden, under the window, said Julien, so that I can have the pleasure of seeing them – make them talk.

– Yes, yes, cried Mme de Rênal, running out.

Soon she returned with some oranges and biscuits, and a bottle of Malaga wine; it had been impossible to steal any bread.

– What's your husband doing now? asked Julien.

– He's writing out schedules for bargains with the peasants.

But eight o'clock had now struck and the house had become full of bustle. If Mme de Rênal was not visible they would search for her everywhere; she had to leave him. Soon she came back, defying prudence, bringing him a cup of coffee; she was worried that he might die of hunger. After breakfast she succeeded in bringing the children under the window of Mme Derville's room. He found them much grown, but they had acquired a common air, or maybe his perceptions had changed.

Mme de Rênal talked to them of Julien. The older one spoke warmly and with regret for their old tutor; but it seemed that the young ones had almost forgotten him.

M. de Rênal did not go out that morning; he was ceaselessly up and down stairs in the house, busy making deals with some peasants to whom he was selling his crop of potatoes. Until lunchtime Mme de Rênal could not find a moment to devote to her prisoner. When lunch was announced and served she had the idea of stealing a plate of hot soup for him. As she noiselessly approached the door of the room he occupied, carefully carrying the plate, she found herself face to face with the servant who had hidden the ladder that morning. At that moment he was advancing down the corridor, also noiselessly, and as though listening. Probably Julien had carelessly been walking about. The servant made off, rather shamefaced. Mme de Rênal entered Julien's room boldly; this encounter had made him anxious.

– You're afraid, said she to him; for myself I can face any danger in the world without blinking. I fear only one thing, and that's the moment when I'll be alone after you've gone; and she ran out of the room.

– Ah! said Julien, inspired, remorse is the only threat that can daunt this sublime spirit!

At last it was evening. M. de Rênal went to the casino. His wife, having announced the onset of a frightful migraine, retired to her own quarters, speedily sent Élisa away and then got up quickly to open to Julien.

He felt that he really was dying of hunger. Mme de Rênal went down to the pantry to look for bread. Julien heard a loud cry. Mme de Rênal returned and told him that, having gone into the pantry without a light, approaching a sideboard where the bread was piled up and extending her hand, she had touched a woman's arm. It was Élisa who had let out the cry Julien had heard.

– What was she doing there?

– Stealing a few sweets, or maybe spying on us, said Mme de Rênal with total indifference. But luckily I found a pâté and a large loaf.

– What've you got there then? asked Julien, pointing to her apron pockets.

Mme de Rênal had forgotten that since lunchtime these had been full of bread.

Julien clasped her in his arms with intense passion; never had she seemed so beautiful to him. Even in Paris, he told himself confusedly, I shall never meet a greater soul. She had all the awkwardness of a woman unused to attentions of this sort, and at the same time the genuine courage of a person who fears only perils of a different order, perils terrible in quite other ways.

Just as Julien was hungrily eating his supper and his lover teasing him on the simplicity of his meal – for she had a horror of speaking seriously – the door was all of a sudden rattled violently. It was M. de Rênal.

– Why have you shut yourself in? he cried.

Julien had only just time to slide under the sofa.

– What? you're fully dressed, said M. de Rênal coming in, you're eating supper and have locked the door!

On an ordinary day this questioning, phrased with characteristic conjugal abruptness, would have upset Mme de Rênal; but she saw that her husband had only to lower his head a little to see Julien – for he had thrown himself into the chair opposite the sofa where Julien had been sitting only a moment before.

The migraine served as an excuse for everything. While her husband went on to recount at length the details of a pool he had won in the billiard room of the casino – a pool of nineteen francs, by God! he added – she caught sight of Julien's hat on a chair three paces in front of them. Her coolness became the greater. She started to undress herself and at a certain moment, passing swiftly behind her husband, threw a dress over the chair with the hat.

At last M. de Rênal went away. She asked Julien to continue with his account of his life at the seminary – yesterday I couldn't listen to you, all the time you were talking I was preoccupied with how to brace myself to send you away.

She was carelessness personified. They talked very loud; and it might have been two in the morning when they were interrupted by a violent knock on the door. It was M. de Rênal again.

– Quickly! – open to me, there are burglars in the house! said he – Saint-Jean found their ladder this morning.

– This is the end of it all, cried Mme de Rênal, throwing herself into Julien's arms. He's going to kill us both, he doesn't believe in any burglars; I'm going to die in your arms, far happier in my death than ever I was in life. She responded not at all to her husband, who was becoming furious, and hugged Julien passionately to her.

– You must save Stanislas's mother! said he with a look of command. I shall jump into the courtyard from the closet window and escape through the garden – the dogs'll know me. As soon as you're able, bundle up my clothes and throw them into the garden. Meanwhile, let them break the door down. Above all, no confessions, I forbid it – it's much better that he has suspicions, not certainties.

– You'll kill yourself jumping! was her sole reply, and her sole concern.

She went to the closet window with him; then she had time to hide his clothes. At last she opened to her husband, who was boiling with rage. He looked round the room and round the closet without saying a word, then disappeared. Julien's clothes were thrown to him, he grabbed them and ran swiftly to the bottom of the garden on the banks of the Doubs. As he ran he heard a bullet whistle past, and immediately the crack of a gun.

That isn't M. de Rênal, he thought, he's too poor a shot for that. The dogs were running silently at his side, and a second shot must have shattered the leg of one of them since he started to cry piteously. Julien leapt the wall of a terrace, made about fifty feet under cover, and started to fly in another direction. He heard voices shouting to each other, and distinctly saw the servant who was his enemy letting off a shot; a farmer arrived to fire from the other side of the garden as well, but by that time Julien had reached the Doubs, where he put on his clothes.

An hour later he was a league from Verrières, on the road to Geneva; if they're suspicious, thought Julien, it's on the Paris road they'll search for me.

END OF THE FIRST VOLUME

BOOK TWO

She's not pretty, she's not wearing rouge.

SAINTE-BEUVE[1]

BOOK TWO

CHAPTER THE FIRST

The Pleasures of the Countryside

O rus quando ego te adspiciam!

VIRGIL[1]

— Monsieur is no doubt waiting for the mail coach to Paris? said the host of an inn where he had stopped to have breakfast.

— Either today's or tomorrow's, it doesn't matter much to me, said Julien.

The mail coach arrived while he was pretending indifference. There were two free places.

— What! it's you, my poor Falcoz, cried a passenger who was arriving from the Genevan side to the man mounting the coach at the same time as Julien.

— I thought you'd settled down near Lyon, replied Falcoz — in a beautiful valley by the Rhône.

— Settled down nicely. I'm running away.

— What! you — running away? you, Saint-Giraud, with your judicious air! — you've committed some crime? said Falcoz, laughing.

— My God, I might as well have. I'm running away from the frightful life one leads in the provinces. As you know, I love the freshness of the woods and the calm of the meadows; you've often accused me of being romantic. All my life I've never wanted to hear about politics, but politics is driving me away.

— But what party are you?

— None — and that's what's done for me. Here's my political creed: I love music and painting; a good book is a significant happening for me; I'm going to be forty-four years old. How long do I have to live? Fifteen, twenty, thirty years more or less? All right! I hold that

243

in thirty years' time ministers will be a little more skilled, but exactly as honest as they are today. I use the history of England as a mirror for our future. You'll always find a king who wants to extend his prerogative; always find rich provincials who are kept awake at night by ambitions to be a deputy, and by the glory and those hundreds of thousands of francs that Mirabeau got for himself:[2] they call it being liberal and loving the people. You'll always find the Ultras fired up by the desire to be a peer or a Gentleman of the Chamber. Everybody wants to busy themselves steering the ship of state, because it's so well paid. So will there never be a little bit of space for a simple passenger?

— Well, well, it ought to be a very comfortable one for a peaceful character like yours. Was it these last elections that forced you out of your province?

— My trouble harks further back.[3] Four years ago I was forty, and I had five hundred thousand francs; today I'm four years older and probably fifty thousand francs poorer — I'm about to lose that in the sale of my château at Montfleury, a wonderful site.

In Paris I was fed up with that perpetual posturing that's forced on one by what you call nineteenth-century civilization. I yearned for benevolence and simplicity. I bought some land in the mountains near the Rhône — and you know earth hasn't anything to show more fair.

For the first six months the local curé and the minor gentry paid court to me; I gave a dinner for them. — I have left Paris, I said to them, in order to have neither to talk about nor hear about politics. As you know, I subscribe to no journals. The fewer letters the postman brings me, the better I like it.

This wasn't to the curé's taste; soon I'm the object of a thousand importunate demands, schemes, etc. I wanted to give two or three hundred francs a year to the poor, and so demands come in for donations to religious associations: those of St Joseph, the Virgin, etc. — I refuse — so hundreds of insults follow. I'm stupid enough to be angry. I can no longer go out in the morning to enjoy the beauty of our mountains without finding some tiresome circumstance to distract me from my dreams and give me a disagreeable reminder of mankind and its malice. At the Rogationtide processions, for example

– whose chant pleases me (it's probably an ancient Greek melody) – they won't bless my fields because the curé said they belong to an infidel. A pious old peasant woman's cow dies, she says it's because it has been near a pond that belongs to the unbelieving me, a free thinker from Paris – and a week later I find all my fish belly upwards, poisoned with lime. Deceit surrounds me in every shape. The Justice of the Peace, a decent fellow but afraid for his job, finds against me every time. Rural peace is hell for me. Once it's clear that I've been abandoned by the curé, the head of the Congregation in the village, and am not supported by the retired captain, head of the liberals, everyone falls on me, down to the mason I've kept in work for a year, down to the wheelwright who tried to get away with cheating me when he fixed my ploughs.

So as to get a foothold to win at least some of my lawsuits, I make myself into a liberal; but, as you just said, these diabolical elections came along, and my vote was asked for . . .

– For some unknown?

– Not at all, for a man I knew only too well. I refused – a terribly rash thing to do! – and from that moment, with the liberals on my back as well, my position became intolerable. I think that if it had entered the curé's head to accuse me of having murdered my servant, there would have been twenty witnesses from both of the parties who would have sworn that they had seen the crime.

– You wanted to live in the country without catering to the passions of your neighbours, without even listening to their chatter. What a mistake . . .

– Well, it's made up for at last. Montfleury is for sale, I'll lose fifty thousand francs if I have to, but I'm overjoyed, I'm leaving that hell of hypocrisy and scheming. Now I'm looking for solitude and rural tranquillity in the only place they exist in France, on the fourth floor overlooking the Champs-Élysées. And I'm still trying to make up my mind whether to begin my political career by supplying the bread to be blessed in the parish of Roule.[4]

– None of this would have happened to you under Bonaparte, said Falcoz, his eyes glinting with indignation and regret.

– Well, yes, maybe, but why didn't he know how to stay put,

your Bonaparte? — all that I'm suffering today, it's him who caused it.

Here Julien's attention redoubled. He had realized from the first that this Bonapartist Falcoz was the old childhood friend who had been repudiated by M. de Rênal in 1816, and that the philosophic Saint-Giraud must be the brother of that chief secretary to the prefecture of — who knew how to have municipal property let to him on such advantageous terms.

— And all of it, it's your Bonaparte's work, continued Saint-Giraud. An honest fellow, inoffensive as can be, forty years old and in possession of half a million francs, cannot set himself up in peace in the provinces; Bonaparte's nobles and priests chase him away.

— Ah! don't speak ill of him, cried Falcoz, France's prestige among the nations has never been pitched so high as during the thirteen years of his reign. And there was a grandeur then in everything one did.

— Your emperor, devil take him, replied the man of forty-four, was great only on the battlefield, and when he reconstituted the finances around 1802. What can one say about his behaviour after that? With his chamberlains, his pomp and his receptions at the Tuileries, he created a new version of all the idiocies of the monarchy. It was a revised version, and it might have served for a century or two. The nobles and the priests have reverted to the old style, but they haven't the fist of iron needed to sell it to the public.

— Listen to the ex-printer's style!

— Who was it hounded me from my land? continued the printer angrily. The priests that Napoleon recalled by his Concordat — instead of treating them like doctors or lawyers or astronomers, and seeing them just as citizens without bothering about how they earned their living. And where would those insolent gentry be today if Bonaparte hadn't made them barons and counts? No, the fashion for such things had gone. Next to the priests it was those petty country nobility who riled me so much, and forced me to become a liberal.

This conversation was endless; its subject will preoccupy France for another half century. Since Saint-Giraud kept on saying that it was impossible to live in the provinces, Julien modestly proposed the example of M. de Rênal.

– Good Lord, young man, you're a fine one! cried Falcoz; he's become the hammer to avoid being the anvil – and a terrible hammer at that. But I see him being outflanked by Valenod. D'you know that scoundrel? He's the real thing. What'll your M. de Rênal say when he sees himself thrown out one of these fine days and Valenod put in his place?

– He'll be left face to face with his own crimes, said Saint-Giraud. So you know Verrières, do you, young man? Very well! Bonaparte, Heaven confound him, made possible the reign of Rênal and Chélan, which now ushers in the reign of Valenod and Maslon.

This conversation about dismal political intrigues dismayed Julien, and distracted him from his deep dreams of pleasure.

He was not particularly conscious of his first sight of Paris, glimpsed in the distance. The construction of castles in Spain woven round his future struggled with the still vivid memories of the twenty-four hours he had just spent in Verrières. He swore to himself never to abandon his lover's children, and to drop everything to go to their rescue if the high handedness of the clergy precipitated a republic and the persecution of the nobility.

What would have happened on the night of his arrival at Verrières if, when he had propped his ladder against Mme de Rênal's bedroom window, he had found the place occupied by a stranger, or by M. de Rênal?

But also what bliss, the first two hours, when his mistress really did want to send him away, and when he pleaded his cause seated beside her in the darkness! A soul like Julien's is pursued by such memories throughout life. The rest of their interview was already becoming confused with the first epoch of their love fourteen months before.

Julien was awoken from his profound reverie by the coach coming to a stop. They had just entered the courtyard of the post office in rue J. J. Rousseau. – I wish to go to Malmaison,⁵ said he to a cab which drew up.

– At this time of day, monsieur, to do what?

– What's that to you! Drive on.

All true passion has an end only in itself. That is why passions are so absurd in Paris, it seems to me, where one's neighbour is always insisting that one thinks so much about him. I refrain from writing of Julien's transports of feeling at Malmaison. He wept. — What! In spite of those hideous white walls built this year, cutting the park into bits? — Yes, monsieur; since, for Julien, as for posterity, there is nothing dividing Arcoli, St Helena and Malmaison.

That evening Julien hesitated a good deal before venturing in to a playhouse; he had curious ideas about these places of perdition.

His deep-rooted mistrustfulness inhibited him from admiring the Paris living around him; he was moved only by the monuments left by his hero.

So here I am at the centre of intrigue and hypocrisy! Here reign the patrons of the Abbé Frilair.

On the evening of the third day, curiosity defeated his plan of getting to see everything before presenting himself to the Abbé Pirard. This priest coldly explained to him the kind of life that awaited him in M. de La Mole's household.

— If at the end of a few months you are not found to be useful, you will go back to the seminary, but by the front door. You're going to lodge with the Marquis, who is one of the greatest noblemen in France. You'll wear a black suit, but like someone in mourning, not an ecclesiastic. I insist that, three times a week you go to pursue your theological studies at a seminary to which I'll introduce you. Every day at noon you'll settle down in the Marquis's library. He expects to employ you in preparing letters for his lawsuits and other business. He'll jot a couple of words in the margin to indicate the kind of response to be made to every letter he receives. I've undertaken that by the end of three months you'll be competent to compose the answers, so that out of a dozen you present for the Marquis's signature he will be able to sign eight or nine. At eight o'clock each evening you'll tidy the office up, and at ten you'll be free.

It's possible, Abbé Pirard continued, that some old lady or soft-spoken man will dangle great advantages in front of you, or even shamelessly offer you gold, to get a look at the letters the Marquis receives . . .

— Ah! Monsieur! cried Julien, flushing.

– It's odd, said the Abbé, with a bitter smile, that, poor as you are, and after a year in the seminary, you're still capable of righteous indignation. You must really have been blind!

Could it be the workings of his blood? said the Abbé softly, as if talking to himself. What's strange, he added, looking at Julien, is that the Marquis knows you . . . I don't know how. He'll give you a salary of a hundred louis to start with. He's a man who acts solely on impulse, that's his failing; he'll compete with you in childishness. If he's satisfied, your salary could rise eventually to eight thousand francs.

But you must be fully aware, resumed the Abbé in a sharp voice, that he's not going to give you all that money for your pretty face. You've got to be useful. If I were you, I'd talk very little and, above all, never talk about what you don't understand.

Oh! said the Abbé, and I've obtained some information for you; I'd forgotten M. de La Mole's family. He has two children, a daughter and a son of nineteen, the height of elegance, and a kind of madman who doesn't know at noon what he'll do at two. He has wit and some courage; he fought in Spain. The Marquis hopes, goodness knows why, that you'll make friends with this young Comte Norbert. I've said that you're a great Latinist – perhaps he counts on your teaching his son some readymade phrases about Cicero and Virgil.

In your place I'd never allow myself to be chaffed by this exquisite young man; and, before you respond to his advances – no doubt they'll be perfectly polite, if a little spoilt by irony – I'd make him repeat them more than once.

I won't conceal from you that this young Comte de La Mole is sure to despise you at first, for you're nothing but a petit bourgeois. He's descended from a courtier who had the honour to have his head struck off in the Place de Grève on 26 April 1574 for a political intrigue. You – you're the son of a carpenter from Verrières, and furthermore paid wages by his father. Ponder the difference and study the history of this family in Moreri;[6] all the flatterers who dine at their house make what they call delicate allusions to it from time to time.

Take care how you respond to the pleasantries of M. le Comte

Norbert de La Mole, major of Hussars and future peer of France, and don't come running to me for sympathy in the future.

— It seems to me, said Julien, flushing deeply, that I ought not even to talk to a person who scorns me.

— You've no notion of that kind of scorn; it'll show itself only in exaggerated compliments. If you're a fool, you'll let yourself believe them; if you wish to make your fortune you ought to let yourself believe them.

— The day that all this ceases to appeal to me, said Julien, will I be thought ungrateful if I return to my little room, number 103?

— Doubtless all the family toadies will slander you, but then I'll appear on your behalf myself. *Adsum qui feci*.[7] I'll say your decision was prompted by me.

Julien was distressed by the sharp, almost malicious, tone he felt in M. Pirard's speech; it spoilt this last remark entirely.

The truth was that the Abbé had erected conscientious scruples about loving Julien, and that it gave him a kind of religious dread to involve himself in the fate of another person.

— You'll also encounter, he added — with the same ill grace, and as though performing a painful duty — you'll encounter Madame la Marquise de La Mole. She's a large, fair-haired woman, pious, lofty, perfectly polite, and still more perfectly undistinguished. She's the daughter of the old Duc de Chaulnes, notorious for his aristocratic prejudices. This great lady is a sort of abstract, in high relief, of the fundamental characteristics of women of her rank. She won't conceal — not she — that to have ancestors who went on a Crusade is the sole quality she admires. Money comes only a long way after that. That surprises you? We're no longer in the provinces, my friend.

In her salon you will meet plenty of great nobles who will talk about our princes in oddly frivolous tones. As to Madame de La Mole, she respectfully lowers her voice when she mentions a prince or, above all, a princess. I don't advise you to speak of Philip II or Henry VIII as monsters in front of her. They were *kings*, and that gives them inalienable rights to the respect of all, and above all to that of those of no birth, like you and me. However, added M. Pirard, we're priests — for she'll take you for one — and under this appellation she considers us as lackeys essential to her salvation.

— Monsieur, said Julien, it seems to me that I shan't be in Paris long.

— Well, we'll see; but understand that for a man of our cloth there's no road to fortune except through the high nobility. And because of that — at least, to me — inexplicable quality you have in your make-up, if you aren't a success you'll be persecuted; there's no middle way for you. Make no mistake. People see that it gives you no pleasure when they address you; in a social nation like this one you're bound to suffer if you don't command respect.

What would have become of you at Besançon without this whim of M. de La Mole? One day you'll realize the extent of the extraordinary nature of what he's done for you and, if you aren't a monster, you'll feel an eternal gratitude to him and his family. How many poor clerics, more learned than you, have lived for years in Paris with their fifteen sous for mass and their ten sous for making an argument at the Sorbonne! ... D'you remember what I told you last winter of the first years of that rogue Cardinal Dubois?[8] Does your pride lead you, by any chance, to imagine that you're more talented than he was?

I myself, for example, a peaceable and middling kind of fellow, I counted on spending my last years in my seminary; I'd been childish enough to become attached to it. Very well! I was about to be thrown out when I handed in my resignation. D'you know how big my fortune was? I had five hundred and twenty francs in capital, neither more nor less; not a friend, and hardly two or three acquaintances. M. de La Mole, whom I'd never seen, whisked me out of this nasty spot; he had only to say a word and they gave me a living where all the parishioners are well-to-do, above the coarser vices, and where the emolument shames me, it's so little proportionate to the work I do. — I only lecture you so long like this to get a little ballast into that head of yours.

A final word: I have the misfortune to be short-tempered; it's possible that you and I will cease to be on speaking terms.

If the Marquise's haughtiness or her son's tiresome pleasantries should really make the household intolerable to you, I advise you to go and complete your studies in some seminary thirty leagues from Paris, and preferably in the north rather than the south. There's more of civilization in the north, and less injustice; and, he added, lowering his voice, I must confess, the neighbourhood of the Paris press frightens petty tyrants.

If we continue to find pleasure in one another's company, and the Marquis's household still doesn't suit you, I offer you a place as my assistant vicar, and I'll go halves with you in what the living yields. I owe you that, and more – he added, interrupting Julien's thanks – for the extraordinary offer you made me at Besançon. If, instead of my five hundred and twenty francs I'd possessed nothing, you would have saved me.

The Abbé's voice had lost its biting tone. To his great shame, Julien felt tears coming to his eyes; he was dying to throw himself into the arms of his friend; he couldn't stop himself saying, in the most manly tones he could manage:

– I've been hated by my father from the cradle; that's one of my great misfortunes; but I'll no longer complain of my luck, for I've found another father in you, monsieur.

– Very well, very well, said the Abbé embarrassedly; then, finding a formulation most appropriate to the director of a seminary – you must never say luck, always say Providence.

The fiacre pulled up; the coachman lifted the bronze knocker on an immense door: it was the Hôtel de La Mole; and these words were to be read in black marble above the door so that passers-by could be in no doubt.

This display displeased Julien. They were so scared of Jacobins! They imagined Robespierre and his tumbrils behind every hedge – so much so that they were often absurd – and then they advertised their house so that if there was an uprising the mob would recognize it and pillage it. He communicated this thought to the Abbé Pirard.

– Ah! poor child, you'll soon be my assistant. What a dreadful idea to come to you!

– I find nothing more obvious, said Julien.

The gravity of the porter and above all the cleanliness of the courtyard struck him with wonder. It was a fine sunny day.

– What magnificent architecture! he remarked to his companion.

He was appreciating one of those very flat-fronted mansions on the Faubourg Saint-Germain, built about the time of the death of Voltaire. Never have fashion and beauty been so far removed from one another.

CHAPTER 2

Entry into the World

An absurd and touching memory: the first salon in which
one appeared on one's own at the age of eighteen! – the
very glance of a woman was sufficient to frighten me. The
more I tried to please, the more awkward I became. I
conceived all the most mistaken ideas; either I let down my
guard for no reason, or I thought a man an enemy simply
because he looked at me seriously. But even then, in the
depths of terrible shyness, how very fine a fine day was!

KANT[1]

Julien stood overwhelmed in the middle of the courtyard.

– Do try to look like a reasonable being, said Abbé Pirard; you
have those grisly notions, and then you behave just like a child!
Where's Horace's *nil mirari* (no enthusiasm)?[2] Remember that the
nation of lackeys you see living here will want to make fun of you;
they'll view you as an equal, unjustly set over them. Beneath their
friendly manners, their good advice, the wish to set you right, they'll
want to lead you into some gross blunder.

– I defy them to, said Julien, biting his lip, and with all his distrust
flooding back.

The salons on the first floor that these gentlemen passed through
before reaching the Marquis's study would seem to you, dear reader,
as depressing as they were magnificent. Should someone make you
a present of them as they stand, you would refuse to live there; they
are the natural home of yawns and tedious disquisitions. They
redoubled Julien's enchantment. How, thought he, could anyone be
unhappy living in so splendid a setting!

Eventually our gentlemen came to the ugliest room in this opulent suite, where scarcely any daylight entered; there they found a thin little man, with lively eyes and wearing a blond periwig. The Abbé turned to Julien and introduced him. It was the Marquis. Julien hardly recognized him, for his manner was so civil. This was no longer the grandee with so lofty an air he had seen at the abbey of Bray-le-Haut. Julien thought that his periwig had much too much hair in it, and spurred on by that impression he was not shy at all. This descendant of the friend of Henri III seemed to him at first to cut a poor figure. He was extremely thin, and fidgeted too much. But he soon discovered that the Marquis manifested a courtesy even more agreeable than that of the Bishop of Besançon himself. The audience lasted no more than three minutes. As they were leaving, the Abbé said to Julien:

— You stared at the Marquis as though he were a painting. I'm no great hand at what these people here call politeness — soon you'll know more than I do — but the intensity of your glare did not seem very polite to me.

They had got up into the fiacre again; then the coachman pulled up at the edge of the boulevard; the Abbé conducted Julien into a large suite of rooms. Julien noticed that there was no furniture. He was inspecting a magnificent gilded clock — decorated with a subject he found highly indecent — when he was approached by an extremely elegant gentleman with a smiling air. Julien made him a half bow.

The gentleman smiled and laid his hand on his shoulder. Julien started and jumped backwards. He reddened in anger. The Abbé Pirard, despite his gravity, laughed till he wept. The gentleman was a tailor.

— I give you your freedom for forty-eight hours, the Abbé said as they left; not until then can you be presented to Madame de La Mole. Someone else might watch over you in these first days of your stay in this new Babylon as if you were a young girl. But damn yourself straight away, if you are to be damned, and I'll be freed from my weakness in thinking of you. The day after tomorrow the tailor will bring you two suits; give five francs to the boy who fits them. But otherwise don't let these Parisians hear the sound of your voice. If you say a single word they'll discover how to make fun of you. It's their particular gift. The day after tomorrow, come to me at midday . . . Go ahead, damn yourself . . . I forgot, go and order some boots, some shirts and a hat at the addresses listed here.

Julien looked at the writing on the list.

– It's the Marquis's own handwriting, said the Abbé; he's an energetic man who foresees everything – he'd rather that than issue orders. He's employing you close to him so that you can spare him that kind of chore. Have you the intelligence to carry out efficiently all that this mercurial man will suggest by a word or two? The future will tell: take care!

Julien went without a word to the craftsmen whose addresses were listed; he observed that they received him with respect, and that the bootmaker, entering his name in the ledger, wrote M. Julien de Sorel.

At the cemetery of Père-Lachaise a gentleman who appeared most obliging, and even more frank in his conversation, offered to show Julien the tomb of Marshal Ney, whom prudent policy has denied the honour of an epitaph.[3] But on parting from this liberal, who with tears in his eyes had almost clasped him to his bosom, Julien found his watch missing. It was on the following day at noon that – richer for this experience – he presented himself to Abbé Pirard, who inspected him closely.

– Perhaps you'll become a fop, said the Abbé severely. Julien had the look of a very young man in deep mourning; in truth he looked very fine, but the good priest was himself too provincial to see that Julien still retained that movement of the shoulders that only provincials think both elegant and important looking. When the Marquis saw Julien he judged of his graces so differently from the Abbé that he asked him:

– Would you have any objection to M. Sorel taking dancing lessons?

The Abbé stood transfixed.

– No, he replied at last, Julien isn't a priest.

Running two steps at a time up a little hidden stair, the Marquis himself installed our hero in a pretty attic mansard giving on to the mansion's enormous gardens. He asked him how many shirts he had ordered from the shirtmaker.

— Two, replied Julien, awed to find so great a man descend to these details.

— Very good, said the Marquis with a serious air and a short and authoritative voice that impressed Julien — very good! Order another twenty-two. Here's the first quarterly instalment of your salary.

Coming down from the attic, the Marquis called out to an old man: Arsène, he said, you will look after M. Sorel. A few minutes later Julien found himself alone in the magnificent library; it was a delightful moment. So as not to be discovered in his emotional state he went to hide himself in a small dark corner; from there he rapturously contemplated the shining backs of the books: I'll be able to read them all, he said to himself. And how could I not like it here? M. de Rênal would have thought himself eternally dishonoured by doing a hundredth part of what the Marquis de La Mole has just done for me.

But let's look at the copying that has to be done . . . This work completed, Julien ventured to approach the books; he could scarce control his joy on finding an edition of Voltaire. He ran to open the library door so as not to be caught unawares. Then he gave himself the pleasure of opening each one of the eighty volumes. They were magnificently bound, the best work of the best bookbinder in London. Nothing more was needed for Julien's cup to run over.

An hour later the Marquis came in, looked at the copies, and saw with amazement that Julien wrote 'that' with two 't's at the end, *thatt*. So everything the Abbé has told me about his learning is just a fantasy! Most put out, the Marquis gently said to him:

— You're not sure of your spelling?

— That's perfectly true, said Julien, without beginning to realize the damage he was doing himself; he was reassured by the Marquis's kind tones, which put him in mind of M. de Rênal's harsh ones.

It is just a waste of time, this experiment with a little abbé from Franche-Comté, thought the Marquis; but I had such need of a reliable man!

— 'That' is written with only one 't' at the end, he said; when your copies are finished, look up the words you're not certain of in the dictionary.

At six o'clock the Marquis sent for him, and glanced at Julien's boots with evident distaste: It's my mistake, I haven't told you that every day at 5.30 you must get dressed.

Julien stared at him without understanding.

– I mean, put on stockings. Arsène will remind you; today I'll make your excuses.

Having said this, M. de La Mole conducted Julien into a salon resplendent with gold leaf. M. de Rênal, on comparable occasions, had always doubled his pace to have the distinction of going through the door first; so this petty vanity in his old patron caused Julien to stumble on the Marquis's heels, and give the latter considerable pain from his gout – Ah! he's even more of a booby than I'd bargained for, he said to himself. He presented him to a tall woman of imposing appearance. It was the Marquise. Julien had the impression of an insolent air, rather like that of Mme de Maugiron, wife of the Sub-prefect at Verrières, when she went to the St Charles day dinner on 4 November. Somewhat confused by the great splendour of the salon, Julien did not hear what M. de La Mole was saying. The Marquise scarcely deigned to look at him. There were several men in the room, among whom Julien recognized with indescribable pleasure the young Bishop of Agde, who had condescended to speak to him some time ago at the ceremony at Bray-le-Haut. Doubtless this young prelate was alarmed by the tender gaze that Julien's shyness fixed upon him, and he did not trouble to acknowledge this provincial.

The men gathered in the salon seemed to Julien somewhat melancholy and constrained; people speak softly in Paris, and do not exaggerate small matters.

At about 6.30 a handsome young man with a moustache, very pale and very slight, came in; he had an extremely small head.

– You always keep people waiting, said the Marquise, whose hand he was kissing.

Julien understood that this was the Comte de La Mole. From the first he found him charming.

Is it possible, he asked himself, that this can be the man whose aggressive jocularity will drive me from this house!

From looking Comte Norbert over, Julien registered that he was wearing boots and spurs; and I – I should be in pumps, obviously, as an inferior. They went to table. Julien heard the Marquise saying something in a severe tone, raising her voice slightly. Almost at the same moment he noticed an extremely fair-haired and very shapely young woman about to sit down opposite him. She did not attract him at all; nevertheless, on looking attentively at her, he thought he had never seen such beautiful eyes; but they promised great coldness of heart. As time passed, Julien detected in them an expression of bored inquisitiveness, together with a consciousness of the obligation to be impressive. Mme de Rênal, too, has very lovely eyes, he thought, everyone compliments her on them; and they have nothing in common with these. Julien did not know enough to realize that it was the fire of wit that shone from time to time in the eyes of Mlle Mathilde, as he heard her called. When Mme de Rênal's eyes sparkled it was with the fire of passion, or from generous indignation at hearing of some wicked action. Towards the end of the meal, Julien hit on a word to express the type of beauty that Mlle de La Mole's eyes possessed: they are scintillating, he said to himself. Otherwise she was cruelly like her mother, whom he liked less and less, and he stopped looking at her. By contrast, Comte Norbert seemed to him admirable in every way. Julien was so taken with him that he had no notion of being envious and hating him for being richer and better born than he.

Julien noticed that the Marquis seemed bored.

Around the time the second course was served he said to his son:

– Norbert, I must ask you for your good will towards M. Julien Sorel, whom I am just about to take on my staff, and of whom I intend to make something, if *thatt's* possible.

– He's my secretary, he remarked to his neighbour, and he writes 'that' with two 't's.

Everyone glanced at Julien, who bowed his head perhaps a little too emphatically towards Norbert; but in general people were satisfied by his appearance.

The Marquis must have talked of the kind of education Julien had received, for one of the guests started on the subject of Horace: it was precisely in talking about Horace that I succeeded with the Bishop of Besançon, said Julien to himself – apparently this is the only author they know. From that moment on he was in control of himself. The achievement was easy because he had just decided that Mlle de La Mole could never be a woman to his eyes. Ever since the seminary he had defied men to do their worst, and that made it difficult for them to frighten him. He would have enjoyed perfect self-possession if the dining room had been less magnificently furnished. In fact, there was a pair of mirrors, each eight feet high, and in which he could sometimes glimpse his adversary talking about Horace, that still made him nervous. For a provincial, his sentences were not too long. He had fine eyes whose brilliance was enhanced by the tremulous fire of his shyness, or by the pleasure it generated in him when making a good reply. He was found to be agreeable. This kind of examination injected some interest into the solemn dinner. The Marquis signalled to Julien's opponent to press him hard. Is it possible that he knows something? he wondered.

In the process of answering Julien hit upon new insights, and lost enough of his nerves to display, not perhaps wit – an impossibility for someone ignorant of the current Paris way of speaking – but ideas that, though delivered without grace and not quite to the point, did demonstrate that he knew Latin perfectly.

Julien's opponent was a member of the Academy of Inscriptions who by chance knew Latin; finding Julien a very good scholar, he dismissed his scruples about making him blush and tried to push him really hard. In the heat of combat Julien at last forgot the magnificent furnishings of the dining room, and produced ideas about the Roman poets that his interlocutor had never read anywhere. As an honest man he gave the secretary credit for them. By good luck they embarked on a discussion as to whether Horace had been rich or poor: a pleasant man, pleasure loving, carefree, writing verse to amuse himself like Chapelle, the friend of Molière and La Fontaine; or a poor devil of a poet laureate following the Court and composing odes for the King's birthday like Southey, Lord Byron's accuser.

There was talk of the state of society under Augustus and under George IV: two periods when the aristocracy had been all powerful; although in Rome they had seen their power wrenched from them by Maecenas, who was a mere knight, whereas in England they had reduced George IV almost to the condition of the Doge of Venice. This discussion seemed to rouse the Marquis from the state of torpor or boredom into which he had been plunged at the beginning of the meal.

Julien knew nothing of the modern names, such as Southey, Lord Byron, George IV – he was hearing them pronounced for the first time. But no one could fail to observe that whenever it was a question of what had happened in Rome, and about which information could be deduced from the works of Horace, Martial, Tacitus, etc., he displayed unchallengeable superiority. Julien blithely expounded several ideas which he had taken from the Bishop of Besançon in their famous discussion; these were not the least to be admired.

When they were tired of talking about poets, the Marquise, who made it a rule to like everything that amused her husband, deigned to look at Julien. – This young abbé's awkward manners perhaps conceal a learned man, said the Academician seated next to her; and Julien partly overheard these words. Readymade phrases suited the temperament of the mistress of the house; she adopted this one about Julien, and thought herself well advised to have invited the Academician to dinner. He will entertain M. de La Mole, she thought.

CHAPTER 3

First Steps

> This immense valley, full of brilliant lights and so many
> thousands of people, dazzles my sight. Not one of them
> knows me, all are my superiors. My head swims.
>
> *Poemi dell av.* REINA[1]

Very early next morning Julien was copying letters in the library
when Mlle Mathilde entered by a little private door cleverly concealed
by the spines of books. While Julien was marvelling at this device,
Mlle Mathilde appeared very much surprised and rather put out to
find him there. With her hair in curling papers she seemed to Julien
to have a hard look, haughty and almost masculine. Mlle de La Mole
had the secret habit of abstracting books from her father's library
without it being noticed. Julien's presence frustrated her purpose this
morning, and that irritated her all the more because she had come
to find the second volume of Voltaire's *Princess of Babylon* – such
a suitable complement to her eminently monarchical and religious
education, a masterpiece of the Sacred Heart! Already, at the age of
nineteen, this poor girl required the spice of wit for a novel to interest
her.

At around three o'clock Comte Norbert visited the library; he
had come to look at a newspaper in order to talk politics that
evening, and was most pleased to meet Julien, whose existence
he had forgotten. He behaved delightfully; he suggested they ride
together.

– My father gives us leave until dinner time.

Julien took note of this 'us' and found it charming.

– Good heavens, my lord, if it was a question of felling an

eighty-foot tree, squaring it off and cutting it up into planks, I'd acquit myself well enough, I dare say; but getting on a horse, I've done that only six times in my life.

– Good, this will be the seventh, replied Norbert.

Actually, Julien recalled to himself the entry of the King of — into Verrières, and believed that he rode very well. But, returning from the Bois de Boulogne, and trying to avoid a cab right in the middle of the Rue du Bac, he fell and was covered in mud. A good thing he had two suits. At dinner the Marquis, wishing to pay him some attention, enquired about the outing; Norbert hastened to reply in generous terms.

– Monsieur le Comte is extremely kind to me, put in Julien, I thank him for it, and feel its value to the full. He was kind enough to lend me the prettiest, most docile of his horses; but even he couldn't attach me to it, and for want of that precaution I fell down plump in the middle of that long street by the bridge.

Mlle Mathilde vainly tried to stifle a burst of laughter, and then, in her indiscretion, asked for details. Julien supplied them with great candour; he displayed grace without being aware of it.

– I augur well for this little priest, remarked the Marquis to the Academician; a provincial being straightforward in such a situation. I've never seen that and won't see it again; and, even more, he's talking about his misfortune in front of *women*!

Julien put his listeners so much at ease about his misfortune that at the end of dinner, when the conversation in general had taken another direction, Mlle Mathilde demanded her brother's account of the unhappy event. Her questions being prolonged, and Julien having met her eyes several times, he had the courage to reply directly, even though he had not been asked, and all three of them ended up laughing as though they had been three young people from a village in the depths of the country.

The following day Julien went to attend two classes in theology, and then returned in order to copy some twenty letters. He found a young man seated next to him in the library, carefully dressed but of disagreeable appearance and with an envious face.

The Marquis came in.

– What are you doing here, M. Tanbeau? he asked the newcomer severely.

– I thought . . . replied the young man, with an obsequious smile.

– No, monsieur, you *did not think*. This is an attempt to impose, but it is not a success.

Young Tanbeau got up furiously and departed. He was the nephew of M. de La Mole's Academician friend, and had determined on a literary career. The Academician had persuaded the Marquis to take him on as a secretary. Tanbeau, who worked in a room apart, had learned of the favour shown to Julien, wished to share it and, that morning, had come to set up his desk in the library.

At four o'clock Julien ventured, after some hesitation, to present himself at Comte Norbert's quarters. The latter was about to go riding and was embarrassed by this, though perfectly polite.

– I believe, he said to Julien, that you will soon be going to a riding school; and after a few weeks I will be delighted to ride with you.

– I wish to have the honour of thanking you for all the kindness you have shown me; and believe me, monsieur, added Julien with a very serious air, I feel much obliged to you. If your horse isn't hurt through my clumsiness yesterday, and if it's free, I'd very much like to ride today.

– Good Lord, my dear Sorel, then on your own head be it. Let's assume I've made all the objections prudence demands; the fact is that it's now four o'clock and we have no time to lose.

Once on horseback:

– What do you do to stop falling off? Julien asked the young Comte.

– Lots of things, replied Norbert, bursting into laughter: sit up straight, for example.

Julien broke into a fast trot. They were in the Place Louis XVI.[2]

– Hey! you young maniac, cried Norbert, far too many carriages here, and what's more, driven by idiots! Once you're down, their tilburies will run over you; they're never going to ruin their horses' mouths by pulling them up short.

Twenty times Norbert saw Julien about to fall; but the outing

finished without incident at last. Coming back in, the young Comte
said to his sister:

— Allow me to present you a real bold spark!

At dinner, addressing his father from one end of the table to the
other, he praised Julien's courage; it was the only thing in his riding
that could be praised. That morning, the young Comte had overheard
the men grooming the horses in the courtyard taking Julien's fall as
a pretext for pitiless ridicule.

Despite so much kindness, Julien felt himself very much isolated
in this family. All its customs seemed alien to him, and he was always
making mistakes. His blunders were the footmen's delight.

Abbé Pirard had left for his parish. If Julien is a broken reed let
him perish, thought he; if he's a man of spirit let him manage his
affairs for himself.

CHAPTER 4

The Hôtel de La Mole

> What does he here! does it please him? does he think he
> pleases? RONSARD[1]

If everything in the aristocratic salon of the Hôtel de La Mole seemed
strange to Julien, this young man, pale and dressed in black, seemed
strange in his turn to those who condescended to notice him. Madame
de la Mole suggested to her husband that he be sent off on some
assignment on the days they had invited certain personages to dine.

– I very much want, replied the Marquis, to pursue this experiment
to the end. Abbé Pirard would have it that we're wrong to shatter
the self-esteem of people we admit to our household. *One can only
lean on something which offers resistance*, etc.[2] This one stands out only
because no one knows his face – otherwise he's a deaf mute.

To get my bearings, said Julien to himself, I must write down the
names of the people I see coming into the salon, with a brief sketch
of their character.

First on his list he put five or six friends of the house who made
up to him on the offchance, thinking him a favourite through the
Marquis's whim. They were poor creatures of varying degrees of
sycophancy; but it must be said in defence of the kind of men one
finds in aristocratic salons nowadays that they were not equally
sycophantic to everyone. There were those among them who would
let themselves be bundled about by the Marquis, but would rebel
against a hard word from Mme de La Mole.

There was an excess of pride and an excess of boredom deep in
the characters of the heads of the family; they were too used to
relieving their boredom by being insulting to be able to hope for

genuine friends. However, except on rainy days and in
furious ennui, which were rare, their manners were al\
cably fine.

If the Hôtel de La Mole had happened to be deserted b\
or six hangers-on who had evinced such paternal feeling .... Julien,
the Marquise would have been exposed to long hours of solitude;
and, in the eyes of women of that rank, solitude is frightful: it is the
sign of *disgrace*.

The Marquis's behaviour toward his wife was exemplary; he made
sure that her salon was adequately embellished with guests; not,
however, with peers – for he found his new colleagues[3] not well
enough born to be in his house as friends, and not amusing enough
to be admitted as subordinates.

It was very much later on that Julien plumbed these secrets.
Political manoeuvring, which is the great staple of conversation
amongst the middle classes, is mentioned only in moments of emergency in the circles of a marquis.

The imperative need to be amused is so powerful – still in this
century of disillusion – that even on the days when there was a
dinner party the Marquis had hardly left the salon when everyone
else would flee. So long as one did not make light of God, the clergy,
the King or holders of office, or artists sponsored by the Court or
any established institution; so long as one had nothing good to say
about Béranger,[4] or the opposition papers, or Voltaire, or Rousseau,
or of anything that made for a little free speech; so long, above all, as
one never mentioned politics, one could freely discuss anything at all.

Not even an income of 100,000 francs, or a blue riband, can prevail
against a salon constituted like this. The slightest vital idea would
seem glaringly vulgar. Despite elevated taste, perfect courtesy and
the desire to please, boredom was imprinted on every face. The
young men who came to pay their respects, fearful of saying anything
that could be suspected of thought, or that betrayed forbidden
reading, would, after making a few highly elegant observations on
Rossini and the weather, fall silent.

Julien noticed that the conversation was usually kept alive by two
vicomtes and five barons whom M. de La Mole had known during

..ıe Emigration. These gentlemen each enjoyed an income of 6,000 or 8,000 livres; four subscribed to *La Quotidienne*, and three to the *Gazette de France*.[5] One of them always had some anecdote about the château to tell, in which the word *admirable* was not long absent. Julien observed that he had five crosses, whereas the others had an average of three.

By way of compensation, ten lackeys in livery decorated the antechamber, every quarter of an hour all evening tea or ices were served; and, at midnight, a kind of supper with champagne.

That was why Julien sometimes stayed until the end; for the rest he found it almost unbelievable that anyone should take the ordinary conversation in this brilliantly gilded salon seriously. Sometimes he would look at those to whom he spoke to see if they were themselves parodying what they said. My own M. de Maistre, whom I know by heart, he thought, has said all this a hundred times better – and even then he's pretty boring.

Julien was not the only one to be conscious of this moral asphyxia. Some consoled themselves by eating lots of ices; others by the pleasure of being able to say for the rest of the evening: I've just come from the Hôtel de La Mole, where I heard that Russia, etc.

Julien learned from one of the house dependants that it was less than six months ago that Mme de La Mole had rewarded more than twenty years' assiduous attendance by making a prefect of poor Baron Le Bourguignon, who had been a sub-prefect ever since the Restoration.

This great event had re-tempered all these gentlemen's zeal; they had been easily aggrieved in the past, now nothing could aggrieve them. Only occasionally was a lack of courtesy apparent, but already Julien had overheard two or three petty exchanges between the Marquis and his wife at the dining table that could wound their immediate neighbours. These noble personages did not in the least dissimulate the scorn they felt for those who did not come from families who *rode in the carriages of the King*. Julien observed that the word *crusade* was the only one that imparted a deeply serious look to their expressions, mingled with respect. Everyday respect was always tinged with condescension.

In the midst of this splendour and this ennui Julien was fascinated only by M. de La Mole; with pleasure he heard him protest one day that he had nothing to do with the advancement of poor Le Bourguignon. It had been a compliment to the Marquise: Julien knew the truth through the Abbé Pirard.

In the Marquis's library one morning the Abbé was working with Julien on the eternal lawsuit with de Frilair:

— Monsieur, said Julien suddenly, is dining with Mme la Marquise every day one of my duties, or is it a favour being shown me?

— It is a signal honour! replied the Abbé, scandalized. M. N——, the Academician, who has assiduously paid court here for fifteen years, has never once been able to obtain it for his nephew M. Tanbeau.

— For me, monsieur, it's the most painful part of my work. I was less bored at the seminary. I've noticed even Mlle de La Mole yawning at times, though she ought to be used to the blandishments of the family clients. I'm afraid of falling asleep. I implore you to get me permission to go to some little inn and dine for forty sous.

The Abbé, truly a self-made man, was very positive about the honour of dining with a great lord. While he was trying to force himself to comprehend Julien's feelings, a little sound made them turn their heads. Julien realized that Mlle de La Mole had been listening. He blushed. She had come in search of a book, and had heard everything; she conceived some respect for Julien. This one isn't on his knees, she thought, like that old priest. God! how ugly that one is.

At dinner Julien did not dare look at Mlle de La Mole, but she had the kindness to say something to him. That day they were expecting a lot of company, and she asked him to stay. Young ladies in Paris don't much care for middle-aged men, especially when they are carelessly dressed. Julien did not need to be especially sharp to make out that those of M. Le Bourguignon's associates who had stayed on in the salon had the honour to be the usual recipients of Mlle de La Mole's satirical remarks. That day, whether or not it was affectation on her part, she was merciless to bores.

Mlle de La Mole was the centre of a little group that formed behind the Marquise's enormous armchair almost every evening. Stationed there were the Marquis de Croisenois, the Comte de Caylus, the Vicomte de Luz and two or three other young officer friends of Norbert or his sister. These gentlemen sat on a large blue sofa. At the end of the sofa opposite to that occupied by the brilliant Mathilde, Julien sat in silence on a little and rather low cane-bottomed chair. This modest position was the envy of all the hangers-on; Norbert considerately sanctioned the presence of his father's young secretary there by addressing a remark to him or mentioning his name two or three times each evening. That evening Mlle de La Mole asked him the height of the mountain on which the citadel of Besançon was built. Julien was quite unable to say whether this hill was higher or lower than Montmartre. He often laughed heartily at what was said in the little group; but felt himself incapable of coming out with anything comparable. It was like a foreign language he could understand, but was unable to speak.

That evening Mathilde's band conducted continuous hostilities with the people entering the vast salon. The clients of the house were picked on first, as being more familiar. One may be sure Julien was attentive; everything interested him – the subjects chosen and the style of raillery.

– Ah! there's M. Descoulis, said Mathilde, he's no longer wearing a wig; does he expect to get a prefecture by his genius? He's showing off the bald forehead he claims is full of elevated thoughts.

– He's a fellow who knows everyone on earth, said the Marquis de Croisenois; he also frequents my uncle the Cardinal. He is able to keep up the illusion with every one of his friends for years on end, and he has two or three hundred friends. He knows how to feed friendship, that's his talent. You may see him, just as you see him there, at the door of one of his friends at seven o'clock on a winter's morning, already spattered with mud.

He explodes from time to time and then writes seven or eight quarrelsome letters. Then he makes peace, and there are seven or eight letters full of friendly effusions. But it is in the frank and sincere confidences of a true gentleman whose heart has no secrets that he most excels. That manoeuvre comes in when he has a favour to ask. One of my uncle's vicars-general is wonderful when he recounts M. Descoulis's career since the Restoration. I'll bring him along to you here.

– Bah! I don't believe in such tales; it's professional jealousy between petty men, said the Comte de Caylus.

– M. Descoulis has a name that will go down in history, retorted the Marquis; with the Abbé de Pradt and MM. de Talleyrand and Pozzo di Borgo[6] he helped bring about the Restoration.

– The man has had control of millions, said Norbert, and I can't imagine why he comes here to be paid off by my father's epigrams, which are often frightful. The other day he cried out – from one end of the table to the other – My dear Descoulis, how many times have you betrayed the trust of your friends?

– But is it true that he has betrayed people? asked Mlle de La Mole. I wonder who hasn't been a traitor?

– Ahah! said the Comte de Caylus to Norbert, so you've got M. Sainclair, the famous liberal, in your house; what the devil's he doing here? I must go over and talk to him, and get him to talk; they say he's so witty.

– But how is it your mother can receive him? asked M. de Croisenois. He has such extravagant ideas, he is so generous, so independent . . .

– Look there, said Mlle de La Mole, there's the independent man bowing down to the ground in front of M. Descoulis and taking his hand. I almost thought he'd carry it to his lips.

– Descoulis must be better placed with the powers that be than we thought, replied M. de Croisenois.

– Sainclair comes here to get into the Academy, said Norbert; Croisenois, see how he greets Baron L—.

– It'd be less base if he got on his knees, put in M. de Luz.

– My dear Sorel, said Norbert, you're an intelligent fellow, but since you've just come down from the mountains, do remember never to greet anyone as that great poet does, even if they were God the Father.

– Ah! here's the prince of wits, M. le Baron Bâton, said Mlle de

La Mole, lightly imitating the tones of the footman who had just announced him.

– I believe even the servants laugh at him. What a name, Baron Bâton! cried M. de Caylus.

– But what's in a name? he asked us the other day, replied Mathilde. – You must imagine the Duc de Bouillon⁷ being announced for the first time – the only thing people need as far as I'm concerned is to get used to it . . .

Julien left the neighbourhood of the sofa. Still not very alert to the delicious subtleties of light-hearted badinage, he thought that for a joke to be amusing it should be founded on some sense. He saw nothing more in the conversation of these young people than a tone of universal denigration, and he was shocked. His provincial, or English-style, scrupulousness went so far as to detect envy in it – in which he was certainly mistaken.

Comte Norbert, he said to himself, whom I've seen making three drafts of a twenty-line letter to his colonel, would be delighted if in his entire life he could produce a single page like one of M. Sainclair's.

Moving round without being noticed because of his lack of importance, Julien approached several groups in turn; he followed Baron Bâton at a distance, hoping to hear him talk. This extremely witty man seemed uneasy, and Julien saw him rally somewhat only when he had found three or four arresting things to say. It seemed to Julien that this kind of wit required space.

The Baron had not the capacity to produce epigrams; in order to shine he needed at least four sentences of six lines each.

– *That man doesn't converse, he discourses*, said someone behind Julien. He turned, and flushed with pleasure when he heard Comte Chalvet named. This is the shrewdest man of the age. Julien had often found his name in the *Memorial of St Helena* and in the fragments of history dictated by Napoleon. Comte Chalvet was concise in his speech; his remarks were like lightning – exact, lively and profound. If he spoke about something the subject moved a step onward as he spoke. He brought facts to bear, and to hear him was a pleasure. Otherwise, politically, he was a blatant cynic.

– I'm an independent myself, he was saying to a gentleman

wearing three decorations, and whom he was apparently mocking. Why should I be of the same opinion today as I was six weeks ago? In that case my opinions would be my tyrants.

Four solemn young men, standing round him, frowned; these gentlemen did not admire a bantering tone. The Comte saw that he had gone too far. Happily, he noticed the honest M. Balland, honest as Tartuffe. The Comte engaged him in conversation: people gathered round and realized that poor Balland was about to be sacrificed. By virtue of the power of moral postures and moralizing – although he was terribly ugly, and after an early career that it would be a delicate matter to relate – M. Balland had married a very rich woman, now dead; then another very rich woman who is not seen in society. He rejoices, in all humility, in an income of 60,000 francs, and has flatterers himself. Comte Chalvet talked to him about all this, and without mercy. Soon there was a circle of thirty around them. Everyone smiled, even the solemn young men – who are the hope of the age.

Why does he come to M. de La Mole's, where he is obviously a laughing stock? wondered Julien. He went up to the Abbé to ask him.

M. Balland slipped away.

– Good! said Norbert, there's one of my father's spies gone; that leaves only the little cripple Napier.

Is that the answer to the puzzle? wondered Julien. But in that case, why does the Marquis receive M. Balland?

The severe Abbé Pirard was standing frowning in a corner of the salon, listening to the footman announcing guests.

– So, said he like Basilio,[8] it's a den of thieves. I see only men of ill repute entering in.

The severe Abbé did not really know how high society worked. But, through his Jansenist friends, he had very precise information about those men who only got into salons through their extreme cleverness in the service of any or all parties, or by their scandalous fortunes. For a few minutes this evening he replied from the fullness of his heart to Julien's urgent questions – then pulled up short, horrified to have always bad things to say of all, and imputing this as a sin in himself. Irritable, a Jansenist, and believing in the Christian duty to be charitable, his life in society was a struggle.

— What a face that Abbé Pirard has! said Mlle de la Mole as Julien neared the sofa again.

Julien felt irritated by this, but none the less she was right. M. Pirard was without question the most honest man in the room, but his acne-ridden red face, agitated by the stings of conscience, made him hideous just then. Look at him, thought Julien, then believe in the idea of physiognomy! It's just when Abbé Pirard's delicate sensibility is accusing him of some trifling fault that he looks atrocious; while on the face of Napier, who everyone knows is a spy, one reads pure happiness and tranquillity. Abbé Pirard had, however, made great concessions to his rôle; he had engaged a servant, and was very well dressed.

Julien noticed something unusual going on in the salon: all eyes were turned towards the door, and there was a sudden hush. The footman announced the celebrated Baron de Tolly, on whom the elections had recently focused the public gaze. Julien stepped forward to obtain a clear view of him. The Baron presided over an electoral college: he had had the brilliant idea of conjuring away the little slips of paper bearing the votes for one of the parties — but in compensation he had duly replaced these with other little bits of paper bearing a name more agreeable to him. This decisive manoeuvre was noticed by some of the electors, who hastened to present their compliments to Baron de Tolly. The good fellow was still pale as a result of this great affair. Some ill-constituted minds had mentioned the galleys. M. de La Mole received him coldly. The poor baron took himself off.

— If he leaves us so soon, it is to go and see M. Comte,[9] said Comte Chalvet, and there was laughter.

In the middle of this sprinkling of great lords, who had little to say, and of intriguers — most of them compromised, but all men of wit — who that evening appeared in succession in M. de La Mole's salon (there was talk of him getting a ministry), little Tanbeau was entering the lists for the first time. If his perceptions still were not very acute, he made up for this, as will be seen, by the vehemence of his language.

– Why not condemn that fellow to ten years in prison? he was
arguing when Julien neared his group; the bottom of a deep ditch is
where reptiles should be kept – one should put them there to die in
the dark, otherwise their venom rises and is even more dangerous.
What's the point of sentencing him to be fined a thousand écus? He's
poor, very well, so much the better; but his party will pay it for him.
It should be a 500-franc fine and ten years in a dungeon.

Good Lord! what monster can they be talking about? wondered
Julien, amazed at his colleagues' violent tone and abrupt gestures.
The little thin, taut face of the Academician's favourite nephew was
hideous as he spoke. Julien soon discovered that they were talking
of the greatest poet of the day.[10]

– Ah, you monster! cried Julien half aloud, and generous tears
moistened his eyes. Ah, you little scrub! he thought, I'll pay you
back for those remarks.

This, though, thought he, is the forlorn hope of the party of which
the Marquis is one of the chiefs. And the illustrious man he libels, how
many crosses, how many sinecures wouldn't he have accumulated, if
he had sold himself, I won't say to the feeble ministry of M. de
Nerval,[11] but to one of those moderately honest ministers we've seen
succeed him?

The Abbé Pirard signalled to Julien in the distance; M. de La Mole
had just been saying something to him. But when Julien – who at
that moment was listening with lowered eyes to the sighings of a
bishop – was at last free and could go up to his friend, he found
himself forestalled by the abominable little Tanbeau. This little
monster detested the Abbé as the source of Julien's favour, and so
had come to woo him.

When will death deliver us from the body of this ancient corruption?[12]
It was in these terms, with biblical force, that the little literary man
was just then speaking of the estimable Lord Holland.[13] His gift was
that he was very well versed in the biographies of living persons,
and had recently made a rapid survey of all those who might aspire
to some influence over the new king of England.[14]

The Abbé Pirard moved into a neighbouring room. Julien followed him: – I must warn you that the Marquis doesn't like scribblers.

Know Latin and Greek, and the history of the Egyptians and the Persians and so forth, if you can manage it, and he'll honour and support you as a scholar. But don't go and write a single page of French, above all on serious matters above your station, or he'll call you a scribbler and think you're a bad omen. How is it that, living in a great nobleman's house, you don't remember what the Duc de Castries said about d'Alembert[15] and Rousseau: Those people like to call everything into question, but they don't have a thousand francs a year.

Everything leaks out, thought Julien, here just as in the seminary! He had written nine or ten passionate pages: a kind of historical eulogy of the old Surgeon-major, who, he claimed, had made a man of him. And this little notebook, said Julien to himself, has always been locked with a key! He went up to his room, burnt his manuscript and returned to the salon. The clever rogues had now gone, and only the gentlemen wearing decorations remained.

Around a table that the servants had just brought in, fully laid out, were seven or eight ladies aged between thirty and thirty-five, all very well-born, very pious and very affected. The dazzling Maréchale de Fervaques came in, making excuses about the lateness of the hour. It was gone midnight; she took her place next to the Marquise. Julien was deeply affected; she had the eyes and the look of Mme de Rênal.

Mlle de La Mole's group was still full of people. She was engaged with her friends in mocking the unfortunate Comte de Thaler.[16] He was the only son of that eminent Jew famous for the riches he had acquired in furnishing money for kings to make war on the people. This Jew had just died leaving his son an income of 100,000 francs a month, and a name unfortunately too well known. So singular a position called for great simplicity of character or great force of will.

Unfortunately the Comte was no more than a decent fellow dressed up in all kinds of pretensions inspired in him by his flatterers.

M. de Caylus maintained that someone had implanted in him a determination to demand the hand in marriage of Mlle de La Mole (to whom the Marquis de Croisenois, who was due to become a duke with an income of 100,000 livres, was paying court).

— Ah! don't accuse him of having determination, said Norbert pityingly. Perhaps what this poor Comte lacked most of all was that very ability to be determined. This side of his character made him worthy to be a king. Constantly asking everyone's advice, he did not have the resolution to follow any to its end.

His physiognomy would have been enough by itself, observed Mlle de La Mole, to give her eternal joy. It was a curious mixture of uneasiness and disappointment; but at one time or another one could discern gusts of self-importance there, and the cutting tone that the richest man in France ought to adopt – above all when he is good-looking enough and not yet thirty-six. He is timidly insolent, said M. de Croisenois. The Comte de Caylus, Norbert and two or three of the young men with moustaches made fun of him as freely as they liked without his noticing it, and eventually sent him away as one o'clock sounded:

– Are those your famous Arab horses you're keeping waiting at the door in this weather? Norbert asked him.

– No, it's a new, very much less costly equipage, answered M. de Thaler. The left-hand horse cost me five thousand francs, and the one on the right isn't worth more than a hundred louis; but I beg you to believe that he's only harnessed at night. His trot is exactly equal to the others'.

Norbert's remark made the Comte think that it was quite the thing for a man like him to have a passion for horses, and that he should not let his get wet. He went out, and those gentlemen left a moment later, still mocking him.

So, thought Julien, listening to their laughter on the stairs, it has been granted me to see the other extreme to my situation! I haven't twenty louis in income, and I find myself standing next to this man who has twenty louis an hour, yet they make fun of him . . . A sight like that cures one of envy.

CHAPTER 5

Sensitivity, and a Pious Lady

> Any vital idea has an air of vulgarity there, so completely
> are they used to monotonous talk. Woe to him who has an
> inventive way of speaking!   FAUBLAS[1]

When, after several months of trial, the house steward handed him
his salary for the third quarter, this is the stage Julien had reached.
M. de La Mole had ordered him to attend to the administration of
his lands in Brittany and in Normandy. Julien made frequent journeys
there. He was put in charge of the correspondence relating to the
famous lawsuit with the Abbé de Frilair. He had been briefed on this
by M. Pirard.

On the basis of the brief jottings the Marquis scribbled in the
margins of all kinds of paperwork that came in, Julien composed
letters that were nearly always passed as fit for signature.

At the theological school his teachers complained of his limited
application, but none the less regarded him as one of their most
distinguished pupils. These varying tasks, undertaken with all the
eagerness of unassuaged ambition, had very quickly robbed Julien
of the fresh complexion he had brought from the provinces. In the
eyes of his young comrades in the seminary his pallor was a merit;
he found them less spiteful, much less subservient to mere cash, than
those at Besançon; they believed him afflicted by consumption. The
Marquis had supplied him with a horse.

Nervous of being encountered while out riding, Julien had told
them that this exercise had been prescribed him by the doctors. Abbé
Pirard had introduced him to several Jansenist societies. Julien was
amazed; the idea of religion was inextricably linked in his mind with

those of hypocrisy and the desire for financial gain. He was impressed by these stern and pious men who had no thought of money. Several of the Jansenists had taken a liking to him and gave him advice. A new prospect opened up before him. Among the Jansenists he got to know a certain Comte Altamira who was almost six foot tall, a liberal who had been sentenced to death in his own country, and very pious. This strange contrast between religious devotion and the love of liberty astounded him.

Julien's relations with the young Comte had chilled. Norbert thought he had reacted too sharply to some of his friends' pleasantries. Having once or twice failed to behave appropriately, Julien had resolved never to say another word to Mlle de La Mole. In the Hôtel de La Mole they were always perfectly polite to him, but he felt himself to have declined in favour. His provincial common sense explained this phenomenon by the popular saying, *What's beautiful is what's new*.

Perhaps he was a little more perceptive than he had been in the first few days or, rather, perhaps the first enchantment with Parisian urbanity had faded.

From the moment he finished his work each day he became prey to a deadly boredom, such was the dessicating effect of that courtesy which characterizes high society – admirable in itself, but so regulated, so closely graduated according to one's standing. Any even slightly sensitive heart can perceive its artifice.

Undoubtedly the provinces can be accused of commonness of tone and lack of polish, but at least people there show some warmth in their responses. At the Hôtel de La Mole Julien's pride was never attacked; but frequently, at the close of day, he would feel an urge to burst into tears. A waiter in the provinces takes an interest in you should you suffer a mishap while entering his café; and if that mishap has in it something embarrassing to your pride, he will, while commiserating with you, come back to the word that torments you over and over again. In Paris they take the trouble to conceal their laughter, but you are always treated as a stranger.

We may pass in silence over a crowd of little adventures that would have made Julien ridiculous, if, in a sense, he had not been beneath ridicule. An absurd over-sensitivity led him into thousands of awkward mistakes. All his recreations were defensive: he practised with a pistol every day, and he was one of the leading pupils at the most celebrated masters at arms. Whenever he had a moment to spare, instead of using it for reading as he would have in the past, he ran to the livery stables and demanded the most vicious horses. In his outings with the riding master it was almost a matter of course for him to be thrown to the ground.

The Marquis was well satisfied with his persistent working habits, his discretion and his intelligence, and gradually confided to him the conduct of all business that was slightly difficult to disentangle. At the odd times when his lofty ambitions allowed him some scope for it, the Marquis conducted his business affairs shrewdly – being in a position to keep up with new developments, he was able to gamble with success. He bought houses and woodlands – but he easily became riled. He gave away hundreds of louis, then sued for hundreds of francs. Rich men of high spirit look to business transactions for amusement, not for results. The Marquis needed a chief of staff who could instil a clear and comprehensible order into all his financial affairs.

Although of so gravely constrained a temperament, Mme de La Mole sometimes mocked Julien. Great ladies are horrified by the *unpredictability* that sensibility can produce; it is at the opposite pole to decorum. On two or three occasions the Marquis came to his defence – if he is ridiculous in your salon, he triumphs when he is at his desk. For his part, Julien believed that he had discovered the Marquise's secret. She condescended to take an interest in everything from the moment that the Baron de La Joumate was announced. He was a frigid creature, of inscrutable physiognomy. He was short, dainty, ugly, very well dressed, spent his life at the château, and normally had nothing to say about anything. That reflected the cast of his mind. Mme de La Mole would have been rapturously happy, for the first time in her life, if she could have gained him as a husband for her daughter.

CHAPTER 6

A Matter of Pronunciation

> Their lofty task is to pronounce calmly on the little happen-
> ings in the everyday life of nations. Their wisdom should
> forestall excessive anger over trivial things, or over events
> that rumour transfigures when it noises them abroad.
>
> GRATIUS[1]

For a man who was newly launched in the world, and whose pride
forbade him to ask any questions, the idiocies into which Julien
lapsed were not too terrible. One day, when a sudden shower
had propelled him into a café on the rue St-Honoré, a tall man in
a beaver overcoat, surprised at his gloomy glare, glowered back at
him in turn – just as Mlle Amanda's lover had done long ago in
Besançon.

Too often had Julien reproached himself with having let that first
insult pass for him to put up with such a look now. He demanded an
explanation. The man in the overcoat immediately showered him
with the lowest kind of insults: everyone in the café gathered round;
passers-by stopped at the door. With the wariness of a provincial,
Julien always carried some little pistols with him; now his hand in
his pocket gripped them convulsively. Nevertheless he restrained
himself, and limited himself to saying to his man, time after time:
Sir, your address? You are despicable.

The persistence with which he stuck to these five words impressed
the throng.

– Be damned! the other fellow who talks so freely should at least
give him his address. The man in the overcoat, hearing this verdict
repeated so often, threw five or six visiting cards in front of Julien's

281

nose. Fortunately none of them hit his face – he had decided to use the pistols only if he were assaulted. The man took himself off, not without wheeling round from time to time to shake his fist in menace and let out more insults.

Julien found himself bathed in sweat. So, the lowest type has the power to do this to me? How can I eradicate such shameful sensitivity?

Where could he find a second? He had no friend. He had met a lot of people; but without exception they always drifted away from him after six weeks of acquaintance. I am an unsociable creature, and now I am cruelly punished for it, thought he. Eventually he had the idea of seeking out a former lieutenant of the 96th called Liéven, a poor devil with whom he had often fenced. Julien told him the whole story.

– I'll certainly be your second, said Liéven, but on one condition: if you don't wound your man, then you will fight me – in the same session.

– Agreed, replied Julien delighted, and they went in search of M. C. de Beauvoisis at the address shown on his cards, which was deep in the Faubourg St-Germain.

It was seven in the morning. It was not until he was sending in his name at the door that it occurred to Julien that this might be that young relative of Mme de Rênal, formerly employed by the Ambassador to Rome, or to Naples, who had given a letter of recommendation to the singer Geronimo.

Julien had given one of the cards thrown at him the previous day to the tall footman, together with one of his own.

He and his second were made to wait three long quarter hours; at last they were ushered into an extremely elegant apartment. Here they met a tall young man dressed up like a tailor's model; his features showed the perfection, and the blankness, of the ancient Greek ideal. His extraordinarily narrow head sported a pyramid of the most beautiful blond locks. These were very carefully dressed, not a curl straying out of place. It was to have his hair done like this, thought the lieutenant of the 96th, that this fop has kept us waiting. The parti-coloured dressing gown, the morning trousers, everything down to the embroidered slippers, was perfectly right and wonderfully arranged. His physiognomy, noble and vacant, spoke of thoughts that would be infrequent and then conventional: all suggested the ideal of the agreeable gentleman, a horror of the spontaneous and the hearty, and a vast deal of gravity.

Julien, to whom the lieutenant of the 96th had pointed out that keeping them waiting like this, after having coarsely thrown his cards in his face, was an added insult, walked brusquely into M. de Beauvoisis's quarters. He intended to be insolent, but was anxious nevertheless to act with perfect decorum.

Yet he was so struck by M. de Beauvoisis's gentle manner, by his air which was at once both formal, self-confident and complacent, by the admirable elegance that surrounded him, that in the twinkling of an eye he lost any idea of aggression. This was not his man of yesterday. His amazement at finding so distinguished a being in place of the coarse creature he had met in the café was so great that he could not think of a word to say. He presented one of the cards that had been given him.

– It is my name, said the fashionable man on whom Julien's black coat, worn at seven o'clock in the morning, made a rather poor impression; but I don't understand, the honour . . .

The manner in which these last words were pronounced revived some of Julien's temper.

– I've come to fight you, monsieur – and without delay he explained the whole situation.

M. Charles de Beauvoisis, having given it his mature consideration, was quite satisfied by the cut of Julien's black coat. It is by Staub, that is obvious, he said to himself while listening to Julien speaking; the waistcoat is in good taste, his boots are very well made; but, on the other hand, this black coat in broad daylight! . . . That would be to avoid a pistol ball more readily, said the Chevalier de Beauvoisis to himself.

From the moment he had provided himself with this explanation, he reverted to perfect courtesy, almost as though Julien was his equal. Their interview was quite long, for the affair was delicate; but eventually Julien was unable to resist the plain facts. The exquisite in front of him had no resemblance at all to the gross fellow who had insulted him the previous day.

Julien felt a tremendous reluctance to depart, and drew out his explanations. He was studying the contained poise of the Chevalier de Beauvoisis – for this is how he spoke of himself, being shocked when Julien called him simply 'monsieur'.

Julien wondered at his gravity, mingled with a certain understated dandyishness that never left him for an instant. He wondered at the singular way his tongue moved while saying things . . . But in the end there was not the slightest reason in all this for picking a quarrel with him.

With the very best grace, the young diplomat offered to fight, but the former lieutenant of the 96th, sitting there for an hour with his legs apart, hands on thighs and elbows out, pronounced that his friend M. Sorel was not so constituted as to want to quarrel with a man, in the German fashion, simply because that man had had his visiting cards stolen.

Julien departed in very ill humour. The Chevalier de Beauvoisis's carriage was waiting in the courtyard, in front of the portico; by some chance Julien raised his eyes and recognized the coachman as his man of the day before.

It was the work of an instant to see him, grab him by his greatcoat, drag him from his seat and shower him with blows from his whip. Two footmen came to their colleague's defence; some punches landed on Julien: at that moment he cocked one of his pocket pistols and fired at them; they took to their heels. All was over in a moment.

The Chevalier de Beauvoisis was descending the stairs with a most pleasing gravity, repeating in his lordly fashion: What's going on? What's going on? He was clearly much intrigued, but diplomatic dignity forbade him from showing too great an interest. When he understood what had happened, hauteur continued to struggle in his face with the lightly humorous self-possession that should never be absent from the countenance of a diplomat.

The lieutenant of the 96th perceived that M. de Beauvoisis would be pleased to fight: he wished, a diplomat himself, to keep the advantage of the initiative for his friend. – Now, he cried, we have the makings of a duel! – Indeed, I believe that is so, replied the diplomat.

– That scoundrel is dismissed, he said to his servants; someone else get on the box. The carriage door was opened: the Chevalier absolutely insisted on doing the honours for Julien and his second. They set off to find a friend of M. de Beauvoisis, who advised them of a secluded spot. During their journey the conversation was extremely pleasant. The only oddity was that the diplomat was in his dressing gown.

These gentlemen, thought Julien, though they are very aristo-cratic, are not at all dull like the people who come to dine at M. de La Mole's; and I see why, he added a moment later – they feel it is all right not to be prudish.

They were talking about some dancers who had had a great public success at a ballet the previous evening. The gentlemen alluded to some spicy details about which Julien and his second, the lieutenant of the 96th, knew nothing whatsoever. Julien was not so stupid as to pretend to know; with a good grace he admitted his ignorance. His candour pleased the Chevalier's friend – he told them the stories replete with details, and told them very well.

One thing impressed Julien greatly. The carriage was delayed for a moment by an altar of repose that was being put up in the middle of the street for the Corpus Christi procession. The gentlemen allowed themselves several jokes; and according to them the curé was an archbishop's son. In the mansion of M. de La Mole, who wanted to be a duke, no one would ever dare say anything like that.

The duel was over in a moment: Julien received a ball in the arm; they dressed it with handkerchiefs; they damped these with brandy; and the Chevalier de Beauvoisis very politely begged to be allowed to take Julien home in the same carriage by which they had come. When Julien mentioned the Hôtel de La Mole the young diplomat and his friend exchanged glances. Julien's fiacre was available, but he found the conversation of these gentlemen infinitely more amusing than that of the worthy lieutenant of the 96th.

My God! a duel – is that all it is! thought Julien. How very lucky to have found that coachman again! How awful for me if I had had to go on enduring that insult in the café! The amusing conversation had scarcely been interrupted. Julien saw then that diplomatic affectations had some value.

So, he said to himself, tedium is not inevitable in a conversation between well-born people! These two joked about the Corpus Christi procession, feeling free to tell extremely scabrous anecdotes full of vivid details. The only thing totally absent was any talk of politics, which was more than compensated for by their graceful tone and the perfect aptness of their phrasing. Julien felt a powerful attraction to them. How happy I would be to see more of them!

Hardly had they parted than the Chevalier de Beauvoisis hurried off to get some information about Julien: what he discovered was not impressive.

He was most curious to get to know this man. Could he decently call on him? The few things he was able to learn were not encouraging.

– All this is too frightful! said he to his second. I can't possibly confess that I've fought with someone who is a mere secretary of M. de La Mole – and also that it was because my coachman stole my visiting cards. – There's certainly scope for ridicule.

That same evening, the Chevalier de Beauvoisis and friend put it about all over the town that this M. Sorel, in other respects an impeccable young man, was the natural son of one of the Marquis de La Mole's intimate friends. This fact was accepted without difficulty. Once it was established, the young diplomat and his friend condescended to visit Julien several times during the fortnight he was confined to his room. Julien let slip that he had never been to the opera in his whole life.

– That's shocking, they said to him, it is the only place to go; your first outing must be to *Le Comte Ory*.[2]

At the opera, the Chevalier de Beauvoisis introduced him to the famous singer Geronimo, who was then having a colossal success.

Julien almost wooed the Chevalier; he was enchanted by the young man's mingling of respect for his own importance, mysterious portentousness and foppery. For instance, the Chevalier lisped slightly because he had the honour of often being in the company of a great lord who had this disability. Never before had Julien met, united in the same person, such amusing absurdity and such perfection of manners that a poor provincial would certainly have to copy.

He was seen at the opera with the Chevalier de Beauvoisis; the friendship got him talked about.

– Well, well! said M. de La Mole to him one day, so you are now the natural son of a rich gentleman in Franche-Comté, an intimate friend of mine?

The Marquis cut Julien short when he tried to protest that he had not contributed to confirming this rumour in any way.

– M. de Beauvoisis didn't want to have fought a carpenter's son.

– I know, I know, said M. de La Mole; it's now up to me to give substance to the tale, which suits me. But I have a favour to ask of you – and which will cost you no more than a half hour or so of your time: on every day when they give an opera, at half-past eleven, go and stand in the vestibule while high society comes out. I still see some provincial mannerisms in you occasionally, it is important that you get rid of them; anyway it is not at all a bad thing that you should know, at least by sight, the great personages to whom I might one day send you on assignment. Look in at the ticket office and make yourself known; they will give you a pass.

CHAPTER 7

An Attack of Gout

> And I was promoted, not on my merits, but because my
> master had the gout.   BERTOLETTI[1]

Perhaps the reader is surprised at this free and almost friendly tone;
we have omitted to mention that for the last six months the Marquis
had been kept at home by an attack of gout.

Mlle de La Mole and her mother were at Hyères, staying with the
Marquise's mother. Comte Norbert saw his father fleetingly only;
they were on excellent terms, but had nothing to say to one another.
M. de La Mole, reduced to the company of Julien, was amazed
to discover that he possessed some ideas. He made him read the
newspapers. Soon the young secretary was capable of excerpting
interesting passages. There was a new paper the Marquis abhorred;
he had sworn never to read it, yet he mentioned it every day. Julien
laughed. The Marquis, exasperated with modern times, set him to
reading Livy; Julien's improvised translation from the Latin text
entertained him.

One day the Marquis addressed him in the tone of overelaborate
politeness that Julien often found irksome:

– Permit me, my dear Sorel, to make you the gift of a blue coat:
when it is convenient to you to put it on and call on me, you will, in
my eyes, be the younger brother of the Comte de Chaulnes – that is
to say, the son of the old Duke, my friend.

Julien did not really understand what this purported; that very
evening he hazarded a visit dressed in blue. The Marquis treated him
as an equal. Julien's heart was quite capable of appreciating genuine
politeness, but he had had no idea of its nuances. Before this little

288

game of the Marquis he would have sworn it was impossible to be treated by him with greater courtesy. What an admirable gift! he said to himself – and, when he rose to leave, the Marquis made his apologies for being unable to see him out, because of his gout.

A curious idea started to worry Julien: Can he be making fun of me? He went to ask the advice of Abbé Pirard, who, less polite than the Marquis, answered only by giving a whistle and then changing the subject. The following morning Julien presented himself to the Marquis, attired in black and carrying his portfolio of letters ready for signature. He was received in the old manner. That evening, blue-coated, there was a different tone again and quite as much politeness as the night before.

– Since these visits which you have been so kind as to make to a sick old man don't bore you too grievously, you might tell me about all the little events of your life – but frankly, without thinking of anything else and telling the tale clearly and entertainingly. For it is essential to be amused, continued the Marquis; that's the only real thing in life. A man can't save my life in battle every day, or make me a present of a million; but if I had Rivarol[2] here, next to my couch, every single day he would spare me an hour of pain and boredom. I knew him well at Hamburg during the Emigration.

And the Marquis told Julien anecdotes of Rivarol and the citizens of Hamburg, who used to meet in groups of four so as to work out the meaning of his witticisms.

Thrown back on the society of this young abbé, M. de La Mole desired to liven him up. He felt himself bound to tease Julien's pride. Since the truth was being demanded of him, Julien resolved to tell it to the full – but keeping back two things: his fanatical admiration for a name that would annoy the Marquis greatly, and his perfect lack of belief, which did not look at all good in a future priest. His little entanglement with the Chevalier de Beauvoisis came just at the right moment. The Marquis laughed till he cried at the scene in the café on the rue St-Honoré – with the coachman overwhelming him with filthy insults. It was a time of perfect frankness in the relations between patron and protegé.

M. de La Mole developed a great interest in this singular individual.

To begin with, he indulged Julien's ridiculous characteristics in order to be entertained by them; soon, though, he found it more amusing to correct, unobtrusively, the young man's odd ways of seeing things. Other provincials who come to Paris admire everything, reflected the Marquis; this one detests everything. They develop far too much affectation, he too little, and idiots take him for an idiot.

The attack of gout was prolonged by the excessive winter cold, and lasted several months.

One can become very fond of a beautiful spaniel, said the Marquis to himself, why should I be so ashamed of becoming fond of this little abbé? – he's an original. I treat him like a son; very well! where's the harm in that? The whim, if it persists, could cost me a diamond worth five hundred louis in my will.

Once the Marquis had understood his protégé's firm character, he began to entrust him with some new business every day.

Julien realized with dismay that this grand seigneur sometimes gave him contradictory instructions on the same subject.

That could be dangerously compromising. So Julien no longer proceeded without bringing along a register in which he wrote decisions down, then had the Marquis initial them. Julien had hired a clerk to transcribe decisions relative to each piece of business in a special file. The file also contained copies of all letters.

At first, this idea seemed the height of absurdity and tedium. But in less than two months the Marquis felt its advantages. Julien suggested to him that they engage a clerk from a bank, who should make it his business to record in double entry all the credits and debits relating to the estates with whose administration Julien had been charged.

These measures so clarified his own affairs for the Marquis that he was able to undertake two or three new speculations without the help of his broker, who perpetually stole from him.

– Take three thousand francs for yourself, he said one day to his young minister.

– My behaviour might be made into a scandal, monsieur.

– Then what would you do? demanded the Marquis testily.

– You might be so kind as to make a formal agreement, and write it in the register in your own hand; this agreement would allow me a sum of three thousand francs. Besides, it was M. l'Abbé Pirard who had the idea of all that accounting. The Marquis – with a bored expression, like that of the Marquis de Moncade listening to his steward M. Poisson[3] reading his accounts – wrote out the agreement.

In the evenings, when Julien appeared in his blue coat, there was never any question of business. The Marquis's kindnesses so cosseted our hero's ever vulnerable self-esteem that soon, despite himself, he felt a sort of attachment to the pleasant old man. It was not that Julien was *receptive* in the Parisian sense of the word; but he was not a monster, and no one, since the death of the old Surgeon-major, had showed him so much kindness. He was amazed to realize that the Marquis displayed a courteous tactfulness with regard to his feelings that he had never found in the old Surgeon-major. Eventually he understood that the Surgeon was prouder of his cross than the Marquis of his blue riband. The Marquis had had a lord for a father.

One day, as the morning's session drew to a close, Julien, dressed in black coat and there for business, so amused the Marquis that he kept him on for two more hours, and was absolutely determined to present him with some bank notes his broker had just brought in from the Stock Exchange.

– I trust, M. le Marquis, that I shall not depart from the profound respect I owe you if I beg to put in a word?

– Speak on, my friend.

– That M. le Marquis deigns to allow me to refuse this gift. It is not to the man in black that it is offered, and it would altogether inhibit the manners so very kindly tolerated in the man in blue.

He bowed most respectfully, and went out without looking back.

This piece of behaviour intrigued the Marquis. That evening, he told the Abbé Pirard about it.

– I must confess something to you at last, my dear abbé. I know about Julien's birth, and I authorize you to fail to keep this confidence a secret.

His behaviour this morning was noble, thought the Marquis, and I'm taking it upon myself to ennoble him.

Shortly after this, the Marquis was at last able to go out of doors.

– Go and spend two months in London, said he to Julien. Special couriers, and others, will bring you the letters I receive, together with my notes on them. You can prepare the answers and send them back to me – putting in each letter with the reply. I have worked out that the delay will be only five days.

Whilst travelling in the post coach on the road to Calais, Julien was amazed at the futility of the supposed business on which he was being sent.

We will pass in total silence over the feelings of hatred, almost horror, with which he stepped on English soil. We know about his infatuation with Bonaparte. In each officer he saw a Sir Hudson Lowe, in each great lord a Bathurst,[4] ordaining the infamies on St Helena and receiving a ten-year ministry for his reward.

In London he at last understood the higher forms of foppery. He made friends with the young Russian aristocrats, who initiated him.

– You have been predestined for the life, my dear Sorel, they told him, you possess naturally that glacial air, a *thousand leagues from the feelings of the moment*, that we must try so hard to adopt.

– You haven't understood your century, Prince Korasoff told him: *Always do the opposite of what is expected of you.*[5] That, upon my honour, is the only religion of the times. Don't be wild or affected, because people always expect wildness and affectation, and therefore the precept wouldn't be borne out.

Julien covered himself in glory one day in the Duke of Fitz-Folke's house, where he had been invited together with Prince Korasoff. They were kept waiting for an hour. The manner with which Julien conducted himself amongst the twenty or so others also waiting is still talked about by young secretaries to the embassy in London. He had an inimitable air.

Despite his friendship with the dandies, he wanted to visit the celebrated Philip Vane[6] – the only philosopher England has produced since Locke. He found him doing his seventh year in prison. The aristocracy does not trifle in this country, Julien reflected; what's more, Vane is dishonoured, vilified, etc.

Julien found him in the best of spirits; the aristocratic fury against him banished boredom. That, said Julien, leaving the prison, is the only cheerful man I have met in England.

The concept that is most useful to tyrants is the concept of God, Vane had said to him . . .

We suppress the rest of his system as being *cynical*.

Then, when he got back:

— What amusing idea have you brought me from England? M. de La Mole asked him . . . He was silent. — What idea have you brought, amusing or not? the Marquis insisted sharply.

— *Primo*, said Julien, the most sensible Englishman is mad for an hour a day; he is haunted by the demon of suicide, which is the national deity.

Secundo, Wit and genius lose twenty-five per cent of their value on landing in England.

Tertio, There is nothing in the world so beautiful, lovable and moving as the English countryside.

— It's my turn now, said the Marquis:

Primo, why did you go and remark at the Russian Ambassador's that there are three hundred thousand men of twenty-five in France passionately wanting war? — did you imagine that that would please the monarchs?

— One doesn't know what to do when talking to our grand diplomats, replied Julien. They have a passion for starting serious discussions. If you stick to journalistic commonplaces, you pass for a fool. If you allow yourself something true and novel, they're astounded, don't know how to answer and at seven o'clock next morning they cause you to be informed by the First Secretary of the Embassy that you have been tactless.

— Not at all bad, said the Marquis, laughing. Nevertheless I am prepared to wager, monsieur the philosopher, that you haven't worked out what you went to England to do.

— I beg your pardon, replied Julien; I went there to dine once a week with the ambassador of the King, who is the most courteous of men.

— You went there to find that cross you see there, said the Marquis. I don't want you to leave off your black coat, but I have become used to the more entertaining relation I've cultivated with the man in blue. Until further orders, make sure you understand this: when I see this cross, you will be the younger son of my friend the Duc de Chaulnes, who, without his knowing it, has been practising diplomacy for the last six months. Now take notice, added the Marquis, with an extremely serious air, and cutting short any manifestations of gratitude, that I have no wish at all that you move out of your station in life. That's always a mistake, and as great a misfortune for the patron as for the protegé. When my lawsuits begin to bore you, or you no longer suit me, I will ask for a fine living for you, like that of our friend the Abbé Pirard – and *nothing more*, added the Marquis in a very dry voice.

This cross set Julien's pride at rest; he talked much more readily. He less often felt offended, and less often thought himself the target of those kinds of remark, capable of being interpreted as less than polite, that can easily escape anyone in a lively conversation.

To this cross he owed also a remarkable visit; this was from M. le Baron de Valenod, who had come to Paris to present his thanks for his baronetcy to the Minister, and to negotiate with him. He was about to be appointed Mayor of Verrières, replacing M. de Rênal.

Julien laughed to himself heartily when M. de Valenod led him to understand that it had just been discovered that M. de Rênal was a Jacobin. The reality was that in the impending new elections the new baron was the Minister's candidate, and that within the electoral college of the department, which in truth was very Ultra, M. de Rênal was being supported by the liberals.

It was no good at all Julien trying to find out anything about Mme de Rênal; the Baron appeared to remember their ancient rivalry and was impenetrable. He ended by asking for Julien's father's vote in the coming elections. Julien promised to write to him.

– You ought, Monsieur le Chevalier, to introduce me to M. le Marquis de La Mole.

In fact, *I ought to do it*, thought Julien; but such a scoundrel! . . .

– To tell you the truth, he answered, I'm too junior a personage in the Hôtel de La Mole to take it upon myself to introduce anyone.

Julien told the Marquis everything: that evening he reported

Valenod's ambition, as well as his career and actions since 1814.

– Not only, M. de La Mole replied in a very serious tone, not only will you introduce me to the new baron tomorrow, but I will invite him to dinner the day after. This fellow shall be one of our new prefects.

– In that case, replied Julien coolly, I request the post of Director of the Poorhouse for my father.

– First class! said the Marquis, becoming very cheerful again. Granted; I had expected a sermon. You are growing up.

M. de Valenod informed Julien that the holder of the lottery concession in Verrières had just died: Julien thought it would be amusing to give the place to M. de Cholin, that old cretin whose petition he had long ago found in M. de La Mole's room. The Marquis laughed heartily at the petition, which Julien recited to him while arranging for him to sign the letter requesting the position from the Ministry of Finance.

Hardly had M. de Cholin been appointed when Julien learned that a departmental deputation had begged the place for M. Gros, the celebrated geometrician: this generous man had an income of no more than 1,400 francs, yet had lent 600 each year to the dying concessionaire to help him support his family.

Julien was astounded at what he had done. But that is nothing, he said to himself, it will be necessary to do a great many other injustices if I am to succeed – and to know how to cloak them under fine sentimental phrases. Poor M. Gros! He is the one who deserves a cross; it's I that have it, and I must behave in the spirit of the government that gave it me.

CHAPTER 8

What Decoration Confers Distinction?

Your water does not refresh me, said the thirsty Genie.
— Yet it's the coolest well in all Diar Békir.   PELLICO[1]

One day Julien got back from Villequier, a charming estate on the banks of the Seine which was of especial interest to M. de La Mole because it was the only one of all his estates that had been held by the celebrated Boniface de La Mole. At the hôtel he found the Marquise and her daughter, just returned from Hyères.

Julien was a dandy by now and understood the fine points of Parisian life. He displayed a perfect coldness toward Mlle de La Mole. He seemed to have no recollection whatever of the occasion on which she had so gaily interrogated him about the details of his ways of tumbling off a horse.

Mlle de La Mole found him taller and paler. There was no trace of the provincial left in his bearing or his turn-out; but this was not so with his conversation: in that one still noticed something too earnest, too positive. Yet in spite of this thoughtful element, his speech was, thanks to his pride, in no way that of an inferior; one simply felt that he still considered too much to be of importance. But one saw that he was a man who would uphold what he said.

— He lacks lightness of touch, but not intelligence, remarked Mlle de La Mole while teasing her father about the cross he had given Julien. My brother has been asking for one for eighteen months — and he is a de La Mole!

— Yes; but Julien is capable of the unexpected, which is never the case with the de La Mole you mention.

M. le Duc de Retz was announced.

Mathilde found herself seized by a yawning she could not control; she became conscious yet again of the antique gildings in her father's salon, and of its ancient inhabitants. She conjured up a completely tedious image of the life she was about to resume in Paris. Even though at Hyères she had pined for the city.

And yet I am nineteen! thought she: according to all these boobies with gilded edges it is the age to be happy. She was glancing at nine or ten volumes of new verse that had piled up on a side table during their absence in Provence. She was unfortunate enough to be cleverer than MM. de Croisenois, de Caylus, de Luz and her other friends. She could predict everything they were going to say to her about the fine sky of Provence, poetry, the South, etc., etc.

Those lovely eyes, in which breathed the deepest ennui – and still worse, a despair of ever finding pleasure – paused on Julien. At least he is not precisely the same as everyone else.

– M. Sorel, said she, in the lively, clipped and completely non-feminine voice used by young women of the upper class, M. Sorel, are you going to be at M. de Retz's ball tonight?

– Mademoiselle, I haven't had the honour of being introduced to M. le Duc. (It was as if these words and that title scorched the lips of the haughty provincial.)

– He has charged my brother with bringing you along; and if you were to come, you could tell me some little things about the estate at Villequier; there is some question of us going there in the spring. I'd like to know if the château is habitable, and if it is as pretty round there as it is said to be. So many reputations are fraudulent!

Julien did not reply.

– Come to the ball with my brother, she added in the driest tone.

Julien gave a respectful bow. – So, even at a ball, I must be accountable to all members of the family. Aren't I paid to be a manager of business affairs? In his ill temper he added: God knows if what I say to the daughter won't contradict the plans of the father, the brother, the mother! It is really like the court of a sovereign prince. You have be a perfect nullity, and yet never give anyone the right to complain.

How I dislike that big girl! thought he, watching Mlle de La Mole as she walked away, her mother having called her over to present her to some women friends. She is outrageously fashionable, her dress is almost falling off her shoulders . . . she is even paler than before she went away . . . How colourless her hair is, through being so excessively fair. You could say light goes right through it. What haughtiness in that way of greeting people, in her gaze! What queenly gestures!

Mlle de La Mole had just called to her brother as he was leaving the salon.

Comte Norbert came up to Julien:

— My dear Sorel, said he, where d'you wish me to pick you up at midnight for M. de Retz's ball? He expressly charged me to bring you.

— I am well aware to whom I owe such kindness, replied Julien, bowing almost to the ground.

His ill temper, unable to find anything to fix on in the tone of politeness, and even of interest, with which Norbert had addressed him, started to vent itself on the reply that he, Julien, had made to this obliging offer. He found it contained a deal too much humility.

That evening, arriving at the ball, he was impressed by the magnificence of the Hôtel de Retz. The courtyard was covered by an immense tent of crimson canvas, dotted with golden stars: nothing could be more elegant. Under this canopy the courtyard had been turned into a wood of blossoming orange trees and oleanders. Their pots had been deeply enough buried for the oranges and oleanders to appear to spring from out the ground. The path through which the coaches arrived was strewn with sand.

To our young provincial this whole arrangement seemed wonderful. He had had no notion of such splendour; in an instant his excited imagination was a thousand miles away from ill humour. In the coach on the way to the ball Norbert had been full of cheer, while Julien took a black view of everything; hardly had they entered the courtyard than these roles were reversed.

Norbert noticed only the few details that, in the midst of such magnificence, had not been perfectly done. He estimated the cost of each detail, and Julien saw that when he arrived at a high total he showed something like jealousy, and became cross.

As for him, he was beguiled, admiring and almost made nervous by the strength of his emotion as he arrived in the first of the rooms used for dancing. There was pressure to move on to the door of the second room, but the crowd was so packed that it was impossible for him to go further. The second salon was decorated in the style of the Alhambra in Granada.

– She's the queen of the ball, you must admit it, said a young moustachioed man whose shoulder was pushing into Julien's chest.

– Mlle Fourmont, who has been the prettiest girl the whole winter, replied his neighbour, knows that she has been relegated to second place: see her strange expression.

– In truth she's jamming on all her sail to be winning. Look – look at that gracious smile just at the moment she's dancing apart in the quadrille. Upon my honour, it's incredible.

– Mlle de La Mole seems thoroughly superior to the pleasures of her triumph – which she is all too well aware of. One might say she is nervous of charming the people she talks to.

– Excellent! That is the art of being seductive.

Julien's efforts to catch a glimpse of this enchanting woman were useless; seven or eight men taller than him blocked his view.

– There's a vast amount of flirtatiousness in that haughty reserve, declared the young man with the moustaches.

– And those great blue eyes lowered so slowly just at the moment one thinks they will give her feelings away, continued his neighbour. My word, nothing so artful.

– See how ordinary the lovely Fourmont looks beside her, added a third.

– That air of reserve is just as if to say: How many delights could I set out before you, were you the man worthy of me!

– And who could be the man worthy of the sublime Mathilde? said the first: some sovereign prince, handsome, witty, well built, a hero in the wars and about twenty years old?

– The natural son of the Emperor of Russia ... to whom, in honour of this marriage, they had given a sovereign state; or quite simply the Comte de Thaler, looking like a dressed-up peasant ...

The door became unblocked, and Julien was able to pass through.

Since these tailor's dummies find her so remarkable it might be worth the trouble to inspect her, he thought. Let me see what it is these people regard as perfection.

As his gaze travelled round in search of her, Mathilde glanced at him. My duty calls, said Julien to himself; but the only ill temper now was in his expression. His curiosity led him to step forward with a pleasure that Mathilde's dress, cut so extremely low on her shoulders, speedily increased – really in a way not very gratifying to Julien's pride. There is something essentially youthful in her beauty, he thought. Five or six young men, amongst whom Julien recognized those he had heard at the door, were between them.

You, monsieur, who have been here all winter, she called to him, is this really the finest ball of the season?

He made no reply.

– This Coulon[2] quadrille seems excellent to me; and these ladies dance it perfectly. The young men turned round to see who could be the lucky fellow from whom she absolutely insisted on getting an answer. It turned out not to be an encouraging one.

– I couldn't possibly be a judge of that, mademoiselle; I spend my life scribbling: this is the first ball of such splendour I have ever seen. The young men with moustaches were scandalized.

– You're a wise man, M. Sorel, she replied, with an even more marked interest; you view all these balls, all these parties, as Jean-Jacques Rousseau did. Such follies amaze you, but do not seduce you.

A mere name[3] succeeded in stifling the fires of Julien's imagination, and chased all illusions from his heart. His mouth assumed a perhaps exaggerated expression of disdain.

– Jean-Jacques Rousseau, he replied, is nothing but a fool when he takes it upon himself to pronounce upon the great world; he understood nothing about it, and brought to it the heart of an upstart lackey.

– He wrote *The Social Contract*, said Mathilde with veneration.

– In the middle of preaching about a republic and the downfall of the royal state, this upstart goes wild with happiness if a duke alters the direction of his after-dinner stroll to accompany one of his friends.

– Ah! yes, the Duc de Luxembourg at Montmorency going with a certain M. Coindet on the way to Paris . . .[4] replied Mlle de La Mole with the unrestrained relish of a first taste of pedantry. She was intoxicated by her erudition, a little like the Academician who discovered the existence of King Feretrius.[5] Julien continued to look cutting and severe. Mathilde had had a burst of enthusiasm; her companion's coldness disconcerted her deeply. She was all the more put out because it was she who was accustomed to producing this effect on others.

Just then the Marquis de Croisenois was eagerly trying to reach Mlle de La Mole's side. He was held up temporarily three steps away, unable to get to her through the crush. He gazed at her while smiling at the obstacle in his way. In front of him was the young Marquise de Rouvray, a cousin of Mathilde. She was leaning on the arm of her husband, to whom she had been married only a fortnight. The Marquis de Rouvray, also very young, was showing all of the fatuous amorousness that grips a man who, having made a marriage of convenience entirely organized by lawyers, discovers a perfectly beautiful being. M. de Rouvray would become a duke on the death of his very aged uncle.

While the Marquis de Croisenois, unable to get through the crowd, looked humorously at Mathilde, she let her heavenly blue eyes dwell on him and his neighbours. What could be more banal, said she to herself, than this whole group? Here's Croisenois, who wants to marry me; he is gentle, polished and has perfect manners like M. de Rouvray. If it weren't for the boredom these gentlemen generate they would be perfectly amiable. He, too, would take me to a ball with the same controlled and satisfied expression on his face. A year after the marriage, my coach, my horses, my gowns, my château twenty leagues from Paris, all that would be as fine as it possibly could be, everything that could be needed to make a parvenue die with envy, a Comtesse de Roiville, for example; and after that . . . ?

Mathilde found the very prospect tedious. The Marquis de Croisenois succeeded in reaching her and speaking to her, but she dreamt on without listening. The sound of his words was lost to her in the general murmur of the ball. Her eyes mechanically followed Julien, who had parted from her with an air that was respectful, but aloof and discontented. In a corner far from the circulating mass, she noticed Comte Altamira, a man of whom the reader has already heard, under sentence of death in his own country. In Louis XIV's time one of his ancestors had married a Prince de Conti; and the memory of this gave him some small protection against the Congregation's police.

So far as I can see, thought Mathilde, a sentence of death is the only thing that confers distinction on a man: it is the only thing no one ever buys.

Ah! what a fine epigram I have just produced! What a pity it didn't occur to me when it would have done me honour! Mathilde had too much taste to introduce a witticism prepared in advance into a conversation; but she also had too much vanity not to be delighted with herself. An air of satisfaction replaced the bored expression on her face. The Marquis de Croisenois, who had been talking to her throughout, believed he was seeing his own success, and redoubled his eloquence.

What could some carping critic say against my epigram? Mathilde asked herself. I would reply to them: the title of baron, of vicomte, can be bought; a cross can be given; my brother is just about to get one, and what has he ever done? A rank can be obtained. Ten years in a garrison, or a relative in the War Ministry, and a man becomes head of a squadron like Norbert. A great fortune! . . . that's still the most difficult and therefore the most meritorious. And – this is amusing! – it is the exact opposite of what they say in books . . . Oh, all right! for a fortune you may marry M. Rothschild's daughter.

My saying really has depth. A sentence of death is still the only thing no one has ever thought of applying for.

– Do you know Comte Altamira? she asked M. de Croisenois.

She had the air of coming back from so far away, and this question was so little related to anything the poor marquis had been talking about for the last five minutes, that it gave his affability a jolt. Yet he was a man of wit, much renowned.

Mathilde has some eccentricity, thought he; it is a disadvantage – but she would confer such a fine social position on her husband! I don't know how this Marquis de La Mole does it; he is allied to the best men in all the parties; he is a man whom nobody can overshadow. And what's more, this eccentricity of Mathilde's may pass for genius. With high birth and plenty of money, genius is never absurd – and then what distinction it can bestow! At other times, when she cares to be, she is so adept at that mingling of wit, individuality and aptness which constitutes perfect charm . . .

Since it is difficult to do two things well at the same time, the Marquis replied to Mathilde in a vacant manner, and as if reciting a lesson:

– Who doesn't know poor Altamira? And he told her the story of his failed conspiracy, inept and absurd.

– Absurd indeed! said Mathilde as though speaking to herself – nevertheless he did do something. I want to see a man; bring him to me, said she to the disconcerted marquis.

Comte Altamira was one of the more vocal admirers of Mlle de la Mole's haughty and almost insulting manner; according to him, she was one of the most beautiful creatures in Paris.

– How lovely she would be on a throne! he said to M. de Croisenois; and he made no objection to being led over to her.

There is never a shortage of people in society who would like to insist that nothing is in such bad taste as conspiracy – it has a Jacobinical odour. And what is more dismal than a failed Jacobin?

Like M. de Croisenois, Mathilde viewed Altamira's liberalism satirically, but she listened with pleasure.

A conspirator at a ball, thought she, what a pretty contrast. In this example, with his black moustachios, she thought she might find the features of a lion in repose; but soon discovered that his mind had only one guiding principle: *utility, the admiration of utility.*[6]

This young comte thought nothing worthy of his attention unless it was capable of delivering government by two chambers to his native land. He gladly forsook Mathilde, the most seductive woman at the ball, because he had noticed the entry of a Peruvian general.

Despairing of Europe, poor Altamira was reduced to thinking that when the states of South America became strong and powerful they might be able to deliver the liberty that Mirabeau had exported there back to Europe.[7]

A little eddy of young gentlemen with moustaches was approaching Mathilde. She clearly realized that she had not put her spell on Altamira, and found herself piqued by his departure; she saw his dark eyes sparkle as he talked to the Peruvian general. Mlle de La Mole studied the young Frenchmen with that deep and earnest gaze none of her rivals could match. Which of them, she wondered, could get himself sentenced to death, even supposing all the circumstances favoured him?

Her strange stare flattered those of little wit, but made the others uneasy. They dreaded the explosion of some witticism, biting and hard to answer.

High breeding gives a hundred advantages, the absence of which offends me, reflected Mathilde: I see this in Julien's case; but it enfeebles those qualities of the soul which allow one to become sentenced to death.

Just at that moment someone next to her remarked: This Comte Altamira is the second son of the Prince of San Nazaro-Pimentel – it was a Pimentel who attempted to save Conradin,[8] who was beheaded in 1268. They are one of the noblest families in Naples.

There! said Mathilde to herself, that bears out my maxim brilliantly: high birth destroys the force of character without which one cannot get sentenced to death! So I am destined not to be very clever this evening. And since I am nothing but a woman like any other, very well, then – I must dance. She gave way to the solicitations of the Marquis de Croisenois, who for the last hour had been urging her to do the *galope*. To distract herself from her failure as a philosopher Mathilde set out to be completely bewitching – and M. de Croisenois was enchanted.

But neither the dance itself nor the wish to please one of the most handsome men at Court – nothing could divert Mathilde. It was impossible to have a greater success. She was queen of the ball, she saw that, but she saw it with indifference.

What a flat existence I would live with a creature like Croisenois! she said to herself as he led her back to her place an hour later . . .

Where will I ever find joy? she added sadly, if after being absent for six months I don't experience it right in the middle of a ball that's the envy of every woman in Paris? And furthermore, I am surrounded by the homage of a company I cannot imagine being better composed. There are no bourgeois elements here except for a few peers and one or two Juliens, perhaps. And then, added she with increasing distress, what advantages has fate not granted me? High birth, wealth, youth! – alas! everything save happiness.

The most dubious of my assets, moreover, are those about which they have been talking to me all evening. Intelligence, I believe in that, for it is obvious that I frighten them all. If they dare raise a serious subject, then at the end of five minutes' conversation they arrive panting, as though they have made a great discovery, at whatever it is I have been saying for the last hour. I am beautiful, I have the asset for which Mme de Staël[9] would have sacrificed everything – and yet it is a fact that I am dying of boredom. Is there any reason I should be less bored when I have changed my name for that of the Marquis de Croisenois?

But, dear God! she added, almost wanting to weep, isn't he a perfect young man? The masterwork of modern upbringing; you can hardly look at him without his finding something agreeable and even witty to say; and he is brave . . . But that Sorel is most peculiar, she said to herself, and her eyes exchanged their melancholy expression for one of annoyance. I made it clear that I had something to say to him, and he has not deigned to return to me!

CHAPTER 9

The Ball

> The luxuriousness of the dresses, the glitter of the candles,
> the scents: so many shapely arms and lovely shoulders! the
> flowers! Rossini's exhilarating tunes, Ciceri's paintings! I'm
> transported quite beyond myself!   *Useri's Travels*[1]

You're in a bad mood, the Marquise de La Mole said to her; I must
tell you, that is not at all gracious at a ball.

— It's just that my head aches, replied Mathilde with a disdainful
glance, it's too hot in here.

At that moment, as if to justify Mlle de La Mole, the elderly Baron
de Tolly was taken ill and collapsed; they had to carry him out.
There was talk of apoplexy — a very disagreeable incident.

Mathilde paid no attention at all. It was a fixed principle with her
never to show interest in old people or in anyone else likely to say
dreary things.

She started to dance in order not to hear talk of apoplexy — of
which in fact this had not been a case, since the Baron reappeared
the day after next.

And still M. Sorel had not come, she said to herself after she had
finished dancing. Her eyes were almost setting off in search of him
when she spotted him in another room. It was astonishing — he
seemed to have lost the air of impenetrable coldness so natural to
him; he no longer looked like an Englishman.

He is talking to Comte Altamira — my condemned man! exclaimed
Mathilde to herself. His looks are full of sombre fire; he seems like a
prince in disguise; his air is prouder than ever.

Julien was walking towards where she was, all the time talking to

306

Altamira; she stared fixedly at that face, searching there for those high qualities that might earn a man the honour of being sentenced to death.

As they went past her:

– Yes! – he was saying to Comte Altamira – Danton truly was a man!

Gracious Heavens! could he become a Danton? Mathilde asked herself; but he has so noble a face, and that Danton was horribly ugly – a butcher, I believe. Julien was still quite close to her, and she did not hesitate to call over to him; she was proudly conscious that, for a young lady, she was asking a very unusual question.

– Danton: he was a butcher, was he not? she said.

– In the eyes of certain individuals, yes, replied Julien with an expression of very ill-disguised disdain, his eyes still glowing from his talk with Altamira – but, unfortunately for well-bred people, he was a lawyer at Méry-sur-Seine; which is to say, mademoiselle, he added with a malicious look, that he started off in life like several of the peers I see here. But it is true that in the eyes of beauty Danton had an enormous disadvantage, for he was extremely ugly.

These last words came out rapidly, in an extraordinary way, which most certainly was not at all polite.

Julien paused for a second, the top of his body leaning forwards slightly in a stance of assertive humility. He seemed to be saying: I am paid to answer you, and I must live on what I am paid. He did not deign to lift his eyes to Mathilde. She, with her lovely eyes opened extraordinarily wide, and fixed upon him, looked as though she was his slave. At last, as the silence persisted, he gave her a glance like a valet gives his master when awaiting orders. Although his eyes now fully met Mathilde's, fixed on him still in their strange gaze, he turned and went off with marked haste.

He, who really is so handsome, thought Mathilde, emerging at last from her trance – he to pronounce a eulogy on ugliness! Never a reference to himself! He's not like Caylus or Croisenois. This Sorel has something of the air my father puts on when he imitates Napoleon so brilliantly at a ball. She had forgotten Danton entirely. – I am certainly very bored this evening. She seized her brother's arm and, to his great discomfiture, forced him to stroll around the ballroom with her. She had had the idea that she might follow the conversation between Julien and the man sentenced to death.

The crush of people was very great. She succeeded in rejoining them, however, just as Altamira, two paces in front of her, was stepping up to a tray to take an ice. He was talking to Julien, his body half turned away. He had noticed an arm in an embroidered sleeve taking an ice just next to his. The braid on it seemed to catch his attention; he turned right round to see what dignitary the arm belonged to. Immediately his eyes, so noble and candid, took on an expression of mild disdain.

— You see this man, he said in a slight undertone to Julien; he is the Prince d'Araceli, ambassador from ——.[2] This morning he demanded my extradition from M. de Nerval, your Minister for Foreign Affairs. Look – down over there playing whist. M. de Nerval is quite inclined to give me up, because we surrendered two or three conspirators to you in 1816. If someone does hand me over to my king I will be hanged within twenty-four hours. And it will be one of those fine young gents in moustaches who will betray me.

— The scoundrels! cried Julien, half out loud.

Mathilde lost no word of this conversation. Boredom had fled.

— Not such great scoundrels, replied Comte Altamira. I've spoken about my own case to impress you with a vivid example. But now look at the Prince d'Araceli; every five minutes he glances at his Golden Fleece; he can't get over the pleasure of seeing that bauble on his own breast. The poor fellow is nothing more than an anachronism. A hundred years ago the Fleece was a signal honour, but then it would have been miles over his head. These days, among well-born people, you have to be an Araceli to be so enchanted with it. He would have seen a whole town swing to get it.

— And is that the price at which he did get it? asked Julien anxiously.

— Not literally, answered Altamira coolly; perhaps he caused thirty or so wealthy squires, thought of as liberals in his country, to be thrown into the river.

— What a monster! Julien insisted.

Mlle de La Mole, who was leaning her head forward with the

liveliest of interest, pressed so close that her wonderful hair almost touched his shoulder.

– You're very young! replied Altamira. I mentioned to you that I have a married sister in Provence; she's still pretty, she's good, and she's mild; she is an excellent mother to her family, faithful in all her duties, pious but no fanatic.

What's this leading up to? wondered Mlle de La Mole.

– She's happy, continued Comte Altamira; she was happy in 1815. At that time I was in hiding there, on her estate near Antibes; very well, then – the moment she heard of the execution of Marshal Ney she started to dance!

– How's that possible? cried Julien, dumbfounded.

– It's the partisan spirit, replied Altamira. There aren't any true passions left in the nineteenth century: that's why there's so much boredom in France. One does the cruellest things imaginable, but without the sensation of cruelty.

– So much the worse! said Julien; at least when one commits crimes it should be done with enjoyment; there's nothing else good about them, and even that only slightly redeems them.

Mlle de La Mole, oblivious of everything she owed to her dignity, had now placed herself almost completely in between Altamira and Julien. Her brother, who, being accustomed to obey her, had given her his arm, was gazing around elsewhere in the salon and, to avoid seeming ridiculous, had assumed an air of having been held up by the crowd.

– You're right, said Altamira; people do everything without pleasure and without any memory of what they've done – even atrocities. I could show you maybe as many as ten men at this ball who will be damned as assassins. They've forgotten about it, and so has everyone else.[3]

A lot of these types are moved to tears if their dog breaks a leg. At Père-Lachaise, when flowers are strewn upon their graves – as you so agreeably put it in Paris – we'll be told that all the virtues of the knights of old were revived in them, and there will be talk of the great deeds of an ancestor who lived in the time of Henri IV. If, in spite of the good offices of the Prince d'Araceli, I am not hanged, and if I am ever able to avail myself of my fortune in Paris, I would be pleased to entertain you to dinner with nine or ten assassins, full of honours and strangers to remorse.

At that dinner you and I would be the only ones innocent of blood, but I'd be scorned and almost hated as a bloodstained Jacobin, and you simply despised as a man of the people intruding into good company.

— Nothing could be truer, said Mlle de La Mole.

Altamira looked at her in amazement, Julien did not condescend to give her a glance.

— Take note that the revolution of which I found myself at the head, continued Comte Altamira, failed to succeed simply because I was unwilling to see three heads roll, and distribute among our supporters the seven or eight million that happened to be in a chest to which I had the key. My king, who is today burning to have me hanged — and was on intimate terms with me before the uprising — would have given me the grand sash of his Order if I had let those three heads roll and distributed the money from the chests — for I would have won at least a half success, and my country would have had a charter, such as it was . . . But that's how the world goes — it's a game of chess.

— At that time, replied Julien, his eyes gleaming, you didn't know the rules of the game; but now . . .

— I'd let the heads roll, you'd have me say, and cease being a Girondin[4] as you hinted the other day? . . . I'll answer that, said Altamira sadly, when you've killed your man in a duel — which is a lot less ugly than handing him over to the headsman.

— My God! said Julien, but the end justifies the means; if, instead of being a mere grain of sand, I had some power, I'd hang three men to save the lives of four.

His eyes shone with the fire of principle and scorn for vain human judgements; they met those of Mlle de La Mole just next to him, and this scornful look, far from changing into a gracious or civil air, seemed to intensify.

She was extremely disturbed; but it was no longer in her power to overlook Julien; she moved away in vexation, taking her brother with her.

I must have some punch and dance a great deal, she said to herself; I must choose the most appropriate person, and at all costs make an impression. Ah good, here's the Comte de Fervaques, famous for his impertinence. She accepted his invitation; and they danced. It's a matter of finding out, thought she, which of us two will be the more insolent, but for me to tease him properly I must make him talk . . . Soon all the rest of those in the dance were dancing only as a formality. No one was willing to miss one of Mathilde's piquant repartees. M. de Fervaques became upset, and, only being able to produce fine phrasing as opposed to fresh ideas, began to sulk; Mathilde, in a temper, was cruel to him, and antagonized him completely. She danced until dawn, and at last retired horribly worn out. But in the carriage her little remnant of energy was used in making herself wretched and uncomfortable. She had been despised by Julien, and was unable to despise him in return.

Julien was overwhelmed by happiness – enchanted unawares by the music, the flowers, the beautiful women, the pervading elegance and, above all else, by his imagination, which dreamt of distinction for himself and liberty for all:

– What a beautiful ball! said he to the Comte – Nothing was lacking.

– Ideas were lacking, replied Altamira.

And his face betrayed the kind of disdain that is all the more telling because one realizes that politeness imposes on one an obligation to hide it.

– You are here, Monsieur le Comte. Isn't that ideas, and ideas which are still conspiring?

– I'm here for my name. But in your salons they detest ideas. They must never be raised above the level of a vaudeville couplet – although then they are rewarded. But if a thoughtful man injects energy and novelty into his remarks you call him a *cynical dog*. Isn't that what one of your judges called Courier?[5] You put him in prison, just like Béranger. With you anyone with a distinguished mind is thrown to the police courts by the Congregation; and good Society applauds.

The truth is that your decaying civilization prizes conventionality above all else . . . You never raise yourselves higher than military gallantry; you produce a Murat[6] but never a Washington. I see only vanity in France. A man who thinks while he talks is likely to come out with something rash, and his host gets the idea he has been dishonoured.

At that moment the Comte's carriage, which was returning Julien, pulled up in front of the Hôtel de La Mole. Julien was in love with this conspirator. Altamira had made him the following magnificent compliment, evidently produced by deep conviction: You don't possess the frivolity typical of France, and you understand the principle of *utility*.

Now it happened that just the night before last Julien had been to see M. Casimir Delavigne's tragedy, *Marino Faliero*.[7] – Wasn't Israel Bertuccio a greater figure than all those Venetian nobles? our rebellious plebeian asked himself; and yet they were men whose noble lineage can be traced back to the year 700, a century before Charlemagne, while all the best born of those who were at M. de Retz's ball this evening only go back, and even then most lamely, to the thirteenth century. Well, good! in the midst of those Venetian nobles, so very high born, it is Israel Bertuccio one remembers.

A conspiracy annihilates all the titles produced by the arbitrary decisions of society. In it a man instantly assumes the rank given him by his manner of envisaging death. Intelligence itself loses its sway . . .

Where would Danton be today, in the age of Valenod and de Rênal? – not even a deputy crown prosecutor . . .

But what am I talking about? – he would have sold himself to the Congregation; he would be a minister, for even the great Danton stole. Mirabeau sold himself, too. Napoleon grabbed millions in Italy – without them he would have been pulled up short, like Pichegru. La Fayette[8] alone never stole. Must one steal? must one sell oneself? wondered Julien. The questions pulled him up short. He spent the rest of the night reading the history of the Revolution.

The following day, working on his letters in the library, he could think of nothing but Comte Altamira's conversation.

In fact, he said to himself after a long reverie, if the liberals in Spain[9] had been willing to commit a few crimes on the people's behalf, they would not have been swept aside with such ease. They were conceited children, chatterers . . . exactly like me! Julien cried suddenly, as if waking up with a start.

What difficulty have I ever overcome that gives me the right to judge those poor devils, who at least, for once in their lives, have dared, have started to take action? I am like a man who gets up from the table and cries: Tomorrow I won't be having dinner; but this won't stop me from being as strong and as quick as I am today. But who can tell how he will turn out halfway through a great course of events? . . .

Such elevated thoughts were interrupted by the unexpected presence of Mlle de La Mole, who was coming into the library. Julien was in a state of such elation from his admiration for the great qualities of Danton, Mirabeau and Carnot[10] – men who had known how not to be suppressed – that his gaze rested on Mlle de La Mole, but without his being conscious of her, without greeting her, practically even without seeing her. When, at last, his great staring eyes did register her presence, the light died out of them. Mlle de La Mole saw this with bitterness.

It was in vain that she asked him for a volume of Vély's *History of France*, which was stored on the topmost shelf and obliged Julien to go to find the larger of the two ladders. Julien had gone up the ladder; he had looked for the volume; had given it to her – but still remained incapable of thinking about her. While he was carrying the ladder back in this trance-like state his elbow struck one of the panes of glass in the bookcase; the tinkle of glass falling on to the parquet at last brought him to his senses. He hastened to excuse himself to Mlle de La Mole; he endeavoured to be polite – but was nothing more than polite. Mathilde plainly saw that she had disturbed him, and that he would much rather go on thinking about what preoccupied him before her arrival than talk to her. After a long look at him she slowly walked away. Julien studied her as she went. He delighted in the contrast between today's simplicity of dress and the sumptuous elegance of the previous evening. Almost as striking was the difference between her two facial expressions. The young lady who had been so lofty at the Duc de Retz's ball had now an almost supplicating look. Definitely, said Julien to himself, that black gown shows off the beauty of her figure more strikingly. She has the bearing of a queen: but why is she in mourning?

If I ask someone the reason for the mourning, it will turn out to be yet another social blunder. Julien had now emerged completely from the depths of his enthusiastic dreams. I must re-read all the letters I wrote this morning; God knows what missing words and what stupidities I will find there. As he was attentively scanning the first of them he heard the rustle of a silken dress just next to him; he quickly turned round; Mlle de La Mole was two steps from his table, laughing. This second interruption irritated Julien.

Mathilde herself was becoming acutely conscious that she meant nothing to this young man; the laugh was to conceal her embarrassment, and it succeeded.

– Clearly you are thinking about something very interesting, M. Sorel. Can it be some strange story of the conspiracy that has sent M. le Comte Altamira to us in Paris? Do tell me what it is about; I'm burning to know; I'll be discreet, I swear! She was amazed to hear herself saying this. What? she pleading? with an employee! Her embarrassment growing, she added, with a little humorous air:

– What's happened to turn you, normally so frosty, into an inspired being, a type of Michelangelo prophet?

This lively, tactless questioning hurt Julien deeply and revived his delusions in full force.

– Was Danton right to steal? he asked her sharply, with an air that became fiercer and fiercer. Ought the revolutionaries in Piedmont and in Spain to have made the people guilty of their crimes? Ought they to have given away all the places in the army, all the decorations, even to men who did not deserve them? Didn't the decorated men dread the return of the King? Was it necessary to loot the treasury at Turin? In a word, mademoiselle, said he, approaching her with a terrifying look, ought he who wishes to banish ignorance and crime from the world go through it like a tempest, dealing out evil at random?

Mathilde took alarm at this, was unable to stand up to his gaze and recoiled two steps. She stared at him for a moment; then, ashamed of her fear, daintily sped from the library.

CHAPTER 10

Queen Marguerite

> Love! In what madness do you fail to make us find some
> delight?   *Letters of a* PORTUGUESE NUN[1]

Julien went on re-reading the letters. When the bell for dinner
sounded: How ridiculous I must have seemed in the eyes of that
Parisian doll! he said to himself, and how foolish of me to tell her
what I really think! But maybe not so foolish. On this occasion the
truth was worthy of me.

Why come and interrogate me on intimate matters like that? And
from her that question was indiscreet. It wasn't at all the thing. My
views on Danton are no part of what her father pays me for.

When he entered the dining-room Julien was distracted from this
bad mood by the sight of Mlle de La Mole's full mourning, which
struck him the more since no one else in the family was in black.

After dinner he felt completely freed from the fit of enthusiastic
dreaming that had gripped him all day. By good fortune, the Academician who knew Latin was at the meal. There's the man least likely
to find me ridiculous, said Julien to himself, if, as I assume, my
puzzlement about Mlle de La Mole's mourning is just awkwardness.

Mathilde was gazing at him with a strange expression. Yes, here
is an example of that coquetry of women in this part of the world
Mme de Rênal described to me, said Julien to himself. I wasn't at all
pleasant to her this morning, I didn't give way to her whimsical
leisure for talk. So I enhanced my value in her eyes. No doubt there
will be the devil to pay later. Her disdainful hauteur will know all
too well how to take revenge. Let her do her worst. What a difference
to the woman I have lost! What charming naturalness there! What

simplicity! I knew her thoughts before she knew them herself; I watched them grow; my only rival in her heart was the dread of her children's death – a reasonable and natural fear, lovable even to me who suffered from it. I've been an idiot. Those notions of Paris I had dreamed up ruined my appreciation of that sublime woman.

Great God, what a difference! What have we here instead? A sterile and haughty vanity, all the shades of self-satisfaction, nothing else whatever.

They rose from table. I must not let my Academician be caught by someone else, said Julien to himself. He went up to him as they were going into the garden, assumed a gentle and submissive air and joined in with his indignation against the success of *Hernani*.[2]

– If only it were still the times of the *lettres de cachet*![3] . . . said he.

– Then they wouldn't have dared, cried the Academician with a gesture worthy of Talma.[4]

Pointing at a flower, Julien quoted a few words of Virgil's *Georgics* and opined that nothing equalled the Abbé Delille's translation. In short, he flattered the Academician in every way possible. After which, with a more casual air:

– I imagine, said he, that Mlle de La Mole has received an inheritance from some uncle or other, for whom she is wearing mourning.

– What! you're a member of the household and don't know about her fantasy? In truth, it's very odd that her mother permits her such things; but, between ourselves, it isn't exactly by force of character that they distinguish themselves in this establishment. Mlle de La Mole has enough for all of them, and leads them by the nose. Today it is 30 April! And the Academician stopped and looked at Julien with a knowing air. Julien smiled as intelligently as he could.

What connection can there be between leading the establishment by the nose, wearing a black dress and the thirtieth of April? he wondered. I must be even dimmer than I thought.

– I must confess . . . said he to the Academician, still looking questioningly at him.

– Let's take a turn around the garden, replied the Academician, in raptures at seeing the chance to tell a long tale in an elegant fashion. What! – Is it really possible you don't know what happened on the thirtieth of April 1574 . . . ?

– Whereabouts? asked Julien, astonished.

– In the Place de Grève.

Julien was still too confused for this information to be much help to him. His curiosity, and the anticipation of some tragic interest – so congenial to his own character – gave him the shining eyes a storyteller passionately loves to see in a hearer. Delighted to find a virgin ear, the Academician recounted to Julien at length how on the thirtieth of April 1574 Boniface de La Mole, the best-looking young man of his day, and his friend Annibal de Coconasso, a Piedmontese gentleman, had their heads cut off on the Place de Grève. La Mole was the adored lover of Queen Marguerite of Navarre.[5] – And take note, added the Academician, Mlle de La Mole is called *Mathilde-Marguerite*. La Mole was simultaneously the Duc d'Alençon's favourite and the intimate friend of the King of Navarre – his mistress's husband, later Henri IV. On Shrove Tuesday of that year, 1574, the Court had found itself at Saint-Germain, with the poor King Charles IX on his death bed. La Mole proposed to rescue his friends the princes, whom the Queen, Catherine de Medici,[6] was keeping prisoners at Court. He gathered 200 horsemen under the walls of Saint-Germain – the Duc d'Alençon panicked – and La Mole was thrown to the headsman.

But what really moves Mlle de La Mole, as she told me herself – seven or eight years ago, when she was only twelve, for she has such a head, such a head! . . . And the Academician raised his eyes to heaven. What struck her in this political catastrophe was that Queen Marguerite de Navarre, in hiding at a house on the Place de Grève, had been bold enough to get someone to beg the head of her lover from the headsman. And the following night, at midnight, she proceeded to take this head in her carriage and inter it herself in a chapel at the foot of the hill at Montmartre.

– Incredible! cried Julien, enthralled.

– Mlle Mathilde despises her brother because, as you can see, he does not care one bit about all this ancient history, and never wears mourning on the thirtieth of April. Ever since that famous execution,

and to commemorate La Mole's intimate friendship with Coconasso
– this Coconasso, Italian as he was, being called Annibal – all the
men of the family have taken that name. And, added the Academician,
lowering his voice, the said Coconasso was, on the testimony of
Charles IX himself, one of the cruellest assassins of the twenty-fourth
of August 1572.[7] But how is it possible, my dear Sorel, that you know
nothing of these things – you who eat your meals in this house?

– So that's why, twice during dinner, Mlle de La Mole addressed
her brother as Annibal. I thought I hadn't heard properly.

– It was a reproach. It's strange that the Marquise puts up with
such follies . . . That grand girl's husband will see some pretty tricks!

This dictum was followed by five or six satirical remarks. The
delight in being in the know that shone in the Academician's eyes
startled Julien. Here we are, two servants busy chewing over their
masters, thought he. But nothing surprises me about this man from
the Academy of Inscriptions. Julien had caught him one day on his
knees in front of the Marquis de La Mole; he was begging for a
tobacco dealership for a nephew in the provinces.

That evening, one of Mlle de La Mole's little lady's maids, who
was making up to Julien just as Élisa had once done, gave him to
understand that her mistress's mourning really was not worn to
attract attention. Her fantastic behaviour derived from something
deep in her character. She genuinely adored this La Mole, beloved
lover of the most intelligent queen of her age, who had died trying
to ensure the liberty of his friends. And what friends! The premier
Prince of the Blood, and Henri IV.

Accustomed to the perfect naturalness that shone forth in all Mme
de Rênal's conduct, Julien saw nothing but affectation in all the Parisian
ladies; and even when he was only the slightest bit disposed to gloom,
found nothing to say to them. Mlle de La Mole formed an exception.

He began to refrain from interpreting the style of beauty belonging
to an aristocratic bearing as evidence of aridity of feeling. He held
long conversations with Mlle de La Mole, who would sometimes
stroll the length of the garden with him after dinner in front of the
open salon windows. One day she told him that she was reading
d'Aubigné's *History* and Brantôme.[8] Very striking reading, thought

Julien; yet the Marquise doesn't allow her to look at Walter Scott's novels.

One day, her eyes flashing with a pleasure that showed the sincerity of her admiration, she told him that she had just read in l'Étoile's *Memoirs*[9] of the feat of a young woman in the reign of Henri III: finding her husband unfaithful, she stabbed him to death with a poniard.

Julien's pride was flattered. A young woman surrounded by such deference, and who, according to the Academician, took the lead in the household, was condescending to converse with him in a manner almost like that of a friend.

I must be deceiving myself, he thought soon; it isn't really familiarity, I'm only like a confidant in a tragedy – it's her need to express her thoughts. In this family I pass for well read. I must go and read Brantôme, d'Aubigné, l'Étoile. Then I'll be able to match some of the anecdotes Mlle de La Mole tells me. What I must do is to get beyond this role of passive confidant.

Little by little his conversations with this girl, whose bearing was so imposing yet at the same time so easy, became more interesting. He forgot his sad role as a resentful plebeian. He found her well informed, indeed intelligent. Her opinions in the garden were very different from those she professed in the salon. With him she sometimes showed an enthusiasm and a candour that were diametrically opposite to her habitual air of cold hauteur.

– The Wars of the League[10] are the Heroic Age in France, she said to him one day, her eyes sparkling with spirit and enthusiasm. Then every man fought for something he definitely wanted, for the triumph of his faction, and not just dully so as to win a cross, as in your emperor's time. You must admit that there was less egotism and petty-mindedness. I love that age.

– And Boniface de La Mole was its hero, he replied.

– At least he was loved as it must be sweet to be loved. What woman living now would not be appalled to touch the severed head of her lover?

Mme de La Mole called her daughter away. Hypocrisy, to be of any use, must keep itself concealed; and Julien, as one can see, had made a kind of half-confidence to Mlle de La Mole about his admiration for Napoleon.

That's the immense advantage they have over us, said Julien to himself as he was left alone in the garden. The history of their ancestors raises them above common feeling, and they do not have to be always worrying about making a living. What misery! he added with bitterness, I'm not fit to talk about these great subjects. My life is just a succession of hypocritical poses – for I haven't a thousand francs a year to feed myself.

– What are you dreaming about now, monsieur? demanded Mathilde, running out again.

Julien was sick of despising himself. Out of pride, he told her his real thoughts. He blushed hotly for speaking of his poverty to a young woman who was herself so rich. By his lofty tone he hoped to make it clear that he asked for nothing. Never had he seemed so attractive to Mathilde; she found in him the expression of a sensibility and candour he so often lacked.

Less than a month after this, Julien was walking pensively in the garden of the Hôtel de La Mole; but his face no longer wore the expression of hardness and intellectual arrogance that the persistent sense of his own inferiority stamped on it. He had just been seeing Mlle de La Mole back to the door of the salon, she having professed to have hurt her foot while running with her brother.

She leaned on my arm in so marked a fashion! said Julien to himself. Am I just being a conceited fool, or can it be true that she has an affection for me? She listens so tenderly even when I go on to her about all the ups and downs of my pride! She, who shows such haughtiness to everyone else! In the salon they would be astounded if they saw that expression. I am sure she never shows anyone else so sweet and kind an air.

Julien tried not to exaggerate this strange friendliness. To himself he compared it with an armed truce. Every day on meeting her again it was almost as if they asked one another: Well, are we friends or foes today? before reverting to the almost intimate terms of yesterday. Julien had realized that if he let this haughty girl offend him with impunity even once, all would be lost. If I have to quarrel, wouldn't it be better straight away, in defending the legitimate interests of my pride, than in having to counter the marks of scorn bound to follow swiftly on the slightest concession detracting from what's due to my personal dignity?

Many times, on days when she was in ill humour, Mathilde tried to take a haughty aristocratic tone with him; she could inject a rare subtlety into such experiments, but Julien rudely rebuffed them.

One day he brusquely interrupted her with: Has Mlle de La Mole any orders to give her father's secretary? He is obliged to hear her orders and carry them out with all respect; but otherwise has nothing to say to her. He is not paid to tell her his thoughts.

Such a mode of existence, and the suspicions peculiar to Julien, dissipated the ennui that pervaded this salon in his mind — so magnificent a place, but a place where everyone was frightened of something, and where it was not done to joke about anything.

It would be so amusing if she loved me! But whether she loves me or not, Julien added, I have as an intimate confidante a clever girl at whose feet I see the whole household tremble — and no one more so than the Marquis de Croisenois. That young man who is so polite, so gentle, so brave and who unites in himself all those advantages of birth and fortune a single one of which would set my heart at ease! He is madly in love with her, he wants to marry her. Think of all the letters M. de La Mole has had me write to the two lawyers arranging the contract! And I, knowing myself to be so inferior with my pen in my hand, I, two hours later, here in the garden, triumph over this extraordinarily amiable young man: for really her preferences are striking, obvious. Possibly she also hates the future husband in him. She has enough pride for that. And the kindnesses she shows me I receive in my capacity as a confidential servant.

But no, either I'm mad or she is setting herself at me; the more coldly and respectfully I treat her, the more she seeks me out. This could be a pose she has taken up, an affectation; but I see her eyes brighten when I appear unexpectedly. Do even Parisian women know how to simulate that? What does it matter to me! I've got appearances on my side — let's embrace appearances. My God, how beautiful she is! How her great big blue eyes enchant me, seen close up and gazing at me as they so often do! How different this spring is from last year's, when I lived a miserable existence, sustaining myself by force of character in the midst of three hundred dirty and spiteful hypocrites! And I almost as spiteful as they were.

In his distrustful moods Julien would think: This young woman is playing with me. She is in league with her brother to mystify me. But then she has such an air of despising that brother's lack of energy! He is brave, that's all, she says. He does not have a thought that dares to defy the fashion. It is always up to me to take up his defence. A girl of nineteen! At that age could anyone possibly be faithful every instant of the day to the hypocritical code they lay down for her?

On the other hand, when Mlle de La Mole fixes her great blue eyes on me in a certain peculiar manner, Comte Norbert always leaves us. I find that suspicious; oughtn't he to be indignant that his sister makes so much of a *domestic* in their household? For I have heard the Duc de Chaulnes speak of me as that. At this memory anger drove out any other feeling. – Is it a love of antiquated language in that maniacal duke?

All right! she is pretty, went on Julien with a tigerish look. I'll have her, then I'll be off, and woe betide anyone who tries to stop me!

This idea became Julien's sole preoccupation; he could think of nothing else. His days passed by like hours.

Whenever he tried to busy himself with some serious business, his thoughts would drop away, and he would come to his senses a quarter of an hour later, his heart beating, his head confused, dreaming on this theme: Can it be that she loves me?

CHAPTER II
The Tyranny of a Girl!

I admire her beauty, but I fear her wit. MÉRIMÉE[1]

If Julien had devoted as much time to analysing what went on in the salon as he spent exaggerating Mathilde's beauty, or in enraging himself against her family's natural hauteur – which she put aside for his benefit – he would have understood in what her dominion over all around her consisted. From the moment anyone displeased Mlle de La Mole she would punish them with a witticism so well designed, so finely chosen, so apparently decorous yet piercing so near to the nerve, that the more one thought about it the greater its sting. Gradually it would become excruciating to afflicted pride. Since she cared not a jot for most of what the rest of her family so earnestly desired, to them she always seemed to have perfect poise. The salons of the aristocracy are good to talk about once one has emerged from them, but that is all; courtesy just on its own is impressive only for the first few days. Julien had experienced this: after the first enchantment, the first incredulity. Courtesy, he said to himself, is merely the absence of the resentment caused by bad manners. Mathilde was frequently bored; perhaps she would have been bored anywhere. At such times, to sharpen an epigram was an amusement to her, a real pleasure.

Perhaps it was in order to have some victims a little more entertaining than the principal members of her family, or the Academician and the five or six lesser family courtiers, that she had raised the hopes of the Marquis de Croisenois, the Comte de Caylus and two or three other young men of the first rank. For her they were nothing but fresh subjects for an epigram.

We confess with reluctance, for we are very fond of Mathilde, that she had allowed herself to receive letters from several of these, and had on occasion replied. We hasten to add that this young person was an exception to the customs of the time. Generally speaking, one would not reproach the pupils of the noble Convent of the Sacred Heart, for lack of prudence.

On one occasion the Marquis de Croisenois returned to Mathilde a somewhat compromising letter she had written to him the day before. He hoped this demonstration of his great discretion would advance his cause considerably. But indiscretion was what delighted Mathilde in her letter writing. Her pleasure was to play with her fate. She did not speak to him for six months.

She was amused by her letters from these young men; but she came to think that they were all alike. It was always the most profound passion, always the greatest melancholy.

– They are all the same impeccable paladins, ready to set sail for the Holy Land, she said to her cousin. Can you imagine anything more insipid? And these are the letters I'm going to get for the rest of my life! Letters like this only change in kind every twenty years, according to the type of occupation that is in fashion. They would have been less wishy-washy under the Empire. In those days young men in Society had seen or carried out actions that had some real grandeur. My uncle, the Duc de N——, had been at Wagram.[2]

– What intelligence is needed to give a slash with a sabre? And when they have done that they talk about it so much! replied Mlle de Sainte-Hérédité, Mathilde's cousin.

– Yes, well! those stories please me. To be in a *first-rate* battle, one of Napoleon's battles where ten thousand soldiers were slain, that shows courage. Exposing oneself to danger elevates the soul and delivers it from the ennui into which my worshippers seem plunged; and this ennui – it's catching. Which among them has any idea of doing anything out of the ordinary? They seek to obtain my hand – a colossal deed! I am rich and my father can advance his son-in-law. Oh! – if only he could find one who was the slightest bit amusing!

Mathilde's lively, precise and colourful way of seeing things impaired her language, as one can see. Often something she came out with was a blemish in the eyes of her polite friends. They could almost have said, had she been a less fashionable person, that her talk was a little too lively for feminine delicacy.

She, on her side, was most unjust to the handsome young knights who filled the Bois de Boulogne. She envisaged the future, not with terror, which would have been an animated feeling, but with a distaste very rare for her age.

What was there for her to desire? Riches, high birth, intelligence, the beauty that was attributed to her and in which she believed – all had been heaped on her by the hand of fate.

Such was the state of mind of the most envied heiress in the Faubourg Saint-Germain when she started to feel pleasure in taking her walks with Julien. She was astonished at his pride; she admired the adroitness of this little bourgeois. He will know how to get made a bishop, like the Abbé Maury,[3] she said to herself.

Soon the genuine and unaffected resistance with which our hero greeted many of her ideas came to interest her; she reflected on it; she told her confidante about the conversations in the greatest detail, and discovered that she could never quite convey their true atmosphere.

All at once an idea lit up within her: I have the happiness of being in love, she said to herself one day, with an incredible thrill of delight. I'm in love, I'm in love, it's obvious! A beautiful and lively young woman of my age, where else should she experience strong feelings if it is not by being in love? I've done my best, but I will never be in love with Croisenois, Caylus and *tutti quanti*. They're perfect, perhaps too perfect; at any rate, they bore me.

She mentally reviewed all the descriptions of passion she had read in *Manon Lescaut*, *La Nouvelle Héloïse*, *Letters of a Portuguese Nun*, etc., etc. There could be no question, certainly, of anything less than a grand passion; a trifling love was unworthy of a girl of her age and birth. She could give the name of love only to that heroic sentiment one met in France in the times of Henri III and Bassompierre.[4] Such love as that would never admit base impediments, but, very far from it, would lead one to go on and do great things. – What a misfortune for me that there isn't a real Court like that of Catherine de Medici or Louis XIII! I feel myself up to the level of everything that is boldest and most magnificent. What wouldn't I be capable of with a king who was a man of spirit, like Louis XIII, sighing at my feet! I would lead him into the Vendée,[5] as Baron de Tolly so often says, and from there he would reconquer his kingdom; then no more Charter . . . and Julien would be behind me. What does he lack? – a name and a fortune. He would make a name, he would acquire a fortune.

Croisenois lacks nothing, and in his whole life he will never be anything more than a duke, half-Ultra, half-liberal, an indecisive figure always avoiding extremes, and *therefore always ending up second*.

What grand enterprise has not been *an extreme* at the moment of its inception? Only when it is accomplished do commonplace people realize that it is possible. Yes, it is love with all its marvels that will reign in my heart; I feel it in the fire that courses through me. Heaven owes me this favour. It cannot be for nothing that all these advantages have been heaped on a single being. My happiness will be worthy of me. None of my days will be a cold reproduction of the one before. Already there is a degree of grandeur and audacity in daring to love a man placed so far distant from me on the social scale. We'll see – will he go on deserving me? At the first weakness I detect in him, I will abandon him. A young woman of my birth, and with the chivalric nature people are good enough to attribute to me [this was one of her father's dictums], must not behave like an idiot.

And isn't that just the role I would be playing if I should love the Marquis de Croisenois? I'd provide a new version of the placid content that I despise so utterly in my cousins. I know in advance all the poor marquis would say to me and all that I'd say in reply. What good is a love that makes you yawn? – I might as well become an eternal churchwoman. I'd have a celebration at the signature of my marriage contract – just like that of my young cousins – where all the heads of the families would shed a tender tear if, that is, they had not been put out of sorts by a final condition introduced into the contract by the opposing lawyer the night before.

CHAPTER 12

Will He be a Danton?

The need for nervous excitement, that is what characterized
the beautiful Marguerite de Valois, my aunt, who soon
married the King of Navarre – the one we now see reigning
in France bearing the name of Henri IV. The whole secret
of this princess's delightful character lay in her need to take
risks; from this derived, from the age of sixteen onwards,
her quarrels and reconciliations with her brothers. Now,
what can a young woman take risks with? With the most
precious thing she has: her honour, her reputation for the
rest of her life.   *Mémoires* of the Duc d'Angoulême,
natural son of Charles IX[1]

Between myself and Julien there is no signing of contracts, no lawyer;
all is heroic, all will be the fruit of chance. Save for noble birth, which
he lacks, it is the love of Marguerite de Valois for the young La Mole,
the most remarkable man of his time. Is it my fault that the young men
at Court are such slaves to the *conventional*, and turn pale at the very
idea of any adventure that is the least bit exotic. For them, a little tour
round Greece or to Africa[2] is the height of audacity, and even then
they wouldn't know how to proceed except in a group. From the
moment they find themselves alone they are terrified, not of the lance
of the Bedouin, but of ridicule – and that fear drives them to distraction.

By contrast, my dear little Julien cares only to act on his own.
Never, for this exalted being, the slightest notion of looking for
support and help from others! – he despises others, and because of
that I do not despise him.

If, being poor, Julien was nobly born, my love would be nothing more than a common stupidity, a banal misalliance; I wouldn't want it; it would lack the hallmarks of a grand passion – the vastness of the difficulties to be overcome, and the dark uncertainty of events.

Mlle de La Mole was so preoccupied with these fine sentiments that the following day, without thinking of it, she boasted about Julien to the Marquis de Croisenois and her brother. Her eloquence went so far that it riled them.

– Be on your guard against that young man, he has far too much energy, cried her brother; if the revolution were to begin again he would have us all guillotined.

She refrained from a direct retort, and hurriedly set to teasing her brother and the Marquis de Croisenois about the fear that energy produced in them. At bottom it was no more than the fear of encountering the unexpected, simply the terror of being taken aback by the unexpected . . .

– Always, gentlemen, always the fear of ridicule, the monster that unhappily died in 1816.

M. de La Mole used to say that in a country that has two parties ridicule can no longer exist. His daughter had understood this idea.

– So you see, gentlemen, she said to Julien's opponents, you will have been scared stiff all your lives, and afterwards you will be told:

It wasn't a wolf, 'twas nothing but its ghost.[3]

Shortly after that Mathilde left them. Her brother's remark had filled her with horror; it worried her deeply. However by the next day she divined in it a most delectable form of praise.

In this century when all energy is dead Julien's energy frightens them. I will tell him what my brother said; I would like to see the response he makes. But I will choose one of those occasions when his eyes are shining. Then he won't be able to lie to me.

– He will be a Danton! she added to herself after a long and rambling reverie. Very well, the revolution will begin anew. What part will Croisenois and my brother play then? It is written out for them in advance: sublime resignation. They will be heroic sheep, allowing their throats to be cut without saying a word. In dying, their sole worry will still be about whether it is in bad taste. But if he had the slightest hope of getting away my little Julien would blow out the brains of any Jacobin who tried to arrest him. He is not frightened of being in bad taste, not he.

These last words made her thoughtful; they reawakened painful memories, and took away all her confidence. They reminded her of jokes made by MM. de Caylus, de Croisenois, de Luz and her brother. These gentlemen had unanimously picked on Julien's *priestly* air: humble and hypocritical.

— Ah, but, she added suddenly, her eyes sparkling with joy, the sheer amount of such gibes and their bitterness proves that, in spite of them, he is the most distinguished man we have seen this winter. What do his faults signify, his absurdities? He has greatness, and they — otherwise so kind and indulgent — are shocked by it. He well knows that he's poor and must study to be a priest; they are army officers and do not need to study; it's so much easier.

Also, in spite of all the handicaps imposed on him by his perpetual black coat and that priestly look, which he's obliged to assume, poor boy, under pain of starving to death, his talents frighten them — nothing could be more obvious. And the priestly physiognomy — it's no longer noticeable the moment we're alone together for a few minutes. Again, whenever these gentlemen say something they think is subtle or original, isn't their first glance always at Julien? I've noticed that most definitely. Moreover, they know very well that he never addresses a word to them without being asked. It's only with me that he starts a conversation; he thinks I have an elevated soul. He replies to their objections only insofar as politeness requires. He goes back to a deferential pose directly. With me he will argue for hours on end, he isn't sure about his ideas so long as I have the slightest objection to them. In any case, the whole of the winter we've had no pistol shots; words have been the only means of attracting attention. Very well, then — my father, a superior man who is carrying the fortunes of our house ever higher, respects Julien. All the rest hate him, but nobody despises him save my mother's pious friends.

The Comte de Caylus had, or pretended to have, a great passion for horses; he spent his life in his stables, and would often dine there. This great passion, together with the habit of never indulging in laughter, made him much respected among his friends: he was the eagle of the little group.

As soon as they were assembled behind Madame de La Mole's sofa the following evening, Julien not being present, M. de Caylus, supported by Croisenois and Norbert, sharply attacked Mathilde's high estimation of Julien – and this without provocation, almost as soon as he saw Mlle de La Mole. She saw through this manoeuvre from a mile off, and it pleased her.

These people are all in league, she said to herself, against a man of talent who hasn't ten louis in income, and is unable to answer them unless he is asked a question. They are scared of him even under his black coat. What would it be like if he were wearing epaulettes?

She had never been so brilliant. From the very first skirmishes she overwhelmed Caylus and his allies with pleasant sarcasms. When the fire of sallies from these glamorous officers had been dampened:

– If tomorrow, she said to M. de Caylus, some rustic lord from the mountains of the Franche-Comté realized that Julien was his natural son, and gave him a name and a few thousand francs, in six weeks he would have moustaches like you, gentlemen; in six months he would be an officer of the Hussars like you, gentlemen. Then the greatness of his character would no longer be a matter for ridicule. I see you are being reduced, Monsieur-the-Future-Duke, to that hoary and mistaken old argument about the superiority of the Court nobility over that of the provinces. But where would you be if I were to push that point to its conclusion – if I was malicious enough to give Julien a Spanish duke for a father, a prisoner-of-war at Besançon in Napoleon's time who, through a scruple of conscience, recognized him on his death bed?

All these suppositions about illegitimate birth were found to be in rather poor taste by MM. de Caylus and de Croisenois. That was all they saw in Mathilde's argument.

However much Norbert was used to being ruled by his sister, she had spoken out so openly that he now assumed an air of severity that fitted rather ill, it must be said, with his kindly and pleasant countenance. He ventured to say a few words.

– Are you unwell, my dear? replied Mathilde with a serious little air. You must be in rather a poor way to answer banter with morality. Moralizing from you? Are you looking for a post as a prefect?

Soon Mathilde forgot all about the Comte de Caylus's air of irritation, Norbert's ill humour and M. de Croisenois's silent despair. For she must deal with a dreadful notion that came to fasten on her mind.

Julien is sincere enough with me, said she to herself; at his age, being so low in fortune, made miserable as he is by an astonishing ambition, a man needs a woman friend. I, perhaps, am that friend; but I see no love in him. With his bold temperament he would have spoken to me of any love.

This uncertainty, this internal debate, which from then on took up Mathilde's every moment, and concerning which she found new arguments each time Julien spoke to her, entirely chased away those fits of boredom to which she was so liable.

At the Convent of the Sacred Heart, as the daughter of a man of intellect who might become a minister and give the clergy back their woodlands,[4] Mlle de La Mole had been the object of the most excessive flattery. The harm done by this can never be mended. They had persuaded her that, because of all her advantages of birth, fortune, etc., she ought to be happier than other girls. Such an idea is the source of the ennui of princes and all their follies.

Mathilde had not escaped from its baneful influence. However much intelligence one has, at ten years old one cannot be on one's guard against a convent full of flatteries, especially ones that are apparently well founded.

From the moment she decided that she loved Julien she was no longer bored. Every day she would congratulate herself on her decision to allow herself a grand passion. Such an amusement has many dangers, thought she. So much the better! – a thousand times better!

Without a grand passion I was dying of boredom at the finest time of my life, from sixteen to twenty. I have already wasted my best

years – obliged to derive my only pleasures from listening to the
chatter of my mother's friends, who, I gather, were not entirely as
strict at Coblenz[5] in 1792 as their words would suggest today.

It was while these looming uncertainties preoccupied Mathilde
that Julien was unable to interpret the long gazes she cast upon him.
He registered clearly enough, though, the great increase of coldness
in Comte Norbert's manners and the fresh outbursts of haughtiness
in those of MM. de Caylus, Luz and de Croisenois. He was used to
these. Sometimes such unpleasant experiences would occur at the
end of an evening when he had shone with more brilliance than
befitted his station. If it hadn't been for the marked welcome extended
to him by Mathilde, and the curiosity the whole set inspired in him,
he would have avoided accompanying those glamorous moustachioed
young men when they attended Mlle de La Mole into the garden
after dinner.

Yes, I cannot possibly pretend to myself, thought Julien, that Mlle
de La Mole doesn't gaze at me in a strange way. Yet even when those
beautiful blue eyes which follow me are opened wide in the least
guarded fashion, I always see a critical element in their depths, an
element of detachment and mischievousness. Can this possibly be
love? What a contrast to the gaze of Mme de Rênal!

One evening after dinner, Julien, who had gone with M. de La
Mole into his office, was quickly returning to the garden. As, without
thinking about it, he approached Mathilde's group, he overheard a
few words ring out quite loud. She was teasing her brother. Julien
heard his own name pronounced twice. He came into view; a profound silence suddenly descended, and efforts to break it were useless.
Mlle de La Mole and her brother were too heated to find another
topic of conversation. MM. de Caylus, de Croisenois, de Luz and
their friends seemed to Julien to have turned to ice. He took himself
off.

CHAPTER 13

A Plot

Desultory remarks, meetings brought about by chance, are
transformed into the strongest possible proofs in the eyes
of a man of imagination if he has some fire in his heart.

SCHILLER[1]

The next day he surprised Norbert and his sister talking about him
again. As he appeared, a dead silence fell, just like yesterday. His
suspicions overflowed. Do these charming young people scheme to
make a fool of me? It must be confessed that is much more likely,
much more natural, than Mlle de La Mole's supposed passion for a
poor devil of a secretary. In the first place, do people like these have
passions? Mystification is their *forte*. They are jealous of my poor
little superiority with words. Being jealous is always one of their
weaknesses. Under this hypothesis, everything becomes clear. Mlle
de La Mole wants to persuade me that she favours me simply so as
to offer me as an amusement for her suitor.

The cruel suspicion completely altered Julien's moral standpoint.
It met with a germ of love in his heart that it had no difficulty in
destroying. This love was based solely on Mathilde's rare beauty,
or rather on her regal manners and wonderful dress style. In such
things Julien was still no more than a parvenu. A pretty Society
woman is the phenomenon, we are assured, that most amazes an
intellectually gifted peasant when he rises into its upper ranks. It
certainly wasn't Mathilde's character Julien had been dreaming of
those preceding days. He had sense enough to realize that he knew
nothing whatsoever of her character. All of what he saw might well
be only a surface.

For instance, Mathilde would not have missed Mass on Sunday for anyone in the world; she accompanied her mother to church almost every day. If some rash guest in the salon of the Hôtel de La Mole forgot where he was and allowed himself even the remotest allusion to a satirical remark against the real or supposed interests of Throne and Altar, Mathilde instantly assumed an icy seriousness. Her look, so piercing, took on all the impenetrable hauteur of an old family portrait.

Yet Julien was sure that she always kept two or three of Voltaire's most free-thinking works in her room. He himself often took a few volumes from the fine edition with the splendid binding. He concealed their absence by separating each volume a little from its neighbour, but it wasn't long before he realized that someone else read Voltaire, too. He employed a trick from the seminary, and placed horsehairs across those volumes he supposed might interest Mlle de La Mole. They went missing for weeks at a time.

M. de La Mole, exasperated with his bookseller, who kept on sending him all the *bogus Memoirs*,[2] commissioned Julien to buy anything new that was at all stimulating or outrageous. But, to prevent any toxic effects seeping through to the household, the secretary was instructed to put them in a little bookcase in the Marquis's own chamber. He soon became certain that these new books had only to be hostile to the interests of Throne and Altar for them to be not long in disappearing. It definitely wasn't Norbert who was reading them.

Overestimating the importance of this, Julien credited Mlle de La Mole with duplicity worthy of a Machiavel. Such imputed wickedness was an attraction in his eyes, almost the only charm of character she had for him. Boredom with hypocrisy and virtuous discourses drove him to this extremity.

He was working his own imagination up rather than being carried away by love.

It was after losing himself in dreams of Mlle de La Mole's elegant figure, of the wonderfully fine taste of her clothing, the whiteness of her hands, the beauty of her arms, the *disinvoltura*[3] manifest in all her movements, that he found himself in love. Then, to complete the spell, he thought of her as a Catherine de Medici. Nothing was too deep or too wicked for the character he gave her. It was the ideal that he had admired in his youth – of Maslon, of Frilair, of Castanède. It was for him, in short, the ideal of Paris.

Has there ever been anything more absurd than a belief in the profundity or the wickedness of the Parisian character?

It is quite possible that this *trio* are making a fool of me, thought Julien. And one would have understood little indeed of his character if one could not already imagine the sombre and chill expression his looks then took on in response to Mathilde's. Bitter irony rebuffed the friendly assurances that an astonished Mlle de La Mole dared twice or thrice to offer him.

Piqued by this sudden strangeness, the young girl's heart, naturally cold, bored and attuned to intellect, became as passionate as it was in her nature to be. But there was also much pride in Mathilde's character, and the birth of an emotion that would make all her happiness depend on another was accompanied in her by a sombre sadness.

Julien had already learned enough since he had come to Paris to be able to discern that this was not the dried-up sadness of ennui. Instead of being eager for evening parties, for shows and all manner of distractions as she had been before, she now avoided them.

Music sung by French singers bored Mathilde to death, yet Julien, who had made it his duty to wait at the exit of Society from the Opera, noticed that she had herself taken there as often as possible. He thought he discerned that she had lost a little of that perfect poise that shone in all her doings. Sometimes she replied to her friends with witticisms rendered outrageous by their biting force. It seemed to him that she was particularly down on the Marquis de Croisenois. – That young man must be madly in love with money not to drop the girl right away, however rich she might be! thought Julien. And as for himself, offended at outrages offered to masculine dignity, he redoubled his coldness towards her. Often he went so far as to answer her in a way that was scarcely even polite.

But however resolute he was in avoiding being beguiled by Mathilde's displays of interest, on certain days these were so marked that – the scales beginning to fall from his eyes – Julien found her so attractive as for it to be at times embarrassing.

The skill and the persistence of these young Society people will end up by triumphing over my small fund of experience, he said to himself; it is time to depart and put a stop to all this. The Marquis had just charged him with the administration of a number of small estates and houses he owned in the lower Languedoc. A journey there was necessary: M. de La Mole reluctantly consented to it. Save in matters of his high ambitions, Julien had become his second self.

When all is said and done they haven't managed to trap me, said Julien to himself as he prepared for his departure. Whether the jokes Mlle de La Mole makes to these gentlemen are genuine or simply designed to give me confidence, still I have amused myself with them.

If there is no conspiracy against the carpenter's son, then Mlle de La Mole is incomprehensible – but to the Marquis de Croisenois at least as much as to me. Yesterday, for example, her bad temper was certainly real, and I had the pleasure of seeing a young man who is as noble and rich as I am penniless and plebeian bucked in my favour. That's the finest of my triumphs; it will cheer me up as I speed in my post chaise through the plains of the Languedoc.

He had kept his departure a secret, but Mathilde knew better than he that he was leaving Paris the next day, and leaving for a long time. She resorted to a terrible headache, made worse by the stuffy air in the salon. She walked much in the garden, and there her bitter wit so harried Norbert, the Marquis de Croisenois, Caylus, Luz and some other young men who had dined at the Hôtel de La Mole, that she compelled them to leave. She gazed at Julien strangely.

This look of hers is perhaps part of some play-acting, thought Julien – but this quick breathing, all this emotion! Bah! he said to himself, who am I to judge all these things? I am dealing with one of the most sublime and subtle women in Paris. That quick breathing which was just about to move me – she will have studied it from Léontine Fay,[4] whom she admires so much.

They had been left alone; the conversation most patently languished. – No! Julien feels nothing for me, said Mathilde to herself, genuinely miserable.

As he was taking leave of her, she gripped his arm hard:

– This evening you will get a letter from me, she said in a voice so altered as to be unrecognizable.

The circumstance quite suddenly moved Julien.

– My father, she continued, has a proper estimate of the services you render him. *You must* not leave tomorrow; find an excuse. And she departed at a run.

Her figure was charming. It would be impossible to have a prettier foot, and she ran with a grace that enchanted Julien; but can you guess what his second thought was after she had suddenly disappeared? He was offended at the imperative tone with which she had brought out the phrase *you must*. Louis XV, too, at the moment of his death, was deeply annoyed at the phrase *you must* clumsily used by his leading physician, and Louis XV was no parvenu.

An hour later, a footman handed a letter to Julien; it was quite simply a declaration of love.

There's not too much affectation of manner, said Julien to himself, attempting, through literary criticism, to contain the joy that rucked up his cheeks and forced him to laugh in spite of himself.

At last – me! he suddenly cried, his feelings being too strong to be contained – me, a poor peasant, to have here a declaration of love from a great lady!

And, for me, that really isn't too bad, he added, controlling his jubilation as much as he could. I have managed to maintain my proper dignity. I have never said I loved her. He started to study the shape of the handwriting; Mlle de La Mole had a fine, small, English-style hand. He needed to have some physical occupation to distract himself from a joy that verged on delirium.

Your departure obliges me to speak . . . It would be beyond my capability to see you no more.

A thought now struck Julien like a revelation, interrupting his examination of Mathilde's letter and redoubling his joy. I have got the better of the Marquis de Croisenois, he cried – I, who say only serious things! And he so handsome! He has moustaches and a charming uniform; he always finds something to talk about, timed just right, some witty or subtle remark.

Julien experienced a spasm of delight; he wandered at random in the garden, ecstatic with happiness.

Later he went up to his office and had himself announced to the Marquis de La Mole, who luckily had not yet gone out. He easily demonstrated to him, showing him some papers stamped as from Normandy, that the care of the Norman lawsuits obliged him to put off his departure for the Languedoc.

– I am very pleased you are not going, said the Marquis, when they had finished talking of business, *I like seeing you here.* Julien went out; this remark made him uncomfortable.

And as for me, I am about to seduce his daughter! – and maybe make her marriage to the Marquis de Croisenois, the delight of his future, impossible: if he doesn't get a dukedom at least his daughter would have a *tabouret.*[5] It came to him that he might leave for the Languedoc in spite of Mathilde's letter, in spite of the explanation given to the Marquis. This flash of virtue evaporated very quickly.

How good I am being, he said to himself; for me, a pleb, to take pity on a family of this rank! Me, whom the Duc de Chaulnes labels a domestic! How does the Marquis make his vast fortune bigger? By selling his stocks when he learns at the château that there might be the semblance of a *coup d'état* tomorrow. And for me – thrown down by hard-hearted Providence into the lowest rank, I to whom a noble heart has been given and not even a thousand francs in income, that is to say, not enough for bread, *literally not enough for bread* – I to refuse an offered pleasure! A clear spring sent to quench my thirst in this burning desert of mediocrity that I cross so painfully! By God, not so stupid; each for himself in this desert of egotism that men call life.

And he recalled the many disdainful stares fixed on him by Mme de La Mole, and above all by *those ladies,* her friends.

The pleasure of triumphing over the Marquis de Croisenois completed the rout of this dim recollection of virtue.

How I'd like him to lose his temper! said Julien; with what assurance I'd give him a thrust of the rapier now. And he made the gesture of a thrust in the *seconde* position. Before this I was a little clerk, basely exploiting my little portion of courage. Since this letter, I am his equal.

Yes, said he with tremendous relish and bringing his words out with deliberation, our merits, the Marquis's and mine, have been weighed in the balance, and the poor carpenter from the Jura has prevailed.

Good! he cried to himself, I have found the key to my answer there. Don't go and think, Mlle de La Mole, that I have forgotten my position in life. I will make you understand and really feel that it is for a carpenter's son that you are deceiving a descendant of the celebrated Guy de Croisenois, who followed St Louis on a crusade.

Julien could not contain his joy. He was obliged to go down into the garden. His room, into which he had locked himself, seemed too narrow for him to breathe.

Me, a poor Jura peasant, he repeated to himself constantly, me condemned to always wear this dreary black costume! Alas! – twenty years ago I would have been in a uniform like them! Then, a man like me was either dead or a *general at thirty-six*. The letter, which he gripped tightly in his hand, endowed him with the figure and stance of a hero. Nowadays, it is true, encased in that black costume a man may have a hundred thousand francs a year by the age of forty, and the blue riband, like M. the Bishop of Beauvais.

Well, good! he said to himself, laughing like Mephistopheles, I am cleverer than they are; I know how to choose the uniform of my century. And he felt his ambition and his affection for the ecclesiastical habit increase vastly. How many cardinals, who have been baser born than me, have been in government! – my compatriot Granvelle,[6] for example.

Little by little, Julien's agitation calmed down; prudence resurfaced. Like his master Tartuffe, whose role he knew by heart, he said to himself:

> I may see in these words a plain pretence . . .
> I'll put no trust in these flatt'ring remarks,
> Until a few of *her* favours for whom I repine
> Arrive to confirm what they tell me is mine.
>
> *Tartuffe*, IV. v

Tartuffe was also ruined by a woman, and he was as good as the next man . . . My answer may perhaps be shown around . . . for which we will find this redress, he went on, enunciating his words slowly and in accents of contained ferocity – we will begin with the liveliest phrases from the sublime Mathilde's letter.

Yes, but some of M. de Croisenois's footmen might jump on me and grab the original.

No, I am well armed, and I'm in the habit, as they know, of firing on footmen.

Very well! one of the men is brave; he hurls himself on me. He has been promised a hundred Napoleons. I kill him or wound him, that's fine, it is just what they're looking for. They chuck me in prison, completely within the law; I appear in the police courts and they send me, with perfect justice and equity on the part of the judges, to keep company in Poissy with MM. Fontan and Magallon.[7] There I sleep higgledy-piggledy with four hundred beggars . . . And I should pity these people? he cried, getting up impetuously. Have they any pity for the Third Estate[8] when they get hold of them? This thought was the last gasp of that gratitude to M. de la Mole which had, in spite of himself, been nagging at him till then.

Softly, softly, gentle sirs, I see this little Machiavellian ploy; Abbé Maslon or M. Castanède at the seminary could not have done better. You pinch the letter of *provocation* from me, and I become the second volume to Colonel Caron at Colmar.[9]

But hold on a moment, gentlemen, I am going to send the fatal letter in a well-sealed packet to M. the Abbé Pirard to secure it for me. There's an honest man, a Jansenist, and as such not to be tempted by financial reward. Yes, but he opens letters . . . It's Fouqué I must send it to.

It must be confessed that Julien's look was terrible, his physiognomy hideous; he breathed unalloyed wickedness. He was the miserable individual at war with all society.

To arms! cried Julien. And he cleared the flight of steps at the front of the hôtel at a single bound. He went into a letter-writer's booth at the corner of the street, frightening him. – Copy this, he said, handing him Mlle de La Mole's letter.

While the writer was working on it, he himself wrote to Fouqué; he begged him to hold a precious security for him. But, said he breaking off, the secret bureau at the post office will open my letter and give you what you are looking for . . . No, gentlemen. He went to buy an enormous Bible at the Protestant bookseller, hid Mathilde's letter very neatly in its covers, had it all wrapped up, and so off went his parcel by the post diligence, addressed to one of Fouqué's employees whose name no one in Paris knew.

This done, he returned, joyful and brisk, to the Hôtel de La Mole. Now *for us*! he cried, locking his door and throwing off his coat:

Very well! Mademoiselle, he wrote to Mathilde, so it is Mlle de La Mole who, by means of Arsène, her father's servant, has had conveyed a most seductive letter to a poor carpenter from the Jura, doubtless to play upon his simplicity . . . And he transcribed the most striking phrases from the letter he had just received.

His own letter would have done honour to the diplomatic caution of M. le Chevalier de Beauvoisis. It was not yet ten o'clock; Julien, intoxicated by happiness and a feeling of his own power – so novel a feeling for this poor devil – proceeded to the Italian opera. He heard his friend Geronimo sing. Music had never exalted him to such a level. He was a God.[10]

CHAPTER 14

Reflections of a Young Lady

How many perplexities! How many nights passed without
sleep! Good God! shall I make myself despicable? He
himself will despise me. But he's going, he's leaving.

ALFRED DE MUSSET[1]

It was not without an inner struggle that Mathilde had written.
Whatever might have been the beginnings of her interest in Julien,
such interest soon overcame the pride that had ruled unchecked in
her heart ever since she had been conscious of her own existence.
For the very first time, this cold, high soul was carried away by
passionate feeling. But if feelings now dominated her pride, they
remained faithful to the forms that pride had shaped. Two months
of struggle and new sensations renewed, so to speak, her entire moral
being.

Mathilde believed that she could see happiness. And this vision,
which is all powerful in courageous spirits when allied to superior
intelligence, had a long struggle with her sense of dignity and
her ordinary feelings of duty. On one occasion she went to see her
mother at seven o'clock in the morning and begged her to let her
take refuge at Villequier. The Marquise did not deign even to reply,
and advised her to go back to bed. This was her last effort at common
prudence and deference to received ideas.

Fear of wrongdoing and of offending things held sacred by the
likes of Caylus, de Luz and Croisenois had little power over her;
such people didn't seem made to understand her; she would have
consulted them had it been a question of purchasing a carriage or an
estate. Her real terror was lest Julien be dissatisfied with her.

Perhaps he too has only the outward appearance of a superior man?

She abhorred lack of character – this was her great objection to the handsome young men surrounding her. The more they mocked gracefully at everything which deviated from the fashion, or which in pretending to follow it followed it clumsily, the more diminished they became in her eyes.

They were brave – and that was all. And even so, she asked herself, how do they show their bravery? In a duel. But a duel is no more than a ritual. Everything is known in advance, even down to what should to be said when one falls. Lying on the grass, one's hand placed on one's heart, there must be a magnanimous pardon for one's adversary and a message for a beauty who is often imaginary – or who, for fear of arousing suspicion, goes to a ball on the day of one's death.

A man may brave danger at the head of a squadron glittering with steel, but what of danger that is lonely, strange, unexpected and truly ugly?

Alas! sighed Mathilde to herself, it was at Henri III's Court that men were to be found as great in their character as they were in their birth! Ah! if Julien had been at Jarnac or Moncontour,[2] I would have no further doubts. In that era of vigour and prowess, Frenchmen weren't men of straw. The day of battle was often the day of least perplexity.

Their life was not all wrapped round like an Egyptian mummy, in an envelope common to all, and always uniform. Yes, she went on, there was more genuine courage in finding one's way back alone at eleven at night from the Hôtel de Soissons when Catherine de Medici lived there, than there is in rushing off to Algeria today. A man's existence was a succession of risks. Now civilization has banished chance, there is no more of the unexpected. If it comes up in ideas there aren't enough epigrams to throw at it; if it comes up in action no amount of cowardice is enough to cope with our fears. Whatever idiocy fear drives us to – it's excused. Degenerate and tedious age! What would Boniface de La Mole have said if, on raising his severed head from out of his tomb in 1793, he had seen seventeen of his descendants let themselves be rounded up like sheep and guillotined two days later? Death was certain, but it would have been bad form to defend oneself and kill a few Jacobins. Ah! in the heroic age in France, in Boniface de La Mole's time, Julien would have been the commander of a squadron and my brother a young priest of exemplary life, with wisdom in his look and moderation on his tongue.

A few months previously, Mathilde had despaired of meeting anyone even a little out of the common mould. She had found some pleasure in allowing herself to write to some few young men in Society. This daring act, so unconventional, so rash for a girl, could have stained her reputation in the eyes of M. de Croisenois, of the Duc de Chaulnes, her maternal grandfather, and of the whole clan of de Chaulnes – who, seeing her marriage plans disrupted, would have wanted to know the reason why. At that time, on the days she had written a letter, Mathilde had not been able to sleep. Yet these had only been answers.

Now she was daring to say that she was in love. She was writing *first* (what a terrible word!), and to a man on the lowest level of Society.

Such circumstances, if discovered, would certainly lead to eternal dishonour. Which of the women frequenting her mother's house would dare take her part? What formulas could be supplied for them to repeat in order to deaden the blow from the fearsome derision of the salons?

Even to speak was appalling – but to write! *There are things one does not write*, cried Napoleon on learning of the capitulation at Baylen.[3] And it was Julien who had told her of that remark, as though giving a lesson in advance!

But all this counted for nothing as yet; Mathilde's suffering had other causes. Oblivious of the terrible effects on Society, the ineffaceable stain so saturated with scorn – for she was outraging her caste – Mathilde was now involved in writing to a being of quite a different nature from men like Croisenois, de Luz or Caylus.

The depth, the *unknowable*, in Julien's nature would have frightened her even in forming a commonplace relationship with him. And now she was in the process of making him her lover, even her master!

Where might his demands not reach if ever I allow him claims on me? Ah well! I shall say with Medea: *In the midst of so many dangers, MYSELF remains to me.*[4]

Julien had no reverence for nobility of birth, she believed. What was much more, he had perhaps no love for her!

In these last moments of agonizing doubt she was visited by ideas of feminine greatness. In the destiny of a girl like me, cried Mathilde impatiently, everything should be distinctive. So that now the pride instilled in her from her cradle militated against her virtue. It was just then that Julien's departure precipitated everything.

(Happily, such characters are extremely rare.)

That evening, very late, Julien had the malice to send a very heavy trunk down to the porter; to carry it he called the footman who was courting Mlle de La Mole's chambermaid. This manoeuvre may have no result at all, he said to himself, but if it succeeds she will think I have gone. He went to sleep very cheerful at his own joke. Mathilde did not close her eyes.

Next day, extremely early in the morning, Julien left the hôtel without being noticed, but returned before eight.

He was scarcely in the library before Mlle de La Mole appeared at the doorway. He handed her his answer. He thought it his duty to speak to her – nothing could be more appropriate, at least – but Mlle de La Mole did not want to hear him, and disappeared. Julien was delighted with this, he had not known what to say.

If this isn't all just a game agreed with Comte Norbert, it is clear that the baroque love so high-bred a girl has taken it into her head to have for me has been fired by the coldness of my looks. I'll be a little more stupid than likely if I ever let myself be carried away enough to develop a taste for this great fair-headed doll. This reasoning left him colder and more calculating than ever.

In the battle that's being mounted, he went on, pride of birth will be like a high ridge constituting a military position between us. It's up there that one must manoeuvre. I've done very ill staying in Paris; if it is all nothing but a game, then the putting-off of my going degrades me and exposes me. What danger would there have been in leaving? For if they are mocking me, I would have been mocking them. If her interest in me has some substance, I would have increased it a hundredfold.

Mlle de La Mole's letter had given Julien's vanity such vivid pleasure that, taken up with laughing over what had happened, he had neglected to think seriously of the advantages of departure.

It was an inherent flaw in his character to be extremely sensitive to his own failings. He was much put out by this one, and was hardly sensible any longer of the incredible victory that had preceded this minor setback when, at about nine o'clock, Mlle de La Mole appeared in the library doorway, threw a letter in his direction and fled.

It seems as though this is going to be a novel in letters, said he, retrieving it. The enemy makes a false step, and now I will give them coldness and virtue in return.

A definite answer was demanded from him in a high tone that increased his inner satisfaction. For two pages on end he gave himself the pleasure of mystifying anyone who should be trying to mock him and, towards the end of his reply, for a further tease, he announced his decision to depart the following morning.

This letter complete: The garden will serve for sending it, he thought, and out he went. He looked up at the window of Mlle de La Mole's room.

It was on the first floor next to her mother's apartment, but below was a large mezzanine.

The mezzanine was so lofty that, walking letter in hand in the avenue of limes beneath it, Julien could not be seen from Mlle de La Mole's window. The arch made by the limes, very beautifully shaped, obscured the view. But what now! Julien exclaimed to himself – another piece of rashness! If someone plans to make a fool of me, letting myself be seen with a letter in my hand is playing into enemy hands.

Norbert's room was exactly above his sister's, and if Julien were to step out of the vault formed by the shaping of the lime branches, the Comte and his friends would be able to follow all his movements.

Mlle de La Mole appeared behind her window; he half showed her his letter; she nodded her head. Immediately Julien started hurriedly back for his own room, and on the great staircase ran by chance into the beautiful Mathilde, who seized the letter with perfect aplomb, and laughter in her eyes.

What passion there was in poor Mme de Rênal's eyes, said Julien to himself, when, after six months of intimacy, she brought herself to take a letter from me! I don't believe that in her whole life she looked at me with laughter in her eyes.

He did not expound the rest of his response to himself as closely; was he perhaps ashamed of the futility of his motives? But what a difference, too, his thought continued, in the elegance of the morning gown, in the elegance of her whole demeanour! Seeing Mlle de La Mole thirty feet away, a man of taste would know what rank she occupied in Society. That's what one might call virtue by demonstration.

Making such little jokes, Julien was still not admitting all of his thoughts to himself; Mme de Rênal had had no Marquis de Croisenois to sacrifice to him. He had had for a rival only that ignoble Sub-prefect M. Charcot, who got himself called Maugiron because there were no more Maugirons.

At five o'clock Julien received a third letter; it was thrown at him through the library door. Again Mlle de La Mole fled. What a mania for writing! he said, laughing – when one might so easily talk! The enemy wishes to have my letters, that's obvious, and lots of them! He was in no hurry to open this last. Yet more elegant phrases, thought he; but as he read he went pale. There were eight lines only.

I need to talk to you: I must talk to you this evening; after midnight on the stroke of one, be in the garden. Take the gardener's long ladder beside the well; put it up to my window and climb into my room. There's a moon: that doesn't matter.

CHAPTER 15

Is It a Plot?

> Ah! how cruel is the interval between the conception of a
> great project and its execution! How many vain terrors!
> How many hesitations! Life is at stake. – Much more is at
> stake – Honour!   SCHILLER[1]

This is getting serious, thought Julien . . . and a bit too obvious, he
added after some thought. Well now! this lovely young miss can talk
to me in the library with a freedom that is, Heaven be praised,
complete – the Marquis never comes here, for fear I'd show him
some accounts. And well now! M. de La Mole and the Comte Norbert,
the only ones who do ever come here, are out almost all day; one
can easily find out when they get back to the hôtel – yet this sublime
Mathilde, for whose hand a sovereign prince would not be too grand,
wants me to do something appallingly rash!

It is obvious – someone wants to ruin me, or make a fool of me
at least. First they tried to destroy me through my letters; these turn
out to be cautious; so all right! – they need an action that is clearer
than the day. These fine young gents must think me very stupid or
very vain. The devil! to climb like that twenty-five feet up on a
ladder to the first floor in full moonlight! – there will be plenty of
time to see me, even from the neighbouring houses. I'll look lovely
on my ladder! Julien went up to his room and, whistling, started to
pack his trunk. He was determined to depart, not even replying.

But this wise resolution could not calm his heart. If by any chance,
he said to himself, closing his trunk, Mathilde is acting in good faith!
– then in her eyes I will be playing the part of a total coward. And
me, I'm not well born, so I must show fine qualities, cash down,

without flattering presuppositions, spelt out in eloquent deeds . . .

He spent a quarter of an hour in reflection. What's the good of denying it? said he at last; I'd be a coward in her eyes. I'd lose not only the most brilliant young woman in high society, as they were all saying at M. the Duc de Retz's ball, but also the divine gratification of seeing the Marquis de Croisenois, son of a duke, and who will be a duke himself, sacrificed to me. A charming young man who has all the qualities I lack – a ready wit, birth, fortune . . .

Regret for this would dog me for the rest of my life – not for her, there are lots of mistresses to be had! – but . . . there's only one honour! as old Don Diego[2] says, and here, clearly and unambiguously, I am backing off from the first danger offered me; for the duel with M. de Beauvoisis turned out to be a joke. This is completely different. I might be shot point blank by a servant, but that's the least of the dangers; I could be dishonoured.

This is getting serious, my lad, he added with the gaiety and the tones of a Gascon.[3] It is a question of *honour*. A poor devil cast as low as me by fortune won't ever have such a chance again; I may have my successes, but they will be lesser things . . .

He pondered for a long time, walking headlong up and down, pulling up short from time to time. Someone had put a magnificent marble bust of Cardinal Richelieu in his room and it attracted his attention in spite of himself. This bust seemed to be staring at him with an austere glare, and as though reproaching him for lacking that audacity which should be natural to the French character. In your time, great monsieur, would I have hesitated?

At the worst, Julien said to himself at last, supposing that all this is a trap, it is extremely murky and much more compromising for a young woman. They know I am not a man who will keep quiet. Then they will have to kill me. That would have been fine in 1574, in Boniface de La Mole's day, but today they would never dare. These people are not the same. How envious people are of Mlle de La Mole! Her shame would immediately echo through four hundred salons, and with what relish!

The servants chatter among themselves about the marked preference I am shown, I know, I've heard them . . .

On the other hand, her letters! . . . they might think I carry them on me. Surprised in her room, they could take them from me. It would be a matter of two, three, four men, how would I know? But those men – where would they get them from? where can you find discreet servants in Paris? The Law would surely scare them off . . . Good Lord! – Caylus, de Croisenois and de Luz themselves. The moment itself, and the foolish figure I would cut among them, that would be what has tempted them. Beware the fate of d'Abailard,[4] Monsieur the Secretary!

Ah well, my God! Messieurs, you will carry the marks I can make, I will strike at the face like Caesar's troops at Pharsalia . . .[5] As to the letters, I can put them in a safe place.

Julien made copies of the last two of these, hid them in a volume of the beautiful Voltaire in the library, and himself took the originals to the post.

When he returned: What madness I am running into! he thought with fear and amazement. It had been a quarter of an hour since he had squarely faced the action of the coming night.

But, if I refuse, I will despise myself ever afterwards! My whole life long this affair will be a great area of doubt, and for me a doubt like that is the cruellest misery. Didn't I suffer it apropos of Amanda's lover! I know I would far more easily forgive myself a clear-cut crime; once that had been confessed I could put it out of my mind.

What! Shall I have been rival to a man bearing one of the most illustrious names in France, and shall I myself blithely declare that I am his inferior! At bottom it is cowardice not to go. That word decides everything, cried Julien, rising to his feet . . . and anyway she is so very pretty!

If this isn't a piece of treachery, what madness she is running into for me! . . . If it is a trick, by God, messieurs! it is up to me to make the joke serious, and that is what I will do.

But what if they pin my arms back the moment I get into the room; they may have installed some ingenious device there!

It's like a duel, he said laughing to himself – my master-at-arms says there's a parry to every thrust, but that the good Lord, who desires an end, so orders it that one of the two forgets to parry.

Anyway, here's something to reply with: he took his pocket pistols and, though the priming was fresh, renewed it.

There were still some hours to wait; in order to be doing something, Julien wrote to Fouqué:

My friend, don't open the enclosed letter except in case of accident, and if you should hear it said that something strange has happened to me. Then rub out the proper names in the manuscript I am sending you, and make eight copies to send to newspapers in Marseilles, Bordeaux, Lyons, Brussels, etc.; ten days later have this manuscript printed, send the first copy to M. the Marquis de La Mole; and a fortnight afterwards scatter the other copies in the streets of Verrières at night.

This little justificatory memoir, cast in the form of a narrative which Fouqué was to open in case of accident, Julien made as little compromising as possible for Mlle de La Mole, but even so it showed her position most exactly.

Julien was just sealing his packet when the dinner bell sounded; it made his heart beat. His imagination, full of the tale he had just composed, felt a tragic foreboding. He saw himself seized by servants, garrotted, led down to a cave with a gag in his mouth. There a servant stood close guard over him and, should the honour of a noble house demand that the adventure have a tragic end, it would be easy to finish things with one of those poisons that leave no trace; then they could say that he had died of an illness and carry him dead back to his room.

Moved like a writer of plays by his own tale, Julien felt real fear as he entered the dining-room. He looked at the servants in their formal livery. He studied their physiognomy. Which of them have been chosen for tonight's expedition? he asked himself. Memories of the Court of Henri III are so present in this family, so often invoked, that, if they thought themselves outraged, they would be more drastic than other people of their rank. He gazed at Mlle de La Mole in order to decipher her family's plans from her eyes; she was pale, and her physiognomy had altogether taken on the cast of the Middle Ages. Never had he thought her air so grand, she was truly beautiful, truly impressive. He almost fell in love. *Pallida morte futura*,[6] said he to himself (her pallor tells of great designs).

It was without any effect that he showed himself walking about for a long time in the garden after dinner; Mlle de La Mole did not appear. To have spoken to her just then would have lifted a great weight from his heart.

Why not confess it? He was afraid. Since he had decided to act he had abandoned himself to this feeling without shame. So long as I find the necessary courage at the point of action, he told himself, what does it matter what I feel now? He went to reconnoitre the position of the ladder, and try its weight.

This is an instrument, he said to himself laughing, that I am fated to employ! here as at Verrières. What a difference! At that time, he added with a sigh, I wasn't obliged to distrust the person for whom I exposed myself. And what a difference in the degree of danger!

If I had been killed in M. de Rênal's garden there would have been no dishonour in it at all for me. They could easily have made my death a mystery. Here, what terrible tales they will come to tell in the salons of the Hôtel de Chaulnes, the Hôtel de Caylus, the Hôtel de Retz, etc. – everywhere, eventually. For posterity, I will be a monster.

For two or three years anyway, he added gaily, laughing at himself. But the idea crushed him. And me, who will be able to defend me? Supposing Fouqué does have my posthumous pamphlet printed, that will only be another source of shame. What! I'm received into a household, and as repayment for the hospitality I receive, the kindnesses with which I have been showered, I print a pamphlet about what has happened! I assault the honour of their women! Ah! a thousand times better to have been a dupe!

That evening was frightful.

CHAPTER 16

One in the Morning

The garden was very large, laid out a few years since in
perfect taste. But the trees were more than a hundred years
old. Something of the countryside was to be found there.

MASSINGER[1]

When eleven o'clock sounded he was on the point of penning a
counter-instruction to Fouqué. He was careful to make a noise as he
locked his door, as though he were shutting himself in. He set off
stealthily to see what was going on throughout the house, particularly
on the fourth floor where the servants lived. Nothing was out of the
ordinary. One of Mme de La Mole's lady's maids was giving a party
and the servants were drinking their punch with great gaiety. People
laughing like that, thought Julien, aren't going to be taking part in a
night-time expedition – if they were they'd be much more subdued.

Eventually he stationed himself in a dark corner of the garden. If
their idea is to hide themselves from the household servants, they
will see to it that the men detailed to surprise me come in over the
garden wall.

Should M. de Croisenois keep a cool head in this affair, he ought
to think it less compromising for the young woman he wants to
marry if I'm caught before I get into her room.

He made a very precise military reconnaissance. It's a matter of
my honour, he thought; if I lapse into some blunder I will find it no
excuse later to tell myself that I hadn't thought about it.

The weather was dismayingly serene. The moon had started to
rise around eleven – at half-past midnight it fully illuminated that
part of the hôtel which gave on to the garden.

353

She's crazy, said Julien to himself; as one o'clock sounded there was still a light in Comte Norbert's windows. Julien had never been so full of fear, he saw only the enterprise's danger and felt no enthusiasm for it at all.

He went to get the huge ladder, waited five minutes to allow time for a possible cancellation, and at five past one leant the ladder against Mathilde's window. He climbed softly up, pistol in hand, amazed not to have been attacked. As he got up to the window she opened it noiselessly.

— So you are here, monsieur, said Mathilde with great emotion; I have been following your movements for the last hour.

Julien was extremely embarrassed, he had no idea how to behave, he felt not the slightest love. In his embarrassment he thought he must be bold, and tried to put his arms round Mathilde.

— For shame! said she, pushing him away.

Quite content to be rebuffed, he hastily glanced around him: the moon was so brilliant that the shadows cast in Mlle de La Mole's room were perfectly black. She could easily have men hidden here without my seeing them, he thought.

— What have you got in the pockets at the side of your coat? enquired Mathilde, very pleased to see something to talk about. She was suffering strangely; all those feelings of reticence and timidity so natural to a well-born girl had resumed their power, and they tormented her.

— All sorts of arms and pocket pistols, answered Julien, no less relieved to have something to say.

— The ladder should be drawn up, said Mathilde.

— It's enormous, it could smash the windows of the salon below, or of the mezzanine.

— We mustn't break the windows, replied Mathilde, attempting an ordinary conversational tone without success — it seems to me you might lower the ladder using a rope fastened to the top rung. I always have a supply of ropes in my room.

And this is a woman in love! thought Julien, she dares to say she's in love! — such coolness, such good sense about precautions, clearly tells me that I am not triumphing over M. de Croisenois as I stupidly believed, but that I am simply his successor. But really, what's the matter with that! Is it as though I'm in love with her? — I do triumph over the marquis in this sense, that he'll be furious to have a successor, and even more furious that his successor is me. How haughtily he looked at me yesterday evening at the Café Tortoni, pretending not to recognize me! and how sniffily he greeted me then, when he couldn't avoid it!

Having fastened a rope to the last rung of the ladder, Julien let it down gently, leaning a long way out over the balcony to make sure it didn't touch the windows. A fine moment to get rid of me, he thought, should someone be hidden in Mathilde's room; but a profound silence continued to reign all around.

The ladder touched the ground and Julien managed to lay it in the bed of exotic flowers that ran the length of the wall.

— What will my mother say, said Mathilde, when she sees all her beautiful plants destroyed! . . . The rope must be thrown down, she added with great self-possession. If someone were to see it leading back up to the balcony that would be hard to explain.

— And how me get away? said Julien in a joking tone, affecting Creole speech. (One of the lady's maids had been born in San Domingo.)

— You, you to go by de door, said Mathilde, delighted by the idea.

Ah! how much this man deserves all my love! thought she.

Julien was just letting the rope fall away into the garden when Mathilde grasped his arm. He thought himself in the hands of an enemy and spun round swiftly, drawing a dagger. She had thought she had heard a window being opened. They stood stock still, holding their breath. The moon shone full on them. The sound wasn't repeated, and there was no further reason for anxiety.

Then their embarrassment, great on both sides, flooded back again. Julien made sure that all the bolts of the door were shot to; he seriously thought of looking under the bed, but did not dare; one or two footmen could have been stationed there. Eventually, scared that he might reproach himself later, he did take a look.

Mathilde had relapsed into all the torments of extreme shyness. She was horrified at her situation.

At last – What did you do with my letters? she said.

Here's a fine chance to disconcert those gentlemen if they are listening – and avoid a battle! thought Julien.

– The first is hidden in a big Protestant Bible that was taken a long way from here by yesterday's post diligence.

In going into these details he spoke up very distinctly, so as to be heard by anyone who might be hidden in two great mahogany wardrobes that he had not dared inspect.

– The other two are in the post, going the same way as the first.

– Really, good God, why all these precautions? asked Mathilde, amazed.

Why on earth should I lie? thought Julien, and he told her of all his suspicions.

– Ah! that's the reason for the coldness of your letters! cried Mathilde, addressing him as *tu*,[2] though in accents that were more distraught than tender.

Julien did not notice this subtle distinction of tone. The intimacy of her language went right to his head, or at least his suspicions evaporated; he ventured to clasp this girl, so beautiful and so awe-inspiring, to him in his arms. He was only half pushed away.

Just as in Besançon with Amanda Binet long ago he consulted his memory and brought out several of the finest phrases from *La Nouvelle Héloïse*.[3]

– You really do have the heart of a man, she replied, without listening much to these formulations; I admit I wished to test your courage. Your suspicions at first – then your resolution – show that you are even more intrepid than I thought.

Mathilde was making an effort with the *tu* forms, she was obviously more intent on this unfamiliar way of speaking to him than with the substance of what she said. The intimate vocabulary, lacking any note of tenderness, now gave Julien no pleasure at all; he was amazed at this absence of happiness, so in order to feel happy he at last resorted to logic. He saw himself as esteemed by this proud young woman, who never allowed herself unqualified praise; and with the help of such reasoning arrived at a state of pleasant self-approval.

It was not, it was true, that rapture of the soul he had sometimes experienced with Mme de Rênal. There was nothing tender in his feelings these first moments. It was rather the sharper pleasure of ambition – and Julien was above all ambitious. He talked some more about whom he suspected, and the precautions he had contrived. While talking, he was thinking of ways in which he might exploit his victory.

Mathilde, still much embarrassed, and with an air of being thoroughly abashed by what she had brought about, seemed delighted to find a topic of conversation. They discussed ways of seeing one another again. Julien rejoiced mightily in his cleverness and daring, of which he offered further proofs while talking. They had to deal with very clear-sighted men, little Tanbeau was certainly a spy, but he and Mathilde were not without some skills themselves.

What could be easier than to meet in the library, to arrange everything?

– I can appear in any part of the house without arousing suspicion, added Julien, almost to the extent of going into Mme de La Mole's room itself. It was essential to go through there to reach her daughter's room. If Mathilde preferred that he always arrive by ladder, it was with a heart rapturous with delight that he would expose himself to this trifling danger.

Listening to him talk, Mathilde was shocked at this air of triumph. So, then, he's my master! she said to herself. She was already a prey to remorse. Her mind was horrified at the unheard-of folly she had just committed. If she had had the power she would have annihilated both herself and Julien. When she had quietened her remorse by force of will, she was made wretched by her feelings of shyness and offended modesty. She had not foreseen her present frightful state at all.

None the less I must talk to him, she told herself at last, it is the done thing, one talks to one's lover. So then, in fulfilment of a duty, and with far more tenderness in the words chosen than in the tone of her voice, she told him of the various resolutions concerning him she had come to in the last few days.

She had resolved that if he did dare come to her with the help of the gardener's ladder, as she had ordered, she would belong to him

357

entirely. But never had such tender things been said in a tone of such frigid politeness. Up to then their meeting had been as cold as ice. It was enough to make one detest love. What a lesson in morals for a young woman! Was it worthwhile ruining her future for such a moment?

After long-drawn-out doubts and hesitations, which to a superficial observer would have seemed born of a most decided hatred – so hard it is for even so strong a will to overcome the feelings of what a woman owes herself – Mathilde ended by becoming his complaisant mistress.

The truth is that their raptures were somewhat *willed*. Passionate love remained more of a model for imitation than a reality.

Mlle de La Mole believed herself to be doing a duty to herself and to her lover. The poor fellow, she said to herself, has accomplished a deed of great daring, he ought to be made happy – if he is not, it is a failure of character on my part. But she would gladly have paid the price of an eternity of unhappiness to escape the cruel necessity she found herself in.

Despite the awful violence she did herself, she remained in perfect control of what she said.

No expressions of regret, no reproaches spoiled the night – which Julien felt as more strange than joyful. What a difference, great God! to his last 24-hour stay in Verrières! These wonderful Paris ways have found the secret of ruining everything, even love, he said to himself with extreme injustice.

He made these reflections while standing upright in one of the mahogany wardrobes in which he had been put when the first sounds were heard in the next apartment – that of Mme de La Mole. Mathilde followed her mother to mass, the maids soon left the apartment and Julien easily escaped before they came back to finish their work.

He got on his horse and sought out the loneliest spots in the woods near Paris. He was much more bemused than happy. The happiness that did from time to time invade his soul was that of a young second lieutenant who, as a result of some amazing action, had instantly been made colonel by the Commander-in-Chief; he felt himself to be transported to a great height. All that had been above him

yesterday was now on a level with him, or even below. In proportion
to the distance as he got further away, Julien's happiness gradually
increased.

If there was an absence of tender feeling in his soul this was
because, however odd the word may seem, in all her behaviour
towards him Mathilde had been performing a duty. There had been
nothing unexpected for her in all the night's events except the misery
and shame she found in place of the perfect bliss they talked about
in novels.

Have I deceived myself, can it be that I'm not in love with him at
all? she wondered.

CHAPTER 17

An Old Sword

I now mean to be serious; – it is time,
Since laughter now-a-days is deem'd too serious
A jest at vice by virtue's called a crime.

DON JUAN, canto XIII[1]

She did not appear at dinner. In the evening she came into the salon for a moment, but did not look at Julien. Such behaviour seemed strange to him – but I don't know their ways, thought he, she will be able to provide me with good reason for all this. Nevertheless, driven on by extreme curiosity, he studied the expression on Mathilde's face; he could not conceal from himself that she wore a contained and hostile look. Surely this wasn't the same woman who last night felt, or pretended to feel, transports of happiness too excessive to be real.

The next day, the day after that, the same coldness on her part; she did not look at him; she did not notice his existence. Devoured by a most lively anxiety, Julien was now a thousand miles away from the feelings of pure triumph that had rushed through him on the first day. Could it by any chance, he asked himself, be a return to virtue? But the word was rather too bourgeois for the haughty Mathilde.

In the everyday situations in life she does not believe in religion at all, he thought, she values it as being extremely useful to the interests of her class.

But might not it be simple feelings of delicacy that reproach her so vividly for her lapse? Julien was sure that he had been her first lover.

But, he said to himself at other moments, one has to admit that there is nothing naive, or simple, or tender in her whole mode of life; I have never seen her haughtier than just now. Does she despise me? It would be just like her to reproach herself with what she has done for me solely on account of the lowness of my birth.

While Julien, filled with assumptions gleaned from books and from his memories of Verrières, was going on the illusory ideal of a tender mistress who ceases to think of her own existence the moment she makes her lover happy, Mathilde's vanity was enraged at him.

Since she had not been bored for two months, she no longer dreaded boredom; so, without in the least suspecting it, Julien had lost his great advantage.

I have provided myself with a master! said Mlle de La Mole to herself, victim to the blackest remorse. He is full of honourable sentiments, very well then; but if I push his vanity to its end he will avenge himself by making the nature of our relations known. Mathilde had never had a lover before, and in this, the time of life that provides some tender illusions for even the driest of souls, she was prey to the most bitter reflections.

He wields immense power over me since he rules by terror and can punish me atrociously if I provoke him. This idea alone was enough to drive Mlle de La Mole to insult him. Daring was the prime quality of her character. Nothing could so well furnish her with some agitation, and offer a relief to her endlessly renewed stock of boredom, as the sensation that she was setting her whole existence upon the toss of a coin.

On the third day, after dinner, and since Mlle de La Mole persisted in avoiding his glance, Julien followed her, in spite of herself, into the billiard room.

– Ah, so, monsieur, you think you have acquired some rather powerful rights over me, she said with barely contained anger, since, quite against my most clearly indicated wishes, you insist on talking to me? ... D'you realize that no one in the whole world has ever dared as much?

Nothing could be more amusing than the conversation between

these two lovers, who, without suspecting it, were fired by the most vivid feelings of mutual hatred. As neither of them had a long-suffering nature, and in any case both were used to the customs of polite society, they soon came to the point of declaring openly that they had quarrelled for ever.

— I swear eternal secrecy to you, said Julien, and I will even add that I would never address another word to you if it weren't that your reputation would suffer from too marked a change. He bowed respectfully and departed.

He managed to carry out what he thought was his duty quite painlessly; he was certainly far from believing himself much in love with Mlle de La Mole. Assuredly he had not loved her three days previously, when he had stood hidden in the great mahogany wardrobe. But, from the moment he saw himself as having quarrelled with her for ever, all was rapidly transformed within him.

His pitiless memory began to go back again over the slightest details of that night which in reality had left him so cold.

In the very night following the declaration of eternal separation, Julien almost went mad on finding himself forced to admit that he adored Mlle de La Mole.

Terrible struggles followed on this discovery: all his feelings were thrown into total confusion.

Two days later, in place of behaving proudly to M. de Croisenois, he could almost have embraced him, melting with tears.

The experience of a continuing unhappiness provided him with a glimmer of common sense; he decided to leave for the Languedoc, packed his trunk and went to the postal depot.

He felt himself near to swooning when, on arriving at the coach office, he was told that by an odd chance there was a place on the Toulouse mail the following day. He reserved it and returned to the Hôtel de La Mole to announce his departure to the Marquis.

M. de La Mole was out. More dead than alive, Julien went to wait for him in the library. Imagine his feelings on finding Mlle de La Mole already there!

Seeing him come in, she assumed an air of hostility that he could not possibly misinterpret.

Transported by misery, dazed by surprise, Julien had the weakness to bring out, in the tenderest and most heartfelt manner – Then you don't love me any more?

– I'm horrified at having given myself to the first comer, answered Mathilde, weeping tears of rage against herself.

– *To the first comer!* exclaimed Julien, and he sprung to an antique medieval sword which was kept in the library as a curiosity.

His pain – which he had thought extreme when he spoke to Mlle de La Mole – had now been increased a hundredfold by the tears of shame he saw her shed. He would have been most happy to have had the power to kill her.

Just as he succeeded, with some difficulty, in drawing the sword from its ancient scabbard, Mathilde, delighted at so novel a sensation, advanced proudly towards him; her tears had dried up.

The image of the Marquis de La Mole, his benefactor, came vividly to Julien's mind. And I am about to kill his daughter! he cried to himself – How appalling! He made as if to throw the sword from him. Certainly, he thought, she is going to burst out laughing at the sight of this melodramatic gesture – and the thought helped him regain complete possession of himself. He examined the ancient blade attentively, as though looking for a speck of rust, then put it back in its scabbard and, with the greatest of calmness, hung it up again on its gilded brass nail.

The whole of this episode, much drawn out towards the end, had lasted a good minute; Mlle de La Mole stared at him in astonishment. I have just been on the point of being slain by my lover! she said to herself.

The idea carried her off to the finest days of the age of Charles IX and Henri III.

She stood stock still in front of Julien, who had just replaced the sword; she gazed at him with eyes no longer full of hatred. It must be admitted that she was wonderfully appealing at that moment, and certainly no woman ever less resembled a Parisian doll (Julien's favourite word of criticism of the women thereabout).

I'm going to fall back into some weakness for him, thought Mathilde; then immediately he will think himself my lord and master

– after a relapse – and at the precise moment I have just taken a firm line with him. She fled.

My God! how beautiful she is! said Julien, watching her run out; there goes the creature who threw herself into my arms with so much fervour less than a week ago ... And those moments will never return! And it's my fault! And while so extraordinary a thing was happening to me – one of such vital concern – I did not even feel it at all vividly! ... I have to acknowledge that I was born with a very dull, a most wretched temperament.

The Marquis appeared; Julien hastened to announce his departure.

– Where for? asked M. de La Mole.

– For the Languedoc.

– Oh no, I beg your pardon, you are reserved for higher things, and if you leave it will be for the north . . . I – to use a military term – I will even confine you to the hôtel. You will oblige me by never being more than two or three hours away, I may need you from one moment to the next.

Julien bowed, and, amazing the Marquis, went out without saying a word; he was incapable of speech, and shut himself up in his room. There he was free to exaggerate all the terrible cruelty of his fate.

So, thought he, I can't even get away! Heaven knows how many days the Marquis will keep me in Paris – great God! what will become of me? And not a single friend whose advice I can ask: Abbé Pirard wouldn't let me finish my first sentence, Comte Altamira would suggest I join in some conspiracy.

And yet I'm going mad, I feel it; I am going mad!

Who can guide me, what will become of me?

CHAPTER 18

Cruel Moments

And she confesses it to me! She describes it down to the
smallest detail! Her lovely eyes, fixed upon mine, express
the love she felt for another! SCHILLER

Ecstatic, Mlle de La Mole could dream of nothing but the bliss of
having been on the point of being slain. Since he almost killed me,
she went so far as to say to herself, he deserves to be my master.
How many fine young Society gentlemen would have to be fused
together to produce so passionate an impulse?

It must be admitted he was extremely handsome when he got up
on the chair to put the sword back exactly in the picturesque place
given it by the interior decorator! It wasn't so very foolish of me to
love him, after all.

If she had been offered just then some reasonable way of reconciliation, she would have grasped it with pleasure. Julien, locked into
his room with a double turn of the key, was prey to the most violent
despair. In his wild rush of ideas he thought of throwing himself at
her feet. If, rather than keeping himself closeted apart, he had
wandered around the garden and house ready to take advantage of
anything that transpired, he might perhaps have instantly turned his
frightful unhappiness into the keenest joy.

Yet the same adroitness we are reproaching him for lacking would
have precluded the sublime impulse to grasp the sword which, at that
very moment, was making him so attractive to Mlle de La Mole. Her
caprice, which was favourable to Julien, lasted throughout the day;
Mathilde conjured up for herself a delightful image of the brief hours
during which she had loved him, and regretted them.

Actually, she said to herself, so far as this poor boy could tell, my passion for him lasted only from an hour after midnight, when I saw him arrive by ladder with all his pistols in the side pocket of his coat, until eight in the morning. It was a quarter of an hour after, while hearing mass at St-Valère, that it occurred to me he was going to assume himself my master, and that he might well try to force me to obedience by terror.

After dinner, far from avoiding Julien, Mlle de La Mole talked to him, and in a manner encouraged him to follow her into the garden; he obeyed. This was the proof she required. Without being fully aware of it, Mathilde was letting herself yield to the love that was once more stirring within her. She found an intense pleasure in walking beside him, and glanced curiously at those hands which had that morning grasped the sword to kill her.

After an action like that, after all that had happened between them, there could be no question of conversation in their former mode.

Little by little Mathilde started speaking to him confidingly about the state of her heart. She took a curiously voluptuous delight in this sort of talk; she proceeded to tell him of the passing enthusiasms she had felt for M. de Croisenois, for M. de Caylus ...

– What! For M. de Caylus, too! exclaimed Julien – and all the bitter jealousy of an abandoned lover burst out in this phrase. Mathilde saw that this was so, and was not at all displeased.

She continued to torture Julien, setting her former feelings before him in the most graphic fashion, and in tones of the most intimate conviction. He saw that she was evoking something present before her eyes. He had the pang of realizing that she was discovering things about her own heart even as she talked.

Jealous anguish can go no further.

To suspect that a rival is loved is cruel enough as it is, but to have the love he inspires told over in detail by the woman you adore is undoubtedly the depth of misery.

Oh, how thoroughly Julien was punished then for the surges of pride that had led him to promote himself above Caylus and Croise-nois! With what inner and heartfelt misery did he magnify the least of their advantages! With what ardent sincerity did he despise himself!

Mathilde seemed to him adorable — words are inadequate to express his overflowing admiration. Walking beside her he kept stealing glances at her hands, her arms, her queenly bearing. He was on the point of falling at her feet, overwhelmed by love and by misery, and crying: Take pity!

And this creature who is so beautiful, so superior to everything, who once loved me, will undoubtedly soon be in love with M. de Caylus!

Julien could not doubt Mlle de La Mole's sincerity; all she said too evidently had the ring of truth. And — so that his misery should be absolutely complete — there were times when, because she was so strongly involved in describing feelings she had once had for M. de Caylus, Mathilde came to speak of him as though she was really in love with him. There was certainly love in her tones of voice, and Julien heard them clearly.

A flood of molten lead could have been poured into his breast and he would have suffered less. Having come to this extremity of misery, how could the poor boy possibly guess that it was precisely because she was speaking to him that Mlle de La Mole found such pleasure in mentally reviewing the romantic inclinations she once felt for M. de Caylus or M. de Luz?

Nothing could do justice to the miseries Julien suffered. In that very same lime avenue where a few days before he had waited for one o'clock to strike before climbing into her room, he now heard elaborate confidences about love felt for others. A human being could not be subjected to a higher degree of distress.

This species of cruel intimacy lasted a good week. Sometimes Mathilde appeared to seek out opportunities to talk to him, sometimes she simply did not avoid them; and the subject of conversation to which they both seemed to revert with a kind of awful relish was the recital of the emotions she had experienced for other men: she told him of the letters she had written, she even recalled actual words for him, quoted entire phrases. Towards the end she seemed to contemplate Julien with a sort of malicious delight. His sufferings gave her keen pleasure.

One sees that Julien had no experience of life, had not even read novels; had he been a little less awkward, and had he managed, with a certain self-confidence, to say to this girl whom he so much adored and who treated him to such strange intimacies: – Confess that, though I may not be worth so much as these gentlemen, nevertheless it is me you love ... perhaps she would have been pleased that he read her aright; or at the least his success would have depended entirely on the grace with which he expressed this idea, and the moment he chose. But, be that as it may, he was emerging well, and to his credit, from a situation that was becoming monotonous in Mathilde's eyes.

One day Julien, lost in love and misery, said to her – So you don't love me any more, I who adore you! It was almost the greatest mistake he could have made.

In a single flash the remark destroyed all the pleasure Mlle de La Mole found in revealing the state of her heart to him. She was just beginning to be amazed that, after all that had happened, he was not offended by her stories – she was going so far as to speculate, at the very moment he made his stupid remark, that perhaps he no longer loved her. No doubt pride has extinguished his love, she said to herself. He is not a man to see people like Caylus, de Luz, and Croisenois – whom he allows are so much his social superiors – set with impunity over him. No, I shan't see him at my feet much longer!

In the days preceding this Julien had, in his artless misery, frequently heaped heartfelt praise on these gentlemen's outstanding qualities; he even exaggerated them. Mlle de La Mole hadn't missed this detail; she had been much surprised by it, but she had not worked out the reason for it. By praising a rival he thought beloved, Julien's distracted soul aspired to partake a little in his happiness.

His frank but profoundly stupid remark changed all this immediately; Mathilde, certain that she was loved, despised him utterly.

She was walking with him when the disastrous remark was made; she left him, and her parting glance expressed the most devastating contempt. Returning to the salon, she did not look at him again all evening. The next day her whole heart was filled with scorn; there was no longer any question of her entertaining the impulse that for a week had given her such pleasure in treating Julien as a most intimate friend; the sight of him offended her. Mathilde's sensation was almost one of disgust; nothing could express the colossal distaste she experienced whenever she set eyes on him.

Julien had not understood anything at all of what had been happening in Mathilde's heart for the past week, but he was conscious of her scorn. He had the good sense to be seen by her as rarely as possible, and never to look at her.

But it was not without a mortal ache that he virtually deprived himself of her company. He thought he could sense his misery becoming even greater because of it. A man's emotional courage surely cannot possibly reach further than this, he said to himself. He spent his time at a little window in the eaves of the hôtel; the shutter was carefully put to, and from there he could at least see Mlle de La Mole when she appeared in the garden.

Imagine what he felt when he saw her strolling there after dinner with M. de Caylus, M. de Luz or some other young man for whom she had confessed she once felt some light romantic fancy?

Julien had never conceived of such an intensity of suffering; he was on the point of crying out loud; this resolute soul was at last thrown into sheer chaos from its foundations up.

Any thoughts not related to Mlle de La Mole became odious to him; he became incapable of composing the simplest letters.

– You aren't in your right mind, said the Marquis.

Julien, trembling that he might be found out, pleaded illness, and his plea convinced. Fortunately for him, the Marquis teased him at dinner about his coming journey: and Mathilde realized that this might be a very long one. Julien had been avoiding her now for several days; and the brilliant young men who possessed all that was lacking in this pale and sombre creature she had once loved no longer had the power to distract her from her dreams.

An ordinary girl, she said to herself, would have sought out the man she preferred from amidst the young men who attract everyone's attention in the salon; but one of the marks of genius is not to allow its preferences to trail along in the rut of the ordinary.

As the companion of a man like Julien, though he lacks a fortune like mine, I would perpetually excite attention, I would never go through life unnoticed. Far from endlessly worrying about revolution, like my cousins who daren't tell off a postilion who drives them badly for dread of the people, I'd be certain to play a part – and a great part: for the man I have chosen has character and boundless ambition. What does he lack? Friends? Money? I'd supply all that. But in her mind she was treating Julien as an inferior being, who could be made to love at will.

CHAPTER 19

The Opéra Bouffe[1]

> *O, how this spring of love resembleth*
> *The uncertain glory of an April day,*
> *Which now shows all the beauty of the sun*
> *And by and by a cloud takes all away.*
>
> SHAKESPEARE[2]

Taken up with the future and the unusual part she hoped to play in it, Mathilde soon began to look back with regret on the dry, metaphysical discussions she had so often had with Julien. When weary of such lofty thoughts, she sometimes regretted also the moments of happiness she had shared with him – these latter memories were not free from remorse, and at certain times she was overwhelmed by this.

But if one does have a moment of weakness, she said to herself, it is due to the dignity of a girl like me to fail in her duty only for a man of merit; it cannot be said that his handsome moustaches seduced me, or his grace on a horse, but rather his profound discussions of the future that awaits France, his ideas about the parallel that the events which may soon sweep over us could have with the revolution in England in 1688. I may have been seduced, she retorted to her remorse – I'm only a feeble woman – but at least I have not been led astray by superficial charms, like a doll.

If there is a revolution, why shouldn't Julien Sorel play the part of Roland, and I that of Mme Roland?[3] I'd much prefer her role to that of Mme de Staël: in our century immoral goings-on will be a hindrance. Certainly no one will be able to reproach me with a second attack of weakness; I would die of shame.

It must be confessed that Mathilde's reflections were not always so serious as the thoughts we here transcribe.

She would gaze at Julien and discover a graceful charm in his slightest action.

Undoubtedly, she said to herself, I have succeeded in extirpating there even the slightest idea that he possesses any rights.

The look of suffering and deep passion with which the poor fellow told me that he loves me, about a week ago, demonstrates that clearly enough; it must be admitted that it was very odd of me to be so annoyed at his saying something that burned with such respect, such passion. Aren't I his wife? It was a very natural thing to say, and it must be admitted that he was being very amiable. Julien was still able to love me after all those endless conversations in which I spoke to him exclusively, and I admit with great cruelty, of the little romantic inclinations that the boring life I lead induced me to have for the Society men of whom he is so jealous. Ah! if only he knew how little danger they pose to me! How unsubstantial they seem compared to him — all mere reproductions of one another.

While making these reflections Mathilde was randomly sketching with her pencil on a page in her album. One of the profiles she had just finished amazed her, delighted her: it captured Julien in the most striking way. This is the voice of Heaven! here's a miracle of love! she cried out to herself with rapture: I have made his portrait without meaning to.

She dashed back to her room, shut herself in, and applied herself in earnest, trying seriously to do a portrait of Julien — but without success; the profile sketched at random remained the best likeness; Mathilde was delighted with this, she saw in it plain proof of a grand passion.

She did not relinquish her album until very late, when the Marquise had her called to go to the Italian opera. Then she had only one aim — to catch sight of Julien so that she could arrange for her mother to get him to accompany them.

He did not appear; the ladies had only commonplace people in their box. All through the first act of the opera, Mathilde dreamed in great gusts of passion of the man she loved; but in the second a certain formulation on the subject of love, sung, it must be admitted, to a melody worthy of Cimarosa, pierced her heart. The heroine of the opera sung: *I must punish myself for my excess of love, too much do I love him!*

The moment she heard this divine cantilena all else in the world vanished for Mathilde. Someone spoke to her, she did not reply; her mother scolded her, hardly could she return her look. Her ecstasy reached a plane of exaltation and passion comparable to the most violent bouts of emotion Julien had suffered on her behalf during the last fortnight. The cantilena, full of marvellous grace, in which was set the sentiment that seemed so strikingly applicable to her own situation, held her attention every moment she was not thinking directly about Julien. Thanks to her love of music, she became that evening as Mme de Rênal always was when thinking of Julien. Love generated in the mind is doubtless more intelligent than true love, but it has only flashes of enthusiasm; it is too conscious of itself, it constantly appraises itself; far from scattering the thoughts, it is constructed by the power of thought alone.

On returning to the house Mathilde pretended – in spite of all that Mme de La Mole might say – to have a fever, and spent part of the night replaying the cantilena over and again on her piano. She sung the words of the famous air that had so struck her:

Devo punirmi, devo punirmi,
Se troppo amai, etc.[4]

The result of this night of madness was that she became convinced that she had succeeded in conquering her love. (This page will do damage to its unfortunate author in more ways than one. Frigid souls will accuse him of impropriety. But he does no injury to those young women who shine in the Paris salons now by supposing that any one of them is susceptible to the wild impulses that degrade Mathilde's character. This character is completely imaginary, and, what's more, is imagined quite apart from those social customs that will assure the civilization of the nineteenth century so distinguished a place amongst the ages.

It certainly was not prudence that was lacking in the young girls who ornamented this winter's balls.

Indeed I don't think one can accuse them of being a great deal too scornful of a brilliant fortune, horses, fine estates and all the things that assure an agreeable position in the world. Far from all these advantages generating nothing but boredom, they are in general the objects of a most constant desire, and if there does exist a passion in those hearts it is for them.

Nor is it any longer love that directs the careers of reasonably talented young men like Julien; these attach themselves with bands of steel to some coterie, and when that coterie prevails, all Society's good things are rained upon them. This is bad news for the educated man who is not a member of any coterie – people will censure him even for the small and uncertain successes he has, and the superior virtues will triumph as they rob him. Ah, sir! a novel is a mirror travelling down the road.[5] Sometimes it reflects the blue of the heavens to the eye, sometimes the mud of the filthy puddles on the road. And he who carries the mirror in his pack will be blamed for being immoral! His mirror shows the filth, and you blame the mirror! Much better blame the high road where the puddles are, and better still the inspector of roads who lets the water gather and the muddy puddles collect.

Now that it is clearly agreed that Mathilde's character is impossible in our age – which is no less prudent than it is virtuous – I am not so scared of giving offence when I continue with the tale of this amiable young woman's follies.)

All day next day she was on the watch for opportunities to assure herself that she had indeed triumphed over her mad passion. Her chief aim was to be as unpleasant as she could to Julien; but none of his movements escaped her.

Julien was too unhappy, and above all too agitated, to detect so complicated an evolution of passion, and still less could he divine in it all that might be favourable to him: he was its victim; his misery had perhaps never been so extreme. His actions were so little under the direction of his intellect that if some disillusioned philosopher had said to him: *Try to take a swift advantage of dispositions that could be favourable to you; in this kind of mentally generated love, the kind one sees in Paris, the mode of behaviour doesn't remain constant for more than two days at a time*, he wouldn't have understood him. But even so, worked up as he was, Julien retained his honour. His prime duty was discretion, and he understood that. To ask advice, to tell his sufferings to the first comer, would have been a relief comparable to that of some poor fellow crossing a burning desert to whom Heaven grants a drop of cold water. He saw that danger, he was afraid that he might respond to an inquisitive questioner with a flood of tears; he shut himself up in his room.

He gazed at Mathilde walking for a long time in the garden; when at last she had left it, he came down; he went up to a rose bush from which she had plucked a flower.

The night was overcast, and he could give way to his misery freely, without fear of being seen. It was quite obvious to him that Mlle de La Mole loved one of those young officers with whom she had just been talking so gaily. Once she had loved him, but then she had realized how little merit he had.

And truly I do have so little! Julien said to himself with complete conviction; all in all I am a pretty dull creature, very common, extremely tedious to others and pretty intolerable to myself. He was mortally weary of all his good qualities, of all the things he had eagerly loved; and in this state of *inverted imagination* he undertook to evaluate existence through his imagination. This is the mistake of a superior man.

Several times the idea of suicide occurred to him; it was a most attractive image, as of a sweet relief; it was the glass of water offered to the wretch dying of thirst and heat in the desert.

My death would increase the contempt she feels for me! he cried. What a memory I will leave behind me!

The only resource left to a human being fallen into the last abyss of wretchedness is courage. Julien had not enough imaginative fire remaining to tell himself – You must dare; but as he looked past the shutters at the window of Mathilde's room he saw that she was putting out her light: he pictured this charming room which he had seen, alas! but once in his life. His imagination could go no further.

One o'clock sounded; there was but an instant between hearing the stroke of the clock and saying – I'm going up the ladder.

This was his flash of inspiration; excellent reasons crowded after. – Could I be more miserable! he cried. He hurried to the ladder – the gardener had chained it up. With the help of the hammer of one of his little pistols – which snapped – Julien, fired now by superhuman strength, twisted one of the links that held the ladder; in a few moments he had it under control and put it up against Mathilde's window.

She will be angry, she will heap scorn on me – what does it matter? I'll give her a kiss, a final kiss, I'll go up to my room and kill myself . . . my lips will touch her cheek before I die!

He flew up the ladder, he rapped on the shutter; after a few moments Mathilde heard him; she tried to open the shutter, but the ladder stopped her; Julien grabbed the iron hook meant to keep the shutter open, and, risking pitching down a thousand times, gave a violent heft to the ladder which moved it a little. Mathilde could open the shutter.

He threw himself inside more dead than alive:

– So it's you, dear one! she said, throwing herself into his arms . . .

Who could describe the excesses of Julien's happiness? Mathilde's was almost as great.

She inveighed against herself, denounced herself to him.

– Punish me for my wicked pride, she said to him, her arms hugging him so that he could scarcely breathe; you are my master, I am your slave, on my knees I must crave your pardon for trying to rebel. She left his arms and threw herself at his feet. Yes, you are my master, she went on, intoxicated by love and delight; reign for ever over me, punish your slave harshly if she tries to rebel.

In another moment she tore herself from his arms, lit the candle, and Julien had the greatest difficulty in the world in preventing her from cutting off all her hair on one side.

– I want to be able to remind myself, she told him, that I am your servant: if ever vile pride should lead me astray, show me this hair and tell me: it's no longer a matter of love, it's not a question of whatever mood your soul may feel just now, you have sworn to obey, obey on your honour.

But it would be wiser to have done with the description of such a pitch of distraction and felicity.

Julien's virtue was equal to his happiness; I must climb back down the ladder now, he told Mathilde when he saw daylight appearing on the distant eastern chimneys beyond the garden. The sacrifice I'm imposing on myself is worthy of you – I'm depriving myself of some hours of the most amazing happiness the human soul could possibly enjoy – it is a sacrifice I make to your reputation: if you see into my heart you will do justice to the violence I am inflicting upon myself. Will you always be for me as you are now? But honour calls, and that's enough. You should know that from our first meeting, not all the suspicions were directed against thieves. M. de La Mole has set a watch in the garden. M. de Croisenois is surrounded by spies, they know what he does every night . . .

At this idea Mathilde burst out laughing. Her mother and one of the serving women were woken up – all of a sudden they called to her through the door. Julien looked at her; she turned pale as she scolded the chambermaid, and did not deign to return a word to her mother.

– But if they think of opening the window they will see the ladder! said Julien.

He clasped her once more in his arms, threw himself upon the ladder and slid rather than climbed down it; in an instant he was on the ground.

Three seconds later the ladder was under the limes in the alley, and Mathilde's honour saved. Coming to his senses, Julien found that he was all covered in blood and almost naked: he had hurt himself in sliding down so precipitously.

His intense happiness had restored all the vigour of his character: had twenty men come on him at that moment, attacking them single-handed would have merely been an additional pleasure. Fortunately, his military prowess was not put to the test: he stowed the ladder in its usual place; he replaced the chain that fastened it; he did not forget to smooth over the marks the ladder had left in the beds of exotic flowers below Mathilde's window.

As he ran his hand in the dark over the damp earth, making sure the prints were entirely effaced, he felt something fall on to his hands

– it was a whole side of Mathilde's hair that she had cut off and thrown down to him.

She was at her window.

– That is what your servant presents to you, she said quite loudly, the mark of eternal obedience. I abjure the use of my reason – be my master.

Julien, overcome, was on the point of picking up the ladder and climbing up to her again. In the end reason prevailed.

Getting back into the hôtel from the garden was not an easy matter. He succeeded in breaking in via a cellar door; once in the house he was obliged to force the door of his own room as quietly as possible. In his confusion he had left everything in the little room he had just got out of so fast, even down to the key in his coat pocket. If only, he thought, she remembers to hide all those material remains!

At last, exhaustion overcame happiness and, as the sun was rising, he fell into a deep slumber.

The lunch bell had great difficulty in waking him; he appeared in the dining-room. Soon afterwards, Mathilde came in. Julien's pride had a moment of pure joy in seeing the love that sparkled in the eyes of this young woman, so beautiful and so surrounded by homage; but soon his prudence felt cause for alarm.

Under the pretence of having had little time for her coiffure, Mathilde had done her hair in a way that let Julien see at first glance the full extent of the sacrifice she had made for him in cutting it the previous night. If so beautiful a countenance had been capable of being ruined by anything, Mathilde would have succeeded in ruining it; one whole side of her lovely ash blonde hair was cut to within half an inch of her head.

At lunch Mathilde's whole behaviour was in accord with this primary rash act. It was as though she had set out to let the whole world know of her mad passion for Julien. It was fortunate that on that particular day M. de La Mole and the Marquise were much preoccupied with some impending promotions to the Blue Riband in which M. de Chaulnes had not been included. Towards the end of the meal it occurred to Mathilde, talking to Julien, to call him *my master*. He flushed to the whites of his eyes.

Whether by chance, or at the instance of Mme de La Mole, Mathilde was not left alone for a moment that day. In the evening, however, while passing from the dining-room to the salon, she found a chance to say to Julien:

– Are you going to think this is an excuse on my part? Mama has just decided that one of her women will spend all night in my apartment.

The day went by in a flash. Julien was at the peak of his happiness. From seven o'clock the next morning he installed himself in the library; he hoped that Mlle de La Mole would deign to appear there; he had written her an infinitely long letter.

He did not catch sight of her until several hours later, at lunch. Today her hair was done up with the greatest care; the place where the locks were cut off had been concealed with a miraculous art. She looked at Julien once or twice, but with calmly polite eyes – there was no question of calling him *my master*.

Julien's astonishment affected his breathing ... Mathilde was reproaching herself with almost everything she had done for him.

On mature consideration she had decided that he was a person who – though not entirely commonplace – did not stand out from the ranks sufficiently to deserve all the wild acts of folly she had dared commit for him. And altogether she was scarcely thinking of love; that day she was tired of love.

As for Julien, the pitchings of his heart were those of a boy of sixteen. Terrible doubt, astonishment and despair filled it by turns throughout the whole of lunch, which seemed to him to go on for an age.

As soon as he could decently get up from table he dashed, rather than ran, to the stable, saddled his horse himself and set off at a gallop; he dreaded shaming himself through some weakness. I must deaden my heart through physical weariness, he said to himself, galloping through the woods of Meudon. What have I done, what have I said, to deserve such a fall from grace?

I must not do anything or say anything today, he resolved as he returned to the hôtel, I must be as dead physically as I am morally. Julien is no longer alive, it is his corpse that still stirs.

CHAPTER 20

The Japanese Vase

His heart does not at first comprehend the extremes of his
    misery; it is confused rather than carried away. But as
    reason returns, so he feels the depth of his misfortune. All
    life's pleasures are as if annulled for him, he can feel only
    the sharp points of the despair that lacerates him. But what
    use is it to speak of physical suffering? What suffering
    felt only in the body can compare with this?

JEAN-PAUL[1]

The bell for dinner was sounding, Julien had only just time to dress;
in the salon he found Mathilde, who was giving her brother and M.
de Croisenois all sorts of good reasons not to go and spend the
evening with Mme la Maréchale de Fervaques at Suresnes.

She could hardly have been more agreeable to them, and more
winning. After dinner MM. de Luz, de Caylus and a number of their
friends appeared. It seemed that Mlle de La Mole had gone back to
the observance of a strict propriety as well as to the cult of sisterly
devotion. Although the weather that evening was pleasant, she
insisted on not going into the garden; she wanted no one to be far
from the armchair in which Mme de La Mole was settled. The blue
sofa became the centre of the circle, as in winter.

Mathilde had taken a dislike to the garden, or at least it seemed to
her utterly tedious: it was bound up with memories of Julien.

Unhappiness diminishes wit. Our hero had the awkwardness to
linger on the little straw chair that had once seen such brilliant
triumphs. Today no one at all spoke to him; his presence went as
though unnoticed, or worse. Those of Mlle de La Mole's friends who

were seated near him at the end of the sofa affected to turn their backs on him, or so at least he thought.

It's a disgrace at Court, thought he. He decided to spend a moment considering those who assumed they could overwhelm him with disdain.

M. de Luz's uncle had an important position around the King, with the result that this handsome officer opened his remarks to anyone who engaged him in conversation with the following striking titbit: his uncle had started for Saint-Cloud at seven o'clock, and he believed he would sleep there that night. This detail was introduced with all the semblance of casual geniality, but introduced it always was.

In scrutinizing M. de Croisenois under the severe gaze of his own unhappiness, Julien marked the extreme influence that this good and amiable young man allowed to occult forces. This was so much the case that he became saddened and annoyed if he saw an event of any importance attributed to simple and purely natural causes. There's a touch of lunacy here, thought Julien. His character has a striking resemblance to that of the Emperor Alexander[2] as Prince Korasoff described him to me. During the first year of his stay in Paris poor Julien – fresh from the seminary and dazzled by the graces, so new to him, of these agreeable young men – had been able to do nothing but admire. Their true character was only beginning to reveal itself to his eyes.

I'm playing an unworthy part here, he decided suddenly. It was now a question of quitting his little straw chair in a way that would not appear too gauche. He tried to improvise, demanding new efforts from an imagination that was wholly preoccupied elsewhere. He was compelled to fall back on memory – his memory being, it must be admitted, ill furnished with this kind of resource. The poor fellow still had very little social poise, so it was with the last degree of awkwardness, noticeable to all, that he rose to leave the salon. Misery was apparent in his whole demeanour. For three-quarters of an hour he had been playing the part of an unwanted underling, of whom no one bothers to conceal their opinion.

The critical observations he had just been making of his rivals prevented him from taking this misfortune too tragically; he possessed the memory of what had happened two evenings ago to sustain his pride. Whatever their advantages over me, thought he, walking into the garden by himself, Mathilde has never been to any one of them what she has condescended to be for me twice in my life.

His perspicacity went no further. He had no understanding at all of that strange creature whom chance had now made absolute mistress of his entire happiness.

The next day he spent trying to kill his horse and himself with fatigue. In the evening he made no further attempt to approach the blue sofa – to which Mathilde remained devoted. He noticed that Comte Norbert did not even deign to look at him when they ran across one another in the house. He must be doing himself unusual violence, he thought, he's naturally so polite.

Sleep would have been bliss to Julien. In spite of his physical tiredness, irresistibly seductive memories began to course through his mind. He had not the wit to see that by his grand excursions on horseback through the woods and environs of Paris – which acted only on himself and not at all on Mathilde's heart and brain – he was abandoning the disposal of his fate to chance.

It seemed to him that one thing alone could offer infinite solace to his torment: to speak to Mathilde. Yet what could he dare say to her?

He was deep in reveries of this at seven o'clock one morning when he suddenly saw her come into the library.

– I know you wish to speak to me, monsieur.

– Great God! Who told you that?

– I know it, what does it signify how? If you're lacking a sense of honour, you can ruin me, or at least try to; but that danger, which I don't think is real, certainly won't prevent me from being sincere. I don't love you any more, monsieur – my wild imagination has been deceiving me . . .

At this frightful blow, engulfed in love and misery, Julien tried to make excuses for himself. Nothing could be more absurd. To excuse oneself for not being liked? But what he did was no longer dictated by reason. A blind instinct prompted him to postpone the decision of his fate. It seemed to him that so long as he kept talking, matters were not yet at an end. Mathilde did not listen to what he said, the sound of his words irritated her, she could not believe he had the audacity to interrupt her.

That morning she was suffering in equal parts from remorse derived from virtue and remorse derived from pride. She was prostrated somehow by the awful idea of having given this little abbé, the son of a peasant, rights over her. It is almost, she said to herself at the moments when she exaggerated her woes, as if I could reproach myself for a lapse with one of the footmen.

In daring, proud natures it is but a single step from anger against oneself to fury with others; in such cases, transports of rage become an intense pleasure.

Mlle de La Mole arrived very swiftly at the point of loading Julien with the most terrible expressions of scorn. She had a powerful wit, and this wit excelled at the art of torturing other people's sense of their own worth, inflicting cruel wounds on it.

For the first time in his life, Julien found himself subjected to the workings of a superior mind fired with violent hatred for him. Far from it even remotely occurring to him to defend himself, he began at that moment to despise himself. Hearing himself heaped with such cruel expressions of scorn, calculated with so much intelligence as to destroy any good opinion he might have of himself, it seemed to him that Mathilde was right, and she was not saying enough.

On her side Mathilde discovered a delicious proud pleasure in punishing both herself and him for the adoration she had felt a few days before.

She had no need to invent the cruel things she said to him with such satisfaction, or think them for the first time. She had only to repeat what that part of her heart hostile to love had been advocating for the past week.

Each word increased Julien's terrible suffering a hundredfold. He made as if to run away – Mlle de La Mole restrained him with an authoritative grip on his arm.

– Please be so good as to realize, he said to her, that your voice is very loud, you can be heard in the next room.

– And what does that matter? Mlle de La Mole replied arrogantly – Who will dare tell me they've heard me? I want to set your petty pride aright for ever concerning any notions it may have developed on my account.

When Julien was able to escape from the library he was so shaken that he felt his unhappiness less acutely. Oh well, she doesn't love me any longer, he repeated out loud, as if to inform himself of his situation. It appears that she has loved me for a week or ten days – but for myself, I will love her all my life.

Is it really possible that she meant nothing! was nothing at all in my heart only a few days ago?

Raptures of pride flooded Mathilde's heart; so she had been able to break away for ever! Triumphing so completely over so strong an attraction made her perfectly happy. Now this little gentleman will understand once and for all that he has not, and will never have, any power over me. She was so pleased that at that moment she really had no love left.

After so appalling, so humiliating a scene, love would have become impossible to anyone less impassioned than Julien. Without losing her dignity for a single moment Mlle de La Mole had made a number of disagreeable remarks to him that were so finely calculated as to appear true, even when recalled with a cool head.

The conclusion Julien at first drew from so astounding a scene was that Mathilde's pride was infinite. He was firmly convinced that everything was over between them for ever – yet at lunch next day he was awkward and constrained in front of her. This was a lapse he could not have been reproached with up until then. In little things, as in great, he was used to know precisely what he ought and wanted to do, and to do it.

That same day after lunch, when fetching from a side table at Mme de La Mole's request a seditious, albeit rather rare pamphlet her priest had brought her in private that morning, Julien knocked over an old blue porcelain vase, the ugliest thing in the world.

Mme de La Mole leapt up with a cry of distress and came to inspect the fragments of her beloved vase more closely. It was old Japanware, she said – it came down to me from my great aunt the Abbess of

Chelles; it was a gift from the Dutch to the Regent, the Duc d'Orléans, who gave it to his daughter . . .

Mathilde had followed her mother, delighted to see the destruction of this blue vase, which she thought horribly ugly. Julien was silent and only slightly ruffled; he noticed Mlle de La Mole just next to him.

– This vase, he said to her, is destroyed for ever, so it is exactly like a feeling that once ruled over my heart; I beg you to accept my apologies for all the stupid things it made me do; and he went out.

– One might really think, said Mme de La Mole as he went, that that M. Sorel is proud and happy with what he's just done.

This remark penetrated straight through Mathilde's heart. It is true, she said to herself, my mother has seen it correctly, that is what he really feels. Only then did the joy of the scene she had created with him the previous day fail within her. Ah well, it's all over, she said to herself with apparent calm; what remains is a great lesson for me; it was a terrible blunder, humiliating! It will teach me wisdom for the rest of my life.

Why wasn't what I said true? thought Julien, why is the love I have for this mad girl still tormenting me?

This love, far from being extinguished as he hoped, made rapid progress. She's mad, it is true, he said to himself, but is she less adorable? Is it possible to be prettier? Aren't all the most glittering attractions that can possibly be produced by the most elegant civilization marvellously united in Mlle de La Mole? Memories of past happiness swept over Julien and rapidly destroyed all his rational efforts.

Reason struggles in vain with memories of this kind; its stern efforts serve only to enhance their charm.

Twenty-four hours after the breaking of the old Japanware vase, Julien was decidedly one of the most miserable of men.

CHAPTER 21

The Secret Note

> For I've seen all I tell you of; and if I might have been
> deceived in the seeing, most certainly I don't deceive you
> in recounting it.   *A letter to the author*[1]

The Marquis sent for him. M. de La Mole seemed rejuvenated, his
eye was sparkling.

– Let's talk a little about your memory, he said to Julien – it's
said to be prodigious! Would you be capable of learning four pages
by heart and then going to recite them in London? And that without
changing a single word! . . .

The Marquis was distractedly rustling through the pages of that
day's *Quotidienne*, and unsuccessfully trying to conceal an air of great
seriousness – like none Julien had seen him wear, even when the
Frilair lawsuit was in question.

Julien had by now enough worldly experience to realize that he
should seem completely taken in by the light-hearted manner on
display.

– That issue of *La Quotidienne* isn't too amusing perhaps; but by
tomorrow morning, if Monsieur the Marquis allows me, I shall have
the honour of reciting it to him complete.

– What, even the announcements?

– Most exactly, and without omitting a single word.

– Can you give me your word on that? replied the Marquis with
sudden gravity.

– Yes, monsieur, and only a fear of failing to keep it could affect
my memory.

– It's merely that I forgot to ask you that question yesterday: I won't now ask you to swear never to repeat what you're about to hear; I know you too well to insult you so. I've already vouched for you, and I'm going to take you to a salon where twelve gentlemen meet; you'll be taking notes on what each of them has to say.

Don't be alarmed, it won't be just a confused conversation, everyone will speak in his turn – I don't mean to say in good order, added the Marquis reviving his natural light and witty tone. While we're talking you will scribble down twenty pages or so; you will come back here with me and we will reduce those twenty pages to four. And those are the four pages you will recite to me tomorrow morning instead of a whole number of *La Quotidienne*. Then immediately you'll be off; you will have to travel by post – like a young man in pursuit of his pleasures. Your aim will be to go unnoticed by anybody. Then you'll find yourself at the side of a great personage. There, more skill will be required. It's a question of deceiving everybody surrounding him, since among his secretaries, among his servants, are people in the pay of our enemies lying in wait to intercept our agents as they pass. You will carry with you an unobtrusive letter of recommendation.

The very moment His Excellency looks at you, you will draw out my watch – this one you see here, that I will lend you for the journey. Take it with you now, that's so much done anyway, and give me yours.

The Duke himself will condescend to take down at your dictation the four pages you have by heart.

That done, but not before – note that well – you may, if His Excellency asks you, tell him about the meeting you are about to attend.

One thing that might prevent your being bored during your journey is that between Paris and the Minister's place there are people who would like nothing better than to take a shot at M. the Abbé Sorel. Then, well, his mission is over and I predict a long wait – for, my dear fellow, how will we know you are dead? Your zeal couldn't stretch to imparting that.

Run along now quickly, and buy yourself a complete outfit, continued the Marquis, serious again. Dress in the fashion of about two years ago. This evening you should appear a trifle unsmart. On the journey, on the other hand, you will be as usual. Does this surprise you, does your suspicious mind see the point? Yes, my friend, one of the revered personages whose opinions you're going to hear is fully capable of sending on information by means of which, at some excellent inn where you've ordered supper one evening, you might well be served a dose of opium – or worse.

– It would be best, said Julien, to go thirty leagues round about, not taking the direct way. This concerns Rome, I suppose . . .

The Marquis took on an air of displeased hauteur that Julien had not seen so pronounced since Bray-le-Haut.

– You'll learn that, monsieur, when I judge it appropriate to tell you. I don't care for questions.

– Oh, it wasn't one; I do assure you, monsieur, I was thinking out loud, replied Julien effusively – I was searching my mind for the safest route.

– Yes, it seems your mind was indeed far away. Never forget that an ambassador, and especially one of your age, should never seem to force a confidence.

Julien was mortified; he was in the wrong. His pride looked for an excuse, but could find none.

– Then learn from this, added M. de La Mole, that a man always gets emotional when he has made some stupid mistake.

An hour later, Julien was in the Marquis's anteroom in the guise of an inferior, with outmoded coat, a cravat of only doubtful whiteness and something of the pretentious little cad in his whole appearance.

On seeing him the Marquis burst out laughing – and only then was Julien properly vindicated.

If this youngster should let me down, said the Marquis to himself, whom could I trust? Yet, when it comes to the point, one has to trust someone. My son and his brilliant friends of the same vein have courage, and loyalty enough for a hundred thousand; if it came to a fight they'd perish on the steps of the Throne – and they do know how to do things . . . except in what's needed just now. Devil take me if I can see one among them who would be able to learn four pages by heart and travel a hundred leagues without being detected. Norbert knows how to die as his ancestors have died – but that's a conscript's virtue, too . . .

The Marquis sank into a deep reverie: And even in getting killed, said he with a sigh, maybe this Sorel would know how to behave just as well as him . . .

– Let's get in the carriage, said the Marquis, as if banishing untimely thoughts.

– Monsieur, said Julien – while my costume here was being got ready I learned the first page of today's *Quotidienne* by heart.

The Marquis took the paper. Julien recited it without getting a single word wrong. Good, said the Marquis – very much the diplomat that evening – all this time the young fellow isn't noticing what streets we're going through.

They arrived in a large salon of rather dreary aspect, part panelled and part hung with green velour. In the middle of the room a scowling footman had just installed a dining table, which he then transformed into a work table by means of a huge cloth – the detritus of some ministry or other, all stained with ink.

The master of the house was an enormous man whose name was never mentioned; Julien thought he had the look and easy address of a man who would put up with much.

At a sign from the Marquis, Julien remained at the lower end of the table. There, to put a face on things, he set about sharpening some quills. Out of the corner of his eye he counted seven men talking, though he saw them only from the back. Two seemed to address M. de La Mole as an equal, the others with more or less deference.

A new personage entered without being announced. It is most peculiar, thought Julien, that nobody is announced in this salon. Is this a precaution taken in my honour? Everyone rose to receive the newcomer. He wore the same extremely distinguished decoration as two or three of those already in the salon. They were conversing in low tones. In assessing the newcomer Julien was reduced to what he could glean from his features and dress. He was short and stout, with a high colour, a gleaming eye and no expression other than the wicked flicker of a wild boar.

Julien's attention was abruptly diverted by the arrival, almost immediately afterwards, of a wholly different personage. This was a very tall and thin man wearing two or three waistcoats. His glance was kindly, his manner courteous.

That's so like the Bishop of Besançon's style, thought Julien. This man evidently belongs to the Church, he doesn't seem more than fifty or fifty-five, and it would be impossible to look more paternal.

The young Bishop of Agde appeared, and seemed astonished when, looking round at the company, his eye fell on Julien. They had not exchanged a word since the ceremony at Bray-le-Haut. This look of surprise embarrassed and irritated Julien. What then! said he to himself, will possessing an acquaintance with someone always fall out to my disadvantage? All these grand seigneurs whom I've never set eyes on before don't intimidate me in the least, and then that young bishop's glance freezes me! It has to be admitted I am a very peculiar kind of person, and most unfortunate.

Soon a little man, very dark, came in with much fuss and bother, and commenced talking as soon as he was inside the door; he had a yellowish complexion and a rather wild air. From the moment of this remorseless talker's entry, groups began to form, seemingly to avoid the tedium of having to listen to him.

Moving away from the fireplace they started to drift down to the bottom of the table where Julien was established. His air became more and more flustered; for in the end, try as he might, he could not help but hear them, and, even with his slight experience, understand the importance of what they so openly discussed – and also how much these grandees now before his eyes should have ensured that it remained secret!

Already, working as slowly as possible, Julien had sharpened twenty quills; this resource now failed him. He vainly looked to M. de La Mole's eye for an instruction; the Marquis had forgotten him.

What I'm doing is absurd, said Julien, sharpening his quills; but men with such commonplace-seeming physiognomies, who entrust themselves or are entrusted by others with such great matters, must be very much on edge. My look, unfortunately, has in it something questioning and a little disrespectful that would doubtless annoy them. If I lower my eyes markedly it will look as though I am storing up what they say.

His embarrassment was extreme, he was hearing some singular things.

CHAPTER 22

The Discussion

The Republic – for each man nowadays who would sacrifice everything to the public good, there are some thousands and millions thinking of nothing but their own enjoyments, their vanity. In Paris a man is valued not for his virtue, but on account of his carriage. NAPOLEON, *Memorial*

The footman rushed in calling out: Monsieur le Duc de —[1]

– Be quiet, you're nothing but a fool, said the Duke as he entered. He said this so adeptly, and with such majesty, that Julien could not help but think that the art of being angry with a lackey must be this great man's whole attainment in life. Julien raised his eyes and immediately lowered them again. He had divined the importance of this new arrival so accurately that he trembled in case his glance had been indiscreet.

The Duke was a man of fifty, dressed like a dandy, and advancing with a springing step. He had a narrow head with a large nose and a curved face held forward; it would have been difficult to appear at once so noble and so insignificant. His arrival was the signal for the meeting to begin.

Julien's physiognomical observations were abruptly interrupted by the voice of M. de La Mole. – May I present to you M. l'Abbé Sorel? said the Marquis; he has the gift of an astounding memory; it was only an hour since that I informed him of the mission with which he may be honoured, yet, to furnish proof of his powers, he has learned the first page of *La Quotidienne* off by heart.

– Ah! the news from abroad about poor N——, said the master of the house. He hurriedly took up the newspaper and, gazing at Julien

392

with an air that was comical in its effort to seem imposing, said to him: Speak on, monsieur.

There was profound silence, all eyes were fixed on Julien. He recited so proficiently that at the end of twenty lines the Duke interrupted – That's enough. The little man with the wild boar eyes sat down. He was evidently the president, for hardly was he seated than he indicated a little card table to Julien, and signed for him to bring it up next to him. Julien settled himself there with the necessary writing materials. He counted twelve men around the green cloth.

– Now, M. Sorel, retire into the next room, said the Duke, and we'll send for you.

The master of the house took on a very worried air: The shutters aren't closed, he told his neighbour in a low tone. And – It's no use looking out of the window – he foolishly called out after Julien.

Well, here I am more or less thrust into a conspiracy, thought the latter. Luckily it's not the kind that leads to the Place de Grève.[2] Even if there was some danger, I owe the acceptance of it, and more, to the Marquis. I'll be delighted if I am given the chance to atone for all the suffering my foolish actions may one day cause him!

While continuing to dwell on his follies and his unhappiness, he studied the place so as never to forget it. Only then did he recall that he had not heard the Marquis tell the footman the name of the street – and that the Marquis had ordered a cab, something he never normally did.

Julien was left alone with his thoughts for a long time. He was in a salon hung with red velour with ample gold stripes. On a table there stood a great ivory crucifix, and on the chimneypiece was M. de Maistre's *Du Pape*,[3] with gilt edges and a magnificent binding. So as not to seem to be listening, Julien turned its pages. From time to time voices were raised in the next room. At last the door opened and he was called in.

– Remember, messieurs, said the president, that from this moment we're talking in front of the Duc de ––. This gentleman here, he went on, gesturing towards Julien, is a young Levite devoted to our holy cause, who, with the help of his astounding memory, can easily repeat everything we have to say, down to the last detail.

It is now that gentleman's turn to speak, he said, indicating the personage with the fatherly look, and who was wearing three or four waistcoats. Julien thought it might have been more natural to call the gentleman with the waistcoats by name. He took some paper and wrote extensively.

(Here the author had wished to put in a page full of dots. – That would show very little grace, said the editor, and if so frivolous a piece of writing lacks grace it is fatal.

Politics, retorts the author, is a millstone tied to the neck of literature, and drowns it in less than six months. Politics in imaginative work is like a shot in the middle of a concert. The noise is deafening but it imparts no energy. It doesn't harmonize with the sound of any other instrument. Such political talk mortally offends half of one's readers – and bores the other half, who, in a different context, in the morning paper, find such things interesting and lively . . .

If your characters don't talk politics, replies the editor, this is no longer France in 1830, and your book is not the mirror you pretend it to be . . .)

Julien's record of what was said ran to twenty-six pages; what follows is a very colourless version; for, as usual, it is necessary to suppress the ridiculous bits – the excesses of which would seem odious and barely credible (witness the *Legal Gazette*).[4]

The gentleman in the waistcoats with the paternal air (perhaps he was a bishop) smiled frequently and, as he did so, the orbs beneath his fluttering lids took on a strange brilliance and a less wavering gaze than usual. This personage, invited to speak first before the Duke (but what Duke? wondered Julien) – and seemingly in order to expound the state of opinion and to play the part of a general advocate – seemed to Julien to fall into the uncertainties and failures to reach firm conclusions with which such magistrates are often taxed. As the discussion went on, the Duke himself went so far as to criticize him for this.

After delivering several sentiments of a moral and pleasing nature, the man in the waistcoats said:

– Noble England, under the guidance of a great man, the immortal

Pitt, spent forty thousand million francs counteracting the Revolution. If the meeting will allow me to touch with some frankness on a melancholy subject, England didn't sufficiently understand that with a man like Bonaparte, above all when there is nothing to oppose him with but a host of good intentions, nothing could be decisive but personal methods . . .

– Oh! another speech in praise of assassination! said the master of the house with a worried look.

– Spare us your sentimental remarks, cried the president testily; his wild boar eye glittered ferociously. Go on, he said to the man with the waistcoats. His cheeks and forehead were reddening.

– Noble England, continued the speaker, is now exhausted, for every Englishman, before he can buy his daily bread, is forced to pay the interest on the forty thousand million francs used against the Jacobins. England no longer has Pitt . . .[5]

– She does have the Duke of Wellington, said a military personage, assuming a very important air.

– Gentlemen! silence, if you please, cried the president; if we go on with these disputes it will have been pointless to have introduced M. Sorel.

– We're aware that monsieur abounds with ideas, said the Duke irritably, glaring at the interrupter, who had been a general under Napoleon. Julien understood that this remark contained some highly offensive personal allusion. Everyone smiled; the renegade general seemed incensed.

– There is no longer a Pitt, messieurs, continued the speaker, putting on the discouraged air of a man who despairs of making his hearers see reason. Even were there a new Pitt in England, you cannot fool the people in the same way twice . . .

– That's why a conquering general, a Bonaparte, is an impossibility for France in future, cried the interrupting soldier.

On this occasion, neither the president nor the Duke ventured a protest – though Julien thought he could see in their eyes how very much they were tempted. They lowered their gaze, and the Duke contented himself with sighing so that all could hear.

But the speaker had been riled.

– People are eager to see me finish, said he heatedly, suddenly abandoning the smiling politeness and measured tones that Julien judged to be the true expression of his character: People are eager to see me finish; they take no account at all of the efforts I am making not to offend the ears of a single person, however long those might be. Well then, messieur, I shall be brief.

So, I assure you in the crudest terms: England hasn't a penny left in the service of the good cause. Supposing a Pitt were to return, even all his genius would not succeed in fooling the small freeholders of England, for they know that the brief campaign of Waterloo alone cost them a thousand million francs. Since you require plain talk, the speaker added, working himself up more and more, I assure you: *You must help yourselves* – for England hasn't a guinea to spare you, and when England doesn't pay, Austria, Russia and Prussia – who have only courage and no money – will be capable of waging no more than one, perhaps two, campaigns against France.

One might hope that the young soldiers the Jacobins could raise would be beaten in the first campaign, and maybe in the second; but in the third – yes, let me appear revolutionary to your prejudiced eyes – in the third you will encounter the warriors of 1794, not the enlisted peasants of 1792.

Here interruptions were heard from three or four sides at once.

– Monsieur, the president said to Julien, go into the next room and make a fair copy of the first part of the minute you have written. Julien went out, much regretting having to do so. The speaker was just about to consider probabilities he had often thought about himself.

They're afraid I might laugh at them, he reflected.

When he was called back again M. de La Mole was speaking, with an earnestness that seemed to Julien, who knew him, extremely amusing:

. . . Yes, messieurs, it is of this unhappy people above all that one may ask: – Will this be a god, a table or a basin?

It will be a God! cried the fabulist.[6] And it is to you, messieurs, that this saying – so noble and so profound – applies specially. Act for yourselves, and then that noble France, almost like the one our ancestors created and which we ourselves saw before the death of Louis XVI, may reappear.

England, her noble lords at least, loathes ignoble Jacobins just as much as we do: without English gold, Austria, Russia and Prussia can manage only two or three battles. Will that be enough to lead to a benign occupation, like the one that M. de Richelieu dissipated so foolishly in 1817?[7] I don't think so.

At this point there would have been an interruption, but this was stifled by a universal *Shush*! It had again originated from the former general of the Emperor, who was yearning for a Blue Riband and wanted to establish his position among the contributors to the Secret Note.

– I don't think so, repeated M. de La Mole after the disturbance. He enunciated the *I* with an insolent hauteur that charmed Julien. Well played! he said to himself, while making his pen fly along almost as fast as the Marquis's words. With one well-placed phrase, M. de La Mole has annihilated that turncoat's twenty campaigns.

– It is not to foreigners alone, continued the Marquis in very deliberate tones, that we should owe a new military occupation. All those young men who write inflammatory articles in the *Globe*[8] might well produce three or four thousand young captains from among whom could emerge a Kléber, a Hoche, a Jourdan, a Pichegru[9] – though less well intentioned.

– We hadn't the sense to honour that fellow sufficiently, said the president, we should have made him immortal.

– In the end there must be two parties in France, resumed M. de La Mole. Not just two parties in name, but two parties very precisely divided, sharply demarcated. Let us be aware of what we must crush. On one side there stand the journalists, the electors, public opinion – in a word, youth and all that it admires. While that drowns itself in the din of its own empty words, we have the certain advantage of being sustained by the budget.

Here there was another interruption.

– You then, monsieur, replied M. de La Mole to the interrupter with admirably lofty ease, since the word shocks you, you are not sustained, rather you devour the 40,000 francs from the state budget and the eighty thousand you get from the Civil List.

And, very well then, monsieur, since you force me to it, I will be so bold as to take you for an example. Like your noble ancestors who followed St Louis on crusade, you should be able to show us, on account of these hundred and twenty thousand francs, a regiment, a company or – what do I say! – half a company, even if it were only fifty men devoted though life and death to the good cause and prepared to fight. As it is, you have just a handful of lackeys who, if there were an uprising, would frighten no one but yourself!

The Throne – the Altar – the nobility could perish tomorrow, messieurs, so long as you haven't created a force of five hundred *dedicated* men in each department; and I mean dedicated – not just with all the gallantry of the French, but with a Spanish constancy, too.

Half this body should be made up of our sons, our nephews – of true gentlemen, in short. And each of these should have at his side, not a loquacious little bourgeois ready to hoist the tricolour cockade if 1815 came round again, but a good peasant, simple and straightforward like Cathelineau;[10] his own gentleman would have instructed him in the cause – ideally they would have been suckled together as foster brothers. Let each of us sacrifice a *fifth* of his income to the raising of this dedicated band of five hundred men per department. That's when you will be able to count on a foreign occupation. No foreign soldier is going to come in even as far as Dijon if he can't count on finding five hundred friendly soldiers in each department.

Foreign kings will listen to you only when you can tell them of twenty thousand gentlemen ready to take up arms and open the gates of France. The task is very painful, you say? – Messieurs, our own heads are the reward. Between the liberty of the press and our class's very existence there is war to the death. Change yourselves into manufacturers, peasants – or take up the gun. Be timid if you wish, but don't be stupid; open your eyes.

In the words of the Jacobin song, I adjure you – *Form your battalions!* Then some noble GUSTAVUS ADOLPHUS[11] may appear, who, stirred by the imminent threat to the monarchic principle, will swoop down from his own realm a thousand miles away and do for you what he did for the Protestant princes. Do you choose to go on talking and doing nothing? Within fifteen years there will be nothing but presidents of republics throughout Europe – not a single king. And with these four letters K-I-N-G will vanish both priests and the higher classes. I see nothing but *candidates* wooing unwashed *majorities*.

It's all very well saying that just now in France there isn't a qualified general, known and admired by all, that the army is organized solely in the interests of Throne and Altar, or that it is stripped of all its veterans while every Prussian and Austrian regiment numbers fifty NCOs who have been under fire.

There are two hundred thousand young townsmen out there who are in love with war . . .

– Enough of such unpleasant truths, interrupted a solemn personage in imposing tones – apparently a man of high ecclesiastical rank, for M. de La Mole smiled pleasantly instead of being annoyed, a sure indication to Julien.

– Enough of such unpleasant truths. Messieurs, we may sum up: a man who must have a gangrened leg cut off is in a poor position to tell his surgeon that the leg is perfectly healthy. If you will allow the expression, messieurs, the noble Duke de —[12] is the surgeon we need . . .

There, at last, the vital name has been pronounced, thought Julien; so it's towards the — that I'll be galloping tonight.

CHAPTER 23

The Clergy, Woodlands, Liberty

The first law of all being is self-preservation, it is to live.
You scatter hemlock and expect to see the ripening corn!

MACHIAVELLI

The solemn personage continued to speak; one could see he knew the subject: with a mild and moderate eloquence that appealed vastly to Julien he expounded the following important truths:

1. England has not a guinea at our disposal; economy and Hume are all the fashion there. The *Saints* themselves won't give us any money, and M. Brougham would laugh at us.[1]

2. It is impossible to get more than two campaigns out of the kings of Europe without English gold; and two campaigns are not enough against the liberal bourgeoisie.

3. The necessity of forming an armed party in France – without which the European monarchic principle will not hazard even two such campaigns.

The fourth point, which I venture to suggest is plain, is this:

The impossibility of forming an armed party in France without the clergy. I boldly assert this because, messieurs, I am going to prove it to you. It is necessary to concede everything to the clergy –

1. Because they work away night and day in this business, and are guided by men of the highest abilities, established far away from storms, three hundred leagues from your frontiers . . .

– Ah! Rome, Rome! cried the master of the house.

– Yes, monsieur, *Rome*! replied the Cardinal proudly. What-ever the more or less clever jokes that were fashionable when you were young, I can tell you plainly that now, in 1830, it is the clergy alone, guided from Rome, who speaks to the little people.

Fifty thousand priests all reciting the same form of words on the day their leaders tell them to, and the people – who, after all, furnish the troops – will be more moved by their pastor's voices than by all the trivial verses[2] in the world . . . (This personal reference excited some murmurs.)

The clergy have an intelligence that outstrips yours, went on the Cardinal, raising his voice; all the steps you've taken towards your great aim, *to have an armed party in France*, have already been taken by us . . . Here some facts were adduced . . . Who sent eighty thousand guns to the Vendée? . . . etc., etc.

– So long as the clergy is still denied its woodlands, it possesses nothing. At the first sign of war, the minister of finance will write to his agents that there's no more money except for the parish priests. At bottom, France is not a nation of believers, and she loves war. Whoever gives it to her will be doubly popular, for to make war is to starve the Jesuits, as the vulgar saying goes; and to make war is also to free those monsters of pride, the French, from the menace of foreign intervention.

The Cardinal was heard with approval . . . It was essential, he said, that M. de Nerval[3] left the ministry, because his name caused needless irritation.

At this remark, everyone rose and started talking at once. They will send me out again, thought Julien; but even the canny president himself had forgotten the presence – the very existence – of Julien.

All eyes became focused on a man Julien recognized. It was M. de Nerval, the First Minister, whom he had glimpsed at M. de Retz's ball.

Confusion was at its height, as the newspapers say in reporting on the Chamber. At the end of a long quarter of an hour silence began to be restored.

Then M. de Nerval rose and, with an apostolic air – I won't pretend to you, he said in a strange voice, that I do not hold fast to my ministry.

It has been pointed out to me, messieurs, that my name redoubles the strength of the Jacobins by turning many moderates against us. For that, I would be most willing to resign; but the ways of the Lord are discerned only by a few; and – he added, looking fixedly at the Cardinal – I have a mission; Heaven has said to me: You will either carry your head to the scaffold or you will re-establish the monarchy in France and reduce the Chambers to the condition of a *Parlement* under Louis XV – and, messieurs, *that I will do*.

He ceased, he reseated himself; a great silence fell.

What a fine actor, thought Julien. He was falling into the mistake, as usual, of attributing too much intelligence to other people. Inspired by the evening's animated debates, and above all by the heartfelt nature of the discussion, M. de Nerval really did at that moment believe in his mission. For all his great courage, the man lacked any common sense.

During the silence that followed the fine assertion – *that I will do*, midnight sounded. Julien found something impressive and solemn about the striking of the clock. He was moved.

The discussion shortly began again with increasing zest, and above all with unbelievable naivety. These people will have to dispose of me by poison, Julien reflected at certain moments. How can they say such things in front of a plebeian?

Two o'clock struck, and still they were talking. The master of the house had fallen asleep long since; M. de La Mole was obliged to ring for fresh candles. The Minister, M. de Nerval, had left at a quarter to two – not without having frequently studied Julien's face in a mirror that hung near him. His departure seemed to make everyone easier.

While the candles were being renewed: – God knows what that man will go and tell the King! said the man in waistcoats in a low voice to his neighbour. He could make us seem rather absurd and wreck our future.

You must admit he shows an extraordinary fatuity, even effrontery, to show himself here. Before he became a minister he was one of us; but a portfolio changes everything, swallows up all a man's concerns, he ought to feel that.

Scarcely had the Minister gone out than Bonaparte's ex-general closed his eyes. Then he mentioned his health, his wounds, looked at his watch and departed.

– I'll wager, said the man in waistcoats, that the General runs after the Minister; he's going to excuse himself for being found here and pretend he's here to guide us.

When the drowsy servants had finished setting out new candles:

— Now, messieurs, said the president, we must deliberate and cease trying to argue with one another. Concentrate on the contents of the note that in forty-eight hours will be in front of our faraway friends. There's been talk of ministers. Now M. de Nerval has left, we may ask — What do ministers matter to us? They'll do what we want.

The Cardinal assented to this with a subtle smile.

— Nothing could be easier, it seems to me, than to summarize our position, said the young Bishop of Agde with the strained and focused heat of exalted fanaticism. Up till then he had kept silent; but his eye, as Julien had observed, though calm and gentle at first, had lit up after the first hour's debate. Now his soul erupted like lava from Vesuvius.

— From 1806 to 1814, said he, England's only mistake was not to undertake direct and personal action against Napoleon. From the moment that man had created dukes and chamberlains, from the moment he had established a throne, the mission God confided to him was ended; he was fit only for immolation. Holy Writ teaches us in more than one place the way to be rid of tyrants. (Here there followed several Latin quotations.)

Today, messieurs, it is no longer a man that must be sacrificed, it is Paris. All France copies Paris. To what end do you arm your five hundred men in each department? A hazardous enterprise, and one of which there will never be an end. For what purpose do you involve all France in something peculiar to Paris? It is Paris alone, with its newspapers and its salons, that perpetrates evil — let the modern Babylon perish.

Between the Altar and Paris there must be an end. Such a clash could even further the worldly interests of the Throne. Why did not Paris dare breathe under Bonaparte? Ask the cannon at St-Roch.[4]

It wasn't until three in the morning that Julien left with M. de La Mole.

The Marquis was subdued and tired. For the first time in speaking to Julien there was a note of entreaty in his voice. He asked his word never to reveal the excess of zeal, as he termed it, that he had chanced to witness. Don't speak of it to our foreign friend unless he really insists on knowing what our young hotheads are like. What does it matter to them if the State is overthrown? – they'll be cardinals and can find refuge in Rome. We – in our château – we'll be massacred by the peasantry.

The secret note that the Marquis drew up from the long 26-page minute that Julien had taken was not finished until a quarter to five.

– I'm deadly tired, said the Marquis, and one can see it very clearly in this note, which lacks precision towards the end; I'm more unhappy with it than anything I've done in my whole life. Now then, my dear fellow, he went on, go you and rest for a few hours and, for fear that someone might try to abduct you, I'll come myself and lock your door.

The following day the Marquis took Julien to an isolated château a fair way from Paris. There they were received by some strange figures whom Julien judged to be priests. He was supplied with a passport in a false name – but this at last showed his true destination, of which he had continued to feign ignorance. He climbed into the barouche by himself.

The Marquis had no doubts about his memory – Julien had recited the contents of the secret note several times – but was much afraid that he might be intercepted.

– Above all cultivate the air of a fop travelling to kill time, he confided in a friendly tone as they left the salon. Perhaps there was more than one false friend at our meeting yesterday.

The journey was swift and very sad. Hardly was Julien out of the Marquis's sight than he forgot about the secret note and his mission, and thought of nothing but Mathilde's disdain.

In a village a few leagues outside Metz the postmaster came to inform him that there were no horses to be had. It was ten in the evening; much put out, Julien ordered supper. He walked up and down in front of the door and very gradually worked his way without being noticed into the stableyard. He could see no horses there.

Even so, that fellow's manner was odd, said Julien to himself – his coarse eyes were weighing me up.

As one may see, he was beginning not to believe implicitly everything he was told. He reckoned he might get away after supper and, in order to discover something about his surroundings, left his room to go and warm himself at the kitchen fire. Imagine his joy when he found there Signor Geronimo the famous singer!

Established in an armchair he had had carried next to the fire, the Neapolitan was complaining loudly and making more noise, all on his own account, than the twenty German peasants crowded open-mouthed around him.

– These people will ruin me, he cried to Julien, I've promised to sing tomorrow at Mayence. Seven sovereign princes have rushed there to hear me. But, he added in a significant manner, shall we go out and get a breath of air?

When they were a hundred paces down the road, and could not possibly be overheard, he asked Julien:

– D'you have any idea what's up? This postmaster is a scoundrel. As I was strolling around I gave twenty sous to a little scamp who told me everything. There're more than a dozen horses in another stable at the other end of the village. They're trying to delay some courier or other.

– Really! said Julien innocently.

It was not enough to have found out about this deception, now he had to get away: and in this Geronimo and his friend could not succeed. – We'll have to wait until morning, said the singer at last, they're suspicious of us. Perhaps it's you or me they're after. Tomorrow morning we will order a big meal; then while they're getting it ready we will go for a walk; we'll make our escape, hire some horses and reach the next post station.

– What about your luggage? asked Julien, to whom it had occurred that it might have been Geronimo himself who had been sent to intercept him. There was nothing for it but to eat and go to bed. Julien was still in his first sleep when he was awoken with a start by the voices of two men talking unconstrainedly in his room.

He recognized the postmaster, equipped with a dark lantern. The beam was directed towards the barouche trunk, which Julien had had carried up to his room. At the postmaster's elbow was a man busy delving calmly into the open trunk. Julien could see only the sleeves of his costume, which were black and close-fitting.

It's a soutane, he said to himself, and he gently gripped the little pistols he had placed under his pillow.

– Don't be afeared they'll wake, Monsieur le Curé, said the postmaster. The wine they was served with was that you did yourself.

– I can't find any sign of papers, answered the curé. Masses of linen – scents – pomades and vanities; it's a fashionable young man, obsessed with his pleasures. The emissary must be the other one, the one who pretends to talk with an Italian accent.

The two men got closer to Julien in order to rifle through the pockets of his travelling coat. He was strongly tempted to shoot them as thieves. Nothing could have been less dangerous in its consequences. He was sorely tempted . . . I'd be nothing but an idiot, he said to himself, I'd compromise my whole mission. – This is no diplomat, said the priest, having searched his coat: and he moved off, which was just as well for him.

– If he touches me in my bed, he will sink himself! Julien was thinking; he might well be coming to knife me, and that I will not tolerate.

The curé turned his head, Julien half opened his eyes – imagine his astonishment! it was the Abbé Castanède! In fact, although the two had taken care to speak fairly softly, it had seemed to him from the first that he recognized one of the voices. Julien was seized with a wild desire to rid the earth of one of the lowest of reptiles . . .

– But my mission! he reminded himself.

The curé and his acolyte retired. A quarter of an hour later, Julien pretended to wake up. He called out and roused the whole house.

– I've been poisoned, cried he, I'm suffering appallingly! He needed a pretext to go to Geronimo's aid. He found him half drugged by the laudanum mixed in the wine.

Julien, fearing some trickery of that kind, had drunk chocolate brought from Paris with his supper. He could not succeed in his aim of waking up Geronimo sufficiently to get him to leave.

– You could offer me the whole of the Kingdom of Naples, said the singer, and just now I could not renounce the delights of sleep.

— But the seven sovereign princes!

— Let them wait.

Julien departed by himself, and arrived at the great personage's residence without further incidents. He wasted a whole morning vainly soliciting an audience. Luckily, at about four o'clock, the Duke wished to get some fresh air. Julien saw him come out on foot, and did not hesitate to go up to ask for alms. When he was two paces away from the great man he drew out M. de La Mole's watch, and showed it with obvious intent. — *Follow me at a distance*, he was told without a glance.

A quarter of a league further on, the Duke suddenly turned into a little *café-hauss*. It was in a room of this tenth-rate establishment that Julien had the honour of reciting his four pages to the Duke. When he had finished: *start again and go more slowly*, he was ordered.

The Prince took notes. — *Get to the next post house on foot. Leave your belongings and your carriage here. Go to Strasbourg any way you can, and on the twenty-second of this month* [it was the tenth] *be in this same café-hauss at midday. Don't leave for another half hour. Be silent!*

These were the only words Julien heard. They were enough to fire him with the highest admiration. This is the way, thought he, to conduct business; what would this great statesman say if he had heard those hysterical chatterers three days ago?

Julien gave himself two days to reach Strasbourg; it seemed to him he had nothing to do there. He made a large detour. If that devil of an Abbé Castanède recognized me, he is not the man to lose me ... and how delighted he would be to humiliate me, and manage to wreck my mission!

The Abbé Castanède, chief of police for the Congregation for the whole of the northern frontier, fortunately had not recognized him. And the Strasbourg Jesuits, though extremely zealous, did not think to look very hard at Julien, who, with his cross and blue frockcoat, had all the air of a young military man preoccupied with his personal appearance.

CHAPTER 24

Strasbourg

> Infatuation! You have all love's energy, all its capacity to
> endure sorrow. Only its delightful enchantments, its gentle
> joys, are beyond your sphere. As I watched her sleeping I
> couldn't tell myself – with all her angelic beauty and sweet
> frailties, she is all mine! Here, delivered into my power, is
> she whom Heaven in its mercy created to enchant a man's
> heart.
> *Ode* by SCHILLER

Obliged to spend a week in Strasbourg, Julien tried to distract himself
by dreams of military glory and devotion to his country. Was he,
then, in love? He had no notion; in his harrowed soul he found
Mathilde alone – absolute mistress of his happiness, as of his imagination. He needed the whole strength of his character to save himself
from despair. To think of anything not related to Mlle de La Mole
was beyond him. In the past, ambition, and the simple triumphs of
vanity, had been able to distract him from the emotions inspired by
Mme de Rênal. Mathilde absorbed everything; she pervaded his
entire future.

In this future Julien foresaw failure on every side. This being
whom we have seen so presumptuous at Verrières, so full of pride,
had sunk into an absurd excess of humility.

Three days ago he would have happily done away with Abbé
Castanède, yet in Strasbourg if a child had contradicted him he would
have said that the child was right. In thinking back to the adversaries,
the enemies, he had met in his life, he now always found that he,
Julien, had been in the wrong.

That powerful imagination, which previously had been constantly engaged in painting his brilliant future success, now became his implacable enemy.

The total solitude of a traveller's life augmented the power of this gloomy vision. What a treasure a friend would have been! But, demanded Julien of himself, is there a single heart that beats for me? And even if I had a friend, would I not be bound in honour to perpetual silence?

Dolefully, he wandered out on horseback to the neighbourhood of Kehl; this is a small town on the banks of the Rhine immortalized by Desaix and Gouvion Saint-Cyr.[1] A German peasant showed him the little streams, the tracks, the islets in the Rhine on which the bravery of these great generals has conferred a famous name. Julien, guiding his horse with the left hand, checked with his right the superb map that ornaments Marshal Saint-Cyr's *Memoirs*. A joyful cry made him raise his head.

It was Prince Korasoff, the London friend who, a few months ago, had unveiled to him the first principles of the higher forms of foppery. Faithful to that great mystery, Korasoff – who had arrived in Strasbourg only the evening before, had been an hour in Kehl, and never read a line about the siege of 1796 – began to explain the whole affair to Julien. The German peasant stared with astonishment – he understood enough French to make out the gross blunders into which the Prince fell. Julien's impression was a thousand miles away from that of the peasant – he regarded the gorgeous young man with admiration, and marvelled at his grace on horseback.

How blithe a spirit! said he to himself. How fine the fit of his trousers; how elegantly his hair is cut! Oh, alas! if I'd been like that perhaps she wouldn't have been seized by such aversion after being in love with me for three days.

When the Prince had completed his siege of Kehl: – You've the look of a Trappist, he said to Julien, you're really overdoing the principle of gravity I taught you in London. Perhaps a melancholy air is not the best form; it is an air of ennui that is required. If you're sad, then there must be something you lack, something you haven't succeeded at.

It's showing yourself to be inferior. If you look bored, on the other hand, the fellow who has tried vainly to please you is the inferior. Try to understand, my dear boy, how grave a mistake this is.

Julien threw an écu to the peasant, who had been listening open-mouthed.

– Good, said the Prince, that shows grace, a noble disdain! Excellent! And he set his horse to a gallop. Julien followed him, filled with mindless admiration.

Ah! if I had been like that she would not have preferred Croisenois to me! The more his reason was shocked by the Prince's ridiculous aspects, the more he scorned himself for not admiring them, and thought himself unhappy not to possess them. Self-disgust could go no further.

As they re-entered Strasbourg, the Prince, seeing him genuinely depressed, asked – Ah well, can it be, my dear chap, that you have lost all your money, or are you in love with some little actress?

The Russians imitate French manners, but always at a distance of fifty years. At the moment they are in the age of Louis XV.

Humourous remarks about love brought in response tears to Julien's eyes: why don't I ask this amiable man's advice? he suddenly asked himself.

– Why, yes, my dear fellow, he said to the Prince, here in Strasbourg you find me very much in love – and even forsaken. A delightful woman, living in a nearby town, has dropped me after three days of passion, and the reversal is killing me.

He described Mathilde's actions and character to the Prince, using assumed names.

– Don't bother to go on, said Korasoff: so as to give you confidence in your doctor, I shall finish off the confession. This young woman's husband rejoices in a huge fortune, or – better – she belongs to one of the noblest families in the region. There must be something that she is so proud of.

Julien nodded, he no longer dared speak.

– Very good, said the Prince, there are three rather bitter pills you must swallow without delay.

1. Every day you must see Mme . . . , what is she called?

– Mme de Dubois.

– What a name! cried the Prince, bursting into laughter; but, I do apologize! that's sublime of you. The thing is to see Mme de Dubois every day; above all, don't seem to her to be cold or hurt; remember the grand principle of our age: do the opposite of what's expected. Behave precisely as you did the week before you were honoured with her favours.

– Ah! I was calm enough then, cried Julien despairingly, I thought I was taking pity on her . . .

– Moths are singed in the candle flame, the Prince went on, it's a saying as old as the hills.

2. you see her every day;

3. you pay court to some other woman in the same set, but without giving this the appearance of a passion, d'you see? I won't pretend that your role isn't a difficult one; you're acting a comedy, and if you're seen to be acting you're lost.

– She's so full of intelligence, and I have so little! I'm sunk, said Julien sadly.

– No, you're simply more in love than I thought. Mme de Dubois is deeply preoccupied with herself, as are all women whom Heaven has given too high a rank or too much money. Instead of looking at you, she looks at herself, and therefore she does not even know you. During the two or three spasms of love she has allowed herself on your behalf she has, with a great effort of the imagination, seen in you the hero of her dreams, not you as you really are . . .

But, what the Devil, my dear Sorel! these are elementary points – are you a complete novice? . . .

Parbleu! Let's go into this shop; there's a charming black cravat, it could almost have been made by John Anderson of Burlington Street; give me the pleasure of accepting it, and chucking away for good that sordid black string you have tied around your neck.

Ah, that's it, continued the Prince as they issued from the shop of the leading haberdasher in Strasbourg – what society does your Mme de Dubois move in? Great Heavens! *what* a name! – Please don't be angry, my dear Sorel, it overwhelmed me . . . Well, to whom will you pay court?

– To a first-rate prude, the daughter of an immensely wealthy stocking merchant. She has the most beautiful eyes in the world, and I find them infinitely attractive; she is certainly of the highest rank around here; but in the midst of all her grandeur she blushes and becomes totally confused if someone happens to mention trade and shops. And unfortunately her father is one of the best-known merchants in Strasbourg.

– So if someone talks of *trade*, said the Prince laughing, you can be sure your beauty is thinking of herself and not of you. This absurdity is perfectly divine – and extremely handy; it will stop your having to seem stupid for a single moment in her lovely eyes. Success is guaranteed.

Julien was thinking of Mme la Maréchale de Fervaques, who much frequented the Hôtel de La Mole. She was a beautiful outsider who had married the Marshal a year before his death. Her whole life seemed to have no other object than to bury the fact that she was the daughter of a man of commerce; and in order to amount to something in Paris she had put herself at the head of the party of virtue.

Julien admired the Prince sincerely; what would he not have given to have his affectations! The talk between the two friends went on and on; Korasoff was entranced; never had a Frenchman listened to him for so long. So at last I have reached the stage, the delighted Prince said to himself, of being listened to when instructing my tutors!

– So we are completely agreed, he reiterated to Julien for the tenth time, not even a hint of passion when, in Mme de Dubois's presence, you are talking to the Strasbourg stocking merchant's beautiful young daughter. By way of contrast, use flaming passion when writing to her. Reading a well-written love letter is a prude's sovereign pleasure; it is a moment of release. She is not playing a part, she dares listen to her heart; two letters a day, therefore.

– Never, never! said the demoralized Julien; I'd sooner be ground to pieces in a mortar than compose three phrases; I'm a zombie, my dear chap, you must not expect anything from me. Let me lie by the roadside and die.

– But who said you had to compose three phrases? In my writing case I have six volumes of love letters in manuscript. They are for all varieties of female character – I have some for the strictest virtue. Wasn't it Kalisky who paid court at Richemond-la-Terrasse – you know where I mean, three leagues from London – to the prettiest Quakeress in the whole of England?

When he left his friend at two in the morning Julien was less miserable.

The following day the Prince called in a copyist, and two hours later Julien had fifty-three carefully numbered love letters, tailored to the most sober and sublime virtue.

– There are not fifty-four of these, said the Prince, because Kalisky got himself dismissed; but what does it signify being ill-treated by a stocking merchant's daughter when what you really desire is to work on the heart of Mme de Dubois?

Every day they rode out on horseback; the Prince was mad about Julien. Not being able to think how to testify to his sudden friendship, he ended by offering him the hand of one of his cousins, a rich Moscow heiress. – And once married, he added, with my influence and the cross you wear you will be a colonel within two years.

– But this cross wasn't awarded by Napoleon, very far from it.

– What does that matter, replied the Prince, didn't he invent it? It's still by far the finest in Europe.

Julien was on the point of accepting; yet his duty summoned him back to the residence of the important personage; when saying goodbye to Korasoff he promised to write. He obtained the answer to the secret note he had carried, and hurried back to Paris; but no sooner had he been alone for two successive days than it seemed to him a torment worse than death to leave France and Mathilde. I won't marry the millions Korasoff offers me, he said to himself, but I will follow his advice.

After all, the art of seduction is his speciality; he has thought of nothing else but such affairs for more than fifteen years – for he is thirty now. One could not say he lacks intelligence; he is subtle and knowing; enthusiasm and poetry are an impossibility in such a character; he is acting for another; even more reason that he is unlikely to go wrong.

It must be done, then – I will pay court to Mme de Fervaques.

It is true that she may perhaps bore me a little, but I will be looking into lovely eyes that are so like those eyes that have loved me best in all the world.

She is an outsider; it will be a new type of character to observe.

I'm insane, I'm drowning, I must follow a friend's advice and not think for myself at all.

CHAPTER 25

The Department of Virtue

> But, if I sample this pleasure so prudently and circum-
> spectly, it will no longer be a pleasure. LOPE DE VEGA[1]

Immediately on his return to Paris, having left the study of M. de La Mole – who seemed extremely put out by the dispatches he received – our hero hurried off to see Comte Altamira. To the distinction of having been condemned to death this handsome foreigner added great gravity, and the happiness of being a very pious man; these two merits and – more than anything – the Comte's high birth appealed considerably to Mme de Fervaques, who saw much of him.

Julien gravely informed him that he was greatly in love with her.

– She represents the purest and most elevated virtue, replied Altamira – just a trifle Jesuitical and overemphatic. There are times when I understand every word that she uses, but not the whole sentence. She often gives me the impression that I don't know French as well as I am said to. Being in her company will make you talked about; it will give you some weight in Society. But let's visit Bustos, added Comte Altamira, who had an orderly habit of mind – he is a man who has paid court to Mme la Maréchale.

Don Diego Bustos, while himself not saying a word, like a lawyer in his office, made them explain the matter at length. He had the plump face of a monk, with black moustaches and an unparalleled gravity; none the less he was a staunch *carbonaro*.[2]

– I see, he said to Julien at last. Has the Maréchale de Fervaques had lovers, or has she not? So, is there any hope of your succeeding? – that's the question. I should tell you that, for myself, I failed. But now that I am no longer piqued about it, I reason to myself about her as follows: she is often irritable and, as I will describe to you in a moment, she is pretty vindictive.

I don't detect in her the hot-tempered impatience that is characteristic of genius, and might throw a sort of patina of passion over her every action. On the contrary, it is to a Dutch kind of phlegm and tranquillity that she owes her rare beauty and her wonderfully fresh colouring.

Julien was becoming impatient with the Spaniard's deliberation and imperturbable calm; from time to time, despite himself, a few monosyllables escaped him.

– Do you want to hear me out? Don Diego Bustos asked him gravely.

– Please forgive the *furia francese*;[3] I am all ears, said Julien.

– The Maréchale de Fervaques, then, is much given to hating people; she persecutes without mercy men she has never set eyes on – little lawyers, poor devils of literary men who have written songs like Collé's – you know?

> I'm just crazy
> About my Maisie, etc.

And Julien had to endure a rendering of the whole thing. The Spaniard was more than willing to sing in French.

Never has this divine song been listened to with greater impatience. When it was over, Don Diego Bustos went on – The Maréchale has had the writer of the ditty:

> A lover at an inn one day . . .[4]

thrown out of his post. – Julien was afraid Don Diego might want to sing this through as well. But he contented himself with a critical analysis. The song really was irreligious, scarcely decent.

– When the Maréchale became angry about this song, said Don Diego, I told her that a woman of her rank ought not to read all the idiotic things that are published. Whatever advances are made in piety and sobriety there will always be a literature of the drinking den in France. And when Mme de Fervaques had the author, a poor devil on half pay, deprived of a job worth eighteen hundred francs, I told her: Be careful, you have tackled this versifier with your weapons, he may reply with his rhymes; he will produce a song on virtue. The gilded salons may be on your side, but people who like a laugh will repeat his epigrams. D'you know, monsieur, what the Maréchale replied? – All Paris may see me tread the path of a martyr, for the Lord's sake; it would be a new spectacle for France. The people will learn to respect quality of birth. It will be the finest hour of my life. – And never had her eyes been so beautiful.

– She has superb eyes, cried Julien.

– I see that you are in love ... Well then, Don Diego Bustos continued gravely, she does not possess the hot-tempered constitution which would make her vengeful. If she likes to do harm nevertheless it is because she is unhappy – I suspect an *inner discontent*. Could she be a prude who has tired of her profession?

The Spaniard gazed at him silently for a long moment.

– That's the whole question, he added gravely, and that's where you might derive some hope. I thought about it a lot during the two years I comported myself as her humble servant. The whole future for you, monsieur, who are in love, hinges on this great problem: Is this a prude tired of prudery, and spiteful because she is miserable?

– Or rather, said Altamira, issuing from his profound silence at last, might it be what I've said twenty times? – quite simply, French vanity; it is the memory of her father, the celebrated draper, that makes this naturally melancholy, repressed character so miserable. There would only be one happiness for her – to live in Toledo and be tormented by a confessor who pointed out to her the gaping mouth of Hell every day.

As Julien was leaving – Altamira tells me, said Don Diego, more gravely than ever, that you are one of us. One day you will help us win our liberty back, so I would like to help you in this little diversion. It would be useful for you to know the Maréchale's style – here are three letters written by her.

– I'll go copy them, cried Julien, and bring them back to you.

— And nobody will ever, through you, hear a single word we have said?

— Never, upon my honour! cried Julien.

— So, God be with you! added the Spaniard, and silently led Julien and Altamira out as far as his staircase.

This scene cheered our hero somewhat; he was nearly smiling. So here is the pious Altamira, he said to himself, helping me out in an adulterous enterprise.

During the whole course of this grave conversation with Don Diego Bustos Julien had been conscious of the hours as they struck on the clock at the Hôtel d'Aligre.

Dinner time was approaching, he was to see Mathilde again! He went back in and dressed himself very carefully.

Blunder number one, he said to himself as he started downstairs; the Prince's ordinances must be followed to the letter.

He went back to his room and chose a travelling costume of the simplest kind possible.

Now, thought he, there's the question of how I am to look at her. It was only half-past five, and they dined at six. He decided to go down to the salon, where he found himself alone. The sight of the blue sofa moved him almost to tears; soon his cheeks were aflame. I must become hardened to this susceptibility, he said to himself angrily; it will betray me. He grabbed a paper to keep himself in countenance, and moved three or four times from the salon to the garden and back.

It was only with great trepidation, and when he was thoroughly hidden behind a great oak tree, that he dared raise up his eyes to Mlle de La Mole's window. It was hermetically sealed; he was on the point of swooning, and remained a long time leaning on the oak; then, with wavering step, he went to view the gardener's ladder again.

The link of the chain, forced by him in — alas! — such very different circumstances, had not been repaired. Carried away by a wild impulse, Julien pressed it to his lips.

After having wandered a long time between salon and garden, Julien felt horribly tired; this constituted his first success and he was vividly aware of this. My looks will be dulled, and won't give me away! Little by little, guests began to appear in the salon; the door never opened without Julien's heart taking a terrible bound.

They sat down at table. At last Mlle de La Mole, ever faithful to her custom of keeping people waiting, made an entrance. Seeing Julien, she blushed deeply; she had not been told of his return. Following Prince Korasoff's advice, Julien looked at her hands; they were trembling. Much upset himself by this discovery, he was fortunate enough merely to appear very tired.

M. de La Mole sung his praises. A moment later, the Marquise addressed a word to him, remarked politely on his air of fatigue. Each moment Julien was saying to himself – I mustn't look at Mlle de La Mole too much, no more should my looks avoid her. I must seem as I really was a week before my misfortune . . . He had reason to be satisfied with his success, and stayed in the salon. Now, for the first time he became attentive to the mistress of the house – he devoted all his efforts to engaging the men of her circle in conversation and keeping up a lively flow of talk.

His politeness was rewarded: around eight o'clock Mme la Maréchale de Fervaques was announced. Julien slipped out and quickly reappeared dressed with the greatest care. Mme de La Mole was immensely gratified by this mark of respect and, wishing to show her satisfaction with him, talked to Mme de Fervaques about his journey. Julien set himself down near to the Maréchale, at an angle where Mathilde could not see his eyes. So placed, and following all the rules of the art, he gazed at Mme de Fervaques with the most wide-eyed admiration. A disquisition on this sentiment formed the opening of the first of the fifty-three letters Prince Korasoff had given him.

The Maréchale announced that she was going to the Opéra Bouffe. Julien hurried there himself; he met the Chevalier Beauvoisis, who led him to a box belonging to the Gentlemen of the Chamber, just to the side of Mme de Fervaques's box. Julien gazed at her constantly. I ought to keep a diary of this siege, he said to himself on returning to the hôtel; otherwise I will lose track of my assaults. He compelled himself to write two or three pages on this boring topic, and managed also – a wondrous thing! – almost not to think about Mlle de La Mole.

Mathilde had virtually forgotten all about him while he was away on his journey. After all, he is only a common kind of creature, she reflected, his name will always remind me of the greatest mistake of my life. I must return in good faith to ordinary ideas of propriety and honour; a woman has everything to lose by forgetting them. She showed herself disposed at last to sanction the conclusion of her treaty with the Marquis de Croisenois, which had been ready for so long. He was wild with joy; he would have been greatly astonished if told that at the core of Mathilde's disposition, which now made him so proud, was a feeling of resignation.

On seeing Julien again, all Mlle de La Mole's ideas changed. In truth, that is my husband, she said to herself; if I am returning to notions of propriety in good faith, it is clear that it is him I should marry.

She expected importunings, airs of melancholy on Julien's part; she prepared her responses: for surely he would try to say a few words to her as they left the dinner table. But, far from it, he stayed firmly in the salon, his eyes not turning even towards the garden – God knew with what difficulty! It will be better to have an explanation with him straightaway, thought Mlle de La Mole; she walked into the garden alone – Julien did not appear. Mathilde strolled up and down outside the long salon windows; she saw him completely absorbed in describing to Mme de Fervaques the old castles that crown and give such character to the banks of the Rhine. He was beginning to be quite adept at producing those sentimental and picturesque phrases that pass in certain salons for *wit*.

Had Prince Korasoff been in Paris he would have been very proud: this evening party was exactly as he had predicted.

He would also have approved Julien's conduct in the days following.

An intrigue among the powers behind the throne was about to result in the dispensation of several Blue Ribands; Mme la Maréchale de Fervaques insisted that her great uncle become a chevalier of the order. The Marquis de La Mole entertained the same pretension for his father-in-law; they combined their efforts, and the Maréchale came to the Hôtel de La Mole nearly every day. It was from her that

Julien learned that the Marquis was about to become a minister: he was offering the *Camarilla*,[5] a highly ingenious plan which would do away with the Charter, without fuss and within three years.

If M. de La Mole became a minister, Julien might expect a bishopric; but he saw all these great affairs as through a veil. His imagination grasped them only very vaguely, and in the distance, so to speak. The frightful affliction that was making him behave like a maniac made him see every transaction in life only in its relation to Mlle de La Mole. He calculated that in five or six years he might succeed in making her love him again.

This coolest of heads was thus sunk, as one can see, into a state of complete irrationality. Of all the qualities that had formerly distinguished him he retained only a little firmness. Faithful in all externals to the plan of conduct Prince Korasoff had dictated, he placed himself as near as he could to Mme de Fervaques's chair each evening, but he was finding it impossible to think of a word to say.

The effort he imposed on himself to seem cured in Mlle de La Mole's eyes absorbed all his spiritual force, and he stayed by the Maréchale's side like a scarcely animate creature; even his eyes, as though in the extremities of physical suffering, had lost all their fire.

Since Mme de La Mole's way of seeing things was nothing but a replica of the opinions of the husband who might make her a duchess, for several days she had been lauding Julien's merits to the skies.

CHAPTER 26

Love in the Mind

> There also was of course in Adeline
> That calm patrician polish in the address,
> Which ne'er can pass the equinoctial line
> Of any thing which Nature would express:
> Just as a Mandarin finds nothing fine,
> At least his manner suffers not to guess
> That any thing he views can greatly please.
>
> DON JUAN, canto XIII, stanza 84[1]

There's a touch of lunacy in the way this whole family sees things, thought the Maréchale; they are infatuated with their young Abbé, who only knows how to listen – though with rather fine eyes, it is true.

For his part Julien found in the Maréchale's ways perhaps slightly too perfect an example of that *patrician calm* which suggests an impeccable politeness and, still more, the impossibility of any lively emotion. Unexpected actions, a failure in perfect self-control, would have scandalized Mme de Fervaques almost as much as the absence of a grand manner towards her inferiors. The slightest sign of sensibility would in her eyes be a sort of *moral inebriation*, highly embarrassing and mightily destructive of what a person of her rank owed to herself. Her great pleasure was to talk of the King's last hunting party and her favourite book, the *Memoirs of the Duc de Saint-Simon*[2] – above all, the genealogical sections.

Julien knew the place which, according to the disposition of the lighting, was most congenial to Mme de Fervaques's beauty. He would find himself there in advance of her, but take great pains to turn his chair so that he could not see Mathilde. Amazed at his persistence in hiding from her, the latter left the blue sofa one day and came to work at a little table near the Maréchale's chair. Julien, by peering under Mme de Fervaques's hat, could see her fairly close to. Those eyes, that held his fate at their disposal, at first frightened him, then jolted him violently out of his habitual apathy; he began to talk, and talk very well.

He addressed his words to the Maréchale, but his sole object was to work on Mathilde's soul. His talk became so animated that Mme de Fervaques ended by not understanding what he meant.

This was an initial point in his favour. If it had occurred to Julien to finish it off it with a few mystical German phrases of elevated religiosity and Jesuitical tendencies, the Maréchale might immediately have classed him among those superior men called upon to redeem the time.

Since, said Mlle de La Mole to herself, he has such awful taste as to talk at so great a length to Mme de Fervaques, and with such warmth, I shall not listen any more. She kept her word for the whole of the remainder of the evening, though with difficulty.

At midnight, as Mathilde took up her mother's candlestick to accompany her to her room, Mme de La Mole paused on the stair to deliver a comprehensive eulogy of Julien. This aggravated Mathilde's bad mood; she could not get to sleep. An idea occurred to her which calmed her: what I find despicable might well make him a most deserving fellow in the Maréchale's eyes.

As to Julien, he had now done something; he was less unhappy; his eyes chanced on the portfolio bound in Russian leather in which Prince Korasoff had enclosed his gift of the fifty-three letters. Julien noticed a memorandum at the foot of the first letter: *No. 1 should be sent a week after the first encounter.*

I'm late! Julien cried, it is an age since I met Mme de Fervaques. He immediately set himself to copying this first love letter; it was a homily full of virtuous phrases, and killingly dull; Julien had the good fortune to fall asleep over the second page.

A few hours later, the bright light of day surprised him huddled over his table. Among the most painful moments of his existence was when, each morning as he awoke, he *learned* his misery afresh. On that particular day he finished off his copying almost with a laugh. Was it really possible, he asked himself, to find a young man who writes like this? He counted several sentences nine lines long. At the foot of the original, he saw a note in pencil.

One delivers these letters oneself: on horseback, black cravat, blue frock coat. One hands the letter to a porter with an air of contrition; profound melancholy in one's eyes. If one chances to see a lady's maid, furtively wipe the eyes. Address a word to the lady's maid.

All this was faithfully performed.

What I am doing is pretty impudent, thought Julien, as he issued from the Hôtel de Fervaques – but so much the worse for Korasoff. To dare write to so celebrated a fount of virtue! I will be treated with the utmost scorn, and nothing would amuse me more. At bottom it is the only comedy I could appreciate. Yes, to cover the odious object that I call *myself* with ridicule would divert me. If I believed in myself I would commit some crime or other for the sake of amusement.

For the last month the high point in Julien's existence had been when he put his horse back in the stables. Korasoff had expressly forbidden him, under any pretext whatever, to look at the mistress who had abandoned him. But the gait of this horse, that she knew so well, the way in which Julien tapped his whip on the stable door to call a groom, sometimes tempted Mlle de La Mole to stand behind her window curtain. The muslin was so fine that Julien could see through it. By looking under the brim of his hat in a certain way he could make out Mathilde's form without being able to see her eyes. Consequently, he said to himself, she cannot see mine, so it isn't looking at her at all.

That evening, Mme de Fervaques behaved to him precisely as though she had not received the philosophic, mystical and religious dissertation he had delivered to her porter that morning with so melancholy an air. The previous evening, chance had shown Julien the way to eloquence; he positioned himself so as to be able to see Mathilde's eyes. She, for her part, left the blue sofa an instant after the Maréchale came in – which meant deserting her usual company. M. de Croisenois showed some consternation over this new caprice; his obvious unhappiness relieved the sharpest of Julien's pains.

This unexpected turn in his experience led him to talk like an angel; and, since self-approbation slithers even into hearts that serve as temples of the most august virtue, when she got into her carriage again, the Maréchale said to herself – Mme de La Mole is right, this young priest does have some distinction. It must be that at first my presence intimidated him. In fact, everything one encounters in this house is very frivolous; the only virtues I see are those helped on by advancing years – and they were in great need of the chilling effect of age. This young man has been able to perceive the difference; he writes well, but I am very much afraid that the plea he makes in his letter for enlightenment through my advice is at root nothing but a sentiment that does not recognize its own true nature.

All the same, have not many conversions started so? What makes me augur well of this one is his style, which is different from that of the other young men whose letters I have had occasion to see. It's impossible not to recognize an unction, a profound seriousness and great conviction in this youthful Levite's prose; he has about him the gentle virtue of a Massillon.[3]

CHAPTER 27

The Finest Places in the Church

Services rendered! Abilities! Merit! Bah! – Join a coterie.

TELEMACHUS[1]

It was in this way that the idea of Julien was for the first time associated with that of a bishopric in the mind of a woman who might sooner or later be handing out the finest places in the Church in France. The advantage would hardly have impressed Julien; at that point his thoughts could not rise at all to anything unconnected with his current misery: everything augmented it; the sight of his room, for example, had become insupportable to him. In the evenings, when he came in with his candle, each piece of furniture, each little ornament, seemed to take on a voice sourly proclaiming some new detail of his unhappiness.

But on that particular evening – I'm due for some forced labour, he told himself, as he arrived back in his room more cheerful than he had been for a long time – let's hope the second letter will be as tedious as the first.

It was even more so. What he was copying seemed to him so absurd that he began transcribing it line by line without thinking of the sense.

It's even more magniloquent, he said to himself, than the formal sections of the treaty of Munster[2] my professor of diplomacy had me copy out in London.

It was only then that he remembered the letters from Mme de Fervaques, the originals of which he had neglected to return to the grave Spaniard, Don Diego Bustos. He looked them out; they really were almost as pompously unmeaningful as those of the young

Russian lord. Vagueness was total. In trying to say everything they said nothing. It is the style of an Aeolian harp, thought Julien. In the midst of immensely elevated thoughts on nothingness, death, the infinite, etc., I see nothing genuine but an abominable fear of ridicule.

The type of monologue we have just given in abridged form was repeated for fifteen days on end. To fall asleep transcribing some sort of commentary on the Apocalypse, to go next day with melancholy mien to deliver a letter, to return his horse to stable in the hope of catching a glimpse of Mathilde's dress, to work, to appear at the opera on those evenings Mme de Fervaques did not come to the Hôtel de La Mole – such were the monotonous events of Julien's existence. It was a trifle more interesting when Mme de Fervaques visited the Marquise; then he could glimpse Mathilde's eyes from under a wing of the Maréchale's hat, and could wax eloquent. His picturesque and sentimental speeches began to take on a character at once more striking and more refined.

He knew very well that what he said would be absurd in Mathilde's eyes, but he wanted to impress her with the elegance of his diction. The more that what I say is false, the more I ought to please her, thought Julien; and so, with deplorable boldness, he began to exaggerate certain aspects of nature. He very quickly appreciated that in order not to seem vulgar in the Maréchale's eyes he must above all avoid simple and reasonable ideas. He continued in this way – or cut his elaborations short – according to what he read of success or indifference in the eyes of the two great ladies he must please.

On the whole, this life was less frightful than when his days were spent doing nothing.

But, he said to himself one evening, here am I transcribing the fifteenth of these frightful dissertations – the first fourteen have been faithfully given to the Maréchale's Swiss porter, and I am about to have the honour of filling all the pigeon holes in her bureau – yet she treats me precisely as though I had not written them! What will it all come to? Will my constancy end by boring her as much as it does me? It must be admitted that this Russian, Korasoff's friend, in love with the beautiful Quakeress of Richemond, must have been a terrible fellow in his day – couldn't be deadlier.

Like all mediocre beings whom chance puts in the presence of the manoeuvres of a great general, Julien understood nothing about the assault carried out by the young Russian on the heart of the beautiful English girl. The first forty letters were designed solely to persuade her to forgive the boldness of writing at all. It was essential to persuade this gentle being who, maybe, was infinitely bored, into the habit of receiving letters that were possibly a little less insipid than her everyday existence.

One day Julien was handed a letter; he recognized the coat of arms of Mme de Fervaques, and broke the seal with an eagerness that would have seemed inconceivable a few days before; it was merely an invitation to dinner.

He hurried to consult Prince Korasoff's instructions. Unfortunately, the young Russian had chosen to be as frivolous as Dorat[3] precisely where he should have been simple and intelligible; Julien could not make out the moral stance he should adopt at a dinner with the Maréchale.

The salon was of the utmost magnificence, gilded like the Galerie de Diane in the Tuileries, with paintings in oil on the ceiling. There were light patches in the painting. Julien learned later that the subjects had seemed insufficiently decent to the mistress of house, who had had the paintings corrected. *This age of morality!* thought he.

In the salon he noticed two or three men who had helped to prepare the secret note. One of them, Monseigneur the Bishop of —, the Maréchale's uncle, held the ecclesiastical portfolio, and, it was said, did not know how to refuse his niece. What tremendous strides I have made, said Julien to himself with a melancholy smile, and how indifferent I am to it! See me dining with the celebrated Bishop of —.

Dinner was mediocre and the conversation exasperating. It is like the headings of a bad book, thought Julien. All the greatest subjects of human enquiry are proudly proposed. Listen for three minutes and you have to ask which is the greater – the speaker's bombast or his abominable ignorance.

The reader has no doubt forgotten the little man of letters called Tanbeau, Academician's nephew and future professor, who seemed to have been given the responsibility for poisoning the salon of the Hôtel de La Mole with his low slanders.

It was from this little man that Julien first gathered the idea that it could well be that Mme de Fervaques, while not responding to his letters, viewed the sentiments that inspired them with indulgence. M. Tanbeau's black heart was devastated at the thought of Julien's success; but, on the other hand, a meritorious man cannot, any more than a fool, be in two places at once, and if Sorel becomes the lover of the sublime Maréchale, said the future professor to himself, she will set him up in the Church in some advantageous manner and I will be rid of him at the Hôtel de La Mole.

M. l'Abbé Pirard also addressed long sermons to Julien on his success at the Hôtel de Fervaques. There was *sectarian jealousy* between the austere Jansenist and the Jesuitical, royal regenerationist salon of the virtuous Maréchale.

CHAPTER 28

Manon Lescaut

> Now, once he was properly convinced of the Prior's foolish-
> ness and asininity, he succeeded pretty well in calling white
> black and black white. LICHTENBERG[1]

The Russian instructions imperiously laid down that, in conversation, one should never contradict the object of one's correspondence. One should never, under any pretext, depart from a stance of the most ecstatic admiration; the letters always proceeded on this assumption.

One evening, in Mme de Fervaques's box at the opera, Julien was extravagantly praising the ballet in *Manon Lescaut*.[2] His only reason for doing so was that he found it trivial.

The Maréchale replied that the ballet was very inferior to the Abbé Prévost's novel.

What! thought Julien, astonished and amused, a lady of such lofty virtue praising a novel! Two or three times a week Mme de Fervaques professed the most comprehensive scorn for those writers who, with their insipid works, try to corrupt a younger generation only too prone, alas! to sensual backslidings.

In this immoral and dangerous genre, the Maréchale went on, *Manon Lescaut* occupies, so it is said, one of the highest places. The faults and richly deserved sufferings of a deeply criminal person are there depicted, it is said, with a truth that has a touch of profundity – which did not prevent your Bonaparte on St Helena from pronouncing it to be a book written for lackeys.

This speech gave Julien back all his mental alertness. Someone has been trying to sink me with the Maréchale; they have told her of my enthusiasm for Napoleon. That has piqued her enough for her to

430

yield to the temptation of letting me know of it. This discovery amused him for the whole evening, and it made him amusing. As he was parting from the Maréchale in the vestibule of the opera – Remember, monsieur, said she to him, that it won't do to admire Bonaparte when one admires me; one may at best accept him as a necessity imposed on us by Providence. In any case, that man had insufficient subtlety of soul to appreciate a masterpiece.

When one admires me! reiterated Julien to himself; that's saying nothing – or saying everything. Here is one of those mysteries of language to which we poor provincials are deaf. And his thoughts were suffused with Mme de Rênal as he copied out an interminable letter destined for the Maréchale.

– How is it, she asked him the next day with an air of indifference he thought poorly acted, that you talk to me of *London* and *Richemond* in the letter you wrote to me last evening, it seems, after leaving the opera?

Julien was very embarrassed; he had copied line by line without thinking of what he wrote, and had apparently forgotten to substitute *Paris* and *Saint-Cloud* for *London* and *Richemond* in the original. He ventured on two or three remarks in answer, but saw he had no chance of finishing them; he felt himself about to give way to wild laughter. Finally, as he searched for something to say, he evolved the following – In the exaltation, whilst writing to you, of discussing the most sublime, the greatest considerations of the human spirit, my own soul may well have become distraught.

I'm making an impression, he said to himself, so I can spare myself the tedium of the rest of the evening. He left the Hôtel de Fervaques at a run. Later that evening, looking again at the letter he had copied yesterday, he quickly found the fatal passage where the young Russian wrote of London and of Richemond. Julien was much surprised to find the letter almost tender in tone.

It was the contrast between the seeming lightness of his conversation and the sublime and almost apocalyptic profundity of his letters that was so noticeable. The Maréchale was pleased most of all by the length of his sentences – this isn't the abrupt manner made fashionable by Voltaire, that extraordinarily immoral man! Even though our hero did everything possible to rid his conversation of any kind of good sense, it still had an anti-monarchichal and sceptical flavour that did not escape Mme de Fervaques. Surrounded by personages of impeccable morality, but who often did not produce a single thought the whole evening, this lady was deeply impressed by anything with an air of novelty; but at the same time she felt it her duty to be offended by it. She called this failing *being alert to the signs of the frivolity of the times* . . .

But visiting such salons is only any good when one has something to solicit from them. The total boredom of the life led by Julien, without real interests, will no doubt be shared by the reader. These are the flatlands of our journey.

Throughout the time usurped in Julien's life by this Fervaques episode, Mlle de La Mole needed great self-control not to think about him. Her soul became victim to violent struggles; sometimes she flattered herself that she despised the melancholy young man – but his conversation captivated her in spite of herself. What amazed her above all was its perfect falsity; he said not a word to the Maréchale that was not a lie, or at least an abominable travesty of his way of thinking – which, on almost all subjects, Mathilde knew intimately. This Machiavellianism impressed her. What profundity! she said to herself; what contrast to the windy idiots or common scoundrels, like M. Tanbeau, who hold forth in exactly the same language!

Nevertheless Julien had some terrible times. It was only to perform the most painful duties that he made his daily appearance in the Maréchale's salon. His efforts to play his part ended in his voiding his soul of all energy. Often, at night, and as he crossed the immense courtyard of the Hôtel de Fervaques, it was by sheer force of character and intellectual power alone that he managed to keep himself from sinking into despair.

I vanquished despair in the seminary, he told himself: and yet, what an awful prospect faced me then! I was to make or fail to make my fortune, but in either case I saw myself obliged to pass my whole life in intimate contact with the most despicable and revolting people in the world. The following spring, eleven short months later, I was perhaps the happiest young man of my time.

But, confronted by the terrible reality, these brave arguments were all too often without effect. Each day he saw Mathilde at lunch and at dinner. From numerous letters dictated to him by M. de La Mole he knew her to be on the point of marriage with M. de Croisenois. Already, this amiable young man appeared twice every day at the Hôtel de La Mole; the jealous eye of a discarded lover missed not a single one of these movements.

On getting back to his room after he thought he had seen Mlle de La Mole treat her admirer affectionately, Julien was unable to prevent himself from directing a loving look at his pocket pistols.

Ah! how much more sensible I would be, he said to himself, to wash the marks off my linen and go into some lonely forest twenty leagues from Paris to put an end to this execrable existence! As I am a stranger in that district, my death would remain hidden for a fortnight, and who would think of me after a fortnight?

This reasoning was very wise. But the next day Mathilde's arm, glimpsed between her sleeve and her glove, sufficed to plunge our youthful philosopher into cruel memories that none the less bound him to life. Very well, then! said he to himself, I will follow the Russian policy to its end. But how can it end?

As regards the Maréchale, certainly, after having copied these fifty-three letters, I shall not compose any more for her.

As regards Mathilde, six weeks of this too painful comedy will either make no difference at all to her anger, or will earn me a moment of reconciliation. Great God! I'd die of happiness! . . . And he could not finish his train of thought.

When, after a long reverie, he managed to return to his argument: So, he said to himself, I will obtain a single day of happiness, after which her harshness will start again – based, alas! on the slightness of my power to please her – and I will have no resource left me, I will be ruined, lost for ever . . .

What guarantees, considering her character, could she give me? Alas! the slightness of my merit explains everything. My manners will still lack elegance, my tones of voice will continue to be dull and monotonous. Great God! Why am I me?

CHAPTER 29

Ennui

To sacrifice himself to his passions, very well; but to
passions he does not feel! Oh, wretched nineteenth century!

GIRODET[1]

Having at first read Julien's long letters without any pleasure,
Mme de Fervaques began to conceive an interest in them. But one
thing disconcerted her: What a shame that M. Sorel isn't a proper
priest! One might admit him to some kind of intimacy; but with
that cross and almost bourgeois style of coat, one exposes oneself
to cruel questions – and how could one answer them? She did not
carry the thought through to its end: that a malicious friend might
imagine, and even spread abroad, that this was some remote cousin,
a relative of my father, some tradesman decorated through the
National Guard.

Up until the moment she saw Julien, Mme de Fervaques's greatest
pleasure had been to inscribe the word *Maréchale* next to her name.
And now a parvenue's vanity, morbid and vastly oversensitive,
conflicted with the arousal of her interest.

It would be so simple, said the Maréchale to herself, for me to get
him made a vicar-general for some diocese near Paris! But plain M.
Sorel! – and also some kind of secretary to M. de La Mole! it's too
awful!

For the first time this soul who *shuddered at everything* was touched
by an interest other than her pretensions to rank and social pre-
eminence. Her aged porter noticed that, when he brought a letter
from this handsome young man, the one with so melancholy a mien,
he was sure to see the disappearance of that absent and discontented

air the Maréchale always carefully assumed at the approach of one of her people.

The tedium of a way of life concerned wholly with trying to impress the world – though lacking any heartfelt joy in its own success – had become so intolerable since she had begun to think of Julien, that nothing more was needed for her lady's maids to be spared a whole day's maltreatment than that she spend an hour the evening before with this singular young man. His growing credit survived some very well-calculated anonymous letters. In vain did little Tanbeau supply Messieurs de Luz, de Croisenois and de Caylus with two or three extremely clever calumnies – which these gentlemen were pleased to spread around without looking too hard at the truth of the allegations. The Maréchale, whose mind was not made to deal with such vulgar devices, would tell Mathilde of her doubts, but was always reassured.

One day, after having asked three times whether there were any letters for her, Mme de Fervaques suddenly determined to write a reply to Julien. It was a triumph for ennui. When it came to the second letter, the Maréchale was almost pulled up short by the indecorousness of writing, in her own hand, an address as common as *M. Sorel, c/o M. the Marquis de La Mole.*

– You must, she said to Julien that evening in the driest tone – you must supply me with some envelopes addressed to yourself.

Here I am being made into a lover and valet combined, thought Julien – and when he bowed he took pleasure in making grimaces like Arsène, the Marquis's ancient servant.

That same evening, he brought her some envelopes, and very early next day a third letter appeared: he read five or six lines at the beginning and two or three towards the end. The whole consisted of four pages of small handwriting, densely packed.

Little by little the pleasant habit of writing almost every day became established. Julien responded with faithful copies of the Russian letters, and – such are the advantages of the high rhetorical mode – Mme de Fervaques was not at all surprised at their lack of correspondence to her own letters.

How then would her pride have been chafed if little Tanbeau, who had made himself a voluntary spy on Julien's doings, had been able to inform her that all her letters were thrown at random, seals intact, into his drawer.

One morning the porter was carrying a letter from the Maréchale into the library; Mathilde chanced across this man, and noticed the address and Julien's handwriting. As the porter left, she went into the library; the letter still lay on top of the table; Julien, very busy working, had not put it in his drawer.

— This is what I cannot tolerate, cried Mathilde, grabbing the letter; you have completely forgotten me — I, who am your bride. Your behaviour is appalling, monsieur.

At these words, her pride — astonished by the shocking impropriety of her own action — began to stifle her; she melted in tears, and soon seemed to Julien not to be in a fit state to breathe.

Surprised — confounded — Julien did not clearly discern all that might be happy and auspicious for him in this situation. He helped Mathilde to a seat; she all but abandoned herself to his arms.

The first instant he felt this movement of hers he experienced an extreme of delight; the next he thought of Korasoff — with a single word I could wreck everything.

So painful was the strain imposed by this politic thought that his arms went rigid. I cannot even let myself clasp this supple and delightful body to my breast, or she will scorn me and abuse me. What a terrible character!

And while he cursed Mathilde's nature he loved it a hundred times more; it seemed to him he held a queen in his arms.

Julien's impenetrable coldness vastly augmented the wounded pride eating into Mlle de La Mole's soul. She was far from having the self-possession requisite to discover and read in his eyes what he felt for her at that moment. She could not bring herself to look at him; she trembled in case she might encounter an expression of scorn.

Sitting on the library divan, quite still, and her head turned right away from Julien, she was prey to the most violent anguish that pride and love combined can inflict on the human soul. What atrocious behaviour she had been guilty of!

It was reserved for me — miserable as I am! — to have my grossly indelicate advances repulsed! – and repulsed by whom? added a pride that was wild with misery – repulsed by my father's servant.

– That is what I cannot tolerate, she said aloud.

And, getting to her feet in a fury, she pulled open the drawer of Julien's table, about two feet in front of her. She stopped as if frozen in horror when in it she saw nine or ten unopened letters, similar in every way to the one the porter had just shown her. She recognized Julien's handwriting, more or less disguised, on each of them.

– So, she cried – beside herself – not only are you on good terms with her, but you even despise her. You, a nobody, you despise the Maréchale de Fervaques!

Ah! forgive me, my dearest, she went on immediately, throwing herself on her knees, despise me if you wish, but love me, I cannot exist any longer deprived of your love. And she fell in a dead faint.

So, thought Julien, here she lies – this proud creature – at my feet!

CHAPTER 30

A Box at the Opéra Bouffe

As the blackest sky
Foretells the heaviest tempest.
DON JUAN, canto I, stanza 73

In the midst of these dramatic events Julien was more startled than pleased. Mathilde's insults proved to him how wise the Russian policy had been. *Say little, do little* – it's my only road to salvation.

He lifted Mathilde up and, without a word, set her back on the divan. Little by little she was overcome by tears.

To keep herself in countenance she took Mme de Fervaques's letters in her hands; slowly she unsealed them. She gave a definite nervous start when she recognized the Maréchale's handwriting. She turned over the sheets without reading them; most were six pages long.

– Tell me something at least, said Mathilde at last in pleading tones, but not daring to look at Julien. You know very well I'm somewhat proud; it is the unhappy side of my position in life and, I admit, even of my character; Mme de Fervaques has stolen your heart away . . . Has she made you all the sacrifices which that fatal passion led me to make?

Julien's only response was a gloomy silence. By what right, thought he, can she ask me to commit an indiscretion unworthy of a gentleman?

Mathilde attempted to read the letters; the tears that filled her eyes made it impossible.

She had been miserable for a whole month, but her proud spirit was still far from acknowledging its feelings. This explosion had happened only by chance. For an instant her pride had been overcome by passion and jealousy.

There she was, seated on the divan, almost touching him. He gazed at her hair and her alabaster neck; for a second he forgot what he owed himself; he slid his arm around her waist and almost clasped her to his chest. Slowly she turned her head towards him: he was amazed at the depth of sadness in her eyes – such sadness that he could hardly recall her usual expression.

Julien felt the strength draining from him, so mortally hard was the self-discipline he must impose.

Those eyes, he told himself, if I let myself be swept away by the pleasure of loving them, will almost immediately show nothing but the coldest disdain. Yet at that very moment, in fainting tones and in phrases she had scarcely the strength to bring forth, she was repeatedly assuring him of all her remorse for actions to which she could only have been led by overweening pride.

– I, too, have some pride, said Julien in a barely articulate voice, and his face revealed the extreme of physical prostration.

Mathilde turned swiftly towards him. Hearing the sound of his voice was a joy of which she had almost given up hope. At that moment she recalled her own haughtiness only to curse it – she would have loved to have discovered some unprecedented, unheard-of ways of showing him how much she adored him and detested herself.

– It is probably because of this pride, Julien went on, that you singled me out for a time; it is certainly because of my firm resolution, worthy of a man, that you respect me now. I may feel some love for the Maréchale . . .

Mathilde was trembling; her eyes took on a strange expression. She was about to hear her fate pronounced. Her reaction did not escape Julien – he felt his resolve falter.

Ah! he said to himself, hearing the empty words issuing from his own mouth as though they were a noise from elsewhere; if only I could cover these pale cheeks with kisses – and yet you know not of it!

– I may feel some love for the Maréchale, he went on . . . his voice dwindling away as he spoke – but certainly, I have no definite proof of her interest in me . . .

Mathilde gazed at him: he bore up under her look – he hoped at least that his face betrayed nothing. Passion swept into the innermost recesses of his heart. He had never adored her so much; he was almost as rapt as Mathilde herself. If only she had been able just then to find sufficient courage and poise to exploit this, he would have fallen at her feet and forsworn all his hollow comedy. He had just enough strength to go on talking. Ah! Korasoff, he cried within himself, why aren't you here! how I need a guide on how to behave! Meanwhile, his voice went on:

– In the absence of any other feeling, gratitude would be enough to attach me to the Maréchale; she has shown me indulgence, she has consoled me when I've been scorned . . . And it's impossible to have unquestioning faith in certain appearances, no doubt extraordinarily flattering, but also, perhaps, not very long lasting.

– Ah! great God! cried Mathilde.

– Well! what guarantee could you give me? interjected Julien, in a sharp, firm tone that seemed for a moment to abandon prudent diplomatic forms. What guarantee? – what god! – would tell me that the position you now seem to want to return to me will even exist a couple of days from now.

– The infiniteness of my passion, and my misery if you love me no more, she replied, grasping his hands and turning towards him.

The energetic movement she made just then disturbed her pelerine somewhat: Julien glimpsed her lovely shoulders. Her slightly dishevelled hair brought back a delicious memory . . .

He was on the edge of surrender. One unwary word, he said to himself, and I will once more begin a long succession of days filled with despair. Mme de Rênal contrived to find reasons for acting as her heart dictated – this Society girl allows her heart to feel only when she has reasoned herself into thinking it should.

He saw this truth in a twinkling, and also in a twinkling regained his courage.

He withdrew the hands that Mathilde was pressing in hers, and with a great show of respect moved a little away from her. A man's resolution could not go much further. Then he busied himself with gathering together all the letters from Madame de Fervaques scattered on the divan – and it was with a show of extreme courtesy, so cruel at that point, that he added:

– Mlle de La Mole will deign to allow me to reflect on all these matters. He quickly walked away from her, and left the library; she heard him closing the doors one after the other.

The monster isn't even ruffled, she said to herself . . .

But what am I saying – monster! he is wise, he is prudent, good; it is myself I should blame for more mistakes than I can even imagine.

This way of looking at things persisted. Mathilde was almost happy that day, for she was completely in love; it was as though that soul had never felt a turmoil of pride – and such pride!

She trembled with horror when, in the salon that evening, a footman announced Mme de Fervaques; to her, the man's voice seemed sinister. She could not abide the sight of the Maréchale, and quickly departed. Julien, who was not especially proud of his hard-won victory, was fearful that his looks might betray him, and had not dined in the Hôtel de La Mole.

The further the moment of combat receded, the faster his love and happiness grew; he was already blaming himself. How could I resist her? he asked himself; what if she stops loving me! – a split second can alter that haughty spirit, and it must be admitted that I have treated her abominably.

He felt strongly that he should appear that night in Mme de Fervaques's box at the Opéra Bouffe. She had expressly invited him: Mathilde could not fail but know of his presence, or of his uncivil failure to attend. But, at the start of the evening, despite the evident truth of this argument, he lacked the strength to plunge into Society. By talking he had spoiled half his happiness.

Ten o'clock sounded: it was absolutely necessary for him to show himself.

By good luck, he found the Maréchale's box full of women; he was relegated to a position near the door, and completely hidden by the ladies' hats. This position saved him from any absurdity; the divinely despairing accents of Caroline in the *Matrimonio Segreto*[1]

441

made him melt in tears. Mme de Fervaques saw these tears; they made such a contrast to the masculine firmness of his usual expression that the soul of this Society woman – so long saturated by all the pride of a *parvenue*, and so corroded by it – was touched. The little that remained in her of a woman's heart led her to speak. She wanted the pleasure of hearing his voice in that situation.

– Have you seen the de La Mole ladies, she said to him, they're up in the third tier. Immediately Julien craned out over the theatre, leaning rather discourteously from the front of the box: he saw Mathilde; her eyes were brilliant with tears.

Yet this isn't their day for the opera, thought Julien – what alacrity!

Mathilde had persuaded her mother to attend the Opéra Bouffe, in spite of the unsuitable position of the box that one of their lady flatterers had eagerly offered. She wanted to see whether Julien was spending the evening with the Maréchale.

CHAPTER 31

Make Her Afraid

So this is your civilization's great achievement! You have
transformed love into a commonplace affair. BARNAVE

Julien ran into Mme de La Mole's box. Immediately he encountered
Mathilde's tear-filled eyes; she was crying unrestrainedly – the only
people there were some lesser beings, the woman friend who had
provided the box and men of her acquaintance. Mathilde placed her
hand on Julien's; it was as though she had lost all fear of her mother.
Almost suffocated by tears, she had only one word for him –
guarantees!

Whatever happens, I must not speak to her, said Julien, himself
full of emotion and trying, so far as he could, and under the pretext
provided by the lustre which dazzles the third tier of boxes, to hide
his eyes with his hand. If I do speak she can no longer be in doubt
of the intensity of my feelings – the sound of my voice will betray
me, all could still be lost.

His emotional struggles were still crueller than in the morning,
his soul having had time to rouse itself. He dreaded to see Mathilde's
vanity provoked. Intoxicated by love and desire, he yet managed to
refrain from saying a word.

This is, in my opinion, one of the finest traits of his character; a
man capable of such an effort of self-control should go far – *si fata
sinant*.[1]

Mlle de La Mole insisted that they take Julien back to the hôtel.
Happily, it was pouring with rain. But the Marquise placed him
opposite herself, talking to him incessantly in a way that would have
prevented him from saying a word to her daughter. It was as though

the Marquise was taking care of Julien's happiness; no longer fearful of losing everything through an excess of emotion, he surrendered to it with abandon.

Dare I relate that, on regaining his room, Julien threw himself on his knees, took the love letters given to him by Prince Korasoff and smothered them with kisses?

– Oh, great man! what don't I owe to you? cried he in an extremity of enthusiasm.

Little by little, self-command returned. He compared himself to a general who has just half won a great battle. The advantage is assured, he said to himself – and is immense; but what will happen tomorrow? all could be lost in an instant.

With a passionate gesture he opened the *Memoirs Dictated at St Helena* by Napoleon,[2] and forced himself to read them for two long hours; his eyes alone were doing the reading – but that did not signify; he compelled himself to go on. During this strange exercise, his heart and mind, soaring to the highest possible plane, worked on unconsciously. This is a heart altogether different from that of Mme de Rênal, he was saying to himself – but got no further.

– *Make her afraid*, he cried suddenly, flinging the book away. The enemy will obey me only so far as I frighten him, that's when he daren't despise me.

He paced up and down in his little room, ecstatic with joy. In fact, his rapture had in it more of triumph than of love.

– Make her afraid! he said again proudly, and had cause for pride. – Even in her happiest days Mme de Rênal would always doubt that my love was equal to hers. Now this is a wayward daemon I must subdue, so I really must *subdue it*.

He knew very well that the next morning Mathilde would be in the library from eight o'clock onwards; he did not appear until nine – burning with love, but with his head keeping control of his heart. Scarcely a moment passed without his reminding himself – Keep her on edge, constantly on edge, all the time, with this great uncertainty: Does he love me? Her brilliant position, the flatteries she hears on all sides, allow her to reassure herself *a little too easily*.

He found her pale, calm, seated on the divan, but not in a condition, apparently, to make any kind of movement. She offered him her hand:

– Dear one, I have given offence, it is true; possibly you are angry with me? . . .

Julien had not expected so simple a manner. He was on the point of betraying himself.

– You would like some guarantees, my dear, she went on after a silence she had hoped to see broken; that's only fair. Carry me off, then, let's hurry away to London . . . I will be lost for ever, dishonoured . . . She plucked up sufficient resolve to remove her hand from Julien's in order to cover her eyes; all her soul's promptings towards modesty and feminine virtue had flooded back to her. – Let it be so, then! – dishonour me, she sighed at last, that will be *a guarantee*.

Yesterday, thought Julien, I remained happy because I had the resolution to be hard on myself. After a short silence he was sufficiently in control of his feelings to reply in glacial tones:

– Once we are on the road for London, once dishonoured, to use your expression, who is to say you would love me? – that my presence in the post chaise won't seem to you an insult? I'm not a monster – for people to think I have ruined you would only be fresh misery for me. It is not your position in the world that is the obstacle – unhappily, it is your own nature. Can you answer for yourself that you will love me for a week?

(Ah! if she loved me for a week, just one week, whispered Julien to himself, I would die of happiness. What does the future matter to me, what matters life? – and such happiness could start this very moment, if I chose, it depends on me alone!)

Mathilde saw him looking thoughtful.

– So, then – she said, grasping his hand – I'm completely and utterly unworthy of you.

Julien took her in his arms – but the moment he did so duty's iron hand gripped his heart. If she sees how much I adore her, I shall lose her. And, before withdrawing from her embrace, he reassumed all his manly dignity.

On that and the following days he was able to conceal the intensity

445

of his happiness; there were moments when he even denied himself the pleasure of taking her in his arms.

At other moments a delirium of happiness drove him way beyond that which prudence advised.

In the garden there was a bower of honeysuckle, planted there to conceal the ladder, and it was in the vicinity of this that he had often been used to stand gazing at Mathilde's distant shutters, lamenting her inconstancy. A great oak grew near it, and the trunk prevented his being noticed by indiscreet eyes.

Passing with Mathilde near this spot – so vividly reminiscent of the intensity of his sufferings – the contrast between past despair and present joys proved too much for his temperament; tears welled into his eyes and, carrying his lover's hand to his lips – On this spot I dwelt in thoughts of you; here I would gaze at yonder shutter, and wait whole hours for the blessed moment when I would see it opened by this very hand . . .

His collapse was total. In vivid colours he painted the intensities of his despair at that time – colours too true to have been improvised. In short asides he told of the happiness that now had brought an end to these terrible pains . . .

Great God, what am I doing! said Julien, suddenly coming to himself. I will ruin myself.

In an excess of alarm he thought he already saw less love in Mlle de La Mole's eyes. This was an illusion; but Julien's face quickly altered and took on a deathly pallor. His eyes dimmed for a moment, and an expression of hauteur, not devoid of malice, swiftly replaced that of the truest, most undissembling love.

– What's wrong, my dearest? Mathilde asked with tender concern.

– I'm lying, said Julien irritably, and I'm lying to you. I blame myself for it, and yet, God knows, I respect you enough not to lie. You love me, you are devoted to me, and there's no need for me to trot out fine phrases just to please you.

– Good God! are all those delightful things you have been saying for the last two minutes just fine phrases?

– Yes, dear girl, and I blame myself severely for them. I invented them some time ago for a woman who loved me and who bored me

... It is a failure of my temperament, I freely decry it in myself – forgive me.

Bitter tears flowed down Mathilde's cheeks.

– Whenever I am driven into momentary distraction by some jarring little detail, went on Julien – my terrible memory, which I now curse, offers me this resource, and I tend to abuse it.

– So I have done something to displease you, without knowing? Mathilde enquired with delightful naïveté.

– I remember that passing near this honeysuckle one day you picked a flower; M. de Luz took it from you, and you let him keep it. I was two feet away.

– M. de Luz? That's impossible, replied Mathilde, with the hauteur that came so naturally to her: that's not the sort of thing I do.

– I'm sure of it, retorted Julien sharply.

– Oh well then, it is true, my dear! said Mathilde, sadly lowering her eyes. She knew positively that for many months she had not permitted any such action from M. de Luz.

Julien gazed at her with indescribable tenderness: No, he said to himself, she doesn't love me *any the less*.

That evening she reproached him, laughing, with his penchant for Mme de Fervaques – A little citizen passionate about a would-be grande dame! ... Hearts of that sort are perhaps the only ones my Julien might not succeed in setting on fire. She has made a real dandy of you, monsieur, said she, playing with his hair.

During the time he had believed himself despised by Mathilde, Julien had become one of the best dressed men in Paris. Yet he retained a superiority to other men of that kind; once dressed he gave his appearance not another thought.

A single thing riled Mathilde: Julien continued to copy out his Russian letters and send them to the Maréchale.

CHAPTER 32

The Tiger

Alas! – why these things and not others?

BEAUMARCHAIS[1]

An English traveller tells of the intimate terms on which he lived with a tiger; he had reared it and used to pet it, but always kept a loaded pistol on the table.

Julien gave way to his rapturous happiness only at moments when Mathilde could not see the expression in his eyes. And he conscientiously carried out his duty of saying something harsh to her from time to time.

On those occasions, when Mathilde's intense devotion and her gentleness, which he saw with astonishment, were on the point of robbing him of all mastery of himself, he had the strength to leave her abruptly.

For the first time Mathilde was in love.

Life, which for her had always crawled at the speed of a tortoise, now flew along.

But, since her pride had to break out somewhere, she insisted on rashly exposing herself to every risk love might make her run. Julien himself was prudent; and it was only when danger arose that she refused to yield to his will; but, while submissive before him, and even humble, she showed all the more arrogance towards those in the household who came near her – family and servants alike.

In the evenings in the salon, with sixty people around her, she would call Julien over and talk with him for long periods to one side.

One day little Tanbeau settled himself near them; she asked him to go to the library to find the volume of Smollett[2] which deals with

448

THE TIGER

the revolution of 1688; and, when he hesitated, she added, with an insulting hauteur that was balm to Julien's soul – There's no need to hurry about it.

– Did you see the look on that little monster's face? he asked her.

– His uncle has put in ten or twelve years' service in this salon – if it weren't for that I would have him shooed away immediately.

Her behaviour towards MM. de Croisenois, de Luz, etc., though perfectly polite, was at bottom just as provocative. Mathilde severely regretted all the confidences she had once made to Julien, and the more so in that she did not dare tell him how she had exaggerated the almost entirely innocent interest she had had in these gentlemen.

Despite her very finest resolutions, every day feminine pride persisted in preventing her from explaining to Julien: – It was because I was talking to you that I took pleasure in describing my weakness about not withdrawing my hand when M. de Croisenois, putting his on a marble table, just brushed it.

Nowadays, hardly had one of those gentlemen been talking to her for a few moments than she would find she had a question to put to Julien, and that would become a pretext to keep him by her.

She discovered that she was pregnant, and delightedly informed Julien of the fact.

– Now do you doubt me? Isn't this a guarantee? I am your wife for ever.

The announcement struck Julien with profound astonishment. He found himself within an ace of letting the first principle of his strategy fall away: – How can I be deliberately cold and offensive to this poor girl who is ruining herself for me? – If she showed even the slightest air of suffering he no longer found the resolution, even on those days when the terrible voice of prudence was to be heard, for making any of those cruel remarks so indispensable, in his experience, to the continuance of their love.

– I want to write to my father, said Mathilde to him one day; he is more than a father to me; he is a friend; as such I think it is unworthy of you, and of me, to try to deceive him, if only for a moment.

– Great God! What's that you're going to do? asked Julien, terrified.

– My duty, she replied, her eyes gleaming with joy.

She found that she was more magnanimous than her lover.

– But he will throw me out in disgrace!

– That's his right, and one ought to respect it. I will give you my arm and we will leave in the full light of day, by the carriage entrance.

Julien, abashed, begged her to put it off for a week.

– I cannot, she replied – honour calls, I have come to see my duty; I must do it, and immediately.

– Well! in that case I order you to postpone it, said Julien at last. Your honour is assured – for I am your husband. This crucial step affects us both. I, too, am within my rights. It is Tuesday today; next Tuesday is the day of the Duc de Retz's reception; that evening, when M. de La Mole returns, the porter shall hand him the fatal letter. He dreams of nothing else but making a duchess of you, I'm certain – think of his grief!

– Don't you mean: think of his revenge?

– I may be quite capable of pitying my benefactor, and horrified at doing him harm; but I do not, and will not, be afraid of any man.

Mathilde submitted. This was the first time Julien had spoken authoritatively to her since she had announced the change in her condition; and never had he loved her so dearly. The tender side of his nature seized joyfully on the pretext of her condition to absolve him from having to speak cruelly to her. The confession to M. de La Mole disturbed him profoundly. Was he going to be parted from Mathilde? And, however great the sadness with which she saw him go, would she still be thinking of him when a month had passed?

He had an almost equal dread of the just reproaches the Marquis might make.

That evening he confessed the second cause of his distress to Mathilde, and then, led on by his love, he confessed the first as well.

She changed colour.

– Really! said she, then six months away from me would make you miserable!

– Immensely, it is the only misery in the world that terrifies me.

Mathilde was overjoyed. Julien had played his part so thoroughly that he had succeeded in making her think that of the two it was she that loved the most.

The fatal Tuesday came. On his return at midnight the Marquis found a letter so addressed as to lead him to open it himself, and then only in private.

FATHER

All the bonds of society between us are broken, nothing is left but those of nature. After my husband, you are, and will always be, the being in the world dearest to me. My eyes are filling with tears, I am aware of what pain I shall be causing you, but, in order that my shame shall not be public, and so that you have time to think and to act, I can no longer postpone the confession I owe you. If your affection for me, which I know to be extreme, prompts you to grant me a small pension, I will go to live wherever you choose – in Switzerland, for example – with my husband. His name is so obscure that no one will recognize a daughter of yours in Mme Sorel, the daughter-in-law of a carpenter from Verrières. Yes – that is the name it has given me such pain to write. For Julien, I fear your anger – on the face of it so just. I shan't be a duchess, Papa; but I was aware of that when I fell in love with him; for it is I who loved first, it is I who seduced him. From you I inherit too lofty a soul to let my attention be taken by what is, or seems to me, commonplace. It was uselessly that I, wishing to please you, thought of M. de Croisenois. Why did you place real merit before my eyes? You yourself told me when I returned from Hyères that *this young Sorel is the only creature who amuses me*. Now the poor fellow is afflicted as much as I, if that be possible, by the pain this letter will give you. I cannot prevent your being angry as a father; but love me still as a friend.

Julien respected me. If he sometimes engaged me in conversation, that was solely on account of his profound gratitude to you; for the natural nobility of his character led him never to respond except out of duty to everything that was so far above him. He has a lively and innate feeling for social distinctions. It was I – I confess it to my best friend, blushing – and such a confession would never be made to anyone else – it was I who, in the garden one day, pressed his arm.

Twenty-four hours from now, why should you be angry with him? My fault is irreparable. If you wish it, his assurances of profound respect and despair at having offended you, shall come to you through me. You will see him no more; but I shall go to join him wherever he wishes. That is his right, that is my duty, he is the father of my child. If your generosity inclines to grant us 6,000 francs to live on, I will take them with gratitude: if not, Julien plans to settle in Besançon, where he will set himself up in the profession of master in Latin and literature. Whatever humble rank he starts from, I am certain he will rise. With him, I have no fears of obscurity. If there's a revolution, I am sure of a leading role for him. Could you say that of any of those who asked for my hand? They have fine estates! I cannot think that circumstance alone is a reason for admiring them. Even under the current regime my Julien would attain a high place, if he had a million, and my father's patronage . . .

Mathilde, who knew her father was a man who always acted on his first impulse, had written eight pages.

– What is to be done? Julien said to himself during the time that M. de La Mole was reading this letter. Where lies, first, my duty, and, second, my interest? What I owe to him is enormous: without him I would have been a minor scoundrel, but not scoundrel enough to stop me being hated and persecuted by the rest. He has made of me a figure in the world. My *necessary* rascalities will be: firstly, less frequent, and, secondly, less ignoble. That is better than if he had given me a million. I owe him that cross, too, and the semblance of diplomatic services, that have put me above my equals.

If he were to take up his pen to prescribe my conduct, what would he write? . . .

Julien was abruptly interrupted by M. de La Mole's ancient personal valet.

– The Marquis demands your presence this moment, dressed or not.

Marching along at Julien's side, the valet added in a low voice:
– Be very careful, monsieur – he is beside himself.

CHAPTER 33

The Torments of Weakness

> In cutting this diamond a clumsy jeweller has robbed it of
> some of its brightest gleams. In the Middle Ages — what
> am I saying? — even under Richelieu — the French retained
> the *power to will*.
>
> MIRABEAU[1]

Julien found the Marquis in a fury; perhaps for the first time in his
life, this noble lord became coarse; he heaped on Julien's head all
the insults his tongue could manage. Our hero was disconcerted,
exasperated, but his gratitude remained unshaken. — How many
brilliant projects, long cherished in the depths of his mind, the poor
man now sees suddenly crumbling in ruin before his eyes! But I owe
him an answer, my silence will only fuel his rage. This answer was
provided by the part of Tartuffe.

— *I am no angel*[2] ... I've served you well, you've rewarded me
generously ... I was grateful, but I am only twenty-two ... In this
household no one understood my way of thinking but you and that
lovable creature ...

— Monster! cried the Marquis. Lovable! Lovable! The day you
found her lovable you should have fled.

— I did try; that time when I asked your leave to go to Languedoc.

Tired of pacing up and down in a rage, the Marquis, oppressed
by misery, threw himself into a chair; Julien heard him mutter to
himself: This isn't really a wicked fellow.

— No, not for you I am not, cried Julien, falling to his knees. But
he was much ashamed of this gesture, and swiftly got up again.

The Marquis's wits really were in disarray. At the sight of this
movement, he began again to heap on Julien atrocious insults worthy

of a cab driver. The novelty of these curses perhaps served as a distraction.

— Hey! my daughter calling herself Mme Sorel! What! my daughter not a duchess! Every time these two ideas recurred to him in definite form they tortured M. de La Mole, and his troubled mind spun out of control. Julien was afraid of being attacked.

In lucid intervals, as the Marquis began to accustom himself to his misfortune, he reproached Julien quite reasonably:

— You should have fled, monsieur, he told him . . . Your duty was to flee . . . You're the lowest kind of creature . . .

Julien went to the table and wrote:

For a long time my life has been insupportable, I shall put an end to it. I beg Monsieur le Marquis to accept, as well as my expressions of boundless gratitude, my apologies for the embarrassment my death in his house may cause.

— Monsieur le Marquis may deign to glance at this paper . . . Kill me, said Julien, or have me killed by your valet. It is now one o'clock in the morning — I will go for a walk by the wall at the end of the garden.

— And go to all the devils! cried the Marquis as Julien departed.

— I see, thought Julien; he'd be pleased to have me spare his valet the trouble of my death . . . Let him kill me, that's all right, it is the satisfaction I am offering him . . . But, Heavens! I do love life . . . I owe it to my son.

After the first minutes of his walk — which had been devoted to apprehensions of danger — this idea, clearly present to his imagination for the first time, began to dominate his thoughts.

So novel a preoccupation transformed him into a man of caution. I must get advice as to how to deal with this explosive being . . . His mind is not under his control, he is capable of anything. Fouqué is too far away, and in any case would not understand the heart of a man like the Marquis.

Comte Altamira . . . Could I be sure of perpetual silence? My request for advice must not become a separate action, and so complicate the situation. Alas! that leaves only the gloomy Abbé Pirard . . .

His mind is cramped by Jansenism . . . A scoundrel of a Jesuit would know the way of the world, and be of more use to me . . . M. Pirard is capable of lashing out at the mere mention of the offence.

The genius of Tartuffe came to Julien's aid: Yes, well, what I will do is go and confess myself to him. This was his final decision after having paced up and down the garden for more than two hours. He no longer thought of being surprised by a pistol shot; sleep was stealing over him.

Very early next morning, Julien was several leagues from Paris, knocking at the severe Jansenist's door. He found, to his amazement, that the priest was not too much surprised at his confession.

Perhaps I should blame myself somewhat, reflected the Abbé, more anxious than angry. – Well, I thought I had an inkling of this love affair. My friendship for you, you little wretch, prevented me from warning the father . . .

– But what is he going to do? Julien asked eagerly.

(At that moment he loved the Abbé, and a scene with him would have been most painful.)

I see three outcomes, went on Julien: first, M. de La Mole could arrange for my death – and he described the suicide letter he had left with the Marquis; second, he could have me shot point blank by Norbert, who would challenge me to a duel.

– And you would agree to that? asked the Abbé angrily, springing to his feet.

– Your aren't letting me finish. Certainly I'd never fire on the son of my benefactor.

Third, he could exile me. If he told me: Go to Edinburgh, go to New York – then I'd obey. Then Mlle de La Mole's condition could be covered up – but I shall never allow anyone to suppress my child.

– Which would be, have no doubt about it, the first impulse of that corrupted man . . .

In Paris, Mathilde was in despair. Towards seven o'clock she had seen her father. He had shown her Julien's letter, and she trembled that he might have thought it noble to put an end to his life – and that without my permission! she said to herself, in misery shot through with anger.

— If he is dead, I shall die, she said to her father. It is you who will have brought about his death . . . Perhaps you will be glad of it . . . But I swear on his departed shade that I'll put on mourning straight away, and I'll be *Sorel, the widow* in public — I'll send out the formal announcements, count on that . . . You'll find me neither timid nor base.

Her passion mounted to a pitch of distraction. M. de La Mole was dumbfounded in his turn.

He began to consider events more rationally. At lunch Mathilde did not appear. The Marquis was relieved of an immense burden and, above all, flattered, when he realized that she had said nothing to her mother.

Julien returned on horseback. Mathilde called him, and threw herself into his arms, almost in front of her maid. Julien was not especially pleased with this ecstatic demonstration — he had emerged feeling very diplomatic and deliberate from his lengthy conference with Abbé Pirard. His imagination had been cooled by the calculation of probabilities. With tear-filled eyes Mathilde told him she had seen his suicide letter.

— My father may change his mind; to please me, leave right away for Villequier. Get back on your horse, be out of the house before they rise from table.

Since Julien did not in any way modify his air of chill astonishment, she burst into a fit of tears.

— Do let me take charge of our affairs, she cried in a flurry of emotion, hugging him in her arms. You know only too well that I don't want to part from you. Write under cover of my lady's maid, make sure the address is written in a hand no one knows — and as for me, I'll write you volumes. Adieu! Go!

Julien was wounded by this last word, but he obeyed nevertheless. It is fated, thought he, that, even in their best moments, these people should have the knack of offending me.

Mathilde firmly resisted all her father's *prudent* suggestions. She would not negotiate at all except on her own terms: that she would become Mme Sorel, and live frugally with her husband in Switzerland, or at her father's house in Paris. She vigorously rejected any suggestion of a secret childbed.

– That would let in a possibility of slander, and of my dishonour. Two months after the marriage I will go travelling with my husband, and it will be easy for us to pretend that my son was born at the appropriate time.

This firm stance, greeted at first with outbursts of rage, eventually made the Marquis ponder.

In a relenting moment:

– Here! he said to his daughter, here's the scrip for an income of ten thousand livres, send it to your Julien and let him make it impossible, quickly, for me to ask for it back.

In order to show *obedience* to Mathilde, whose love of command he knew so well, Julien had pointlessly travelled forty leagues: he was at Villequier, regulating the steward's accounts; the Marquis's generosity caused him to return. He went to ask shelter from the Abbé Pirard, who during his absence had become Mathilde's most effective ally. Every time he was questioned by the Marquis he demonstrated that all courses of action other than a public marriage would be criminal in the eyes of God.

– And fortunately, the Abbé would go on, the wisdom of the world is here in accord with religion. Could one rely for an instant, given Mlle de La Mole's fiery nature, on a secrecy she has not imposed upon herself? If the open step of a public marriage isn't taken, Society will talk about this strange misalliance for very much longer. Everything must come out at once, without the least mysteriousness, real or apparent.

– That's true, said the Marquis thoughtfully. By this arrangement, at the end of three days, talk of the marriage would become merely stale news for brainless gossips. We should make use of some great government anti-Jacobin measure to slip it by, undercover in its train.

Two or three friends of M. de La Mole agreed with Abbé Pirard. In their eyes the great difficulty was Mathilde's determined character. But even so, and after all these excellent arguments, the Marquis could not, in his soul, get used to renouncing the hope of a *tabouret* for his daughter.

His memory and imagination were full of those tricks and deceptions of all kinds that had still been possible in his youth. To yield to necessity, to fear the law, seemed an absurd and shameful thing for a man of his rank. He now paid dearly for all those enchanting dreams, indulged for the last ten years, about the future of his cherished daughter.

Who could have foreseen it? he asked himself. A girl of so lofty a character, of such high powers, prouder even than I of the name she bears! – and whose hand, before she was of age, had been asked for by all the most illustrious names in France!

All foresight must be abandoned. This age is destined to bring everything to confusion. We are marching into chaos.

CHAPTER 34

A Man of Intelligence

> The Prefect, coursing along the highway on his steed, said
> to himself: Why shouldn't I become Minister, President of
> the Council, a Duke? Here's how I'd wage war . . . This is
> the way I'd put innovators in irons . . .   *The Globe*

No amount of argument can dissolve the power of ten years' agreeable reverie. The Marquis could not think it rational to be angry, but could not bring himself to forgive. If only, he would occasionally say to himself, this Julien could accidentally die . . . By such means his downcast spirit found scraps of comfort in the most ridiculous of chimeras. And these neutralized the effect of Abbé Pirard's wise counsel. So a month went by without the negotiations moving forward a single step.

In this family affair, as in politics, the Marquis had brilliant insights that, for three days, would fill him with enthusiasm. At such times, the appeal of a plan of conduct was not that it was backed by good arguments – rather, the arguments were good in his eyes only so far as they supported the favoured plan. For three whole days he would strive with all the ardour and enthusiasm of a poet to lead things to a certain point; the next day he would not give the matter another thought.

At first, the Marquis's slow proceedings disconcerted Julien; but, after a few weeks, he began to divine that, in this affair, M. de La Mole had no definite plan.

Mme de La Mole, and the rest of the household, believed that Julien was travelling in the provinces, administering estates; he'd concealed himself in Abbé Pirard's presbytery, and saw Mathilde nearly every day; she would spend an hour with her father every morning, but sometimes they went whole weeks without mentioning the affair that preoccupied them both entirely.

– I've no desire to know where that fellow is, said the Marquis one day – but convey this letter to him. Mathilde read:

The estates in Languedoc yield 20,600 francs. I give 10,600 francs to my daughter, and 10,000 francs to M. Julien Sorel. Be it understood that I give the estates themselves. Instruct the notary to draw up two separate deeds of gift and to bring them to me tomorrow; after which no more relations between us. Ah, monsieur, could I have foreseen all this?

Marquis de LA MOLE

– Thank you very much, said Mathilde gaily. We will go and settle at the château at Aiguillon, between Agen and Marmande. They say the countryside there is as beautiful as it is in Italy.

This gift greatly surprised Julien. He was no longer the severe and cold individual that we have known. The destiny of his son consumed all his thoughts for the future. This unexpected fortune, quite considerable for so poor a man, made him ambitious about it. He envisioned himself as having, between his wife and himself, an income of 36,000 livres. As for Mathilde, all her feelings were taken up with adoration of her husband – for such, in her pride, she always called Julien. Her great, her sole, ambition was to have her marriage recognized. She spent her days exaggerating the high foresight she had shown in linking her fate to that of so superior a man. In her mind personal merit was the fashion now.

The almost continuous separation, the multiplicity of things to be done, the little time left to talk of love, all combined to crown the good effects of the wise policy formerly initiated by Julien.

Mathilde ended by growing impatient at seeing so little of the man she had so genuinely come to love.

In a moment of irritation she wrote to her father, starting her letter like Othello:[1]

That I have preferred Julien to the delights that Society offered M. de La Mole's daughter, my choice sufficiently proves. Those pleasures of prestige and petty vanity are nothing to me. Observe that soon I will have lived separated from my husband for six weeks. That is enough to demonstrate my respect for you. By the coming Thursday I shall quit the paternal roof. Your generosity has made us rich. No one but the estimable Abbé Pirard knows my secret. I shall go to his house; he will marry us – and an hour after the ceremony we will be on the road for Languedoc, and will never reappear in Paris unless you order it. But what cuts me to the heart is that all this could make a succulent piece of scandal to use against me – and against you. The epigrams of a stupid public – might not they force our excellent Norbert to seek a quarrel with Julien? Should that happen – I know him – I would have no control over him at all. We would discover in that soul the outrage of an incensed plebeian. Oh father! I beg you on my knees – come to attend my wedding next Thursday, at M. Pirard's church. The point of any spiteful stories would be blunted, and the life of your only son, and that of my husband, would be preserved, etc., etc.

This letter threw the Marquis's soul into an unfamiliar state of confusion. So, at last, he must come down on *one side or the other*. All his little habits, all his commonplace friends, ceased to influence him.

In these troubled circumstances the ruling features of his character, imprinted in him by the events of his youth, regained all their power. The miseries of the emigration had made him a man of imagination. After having rejoiced for two years in an immense fortune, as well as all the distinctions conferred by the Court, the events of 1790 had cast him into the terrible hardships of the Emigration. This harsh school had transformed his 22-year-old soul. In his depths he felt himself as a transient, camping temporarily in the midst of his current wealth, rather than as a being determined by it. Yet the very same imagination that saved him from suffering the cankers of wealth had left him prey to the foolish obsession of seeing his daughter embellished by a grand title.

At times in the six weeks just passed, the Marquis, impelled by a caprice, had wanted to make Julien rich; poverty seemed to him base – dishonouring to him, M. de La Mole – impossible for the husband

461

of his daughter; he threw money at it. The next day, his mind taking another course, it seemed to him that Julien would understand the mute language of financial largesse, change his name, exile himself to America and write to Mathilde that he was dead to her. M. de La Mole would imagine this letter as already having been written, and start to calculate its effect on his daughter's character . . .

The day that Mathilde's *actual* letter dragged him from such callow dreams, he – having thought for a long time of killing Julien or making him disappear – dreamed of building up a brilliant fortune for him. He was already making him take the name of one of his own estates – so why not pass his peerage on to him? M. le Duc de Chaulnes, his father-in-law, had spoken to him several times, since his only son had been killed in Spain, of a wish to transmit his own title to Norbert . . .

– One cannot deny Julien a singular aptitude for business, daring, perhaps even a touch of *brilliance*, said the Marquis to himself . . . But at the core of this character I find something frightening. That's the impression he makes on everybody, so it must have some substance [the more difficult this substance was to grasp, the more it troubled the old nobleman's imaginative nature].

My daughter said to me very aptly the other day [in a letter that has been suppressed]: *Julien has not affiliated himself to any salon, to any coterie.* So he has not provided himself with any support against me, not the smallest thing to fall back on if I abandon him . . . But is that out of an ignorance of the real nature of Society? . . . I have told him two or three times: There is no real or profitable advancement except through the salons . . .

No, he does not have the cunning genius of a sharp little lawyer who lets slip neither moment nor opportunity . . . Not at all a character like Louis XI.[2] On the other hand, the maxims I notice him using are the reverse of generous . . . I am lost here . . . Does he repeat such maxims to serve as a *dam* to his passions?

Anyway, one thing emerges plainly: he cannot stand contempt – I've got him there.

He has no veneration for high birth, it is true, there's no instinctive respect for us . . . that's a fault; but, even so, a seminarist's soul is usually offended only by lack of gratification and money. He – a very different kind – he cannot abide scorn at any price.

Given a sense of urgency by his daughter's letter, M. de La Mole saw the necessity of making a decision – In the end, the big question is: has Julien been impudent enough to dare pay court to my daughter because he knows I love her more than all the world, and that I have an income of a hundred thousand écus?

Mathilde protests to the contrary . . . No, little monsieur Julien, this is a point on which I am determined to allow myself no illusions.

Is it true love, completely spontaneous? Or is it rather a vulgar ambition to get on so highly in the world? Mathilde is clear-sighted, she has sensed from the first that such a suspicion could ruin him with me, and hence that avowal – that it was she who first realized herself in love . . .

A girl with so haughty a temperament forgot herself so far as to make material advances! . . . To squeeze his arm in the garden, one evening – ugh! As if she had not a hundred more delicate ways to let him know she favoured him.

Qui s'excuse, s'accuse; I don't trust Mathilde . . .

On this particular occasion, the Marquis's reasonings were more conclusive than usual. Nevertheless – habit prevailing – he decided to gain time by writing to his daughter. At that time letters were being written from one side of the hôtel to the other. M. de La Mole was not venturing to argue with Mathilde face to face. He was afraid of cutting everything short by a sudden concession.

LETTER

Beware of committing further follies; here is a lieutenant's commission in the Hussars for M. le Chevalier Julien Sorel de La Vernaye. You see what I am doing for him. Don't oppose me, don't question me. He must leave in twenty-four hours, to report to Strasbourg, where his regiment is stationed. I enclose an order on my banker; I must be obeyed.

Mathilde's love and joy were boundless; she wanted to profit by the victory, and immediately wrote back:

M. de La Vernaye would be at you feet, senseless with gratitude, if he knew all you have condescended to do for him. Yet, in the midst of this generosity, my father forgets me; your daughter's honour is in danger. A single indiscretion could become an eternal stain that an income of 20,000 écus could never erase. I shall decline to send the commission to M. de La Vernaye unless you give me your word that, within the coming month, my marriage will be publicly celebrated, at Villequier. Shortly after that time, which I beg you not to exceed, your daughter will be able to appear in public only under the name of Madame de La Vernaye. How I thank you, dear father, for having rescued me from the name of Sorel, *etc., etc.*

The response was unexpected:

Obey, or I'll take everything back. Tremble, rash girl. I still do not know what manner of man your Julien is, and you yourself know less than I. He must leave for Strasbourg, and take care he does not put a foot wrong. I shall make my wishes known within the fortnight.

So firm an answer amazed Mathilde. *I do not know Julien*: these words threw her into a reverie that soon produced the most enchanting suppositions – though she thought them true. My Julien's spirit does not wear the mean little *uniform* of the salons, and my father cannot believe in his superiority precisely because of *that which* demonstrates it . . .

All the same, if I don't obey this typical little whim of his, I can see the possibility of a public quarrel; any kind of scandal would lower my position in Society, and could make me less attractive to Julien. And after a scandal . . . ten years of poverty – yet only the most glittering opulence can rescue me from ridicule for the oddity of choosing a husband on merit. If I live at a distance from my father, he – at his age – might forget me . . . Norbert would marry an attractive woman, someone clever: the ageing Louis XIV was seduced by the Duchesse de Bourgogne . . .

She decided to obey, but was careful not to tell Julien of her father's letter; his fierce temperament might drive him to some rash act.

When she informed Julien that evening that he was a lieutenant of hussars his joy was boundless. One may conceive of it by remembering that this was his life's ambition, and by considering also the passion that he now had for his son! The transformation of his name struck him with astonishment.

Well, after all, thought he, my romance is at an end – and credit to me alone. I have been able to make myself loved by this monstrously proud being, he added, glancing at Mathilde; her father cannot live without her, nor she without me.

CHAPTER 35

A Storm

O God, give me mediocrity!

MIRABEAU

His soul was rapt; he only half responded to Mathilde's eager displays of tenderness. He remained silent and grave. Never had he seemed so great in her eyes, so adorable. She feared lest some subtle trick of his pride might intervene and upset the whole situation.

She observed that the Abbé Pirard visited the hôtel almost every morning. Had not Julien been able to gather something of her father's intentions from him? Had not the Marquis himself, in a moment of caprice, perhaps written? How could she explain Julien's severe air after a stroke of such great good fortune? She did not dare question him.

She did not dare! – she, Mathilde! From that time on, there was in her feeling for Julien something vague, unpredictable, almost terror-like. This dry soul felt all the passion possible to a creature brought up in the excessively civilized atmosphere that prevails in Paris.

The following day, early in the morning, Julien was at the Abbé Pirard's presbytery. Post horses, hired from the neighbouring depot, arrived in the courtyard drawing a dilapidated carriage.

– An outfit like that isn't quite the thing for you nowadays, said the severe Abbé, with a grudging look. Here's twenty thousand francs, a present from the Marquis; he invites you to spend them in a year – though trying, please, to make yourself as little ridiculous as possible. (In so considerable a sum, thrown to a young man, the priest saw only an occasion of sin.)

The Marquis also says: M. Julien de La Vernaye will have received this sum from his father, to whom it is otherwise needless to refer. M. de La Vernaye will perhaps deem it appropriate to make a gift to M. Sorel, a carpenter at Verrières, who cared for him in his childhood . . . I will take that part of the commission on myself, added the abbé; I have at last persuaded M. de La Mole to settle with that perfect Jesuit, the Abbé de Frilair. His influence is decidedly too much for us. An implicit condition of the agreement will be the tacit recognition of your high birth from the man who rules Besançon.

Julien could no longer repress a surge of joy; he embraced the Abbé – he saw himself as having been acknowledged.

– Come now! said M. Pirard, pushing him away; what is the meaning of this worldly display? . . . As for Sorel and his sons, I shall offer them a pension of five hundred francs a year, in my own name, payable to each of them for so long as I am satisfied with them.

Julien had already become cool and distant. He thanked the Abbé, but in extremely vague terms, and committing himself to nothing. Can it really be possible, he said to himself, that I am the natural son of some grand seigneur, exiled to our mountains by the terrible Napoleon? Every moment the idea seemed to him less preposterous . . . My hatred of my father would be a proof . . . I would no longer be a monster!

A few days after this self-communion, the 15th Regiment of Hussars, one of the most brilliant in the army, was drawn up in battle order on the parade ground in Strasbourg. M. le Chevalier de La Vernaye was mounted on the most beautiful horse in Alsace, which had cost him 6,000 francs. He was enlisted as a lieutenant, without having been a second lieutenant other than on the rosters of a regiment he had never heard of.

From the first day his impassive air, his severe and almost cruel look, his pallor, his imperturbable self-control gave him the makings of a reputation. A little later on, his perfect and reserved courtesy, his skill with pistols and with other weaponry – displayed without too much affectation – banished any notion of overt mockery at his expense. After wavering for five or six days, the general opinion in the regiment declared in his favour. This young man has everything, said the bantering older officers, but youth.

From Strasbourg, Julien wrote to M. Chélan, the former curé of Verrières, who was now approaching the extreme limit of old age:

You will have learned, with a joy I cannot doubt, of the events that have led my family to make me rich. Here are 500 francs, which I beg you to distribute without fuss, and without any mention of my name, among the unhappy people who are as poor now as I once was, and who, without doubt, you now aid as once you aided me.

It was ambition, not vanity, that intoxicated Julien; even so, he gave a great deal of his attention to his external appearance. His horses, his uniforms, his servants' liveries were maintained with a correctness that would have done honour to the punctiliousness of a great English lord. Only just made lieutenant, promoted by patronage a mere two days ago, he was already calculating that in order to be, like all the great generals, commander-in-chief by the age of thirty at the latest, he should be better than a lieutenant at twenty-three. His thoughts were solely of glory, and of his son.

It was in the midst of such unbridled dreams of ambition that he was surprised by a young footman from the Hôtel de La Mole, who presented himself as a courier.

All is lost – wrote Mathilde – Hurry here as fast as you can; sacrifice everything, desert if you have to. As soon as you arrive, wait for me in a cab, next to the little garden gate at No. — in — Street. I will manage to get there to speak to you; perhaps I will be able to smuggle you into the garden. All is lost – without remedy, I fear; count on me, you will find me devoted and firm in adversity. I love you.

Within a few minutes, Julien had obtained leave from his colonel and left Strasbourg at a gallop; but the frightful anxiety that consumed him did not permit him to continue this form of transport any further than Metz. There, he threw himself into a post chaise; and it was with almost incredible rapidity that he arrived at the place arranged, close to the little door of the Hôtel de La Mole gardens. This door was opened, and immediately Mathilde, oblivious to all appearances, threw herself into his arms. Fortunately, it was no later than five in the morning and the street was still empty.

– All is lost; my father, frightened of my tears, left on Thursday night. For where? No one knows. Here is his letter; read it. And she climbed into the cab with Julien.

I could forgive everything except the scheme to seduce you because you are rich. That, unhappy girl, is the frightful reality. I swear to you, on my honour, that I will never consent to a marriage with this man. I will guarantee him an income of 10,000 livres if he is prepared to live far away, beyond the frontiers of France, or, better still, in America. Look at the letter I received in answer to some information I asked for. The impudent fellow himself had advised me to write to Mme de Rênal. Never will I read a single line from you about him. I have conceived a horror of Paris and of you. I advise you to shroud what is about to come to pass in the greatest secrecy. *Sincerely* renounce this vile man, and you will have found a father again.

– Where is Mme de Rênal's letter? asked Julien coldly.

– Here it is, my dear. I didn't want to show it to you without your being prepared.

LETTER

That which I owe to the sacred cause of religion and of morality forces me, monsieur, to the painful step I am about to take in regard to you; an infallible precept ordains that I harm my neighbour at this moment, but so that an even greater scandal may be averted. The woes that I feel must be surmounted by the sentiment of duty. It is only too true, monsieur, that the conduct of this person, about whom you demand the entire truth from me, could have seemed inexplicable or even respectable. Someone might have thought it acceptable to hide, or misrepresent, a part of the reality – prudence might have demanded it, as well as religion. But this conduct of which you desire to know has in fact been extremely reprehensible, more so than I can tell you. Penurious and rapacious, this man has sought to achieve a position for himself and become something in life by means of the most consummate hypocrisy, and by the seduction of a weak and unhappy female. It is a part

of my painful duty to add that I am obliged to believe that Monsieur J—
lacks all religious principle. In all conscience, I am forced to think that one
of his ways of achieving success in a household is to seek out and then
seduce the most influential woman there. Cloaked by a pretence of disinterestedness and by phrases taken from novels, his great and only aim is to
gain control of the master of the house and his fortune. In his wake he
leaves misery and eternal regret, *etc., etc.*

This letter, extremely long and half effaced with tears, was certainly
in Mme de Rênal's hand; she had even penned it more carefully than
usual.

— I cannot blame M. de La Mole, said Julien when he had finished
it; he is just and wise. What father would be willing to give his
precious daughter to such a man! Adieu!

Julien leapt from the cab and ran to his post chaise, which was
drawn up at the end of the street. Mathilde, whom he seemed to have
forgotten, went a few steps in pursuit; but the stares of the tradesmen
going up to the doors of their shops, and to whom she was known,
forced her to retreat precipitately into the garden.

Julien had left for Verrières. During his rapid journey he was
unable to write to Mathilde as he had planned to do, for his hand
made only illegible marks on the paper.

He arrived in Verrières on a Sunday morning. He went to the
local gunsmith, who heaped him with compliments on his recent
good fortune. It was the talk of the district.

Julien had much trouble in making him understand that he required a pair of pocket pistols. At his request, the gunsmith loaded
them.

The *three chimes* were just sounding – a signal well known in
French villages, which, after the various bell ringings of the morning,
announces the imminent start of mass.

Julien went into the new church at Verrières. All the high windows
of the building were veiled with crimson blinds. Julien found himself
a few paces behind Mme de Rênal's pew. It seemed to him that she
was praying with fervour. The sight of this woman who had loved
him so well made his arm tremble to such an extent that at first he

could not carry out his plan. I cannot, he said to himself – physically, I cannot do it.

At that moment, the young cleric serving the mass rang for the *Elevation*. Mme de Rênal bowed her head, and for an instant it was entirely covered by the folds of her shawl. Julien no longer saw her so clearly; he fired one pistol at her and missed; he fired a second shot; she fell.

CHAPTER 36

Melancholy Details

Don't look for any weakness on my part. I have taken my
revenge. I have deserved death, and here I am. Pray for
my soul.   SCHILLER

Julien stood quite still, seeing nothing more. When he recovered
himself somewhat he became aware of the *whole congregation* fleeing
the church; the priest had left the altar. Julien began to walk quite
slowly behind some women who were crying aloud as they went.
One woman, anxious to get out faster than the others, pushed roughly
into him, and he fell down. His feet were caught by a chair knocked
over in the crowd; getting up again he felt a pressure on his shoulder;
it was a gendarme in full uniform, arresting him. Automatically he
tried to get at his pocket pistols, but a second gendarme pinned his
arms.

He was taken to the prison. They entered a room, handcuffs were
put on, and he was left alone, the door being double locked on him;
all this was accomplished very quickly, and he was barely conscious
of it.

– Heavens, it is all over, then, he said to himself quite loudly as
he came to his senses . . . Yes, in a fortnight the guillotine . . . or
killing myself between now and then.

His thoughts stopped there; his head felt as though it had been
violently compressed. He looked to see if anyone was holding him.
After a few moments he lapsed into a profound sleep.

Mme de Rênal had not been mortally wounded. The first ball had
pierced her hat; the second shot was loosed off as she turned. The
ball had struck her on the shoulder and, astonishingly, had been

deflected by the shoulder blade – which had none the less been shattered – against a gothic pillar from which it chipped an enormous stone splinter.

When, after a long and painful dressing of the wound, the surgeon, a grave individual, said to Mme de Rênal that – I would answer for your life as I would for my own . . . she was deeply afflicted.

For a long time she had sincerely desired death. The writing of that letter to M. de La Mole – which had been imposed on her by her current confessor – had given the final jolt to a soul enfeebled by constant, insistent suffering. This suffering was derived from the absence of Julien – her own name for it being *remorse*. The confessor, a virtuous and fervent young priest newly arrived from Dijon, was not deceived.

To die in such a way, but not by my own hand, thought Mme de Rênal, is in no sense a sin. God will perhaps even pardon me for rejoicing in my death. And she dare not complete her thought – that to die by Julien's hand would be the height of felicity.

Hardly was she rid of the surgeon's presence, or of all the friends who had crowded to her, than she called in Élisa, her lady's maid.

– That gaoler, she said to her, blushing deeply, is a cruel man. No doubt he will ill treat him, thinking that would somehow be agreeable to me . . . The thought of it is unbearable. Could you not go to him, as from yourself, and give him this little packet with a few louis in it? You could say that religion forbids that he ill treats him . . . But, above all, he is not to go round talking about any money he has been sent.

It was to the aforementioned transaction that Julien owed his humane treatment by the gaoler at Verrières; this was still M. Noiroud, that perfect ministerial appendage, who we have seen being given such a fine fright by the appearance of M. Appert.

A magistrate appeared at the prison.

– I have caused death, and with premeditation, Julien told him; I bought the pistols and had them loaded by M. —, the gunsmith. Article 1342 of the Penal Code is clear, I deserve death, and I expect it.

The magistrate, astonished by this kind of response, wished to multiply his questions so as to get the accused to *inculpate* himself by his answers.

— But don't you see, said Julien smiling, that I am making myself as guilty as you could possibly desire? Go away, monsieur, you won't miss the prey you are after. You will have the pleasure of passing sentence. But for now, spare me your presence.

There remains one troublesome duty to perform, thought Julien, I must write to Mlle de La Mole.

I have avenged myself — *he told her* — Unfortunately my name will appear in the newspapers, and I shall not be able to depart this world incognito. In two months I shall die. The revenge was atrocious, as is the misery of being separated from you. From this moment I forbid myself to write or to pronounce your name. Never speak of me, not even to my son: silence is the only way to honour me. With the common herd I will go down as an ordinary assassin ... At this supreme moment, allow me to tell you the truth: you will forget me. This great catastrophe — about which I advise you never to say a word to a living soul — will have exhausted, for years to come, all the romantic and highly adventurous elements I have observed in your nature. You were made to live with the heroes of the Middle Ages; now show their firmness of character. What is about to take place should be gone through in secret, without compromising you. You will take a false name, and confide in no one. If the help of a friend is absolutely necessary, I bequeath you Abbé Pirard.

Talk to absolutely no one else, above all not to people of your own class — the de Luzes the Cayluses.

A year after my death, marry M. de Croisenois; I beg this of you — as your husband, I order it. Do not write to me, I should not reply. Much less wicked, as it seems to me, than Iago, I will say with him: *From this time forth I never will speak word.*

No one will ever see me speak or write; you have my last words, as you have my last adoring thoughts.

J. S.

It was after despatching this letter that Julien, having recovered himself a little, felt extremely miserable for the first time. One by one, each of his ambitious aspirations had to be torn from his heart in succession with the powerful sentence: I am going to die. Death in itself was not *horrible* to him. His whole life had been nothing but a long preparation for misfortunes, and he had made sure never to neglect that which passes for the greatest of them all.

What of it! he said to himself, if I was due to fight a great duellist sixty days from now, should I be so feeble as to constantly dwell on it, my soul trembling in terror?

He spent an hour or more trying to achieve a full understanding of himself in this matter.

When he had seen clearly into his soul, and when the truth stood in front of his eyes as precisely as one of his prison bars, he began to think about remorse.

Why should I feel any? I have been atrociously wronged; I have killed, I deserve death, but that is the sum of it. I die having made up my accounts with mankind. I leave no obligation unfulfilled, I owe nothing to anyone; my death has nothing dishonourable about it except as regards its instrument; that by itself, it is true, will richly suffice to shame me in the eyes of the townsfolk of Verrières; but to the eye of the intellect, what could be more contemptible! And one way remains to me of winning their regard – to throw pieces of gold to the people as I go to the scaffold. My memory, linked with the idea of *gold*, will be glorious to them.

Following this piece of reasoning, which after a moment's consideration seemed to him evidently true – Then I have nothing more to do on earth, Julien told himself; and fell into a deep sleep.

About nine that evening, the gaoler awoke him, bringing in his supper.

– What are they saying in Verrières?

– Monsieur Julien, the oath I took in front of the crucifix in the King's court the day I was installed in my office compels my silence.

He said no more, but lingered there. The sight of this vulgar hypocrite amused Julien. I must make him wait a long time, he thought, for the five francs he wants as the price of his conscience.

When the gaoler saw the meal finished without any attempt at bribery:

– The friendship I feel for you, Monsieur Julien, he said in a false, soft voice, compels me to speak – though people do say it is against the interests of justice, for it might help you set up your defence . . . Monsieur Julien, who is a good young gentleman, will be pleased if I tell him that Mme de Rênal is recovering well.

– What's that! She is not dead! shouted Julien, in complete astonishment.

– Ah! You knew nothing about it! cried the gaoler with a stupid air that fast became one of happy greed. – It would only be fair that Monsieur should give a little something to the surgeon who, according to justice and the law, ought not to say anything. But, to oblige Monsieur, I have been to see him, he has told me everything . . .

– All right, yes, yes! – then the wound is not mortal, cried Julien losing patience – can you answer for that on your life?

The gaoler, a giant of six foot, took fright and retreated towards the door. Julien realized that he had adopted the wrong route to get at the truth, seated himself again and threw a napoleon in M. Noiroud's direction.

As the man's account began to convince Julien that Mme de Renal's wound was indeed not fatal, he felt himself being overcome by tears.

– Leave me! he said brusquely.

The gaoler obeyed. Hardly had the door closed than Julien cried out – Great God! so she isn't dead! And he fell to his knees, shedding warm tears.

In this supreme moment, he became a believer. What matter the hypocrisies of priests? can they detract anything from the truth, the sublimity, of the concept of God?

Only then did Julien begin to repent the crime he had committed. Only at this very point, by a coincidence which rescued him from despair, was he relieved from the state of physical restlessness and near madness into which he had been plunged since his departure from Paris for Verrières.

His tears flowed from a generous spring – he had no doubts at all of the sentence that awaited him.

So she will live! he said to himself . . . She will live to forgive me and to love me . . .

Very late next morning, when the gaoler awoke him:

— You must have t'rific nerves, Monsieur Julien — the man said to him — I have been in twice already and did not like to wake you. Here are two bottles of first-rate wine sent you by our curé, M. Maslon.

— What? that scoundrel's still around? said Julien.

— Yes, monsieur answered the gaoler, lowering his voice, but don't speak so loud, it might do you some harm.

Julien laughed heartily.

— At the stage I have reached, my friend, you are the only one who could do me harm — if you stopped being kind and gentle . . . You will be well enough paid, said Julien, interrupting himself and reassuming an imperious air. This air was immediately justified by the gift of a piece of money.

M. Noiroud told over again, and in the greatest detail, all he had learned about Mme de Rênal — but he did not mention Mlle Élisa's visit.

The man was as servile and humble as it was possible to be. An idea crossed Julien's mind: This misshapen giant of a fellow must earn only three or four hundred francs, for his prison isn't at all busy; I can promise him ten thousand if he is willing to flee to Switzerland with me . . . the difficulty would be to convince him of my good faith. The idea of conducting a long colloquy with so vile a being filled Julien with disgust, and his thoughts strayed elsewhere.

By that evening it was too late. At midnight a post chaise came to fetch him. He was much pleased with the gendarmes who escorted him on his journey. When they had arrived at the prison in Besançon next morning they were good enough to lodge him in the upper storey of the gothic keep. He judged the architecture to be of the early fourteenth century; he admired its grace and pointed lightness. Through a narrow gap between two walls on the far side of a deep court he could glimpse a wonderful view.

The next day there was an interrogation, after which he was left in peace for several days. His spirit was calm. He saw nothing in his case that was not straightforward: I intended to kill, I deserve to be killed.

His thoughts did not dwell longer on this argument. The trial, the tiresomeness of appearing in public, the defence – he thought of all these as slight embarrassments, as tedious ceremonies about which there would be time to think when the time came. The moment of death gave him no greater pause – I will think about that after the trial. Life was not at all tedious to him, he looked at everything in a new light, and no longer felt any ambition. He rarely thought about Mlle de La Mole. He was greatly preoccupied by his remorse, and often conjured up the image of Mme de Rênal before his eyes – above all in the silence of the night, disturbed in this high keep only by the murmur of the eagle owl!

He thanked Heaven that he had not dealt her a mortal wound. How amazing! he said to himself, I believed that with her letter to M. de La Mole she destroyed all my future happiness, and now, less than a fortnight after the date of that letter, I no longer give a thought to any of the things that concerned me then ... An income of two or three thousand livres to live out a quiet life in some mountainous retreat, like Vergy ... I was happy then ... And I did not realize my own happiness!

At other moments he leapt out of his chair. – If I had given Mme de Rênal a mortal wound, I would have killed myself ... I need to be sure of that so as not to be horrified by myself.

Killing myself! that is the great question, he thought. These formalistic magistrates, so fierce in pursuit of the poor accused, and who would hang the best of citizens to get their claws on a cross ... I would escape from their power, escape from their insults – dressed up in bad French – that the local paper would call eloquence ...

I may live five or six weeks longer, more or less ... Kill myself! Good Heavens, no! he said to himself a few days later – Napoleon lived on ...

Besides, life is pleasant; this is a tranquil staging place; I have nothing to bore me here, he added, laughing – and he started making a note of the books he wanted sent from Paris.

CHAPTER 37

A Keep

The tomb of a friend.

STERNE[1]

He heard a great disturbance in the corridor; it was not the time of day for visitors to be climbing up to his prison; the eagle owl flew off with a shriek, the door opened and the aged Curé Chélan, all trembling and with his walking stick in his hand, tumbled into his arms.

– Ah! great God! can this be possible, my child ... Monster! I should say.

And the good old man could not manage another word. Julien was afraid he might fall. He had to help him to a chair. Time's hand was weighing heavy on this once so vigorous man. Julien found him no more than the shadow of his former self.

When he had recovered his breath: It was only the day before yesterday I received your letter from Strasbourg, with your 500 francs for the poor of Verrières – they brought it to me in the mountains at Liveru, where I have retired to live with my nephew, Jean. Yesterday I heard of this disaster ... O Heaven! can it be possible! And the old man no longer wept; he seemed deprived of ideas and added mechanically: You will be needing your five hundred, I have brought you them.

– What I need, Father, is to see you! cried Julien, very much moved. I have plenty of money.

But he could no longer get a rational response. From time to time M. Chélan shed a few tears, which trickled silently down his cheek; then he peered at Julien, and seemed as though dazed when he saw him take his hands and carry them to his lips. This physiognomy,

479

once so full of life and used to express the noblest feelings with such power, no longer stirred from out its apathy. Soon a peasant-like fellow came looking for the old man. – He mustn't get over-tired, he told Julien, who realized it was the nephew.

This apparition left Julien plunged into suffering so bitter as to go beyond tears. Everything seemed to him so sad and irremediable; he felt the heart go cold in his breast.

It was the cruellest moment he had suffered since his crime. He had just seen death, and in all its ugliness. All illusions of spiritual grandeur and generous feeling were scattered like clouds before the storm.

This frightful state lasted several hours. Infections of morale call for physical antidotes – and champagne. Julien would have thought it cowardice to have recourse to things of that sort. Towards the end of a horrible day, the whole of which had been spent pacing up and down his narrow prison, he cried: What a fool I am! If it was my fate to die in the same way as others, the sight of this poor old man might well throw me into this terrible state; but a quick death in the flower of my youth is precisely what protects me from that tragic decay.

But however he reasoned, Julien felt softened and upset like any pusillanimous little being, and so was made miserable by this visit.

There was no more rude ambition and grandiosity left in him, no more Roman virtue; death seemed to loom much higher over him, a much less facile thing.

This will be my thermometer, he said to himself. This evening I am ten degrees under the the level of courage required for the guillotine. I had it this morning, that courage. But anyhow, so long as it returns at the right moment, what does it matter! The idea of a thermometer amused him, and eventually served to distract his mind.

When he awoke the next morning he was ashamed of the previous day. – My happiness, my peace of mind are at stake. He almost decided to write to the Public Prosecutor requesting that no one be admitted to see him. But what about Fouqué? he thought. If he decides to take it upon himself to come to Besançon, how miserable he will be!

It was perhaps two months since he had thought of his friend. – I was a great clown at Strasbourg, my thoughts did not go beyond the cut of my coat collar. The recollection of Fouqué preoccupied him, and left him feeling still more softened. He walked up and down agitatedly. Here am I certainly twenty degrees under the level to meet death . . . If this feebleness increases, it would be better to kill myself. What a joy for the Abbé Maslons and the Valenods if I should die like a grovelling wretch!

Fouqué did come; this simple, good man was bewildered by grief. His sole idea, if it can be called one, was to sell all he possessed in order to bribe the gaoler to save Julien. He talked for a long time about the escape of M. de Lavalette.[2]

– You distress me, Julien told him – M. de Lavalette was innocent, but, as for me, I am guilty. Without meaning to, you make me realize the difference . . . But, is that true, really! What? – you would sell all you have? he asked, suddenly becoming alert and distrustful again.

Fouqué, delighted to find his friend responding to his ruling idea, set out in detail, almost to the last hundred francs, what he could get for each of his possessions.

What sublime aspirations in a small country capitalist! thought Julien. How many cheese parings, how many obscure acts of petty stinginess, that made me blush so deeply for him when I noticed them, he would now sacrifice for me! One of those beautiful young men that I used to see at the Hôtel de La Mole – readers of *René*[3] – would have none of his awkwardness, but, except for those who are exceedingly young, and anyway have inherited their money and do not know the value of it, which of those handsome Parisians would be capable of such a sacrifice?

All Fouqué's clumsy speech and awkward movements became as nothing – he threw himself into his arms. Never have the provinces, in comparison with Paris, received a finer homage. Fouqué, delighted at the spark of enthusiasm he saw in the eyes of his friend, took it as a consent to the escape.

This glimpse of the *sublime* gave Julien back all the zest M. Chélan's appearance had taken away. He was still very young; but in my opinion he was a healthy plant. Instead of proceeding from tenderness to guile, as most men do, ripening age would have made his soul quick to feel – he would have been cured of his insane distrust . . . But what use these idle speculations?

The interrogations became more frequent, and this in spite of all the efforts of Julien – whose answers were aimed at shortening the affair: I have killed, or at least tried to kill, and with premeditation, he would repeat day after day. But the magistrate was before all else a stickler for form. Julien's declarations did not shorten the interrogations at all – the magistrate's professional pride had been provoked. Julien was not aware that they had intended to transfer him to a frightful little cell, and that it was only thanks to Fouqué's diplomatic interventions that he was allowed to remain in his pretty room 180 feet up in the air.

M. l'Abbé de Frilair was one of the numerous important people who ordered their supply of firewood from Fouqué. The worthy merchant went straight to the all-powerful Vicar-general. To his inexpressible delight, M. de Frilair told him that, moved by Julien's good qualities and by the services he had rendered the seminary in the past, he planned to speak to the magistrates on his behalf. Fouqué saw a hope of saving his friend, and, bowing down to the ground as he was leaving, he begged that the Vicar-general expend the sum of ten louis on masses praying for the acquittal of the accused.

Fouqué was oddly mistaken. M. de Frilair was no Valenod. He declined, and even tried to intimate to the good young peasant that he would do better to keep his money. Seeing that it was impossible to make himself clear without being indiscreet, he advised him to give the money as alms for the poor prisoners – who did in fact lack for everything.

This Julien is a singular creature – what he has done is inexplicable, reflected M. de Frilair, and nothing should be inexplicable to me . . . Perhaps it would be possible to make a martyr out of him . . . In any case, I will get to the *root* of this affair and maybe find an opportunity to frighten that Mme de Rênal, who doesn't respect us, and in her heart detests me . . . Perhaps in all this I could find a way of staging a sensational reconciliation with M. de La Mole, who has a weakness for this little seminarist.

The agreement about the lawsuit had been signed some weeks previously, and the Abbé Pirard had departed from Besançon, not without having mentioned – on the very day the wretched young man had tried to assassinate Mme de Rênal in the church at Verrières – the mystery surrounding Julien's birth.

Julien could foresee only one disagreeable event likely to come between his present state and death – a visit from his father. He consulted with Fouqué on the idea of writing to the Public Prosecutor and asking to be excused from receiving any visits. This horror of seeing a father, and at such a time, shocked the timber merchant's honest and deeply conventional heart.

He believed he could now see why so many people passionately detested his friend. But out of respect for his misfortune he dissembled the feeling.

– In any case, he answered coldly, such an order for close confinement would not apply to your father.

CHAPTER 38

A Man of Power

> Her movements are so mysterious and her figure so elegant.
> Who can she be?
>
> SCHILLER

The next day the doors of the keep were unlocked very early. Julien was woken with a start.

– Oh, good God! thought he, here comes my father. What a disagreeable business!

At that same moment a woman in peasant dress flung herself into his arms – he could scarcely recognize her. It was Mlle de La Mole.

– My dear wretch, all that your letter told me was where you were. Only when I got to Verrières did I hear of what you call your crime – and that is really a noble act of vengeance, displaying all the loftiness of the heart that beats within this breast . . .

Despite his new reservations about Mlle de La Mole, which in any case he had not very precisely formulated to himself, Julien found her wonderfully attractive. How could he fail to acknowledge, in her whole manner of acting and speaking, a nobility and disinterestedness far beyond anything a petty and vulgar soul could have aspired to? Again he thought it was a queen he loved, and it was with an uncommon elevation of thought and diction that, after a few moments, he said:

– The future was delineating itself very clearly before my eyes. After my death, I had you married to M. de Croisenois, who would have married a widow. And the noble, though rather romantic, soul of this charming young widow – deeply shaken, and converted to a belief in ordinary good sense by a portentous event with great tragic

484

significance for herself — would have condescended to do justice to the very genuine qualities of the young marquis. You would have resigned yourself to being happy in the ways that the world is happy: through deference, wealth, high rank . . . But as it is, darling Mathilde, if your arrival in Besançon is suspected, it will be a mortal blow for M. de La Mole, and I could never forgive myself that. I have already caused him so much grief! That Academician would say that he had nourished a serpent at his breast.

— Well, I will admit I had hardly expected such cool reasoning, such a concern for the future, replied Mlle de La Mole, half angry. My lady's maid, who is almost as cautious as you, got herself a passport, and I have posted down here under the name of Mme Michelet.

— And could Mme Michelet get in to see me here as easily as all that?

— Ahah! so you are still the superior man I chose! First I offered a hundred francs to a magistrate's secretary, who pretended that *my* entrance to this keep was impossible. But, having taken the money, the honest man made me wait — he raised objections — I thought he had the idea of cheating me . . . She paused.

— Well? said Julien.

— Don't be angry, my little Julien, she said, taking him in her arms, I had to tell this secretary man my name — he took me for a young Parisian working woman, in love with the handsome Julien . . . Really, those were his words. I swore to him I was your wife, and I will have permission to visit you every day.

The comedy is come full circle, thought Julien, I have not been able to stop it. And, after all, M. de La Mole is such a grand seigneur that public opinion will easily be able to find excuses for the young colonel who will marry this charming widow. My coming death will cover up everything . . . And he abandoned himself delightedly to Mathilde's love; it was wildly extravagant, it was full of the grandest feelings, it was everything most outlandish. She seriously proposed that she might kill herself at his side.

After these first transports, and when she had feasted on the joys of being with her Julien again, her spirit was suddenly seized with a lively curiosity. She studied her lover, and found him much greater than anything she had imagined. Boniface de La Mole seemed revived in him, but in even more heroical form.

Mathilde consulted the leading lawyers of the district, whom she offended by proffering gold too bluntly — though they ended by accepting it.

She rapidly came to this conclusion: that, at Besançon, in doubtful matters of high importance, everything depended on M. l'Abbé de Frilair.

At first, under the obscure name of Mme Michelet, she found insurmountable difficulties in getting into the presence of this all-powerful Congregationist. But rumours of the beauty of the young dressmaker who had descended, mad with love, from Paris to Besançon to console the young Abbé Julien Sorel began to sweep through the town.

Mathilde hurried round the streets of Besançon on foot. She hoped not to be recognized. But in any case she thought it might not harm her cause to make a great impression on the populace. In her delusion she dreamed that she might stir them up to riot and rescue Julien on his journey to the scaffold. Mlle de La Mole believed she dressed simply, in a mode suitable to a grief-stricken woman; but her style attracted everyone's gaze.

By the time that, after a week of solicitations, she obtained an audience with M. de Frilair, she had become the general centre of attention in Besançon.

However high her courage, the idea of an influential member of the Congregation was so linked in her mind with that of deep and calculated wickedness that she trembled as she rang the bell at the Bishop's gateway. She was hardly able to go on when she had to climb the staircase that led to the Vicar-general's first-floor apartments. The solitude of the Bishop's Palace chilled her. — I might be seated in an armchair, and this chair grasp me by the arms — and I would have disappeared. Who could my maid ask for news of me? The Captain of Gendarmes would be careful not to interfere . . . in this big town I am all alone!

At her first sight of the apartment itself, Mlle de La Mole was reassured. To start with, the door was opened to her by a footman in a very elegant livery. The salon where she was asked to wait glowed with that subtle and delicate luxury – so different from vulgar magnificence – found only in the best Paris houses. And from the moment she saw M. de Frilair approach her with a pleasant and fatherly air, all her notions of atrocious crime evaporated. In his handsome face she did not even find any trace of that strenuous and somewhat rugged virtue which is so antipathetic to Parisian Society. The half-smile enlivening the countenance of this priest who controlled everything in Besançon proclaimed the man of good society, the learned prelate, the capable administrator. Mathilde could have imagined she was in Paris.

M. de Frilair needed only a few moments to lead Mathilde to admit to him that she was the daughter of his mighty adversary, the Marquis de La Mole.

– It is true that I am not really Mme Michelet, she said, reassuming all her habitual hauteur – and the avowal matters little to me since I have come to consult with you, monsieur, on the possibility of facilitating the escape of M. de La Vernaye. In the first place, he is guilty only of a piece of stupidity; the woman he fired at is getting well. In the second, I can give you fifty thousand francs, cash down, to smooth it over with the little people concerned, and can engage myself for double that. In short, my gratitude and that of my family would find nothing at all out of the question for someone who could rescue M. de La Vernaye.

M. de Frilair seemed amazed at the name. Mathilde showed him several letters from the Ministry of War that were addressed to M. Julien Sorel de Vernaye.

– You will understand, monsieur, that my father has made himself responsible for his career. I married him in secret – and my father wishes him to have a high rank before making public what is, for a La Mole, a slightly unusual marriage.

Mathilde noticed that M. de Frilair's air of affability and gentle amusement faded rapidly as he heard these important revelations. A look of subtlety, mingled with profound duplicity, came over his face.

The Abbé was having doubts; slowly he re-read the official documents.

What advantage can I draw from these strange confidences? he was asking himself. Here, at a stroke, I am on terms of intimacy with a friend of the celebrated Maréchale de Fervaques, all-powerful niece of Monseigneur the Bishop of —, who deals out the bishoprics in France ... What I thought of as lying far distant in the future is suddenly here, unforeseen. And it could lead me to the goal of all my desires ...

At first Mathilde was alarmed at the sudden changes in the physiognomy of this powerful man, with whom she found herself isolated in a remote chamber. But come! – she said to herself immediately – wouldn't the worst thing have been to make no impression whatsoever on the cold self-centredness of a priest sated with power and pleasures?

Dazzled by the swift and unexpected route to a bishopric opening before his eyes, and disconcerted by Mathilde's spirit, M. de Frilair had momentarily dropped his guard. Mlle de La Mole saw him almost at her feet, ambitious and nearly trembling with eagerness.

It is all becoming clear, she thought, around here nothing is impossible to a friend of Mme de Fervaques. Despite a feeling of jealousy that still rankled sorely, she had resolution enough to enlarge on the fact that Julien was the Maréchale's intimate friend, and that he met Monseigneur the Bishop of — at her house practically every day.

– If a list of thirty-six jurors were to be drawn by lot, even four or five times in a row, from the leading inhabitants of this department, said the Vicar-general, with the hard light of ambition in his eyes and emphasizing his words, I would think myself extremely unfortunate if out of each list I could not count on nine or ten friends, the most intelligent of the lot. I nearly always have a majority – more even than needed for a condemnation. So you will understand, mademoiselle, how easily I could secure an acquittal ...

The Abbé suddenly pulled up short, as if amazed at the sound of his own words; he was revealing things one never mentioned to the profane.

Then, however, he in his turn dumbfounded Mathilde by informing her that what most surprised and interested Besançon society about Julien's strange adventure was that in the past he had inspired a grand passion in Mme de Rênal, and had for a long time reciprocated it. M. de Frilair easily perceived that this story distressed her greatly.

I have found how to get back at her! thought he. There is a way after all of controlling this headstrong little lady; I was afraid that I might not be able to. To his eyes, her aristocratic and intransigent manner vastly enhanced the exquisite beauty he now found almost pleading before him. He regained all his self-possession, and had no hesitation in twisting the dagger in her heart.

– I shouldn't be surprised, he remarked airily, if in the end we were to find that it was from jealousy that M. Sorel fired a couple of pistol shots at the woman he had formerly so much adored. She is certainly not without attractions, and for some time she has been seeing a lot of a certain Abbé Marquinot de Dijon, a kind of Jansenist – without morals, as they all are.

At his leisure, M. de Frilair voluptuously tormented the heart of this beautiful girl, whose weak spot he had now found.

– Why? said he, fixing burning eyes on Mathilde – why should M. Sorel have chosen a church if it wasn't because his rival was celebrating mass in it at that very moment? Everyone agrees on the boundless intelligence, and the still greater caution, of the lucky man you want to protect. What could have been simpler than to have hidden in Mme de Rênal's garden, which he knows so well? – there, with the virtual certainty of being neither seen, nor stopped, nor suspected, he might have dealt out death to the woman who made him jealous.

This argument, apparently so fair, so plausible, succeeded in undermining all Mathilde's self-possession. Her haughty spirit, though imbued with all the dry perceptiveness that passes in the great world as faithfully representing the human heart, was not made to apprehend readily that joy in scorning all caution which can be so intense for an ardent soul. In the higher ranks of Parisian Society where Mathilde had spent her existence, passion only very occasionally divests itself of prudence – and it is only from a lodging up on the fifth floor that one jumps out of the window.

The Abbé de Frilair was now confident of his power. He gave Mathilde to understand (doubtless he lied) that he could bend the public functionary in charge of Julien's prosecution entirely to his will.

After the lots had been drawn for the thirty-six jurors in the assizes, he would be able to negotiate directly, and in person, with at least thirty of them.

If Mathilde had not seemed so attractive to M. de Frilair he would only have spoken to her so plainly at their fifth or sixth encounter.

CHAPTER 39

Intrigue

> Castres, 1676. – A brother came to assassinate his sister in
> the house next to mine; this gentleman was already guilty
> of one murder. His father had saved his life by secretly
> distributing 500 écus amongst the counsellors.
>
> LOCKE, *Travels in France*[1]

On leaving the Bishop's Palace, Mathilde did not hesitate to send a
courier to Mme de Fervaques; she was not deterred for one moment
by the fear of being compromised. She entreated her rival to obtain
a letter for M. de Frilair, to be written entirely in the hand of
Monseigneur the Bishop of —. She went so far as to beg her to hurry
down to Besançon herself – a heroic action on the part of so haughty
and jealous a spirit.

Following Fouqué's advice, she had the good sense not to mention
these proceedings to Julien. Her presence troubled him enough as it
was. Becoming more scrupulous and sensitive as death approached
than he had ever been before, he felt compunction not only about M.
de La Mole, but also about Mathilde.

What's this! said he to himself – while I am with her I endure fits
of inattention, even of boredom. She is ruining herself for me, and
this is how I repay her! Am I really such a scoundrel? Such a question
would not have detained him long when he was still ambitious; then
the only disgrace he had recognized was the failure to succeed.

His moral unease in Mathilde's presence became the more marked
since he inspired in her at this time the wildest, most extraordinary
passion. She would talk of nothing but the incredible sacrifices she
was eager to make to save him.

Exalted by a sentiment of which she was proud, and that overcame all her arrogance, she was reluctant to let a moment of her life go by without occupying it with some remarkable deed. The strangest projects, most perilous for her, filled all her long talks with Julien. The amply paid gaolers allowed her to do what she liked in the prison. Mathilde's ideas were not confined to the sacrifice of her reputation; she cared little if the whole of Society should know of her condition. Flinging herself to her knees and suing for mercy in front of the King's galloping carriage – compelling the Prince's attention at the risk of being trampled in pieces a thousand times – such was the one of the milder fantasies dreamed up in this bold and exalted imagination. She was confident that her friends in the service of the King would admit her to the reserved sections in the park at St-Cloud.

Julien felt himself hardly worthy of so much devotion – in truth he was weary of heroics. He would have found a simple, naive, even a timid tenderness affecting, whereas, on the contrary, the notion of an audience, of the presence of *others*, was always requisite to Mathilde's haughty soul.

In the midst of all her anguish, all her fears for the life of this lover whom she had no wish to survive, she felt an obscure need to astound Society by the intensity of her love and the sublimity of her undertakings.

Julien was beginning to feel provoked at his incapacity to be moved by all this heroical behaviour. What, then, if he had learnt of all the follies that Mathilde heaped on the head – devoted, but limited and eminently reasonable – of the excellent Fouqué!

The latter did not know quite how to find fault with Mathilde's devotion; he too would have sacrificed his whole fortune and exposed his life to the greatest dangers to save Julien. He was stupefied by the amount of gold Mathilde flung around; and for the first few days he, who had all of the provincial's veneration for money, was deeply impressed by the sums expended.

But as time went on he discovered that Mlle de La Mole's projects were subject to frequent variation, and, to his great relief, he found a term by which to criticize a character that exhausted him so much:

she was *changeable*. From this epithet to that of *hot-headed*, the greatest possible anathema in the provinces, was only a step.

It is strange, said Julien to himself one day as Mathilde was leaving the prison, that so flaming a passion, and one of which I am the object, leaves me so cold! – and two months ago I adored her! I have often read that the approach of death detaches one from everything; but it is frightful to feel ungrateful and be unable to change. Am I then just an egoist? He suffered the most humiliating self-reproaches on this account.

Ambition was dead in his heart – another passion rose on its ashes; he labelled it remorse for having assassinated Mme de Rênal.

Really he was deeply enamoured of her. He found a peculiar happiness when, left absolutely alone and with no fear of being interrupted, he could abandon himself wholly to memories of happy days spent long ago in Verrières and at Vergy. The least details of that past – far too quickly flown – had for him an irresistible freshness and charm. He never gave his success in Paris a thought; he was bored by it.

This disposition, which rapidly grew stronger, was partly guessed at by Mathilde's jealousy. She saw very clearly that she must fight against his love of solitude. Sometimes, in trepidation, she mentioned the name of Mme de Rênal. She saw Julien tremble. Henceforth her passion had no bounds, no measure.

– If he dies, I die after him, she said to herself with all possible sincerity. What will the Paris salons say when they see a girl of my rank adore a doomed lover to such a degree? To find a love like this one must go back to the heroic age; it was passions of this kind that made hearts beat faster in the times of Charles IX and Henri III.

– What! said she to herself with horror, in the midst of the most fervent raptures, and clasping Julien's head to her breast – this fine head is destined to fall! Very well! she went on, inflamed by a heroism not unmixed with happiness – very well, my lips, that now are pressed to these beautiful locks, will themselves be cold less than twenty-four hours after.

The idea of such moments of heroism and terrible voluptuousness held her in an unconquerable grasp. The thought of suicide, so fascinating in itself, and hitherto so distant from this haughty soul, penetrated it and soon ruled there with absolute dominion. No! the blood of my ancestors has not become lukewarm in its descent to me, Mathilde proudly told herself.

— I have a favour to ask of you, her lover said to her one day: put your child out to nurse in Verrières, Mme de Rênal will supervise it.

— That's such a hard thing to say to me ... And Mathilde went pale.

— That's true, and I ask a thousand pardons, cried Julien, emerging from his reverie and taking her in his arms.

After having dried her tears he returned to the thought, but more skilfully. He had given the conversation a melancholy philosophical turn. Now he spoke of the future that for him was so soon to find an end.

— One must admit, dearest love, that passionate loves are a contingency of life, but a contingency met with only by superior souls ... The death of my child would at root be a relief to your family's pride, and that fact will not be lost on their underlings. Neglect will be the fate of this child of misfortune and shame ... I trust that, at a period I would not care to prescribe, but am nevertheless resolute enough to foresee, you will take my parting advice: that you will marry M. le Marquis de Croisenois.

— What! and dishonour myself!

— No dishonour can attach to a name like yours. You will be a widow and the widow of a lunatic, that's all. I will go further: since my crime wasn't in any sense for money it won't dishonour you at all. By that time, perhaps, some enlightened lawgiver will have procured the suppression of the death penalty from the prejudices of his contemporaries. Then some friendly voice may cite an example: Listen, that first husband of Mlle de La Mole's was a madman, but he wasn't wicked, not a villain. It was ridiculous to chop off his head ... So my name won't be infamous — at least, after a certain time ... Your position in the world, your fortune and, if I may say so, your own genius will make M. de Croisenois, by then your husband, play a role he could not aspire to on his own. He possesses only birth and high courage, and these qualities alone, which made a man of parts in 1729, are an anachronism a hundred years later, and only supply a man with pretensions. Different qualities now are needed to lead the youth of France.

You will bring the advantage of your own powerful and enterprising character to the political faction into which you will thrust your husband. You will be the successor to the Chevreuses and the Longuevilles[2] of the Fronde . . . But by then, dearest one, the sacred flame that burns in you will have cooled a little.

– Allow me to say this to you, he added after several other preparatory remarks: in fifteen years you will regard the love you have felt for me as a folly – pardonable, but a folly none the less . . .

All at once he broke off and returned to his musings. He found himself yet again faced with the idea that so shocked Mathilde: fifteen years from now Mme de Rênal will adore my son – and you will have forgotten him.

CHAPTER 40

Tranquillity

> It is because I once was mad that now I am wise. Oh
> philosopher, you who see only things immediately before
> your eyes, how limited are your views! Your vision is not
> fitted to follow the underground workings of the passions.
>
> MME GOETHE

This conversation was cut short by an interrogation, followed by a conference with the counsel entrusted with the defence. These were the only truly disagreeable events in an existence otherwise full of carefree hours and tender reverie.

— It was murder, a premeditated murder, said Julien to judge and counsel alike. I'm sorry about this, messieurs, he added, smiling; but it reduces your task to very little.

After all, said Julien to himself when he had succeeded in ridding himself of these two, it becomes me to be brave, and apparently I must be braver than them. They regard this duel that I am fated to lose as the worst possible evil, as the *King of Terrors*,[1] while I shall give it serious attention only on the day it arrives.

It is because I have experienced a greater unhappiness, went on Julien, philosophizing to himself. My sufferings on my first trip to Strasbourg were a very different affair – then, when I believed myself abandoned by Mathilde . . . And to think how passionately I longed for the perfect intimacy that now leaves me so cold! . . . In fact I am happier alone than when my solitude is shared by this extraordinarily beautiful girl . . .

The counsel, a man of rules and formalities, believed him mad, and thought, like the public, that jealousy had put the pistol in his hand. One day he hazarded to suggest to Julien that this allegation, true or false, would serve as an excellent plea for the defence. But in a twinkling the accused once more became passionate and incisive.

– On your life, monsieur, cried Julien, beside himself with anger, be sure you never let me hear that abominable lie again! The prudent lawyer feared for a moment that he himself might be killed.

He prepared his plea, for the fatal moment was rapidly approaching. Besançon, and the whole department, talked of nothing but this *cause célèbre*. Julien didn't know of this – he had asked that no one should ever tell him things of that sort.

That very day, when Fouqué and Mathilde wished to inform him of certain public murmurs that were extremely likely, they thought, to supply grounds for hope, Julien had cut them off at the first word.

– Leave me to my life of imagination. Your little schemings, your petty details from the real world – more or less galling so far as I am concerned – drag me down from the heights. One dies as one may; myself, I don't wish to think of death except in my own way. What do *others* matter to me! My relations with *others* are to be rudely cut off! I beg you, talk to me no more of those people: it is quite enough for me to see the judge and counsel.

Really, he said to himself, it seems that my destiny is to die in a dream. It should be admitted that an obscure being like myself, sure to be forgotten within a fortnight, would be an absolute fool to start acting a part at this stage . . .

It is curious, though, that I have learned the art of enjoying life only now, when I see its end so near.

He spent these last days strolling on the narrow terrace high up on the keep, smoking some excellent cigars that Mathilde had sent a courier into Holland to obtain, and without suspecting that his appearance every day was awaited by all the telescopes in the town. His thoughts were at Vergy. He never spoke to Fouqué of Mme de Rênal, but on two or three occasions his friend had told him that she was rapidly recovering, and the words echoed in his heart.

While Julien's soul dwelt almost entirely in its ideal realm, Mathilde – occupied with realities as befits an aristocratic heart – had been able to foster the intimacy of the correspondence between Mme de Fervaques and M. de Frilair to such a degree that the potent word 'bishop' had already been pronounced.

The venerable prelate in charge of the list of benefices added a postscript to a letter to his niece: *This poor Sorel is nothing worse than a giddy boy, I hope he will be restored to us*.

On seeing these lines, M. de Frilair was quite delighted. There was no doubt that he could save Julien.

– If it weren't for that Jacobin law – he remarked to Mathilde the day before the drawing of lots for the thirty-six jurors for the session – which demands the making up of an endless list of jurors, and has no real purpose other than to rob well-born men of all their influence, I could have answered for the *verdict*. I certainly got Father N— acquitted.

Next day M. de Frilair was gratified to see that among the names issuing from the urn were five members of the Congregation in Besançon, and, among the strangers to the town, the names of MM. Valenod, de Moirod, de Cholin. – I can answer straight off for these eight jurors here, said he to Mathilde. The first five are machines. Valenod is an agent of mine, Moirod owes everything to me, de Cholin is an imbecile scared of everything.

The newspaper made the jurors' names known throughout the department, and Mme de Rênal, to her husband's inexpressible dismay, said she wished to go to Besançon. The most that M. de Rênal could get her to agree to was that she would not leave her bed, so as not to incur the unpleasant experience of being called as a witness. – You don't understand my position, said the former mayor of Verrières, I'm now a liberal by *defection* as they call it; there's no kind of doubt that that scoundrel Valenod, and M. de Frilair, will have no difficulty in persuading the Prosecutor-general and the judges of anything that might be unpleasant to me.

Mme de Rênal obeyed her husband's order without difficulty. If I were to appear at the Assize Court, she said to herself, it would seem as though I were seeking vengeance.

In spite of all the promises of prudence made to her confessor and to her husband, she had hardly arrived in Besançon before she wrote to each of the thirty-six jurors in her own hand:

I shall make no appearance on the day of trial, monsieur, because my presence might throw disrepute on M. Sorel's cause. I desire only one thing in the world, and this thing passionately – that he be saved. Have no doubt of this: the frightful idea that an innocent man be sent to his death on my account would poison the remainder of my life, and doubtless shorten it. How can you condemn him to death while I myself live? No, there can be no doubt, Society has no right to snatch a man's life away, above all the life of a being like Julien Sorel. Everyone in Verrières knows that he suffers fits of distraction. This poor young man has powerful enemies; but even among his enemies (and how many of them there are!), where is he who would question his admirable gifts and profound learning? This is no ordinary person that you are about to judge, monsieur. During a period of almost eighteen months we all knew him as pious, wise and industrious; only he was afflicted, two or three times a year, with an excess of melancholy which amounted almost to a derangement. The whole town of Verrières, all our neighbours at Vergy where we spent the summer season, my entire family, M. the Sub-prefect himself, appreciated his exemplary piety; he knows the whole of the Holy Bible by heart. Would an impious man apply himself for years to learning the Holy Book? My sons will have the honour of handing you this letter: they are children. If you deign to question them, monsieur, they will be able to supply you with all the details about this young man that might still be needed to convince you of how barbarous it would be to condemn him. Very far from avenging me, you would be dealing out my death.

What can his enemies oppose to this fact? The wound, the result of one of those moments of madness that even my children saw in their teacher, is so little dangerous that after less than two months it allows me to travel from Verrières to Besançon in a post chaise. If I should suspect, monsieur, that you hesitate in the slightest in preserving a person so little guilty from the barbarity of the laws, I will rise from my bed, to which only the orders of my husband confine me, and come to throw myself at your feet.

Conclude, monsieur, that premeditation is not established, and you will avoid having to reproach yourself with the blood of an innocent, *etc., etc.*

CHAPTER 41

The Trial

The district remembered this celebrated trial for a long
time. The feeling running in favour of the accused almost
resulted in a civil disturbance: for his crime was sensational,
yet it was not atrocious. Even if it had been, the young man
was so handsome! His high career, so quickly brought to
an end, further excited tender feeling. Will they condemn
him? the women asked the men of their acquaintance, and
one saw them turn pale as they waited for an answer.

SAINTE-BEUVE[1]

At last the day so much dreaded by Mme de Rênal and Mathilde
arrived.

The unusual look of the town increased their dread, and not even
Fouqué's stolid soul was left quite unmoved. The whole province
had flocked to Besançon to witness the trial of this romantic cause.

For several days there had been no room at the inns. M. the
President of the Assizes had been overwhelmed by demands for
tickets; all the ladies in the town wished to be there at the judgment;
Julien's portrait was hawked up and down the streets, etc., etc.

For this supreme moment Mathilde was holding in reserve a letter
written entirely in the hand of Monseigneur, the Bishop of—. This
prelate, who ruled over the Church in France and appointed bishops,
had condescended to request Julien's acquittal. The day before the
trial Mathilde handed his letter to the all-powerful Vicar-general.

At the end of their interview, as she was leaving, dissolved in
tears, M. de Frilair, emerging from his diplomatic reserve at last, and
almost moved himself, told her: I can answer for the jury's verdict.

Among the twelve charged with examining your protegé's crime — and above all whether there was premeditation — I can count on six who are devoted to my cause, and I will make it clear to them that my translation to a bishopric depends on them. Baron Valenod, whom I created Mayor of Verrières, controls two of his assistant administrators, MM. de Moirod and de Cholin, completely. As it happens, fate has given us two very unsound jurors in this affair; but, even though they're ultra-liberals, they are faithful to my orders in important matters, and I have sent to ask them to vote with M. Valenod. I am assured that a sixth juror, an immensely rich manufacturer — and a loudmouth liberal — secretly covets a contract with the Ministry of War, and he certainly would not want to displease me. I have let him know that M. Valenod has received my final word.

— And who is this M. Valenod? asked Mathilde uneasily.

— If you knew him, you would have no doubt of our success. He is a bold talker, impudent, coarse, made to lead fools. In 1814 I plucked him from the gutter, and I shall make him a prefect. He is capable of having the other jurors beaten up if they don't vote along with him.

Mathilde was somewhat reassured.

That evening another discussion awaited her. To avoid prolonging a disagreeable occasion, whose outcome was in his eyes certain, Julien had resolved not to make a speech.

— My lawyer will speak, that's quite sufficient, he told Mathilde. As it is, I will be exposed as a show to all my enemies for far too long. These provincials have been shocked at the rapid rise to fortune that I owe to you and, believe me, there's not one that doesn't want me condemned — reserving to themselves the right to cry like boobies when I'm led off to my death.

— They want to see you humbled, that's all too true, replied Mathilde, but I don't believe they are cruel. My presence in Besançon, and the spectacle of my grief, has intrigued all the women; your handsome face will do the rest. If you say but a single word in front of the judges the whole courtroom will be behind you, etc., etc.

Next morning at nine o'clock, when Julien had come down from his prison to go to the great hall of the Palais de Justice, it was only with great difficulty that the gendarmes managed to clear a way through the immense crowd packed into the courtyard. Julien had slept well, he was very calm, and felt nothing but a kind of philosophical pity for this envious mob who, without being cruel, were shortly to applaud his sentence of death. He was greatly surprised when — held up more than a quarter of an hour in the middle of the crowd — he was forced to recognize that his presence inspired the public with a tender compassion. He heard not a single unpleasant remark. These provincials, he said to himself, are less spiteful than I thought.

On entering the hall of the court he was struck by the elegance of its architecture. It was pure gothic, and a multitude of little columns had been cut into the stone with the greatest care. He might have been in England.

But soon all his attention was taken by twelve or fifteen pretty women who, seated opposite the accused's dock, filled the three balconies above the examining magistrate and jurors. Turning towards the crowd, he saw that the circular gallery dominating the amphitheatre was full of women: most of them were young, and seemed to him extremely pretty; their eyes were shining, full of concern. In the rest of the hall the crowd was vast; people were struggling at the doors and the guards were unable to impose silence.

When all the eyes searching for Julien became aware of his presence, seeing him come into the slightly raised position reserved for the accused, he was greeted with a murmur of surprise and compassionate interest.

One would have thought him no more than twenty that day; he was very simply dressed, but with a perfect grace; his hair and his brow were charming; Mathilde herself had insisted on presiding over his toilet. Julien's pallor was extreme. Hardly was he seated in the dock than he heard all around him: Gracious! how young he is! . . . But he's no more than a child . . . So much better looking than his portrait.

— Hey, my prisoner, said the gendarme seated on his right, d'you see those six ladies up in that balcony? The gendarme pointed out a little gallery jutting into the amphitheatre over the jurors' places.

There's Madame the Prefect's wife, and next to her – he went on – Mme la Marquise de N——, who is a good friend to you – I overheard her talking to the examining magistrate. After that Mme Derville . . .

– Mme Derville! cried Julien, a lively flush colouring his brow. When she leaves here, he thought, she will write to Mme de Rênal. He was unaware of Mme de Rênal's arrival in Besançon.

The witnesses were heard very quickly. At the first words of the public prosecutor's opening speech two of the ladies seated in the little balcony dissolved in tears. Mme Derville would be far from softening like that, thought Julien. Yet he saw that she was very flushed.

The public prosecutor was creating an effect of pathos, in bad French, on the subject of the barbarity of the crime that had been committed; Julien saw that Mme Derville's neighbours seemed to disapprove strongly of this. Several jurors, apparently acquaintances of these ladies, were speaking to them and appeared to be reassuring them. That cannot but be a good omen, thought he.

Up to that point he had felt himself pervaded with unqualified contempt for all the men taking part in the trial. The public prosecutor's banal eloquence had increased this feeling of distaste. But gradually his soul's barren reserve disappeared before the marks of concern so clearly shown for him.

He was pleased by his counsel's firm demeanour. – Now, no phrasemaking, he muttered to him as he was about to speak.

– All those cadences pilfered from Bossuet[2] and used against you have actually worked in your favour, replied the counsel. In fact, he himself had scarcely been speaking for five minutes when almost all the ladies had their handkerchiefs in their hands. Encouraged, the counsel addressed the jury in strong terms. Julien trembled, he felt himself on the point of tears. Great God! what would my enemies say?

He was about to give way to the softened mood gaining on him when, happily for him, he happened to catch an impudent glance from M. le Baron de Valenod.

That bastard's eyes are all lit up, he said to himself; what triumph in that low soul! Even if my crime had led to nothing but only that,

I would curse it. God knows what he will say about me to Mme de Rênal!

The idea obliterated everything else. Shortly afterwards, Julien was recalled to himself by signs of approval from the public. The lawyer was bringing his plea to an end. Julien remembered that it was the accepted thing to shake his hand. Time had sped by.

Refreshments were brought for the counsel and the accused. It was only then that Julien was struck by a singular phenomenon: none of the women had left the hearing to go to dinner.

— My word, I'm dying of hunger, remarked the counsel — and you?

— Yes, me too, answered Julien.

— Look, there's the Prefect's lady being served her dinner, too, said the counsel, indicating the little balcony. Keep your spirits up, all is going well. The hearing recommenced.

As the president made his summing up, midnight sounded. The president was obliged to pause; in the midst of the tense general silence the reverberations of the clock chimes filled the hall.

Here it is, the beginning of my last day, thought Julien. Soon he felt himself fired by the idea of duty. Up until then he had controlled his feelings, and kept to his resolve to say nothing; but when the President of the Assize asked him if he had anything to add, he rose to his feet. He gazed at Mme Derville's eyes, which, amidst the lights in front of him, seemed to glitter. Can she by any chance be crying? he wondered.

— Gentlemen of the jury,

My horror of contempt, which I thought I could defy at the moment of my death, now forces me to speak. Messieurs, I do not have the honour to belong to your class, you see in me a peasant who is in rebellion against the baseness of his lot.

I ask no mercy of you, continued Julien, his voice becoming firmer. I am under no illusion — death awaits me: it will be a just death. I attempted to shorten the days of a woman who is most worthy of all respect, of all homage. Mme de Rênal had acted like a mother to me. My crime is atrocious, and it was *premeditated*. Therefore I have deserved death, gentlemen of the jury. But even were I less guilty, I now see around me men who, without pausing to think what pity my youth might deserve, will want to punish me and so discourage for ever that class of young men who, born into an inferior class and in one way or another oppressed by poverty, have the good luck to obtain a good education and the audacity to mix in what the arrogance of the rich calls Society.

That is my crime, messieurs, and it will be punished with all the more severity in that, when it comes to it, I am not being judged by my peers. I see there on the jury benches no peasant who has done well, but only indignant bourgeois . . .

Julien went on in this vein for twenty minutes; he said everything he had in his heart; the public prosecutor, who had hopes of winning aristocratic favour, was springing up and down in his seat; but, despite the somewhat abstract turn that Julien had given to the debate, all the women were melted in tears. Mme Derville herself had her handkerchief at her eyes. Before closing, Julien returned to the question of premeditation, to his repentance, to the respect, the boundless filial devotion that, in happier times, he had entertained for Mme de Rênal . . . Mme Derville let out a cry and fainted.

One o'clock chimed as the jurors retired to their room. None of the women had left her place; many of the men had tears in their eyes. At first there were the liveliest discussions; but, little by little, the jury's decision being awaited for a long period, a general fatigue began to diffuse some calm into the assembly. It was a solemn time; the lamps shone less brightly. Julien, who was extremely tired, overheard arguments on the question of whether this delay was a good or a bad sign. He noted with pleasure that everyone spoke in his favour; the jury still did not return, yet not a single woman left the hall.

Just as two o'clock was chiming a great stir was heard. The small door to the jurors' room opened. M. le Baron de Valenod came in with a grave and theatrical step, followed by the rest of the jurors. He coughed, then declared that, on his soul and conscience, the unanimous verdict of the jury was that Julien Sorel was guilty of murder, and of murder with premeditation: this verdict entailed the death penalty; it was pronounced a moment later. Julien looked at his watch, reminding himself of M. de Lavalette; it was a quarter past two. Today is Friday, he thought.

Yes, but it is a happy day for that Valenod, who is condemning me . . . I am too closely guarded for Mathilde to be able to save me as did Mme de Lavalette . . . So, in three days, at this very hour, I shall know what to think about the *Great Perhaps*.

At that moment he heard a cry, and was recalled to events in this world. The women around him were sobbing; he saw that all faces were turned towards a little gallery perched in the top piece of a gothic pilaster. He learned later that this was where Mathilde had hidden herself. As the cry was not repeated, they all turned back again to look at Julien, who the gendarmes were trying to move through the crowd.

Try not to give that imbecile Valenod anything to laugh about, thought Julien. What a sanctimonious and self-satisfied air he had announcing the verdict that means the death penalty! – whereas that poor President of the Assize, even though he has been a judge for years, had a tear in his eye as he sentenced me. What joy for Valenod to get his revenge for our old rivalry over Mme de Rênal! . . . So I will never see her again! It is all done . . . Now a last farewell between us is impossible – I sense that . . . How happy I would have been to let her know of all the horror I feel for my crime!

These words only: I find myself justly condemned.

On leading Julien back into the prison they put him in a room reserved for those condemned to death. He, ordinarily observant of even the most trifling detail, did not realize that they had not taken him back up to his keep. He was dreaming of what he would say to Mme de Rênal if he had the happiness to see her before his last moment. He imagined that she would try to interrupt what he said, and wanted to be able to convey the full force of his remorse from the very first word. After doing what I did, how am I going to convince her that it is her alone that I love? For after all I did try to kill her, out of ambition or from love of Mathilde.

As he got into bed he discovered that the sheets were made of some coarse fabric. The scales fell from his eyes. Ah! I am in a cell, he said to himself – because I have been condemned to death. That is justice . . .

Comte Altamira told me that on the day before his death Danton declared in his great booming voice – That's odd, the verb to guillotine cannot be conjugated in all tenses; one may well say: I will be guillotined, you will be guillotined, but one can never say: I have been guillotined.

Well, why not, Julien's thoughts continued, if there is a life to come? . . . My word, if I meet the God of the Christians I am lost; he is a despot and, like all despots, full of ideas of vengeance; his Bible speaks of nothing but abominable punishments. I have never loved him; I have never even been willing to believe that anyone truly loves him. He is pitiless (and he recalled to himself numerous passages from the Bible). He will punish me in atrocious ways . . .

But if I should meet the God of Fénelon! Perhaps he will

say: Much shall be forgiven thee, for thou hast loved much . . .²

Have I loved much? Ah! I have loved Mme de Rênal, but my conduct has been atrocious. In that, as in everything else, simple, modest virtue has been sacrificed to that which glitters . . .

But then, what prospects they were! . . . colonel of Hussars, if there was a war; secretary of legation during peacetime; then an ambassador . . . for I would have quickly learned everything about public affairs . . . and, even if I had been a mere idiot, could the Marquis de La Mole's son-in-law fear a rival? All my foolish blunders would have been forgiven, or, rather, counted as virtues. A man of distinction, and enjoying the grandest possible existence in Vienna or London . . .

– Not precisely, monsieur – guillotined in three days.

Julien laughed cheerfully at this riposte from within his own mind. Really, a man has two selves within him, he thought. Who the devil dreamed up that spiteful remark?

– All right, then! yes, my friend, guillotined in three days, he retorted to his interrupter. M. de Cholin will hire a window, halving the cost of it with the Abbé Maslon. Well then, as to the cost of hiring this window, which of these two worthy fellows will bilk the other?

A passage from Rotrou's *Venceslas*³ suddenly occurred to him.

LADISLAS: . . . My soul is all prepared.

THE KING (*Ladislas's father*): And so is the scaffold; there bear your head.

A good retort! he thought, and he fell asleep. In the morning he was woken by someone grasping him tightly.

– What – already! exclaimed Julien, opening a haggard eye. He imagined himself to be in the hands of an executioner.

It was Mathilde. – Luckily, she doesn't realize what I meant. And this thought composed him. Mathilde seemed to him altered, as though from six months of illness: in truth she was scarcely recognizable.

– That vile Frilair has betrayed me, she told him, wringing her hands; rage had robbed her of her tears.

– Wasn't I fine yesterday when I spoke out? answered Julien. I was speaking spontaneously – and for the first time in my life! True – it's to be feared that it will also be my last . . .

At this moment Julien was capable of playing on Mathilde's nature with all the confidence of a skilled pianist touching the keys . . . – It is true I don't have the advantages of illustrious birth, he went on, but the lofty spirit of Mathilde was able to raise her lover up to her own level. D'you think even Boniface de La Mole would have stood up better before his judges?

That day Mathilde was unaffectedly tender, like any poor young girl living up on a fifth floor; but she could not get anything more straightforward out of him. He was repaying her, without meaning to, for the torments she had so often inflicted.

No one knows anything about the sources of the Nile, Julien said to himself; it hasn't been granted to the human eye to see the king of rivers in the form of a little stream: in the same way no living eye will see a feeble Julien, primarily because he isn't feeble. Yet my heart is easily touched; if said sincerely, the most commonplace phrase will soften my voice and even make tears flow. How often have barren natures despised me for this failing! They thought I was asking for sympathy – and that is what I cannot stand.

It is said that at the foot of the scaffold Danton was moved by the memory of his wife; but Danton had breathed energy into a nation of light-minded ditherers, and halted the enemy before Paris . . .[4] I am the only one who knows what I could have achieved . . . For everyone else I remain no more than a MIGHT HAVE BEEN.

If Mme de Rênal was here in my cell instead of Mathilde, should I still be able to stay true to myself? In the eyes of Valenod and all the local dignitaries the intensity of my despair and my repentance would pass for an ignoble fear of death; they are so proud, those feeble souls, when their wealth puts them above temptation! Having just condemned me to death M. Moirod and M. de Cholin will have said to one another – Don't you see what it is to be born a carpenter's son! A man can get educated, skilled – but the spirit! – a courageous spirit cannot be acquired . . . Even with my poor Mathilde here, who is weeping now – or rather can weep no more, he added looking at her reddened eyes . . . and then he clasped her in his arms, the sight of such true grief making him abandon his syllogism. – It is likely she has been weeping the whole night long, he said to himself – even so, one day how ashamed she will be at the memory! She will see herself as having been led astray as a young girl by the base reasonings of some plebeian . . . That Croisenois is weak enough to marry her and, my God, he will do well. She will make him play a part,

> To the sway of that firm spirit, great with some design
> The grosser souls of common men must themselves resign.[5]

Well, well! that's amusing: ever since I have been going to die all the verses I have ever known are coming back to mind. That will be a sign of decay setting in . . .

– He's there, in the next room, Mathilde had been repeating in a faint voice. Eventually he paid attention to her. Her voice is weak, thought he, but all her old imperiousness of character is still there in her tone. She keeps her voice low so as not to get angry.

– And who is there? he asked gently.

– Your lawyer, for you to sign your appeal.

– I shall not be appealing.

– What! not appeal, she replied, lifting herself up, eyes sparkling with ire – and why, if you don't mind my asking?

– Because at this moment I feel the courage to die without making myself too ridiculous. And who could assure me that in a couple of months, after a long spell in this damp cell, I will be as well disposed? I foresee interviews with priests – with my father . . . Nothing in the world could be so unpleasant for me. Let me die!

This unexpected contrariness reawoke all the haughty side of Mathilde's nature. She had been unable to see the Abbé Frilair before the hour when the Besançon prison cells opened; and her fury now rebounded on Julien. She adored him; yet, for a long quarter of an hour he faced once again – in her imprecations against his character, her regrets at ever having loved him – the full force of that proud spirit that had overwhelmed him with such devastating insults in the library of the Hôtel de La Mole.

— Heaven owed it to the glory of your race that you be born a man, he answered.

But as for myself, thought he, I would be a real fool to live another two months in this disgusting place, the target of all the derision and humiliation the patrician faction could think up,[6] and having for my sole comfort the imprecations of this hysterical girl ... Oh well, on the day after tomorrow, in the morning, I am to fight a duel with a man famous for his remarkable skill and courage ... — Yes, most remarkable, interjected his Mephistophelean voice – his strokes never fail.

Oh, well, so be it, let it come (Mathilde continued her eloquence). By God, no! he said to himself, I shall not appeal.

This resolve made, he fell into a reverie ... The postman on his rounds will deliver the paper at six as usual; at eight, after M. de Rênal has read it, Élisa will walk in on tiptoe and place it on her bed. A little later she will awake: suddenly, in reading, she will be troubled; her pretty hands will shake; she will read up until these words: *At five minutes past ten he had ceased to exist.*

She will cry hot tears, I know her; it will be nothing that I tried to kill her, all will be forgotten. And the woman whose life I tried to take will be the only one sincerely weeping for my death.

Ah! there's a paradox! he thought – and, for the long quarter of an hour in which Mathilde went on making a scene, he dreamed only of Mme de Rênal. In spite of himself, and although he often replied to what Mathilde was saying, he could not tear his soul away from the thought of the bedroom at Verrières. He saw the Besançon *Gazette* on the orange taffeta counterpane. He saw the pure white hand clutching it convulsively; he saw Mme de Rênal crying ... He traced the course of each tear drop as it ran down her lovely face.

Mlle de La Mole, unable to get anything out of Julien, called in the lawyer. Fortunately he was a former captain in the army of Italy in 1796, where he had been a comrade of Manuel.[7]

For the sake of form, he opposed the condemned man's decision. Julien, wishing to treat him with respect, set out all his reasons.

— My word! a man may well think as you do, the lawyer – whose name was M. Félix Vaneau – ended by saying. But you have three whole days in which to appeal, and it is my duty to return to you each day. If a volcano opens up under the prison in the next two months, you would be saved. You might die of illness, he said, glancing at Julien.

Julien pressed his hand. – Thank you, you are a decent fellow. I will think it over.

And when Mathilde eventually departed with the lawyer, he felt more of warmth towards the lawyer than he did towards her.

An hour later, as he lay sleeping deeply, he was roused by some tears he felt trickling down his hand. Ah! thought he, half-waking, it's Mathilde again. Faithful to her theory, she wants to combat my resolve with tenderness. Bored by the prospect of yet another scene in the Pathetic style, he did not open his eyes. The lines spoken by Belphégor as he flees from his wife[1] ran through his mind.

He heard an unfamiliar sigh; he opened his eyes – it was Mme de Rênal.

– Ah, dearest! I see you again before I die – can this really be happening? he cried, throwing himself at her feet.

But forgive me, lady – he added immediately, his sense returning. – I'm nothing better than a murderer in your eyes.

– Monsieur . . . I have come to implore you to appeal, I know you don't want to . . . Her sobs stifled her, she could not go on.

– Deign to forgive me.

– If you want my forgiveness, my darling, she said, springing up and throwing herself into his arms – appeal against your death sentence straight away.

Julien smothered her with kisses.

– Will you come here and see me every day for those two months?

– I swear to you I will. Every day, unless my husband forbids it.

– I will sign! cried Julien. Heavens above! you forgive me – is it possible!

He folded her in his arms; he was in ecstasy. She let out a little cry.

– It's nothing, she said, only you are hurting me.

– Ach! your shoulder, cried Julien, melting in tears. He drew back a little, and covered her hand in fervent kisses. — Who could have said that this would happen when last I saw you in your bedroom in Verrières . . . ?

— Well, who could have said that I would write that infamous letter to M. de La Mole . . . ?

— You must know that I have always loved you, that I have never loved any one but you.

— Can that be so! cried Mme de Rênal, ecstatic in her turn. She leant over Julien, who was on his knees before her, and for a long time they wept together in silence.

Never in his whole life had Julien had a moment to compare with this.

Much later, when they were capable of speech:

— And this young Mme Michelet, said Mme de Rênal — or rather Mlle de La Mole; for I'm really beginning to believe that strange story!

— It is only true in appearance, replied Julien. She is my wife, but not the one I adore . . .

Interrupting each other over and over again, they succeeded, with great difficulty, in telling each other the things they had not known. The letter sent to M. de La Mole had been composed by the young priest who directed Mme de Rênal's conscience, and then copied out by her.

— What horrors religion has led me into! she exclaimed — and even then I toned down the most frightful parts of that letter . . .

Julien's transports of joy showed how thoroughly he forgave her. Never had he been so wildly in love.

— But I still think of myself as a pious woman, Mme de Rênal assured him as their talk continued. I sincerely believe in God; I believe, too — indeed, it has been proved to me — that the sin I am committing is frightful, but the moment I see you, even after you fired off two pistols at me . . . And at this point, despite her protests, Julien covered her with kisses.

— Let me go now, she continued. I must talk to you sensibly, darling, for fear of missing things out . . . From the moment I set eyes on you, all sense of duty evaporates, I am made up of nothing but love for you – or rather love is too feeble a word. I feel for you what I ought to feel only for God: a mixture of respect, passion, submission . . . Really, I don't know what it is you inspire in me. If you asked me to stab the gaoler the crime would be done before I had given it a thought. Explain that to me clearly before I go – I want to see right into my own heart, for in two months we must leave each other . . . But as to that – do we really have to part? she asked, smiling.

– I take back my word, cried Julien, rising to his feet; I will not appeal against the death sentence if, by poison, the knife, pistols, charcoal fumes – or any other means whatever – you try to end your life, or put it in danger.

Mme de Rênal's expression underwent a sudden change; her eager tenderness was replaced by a deeply thoughtful look.

– Yet . . . if we were to die, just like that? she asked at length.

– Who knows what we would find in another life? answered Julien; torments perhaps, perhaps nothing at all. Can't we just spend these two months together, living in joy? Two months – that's a lot of days. I will be happier than I have ever been!

– Happier than you have ever been!

– Than I have ever been, repeated Julien with delight – and I say to you what I say to myself. Heaven forbid I should exaggerate.

– Your saying it constitutes a command for me, she said with a timid and melancholy smile.

– Very good, then! swear on your love for me, my dearest, to make no attempt on your life, direct or indirect . . . Remember, he added, you must live for my son, whom Mathilde will leave to the servants when she becomes the Marquise de Croisenois.

– I do swear, she answered coolly – but I must have your appeal to take with me, written and signed in your own hand. I shall go to the public prosecutor in person.

– Take care, you will compromise yourself.

– After the business of having come to visit you in prison I will forever be a heroine of gossip in Besançon, and throughout all Franche-Comté, she replied with an air of great affliction. – Propriety's strict bounds have been transgressed . . .[2] I am a woman who has lost her reputation – it is true that it was for your sake . . .

Her voice was so very sad that Julien hugged her with an elation entirely new to him. This was no longer the intoxication of love, it was passionate gratitude. Now, for the first time, he realized the full extent of the sacrifice she had made for him.

Doubtless some charitable being had informed M. de Rênal of the long visits his wife made to Julien in prison; for, after three days, he sent his carriage to her with express orders to return to Verrières at once.

This cruel parting began Julien's day badly. Then, two or three hours later, he was told that a certain conniving priest, who had not however been able to ingratiate himself with the Jesuits of Besançon, had, since the early morning, established himself in the street outside the prison gate. It was raining heavily, and there the man played the martyr. Julien was feeling ill disposed, and this piece of stupidity affected him deeply.

Already that morning he had refused a visit from the priest, but the fellow was determined to obtain Julien's confession, and so make a name for himself among the young women of Besançon with all the revelations he imagined he would receive.

He loudly declared that he was going to spend the day and night at the prison gate; – God has sent me to move the heart of this second apostate . . .[3] And the common folk, intrigued as always by a commotion, began to gather round.

– Yes, my brethren, he said to them, I shall spend the day here, and the night, and all the days and all the nights to come. The Holy Ghost has spoken unto me and I have a mission from on high; 'tis I who must save the soul of this young Sorel. Join ye in my prayers, *etc., etc.*

Julien had a horror of scandal and of everything that might draw attention to himself. He thought of embracing this occasion to leave the world incognito; but he still had some little hope of seeing Mme de Rênal again, and was deeply engulfed in his love for her.

The prison gate was situated on one of the busiest streets. The idea of this muddy priest, stirring up a mob and a scandal, tormented his soul. – And, no doubt, he repeats my name the whole time! The episode was more terrible to him than death itself.

Two or three times, at hourly intervals, he called one of the turnkeys – who was devoted to him – to send to see if the priest was still at the prison gate.

– Monsieur, he is on both knees in the mud, the turnkey told him on each occasion; he is praying out loud and saying litanies for your soul ... Impertinent scoundrel! thought Julien. At that moment, in fact, he could make out a low murmuring sound – the crowd responding to the litanies. To crown his irritation he glimpsed the turnkey moving his lips, repeating the Latin words. – They'm beginnin' to say, the turnkey added, that you must have a most obdurated heart to refuse the succour of this holy man.

Oh, my native land! how sunk in barbarism you still are! Julien cried out within himself, carried away by anger. And he went on thinking out loud without bothering about the turnkey's presence.

– That fellow wants to get in the newspaper, and this is his way of doing it.

Ah! damn provincials! In Paris I wouldn't be forced to put up with these vexations. There they know more about charlatanism.

– Have this holy father come in, he said to the turnkey at last – and great beads of sweat trickled down his brow. The turnkey made the sign of the cross and went out joyously.

This holy father seemed to be horribly ugly, and still more horribly muddy. The chill rain falling increased the darkness and damp in the cell. The priest made as if to embrace Julien, and addressed him as with fervent emotion. The lowest style of hypocrisy was all too obvious; Julien had never been so irritated in all his life.

A quarter of an hour after the priest's entrance, Julien discovered himself to be a total coward. Death for the first time appeared horrible to him. He thought of the state of putrefaction his corpse would be in two days after the execution, etc., etc.

He was on the point of betraying some sign of weakness – or of throwing himself on the priest and strangling him with his own rosary chain – when he had the idea of asking the holy man to go and say a good 40-franc mass for him, that very day.

Since it was almost noon,[4] the priest quickly decamped.

As soon as he had left, Julien began to weep copiously, and wept at the thought of death. Little by little it came to him that if Mme de Rênal had been in Besançon he might have confessed his weaknesses to her . . .

Just at the moment he was regretting the absence of this adored woman most, he heard Mathilde's step.

The worst of being in prison, he thought, is not being able to lock one's door. All that Mathilde said to him was merely an irritant.

She told him that on the day of the trial M. Valenod – by now with his nomination as prefect in his pocket – had dared make a fool of M. de Frilair and give himself the pleasure of condemning Julien to death.

– What was your friend thinking of – M. de Frilair asked me just now – to stir up the petty vanities of this *bourgeois aristocracy* and then attack them! Why mention *caste*? He showed them what to do in their own political interest: those boobies hadn't been thinking about that, they were ready to burst into tears. Then the interests of caste came and blinded them to the horror of condemning a man to death. It has to be admitted that M. Sorel is very raw in this kind of business. If we don't succeed in saving him by means of clemency, his death will be a kind of *suicide* . . .

Mathilde had no need to be careful to guard against telling Julien what she herself hardly suspected: that the Abbé de Frilair, seeing that Julien was lost, thought it might serve his own ambitions to aspire to be his successor.

Almost beside himself with impotent rage and frustration, he told Mathilde: Do go along and hear a mass for me, and give me a moment's peace. Mathilde, already very jealous of Mme de Rênal's visits, and aware of her recent departure, understood the reason for Julien's temper and burst into tears.

Her misery was genuine. Julien saw that, and was only the more irritated. He had an overwhelming desire for solitude, yet how could he obtain it?

At last Mathilde, having tried to soften him with all the arguments she could think of, left him in peace – but almost at the same moment, Fouqué arrived.

– I need to be alone, he told this faithful friend . . . And, when he saw him hesitate: I am making a draft for my plea for clemency . . . and as to the rest . . . if you want to gratify me, don't ever talk of death. If I have need of any particular services on that day, leave me to mention them first.

When at last Julien had gained his solitude, he found himself even more depressed, tremulous, than ever before. The little strength left to his enfeebled spirit had been exhausted in concealing his state from Mlle de La Mole and Fouqué.

Towards evening there came a thought to console him:

If they had told me of my execution this morning, just at the moment death seemed so hideous to me, *the eye of the public would have been a spur to glory*[1] – maybe my gait would have been a little wooden, like that of a nervous fop entering a salon – and a few perceptive people, if there are any in the provinces, would have been able to guess at my weakness . . . but no one *would have seen it*.

He felt himself relieved of a part of his misery. Just now I am a coward, he chanted to himself over and again – but no one will know of it.

The following day an event that was almost more disagreeable awaited him. For a long time his father had been announcing that he would visit; that day, before Julien was awake, the hoary-headed old carpenter appeared in his cell.

Julien felt weak, he expected the most wounding reproaches. To complete his misery, he was that morning feeling a sharp pang of guilt at not having loved his father.

Mere chance, he said to himself while the turnkey was tidying his cell a little, has placed us side by side upon the earth, and we have done almost as much harm to each other as we possibly could. He is coming to deliver the final blow at the moment of death.

Immediately no witnesses were present, the old man's stern harangue began.

Julien was unable to restrain his tears. What shameful weakness! he said to himself furiously. Now he will go around everywhere exaggerating my lack of courage; what triumph for Valenod and for all those dreary hypocrites who reign in Verrières! They are very big in France, they combine all possible social advantages. Up until now, I could at least tell myself that, although they get all the money, it is true, and honours accumulate all around them, yet it is I who possess nobility of heart.

And now here is a witness, whom everyone will believe, and who will testify to the whole of Verrières, and who will exaggerate it, how weak I have been in the face of death! I will have been a coward in an ordeal with which everyone is familiar!

Julien was close to despair. He did not know how to be rid of his father; and to pull off a sham in a way that could fool so astute an old man seemed to him just then quite beyond his powers.

His mind ran rapidly over the possibilities.

— *I've made some savings*! he cried suddenly.

This inspired remark completely altered the old man's expression and Julien's situation.

— How should I dispose of them? Julien continued more calmly: the effect he had produced had dispelled all feelings of inferiority.

The ancient carpenter burned with desire not to let slip any part of this money, some of which Julien seemed to want to give to his brothers. He spoke at length and with passion. Then Julien was able to play with him.

— Ah, well! the Lord inspires me in regard to my will. I shall give a thousand francs to each of my brothers and the rest to you.

— Very good, replied the old man, the rest is due to me; but if God has been merciful in touching your heart, and you want to die a good Christian, you should pay your debts. There is still outstanding the costs of your feed and upbringing — which I advanced you, and which you don't think of . . .

So there is the love of a father! Julien could only repeat to himself, his spirit reduced to tatters, when at last he was alone again. Soon the gaoler reappeared.

– Monsieur, after the family has visited I always bring my guests a bottle of good champagne wine. It is a trifle dear, six francs a bottle, but it cheers you up wonderfully.

– Bring three glasses, replied Julien with childish enthusiasm – and ask in a couple of those prisoners I hear can walking in the cloister.

The gaoler led in two recidivists, just about to be sent back to the galleys. These were two sprightly villains, really remarkable for their cleverness, courage and nerve.

– If you slip me twenty francs, said one of them to Julien, I will tell you the story of my life in detail. It is *delicious*.

– But won't you lie to me? asked Julien.

– Not a bit of it, he answered, my mate there, who is jealous of the twenty, would betray me if I told a lie.

His story was abominable. It was a display of a courageous spirit in which only one passion had survived, the passion for money.

After they had left Julien was no longer the same man. All his rage against himself had vanished. His atrocious suffering, poisoned by the pusillanimity that had preyed on him since Mme de Rênal's departure, had transformed into melancholy.

As I became less deceived by appearances, he said to himself, I would have come to realize that the Paris salons are full of honest folk like my father, or clever rogues like these birds from the galleys. They were absolutely right; salon frequenters never get up in the morning with the urgent question – How am I going to eat? They boast of their own uprightness! then, when called on to a jury, proudly condemn a man who has stolen a silver fork because he feels he is dying of hunger . . .

. . . But when they are at Court, and it is a question of winning or losing some ministerial post, my upright salon dwellers lower themselves to crimes exactly parallel to those that the need to eat inspires in those two convicts . . .

There is no such thing as a *natural right*:[2] that phrase is only an antiquated stupidity very well fitted to the public prosecutor who hounded me the other day, and whose ancestor was enriched by one of Louis XIV's expropriations. There is only a *right* when there is a law forbidding something or other on pain of punishment. Prior to the law, there is nothing *natural* but the strength of the lion, or the needs of a creature who is hungry, who is cold – in a word, *necessity* ... No, the people who get the honours are no more than the scoundrels who have been lucky enough not to be caught red-handed. The prosecutor that society unleashed on me owes his riches to some vileness ... I did commit a deadly assault, and am justly condemned, but, that single deed apart, the Valenod type who condemned me is a hundred times more poisonous to society.

Very well, then! added Julien sadly, but without rancour – despite his avarice, my father is worth more than all those kinds of men. He has never loved me. I am just about to make his cup overflow by disgracing him with a shameful death. This dread of needing money, this exaggerated view of men's malice that is labelled *avarice*, makes him find prodigious matter for consolation in the sum of the three or four hundred louis that I will be able to leave him. One day, on a Sunday, after dinner, he will display his gold to all the envious eyes of Verrières. At this price – his look will challenge them – at this price, which of you wouldn't be delighted to have a son sent to the guillotine?

Julien's philosophy might very well be valid, but it was of a nature to make him welcome death. So passed five long days. He was considerate and gentle to Mathilde, whom he saw to be in a state of the most acute jealous exasperation. One evening he did think seriously of killing himself. His spirit was demoralized by the deep misery into which he had been thrown by Mme de Rênal's departure. Nothing gave him pleasure any more, neither in real life nor in his imagination. Lack of exercise had begun to affect his health and to give him the highly strung yet feeble temper of a young German intellectual. He was losing the manly pride that, with a vigorous oath, rebuts certain unworthy thoughts likely to assail an unhappy soul.

I have loved truth ... Where is truth? ... Everywhere hypocrisy, or at least charlatanism, even among the most virtuous, even among the greatest; and his lips curled with distaste . . . No, man cannot put his trust in man.

Madame de —, when collecting for her poor orphans, told me that a certain prince was about to donate ten louis – it was a lie. But what am I saying? Napoleon on Saint Helena! . . . Pure charlatanism, proclamations in favour of the King of Rome.[3]

Great God! if a man like that – still more at a time when misfortune should have recalled him sternly to his duty – descends to charlatanism, what can we expect from the rest of the species? . . .

Where is truth? In religion . . . Oh, yes, he went on with a twisted smile of violent scorn – in the mouths of Maslon, de Frilair, Castanède . . . Perhaps it is to be found in pure forms of Christianity, where the priests are no more paid than were the Apostles? But St Paul was rewarded by the pleasures of command, of preaching, of making himself talked about . . .

Ah! if only there were a true religion . . . Fool that I am! I see a gothic cathedral, ancient stained glass; my vulnerable heart conjures up the figure of a priest within that window . . . My soul embraces it, my soul has need of it . . . What do I meet but a fop with greasy hair . . . a Chevalier de Beauvoisis, without the charm.

But a true priest, a Massillon, a Fénelon . . . well, Massillon consecrated Dubois[4] – Saint-Simon's *Memoirs* have spoiled Fénelon for me; but, even so, a true priest . . . With him there would be a space in the world where feeling souls could unite . . . We would not all be isolated from one another . . . This good father could talk to us of God. But of what God? Not the God of the Bible, a petty despot, cruel and avid for vengeance . . . rather the God of Voltaire, just, good, infinite . . .

He was disturbed by all his memories of the Bible that he knew by heart . . . But how, whenever *two or three are gathered together*, how to believe in that mighty name GOD, after the frightful way our priests have abused it?

To live in isolation! . . . What torture! . . .

I am getting out of control, and becoming unjust, said Julien to himself, striking his brow. I am in isolation here in this cell; but I haven't *existed in isolation* in the world; I possessed a powerful idea of *duty*. The duty I laid down for myself . . . rightly or wrongly . . . has been like the trunk of a sturdy tree against which I leant during the storm; I wavered, I was shaken . . . But I wasn't swept away.

It is the damp air of this cell that makes me dwell on isolation . . .

But why am I still a hypocrite while I am cursing hypocrisy? It is not death, nor the cell, nor the dank air – it is Mme de Rênal's absence that is crushing me. If, in Verrières, I was obliged to live several whole weeks shut up in the cellars of her house in order to see her, would I have any complaints?

– The influence of my contemporaries is too much for me, he said aloud with a bitter laugh. Alone, talking to myself, two steps away from death, I am still a hypocrite . . . Oh! Nineteenth Century!

. . . A hunter fires a shot in the forest, his prey falls, he darts forward to seize it. His boot strikes an ant-hill two feet high, destroys the ants' burrows, scatters the ants and their eggs far and wide . . . The most philosophical of the ants is quite unable to understand this black mass, immense, terrifying: the hunter's boot, that suddenly smashed into their world with incredible speed, preceded by an astounding noise, accompanied by flashes of reddish fire . . .

Such are death, life, eternity – simple phenomena for those with organs of sense vast enough to comprehend them . . .

A mayfly is born at nine o'clock in the morning on a fine summer's day and dies at five in the afternoon; how should it understand the word *night*? Granted five more hours of existence it would see and understand what night is.

The same with me, I am going to die at the age of twenty-three. Let me have five more years of life to spend with Mme de Rênal.

He started to laugh like Mephistopheles. What idiocy to discuss these grand problems!

First, I am being a hypocrite, as though there was someone here to hear me.

Second, I am failing to live and to love when I have so few days of life left to me . . . Alas! Mme de Rênal is absent from me; perhaps her husband will not let her come back to Besançon and go on dishonouring herself.

That is what is isolating me, not the absence of a God who is just, good, all-powerful, never ill-willed, not at all thirsty for vengeance.

Ah! if such a One existed . . . Alas! I would cast myself at His feet. I have deserved death, I would say to him; but, great God, good God, merciful God, give me back her whom I adore!

By then the night was far advanced. After an hour or two of peaceful slumber, Fouqué came in.

Julien felt himself to be strong and resolute, like a man who sees clearly into his own soul.

I don't want to play such a rotten trick on poor old Abbé Chas-Bernard as to call upon him, he told Fouqué; he would be unable to eat for the next three days. But do try to find me a Jansenist, some friend of M. Pirard who will be impervious to intrigue.

Fouqué had impatiently waited for this opening. Julien now decorously discharged all duties that are due to public opinion in the provinces. Thanks to M. l'Abbé de Frilair, and in spite of this unfortunate choice of a confessor, in his cell Julien was under the protection of the Congregation; if he had acted with a little more enterprise he might even have contrived to escape. But the bad air of his cell was producing its effect, his mental powers were in decline. This made him all the happier when Mme de Rênal did return.

– My first duty is towards you, she said, taking him in her arms; I have put Verrières behind me . . .

Julien had no petty pride with her – he told her all his weaknesses. She responded with all her powers of grace and charm.

Immediately she had left the prison that evening she summoned to her aunt's house the priest who had latched on to Julien as prey; since his dearest wish was to gain credit amongst the young matrons of Besançon high society, Mme de Rênal easily persuaded him to go and perform a novena at the Abbey of Bray-le-Haut.

No words can convey the intensity and wildness of Julien's passion.

By the power of money, and by using and misusing the prestige of her aunt, a lady well known to be of great piety and wealth, Mme de Rênal contrived to visit him twice each day.

At news of this, Mathilde's jealousy reached fever pitch. M. de Frilair had confessed that not even all his influence could brave convention to the extent of gaining permission for her to see her friend more than once a day. Mathilde ordered that Mme de Rênal be followed in order to know of her slightest movements. M. de Frilair exhausted all the resources of a very adroit mind to persuade her that Julien was unworthy of her.

In the midst of all these torments she loved him only the more, and presented him with a horrible scene almost every day.

Julien wished with all his might to act honourably, and to the end, towards the poor young woman he had so strangely compromised; but his uncontrollable passion for Mme de Rênal defeated him at every step. Then, when, by reason of his weak arguments, he was failing to persuade Mathilde of the innocence of her rival's visits, he said to himself: By now the end of the drama must be very near; that is a sort of excuse for me if I cannot manage to dissimulate better.

Mlle de La Mole learned of M. de Croisenois's death. M. de Thaler, that exceedingly rich young man, had allowed himself to make disagreeable remarks on the subject of Mathilde's disappearance; M. de Croisenois had begged him to retract them: M. de Thaler had then shown him some anonymous letters that he had been sent, full of details assembled with such skill that it was impossible for the Marquis not to recognize the truth.

M. de Thaler allowed himself some pleasantries that were not subtle. Wild with rage and misery, M. de Croisenois demanded such heavy reparation that the millionaire preferred a duel. Stupidity won; and one of the most amiable young men in Paris was dead before the age of twenty-four.

This death made a strange and unhealthy impression on Julien's enfeebled mind.

– Poor old Croisenois, he said to Mathilde, he really was very moderate and behaved like a true gentleman towards us; he might well have hated me for the rashness of your behaviour in Madame your mother's salon, and he probably longed to quarrel with me – the hatred scorn provokes is usually ferocious . . .

The death of M. de Croisenois upset all Julien's plans for Mathilde's future; he spent several days trying to persuade her that she should accept the hand of M. de Luz. – He is a shy sort of fellow, not at all a Jesuit, he argued, who will undoubtedly find his own place in the ranks. His ambitions are less brilliant but more persistent than those of poor Croisenois and, with no ducal title in the family, he won't have any difficulty marrying the widow of Julien Sorel.

– And a widow, too, who has a contempt for grand passions, Mathilde coldly commented: for she has lived long enough – after six months! – to see her lover preferring another woman, a woman who is the cause of all their suffering.

– You are unjust; Mme de Rênal's visits will supply some striking phrases to the Paris attorney in charge of my appeal for clemency; he will be able to paint the picture of a murderer being honoured by his victim's care. That should have its effect, and maybe one day you will see me becoming the subject of some melodrama, *etc., etc.*

A burning jealousy with no chance of reparation, a persistent misery that was hopeless (for, even supposing Julien was saved, how could she regain his heart?), a feeling of shame, and her despair at loving this unfaithful lover more than ever, had cast Mlle de La Mole into a gloomy silence from which M. de Frilair's assiduous attentions could not – any more than Fouqué's blunt frankness – draw her out.

As to Julien, save in the moments usurped by Mathilde's presence, he lived for his love and with almost no thought of what was to come. As a curious result of this passion, at its height and with no pretences at all, Mme de Rênal came to share almost equally in his carefree moods and gentle gaiety.

– In the past, Julien said to her, when I could have been so extraordinarily happy during our walks in the woods at Vergy, furious ambition transported my soul to imaginary realms. Instead of me pressing this lovely arm, which was so near to my lips, my heart, the future took me away from you; I was engaged with the innumerable struggles I would have to endure to amass a vast fortune ... No, I would have died quite without knowing the nature of happiness had it not come to you visiting me in this prison.

Two events occurred to trouble this peaceful existence. Julien's confessor, sincere Jansenist that he was, was not anything like sufficient protection against the intrigue of the Jesuits, and, although unaware of it, he became their instrument.

He arrived one day to say that in order to avoid falling into the frightful sin of suicide, it was essential that Julien take all possible measures to obtain clemency. Now, since the clergy had a great deal of influence at the Ministry of Justice in Paris, an easy means offered itself: he must undergo a sensational conversion . . .

– A sensational conversion! repeated Julien. Ah! I have caught you at it too, father, playing the missionary role . . .

– Your youth, the Jansenist replied gravely, the interesting face with which Providence has endowed you, the very motive of your crime, which remains inexplicable, the heroic deeds that Mlle de La Mole has lavished on the cause, everything, in short, up to the astounding friendship shown you by your victim – everything has combined to make you the hero of all the young ladies of Besançon. They have become oblivious of all else, even politics, for your sake . . .

. . . Your conversion would resound in their hearts and make a profound impression. You could be of the greatest service to religion – and as for me, should I hesitate for the frivolous reason that the Jesuits would take the same steps on a like occasion? If that was so, even in this particular case, which has escaped their rapacity, they would still be doing harm! Let it not be so . . . The tears shed at your conversion would cancel out the corrosive effect of ten editions of Voltaire's blasphemous works.

– And what would I have left, replied Julien coldly, when I despised myself? I have been ambitious, I do not wish to blame myself for that – for at that time I was acting according to the customs of the age. And now I live from day to day. But, glancing at the prospect ahead, I would make myself very unhappy indeed, if I slid into such a piece of cowardice . . .

The other incident, affecting Julien in a very different way, originated with Mme de Rênal. I have no idea what scheming friend had succeeded in persuading this naive and timid soul that it was her duty to leave for Saint-Cloud, or to go and throw herself at the knees of King Charles X.

She had made the sacrifice of parting from Julien and, after an effort like that, the distastefulness of making a spectacle of herself –

which at any other time would have seemed worse than death – was nothing in her eyes.

– I will go to the King and openly avow that you are my lover: the life of a man, and of a man like Julien, must override all other considerations. I will say that it was through jealousy that you made an attempt on my life. There are hundreds of examples of young men redeemed in such cases by the humanity of a jury, or of the King . . .

– I will stop seeing you, I will have my prison closed to you, cried Julien, and certainly the next day I will kill myself in despair if you don't swear not to do anything to make a public spectacle of us both. This notion of going to Paris isn't yours. Tell me the name of the scheming female who suggested it to you . . .

Let's be happy in the handful of days left in this short life. Let's conceal our existence; my crime is only too plain. Mlle de La Mole has all the influence there is to be had in Paris, be assured that she will do all that is humanly possible. Here, in the provinces, I have all the rich and influential people against me. What you would do would only further aggravate those rich and, above all, mediocre kind of men for whom life is such an easy matter . . . Don't let's give them anything to laugh at, those Maslons and Valenods – and thousands of others worthier than them.

The foul air of the cell was becoming intolerable to Julien. Fortunately, on the day it was announced to him that he must die, a pleasant sunshine was cheering all the natural world, and Julien was in courageous mood. Walking in the open air was a delicious sensation for him, as is treading on the earth again for the sailor who has been long at sea. Forward then, everything's all right, he said to himself, I don't lack courage at all.

Never had that head been so poetic as at the moment it was to fall. The sweetest hours he had known in the woods at Vergy long ago came crowding into his thoughts with wonderful intensity.

Everything passed off simply, appropriately, and with no affectation on his part.

Two days before, he had said to Fouqué:

– As to what I will feel, I can't answer; this cell, being so sordid, so damp, gives me feverish moments when I don't know myself; but as to fear — no, no one will see this face blench.

He had arranged in advance that, on the morning of the last day, Fouqué should carry off both Mathilde and Mme de Rênal.

— Take them both in the same carriage, he had said. Make sure the post horses keep up a gallop. They will fall into one another's arms, or they will show mortal hatred. In either case, the poor women will be distracted a little from their terrible sorrow.

Julien had exacted a vow from Mme de Rênal that she would live to look after Mathilde's son.

— Who knows? Perhaps we still have some sensation after our death, he had said one day to Fouqué. I would rather like to repose, since repose is the word, in the little cave on the great mountain that looms over Verrières. Many's the time — as I have told you — that, retreating into that cavern at night, my gaze plunging far over the richest provinces of France, ambition has flamed in my heart: that was my passion, then ... Anyway, that cave is dear to me, and nobody could disagree that it is placed so as to fill a philosophic soul with envy ... Very well! these good Congregationists in Besançon will do anything for cash; if you knew how to handle it, they would sell you my mortal remains ...

Fouqué succeeded in this sad bargain. He was spending the night alone in his room next to the corpse of his friend when, to his great surprise, he saw Mathilde come in. Only a few hours earlier he had left her ten leagues from Besançon. Her expression and her eyes were wild.

— I want to see him, she said.

Fouqué had the resolution neither to speak nor to rise. He pointed with his finger at a large blue cloak on the floorboards; in that was wrapped what remained of Julien.

She threw herself on her knees. The memory of Boniface de La Mole and Marguerite de Navarre inspired her, no doubt, with superhuman resolve. Her trembling hands opened the cloak. Fouqué turned away his eyes.

He heard Mathilde walking about rapidly in the room. She lit a large number of candles. When Fouqué summoned up the strength to look at her, she had placed Julien's head on a little marble table in front of her, and was kissing its brow . . .

Mathilde followed her lover to the tomb he had chosen. A large band of priests escorted the bier and, unknown to all, alone in her veiled carriage, she carried on her knees the head of the man she had so dearly loved.

Coming in this way almost to the summit of one of the highest mountains in the Jura, in the depths of the night, and in that little cave now magnificently lit up by innumerable tapers, twenty priests celebrated the service for the dead. All the inhabitants of the little mountain villages that the convoy had crossed followed it, attracted by the singularity of this strange rite.

Mathilde appeared in the midst of them in long mourning robes and, at the end of the service, had many thousand five-franc pieces scattered in the crowd.

Left alone with Fouqué, she insisted on burying her lover's head with her own hands. Fouqué narrowly avoided losing his mind with grief.

By Mathilde's agency this wild cavern was decorated with marble carvings sculpted in Italy at great expense.

Mme de Rênal was faithful to her promise. In no way did she seek to take her own life; but three days after Julien, she died, her children in her arms.

THE END[1]

TO THE HAPPY FEW

APPENDIX A

Stendhal's Epigraphs and Quotations

Stendhal thought that the function of an epigraph was to 'augment the sensation, the emotion of the reader, if there is emotion there', rather than to add philosophical judgements. Many of his epigraphs in this novel (about 80 per cent) seem, therefore, to have been written by him for such suggestive purposes, and then attributed to an appropriate-sounding source – e.g., even before the first paragraph begins there are resonances of Danton and of Hobbes, although not actually the work of Danton or Hobbes. Like Sir Walter Scott, Stendhal is not pernickety about accuracy of citation, and towards the end there tends to be less and less likelihood that the epigraphs are genuine quotations. Perhaps this is the result of authorial insecurity? – but one of the effects is to scatter a kind of secondary cultural prestige around the text. Another is that even the invented voices add to the charm and authority of the work by their suggestion of polyphonic diversity, by the sense they give that a novel is a dramatic mixture as well as a narrator's monologue. George Eliot did something similar on a less extensive scale.

Often, too, these resonances feel and sound the richer for being presented by Stendhal in the language or pretended language of origin. In many cases that language is English, and for this to stand out in the English translation – to register the difference and at the same time spare the reader from having always to apply to a note – I have used italics as an accepted indication of a *foreign language*.

(So often, when the invented epigraphs are attributed to English writers Sterne, Locke etc. – their not being in italics is another indication of their being in French in the original, and therefore unlikely to be genuine.)

This system is applied both to English epigraphs and word or phrases within the text.

There is an amusing discussion of epigraphs in general, though it only just mentions Stendhal, in Kevin Jackson's *Invisible Forms* (London: Picador, 1999).

APPENDIX B

French Currency and Distances in the 1820s

CURRENCY

franc: the standard unit coin, established under Napoleon in monetary reforms, 1797–2002.

centime: one-hundredth of a franc.

sou: 5 centimes (in Besançon dialect, *sol*).

livre: an older, pre-revolutionary name for an amount of about 1 franc. Like the English guinea, it is an idea, not a coin, and tends to be estimated generously, as a round figure, etc. Its name was still preferred by traditionalists.

écu: silver coin worth either 3 or 6 francs.

louis: gold coin worth 20 francs.

napoléon: gold coin worth 20 francs, or sometimes 24 francs.

RELATIVE VALUES

It was an inflationary period when Stendhal was writing. This adds a further difficulty to the notoriously complex enterprise of establishing comparisons with present day values, especially since present day values also constantly shift, upwards. As with most things, a sense of relative values – what sounds a lot and what a little – are usually best inferred from the text, which is very open about money.

However, given the important qualification that in any case different societies pay differently for different things – for example, domestic labour was very cheap in the early nineteenth century, exotic imports very expensive – it may be useful to say that one could multiply every sum by *sixty or thereabouts* to arrive at an estimate of early twenty-first century equivalents.

FOREIGN EXCHANGE

It is estimated, again very roughly, that in 1830 a franc was the equivalent of 1s.3d. in English money (6.25 p.); and therefore c.16 francs = £1; or perhaps less. A little later Thackeray, in *The Newcomes* (1854, but set in the 1830s) has the impoverished Vicomte de Florac say, of the futility of using a still grander title that he has just inherited, that 'Florac has two louis in his pocket, and Montconour exactly forty shillings'.

DISTANCES

A *league* (*lieue*) is, like the livre, a fairly approximate, older, measure. It is just under 3 miles, or about 4 kilometres.

NOTES

EDITOR'S NOTICE

1. *Editor's Notice*: by Stendhal, to the first edition.
2. *great events of July*: The revolution of 1830, also known as the July Days or the Three Days (27–29 July) – was a reaction, at first largely by liberal bourgeois deputies led by Adolphe Thiers, to the rule of Charles X (1757–1836), Louis XVIII's brother and successor since 1824. Under the influence and administration of his minister the Prince de Polignac – a mystical and driven extreme royalist Ultra who had visions of the Virgin Mary, perhaps the model for M. de Nerval in the novel – the King had become narrowly autocratic, almost nervously feudal in pretension.

As in the case of many subsequent revolutions, the course and upshot of that of 1830 were in very many ways not at all what had been foreseen. As in 1789, journalists – who were directly threatened by the government – mobilized (and created) popular feeling, especially in Paris. Barricades were erected, idealists fought, and mobs rioted. At first, on 28 July, Marshal Marmont, 'trying to take the offensive against the barricades' with troops who in any case were unenthusiastic about the Bourbons, 'lost the eastern districts and fell back on the Tuileries; on the 29th, with the Louvre surrounded, he gave the order to retreat'. But now, alarmed at the mass fervour and violence, and remembering 1789, the liberal deputies and Thiers intervened, calling in the aged national hero the Marquis de Lafayette to command the bourgeois Municipal Guard (he had commanded the National Guard in 1789). Together they put down the mobs, avoided the possible radicalism of a new republic and installed the Duc d'Orléans, Louis Philippe, as a constitutional monarch. It is common and easy to scorn Louis Philippe – especially since his reign ended in another revolution in 1848 – but the shadow of Napoleon allowed virtually no glamour to anyone else, and perhaps subsequent history shows that scorn is too easy.

In any case, this revolution fired, and was fired by, 'young France'; the results of its compromise, and the advertised ensuing ethos of 'enrich yourselves', disgusted many of them and became subject matter for some of the very best French fiction writers – Balzac, Stendhal, Flaubert . . . and thus a potent source for the impressions of posterity.

3. *were written in 1827*: This is a piece of local provocation by the author. In fact *The Red and the Black* was put on paper in 1829–30; and, of course, the reader has just been told that it is a chronicle of 1830, now published in November of that year. Possibly the whole note is meant to play down the permanent importance of the political upheaval of July to Stendhal's subject, for what is remarkable and tantalizing in the internal chronology of the novel is that the revolution does not happen. (There is a lively discussion of this in Michael Wood's *Stendhal* (London: Elek, 1971), pp. 65–9.)

BOOK ONE

CHAPTER THE FIRST

A Small Town

1. *Danton*: Not an actual quote from, but in the spirit of, Danton (1759–94), the mighty and often heroic proponent and orator of the French Revolution – the accelerating violence of which led to his own death by the Guillotine.

2. *Hobbes*: Not, of course, an actual quote from Hobbes either, who did not write gnomic verse (though there are some autobiographical verses). But it can be said to have a flavour of his hard-headed political philosophy (I assume that 'thousands' refers to money, unless, possibly, it is an indirect way of opening the novel's contrast between small town and city).

3. *the Franche-Comté*: To a French reader this would have conveyed the sense of a region far from the centre. The Franche-Comté is a spectacular area in the extreme east, next to Switzerland, and became part of the kingdom only in the seventeenth century. It is as north Wales is to an Englishman, though even more remote. There are remarks later in the novel about its people's uncertain grasp of French.

4. *1815 made him Mayor of Verrières*: M. de Rênal is an Ultra (an ultra royalist, hostile to anything to do with the Revolution or Napoleon) who has benefited from the restoration of the Bourbons in that year, and who therefore wants to distance himself from the appearance of the Modern – capital, industry, commerce, etc.

And, as the previous paragraph of the text suggests, mayors in France — because, no doubt, of the different historical evolution of the feudal structure on the Continent — were much less irretrievably bourgeois, middle-class and unaristocratic than in English tradition. This is an important social nuance for this novel. Talleyrand, for example, who was at the heart of European politics for forty years, and whose family was one of the very oldest in France, late in life became Mayor of Valençay for six years.

5. *from Italy by those masons who cross the gorges of the Jura on their way to Paris every spring*: It has been suggested that this is likely to be a covert allusion to the international spread of liberal ideas via Freemasonry.

CHAPTER 2

A Mayor

1. *Barnave*: Antoine Barnave (1761–93) was one of the major orators of the French Revolution, and was involved in apprehending the Royal Family after its flight to Varennes; later, though, he developed royalist sympathies, and was of course guillotined. He came from Grenoble and was known to members of Stendhal's family.

2. *Abbé*: This is a general term used for one of the clerical class, from archishop to seminarist, and not necessarily an ordained priest.

3. *the Army of Italy*: The name of this army of the Revolution, led to legendary successes by General Bonaparte, has a powerful Napoleonic ring, second only to that of the Grand Army. Stendhal was a member of both bodies, and his posting to Italy when he was eighteen was a key event in his development as a young man – see, especially, the first paragraph of *The Charterhouse of Parma* (1839).

4. *Jacobin*: Originally describing the extreme left of the Revolution, the party of Robespierre, of the Terror, and the radical refashioning of human nature by Reason. By extension, anything the least bit radical or left-wing.

5. *Legion of Honour*: The order and its decoration was reluctantly retained by the King at the Restoration in 1815. Balzac says, in *La Rabouilleuse* (1842), that around 1821–2, 'although government policy had been to discredit the order by unlimited conferment, there were still only 53,000 people in France on whom it had been bestowed' (I. 9) – so that its ethos, as here, was still redolent of Napoleon, who had instituted it in 1802.

6. *at the Château*: At the court of Charles X, which was at the Château de St Cloud as well as in the Tuileries.

7. *M. Appert*: A real person. Benjamin Appert was a famous prison reformer and philanthropist. He figures, in a would-be merciful capacity, in one of Stendhal's 'sources', the reports of the trial and execution of Antoine Berthet.

8. *Stendhal's note*: 'An actual remark'.

CHAPTER 3

The Welfare of the Poor

1. *Fleury*: The Abbé (Claude) Fleury (1640–1725) was confessor to Louis XV, and the author of a great *Ecclesiastical History* (1721) which denied extreme papal claims. This is relevant to the following chapter, in that the aged Curé Chélan would have been in this – Gallican – tradition, and therefore vulnerable to younger priests like Maslon, who would be advocates of the fashionable new version of the Ultramontane doctrine, stressing papal authority.

2. Buonaparté's *campaigns . . . voted* no *to the Empire at that time*: *Buonaparté* is a version of the Corsican/Italian spelling of Napoleon's name, used insultingly by political opponents. The Mayor also implies that the Surgeon is one of a tiny minority of died-in-the-wool republicans who had been against the assumption of the imperial title which gave First Consul Bonaparte *some* respectability in monarchist eyes.

3. *écus*: often translated as crowns: worth either three or six francs each.

4. *M. le Duc d'Orléans . . . Mme de Montesson, the famous Mme de Genlis, and M. Ducrest, the force behind the Palais-Royal*: One interesting point about these personages in the present context is that they were all members of the Orléans family (and thus faction), the then head of which, Louis-Philippe, became king in 1830. Perhaps it is ironic that M. de Rênal, an Ultra of the Bourbon persuasion, should honour them so richly in memory.

The Duke of Orléans (1747–93) was an anglophile and the rakish friend of the Prince of Wales (later George IV), who, perhaps in the hope of himself being made a constitutional monarch, proclaimed himself a liberal ('Philippe Égalité'), courted the people with his lavishness, voted for the death of his cousin Louis XVI, and was subsequently himself guillotined.

Mme de Montesson was the lady whom Orléans had secretly married; Mme de Genlis was her niece, a celebrated lady of letters of the *ancien régime*, who supervised the education of the future King Louis-Philippe; and M. Ducrest was her nephew, who transformed the gardens of the Orléans palace in Paris, the Palais-Royal. The palace was already open to the public, but Ducrest conceived and oversaw the addition of what quickly became famous galleries and arcades of smart and lively shops, cafés, bagnios, etc.

CHAPTER 4

Father and Son

1. *E sarà mia colpa/ Se cosi è?*: 'And is it my fault/ that this is so?' Probably not word for word Machiavelli; but Stendhal had admired the playwright and political thinker since his youth, and often quotes or alludes to him. Machiavelli seems to have been particularly attractive to Stendhal's generation in France.

2. *animal*: Abuse from Père Sorel, of course, but it is amusing to note that 'Animal' is one of the approximately 350 aliases Henri Beyle toyed with in his lifetime, and even published under.

3. *Memorial of St Helena*: The *Mémorial de Sainte-Hélène* (1824). This, more usually translated as *The St Helena Chronicle*, sometimes as *Life and Conversations of Napoleon*, is a very extensive and circumstantial record of the experiences and conversation (1815–16) of the deposed Emperor on board ship and at his final place of refuge.

In itself a testimony to the Emperor's capacity to produce the ethos of a fanatical personal devotion, the book was the work of Napoleon's secretary, Comte Emmanuel de Las Cases (1766–1842), formerly a royalist naval officer, then an *émigré* (i.e. an aristocrat fleeing abroad from the Revolution), and the author of an *Historical Atlas*. Las Cases became a kind of Boswell, and his book the Emperor's *apologia*. It is exceedingly rhetorical and partisan; sometimes paranoid and often bumptious; full of special pleading verging on the humbug. Nevertheless its eight volumes, packed with narrative, anecdote and testimonials to the Emperor's magnanimity, genius and humanity, and full of his wisdom about the state and the world, are highly persuasive. The portrait is of a magnetic man of power who is also dignified in adversity, considerate and gentlemanly, serious and witty. Alfred de Vigny, in *Servitude and Grandeur of Arms* (1835), talks of 'fashioning a personality fit to realize the best philosophical models'. And in a reversal of the Emperor's own famous remark that history is written by the victors, the work is famous as 'the keystone of the Napoleonic legend'.

Stendhal treasured his copy of the *Mémorial*, and more than once worked on his own sketches of a life of Napoleon. But, needless to say, he had a very much more complex and ambivalent attitude to his subject. (See, for example, Geoffrey Strickland, *Stendhal: The Education of a Novelist* (Cambridge: Cambridge University Press, 1974), chapter 4.) Though he had served the Emperor well as an administrator, he had been especially dismayed by the transition from republic to empire and the reconstitution of a court. 'In his fiction . . .', says Robert Alter, 'he would engage the Napoleonic phenomenon . . . with a peculiar and forceful conjunction of acute judgement and impassioned sympathy' (London: Allen & Unwin, 1979).

4. *varieties of human physiognomy*: 'physionomie' was a favourite word with Stendhal (and, much more emphatically, Balzac), referring as it does to the late eighteenth-century semi-science of reading the mind's complexion in the face, most famously elaborated by the Swiss intellectual (and, according to Napoleon, 'egregious charlatan') J. K. Lavater (1741–1801) in his *The Art of Knowing Men by Their Physiognomy* (1775).

CHAPTER 5

A Negotiation

1. Cunctando restituit rem – *Ennius*: 'By delaying he restored things' (i.e. the Roman republic). This a phrase quoted by Cato the Elder from the now largely lost works of his friend the epic poet Ennius in praise of the Roman dictator Q. Fabius Maximus's long-drawn-out strategy, in 217 BC, of shadowing Hannibal but not giving battle, which gave Rome time to recover from the terrible defeat at lake Trasimene. After the abandonment of these tactics was followed by the even more shattering defeat at Cannae in 216, they were resumed.

2. *Rousseau's* Confessions: the Swiss-born Jean-Jacques Rousseau (1712–78), the most worshipped and the most despised of Enlightenment philosophers, also a musician, playwright, composer of operas and eloquent novelist, was a father of the theory and psychology of revolution and Romanticism, if sometimes a paranoid and ambivalent one. In *The Social Contract* (1762), he attacked private property and thus the foundations of civil society. It was he who coined the phrase 'Liberty, Equality, Fraternity'; he also stressed the innate virtue of natural Man – Man, now in chains, who must be forced to be free. He was almost deified by the French Revolution – his bust, carved from the stones of the Bastille, was carried in pomp by a procession of soldiers and maidens. He is still a power.

NOTES

In the *Confessions*, published posthumously but much publicized before his death, Rousseau winningly set out to invent a new mode of autobiography in which the whole man – deviousness, faults and all – would be set forth. It is a minute account of a life and character written in an age before 'personality' was taken for granted. He brings out for the first time all the things that since have become the commonplaces of a personal account – for example, that happiness can be felt but not described, etc. With a kind of nervous boldness, he confesses to petty theft, masturbation and all kinds of humiliating failure. Opinions vary as to the true frankness of some confessions: often he protests far too much, in canting tones, to be believed, even by the impressionable; but their intermittent charm is enormous, insidious, and their influence, as here, very great.

One of Rousseau's emphases is on the tender happiness and freedom of his own early childhood, until this was intruded upon by a drastic sense of the injustice of a particular punishment.

Among numerous other aspects and nuances of the *Confessions*, episodes in Book 3 in which the young Rousseau finds himself uneasily between stairs in a noble household perhaps suggest aspects of *The Red and the Black*. The specific repugnance remarked here is shown in a scene in Book VII, when, fresh from the provinces in 1742, Rousseau was trying to interest aristocratic Parisian ladies in his invention of a numerical scheme of musical notation.

We learn in I. 24 here that Julien later also reads at least parts of *La Nouvelle Héloïse*; this is Rousseau's amazingly popular and influential epistolary novel of love, the family and the natural perfectibility of the sentiments of Man, published in 1761.

3. *M. de Maistre's book* Du Pape: Joseph Marie, Comte de Maistre (1753–1821) was the Savoyard diplomat and philosopher, the very antithesis of Rousseau, who became the representative of the king of Sardinia in Russia, and whose most famous work is *Les Soirées de Saint Pétersbourg*. *Du Pape* was published in 1819. It is Ultramontanist, i.e. supports papal absolutism.

Maistre was a genuine reactionary (and therefore a very interesting figure): he was savagely hostile to all enlightenment, all liberal or democratic thought, and a propagandist for extreme, drastic autocracy and the Divine Right of kings. The 'Voltaire of reaction', according to Isaiah Berlin. In spite of – or perhaps because of – the destructive brilliance of his writing, Maistre was considered an ogre by liberals, but even the moderate royalist Alfred de Vigny attacked him memorably and quite fiercely in his *Servitude and Grandeur of Arms* (1835).

NOTES

4. *the bridge at Lodi, of Arcoli and of Rivoli*: Spectacular victories (1796–7) of the young Bonaparte over the Austrians in northern Italy.

5. *Justice of the Peace . . . spy for the Congregation*: A French Justice of the Peace was not, as in England, an unpaid local worthy, but a salaried professional.

Congregations generally are societies of Roman Catholic enthusiasts, clergy and laity; but in this particular usage, in the murky politics of post-Restoration France, a powerful, manipulative, secret, Ultramontanist and Jesuit-inspired network is implied. For a complementary and confirmatory account of the dark and complex workings of a congregation in provincial France – where petty events and feelings produce dire consequences – see Balzac's brilliant *novella* 'The Abbé Birotteau' (1832).

6. *(Le) Constitutionnel*: A newspaper that provided the liberal forum from 1815.

7. *Mme de Beauharnais*: The glittering widow Josephine, whom Napoleon persuaded to marry him in 1796. Crowned empress in 1804, she was divorced by Napoleon in 1809 for reasons of state (getting an heir, the Austrian alliance), but lived on in dignity and charm at Malmaison until 1814.

CHAPTER 6

Ennui

1. *Non so più . . . facio – Mozart*, Figaro: 'I no longer know what I am/ Or what I'm doing'; from Cherubino's aria in act I, scene v of Stendhal's favourite opera.

CHAPTER 7

Elective Affinities

1. *Elective Affinities*: An allusion to *Die Wahlverwandtschaften* (1809) (translated into French as *Les Affinités électives*), Goethe's fictional experiment in which he – with characteristic universalizing intent – seeks to apply the structures and imperatives of chemistry and the cultivation of an estate to human relations. The happy marriage of two wealthy amateurs is disturbed by the coming of two alien factors into their dignified but dilettante existence – an old friend and a young niece, with whom they develop more or less deterministic affinities. It was widely considered an immoral book at the time, but it interested Stendhal. In turn, Goethe admired *The Red and the Black*.

2. *Sacred Heart of Jesus*: Marguerite Marie Alacoque (1647–90, canonized 1920), a French nun of the Visitation Order, was the founder of the devotion of the Sacred Heart of Jesus; it was very popular with the Jesuits and the Congregation after 1815.

3. *Gymnase*: A theatre for comic opera and vaudeville in Paris, opened in 1810, and also know as the *Théâtre de Madame*.

4. *the late Prince de Condé . . . Besenval's* Memoirs: Besenval, a Swiss officer in the French service, published his book of recollections in 1805, and it was regarded by Stendhal as a fine source for customs under the Ancien Régime. The Prince de Condé is probably not the seventeenth-century soldier hero *le Grand Condé*, but much more likely his descendant, who led a counter-revolutionary army in 1792.

5. *La Quotidienne*: An ultra royalist newspaper, founded in 1792.

6. *mezzo termine*: Compromise.

CHAPTER 8

Minor Events

1. *Don Juan*: Lord Byron's comical, satiric and romantic epic (1819–24).

2. *Gabrielle*: Gabrielle de Vergy is the heroine of a complicated thirteenth-century tale, extant in several versions. The core of it is that the Chatelaine Gabrielle's chivalric lover is, Jacob-like, solicited by the Duchess of Burgundy and then forced to reveal his true love after a false accusation of rape by the Duchess. Gabrielle, hearing of this revelation, dies of grief (or suicide), at which her lover kills himself over her body. In later versions of the tale (referred to in I.21, below, and a melodramatic stage version of which Stendhal had seen) the lover dies first and the jealous husband feeds her, unknowing, his heart.

3. *M. Godart's fine work*: J.-B. Godart, *The Natural History of Butterflies in France* (c.1823).

4. *the object of his rapture*: i.e., the *Memorials of St Helena*.

CHAPTER 9

A Rural Evening

1. *M. Guérin's Dido ... Strombeck*: The German artist Baron Strombeck became a friend of Stendhal from 1806.

Guérin's painting of the Queen of Carthage (1817) shows her reclining on her day throne fondling a child. Her sister Anna stands behind her and they are listening entranced to the story of the heroic Aeneas, who sits in front of them wearing a plumed helmet.

2. *Charles the Bold*: The last of the mighty Valois dukes of Burgundy, killed at Nancy in 1477. Otherwise known as Charles the Rash (Téméraire).

3. *Robespierres*: Citizen Maximilien Robespierre (1758–94), the green-eyed, fanatical, sometimes hysterical worshipper of Reason and the Supreme Being who – coming from the provinces – presided over the murderous excesses of the Terror and was himself consumed by it, had, of course, become the last word in revolutionary frightfulness. (Revisionist commentators, from Napoleon himself downwards, have, however, argued that Robespierre was of a scrupulous disposition and not keen to shed blood.)

CHAPTER 12

A Journey

1. *Siéyès*: The shrewd Abbé Siéyès (1748–1836) went from being a vicar-general of the Church to becoming a leading republican theorist and somewhat ambivalent exponent of the rights of man; at the centre of political life and intrigue in the 1790s, he was in the Directorate and, briefly, in 1799, a consul under Bonaparte; after he resigned, he was made a count. He is therefore the adventurous kind of authority Stendhal like to cite, although the scholarly consensus is, again, that Stendhal probably produced this epigram himself.

2. *Like Hercules*: This sounds also – indeed, more – like the choice of Achilles: between a long and prosperous life and an early death conferring immortal glory.

CHAPTER 13

Open Work Stockings

1. *Saint-Réal*: Abbé de Saint-Réal (1639–92) was a historian who in *The Uses of History* (1671) offers the sentiment (not unusual since Herodotus) that history holds up an image to our vices. This is possibly the reason for Stendhal's otherwise random and unlikely attribution of this remark to him. But the remark itself has been material for much earnest comment on realism (even réal-ism) and Stendhal's 'aesthetic'. Many readers will find difficulties in reconciling so simple and so apparently casual a way of defending his possibly provoking material, with the complex, highly selective and defined vision of *The Red and the Black* itself.

CHAPTER 14

English Scissors

1. *Polidori*: Dr William Polidori was the doctor and adventurer who accompanied Byron on his travels. Stendhal had met them in Milan in 1816.
2. *Love . . . seeks them not*: These lines are actually not from Corneille but from another seventeenth-century dramatist, Jean Rotrou, in his *Venceslas* (1647). But the attribution to Corneille of lines that impressed him would perhaps be natural in the reader of the *Memorial of St Helena*, where Napoleon is recorded as saying: 'Tragedy fires the soul, elevates the heart, and is calculated to generate heroes. Considered under this point of view, perhaps, France owes to Corneille a part of her great actions; and, gentlemen, *had he lived in my time, I would have made him a Prince*' (vol. II, p. 250).

CHAPTER 15

The Cockcrow

1. *Blason D'Amour*: This blazon of love, or heraldic riddle, is a piece of medieval French moralizing, heavily stressed by rhyming at each line. Literally:

Love in Latin is *amor*;
From which love comes death,
Forerun by care which gnaws,
Sorrow, tears, deceit, sin, remorse.

CHAPTER 16

The Following Day

1. *Don Juan*, canto 1, stanza 170: Slightly misquoted (there are no elisions, and there is no comma), possibly to suit the French ear.

CHAPTER 17

The First Deputy

1. *the Chamber*: the Chamber of Deputies was the lower house in the *Parlement* under the charter granted at the Restoration in 1814. Its members were appointed by an electoral college, itself elected by the more prosperous or substantial subjects of the King.
2. *battle of Fontenoy*: (1745) The classic battle of eighteenth-century formal confrontation and manoeuvre, in which the French (with some Irish regiments, the legendary 'wild geese') defeated the British and Dutch.
3. *familiar forms of address*: Using *tu* instead of *vous*; like the older English distinction between 'thou' and 'you'. The *salutary institutions*, where such familiarities were permitted, were organized by the Congregation to promote amity between social classes. This, of course, was suspect to the left.
4. *Richelieu*: Most likely (as Roger Pearson says in his detailed discussion of the novel in *Stendhal's Violin* (Oxford: Clarendon Press, 1988)) the great seventeenth-century cardinal (1585–1642), aggrandizer and virtual ruler of France under Louis XIII; the subtle and ruthless creator of the absolutist state. But also quite possibly, with somewhat bathetic effect in context, the Duc de Richelieu (1766–1822), a libertine and wit who twice became Louis XVIII's first minister (see also n. 7 to II. 22).

CHAPTER 18

A King at Verrières

1. *Jansenist*: Jansenists, followers of the Dutch theologian Cornelius Jansen (1585–1638) flourished especially in the seventeenth century, and were a powerful party in the French Church and hence in politics. They originated in enmity to the Jesuits. Their austere Augustinian doctrines stress predestination and salvation by grace alone, and from the outside they look very much like Calvinists. Hence M. Maslon is crying something like: 'A Puritan!' Commentators agree that Stendhal tends to exaggerate the powers of both Jansenists and Jesuits, as organizations at any rate, in the early nineteenth-century state.

2. *at Leipzig and at Montmirail*: Leipzig (1813), the 'battle of the Nations', was a hugely expensive conflict in which Napoleon was eventually defeated by the vastly superior forces of the allies (Austria, Prussia and Russia). It was probably the largest battle fought up until that time. Montmirail was one of a series of cunning lesser victories Napoleon inflicted on the invading allies the following year – this time the Prussians under Blücher.

3. *Duke Charles the Bold*: Charles le Téméraire (1433–77), the last great Duke of Burgundy, presided over one of the great courts of medieval Europe, a centre of learning with a magnificent library which patronized modern poets and writers, and encouraged translations of classical Greek and Latin texts. He died in battle against the French.

4. *sky-blue riband*: The riband of the Order of the Holy Spirit – an extremely exclusive order with only a hundred members. It was founded in 1578 by Henri III (the instigator of the terrible St Bartholomew's Day massacres of Protestants in 1572) and so has strong Counter-reformation, and therefore also Restoration, connotations.

5. *chapelle ardente*: A funeral arrangement of candles round a coffin.

6. *Philip the Good . . . graceful figure of wax*: Philip the Good was Charles the Bold's father, and under them and their immediate predecessors the Duchy of Burgundy ran right through the centre of Europe, from the Netherlands to Switzerland. Their court was more than royal.

It is plausible that such fifteenth-century magnates would revere extravagant pious effigies, though the historical St Clement was not a soldier but a first-century pope.

CHAPTER 19

Thought Brings Suffering

1. *Barnave*: Antoine Barnave (1761–93) was a politician and supporter of the monarchy executed during the revolutionary Terror.

2. *1793 of execrable memory*: 1793 was the year of the Terror in France. The National Guard in Lyons revolted against it, and took reprisals against the Jacobins, killing 200 or so. Hence the siege of Lyons.

CHAPTER 20

Anonymous Letters

1. *Guardate alla pagina 130*: Look at page 130.

CHAPTER 21

Dialogue with a Master

1. *in 1816 you helped with certain arrests*: This is an allusion to a Bonapartist and liberal conspiracy in Grenoble in that year.

CHAPTER 22

Modes of Behaviour in 1830

1. *R(évérend) P(ère) Malagrida*: An Italian Jesuit who returned from thirty years as a missionary in Brazil to help the victims of the great earthquake in Lisbon in 1756, but in 1761 was burnt at the stake by the Inquisition for alleged treason. The remark about language is widely attributed to Talleyrand.

2. *What it is to be a priest*: Apparently the tone of this would have sounded lightly satirical to an 1830s reader, being an allusion to a much-quoted remark of the celebrated liberal clerical reformer, the Abbé Lammenais.

3. acculturate . . . *King Philip*: Stendhal seems to have considered the word

used (*éduquer*) to be pretentious – though he was quite content with *éducation* elsewhere – so a literal translation won't do.

Some modern scholars conjecture that the King Philip in question must be Alexander the Great's father, who, of course, employed Aristotle as a tutor.

4. *last mission*: Catholic propaganda exercise.

5. *Ligorio*: Alfonso Liguori was an eighteenth-century theologian with strong anti-Jansenist views. He was later canonized.

6. *La Fontaine . . . Messire Jean Chouart*: The great seventeenth-century fabulist is, of course, part of traditional French education. The Chouart fable – *The Curé and the Corpse* is about a priest who is speculating on the worldly pleasures to be bought and enjoyed from the profits of the funeral he is about to conduct when he collides with the coffin and ends up sharing the grave.

7. *Gros*: L.-G. Gros (1765–1812) was a real person, a mathematician who had taught the young Stendhal; he was a liberal and a Jansenist.

8. *Crow . . . fox*: Julien is using La Fontaine for his lesson (*The Crow and the Fox* in *Fables choisies* (1668).

9. *chophouse . . . conventional modern delicacy pronounces with such relish*: Because eating at a workaday restaurant would be thought of as a form of slumming it.

CHAPTER 23

The Frustrations of a Public Servant

1. *. . . of a Public Servant*: This varies from the contents page, where it is *. . . of High Places*.

2. *CASTI*: 'The pleasure of holding one's head up high for the whole year is well and truly paid for by certain quarters of an hour which one must endure.' The Abbé Casti was an eighteenth-century Italian moralist and storywriter.

3. *the Charter*: the Bourbon Charter, the Constitution of 1814, could be seen as giving substantial power to local men of substance – as here.

4. *Ladyes alle . . . mad is hee*: Like many Renaissance potentates (e.g. his contemporary, Henry VIII of England) Francis I of France had, or was supposed to have, a literary side. It was part of being a prince. These particular lines attributed to him,

Souvent femme varie
Bien fol qui s'y fie

follow a well-worn literary convention and have become almost proverbial. They have come to the notice of the modern reader through Victor Hugo's incorporation of them – just after this novel – into his play *Le Roi s'amuse* (1832), and their consequent transmutation into Verdi's *Rigoletto* (see the aria 'La Donna è mobile').

5. *M'sieur Noinety-Foive*: M. *Nonante-cinq* – nickname for a reactionary provincial magistrate. It had its origin in a real person, a M. Mérindol of Marseilles, as satirized by the pamphleteer Barthélemy; but signifies something like a cross between Fielding's Squire Western and Dickens's Mr Bumble. There is in particular, of course, the implication of financial chicanery under pressure from the Church.

6. *carta canta*: This paper sings of it.

7. *stramonium*: A then fashionable tonic that acts on the nervous system.

CHAPTER 24

A Capital

1. *siege of 1674*: In that year Besançon, then under Spanish occupation, was besieged by Louis XIV.

2. *Bisontium*: i.e. Besançon (Latin: *Vesontio*). The adjective Bisontine seems to have come to suggest extreme provinciality to Stendhal (see also I, 28).

3. *phrases from* . . . La Nouvelle Héloïse: Rousseau's famous epistolary novel of 1761 is rich in the rhetoric of as yet unconsummated love:

Oh my Julie . . . would that I could spend my days with you in these unknown places, fortunate in our happiness and unbeknownst to the world! Would that I could here collect my whole soul in you alone and become in turn the universe to you! Then your adored charms would enjoy the homage they deserve! Then our hearts would forever savour the delights of love! A long and sweet intoxication would allow us to forget the passing of time . . . (Part 1, letter 23, trans. Judith H. McDowell)

– and so on. Later there are more physical passages. (This language sounds, of course, very much less strained in its context.)

CHAPTER 25

The Seminary

1. *Intelligenti pauca*: Few words are enough for those who understand.

2. *Bossuet, and Arnault, and Fleury*: Bossuet, Bishop of Meaux, was the great preacher at Louis XIV's Court, and a prominent Gallican; Arnault was a leading seventeenth-century Jansenist theologian from the Jansenist headquarters at the monastery of Port-Royal; and Fleury was the ecclesiastical historian whose words are used in the epigraph to chapter 3 above. All, in short, authorities counter to the Congregation and the pro-Papal, Jesuit tendencies associated in this novel with the Abbé Maslon, M. de Frilair, etc.

3. *Vale et me ama*: Farewell and grant me your love.

4. *so many faults ... crimes*: c.f. Alfred de Vigny, Stendhal's younger contemporary, in defence of honour:

This strange, proud virtue is animated by a mysterious vitality, and it stands erect in the midst of all our vices, blending so well with them that it is fed by their energy. (1835)

5. *the Bull* Unam Ecclesiam *of St Pius V*: 'One Church'; Pius V was one of those fierce Counter-reformation popes (1566–72) who might well have promulgated a bull on Church discipline. He was the pope who excommunicated Elizabeth I of England and inspired the campaign against the Turks which resulted in the famous naval victory of Lepanto in 1571. But Stendhal appears to have invented this particular bull; its name might have been suggested by Boniface VIII's *Unam Sanctam* of 1302, which was the highwater mark of papal claims to supremacy over the world.

CHAPTER 26

The World, or What the Rich Don't Have

1. *Young*: An attribution to Edward Young (1683–1765), the English clergyman, poet and moralist and author of the meditative *Night Thoughts* (1742–5). It is in French in the original, and probably written by Stendhal.

2. *a sergeant*: In his edition, P.-G. Castex convincingly comments that the original French *sergent* – would not have meant an NCO, but something like a 'Sergeant-Major General', associated with the High Command.

3. *Siéyès or Grégoire*: For Sieyès, see n. to I. 12. Abbé Grégoire (1750–1831) was Bishop of Blois and became a prominent member of the Convention in the Revolution. He was a sternly Christian theorist of democracy.

4. *Sixtus the Fifth . . . energy and arrogance*: Felice Peretti (1521–90) was a reforming Franciscan preacher and theologian who, on becoming a cardinal in 1570, pretended modest debility so successfully that he was elected as an interim pope in 1585. He then displayed notable energy and reforming zeal.

5. *Abbé Delille*: Jacques Delille (1738–1813), poet and translator of Virgil, who may have given this anecdote to Stendhal personally. He became the epitome of the conventional versifier – the aphorist Chamfort described him as 'a verse mill'.

6. To this Stendhal added his own note: 'See, in the Museum of the Louvre, No. 1130, Francis, Duke of Aquitaine taking off his breastplate and assuming a monk's habit.'

CHAPTER 27

First Experience of Life

1. *DIDEROT*: This quote is not from Denis Diderot (1713–84), the Enlightenment philosopher and novelist whose sceptical playfulness Stendhal much admired – and liked the idea of in this context, no doubt – but is adapted from a memory of Voltaire's mock-heroic epic about Joan of Arc, *La Pucelle d'Orlèans* (1755).

CHAPTER 28

A Procession

1. *arms drill*: There was an anti-ecclesiastical tradition, at least as old as Voltaire, but semi-seriously subscribed to by Stendhal also, that seminaries, Jesuits in particular, trained their pupils in the use of arms in case of insurrections in France.

2. *Incedo per ignes . . . hidden enemies*: This line from Horace means literally, 'I go on through flames.'

3. *Barême*: Celebrated seventeenth-century mathematician who also produced a popular handbook on accounting.

CHAPTER 29

The First Promotion

1. *The Precursor*: *Le Précurseur* was a liberal newspaper published in Lyon.
2. *that* other's *day*: i.e. Napoleon's.
3. . . . *cherished by the people*: This line was inscribed on Henry IV's statue in Paris. It is from Gudin de la Brenellerie's *Eulogy* on Voltaire, and alludes to the latter's *Henriade* (1723).
4. *Benjamin*: i.e. favourite son, after Jacob's last born in the Old Testament.
5. *the Emigration*: Many of the aristocrats who fled the disappropriations of the Revolution and the Terror found themselves poor exiles.
6. *young woman . . . 'Mary Magdalene'*: This refers, possibly sardonically, to the poetess Delphine Gay (1804–55) whose custom was to recite her poems in salons.

CHAPTER 30

An Ambitious Man

1. *Edinburgh Review*: Stendhal greatly admired this famous quarterly magazine, but almost certainly wrote this opinion (in French in the text) himself.
2. *a certain ministry*: An allusion to a movement to appoint an administration of Ultras in early 1828.
3. *in pace*: Latin 'in peace' – referring to the idea that under this euphemism troublesome monks were condemned to punitive or even lethal solitary confinement. *Vade in pace* is the traditional formula used when locking up a prisoner for life.

BOOK TWO

1. *Sainte-Beuve*: The attribution of this favourite paradoxical juxtaposition (see I. 14 and 15) to the writer and, later, famous critic Charles-Augustin Sainte-Beuve (1804–69) seems unlikely. In 1854 Sainte-Beuve wrote one of the first critical reviews of Stendhal's literary career.

CHAPTER THE FIRST

The Pleasures of the Countryside

1. *Virgil*: 'O countryside, when shall I see thee again!' Sounds like the *Georgics*, perhaps, but is actually a mock-serious speech by a city miser from Horace's *Satires*.
2. *Mirabeau got for himself*: Honoré Gabriel Riqueti, Comte de Mirabeau (1749–91) was the reformed libertine aristocrat and political prisoner whose audacity and eloquence in advocating constitutional monarchy dominated the National Assembly of the Third Estate at the beginning of the Revolution. He was a towering and prodigious figure, and, as is hinted, his mediation between the Throne and the Revolution also re-made his fortune.
3. *further back*: Castex points out that this sentence is a quotation from Racine's tragedy *Phèdre* (1677).
4. *Roule*: The church of St Philip de Roule is in the centre of Paris.
5. *Malmaison*: The palace especially associated with Napoleon and Josephine.
6. *Moreri*: A late seventeenth-century historical/biographical dictionary.
7. *Adsum qui feci*: 'Here I am who did it', Virgil, *Aeneid*.
8. *Dubois*: Guillaume Dubois (1656–1723), an apothecary's son, rose to become an all-powerful minister in the Regency of the Duc d'Orléans. He is said to have shared in his master's debaucheries.

CHAPTER 2

Entry into the World

1. *Kant*: It is more than usually unlikely that the lofty and austere transcendental philosopher Immanuel Kant (1724–1804) wrote this. Stendhal was sceptical about the enthusiasm in Paris for Kant's philosophy, and awards him the authorship of what seems a delicate piece of self-parody.

2. *nil mirari . . .*: Strictly *nil admirari* – 'Never enthuse over things' – advice from Horace's *Epistles*.

3. *cemetery of Père-Lachaise . . . Marshal Ney . . . denied . . . an epitaph*: At that time the famous cemetery of Père-Lachaise, opened in 1804, was a fairly popular place to walk.

On Napoleon's return from Elba, Ney had promised to bring him to Louis XVIII in a cage. Instead, he rejoined him and fought with valiant futility at Waterloo. It was one of the scandals and grievances of the time that so famous a soldier was then court-martialled, shot and buried in relative obscurity.

CHAPTER 3

First Steps

1. *Poemi dell av. Reina*: 'Poem by Reina, the lawyer' – Francesco Reina (1772–1826) was a Milanese lawyer and man of letters known and liked by Stendhal.

2. *Place Louis XVI*: Now the Place de la Concorde.

CHAPTER 4

The Hôtel de La Mole

1. *Ronsard*: Pierre de Ronsard (1524–85), the celebrated poet of the Pléiade school, a loose grouping of poets inspired by humanist ideals and classical and Italian models. The quotation, though, was made up by Stendhal.

2. *which offers resistance*: Attributed to Talleyrand (see n. 6 below).

3. *new colleagues*: This supposedly refers to new elevations to the peerage

by Charles X in the late 1820s. In France not every nobleman was a peer.

4. *Béranger*: Pierre-Jean de Béranger (1780–1857) was a liberal patriotic poet and song writer.

5. *La Quotidienne . . . Gazette de France*: Ultra newspapers of slightly differing tendencies.

6. *the Abbé de Pradt and MM. de Talleyrand and Pozzo di Borgo*: All three were at the Congress of Vienna in 1815.

The Abbé de Pradt (1759–1837) was Napoleon's chaplain and unsuccessful ambassador in Warsaw, who reverted to Royalist views in 1814.

Charles-Maurice de Talleyrand (1754–1838), Prince of Benevento, etc., on the surface a bland and cynical aristocrat, wit and libertine, was one of the most talented survivors in history. A young abbot and Bishop of Autun just prior to the Revolution, he became President of the Assembly, a financial and educational reformer, and the disposer of the Church lands to the State; then an émigré to England and America; then foreign minister to the Directory; then Napoleon's right hand in foreign affairs; then, from around 1806, he became disaffected with the Emperor's seemingly insatiable policy of expansion; then, as mentioned here, he became Louis XVIII's foreign minister; then, briefly, his first minister; then, again disaffected, he became a prime mover in the unseating of the Bourbons in favour of Louis Philippe in 1830. Some people think that Comte Chalvet later in this chapter is meant as a sketch of him; others point to his consistent self-enrichment and like to repeat what Napoleon once called him, 'a piece of shit in a silk stocking'; others still love him for his astonishing talents, his constant search for peace, his unfanatical liberal-mindedness and his charm.

Carlo Andrea Pozzo di Borgo (1764–1842) was a Corsican diplomat and devoted enemy of Napoleon, latterly in the Russian service.

7. *de Bouillon*: An old French family. Amusement at his name would be much like amusement at the title of the Earl of Sandwich in England.

8. *like Basilio*: An allusion to *The Marriage of Figaro* (1784) by Beaumarchais (though the phrase is actually used by the character Bartolo). Beaumarchais was generally considered as having a subversive point of view – Napoleon went so far as to say that *Figaro* was 'the Revolution in action'.

9. *M. Comte*: A conjuror and magician.

10. *greatest poet of the day*: A liberal description of Béranger, who in 1828 had been sentenced to a fine of 10,000 francs and nine months in prison for sedition.

11. *M. de Nerval*: A figure in this novel for an Ultra minister, normally taken to be based on the Prince de Polignac.

12. *body of this ancient corruption*: Perhaps a version of St Paul's 'Who shall deliver me from the body of this death?' (Romans 3.24).

13. *Lord Holland*: The famous Whig magnate who had been relatively favourable to the Revolution and to Napoleon.

14. *new king of England*: William IV succeeded his brother George IV in June 1830.

15. *d'Alembert*: Jean d'Alembert (1717–83) was an Enlightenment mathematician and *philosophe*, therefore a subversive.

16. *de Thaler*: A Thaler was a German coin. This is a reference to the Rothschilds, who had furnished money for Louis XVIII's 1823 invasion of Spain in support of a fellow Bourbon.

CHAPTER 5

Sensitivity, and a Pious Lady

1. *Faublas*: Faublas is the hero of Louvet de Couvret's *The Loves of Chevalier Faublas* (1787–90). But this epigraph is actually Stendhal's restatement of a theme from the previous chapter.

CHAPTER 6

A Matter of Pronunciation

1. *Gratius*: Probably a misspelling of Grotius, the seventeenth-century legal theorist and exponent of the law of nations; but probably, also, written by Stendhal.

2. *Le Comte Ory*: Opera by Gioacchino Antonio Rossini (1792–1868). It was given its premiere in Paris in 1828, and was splendidly restaged in 1830.

CHAPTER 7

An Attack of Gout

1. *Bertoletti*: A Piedmontese journalist, and an acquaintance of Stendhal.

2. *Rivarol*: Antoine Rivarol (1753–1801) was a celebrated exquisite and wit of the *ancien régime*. His presence in the German merchant city of Hamburg is quite often taken as an extraordinary piece of incongruity by writers of this time.

3. *Marquis de Moncade . . . M. Poisson*: Characters in *L'École des bourgeois* by Soulas d'Allainval (1728), a popular comedy that was still often produced in the early nineteenth century.

4. *Sir Hudson Lowe . . . Bathurst*: The villains of the *Memorial of St Helena*. Lord Bathurst appointed Lowe as governor of St Helena in 1816. The truth of the details and motivation of their treatment of Napoleon remains controversial.

5. *the opposite of what is expected of you*: This, and what follows, compares interestingly with what Jules Barbey D'Aurevilly has to say in his famous work about Beau Brummel, *Dandyism* (1844):

the most general characteristic . . . of Dandyism, is always to produce the unexpected, that which could not be logically anticipated by those accustomed to the yoke of rules . . . eccentricity is unbridled, wild and blind . . . Dandyism on the contrary, while still respecting the conventions, plays with them.

6. *Philip Vane*: An invented personage, possibly based on the radical journalist Richard Carlile, a disciple of Tom Paine and Francis Place who had spent a (much shorter) stretch in Dorchester prison because of his campaigns for free speech, and was a strident libertarian and atheist, later advocating sexual freedom and contraception, etc.

CHAPTER 8

What Decoration Confers Distinction?

1. *Pellico*: Silvio Pellico (1788–1854) was a tragic poet and prominent liberal who had been imprisoned by the Austrians in the dreaded prison fortress of the Speilberg. Stendhal had known him in Milan.

2. *Coulon*: The brothers Coulon were celebrated dancing masters.

3. *A mere name*: Rousseau, like Julien, could have been thought of as a lackey in a great household.

4. *Duc de Luxembourg at Montmorency . . . on the way to Paris*: An incident in Book X of Rousseau's *Confessions* (1782–9).

5. *King Feretrius*: A famous howler. In 1823 a would-be scholarly journalist – who was an Ultra and therefore a target for the liberals – had misread this obscure word in an ancient Latin text (actually ascribing an attribute to Jupiter) as a proper name, and so discovered a non-person.

6. *utility*: Stendhal had an immense admiration for the *philosophe* Claude Arien Helvetius (1715–71) whose principle of utility so influenced the later English Utilitarians (Bentham, Mill, etc.); though he also thought him a 'chilly being who knew nothing of love, or friendship, or . . . other vital passions'.

7. *Mirabeau had exported there*: Stendhal's note to this is: 'This page, written on the 25th of July 1830, was printed on the 4th of August. (*Editor's Note*).' 25 July 1830 was the date of the four repressive *ordonnances* from Charles X's Council that triggered the Revolution of that year. Stendhal's note may be claiming some kind of prophetic force – but exactly what is unclear.

André Mirabeau (1754–92), Honoré's younger brother who had served in the American War of Independence, may be the Mirabeau being referred to here.

8. *Conradin*: A romantic figure (1252–68), the last of the Hohenstaufen Holy Roman Emperors in Germany, Italy and Sicily, who was executed after being defeated by the royal French adventurer Charles of Anjou.

9. *Madame de Staël*: An energetic, very wealthy and flamboyant progressive intellectual, Germaine de Staël (1766–1817) lived a courageous and colourful life. Her salon in Paris was influential until she fell out with Napoleon; then she gathered a galaxy of talents at Coppet in Switzerland. She knew practically everybody and had many love affairs. Her most famous writings are the two novels *Delphine* and *Corinne*, the pioneering *Reflections on the Relations between Literature and Social Institutions* (1800) and *On Germany* (1807). In the last named she was the first person to use the word 'Romanticism' in the sense it soon came to retain.

CHAPTER 9

The Ball

1. *Useri's Travels*: An invention by Stendhal.

2. *Prince d'Araceli, ambassador from —*: Naples is the obvious place; but the church of Ara Coeli is on the Capitol in Rome.

3. *so has everyone else*: Stendhal's note: 'It is a malcontent who speaks. *Molière's note on* Tartuffe.' The phrase echoes some phrases in the play.

4. *Girondin*: i.e. a moderate revolutionary.

5. *Courier*: Paul-Louis Courier (1772–1825) was a professional soldier and a radical opponent of the Restoration, whom Stendhal knew quite well.

6. *Murat*: Napoleon's great cavalry marshal, eventually King of Naples, was

famous for his courage, dash and display rather than his strategic sense or intellect.

7. *M. Casimir Delavigne's tragedy*, Marino Faliero: In this play of 1829, the liberal element in fourteenth-century Venice, aided by one Israel Bertuccio – 'a humble artisan of the arsenal' – works to overthrow a corrupt oligarchy and make Faliero into the Doge.

8. *Pichegru . . . La Fayette*: Charles Pichegru (1761–1804) was one of the leading revolutionary and directory generals – a 'saviour of the nation' – until he switched sides to the emigrés in 1795.

The Marquis de La Fayette: (1757–1834) was a general and an important reforming politician, a figure of enormous prestige, who fought in the American War of Independence and was the patron and supporter, from a sternly moderate and royalist point of view, of the revolutions of 1789 and of 1830. The latter intervention caused some derision; and not everyone agreed on his qualities. His near-contemporary Talleyrand remarks in his memoirs that 'mediocrities play a part in great events simply because they happen to be there'.

9. *in Spain*: Refers to a revolt suppressed in Catalonia in 1829.

10. *Carnot*: Lazare Nicolas Carnot (1753–1823) was the great organizer and large-scale strategist behind the revolutionary armies, a member of the Directorate, and Napoleon's war minister in 1800. He fell out with Napoleon but came back to organize the armies in 1814. He went into exile at the Restoration.

CHAPTER 10

Queen Marguerite

1. *Letters of a Portuguese Nun*: An anonymous collection of passionate love letters, published in 1669 in French, and purporting to be from a nun betrayed by her lover.

2. *Hernani*: The first night, in February 1830, of Victor Hugo's *Hernani* – a play which deliberately flouted neo-classical rules – was a near riot and a set piece confrontation between Romantic and neo-classical theorizing. Stendhal may have been embarrassed about the play itself.

3. *lettres de cachet*: Letters, granted by the King under the Ancien Régime, which allowed exile or imprisonment upon suspicion. Abolished in 1790.

4. *Talma*: Celebrated neo-classic tragic actor.

5. *Queen Marguerite of Navarre*: Marguerite of Valois (1553–1615) the

glamorous daughter of Henry II, and sister to Francis II, Charles IX, Henry III and the Duc d'Alençon, was married from 1572 until 1594 to the king of Navarre, later the great Henry IV. She was known as *la Reine Margot* and is famous for her elegance, her charm and her writings, particularly her *Memoires*.

6. *Queen Catherine de Medici*: (1519–89) Widow of Henry II, then acting as Regent. This ruthless powerbroker was anxious to prevent a plot to put Alençon on the throne in place of his brother. The principal events here are historical.

7. *the twenty-fourth of August 1572*: The date of the appalling St Bartholomew's Day massacres of Protestants by Catholics throughout France, ordered by Catherine de Medici and Charles IX. The best fictional account of these, and the murky atmosphere preceding them – still horrifying though embedded in a romantic action – can be found in some of the early twentieth-century novels and tales of Stanley J. Weyman, especially *Count Hannibal* (1901).

8. *d'Aubigné's* History *and Brantôme*: Jean d'Aubigné (1552–1630), Henry IV's vice-admiral of Guyenne and Brittany, was an outspoken Protestant poet, satirist and historian of his own time.

Pierre de Brantôme (*c*.1540–1614) was a multi-faceted soldier, courtier and scholar on the Catholic side, whose various *Lives* of his contemporaries constitute one of the period's most vivid literary achievements.

Both tell the story of Boniface de La Mole.

9. *l'Étoile's* Memoirs: Pierre l'Étoile (1546–1611) wrote a journal of life in Paris which includes the reign (1574–89) of Henry III.

10. *Wars of the League*: The Catholic Holy League, dominated by the family of Guise and supported by Spain, was formed in 1584 in response to the threat of a Protestant hegemony led by Henry of Navarre. (It was partly through means of his conversion to Catholicism in 1593 that this prince, having become King Henry IV in 1589, established a more lasting peace in 1598.)

CHAPTER 11

The Tyranny of a Girl

1. *Mérimée*: Prosper Mérimée (1803–70), the author of *Carmen*, etc., was a friend of Stendhal.

2. Wagram: The scene of one of Napoleon's greatest victories, when he

defeated the Austrian army at the village of Wagram, north of Vienna, in July 1809.

3. *Abbé Maury*: Jean-Siffrein Maury (1746–1817) was a celebrated wit, and a ruthless Church careerist who became a bishop and subsequently a cardinal.

4. *Bassompierre*: François de Bassompierre (1579–1646), Henry IV's friend, was a marshal of France and a diplomat who was also a rival of Cardinal Richelieu, famous for his extravagance and his gallantries. He wrote his *Mémoires* while imprisoned in the Bastille.

5. *the Vendée*: The west coast location of the most threatening royalist counter-revolutionary revolts in 1793–6, which were eventually put down with enormous difficulty and an almost genocidal fervour. There was a further Vendéen uprising in 1832, a reaction to the constitutional settlement of 1830, led by the Duchesse de Berri. Indeed, Mathilde's idea here may not be quite so fanciful as it at first sounds: Balzac's narrator in *Les Chouans* (1828) says: 'The involvement of young ladies of noble birth . . . in this war that monarchies were fighting against the spirit of the age was a phenomenon of the times and not one of the least remarkable.'

CHAPTER 12

Will He Be a Danton?

1. *Duc d'Angoulême, natural son of Charles IX*: Charles de Valois (1573–1650), whose mother was Marie Touchet.

2. *Greece or to Africa*: An allusion to the post-Byronic cult of going to the aid of Greek independence; and to the French conquest of North Africa, which was getting under way in 1830 – Algiers fell in July.

3. . . . *nothing but its ghost*: From La Fontaine, *The Shepherd and His Flock*.

4. *their woodlands*: i.e. the Church domains confiscated at the Revolution.

5. *at Coblenz*: This was an important émigré gathering place (where there were the usual reports of loose living, etc.).

CHAPTER 13

A Plot

1. *Schiller*: This is not by the German dramatist and theorist, but seems instead to be a Stendhalian variation, in French, on the theme of Iago's remarks on jealousy in *Othello* III, iii that start 'Trifles light as air . . .'

2. *bogus Memoirs*: There was a short-lived craze for historical memoirs in the late 1820s, inviting exploitation by apocryphal hacks. In Balzac's *The Wild Ass's Skin* (1831–45), set around 1829–30, a literary projector says: 'I'm snowed under with work. I've laid my hands on material for writing some quite curious historical memoirs, but I don't know to whom I can attribute them . . . I have to make haste because memoirs are going out of fashion.'

3. *disinvoltura*: An Italian word for the effect of carefree abandon achieved by elegant persons.

4. *Léontine Fay*: A celebrated actress at the Gymnase theatre.

5. *tabouret*: A folding footstool, the importance of which was that it conferred the right on a duchess to sit down in the presence of the King or Queen at Court.

6. *Granvelle*: Antoine de Granvelle (1517–86) was born in Besançon and became a minister for the Emperor Charles V and his son Philip II of Spain.

7. *in Poissy with MM. Fontan and Magallon*: The editors of a satirical publication, *The Album*, were imprisoned for five years at Poissy in 1824.

8. *the Third Estate*: Julien identifies himself with that class (lawyers, liberal aristocrats, burghers, journalists, ex-priests, etc., etc.) most actively associated with the Revolution.

9. *Colonel Caron at Colmar*: Colonel Caron was executed by firing squad for insurrection in 1822. It was widely held that he had been framed.

10. *a God*: Stendhal's note at this point is *'Esprit per. pré. gui. 11.A.30'* – one of the cryptic notations he seems to have enjoyed, and which scholars have deciphered as a reference to his disappointment at not being given a prefecture by Guizot, the incoming Minister of the Interior after the July Revolution. Thus: *Wit fails. Prefect. Guizot. 11 August 1830*. This was on account, Stendhal believed, of his being too intelligent. We may recall that this Guizot was the celebrated liberal professor of history at the Sorbonne and editor of Shakespeare who later became a first minister of France.

CHAPTER 14

Reflections of a Young Lady

1. *Alfred de Musset*: (1810–57) The Romantic poet, novelist and dramatist who had just published his first book, *Tales from Spain and Italy*, at the age of nineteen.

2. *at Jarnac or Moncontour*: Victories of the armies of the Duc d'Anjou, the future Henri III, over the Protestants in 1569.

3. *at Baylen*: Here, in Andalusia, Napoleonic arms suffered their first major setback when General Dupont wrote out his surrender to a Spanish army in 1808.

4. MYSELF remains to me: A reminiscence of Corneille's *Medea* (1635).

CHAPTER 15

Is It a Plot?

1. *Schiller*: As in the epigraph to II. 13, Schiller's name is put under a Stendhalian pastiche of Shakespeare. It is in French, and is this time based on Brutus's speech in *Julius Caesar*, II, i, starting 'Between the acting of a dreadful thing . . .'

2. *old Don Diego*: A character from *The Cid* (1637) by Corneille.

3. *Gascon*: Gascon gentlemen had a reputation for boastful gallantry and laughing punctilio and alacrity in the code of honour.

4. *Abailard*: Stendhal's spelling of Peter Abelard (1079–1142), the celebrated Nominalist theologian of Paris, author of *Sic Et Non*, whose famous love affair with (and secret marriage to) his pupil, the noble Héloïse, was tragically and brutally ended by her uncle, Canon Fulbert, who cruelly had him castrated. But Héloïse and Abelard survived and, after many further tribulations, he became an abbot and she a prioress, and they were able to make their eloquent correspondence (to which, of course, the title of Rousseau's *La Nouvelle Héloïse* refers) public.

5. *Pharsalia*: Caesar's final battle in 48 BC, against Pompey in their civil war. There is a story that Caesar ordered this tactic as a threat to the aristocratic countenances of his senatorial enemies.

6. *Pallida morte futura*: 'Pale with her impending death' – a description of the tragic Dido in Virgil's *Aeneid*, IV, 643.

CHAPTER 16

One in the Morning

1. *Massinger*: On the back, as it were, of the Romantic enthusiasm for Shakespeare, the names of other English Jacobean dramatists enjoyed prestige at this time. But this passage, in French in the original, is not to be found in Massinger.

2. *addressing him as* tu: This phrase is a translator's addition, the English now unfortunately sounding so old-fashioned (thy, thee, etc.) as to be unusable. (See also I. 30, and for use to servants, n. 3 to I. 17.)

3. *phrases from* La Nouvelle Héloïse: See n. 3 to I. 24.

CHAPTER 17

An Old Sword

1. *Don Juan*, canto XIII: The first stanza of this canto, slightly mispunctuated.

CHAPTER 19

The Opéra Bouffe

1. *Opéra Bouffe*: This was the Italian opera house on the Boulevard des Italiens – a fashionable gathering place, like the Opéra itself.

2. *Shakespeare: Two Gentlemen of Verona*, as in I, 17.

3. *Roland . . . Madame Roland*: Jean-Marie Roland (1734–93) was a Girondin revolutionary, and Minister of the Interior in 1792; he protested against the September massacres and took part in the final power struggle between the Girondins and the Jacobins. His wife, Marie-Jeanne (1754–93) – for whom Stendhal often expressed his admiration – conducted a very celebrated salon, and when imprisoned by the Jacobins prior to her execution in 1793 wrote wonderful letters, as well as her famous *Memoirs* of childhood. When he heard of her death, Roland killed himself with his sword.

4. *Devo punirmi . . . Se troppo amai*: 'I must punish myself, must punish myself/If I've loved too much' – this is not from any known opera; but the

invocation of Cimarosa, one of Stendhal's best-loved composers, clearly
indicates excellence.

5. *a mirror travelling down the road*: The simile in this jaunty, tongue-in-cheek
exposition (which also occurs elsewhere in his works) has often been made
to bear the weight of being taken as an expression of Stendhal's theories of
Realism – even Naturalism – in the novel: this is surprising in view of its
tone, and its position in a text that so clearly depends on a finely tuned, and
most un-mirrorlike, artistic selectiveness.

CHAPTER 20

The Japanese Vase

1. *Jean-Paul*: This is the pen name of J. P. F. Richter (1763–1825),
the brilliantly idiosyncratic Bavarian novelist and humourist who enjoyed
considerable popularity in Germany, France and in England at this time –
his work became a major literary influence on the young Schumann. But
the passage, in French in the original, has not been identified as belonging
to his work.

2. *the Emperor Alexander*: The glamorous young Tsar of Russia (1777–
1825) had made triumphant appearances in Paris and London after the defeat
of Napoleon (there is a very interesting portrait of him in *War and Peace*),
but the reputation of his later years was clouded by reactionary turns and a
reputation for mysticism.

CHAPTER 21

The Secret Note

1. *A letter to the author*: Scholars think that this and the following chapters
allude to rumours in the liberal press in 1829 that Ultra elements in
the government, fearing another revolution, were intriguing with foreign
monarchs concerning a possible pre-emptive intervention in French affairs.
A secret note, or memorandum, was said to have been sent. The figures
who appear are variously identified as sketches of political personalities.

CHAPTER 22

The Discussion

1. *Monsieur le Duc de* — : Note that, though typographically identical, the dash for this duke (perhaps a sketch of the historical Duc de Blacas) conceals a different identity from that of the mysterious minister, duke or prince for whom Julien has to memorize his report – see below.

2. *Place de Grève*: A square in Paris, now Place de L'Hôtel de Ville, which was used as the place of public execution in pre-revolutionary times.

3. *M. de Maistre's* Du Pape: Joseph de Maistre (1755–1821) was an extreme Catholic, royalist and a leading theoretician among the Ultras, who remained a powerful influence on the traditional French Right. His book *Du Pape* (1819) argued the case for papal infallibility.

4. *Legal Gazette*: The *Gazette des Tribunaux*, a daily report of proceedings in the Courts, much read by Stendhal.

5. *no longer has Pitt*: William Pitt (1759–1806) had been dead well over twenty years.

6. . . . . It will be a God! *cried the fabulist*: In 'The sculptor and the statue of Jupiter' by La Fontaine (*Fables*, IX, 6), a sculptor confronts his block of stone, reasons with himself and decides thus.

7. *M. de Richelieu dissipated so foolishly in 1817*: The Duc de Richelieu (1766–1822) was twice appointed Louis XVIII's first minister. During one of these periods the Ultras had sent a much-reported 'Secret Note' recommending continued allied occupation of France after 1815; but by 1818 the Duke had cleared the country of foreign soldiers. Stendhal's intensified version of this incident is a further example of his concentration of Restoration happenings into the supposed timespan of the novel.

8. *the* Globe: *Le Globe* was a radical and Romantic newspaper started in 1824.

9. . . . . *a Kléber, a Hoche, a Jourdan, a Pichegru*: Representatives of the generation of young generals, often of humble birth, who carved out brilliant careers in the defence of revolutionary France. For the last – who changed sides, and whom the President proceeds to praise – see n. 8 to II. 9.

10. *Cathelineau*: A peasant hero of the Vendée, killed in 1793.

11. *Gustavus Adolphus*: The Swedish hero-king of the seventeenth-century Thirty Years War was, of course, the enemy of Roman Catholicism, of Cardinal Richelieu and of France.

12. *the noble Duc de* — : Scholars think this is a veiled allusion to the great

Austrian Chancellor, Prince Metternich (1773–1859), who was the focus of European reactionary monarchical politics in the early nineteenth century, and whose usual residence was in the Grand Duchy of Hesse. And thus that in the next sentence it is to Mainz (Mayence), the capital of Hesse, that Julien assumes he will be sent.

CHAPTER 23

The Clergy, Woodlands, Liberty

1. *economy and Hume ... The* Saints *... M. Brougham*: This is a kind of coded summary of tendencies in England which would be antipathetic to the principles of Holy Alliance monarchical doctrine. Thus: *economy* is probably the new Utilitarian science of political economy; *Hume* is the Scots philosopher David Hume (1711–76) famous for his sceptical reason; the *Saints* represent radical religious dissent; *Brougham* is Lord Henry Brougham (1778–1868), a leading liberal-minded lawyer and statesman.

2. *trivial verses*: Probably a reference to M. de La Mole's quotation from the *Marseillaise* in the previous chapter.

3. *M. de Nerval*: This figure is normally taken to be based on the visionary Ultra, the Prince Jules de Polignac (1780–1847), who was Charles X's great friend and first minister, and whose sweeping ordinances had much to do with sparking off the revolution of 1830.

4. *the cannon at St-Roch*: A reference to the famous 'whiff of grapeshot'. In October 1795, General Bonaparte caused a single small cannon to be fired from near the church of St-Roch by the Tuileries. This was enough to intimidate the National Guards, who were supporting the Directory, and so inaugurated the Consulate.

CHAPTER 24

Strasbourg

1. *Desaix and Gouvion Saint-Cyr*: Heroes of the defence of France against the Austrians in 1796. Saint-Cyr's *Memoirs* of this campaign were published in 1829.

CHAPTER 25

The Department of Virtue

1. *Lope de Vega*: Brilliant and prolific Spanish poet and dramatist (1562–1635). But this remark has not been traced to him, and is in French in the original.

2. *carbonaro*: Member of a secret society of Italian republicans.

3. *furia francese*: An Italian phrase used to describe the shocking onset of French troops in battle after Charles VIII's invasion of Italy in 1494.

4. *A lover at an inn one day*: The whole idea of the prudish beauty persecuting writers of popular verse is said to be based on the severities of Louis XVIII's official mistress, Madame de Cayla, against, among others, Béranger – and Béranger's rather scurrilous reply, glanced at here, insinuating the King's impotence, etc. Mme de Cayla is also said to have caused paintings to be altered in the interests of greater modesty.

5. *the* Camarilla: A Spanish term, like *junta*, *cabal*, etc., applied to the association of Ultras within the government.

CHAPTER 26

Love in the Mind

1. *Don Juan, canto XIII, stanza 84*: Actually stanza 34 – and quoted with slight changes of punctuation. (The final, unquoted, line is – 'Perhaps we have borrowed this from the Chinese'.)

2. *Saint-Simon*: These memoirs of the soldier, courtier and diplomat Louis de Rouvroy, Duc de Saint-Simon (1675–1755), are records of the French Court 1694–1723, and famous for their scathing wit, devastating insight into petty motivation and formidable reverence for the institutions of aristocratic precedence.

3. *a Massillon*: Jean-Baptiste Massillon (1663–1742) was Bishop of Clermont and a celebrated preacher at the courts of Louis XIV, the Orléans Regency and Louis XV.

CHAPTER 27

The Finest Places in the Church

1. *Telemachus: Les aventures de Télémaque* is a fable about the son of Odysseus, written by Archbishop Fénelon (1651–1715) in 1699 to guide Louis XIV's nephew, the young Duc de Bourgogne, in matters of conduct and governance. The King took it as a satire on his Court.

2. *treaty of Munster*: The treaty of Münster was drafted in 1644, at the end of the Thirty Years War, and became a basis of international law.

3. *Dorat*: Claude Dorat (1734–1800) had a reputation for the airy intangibility of his poetic manner.

CHAPTER 28

Manon Lescaut

1. *Lichtenberg*: Georg Christoph Lichtenberg (1742–99) was a physicist, and a stern aphorist – 'the spirit of Chamfort entered into a German professor', according to Stendhal. But this passage is in French in the original.'

2. *Manon Lescaut*: An extremely lavish setting of the famous adventures of Chevalier de Grieux and his fickle Manon was mounted at the Opéra in 1830, with a libretto by Scribe and score by Halévy.

CHAPTER 29

Ennui

1. *Girodet*: Alphonse Girodet (1767–1824) was a painter and literary man, some of whose writings and correspondence were published in 1829.

CHAPTER 30

A Box at the Opéra Bouffe

1. *(Il) Matrimonio Segreto: The Secret Marriage* (1792) by Domenico Cimarosa. In it, the hero marries his employer's daughter.

CHAPTER 31

Make Her Afraid

1. *si fata sinant*: If fate permits. *Aeneid*, I, 19.
2. Memoirs Dictated at St Helena *by Napoleon*: Probably those taken down by General de Montholon and General Baron Gourgaud, and published 1822–7. Although Las Cases was the most important imperial propagandist, these two shared with him, and with Marshal Bertrand, the task of transcribing Napoleon's dictations.

CHAPTER 32

The Tiger

1. *Beaumarchais*: From *The Marriage of Figaro*, V. iii.
2. *Smollett*: The Scottish novelist (1721–71) Tobias Smollett's *History of England* came out in three volumes in 1757–8.

CHAPTER 33

The Torments of Weakness

1. *Mirabeau*: Honoré-Gabriel Riqueti, Comte de Mirabeau (1749–91), revolutionary orator, statesman and polemical writer.
2. *I am no angel*: From *Tartuffe*, III, iii.

CHAPTER 34

A Man of Intelligence

1. *like Othello*: i.e. like Desdemona in *Othello* I, iii! 'That I did love the Moor, to live with him/ My downright violence, and scorn of fortunes/ May trumpet to the world; my heart's subdued/ Even to the utmost pleasure of my lord . . .'

2. *Louis XI*: (1423–83) a king famous for his labyrinthine, amoral, Machiavellian successes, particularly against the power of Burgundy.

CHAPTER 37

A Keep

1. *Sterne*: Laurence Sterne, author of *Tristram Shandy* (1759–67), was very popular with French intellectuals of this period – but this quote is in French in the original and was probably invented by Stendhal.

2. *the escape of M. de Lavalette*: Comte Antoine de Lavalette, an important Napoleonic official, was condemned to death after Waterloo, but escaped to Bavaria by dressing in his wife's clothes. His action of looking at his watch while being sentenced was widely remarked upon.

3. *René*: Chateaubriand's novel of melancholy sensibility (1802).

CHAPTER 39

Intrigue

1. *Locke*, Travels in France: From John Locke's (1632–1704) journal in *The Life of John Locke*, published by Peter, Lord King in 1829. This has been freely translated into French, presumably by Stendhal, and is translated here; but most editors, following the example of Scott Moncrieff (who thanks Vyvyan Holland for pointing the passage out), prefer to print the seventeenth-century original: 'He that endeavoured to kil his sister in our house, had before kild a man, & it had cost his father 500 escus to get him off, by their secret distribution gaining the favour of the Counsellors.'

2. *the Chevreuses and the Longuevilles*: The Duchesses of Chevreuse and of

Longueville were glamorous leading figures in the Fronde – the dangerous aristocratic rebellions against the government led by Cardinal Mazarin during Louis XIV's minority (1648–52).

CHAPTER 40

Tranquillity

1. *the King of Terrors*: A phrase from the Book of Job 18.14 that had been memorably employed by Chateaubriand in *The Genius of Christianity*, (1802).

CHAPTER 41

The Trial

1. *Sainte-Beuve*: Charles Augustin Sainte-Beuve (1804–69) is chiefly remembered as a literary theorist, critic and proponent of Romanticism, though he was also a poet and novelist. Enormously influential in his own day, he is also notorious for his misjudgement of the work of some of his contemporaries, including Stendhal.

2. *pilfered from Bossuet*: Jacques-Bénigne Bossuet (1627–1704), as Bishop of Meaux and tutor to the Dauphin, was one of the most influential figures at the court of King Louis XIV. His sermons and funeral orations are famous for their rhetorical style. (See n. 2, I. 25.)

CHAPTER 42

1. *Chapter 42*: Stendhal left the last four chapters of the novel untitled.

2. *thou hast loved much*: An allusion to Jesus's comments on Mary Magdalene in *Luke* 7. 47.

3. *Rotrou's* Venceslas: Jean Rotrou (1609–50) was a dramatist, a friend and rival of Pierre Corneille. *Venceslas* (1647) was his most successful tragedy.

4. *Danton . . . the enemy before Paris*: Danton's stirring Jacobin oratory put new courage into the revolutionary armies, who defeated the invading Prussians at the crucial battle of Valmy in September 1792.

5. *must themselves resign*: Slight variation on Voltaire's tragedy of *Mahomet* (1742), II, v.

6. *Stendhal's note*: 'This is a Jacobin talking.'

7. *a comrade of Manuel*: Jacques Antoine Manuel (1775–1827), much admired by Stendhal, was a soldier in the revolutionary armies from 1792, and afterwards an outstanding liberal advocate and orator.

CHAPTER 43

1. *lines spoken by Belphégor*: In La Fontaine's Fable *Belphégor* (V. 7) – adapted from Machiavelli – this demon is sent by the King of Devils to investigate marriage; he weds an excessively virtuous wife, and flees back to Hell exclaiming with relief:

> Sire . . . the marriage knot
> Damns as sure as any other state.

2. *have been transgressed*: Another (the fifth) allusion to *Phèdre* (III, i), as detected by Castex.

3. *second apostate*: Probably a reference to the Byzantine Roman Emperor Julian the Apostate (331–63) who tried briefly, after the conversion of Constantine, to return the Empire to paganism.

4. *almost noon*: Masses had to be said before noon.

CHAPTER 44

1. *a spur to glory*: An allusion to Voltaire's heroic-comical poem *La Pucelle* d'Orléans (1755).

2. *as a natural right*: The doctrine of Rousseau, etc., and of much thought to this day.

3. *the King of Rome*: Napoleon's son by Marie-Louise of Austria, Napoleon II (1811–32), was declared King of Rome when he was born; the Emperor had abdicated in his favour in 1814, and again in 1815.

4. *Massillon consecrated Dubois*: This is compromising because Dubois is for Julien the exemplar of a corrupt and worldly prelate. See above, n. 8 to II. 1.

CHAPTER 45

1. *Stendhal's note*: 'The drawback of the reign of public opinion, which in other aspects procures *liberty*, is that it mixes itself up in things with which it has nothing to do; for example: private life. Hence the melancholy in America and in England. To avoid impinging on private life, the author has invented a small town, *Verrières*, and, when he had need of a bishop, a jury, an assize court, he sited them all in Besançon, where he has never been.'